MARY A. LARKIN OMNIBUS

Ties of Love and Hate
The Wasted Years

MARY A. LARKIN

D1627702

sphere

SPHERE

This omnibus edition first published in Great Britain by Warner Books in 2001
Published by Sphere in 2007

Mary A. Larkin Omnibus Copyright © Mary A. Larkin 2007

Previously published separately:

Ties of Love and Hate
First published in Great Britain in 1993 by Judy Piatkus
This edition published by Warner in 1994
Reprinted 1998, 1999, 2001
Reprinted by Time Warner Paperbacks in 2004
Reprinted 2005
Reprinted by Sphere in 2007
Copyright © Mary A. Larkin 1993

The Wasted Years
First published in Great Britain by Judy Piatkus 1992
Published by Warner Books in 1993
Reprinted 1994 (twice), 1995, 1998, 1999
Reprinted by Time Warner Paperbacks in 2002
Reprinted 2005
Copyright © Mary A. Larkin 1992

The moral right of the author has been asserted.

A CIP catalogue for this book is available from the British Library.

ISBN 978-0-7515-4013-0

Papers used by Sphere are natural, recyclable products made from
wood grown in sustainable forests and certified in accordance with
the rules of the Forest Stewardship Council.

Printed and bound in Great Britain by Mackays of Chatham Ltd.
Paper supplied by Hellefoss AS, Norway

Sphere
An imprint of
Little, Brown Book Group
Brettenham House
Lancaster Place
London WC2E 7EN

A Member of the Hachette Livre Group of Companies

www.littlebrown.co.uk

Ties of Love and Hate

To my mother Molly McAnulty

The Falls Road and districts portrayed in TIES OF LOVE AND HATE actually exist and the historic events referred to in the story are, to the best of my knowledge, authentic.

However, I would like to emphasise that the story is fictional, and all characters are purely a figment of my imagination and are not based on any person alive or dead. Any similarity is purely coincidental.

CHAPTER ONE

Belfast, 1907

A thunderous frown on his dark, handsome face, Paul
Mason sat very straight, careful not to crush the girl by his
side. His body swayed to the motion of the tram as it
ground its way up the Grosvenor Road. His thoughts were
in a turmoil. Had he made a terrible mistake? Without
moving his head, he slanted his eyes sideways and
examined the girl sitting next to him, her head turned from
him as she gazed blindly out of the tram window. He noted
the tremors that shook her jaw, the convulsive swallowing
as she strove for control, and an ache swelled in his chest.
The tension eased a bit, replaced by tenderness as he eyed
her small close-fitting hat. Perched forward, on top of the
bright rolls and curls that were the current hairstyle, the
white hat with its provocative eye veil was the only sign
that she was a bride. Her suit was a sombre dark blue and
the bag she clutched in her black-gloved hands was also
black, the fine, soft leather matching the buttoned boots
that encased her small feet. His wife, Mrs Maggie Mason!

That morning, when they had been joined in matrimony,
he had been dizzy with happiness, walking on air, unable
to believe his good fortune. But now doubts haunted his
mind. Now he was afraid he had done the wrong thing.

The light from passing street lamps sent glancing
copper glints across Maggie's thick hair and to divert his
mind from his worries, Paul tried to picture it loose,
hanging about her face in all its glory. They had been
courting six months but he had yet to see a hair out of

place. Indeed, he had barely kissed her! Maggie was just not that kind of girl. She was warm and gentle, and he sensed a deep sensuality in her, but he had been careful, afraid of putting a foot wrong; afraid of losing her.

He would not have dreamt that he could wait six months to make her his own but he had, feeling quite virtuous about it, although temptation had been forever present in the form of Marie Collins. His mind shied away from thoughts of her. He had treated her abominably. Instead of telling her about Maggie, face to face, he had chosen the coward's way out and sent her a letter. What if Maggie should ever find out about Marie? He shrugged mentally. So far as that was concerned, his conscience was clear. After all, he had not told Maggie that she was the first woman in his life; she had never asked. Still, he dreaded the day should she ever find out because until he had met Maggie he had intended to marry Marie, and she had been his in every way but name. To his great shame, he had acted like a cad towards her.

As if aware of his scrutiny, Maggie moved restlessly and this brought her profile further into view. Small straight nose, smooth wide brow, and curved high cheek bones. She was beautiful, and she was his! His wife.

He could also see the ugly red imprint of a hand mark standing out starkly against the whiteness of her skin – the proof of his failure to protect her.

Ah, but sure I never dreamed her da would hit her, he lamented inwardly. She didn't want me with her. Begged me to let her go alone.

In spite of all the arguments in his favour, he felt guilty, ashamed even. He was her husband. He should have been by her side, and then by God no one would have dared lift a hand against her! His fists opened and closed where they lay on his thick, muscular thighs and the anger in him was so great he could hardly contain it as he silently cursed the man who had dared to hit Maggie.

It was with relief that he noticed the Royal Victoria Hospital loom up on the left-hand side of the road, and knew that they were approaching the junction where the

Grosvenor and Springfield Roads were divided by the Falls Road, which ran for miles from left to right.

He leant towards the girl. 'Maggie, this is our stop,' he said gently.

She seemed oblivious to his words and he repeated them, this time accompanying them with a slight squeeze of her arm. She nodded dully. Leaving her to follow, he went to the well of the stairs and lifted out two suitcases, placing them on the platform. Expensive hide cases such as he had never seen in his life before. How had he blinded himself to her wealth? They were so much at one with each other, so much in harmony, he had failed to realise just how far apart they really were. But today his eyes had been opened, indeed they had!

When, with a shudder and a series of jerks the tram ground to a halt, Paul leapt from the platform. Swinging the cases down by the side of the road, he turned and clasped Maggie around the waist, swinging her down beside them. Heedless of the amused eyes and craned necks at the tram windows as it jolted on its way, he held her loosely in his arms and willed her to look at him, his gaze insistent, until at last the thick, dark lashes that fanned her cheeks fluttered then lifted and he saw that her eyes, those pale, silvery eyes that seemed to see into his very soul, were now dark, troubled pools.

Tightening his grip on her, his voice full of pain, he cried, 'Ah, Maggie, Maggie my love, I should have been with you! I shouldn't have let you go alone.'

Wanting to reassure him she tried to smile, blinking furiously to hold back the threatening tears, but in spite of her efforts, one escaped and tumbled down her cheek. Tenderly wiping it away with the pad of his thumb, and cupping her face in his hands, Paul bent and kissed her – a deep kiss, gently parting her lips, seeking some response. But she stood cold and lifeless in his embrace.

The rain started to fall, large drops, splashing on her face, her hat, the suitcases. Paul glared angrily at the sky before placing the smaller of the cases under his arm and proffering his free arm to Maggie.

3

'Even the weather's against us,' he fumed. 'All those weeks of sunshine, and it had to rain today. Our wedding day!'

Conscious of the mucky road, Maggie swept her long trailing skirt and petticoats high, and tucking her other hand under his elbow, walked close by his side down the Falls Road, trying to shake off the misery that engulfed her. The drabness of the buildings that lined the road did nothing to raise her spirits and she realised that she was afraid. Afraid? It was terror that tightened the muscles of her throat, cramped her stomach. With her mind's eye she saw again her father's face full of wrath, heard again his voice roar: 'Love? What do you know of love? A chit of a girl like you! It's infatuation you feel!'

And at the memory, her heart lurched inside her body, making her feel physically sick. Since meeting Paul six months earlier, she had been so sure that they were meant for each other, sure that they were destined to marry, that it had come as a shock to her when today her father had shaken that belief and led her to doubt the depth of her feelings for Paul. Was her father right? Was it infatuation she felt? She did not know.

In despair, her thoughts whirled. She had nothing to compare her feelings for Paul against. Daughter of a councillor, she had lived a sheltered life, dating only one other boy and that when she was barely sixteen. And it had lasted such a short time! A few walks in the park, a few trips to the pictures. And then the heartbreak, the pain! But one thing she did know. Her life had become fuller and richer since meeting this man who was now her husband, and when he was not near, she felt lost.

Breaking in on her thoughts, Paul said with a nod of his head, 'That's the Dunville Park, love. That's where you'll take our children to play.'

A few months earlier he would have said 'kids', but since meeting Maggie he found himself constantly correcting his manner of speaking. He loved to hear Maggie talk. Loved the way she rounded off her words. Her voice was music to his ears, and it made him wish he had been better educated. But he was determined to learn. He intended that their children would have two parents who spoke properly, and he would be taking Maggie further up the Falls Road to live. Up where the professional people dwelled. Waterford Street was just a stop-gap.

Maggie narrowed her eyes against the heavy rain and peered across the road at the park. The trees that loomed wet and bedraggled over the railings seemed to be crying out in sympathy with her. Once again she nodded, despair deepening at the desolation of it all. Paul eyed her anxiously. She had not spoken since leaving the Malone Road an hour ago and he was worried. It was as if she was in a state of shock. Quickening his pace, he turned up Waterford Street, careful to lead her up the side of the road, the cobbled footpaths being too slippery for her high-heeled boots. Maggie was almost running to keep up with him, but in his anxiety to get her indoors, he failed to notice.

He came to a halt outside one of the better-looking houses. The door was painted a dark green and the brass knocker glowed dimly in the gloom. Through the thick, white lace curtains that hung at the window, a fire could be seen burning and the sight warmed Paul's heart as he lifted his hand to the knocker. However, before he could knock on the door it was pulled open by a tall thin woman. Mollie Grahame was fifty-five years old, but Maggie could be forgiven if she thought her much older. Widowed at thirty, she'd had a hard struggle to bring up three sons on her own and it showed in her deeply lined face and snow white hair.

Hiding her concern at the sight of the slight figure clinging to Paul's arm, she cried warmly, 'Come in! Come on in. Isn't it an awful night?' And she ushered them through the small hall and into the kitchen, masking her bewilderment with a smile. She had expected a happy bride and groom; instead, her usually cheerful lodger looked glum and the bride looked like death, with eyes like saucers in a small, pinched face.

5

Clasping the young girl's hands tightly in her own, Mollie said softly, 'So you're Margaret!' and smiled warmly at her. 'Welcome to my home. I hope you'll be happy here.'

The warm greeting brought a wavering smile to Maggie's face and she replied gravely, 'Thank you very much, Mrs Grahame.'

The clear enunciation of her words confirmed Mollie's worst suspicions, having noted the fine serge material of her suit and the soft kid leather of the quality boots. This was no working-class girl! There was breeding here. Careful not to let her expression betray her dismay, she gave Maggie's hands a comforting squeeze and turned to Paul.

'Hang Margaret's coat up to dry, Paul. I'll wet the tea.' And taking a kettle and a griddle of bread from the big black range that ran the length of one wall, she bustled into the scullery, her mind in a whirl. In all the past months when they had been decorating the two upstairs rooms that he rented from her, Paul had not once mentioned the fact that Margaret was upper-class. From his affectionate nickname of Maggie, Mollie had somehow pictured a working-class girl and now she was dismayed. Would Margaret fit in on the Falls Road? Was she a Catholic? Somehow Mollie thought not.

Paul helped Maggie off with her coat and hung it on the banisters that ran along the wall facing the range, the stairs behind rising to the next floor. Then, removing the hat-pin that secured her hat, he lifted it carefully from the bright copper hair and there was reverence in the way he dusted a speck of dirt off its brim before placing it on the dresser. He led his wife to the fireside, where he gently pushed her into the room's only armchair. It was an old chair but she sank gratefully into its comfortable depths, and rested her head against its high back.

Kneeling by her side, Paul undid the tiny buttons along the sides of her soft kid boots and eased them from her feet. Even through her thick ribbed stockings he could feel the chill of her feet and he chafed them gently with his hands, before placing them on the brass fender to warm. A long, drawn out sigh left his lips as he examined her face, pale and drawn, a darkening shadow on her cheek. Leaning forward he caressed the bruised cheek with the back of his hand.

'Ah, Maggie ... I wish I'd went with you! I'll never forgive meself, so I'll not. Never!'

Anxiously, she grabbed his hand, 'It's all right Paul. Everything is going to be all right!' she cried, gripping his fingers reassuringly between her own.

He thought she sounded as if she was trying to convince herself instead of him and his heart sank, but Mollie, returning to the kitchen with a tray in her hands, prevented him from pursuing the matter. Pulling a small table close to Maggie's chair, he gave his landlady a grateful smile and relieved her of the tray.

'Thanks, Mollie.'

As she eyed her, Mollie felt heartache for Maggie, who looked so woebegone, so lost. It was all wrong; this was her wedding day. She should be gay and happy. Her voice gentle, she said consolingly, 'You'll feel better once ye get something warm inside of ye, Margaret.'

'Please call me Maggie. That's what Paul has christened me.'

Then with a tremulous smile, Maggie gazed up at her. The light from the gas mantle above the fireplace fell full on her face and Mollie noticed for the first time the bruised cheek. Mouth agape, her eyes sought Paul's. Reading her mind, he gently shook his head to let her know that he was not the culprit. Relieved, she answered Maggie, 'Of course I will – but only if you'll call me Mollie. No more Mrs Grahame, all right?'

Maggie nodded her agreement. She never wanted to be called Margaret again because Margaret Pierce had died as surely as if they had shot her when her parents had disowned her two hours ago.

Once Maggie was settled, sipping a mug of hot tea, Mollie headed for the scullery, saying over her shoulder, 'Gi'me a shout, Paul, if ye need anything else.'

7

'OK Mollie, thanks. Thanks for everything.'

The hot tea, combined with the heat of the fire, eased some of the tension from Maggie's body and slowly she relaxed. But she refused the griddle scones oozing with jam, when Paul offered the plate to her. She was afraid food would stick in her throat, she was so choked with emotion. However, she showed her gratitude for the sweet, hot tea, clasping the mug in both hands and sipping at it to quench her thirst.

After eating some of the scones and gulping down his mug of tea, Paul rose to his feet and lifted the cases, heading for the stairs.

'I'll put these upstairs, Maggie. You relax there 'till I get a fire goin'.'

'I've already lit a fire in the front room, Paul,' Mollie shouted from the scullery, bringing a pleased smile to his face. Mollie was a treasure, always ready to do a good turn.

'Thanks, Mollie,' he shouted back, and with a reassuring smile at Maggie, climbed the stairs.

Thank God for Bob Smith! He was Mollie's nephew and it was through him that Paul had come to live here. Knowing that Paul was getting married and wanted rooms away from his family, and aware that his Aunt Mollie was short of money since the marriage of her youngest son, he had introduced them and was pleased when they took to each other on sight.

Although Paul loved each and every one of his family, he thought someone of his wife's quiet disposition might find them overpowering. She would have enough adjusting to do living in two rooms, without his family breathing down her neck. Just how much adjusting she would have to do he had not realised until today. Today he had seen Maggie's home for the first time and now wished he had not. It had knocked the heart out of him.

His gaze roamed around the front bedroom, the room that Mollie and he had decorated and made into a sitting room. Somewhere Maggie and he could sit in privacy. He had worked hard to pay for the two small wooden armchairs that flanked the tiny tiled hearth, and the bookcase that graced one corner had been his pride and joy. Bought in Smithfield Market for one and sixpence it had been in an awful state, but week-end after week-end he had worked on it and now it stood restored to all its former glory; rich dark oak gleaming in the dim light. Adorned with his few precious books and some knick-knacks, it held pride of place. The rooms were luxurious by lower Falls Road standards and he had been proud of them. Oh, yes indeed. He had been proud all right! Well, it just went to show that it was right what they said, pride did come before a fall. He had been bursting with pride, could not wait to show Maggie the rooms, but that was before he had seen her parents' house and become aware of just how wealthy they were. Now he felt deflated. He looked about him with distaste, the memory of his wife's home fresh in his mind.

With a groan he muttered, 'In the name of God, what was I thinkin' of? How can I expect Maggie t'live here?'

He wished again that he had not seen her home, large and standing in its own grounds. Much better to have lived in ignorance. He would be in a happier frame of mind now if he had resisted the impulse to take a look at that house.

With a sigh of regret for his own stupidity, he carried the cases into the back bedroom. This room was even smaller! The double bed pushed against one wall took up half the floor space and a battered wardrobe against the opposite wall left just enough room for the white-painted chest of drawers that stood underneath the long narrow window. On top of the chest, beside a wash jug and basin, stood an alarm clock and a candle stick sporting a new candle. Looking around the cramped quarters, his despair grew. Was he daft to bring Maggie here to this? He shook his head and bit on his lip. He needed his head examined, so he did. Since meeting her, he had been walking on cloud nine, thinking love was all that mattered. Now he was not so sure. In fact, he very much doubted that love could bridge the gap between them.

Placing the smaller suitcase on the bed, he rummaged

9

through it until he found a nightdress. It was made of soft white silky material and he felt a surge of desire when he pictured her in it. He spread it lovingly on top of the bright patchwork quilt and, closing the case, hoisted it and its companion up on top of the wardrobe. Maggie could unpack them herself tomorrow morning. Back in the front bedroom he lifted the poker from the tiled hearth and raked at the fire, pleased when the flames brightened the room and warmth embraced the two armchairs. Once more he examined the room and again found it wanting. It was so small, so cramped. Wearily, he pushed his fingers through his hair in a gesture of defeat. Closing his eyes, he delayed a few minutes longer to compose himself before descending the stairs.

He found that Maggie had dozed off. She awoke with a start as he approached her chair. With a hand on her shoulder, he was quick to apologise, 'I'm sorry, love. I didn't realise you were sleepin'.'

Coming from the scullery, Mollie was all sympathy. 'Ah, the poor wee dear! Take her t'bed, Paul. Sure she's all in.' And she bustled about, pulling the small table away from the chair, making room for Maggie to get to the stairs.

She rose slowly to her feet and the look she gave Mollie was apologetic. 'Forgive me for not sampling your scones. They look delicious but I am very tired,' she said softly.

With a wave of her hand, Mollie dismissed the apology. 'It's all right! Never worry yerself. It's a good night's sleep ye need.'

She shot a warning glance at Paul and Maggie went bright red as the implication of the look sank in, but Paul just smiled and said. 'Thanks for everything, Mollie.'

Bidding her goodnight, they climbed the narrow staircase single file. Once in the front room Paul waited anxiously while Maggie looked around. Her heart quailed when she saw how small the room was, and unbidden a picture of her previous spacious bedroom flashed across her mind, but knowing that Paul was watching her reaction to the room, she managed to smile.

10

'It's lovely, Paul. You must have worked hard to have it so nice.'

He sighed with relief, but it was tinged with sadness. Drawing her into the circle of his arms, he removed the combs and clips that held her hair in place and let it cascade down her back in thick waves. Then, stifling a sob, he sank his face into its soft masses and inhaled the perfume that was so much a part of her. She always smelt nice, his Maggie. Nice enough to eat.

His voice muffled, he cried, 'I don't know what I was thinkin' about, bringin' you here. I'm a stupid fool, so I am!'

'Don't! Don't say that!' Her voice was tinged with fear as she drew back and gripped his waistcoat tightly in her fists. He must be strong! He must convince her that they had done the right thing. 'All I need is you, Paul.' A tug at his waistcoat accompanied each word. 'It doesn't matter where we live as long as I'm with you. *You* are all I need. Believe me, you're all I need.'

Sensing the fear that was swamping her, he drew her gently to one of the armchairs and, sitting down, pulled her on to his lap. Arms clasped tightly around her, his cheek pressed against the softness of her hair, he asked, 'Was it very bad, Maggie?', inwardly wincing at the stupidity of the words. Could it have been any worse? Hadn't her da hit her? But he was at a loss what to say or do. He felt so inadequate, so useless.

Sadly, she nodded her head. Gazing into the heart of the fire, she saw again her father's study as it had been earlier that evening. Her father dressed in his old comfortable smoking jacket, busy at his grand oak desk. Her mother kneeling in front of the marble hearth, setting spills and sticks in the grate, preparing to light the fire. The first fire to be lit in a long time, the weather having been sunny and warm for weeks past, but today it had changed. Today had been like a day in November, instead of early August. Her wedding day! Was that an omen? Tears filled her eyes but she fought them back and let her memory run on, reliving word for word the scene in her father's study.

11

The third occupant of the room, her younger brother William, was sitting on the deep seat of the bay window and when she entered the room all three turned to look at her. Some of the emotions she was feeling must have shown on her face because her mother rose slowly to her feet, her head tilted back, brows raised inquiringly, and her father slowly swung right around in his swivel chair until he was facing the door.

'Is anything wrong, Margaret?' Ruth Pierce asked, worried eyes anxiously scanning her daughter's strained face.

'I have something to tell you, Mother.' To her dismay, her voice came out in a squeak, causing her mother to draw back and blink in surprise.

In haste Maggie blurted out. 'I got married this morning.'

Silence. Had they not heard her? She gazed from one to the other, puzzled. Of course they had! Her mother and father remained motionless, as if frozen in time, but William had abandoned his book and moved to the edge of the window-seat, his eyes starting from his head, face agog with suppressed excitement. At last, exchanging a startled glance with his wife, her father rose slowly to his feet, a bemused look on his face. Then, with a shake of his head, as if at some absurdity, he said, 'For a minute there, Margaret, I actually thought you said you were married.' And he laughed softly at the idea.

'I did. I was married this morning.' She was glad to find that when she answered him, her voice was controlled.

'Bah! Don't be silly, Margaret,' her mother cried, her voice full of ridicule. 'You can't just get married like that! The banns must be called. Besides, you need our permission.'

'No, Mother.' She shook her head to emphasise her words. 'I'm twenty-one, I don't need permission, and the banns were called.'

'The banns were . . . the banns were . . .' Her mother's face cleared and she said reproachfully, 'Ah! You're having us on.'

At Maggie's shake of the head her mother muttered, 'But . . . but you don't bother with men!'

She sounded so bewildered and confused, Maggie felt her first misgivings. Had she been wrong not to tell her parents? Paul had begged her to confide in them, to do things right, but she had been convinced that once their marriage was an accomplished fact, once she was Paul's wife, she would stand a better chance of winning them around. She had neglected to tell Paul how much her father disliked Roman Catholics. He would have done all in his power to stop the wedding and he was so strong, so domineering, she was not sure that she would have been able to stand up to him. Now the damage was done and she was Paul's wife. Surely they would accept him, now that he was her husband?

'Hush, Ruth!' her father admonished her mother, then turned a frowning countenance to Maggie. 'If this is a joke, let me warn you that it's in very poor taste.'

When she just mutely shook her head, the frown deepened and he barked at her, 'Well then, girl! Just who the hell did you marry? Eh? Eh? And how the hell did you manage to keep it a secret?'

This startled her. She had never known her father to swear before and she gulped before muttering. 'Paul Mason.'

'Speak up, girl! Hold up your chin! Stop muttering into your chest. I can't hear you.'

Maggie's chin rose proudly in the air as her father taunted her, and she said loud and clear: 'Paul Mason.'

As she watched her father's face screw up in concentration as he tried to put a face to the name, saw him shake his head, perplexed, she again felt doubt. Should she have told them? At last her father spoke.

'I don't know anyone called Paul Mason.'

'I know you don't.' In spite of herself, her voice was shaky as she delivered her blow. 'He's a Roman Catholic.'

There! It was out! The unforgivable. She eyed her father closely, fearful of his reaction, well aware of the animosity he bore the Catholic community. But surely now that she was married he would accept Paul? Oh, he must, he must! After all, Paul was his son-in-law!

'Are you telling me that you were married in the Catholic Church?'

His voice was deceptively calm, but when she nodded in confirmation he advanced slowly towards her and she found herself backing away from him until she could go no further, her way blocked by the closed door. She feared her father. Why, she did not know. He had never lifted his hand to her. Indeed, he paid her very little attention, just vaguely acknowledged her presence with an indulgent smile; a nod of approval when she did something that pleased him. He was too busy preparing William to follow in his footsteps to bother about a mere daughter. Surely it could not make much difference to them who she married? They should be glad to have her off their hands. They were so devoted to each other, they needed no other except William, their son and heir.

In spite of this Maggie had always sensed a ruthlessness in her father and now quaked in her shoes, fear in her heart, as she gazed up at him.

Glaring down at her from his great height, he said in a deceptively kind voice, as if talking to a halfwit, 'Margaret, you know this can never be, don't you?' His head moved slowly from side to side.

Now, her mouth twisted wryly as she recalled how she had gaped up at him. Thinking he did not understand she hastened to assure him: 'You don't understand, Father. Paul and I are married.'

With a wave of his hand he dismissed her words and stated with confidence, 'The marriage can be annulled. If the Pope can decree, as he did, that marriages between Catholics and Protestants are null and void unless they take place in a Catholic Church, then I'll see to it that your marriage is annulled. If it is not consummated, it can be annulled!' Then, eyes bulging with horror, he bellowed, 'Surely you're not pregnant, girl?'

When she just stood mute, he roared. 'Come on . . . tell me! Are you pregnant?'

14

She hesitated, wondering if she should pretend to be pregnant. Would it help her case?

'Well, girl?' His eyes were bulging, face shiny with sweat, as he awaited her reply. 'Answer me!'

This caused her quickly to admit that she was not pregnant, and at her shake of the head he sighed, a sound echoed by her mother.

'You picked the right time to do this, didn't you, Margaret? Tell me, just where did you meet this . . . this . . . what's his name?'

'Paul . . . Paul Mason.'

'Where did you meet him?'

Tense again, she answered him, 'He's a bricklayer. He was working on those buildings on Shaftsbury Square.' She dreaded the next question. Hoped he would neglect to ask it. But no such luck.

With a frown he asked, 'Who introduced you to him?'

Head low, chin almost on her chest, she stood silent and ashamed, not wanting to admit that Paul had picked her up.

Her father's smile held contempt. 'So he picked you up! He . . . picked . . . you . . . up! Ah, Margaret, even after all our warnings, you let a boy pick you up.' His eyes held pity and with sad shake of the head, he added, 'And look at the mess it's landed you in. I hope this will be a lesson to you. Though, somehow, I don't think we'll have much trouble getting rid of Paul.' He leaned forward and gazed intently into her face. 'Do you think for one minute he would have bothered with you if you had been a poor Protestant from the Shankill Road? Eh, do you? Now tell the truth. Do you really think he would have sought you out if you had been poor?'

Head thrown back, chin in the air, she shouted at him to still the doubts that were growing by the minute. 'Paul loves me! He didn't know who you were. That you are rich.'

Soothingly he replied, 'I'm not saying he doesn't love you. Ah, no, Margaret . . . I'm not saying that. You're a beautiful girl. Why, you could have any boy you choose!

15

What I am saying is, it's easy to love where there is money and he didn't have to know who I was. All he had to do was look at your clothes . . .'

Blinded by tears she interrupted him. 'Paul loves me. He's not interested in your money.'

Then her father played his trump card. 'We shall see! We shall see!' A light laugh accompanied his next words. 'Remember Bill Morgan? Eh . . . remember him? Remember how sure you were of his worth?'

Her mouth went dry. Would she ever forget Bill Morgan? Ever forget the pain and humiliation he had caused her? She licked lips that suddenly felt like paper and muttered defensively, 'I was only sixteen when I dated Bill.'

The pain in her voice softened him and he leant forward entreatingly. 'Look, love, let me handle this. Please, love . . . let me send him packing before it's too late.'

'No! I tell you Paul loves me. *He* won't be bought,' she insisted angrily. Oh, but her father knew how to hurt. Bill Morgan had been her one and only boyfriend. A penniless student, he had been bought off with ten pounds. Ten lousy pounds! Probably a fortune to a seventeen-year-old student, but she had trusted him and the bottom had fallen out of her world when her father had told her about their deal. Even though she had not loved Bill, that was what had hurt most – the fact that a callow youth had sold her out – and the hurt had lingered for a long time. For months she had thought that people were pitying her, talking about her behind her back. Then one day she had realised people were too busy living their own lives to worry about Margaret Pierce's broken romance, but it had soured her, made her avoid men, until Paul. Her heart cried out. Paul was different. Wasn't he? Her father had always been able to make her doubt her worth, always made her feel inadequate. Annoyed at her stubbornness, he turned abruptly to her mother.

'Take her to her room, Ruth, and stay with her until John Mortimer comes. He'll advise us. Help us to get this sorted out.'

At this mention of the family solicitor, Maggie turned in anguish to her mother. 'Mam, I love him!' She pleaded silently with her eyes, but no help was forthcoming from that quarter. That was when her father bawled at her.

'Love? Love?' he thundered. 'What does a chit of a girl like you know about love? Eh? It's infatuation you feel! You mark my words. In six months' time, you'll be glad we intervened.'

These words took the wind out of her sails and strengthened the doubts that already assailed her, but turning to open the door, she cried stubbornly, 'Paul loves me, I know he does. I'm going to pack my clothes.'

Before she could pull the door open, her father gripped her roughly by the shoulder and swung her round to face him. Purple with rage, he ground out through clenched teeth: 'Oh, no, you're not. What about us . . . your mother and me? Eh? Have you thought about us at all? What will our friends . . . my fellow councillors . . . think? Have you forgotten about the election? Good Lord, it's barely three weeks away! What if some nosey reporter gets wind of this? Eh? Why, my chances of getting re-elected would be nil.'

Grim-faced, he shook his head. 'No, Margaret. I won't let you do this to me. I won't let you ruin my chances,' he growled, and his fingers bit cruelly into the soft flesh of her shoulder.

At the mention of the election, all fight left her and she hung like a limp rag from his great fist. She had completely forgotten about the election. If she had remembered, she would have known that there was no chance of winning her parents around. It would have been touch and go at any ordinary time, but just before an election? No chance! She had been wasting her time. Disappointment engulfed her. She had thought she stood a fighting chance, but she had been wrong. Engulfed in misery, she shouted the first thing that entered her mind.

'The election! That's all you ever think about, isn't it? Well, for better or worse, I'm married. And I'm staying married. So what about when you have Catholic grandchildren, eh? How will you cover up then?'

She was unprepared for the effect these words had on her father. His hand rose in the air and she knew he was about to strike her, but in her astonishment made no effort to ward off the blow, taking the full force of it and being knocked across the room. When she attempted to rise her head buzzed and dizziness made her sag down again. It was only with William's help that she was able to get up from the floor. Awash with tears, she once again groped for the door handle, only to be brought abruptly to a standstill by the sound of her father's harsh gasping for breath. She turned aghast as his body hit the floor. With her heart thudding so violently against her ribs she was sure they must hear it, she watched anxiously as William turned his father on to his back. She watched him loosen the high stiff collar, and all the while terror kept her frozen by the door.

Her mother was scrabbling frantically in the desk drawer, muttering over and over, 'Oh, where are they? Dear Lord, where are they? Oh, where does he keep them?'

At last she produced a small bottle of tablets. Falling to her knees beside her husband, she tried to force one between his teeth, all the while begging him: 'Come on now, Clive? You know you must put it under your tongue. Come on, love. Put it under your tongue. Please!'

After what seemed an eternity, as Maggie hung to the door handle for support, the harsh ghastly sounds eased and she discovered that she was biting so hard on her lip, she had drawn blood.

She had been aware that her father had a heart condition, but this was the first time she had witnessed an attack and fear gripped her. Would he be all right?

With her husband's head cradled in her lap, her mother glared up. 'See what you've done? You could have killed him! Go on, get out! You . . . you . . .'

'Ah, Mam . . . I'm sorry. I'm so sorry,' she whimpered, weak with relief at seeing the colour returning to her

18

father's face, the blue tinge fade from around his lips. 'I'm so sorry.'

Once more she turned to the door, but a weak gesture of her father's hand caused her to pause. When he spoke his breath was laboured and she had to lean close to hear his whispered words. 'If . . . you leave this house . . . today, Margaret . . . don't ever come back. Do you hear me? Don't . . . ever . . . come . . . back. And tell that . . . that Paul fellow . . . he'll never touch a penny of my money. Do you hear me? Not a penny.'

His wife interrupted him. 'Clive, please save your strength. You need to rest.'

With a weak gesture of his hand, he silenced her and continued, 'He'll not want you without money, Margaret. Mark my words, he'll not want you for long . . . and then what will become of you?'

His eyes held hers. 'If you go, Margaret, I never want to see you again. Never!'

She could see the unspoken plea in his eyes and compassion smote her. She longed to reassure him, to tell him she would stay, but how could she? She was married to Paul. She loved Paul.

Holding him close, Ruth soothed him, 'Hush, love, hush. You must rest.' Completely ignoring Maggie, she turned to William. 'Help me get him to the couch, son.'

Sobs tearing at her throat, Maggie fled from the room, her father's words filling her mind with doubts. Was he right? What if he had died? She went cold at the idea. If he had, she would never have been able to bring herself to stay with Paul. A shiver coursed through her body at the very thought and she started to pack her bags in a fever of impatience; anxious to be with Paul, to seek reassurance. While she was packing, William came and sat on the bed and watched her.

'Will I ever see you again?' he asked.

Her jaw dropped in surprise as she gaped at him. 'Why ever not? You're sixteen! They can't stop you from seeing me.'

He grimaced and jerked his head from side to side at her

stupidity. 'I know they can't.' His voice was sarcastic and leaning forward he stressed, 'But I would not like to cause another attack like that. Let me tell you something . . . that was a bad attack. I've never seen him so bad.'

Face crumpling, tears near the surface, she accused him, 'You should have warned me! I might have killed him.'

'Warned you?' he cried, obviously affronted. 'Hah! I've hardly seen you this last few months.'

At his indignation, she hung her head in shame, knowing that he spoke the truth. She had been wrapped up in her own affairs, thought only of Paul and becoming his wife. How could she have imagined that her parents would accept Paul? She had been a fool. A stupid fool.

'I've just phoned the doctor,' William informed her. 'He's on his way. He has already been out to Father twice this last few months.' William piled on the agony, making Maggie cringe.

'Oh, no! Why didn't you tell me?' she wailed.

Satisfied that he had made his point, William ignored the question and asked, 'Are you really married?'

She nodded and he probed, 'Are you a Roman Catholic now?'

'No. I don't think I shall ever become a Catholic.'

'What's all the fuss about then?'

'Any children I have must be brought up Catholics.'

'Oh.' Now he understood why his father was so upset. There were already enough Catholic children being born every year without his sister contributing to them. The Catholics bred like rabbits. His father had every right to be angry.

Cases crammed to capacity, she pressed them closed and stood looking around the room, a lump rising in her throat. She loved her bedroom, having picked each piece of furniture with love and care. The bed with its lace canopy was her pride and joy, as was the Persian carpet, one of several that her father had had imported. In this room she had dreamed about the future and now she was stepping out into it. Wondering what was in store for her, she felt afraid. Her father had instilled fear and doubt into her mind. With a sigh she lifted the cases and headed for the door. Taking the biggest case from her, William preceded her down the stairs.

In the hall she looked at him appealingly. Pulling her close he whispered. 'Be happy, Margaret, and when you're settled, I'll come and visit you.'

'Really, William? You mean that?'

'Yes!' His answer was abrupt. He pushed her aside and hurried back up the stairs, but catching the glint of tears in his eyes, she guessed that he did not want to appear unmanly.

Once outside the big double doors, she set the cases down and turned for a last look. As she did so, her mother came from the study, closed the door gently and crossed the black and white tiled floor towards her, a finger to her lips.

'Is he all right?'

'Do you care?' Ruth's voice was full of bitterness.

'Ah, Mam, you know I do.'

Ruth gripped her arm tightly and implored. 'Prove it, Margaret! Stay the night and talk it over. You're making a terrible mistake, you really are! You'll live to regret it. Listen to your father and be advised by him. Let us send for John Mortimer.'

'Mam, it's no use! I'm married to Paul, and Mam . . . I love him so much.' She longed for some word of comfort, a sign that she was loved and wished well. However, her mother drew back.

'Why do you think I didn't tell you? I knew in my heart that you would not approve. I knew you would try to stop me. That's why I got married first. I thought if it was an accomplished fact, I would be able to win you around.' Sadness tinged her voice as she added, 'I forgot about the election.'

'Where are you going to live, Margaret?'

The anxious note in her mother's voice warmed her heart a little.

'Paul has two rooms on the Falls Road.'

'The ghettos?'

21

Dismay made Ruth's voice shrill and she pressed a hand to her lips and glanced apprehensively towards the study door before asking in a lower tone, 'Do you know what they are like?'

When Maggie fearfully shook her head, her mother cried distractedly, 'Ah, Margaret, they're awful! Just awful. Long, dingy, narrow streets. Just like rabbit warrens. And there's no hot water, mind . . . and outside toilets.' She pressed her lips together in anguish before continuing, 'Ah, Margaret, Margaret, I give you a month! One month before you want to come home. When poverty comes in the door, love flies out the window. I only hope your father allows you to return. You have let him down badly.'

Chin tilted in the air, Maggie held at bay the fear that gripped her and replied bravely, 'No, Mother, I shall never return unless you accept Paul. And he has a good job. We'll be all right, we'll manage.' Lifting her cases, she turned once more to her mother. 'Mam?'

'Yes?'

'Will you pack the rest of my belongings and I'll send for them?'

Ruth nodded sadly in reply, looking so forlorn Maggie dropped the cases and reached out impulsively to hug her, grimacing when she was quickly shrugged off. She would never be able to understand why her mother had borne two children, she was so lacking in motherly feelings.

Head high, she walked down the drive as sedately as the heavy cases would allow, aware that her mother was watching her. However, once out of sight of the house, she sank down on to a low wall, fearful that her shaking legs would betray her and she would fall.

From the vantage point where he awaited her, Paul observed her sit down on the wall and hastened to her side. Hovering solicitously over her, he asked, 'Are you all right, Maggie?'

When she lifted her head, unwittingly displaying the livid mark on her cheek, his eyes widened.

'The bad bugger! The friggin' bastard! To hit a defenceless girl!' He was spluttering in his rage.

Maggie's mouth dropped open and she gaped up at him in amazement; she had never heard him use such language before.

'Ah, Maggie! I'm sorry, love, but I could murder the bas—' His head nodded in agitation and he clamped his lips tightly together as he tried to stem the flow of angry words. 'I'm sorry, love,' he gulped, and repeated, 'Ah, I'm sorry.'

Conscious of passers-by casting curious glances in their direction, Maggie rose to her feet and touched his arm reassuringly. 'I'm all right. Honestly, I'm all right. Let's go, Paul.' And without a backward glance, she headed down the Malone Road towards town, leaving him to follow.

Paul lifted the cases, but stood undecided. He had never seen Maggie's home; knew in his heart he would be better not seeing it, but against his better judgement he walked a few steps up the drive until the house came into view. It was large and majestic, with lush green lawns and flower beds a riot of colour. A mansion as far as he was concerned. Filled with dismay he hurried after Maggie and the journey to Waterford Street was spent in silence, worry gnawing at both their minds. Had they made a terrible mistake?

As Maggie came back to reality, a convulsive shudder passed through her body. Holding her tighter still, Paul urged her, 'Come on, love, get it out of your system. Tell me all about it.'

She drew back and gazed into his face, needing to see his reaction to her words. 'My father has disowned me. He never wants to see me again.' The depth of her hurt at her parents' rejection came across to him and he could almost taste her fear when she added, 'He says I will never receive a penny of his money.'

Cupping her face in his hands, he held her gaze earnestly.

'Does that worry you, Maggie?'

'The question is . . . does it worry you, Paul?'

'Maggie! Ah, Maggie, do you really think I'm after your da's money?'

Face crumpling, she wailed, 'I don't know what to think! I'm all mixed up.'

Rocking her gently, he urged. 'Hold on to the fact that we love each other, Maggie. That's all that matters. Remember the first time we met?'

She nodded shyly. Oh, yes, she remembered.

He gave an embarrassed laugh. 'When you laughed into my eyes something wonderful happened. It was as if an electric current passed between us. Then you hurried on, leaving me with a foolish grin on my face and my mates taking the mickey out of me.' Again he laughed wryly. 'I wouldn't have thought it could happen like that, but you felt it too, didn't you?' He sounded anxious. He had never asked her before, if she had been bowled over like him.

She nodded and snuggled closer. That look had changed her life. Again and again she had relived the rapture of it, until she could wait no longer. All aquiver, she had walked along Shaftsbury Square, kidding herself that it would not matter if he ignored her. But she need not have worried. Paul had seen her coming and had stood, brick in hand, watching her. Under the smiling glances of his workmates, he had courteously asked her to walk in the Botanic Gardens with her the next day, a Saturday. Shyly, she had agreed, and from then on they had been inseparable.

'Maggie, I knew then that you were too good for me. God . . . I knew you were far above me, an' I knew I'd no right to ask you out, but I thought love could conquer all. I love you so much, I thought love could conquer all. Now I'm not so sure.'

These words caused her to cry out: 'Don't say that! You musn't say that! All I need is you. As long as we're together it doesn't matter where we live.'

The smile they shared was full of love and trust and he said softly, 'Maggie, I really do love you. And, honestly, your da's money never entered into it. And we won't always live here.' His eyes scanned the small room. 'Ah, no! I'll work me fingers to the bone, and one day I'll take you further up the Falls where the houses have bathrooms, an' . . .'

Giving an embarrassed laugh, Maggie interrupted him. 'Speaking of bathrooms, I need to go somewhere.'

Paul pushed her to her feet, laughing gently. 'This, my love, is one of the things you'll have to get used to.' He led the way downstairs. Going to the fireplace, he took a candle in a holder from the mantelpiece, and lighting it from the embers of the dying fire, guided her through the scullery and out into the yard.

'There it is, love. The masterpiece! The "wee" house.'

By the light of the candle she could see that the yard was small and cluttered. The wee house, as Paul called it, was at the bottom of the yard and the space between it and the house was covered over with a makeshift roof, giving protection from the rain. It also housed a mangle, a big tin bath hanging on a nail on the wall, and numerous other odds and ends.

Handing her the candle, Paul said, 'I'll wait here for you,' and took up a stand at the back door. He was glad Mollie was particular about her wee house, keeping it spotlessly clean and white washed. He had been in many a wee house that was a disgrace to its owners, with spiders weaving their webs in every corner. But not Mollie's! No, not Mollie's, and thank God for that.

When she passed through the scullery again, Maggie paused to wash her hands and her eyes widened in surprise when she saw the big brown jawbox. She had never seen anything like it before in her life, and was about to comment on it when Paul, a finger to his lips, stopped her. With a nod at the door leading off the scullery, he mouthed one word, 'Mollie,' and quietly they passed through the kitchen and climbed the stairs to bed.

In the front room Maggie went to the fire and made a big thing of warming her hands. Bed-time could be put off no longer and she wondered how she would be able to get undressed and into bed in front of Paul.

Watching her, he smiled tenderly, went to her and put his arms around her. His hands cupping her breasts, he nuzzled the thick hair away from the nape of her neck and kissed it – soft feathery kisses that sent tremor after tremor coursing through her. 'Maggie, don't be afraid. I won't do anything you don't want me to.'

Gently he turned her to face him and started to undo the tiny pearl buttons down the front of her blouse. Each time his fingers touched her bare skin she flinched, afraid of the emotions raging through her. Would he think her wanton if he became aware of how she felt? Tenderly he eased the blouse off her shoulders, down her arms, and let it fall to the floor. All the while his eyes were seducing her, willing her to let herself go.

Although adequately covered she felt naked as his eyes examined the swell of her breasts above the fine lawn camisole. Then, following the directions of his hands, her skirt fell to the floor, soon to be joined by her petticoats. Bemused, she stepped out of them and allowed him to struggle with the hooks of her corset, even moving accommodatingly to help him, until at last only her stockings, drawers and camisole remained. Only when her breasts were free of the restricting camisole and his dark head lowered towards them did she react in dismay. Surely she should not be letting him do these things? Had she no modesty? What must he think of her?

'Shush, love. It's all right,' he soothed her. 'I promise not to hurt you . . .'

'Please, Paul. I need my nightdress.'

'Maggie, we're married. It doesn't matter that I can see you. We can do . . .'

There was panic in her voice as she pulled the camisole up over her breasts, insisting, 'Paul! I want my nightdress.'

He fought down the hot animal desire that her near naked body had aroused in him and drew a deep breath before saying, 'All right, Maggie. We'll do it your way. I unpacked your nightdress, it's on the bed.' He gave her a slight push towards the backroom door and, thankfully, she escaped into its comforting darkness.

Declining to light the candle, in the dim light from the window, she quickly removed her drawers, camisole and stockings. Naked, she groped about on the bed until her fingers encountered the silky feel of her nightdress. Willing Paul not to come until she was covered, she quickly pulled it over her head. Comforted as its long length covered her nudity, she crept into the big double bed and tried in vain to still her shaking limbs.

When Paul entered the room, he too stripped in the darkness and slipped into bed beside her. Naked! He drew her close, and feeling the maleness of him she cowered away, memories from her last year at school crowding into her mind. Shocked whispers of: 'It's awful! You feel as if you're being torn apart.' She wished her mother had spoken to her about these things but, no, not a word. Not one word!

'Maggie, I'm not goin' to hurt you. Trust me, love. Just let me hold you, and if you just want to sleep . . . well, that's all right with me. We've plenty of time. The rest of our lives. I'm content to wait,' he assured her, his voice soft and caressing, his hands gentle.

Relaxing against the warmth of his body, she confessed. 'I'm nervous, Paul. Sure you won't hurt me?'

'Never, Maggie.' His lips trailed her face, brushed her throat, her breasts. 'Never my love. If you say stop, I will.'

As he kissed and caressed her he only hoped he would not be put to the test. Would he be able to stop if she asked him to? The need for her was so deep. Would he be able to stop? He concentrated on making her aware of her sensuality, glad that it was not his first time. Grateful that Marie had taught him. Aye, and taught him well. As always, thoughts of Marie made him feel ashamed of his treatment of her, but then all rational thought fled as Maggie's response to his caresses sent his pulses racing. As a musician plays his favourite instrument, he slowly, sensuously, with long light strokes, played Maggie's body. Soon, the rhythm of the strokes had her moaning softly.

'Let yourself go, Maggie,' he urged her.

Her lips pressed tightly together and her head moved slowly from side to side.

'Why not?' he asked in bewilderment. 'Don't you love me?'

'The bed's creaking. Mollie will hear.'

A delighted gurgle of amusement was stifled on his lips as her hand covered his mouth, and to Maggie's dismay the bed creaked even louder as he tried to control his mirth.

'Ye see how it is, Maggie? It's creakin' an' I'm only laughin'.'

He felt her body move as she joined in his silent laughter and the bed creaked and groaned in reply. The laughter relaxed her and when he drew her close again, he knew she was his for the taking. He had sensed a deep sensuality in her and he had not been mistaken. Soon her shyness fled and when her hands reached for him, urging him on, returning caress for caress, Mollie was forgotten. In the darkness, all Maggie's inhibitions fled and after the first gasp of pain when he entered her, she gave her all, uncaring that the old bed creaked and groaned as they thrashed about on it, forgetful that Mollie was sleeping (hopefully) in the room below. All was forgotten in the joy of discovering the wonder of love, the delights of Paul's body, the wonderful sensations he was arousing. Every nerve edge was alive, crying out for fulfilment, and when at last he took her, it was on a wave of such passion that even Paul was full of awe. Never before had he experienced such gratification. It made him humble, and aware that love had to be present to create such wonder. Sex alone was just lust; an animal call of the body.

As they lay at peace, savouring the aftermath of the storm they had just experienced, he found himself praying that he would be able to make Maggie happy. That he would be able to make up to her for all that she had given up to become his wife.

Maggie squirmed sensuously, then rolling over on to her back she stretched contentedly. She felt so good! Her eyes opened and closed sleepily – only to open again as she gazed around the small cluttered room in surprise. Then,

28

as memories of the night before came rushing back, she knew why she felt so good and clasped the empty pillow beside her, hugging it.

'Where on earth is Paul?' Even as the thought entered her mind she heard him on the stairs, and fastened her eyes on the doorway to greet him. Feeling cool, she glanced down and was horrified to see that her breasts were bare. Spying her nightdress on the floor, she hurriedly scooped it up and hastily pulled it over her head, remembering with shame how eagerly she had helped Paul remove it the night before. Quick though she was, he was standing at the bedside when her head emerged from the neck of the nightdress, a tray in his hands, teasing laughter in his eyes.

'May I say you're lookin' very demure this mornin', Mrs Mason?'

To her dismay tears filled her eyes. She had acted like a wanton woman the night before; never in her life had she experienced such pleasure. Why, her body still tingled from the memory of it, but was a woman supposed to enjoy it? What about Paul? Was he disappointed in her? Had she been too forward? Did he want a demure wife?

At a loss to understand the different expressions flitting across her face and horrified to see the tears glistening in her eyes, Paul leant forward and whispered urgently, 'Maggie! Look at me!'

At last her eyes, big, grey and beautiful with the tears clinging on the thick lashes, met his, and he cried, 'What's wrong, love?'

She gulped before answering him, 'Do you want a demure wife?'

'Phew!' His breath came out on a sigh. 'You had me worried there! Maggie Mason, I love you, demure or wanton. Sad or happy. I love you so much, so very much, an' I'll do all in my power to make you happy. That's a promise, Maggie.'

Her smile was tremulous. 'Really, Paul? You're not disappointed in me?'

'Really, Maggie! Not even a tiny wee bit disappointed. I love you,' he answered solemnly, trying not to smile.

29

Their eyes met and they gazed enraptured at each other for a long moment, then Paul cried, 'Come on, woman, behave yourself or I'll be tempted t'miss Mass! Sit up an' enjoy the luxury of breakfast in bed.'

With a flirtatious smile, she sat up and, pulling the pillows up behind her back, took the tray on her knee.

'Don't be expectin' this every mornin, mind.' As he relinquished the tray he nodded down towards it. 'Most mornin's I don't have time t'bless meself.'

'Thank you, Paul. I'm starving.'

'Ah, that's what I like to hear. That's the sign of a contented woman. I'm away t'Mass, love. You have a lie in an' when I come back I'll bring you some water to bathe with.'

At the door he paused and then came back. 'Maggie?'

She looked up at him inquiringly.

'Thanks for havin' me,' he muttered, greatly embarrassed.

Overcome with emotion at his humility, she whispered, 'Ah, Paul. Sure I'm the happiest woman in Belfast today.'

'Only Belfast?' A smile tugged at the corner of his mouth and his eyes twinkled. 'I'll have to try harder t'night, so I will.' And with a deep chuckle, he left the room.

While she ate her breakfast Maggie relived the day before. Not the kind of wedding that she had dreamed about. No white dress and walking down the aisle on her father's arm to the strains of the organ. Instead a quick ceremony in the sacristy of the church by a priest who did not try to hide his disapproval. She would be forever grateful to Paul's family for the way they had tried to make the day a memorable one. His parents must have been disappointed, their oldest son marrying a Protestant, but they had rallied round. Although money was scarce, they had arranged a buffet lunch in their home and Bill, Paul's father, and his friend had produced fiddles. The reception had gone with a swing, to the sound of Irish reels. When she had tried to apologise for her quietness, Paul's mother,

Anne, had said sadly, 'Ah, daughter! Sure aren't you alone in a crowd of strangers? Never worry yer head about that.'

Her own parents' reception of her news entered her mind but she pushed it resolutely away. The doubts it had caused had vanished in the night when she had lain in Paul's arms. He loved her, that was all that mattered. Breakfast finished, she decided to fetch her own water to bathe and looked around for her dressing gown. At last she found it, still in the suitcase, and donning it, descended the stairs, tray in hand.

From her stand by the kitchen range, Mollie watched her. Noting the deep rose-coloured quilted dressing gown, she was dismayed. What was Paul thinking of, bringing a girl like Maggie to live on the Falls Road? The neighbours would have a field day when they saw all Maggie's finery. Especially Belle Hanna! She had been pushing her daughter Mary at Paul since he had come to live in Waterford Street, and although a presentable young man like him had been welcomed with open arms by the neighbours, a beauty like Maggie, and a Protestant at that, was a different matter. Jealousy would be rife and Maggie would suffer.

In spite of her misgivings, Mollie greeted her with a smile. 'You're lookin' better this mornin'. Here . . . gimme that tray.'

Clinging fiercely to it, Maggie cried, 'Oh, no, I'll wash these dishes, Mrs Grahame.'

'Not the day ye won't! This is your day off. An', remember, the name's Mollie. Did ye have a good night's sleep?'

Maggie relinquished the tray, and remembering the creaky bed, hot colour swept up her neck and reached her hairline.

'Yes. Yes, I did, thank you, Mollie.' Thinking that she detected a twinkle in Mollie's eyes, she hastened to add, 'Paul is right. He said you were kind.'

It was Mollie's turn to blush and she muttered, 'Away with ye.' And nodding towards a kettle hissing on the range, she added, 'You can have yon kettle of water to bathe with.'

When Maggie lifted the kettle and headed for the stairs, Mollie's voice stopped her in her tracks. 'Maggie?'

She turned, brows arched inquiringly and Mollie said hesitantly, 'I just want to say . . . well, I think you an' I'll get along all right.'

Smiling, Maggie replied, 'So do I, Mollie. If I should ever overstep the mark, please don't hesitate to tell me.' And she climbed the stairs wrapped in happiness. It was going to be all right.

Mollie watched her out of sight, a slight frown on her brow. She sensed that this young girl was a timid soul and feared she would not be able to stand up for herself when the neighbours started mimicking her. And mimic her they would, no doubt about that. If she was a poor waif they'd not be able to do enough for her, but all Maggie's finery would get their backs up. They would be eaten by jealousy, and she would suffer the consequences.

With a sigh Mollie carried the tray into the scullery. Well, they would have to get past her first and she was able for them. Hopefully, everything would pan out all right.

Upstairs, as Maggie washed herself down in the confined space, she wondered when she would next have a bath. Paul had informed her that there were public baths further down the Falls Road, which he used often, but somehow the idea of going into a public place to bathe did not appeal to her. However, Paul and Mollie were clean enough, and if they could manage, so could she.

'Still it won't be easy to adjust to,' she fretted. Then, remembering Paul's arms around her and the pleasures of the night before, she knew it would all be worthwhile.

CHAPTER TWO

The bright weather had returned and after lunch had been consumed Paul insisted that Maggie must come for a walk with him and view her new surroundings. She found that Waterford Street consisted of a row of identical houses, Mollie's being one of them. On the opposite side other streets ran off parallel to the Falls Road and emerged out on to the Springfield Road. Paul led her down one of these, Malcomson Street – named, he informed her, after a mill owner – and on the Springfield Road itself, pointed out to her some of the mills and factories that supplied employment for the neighbourhood. Not the thriving concerns they had been at the end of the last century, but still supplying work for many.

The Blackstaff was the biggest of the mills and facing it was Hughes Bakery, famous for its crusty baps, and beyond that the Springfield Linen Factory.

As she walked down the Springfield Road and then along the Falls Road, by Paul's side, Maggie was glad to find that the shops were not as drab and dingy as she had thought them the night before when it was raining. Indeed, she thought them quite presentable, with their owners advertising their wares with colourful posters for Colman's Mustard, Black Lead, Bovril and numerous other goods. She was honest enough to admit to herself that the great pleasure experienced the night before was probably colouring her view and with this thought she stole a glance at Paul, only to be thrown into confusion as she met his eyes. The smouldering passion she encountered sent the colour rushing to her cheeks and the blood racing in her veins. Paul laughed softly at her blushes and squeezed her arm possessively to his side.

It was the Dunville Park that surprised and pleased Maggie most. It was so unexpected! Sitting surrounded on two sides by terraced houses and on the other two sides by busy roads, it was an oasis of beauty. The rain-drenched trees that had depressed her so the previous night now rustled softly in the light breeze, they and the thick dark laurel bushes that enclosed them a picture to delight the eye. Lush green grass was dotted with huge colourful flower beds and there were two summerhouses where old men could be seen playing dominoes or dozing in the warm sun. At the bottom of the park there was an area for children to play, with swings and slides, and holding pride of place in the centre stood a maypole, with childrens winging on ropes attached to the handles. But it was the fountain, white and majestic, with water tumbling down from the mouths of gargoyles to be recycled in a continuous stream, that made Maggie stand in awe.

'It's lovely, Paul,' she said softly. 'So unexpected.' Then as her eyes strayed further afield, she gasped. 'And a house! Who lives there?'

'That, Maggie, is where the weighbridge master lives. Ye see, on market day you're more likely to get knocked down by a herd of cattle than a tram on the Falls Road, an' that's where they weigh in before goin' on down to the market. An' mind . . . you have to watch your step, 'cause they leave more than their hoofprints behind them, if you get me meanin'?'

With a twinkle in her eye she replied dryly, 'I had noticed.' And lifting her skirts high, displayed slim ankles while grimacing down at the stains on the toes of her boots.

'That'll teach you to look where you're walkin' in future,' Paul teased her, and was rewarded with an impish grin.

As they walked, he was aware of the admiring eyes of

the men and was pleased and happy, greeting one and all with remarks about the weather. In return the men agreed with him, and as they doffed their caps to Maggie, their eyes lingered on the beauty of her face.

For her part, Maggie was apprehensive because in spite of the nods of acknowledgement, she sensed that the women were unfriendly. Observing their dark serviceable skirts and shawls, she felt overdressed and uneasy in her finery, and vowed not to flaunt her beautiful clothes; she wanted to fit in here, to be accepted.

Suddenly it dawned on Paul that the road was crowded, even for a Sunday. Everyone seemed to be heading down towards the town. Where were they going? Then he remembered: the union leaders were holding a meeting today. In the excitement of his marriage, he had forgotten about it. Would Maggie go down with him?

'Maggie ... there's a meeting down-town today. A union meeting ... would you like to go down?'

Headlines from the newspapers flashed across Maggie's mind. Big Jim Larkin speaks to 20,000 people from the Custom House Steps ... The champion of the underdog forms unions of the dockers and carters. The dockers strike for more money ... The town almost at a standstill ...

'Is Big Jim Larkin speaking?'

'I imagine so.'

'Then let's go!'

Soon they were standing mesmerised as speaker after speaker urged the workers to stand firm.

'Fight for your rights! The cost of food has gone up ... we need more money ... a fair wage.' The most eloquent speaker being Big Jim, flamboyant in his ten-gallon hat.

Remembering her mother complaining about the rise in food prices, Maggie could sympathise with the low-paid workers. Her mother had more money to draw on. They had not.

'Do you know something, Maggie? This is history we're makin' here today. Imagine ... Catholics and Orangemen standing shoulder to shoulder fightin' for their rights! Wouldn't it be wonderful if we could all live and work together in harmony?'

Maggie agreed with him but remembering her father's comments about Big Jim, how he had to be stopped and Larkinism stamped out, and knowing that her father was speaking on behalf of many, she doubted if it could ever be.

In spite of her good intentions, her resolution not to let the neighbours worry her, Maggie found the weeks that followed long and tedious. She felt trapped in the small house and found going to the corner shop an ordeal because of the mocking courtesy extended to her. The walls of the house seemed to be closing in on her and she had nowhere to go to escape. She missed the garden at home where, weather permitting, she had sat daily. However, when Paul came home from work each night, her smile was bright and she assured him that she was happy . . . and in his arms she was.

Paul watched and silently applauded her as she strove to adapt to her new way of life. He realised how hard it must be for her and, glad that there was plenty of work in the building trade, as the town flourished and expanded, worked all the overtime he could get, saving every spare penny, determined to buy her a house of her own. Somewhere further up the Falls Road where she would fit in better. Up where the schoolteachers and professional people lived.

He had quickly become aware that Maggie was not being accepted in Waterford Street. She stuck out like a sore thumb in her fine clothes, even though she only wore the oldest of them, and her beauty did not help any. The women envied her and this made them unfriendly. Mollie shielded her all she could, accompanying her to the shops along the Falls Road and frowning down the amused looks, tinged with envy, that greeted them. She endeavoured to cover up the sniggers and snide remarks, but still Maggie suffered.

She discovered that her mother was right. Most of the

streets were like rabbit warrens and even narrower than she had at first thought. She hated the people of the Falls: hated the way they made fun of her, mimicking her behind her back. She found the narrow, dingy streets confining and the mucky cobbled sidewalks were ruining her boots and shoes. Although Mollie assured her that the people of the Falls were warm hearted and friendly and were just jealous of her finery, she did not believe her. Didn't she wear her oldest clothes so as to fit in? No . . . it was she herself that they disliked! Didn't she know that she was unlikeable? Had not her own family been glad to be rid of her? She was lucky to have met Paul. He was her life. During the night she clung to him fiercely, and her days were spent keeping the small house clean while Mollie worked in the mill – even getting down on her knees to scrub the stone floor, something she hated, but felt obliged to do. Not that Mollie expected it of her. Most mornings she managed to scrub the floor herself before going to work, and chastised Maggie for doing menial tasks. But though she disliked the work, it helped to pass the time for Maggie because she was lonely and bored and there was fear in her heart as she pictured the years ahead. Was she doomed always to be an outsider? A misfit?

As Christmas loomed near, Mollie watched her become more and more despondent. Deciding to make a suggestion, she waited until she and Maggie were alone.

'Look, Maggie, I know I shouldn't suggest it. Paul'll be angry at me, but . . .' Her voice trailed off and she bit on her lip. Was she doing the wrong thing? Should she mind her own business?

Needle poised above the piece of embroidery that she was working on, one of her few pastimes, Maggie looked up askance.

Deciding that she had gone too far to back down, Mollie continued, 'Would you not consider gettin' a part-time job?'

Amazement brought an incredulous look to Maggie's face at the question, knowing work in the mills was slack and that half the street was on short time.

'Sure the mills are laying people off,' she retorted, her surprise apparent.

Mouth gaping, Mollie threw her hands high in horror. 'No! Oh, my God, no! Not in the mill! Paul'd never hear tell of you workin' in the mill.' Seeing Maggie's amusement at her reaction, she laughed wryly, drew a deep breath and continued more quietly, 'They've been advertisin' for a part-time worker in the library for a while now an' can't get anybody suitable. An educated girl like you'd get started without any bother.'

Hope brightening her eyes, Maggie slowly straightened up in her chair. 'Oh, Mollie! Do you really think so?'

'I think ye would, but . . . would Paul let ye?'

'Oh!' Maggie slumped down in defeat; Paul would never agree. Then a determined look crossed her face as she straightened up again, her shoulders squared. 'I won't mention it to Paul until I see if they will start me. Then, if they do, I'll just have to make him let me go,' she declared.

Pleased at her enthusiasm, Mollie praised her. 'That's me girl! Never venture, never win. Go try yer luck tomorrow.'

Maggie did and returned aglow. She had got the job.

'No! I will not permit it!' Paul was tight-lipped and adamant when Maggie told him her news.

'Paul, it's just for four hours a day. Please, love. Please let me go.'

Overjoyed to have obtained work, she thought she would die if Paul forbade her to start, but he had his mule-headed look on his face and her heart sank when he cried, 'No! An' that's my last word on the subject.'

Opening her mouth to argue, she caught Mollie's shake of the head and warning look, and closed it again. She would try later when she and Paul were alone. She just had to make him change his mind. She just had to!

That night, as she lay in his arms, she again broached the subject. 'Paul . . . please let me take this job.'

'Ah, Maggie, drop it. It's against my principles. Why,

38

you've never worked in your life an' you're not startin' now.'

'Oh, yes, I have!' she cried.

He gazed at her in amazement. 'I didn't know you ever worked.'

Scrambling over him and out of bed, where she felt at a disadvantage, she stood with hands on hips, glaring at him.

'Oh, but I have! Dear me, I have! I worked from seven every morning until seven every night. And when William was a baby, I baby-sat most nights. Furthermore, I only received my keep and pocket money.' She paused for want of breath and became aware that he was smiling at her.

'You think that funny?' she asked, her eyes flashing green fire.

'You mean, you looked after the house for your parents?' From under raised brows his eyes twinkled and teased her.

Angrily stamping her foot, she asked in a carefully controlled voice, 'You don't call that working?'

'Hell, no, Maggie. Every woman does that.'

Hands still on her hips she leant forward, aware that the low neck of her nightdress gaped away from her body and he could see most of her full breasts, knowing that his desire for her always simmered and flared at the slightest provocation. For a moment she felt shame at the way she was using her body to help win her case, but then hardened her heart. Had not women used their wiles to get their own way since time began?

'Let me tell you something, Paul Mason. I could get a job as a housekeeper any day. Shall I try? Shall I? Just to prove I can.'

He reached out for her, his eyes on her breasts, a smile of anticipation on his lips, but she moved tantalisingly away, saying, 'Well? Answer me. Shall I try?'

The laughter faded from his face and he eyed her under narrowed lids. 'I think you're gettin' away from the point, Maggie. I don't want my wife to work at all.'

39

Her hands left her hips and she clasped them together in front of her. Was she fighting a losing battle?

'Why, Paul? Why? Because of your pride?' She thumped her breast with her fist. 'What about me, eh? Don't I count? I'm bored stiff here on my own all day. Every day the same as the one before.'

His face closed up and she knew she had hurt his pride. 'I beg your pardon. I didn't realise I was so borin',' he said gruffly, and rolling on his side, presented to her a back stiff with resentment.

Instantly she was back in bed, her arms around him, her voice pleading. 'Ah, Paul love, you know you don't bore me. It's just that I'm alone in the house all day, until Mollie comes home from work. The neighbours don't like me and I haven't any friends.'

Hearing the hint of tears in her voice, he slowly turned towards her. Fingers in her hair, he pulled her face close to his. 'The neighbours are jealous,' he whispered against her lips, and kissed her savagely. 'Ah, Maggie ... Maggie. I want to give you so much. So much! And one day I will. I'll buy you a fine house up the Falls. That's a promise!'

His lips trailed her face, her neck, the hollow between her breasts, in his slow sensuous journey of arousal. Biding her time, she returned kiss for kiss, caress for caress, until she knew that if she asked him for the moon he would try to get it for her. Then, still feeling a little ashamed, she whispered, 'Paul? Can I start in the library?'

Aware that he was being manipulated, he smiled wryly. 'Does it really mean so much to you?' And when she nodded vigorously, he crushed her close and she knew she had won.

Carnegie Library, built just a few years earlier, was situated on the Falls Road not far from Waterford Street. It was an imposing pale grey stone building, and Maggie loved the hushed atmosphere in which she worked. The old people had little education and she enjoyed helping them choose books that they would find easy to follow. Soon she had made friends with them. The days spent upstairs in the children's department were her happiest, though. Above all, she had no time to be bored and Paul and Mollie rejoiced to see her so contented.

Paul insisted that she keep her small wage every week so she saved it, determined to make their first Christmas together a happy one.

Mollie planned to spend Christmas Day at the home of her youngest son Brian, and Boxing Day with her other son Bob. This festive season once again awakened longings in her to know what had become of her oldest son and Maggie listened patiently, as yet again she recalled how he had left home one Christmas when he was only seventeen to go to England to make his fortune. Apparently he had kept in touch for some years and Mollie knew he had married and had a son, but since then silence. Convinced he was dead, she mourned for him, her first born, her darling Barney.

Paul's parents had invited them to join the family for their Christmas dinner and although Maggie was glad there was a small corner of her heart grieving because her own family was ignoring her. Even William had not paid the promised visit. Before they'd had a chance to send for Maggie's personal belongings, her mother had packed them and forwarded them to her, causing Paul to remark dryly, 'She's afraid we'll send the coalman's cart for them.'

Picturing the coalman's old shaggy horse and dirty cart trundling up the driveway to rattle to a halt at her parents' home, Maggie had to laugh. Thus she was able to hide from Paul the deep pain she felt at how quickly her parents were washing their hands of her. She had to admit her mother had been generous. As well as Maggie's personal effects, she had sent the bedroom carpet, the bed linens, the oil lamp, and the writing bureau her father had bought her for her twenty-first birthday, causing raised eyebrows and envious looks from the neighbours as they were unloaded from the huge van. But after their arrival, silence. It was as if she was dead. Indeed, her father probably thought of her as dead. How could she have been so foolish to think that her parents would accept Paul?

If only they would give him a chance! She knew that they could not fail to like him. What did it matter that he was a Catholic? But in her heart she knew that it did matter, it mattered very much. A few days after her marriage, she had read a small paragraph in the newspaper about it. Just a short passage, with the bare details. No mention of where the marriage had taken place, nothing to indicate a rift with her family, and she knew that her father had arranged for the passage to be printed. This way, most people would think that her parents had agreed to the wedding and reporters would not be raking about for scandal.

Oh, yes, her father was a resourceful man. He had to be admired for that at least. From the newspapers she later learnt that he had retained his seat on the council and for this she was grateful. She was glad that her marriage had not spoilt things for him, had not interfered with his ambitions. In her heart she wished that things had been different; that she and Paul could visit her home and that her father could have helped Paul to obtain a better job. But, alas, it was obviously not to be, so she must make the best of what she had.

A week before Christmas, with her savings, Maggie bought good presents for Paul's family. Not too expensive, that would only embarrass them, but good. She wanted to show her appreciation for their kindness to her. On Christmas Eve, attending midnight Mass in St Paul's Church with him, she had to admit that the ceremony was beautiful but was glad that Paul put no pressure on her to become a Catholic. She felt uneasy praying to statues and thought that if Catholics really believed God was present in the tabernacle, why were they not more respectful in His presence?

Christmas Day dawned and they awoke to a glittering wonderland. Thick white frost covered the rooftops and lamp posts, just like icing on a cake, and Paul reacted like a young boy.

'Let's walk through the park, Maggie. Eh, love? Sure it'll be like fairyland on a day like this,' he cried, agog with excitement. 'We can catch the tram at the lower stop at Sorella Street.'

Maggie laughingly agreed. Packing the presents into a holdall, they set off in high spirits. She was glad to see Paul so cheerful. He had been so depressed lately because work had been at a standstill for six days on account of the frosty weather. He was worried in case they had to dip too deeply into their savings; his determination to move further up the Falls being stronger than ever. Now that Maggie was working and some of the neighbours, if not exactly friendly, at least acknowledged her, she was content to stay in Waterford Street, but nothing she said could deter Paul. His mind was made up.

As he walked down the road, the cobble stones on the pavement being slippy with frost, Paul was as proud as punch to have Maggie clinging to his arm. Today, in honour of the occasion, she was wearing her finery. Her slim figure was shown off to advantage in a pale grey soft wool suit, the three-quarter length jacket trimmed with fur while she carried a matching fur muff. On her head sat a hat, tilted so much to the front Paul thought it was sure to fall off, in spite of the hat-pins that anchored it. It was also pale grey, with a wide brim and a profusion of white feathers on top. He was well aware of the envy of the men in the district since he had brought Maggie there as his bride, and he knew it was jealousy and fear that kept the women from offering her their friendship. Looking down into the heavily lashed eyes, which were taking their colour from the pale grey of her hat and shining like diamonds, and noting the transparent sheen of her skin and bright copper blaze of her hair, he did not blame them for their caution.

The park did have a fairytale appearance. A snow cap covered each gargoyle's head in the fountain and icicles hung like fangs from their mouths. High in the sky a weak sun teased all the colours of the rainbow from the frost-covered trees, and the stiff frozen grass crunched under their feet as they left the path to go close to the fountain. Rosy-cheeked children, eyes bright with excitement, laughed and played. Seeing them, Maggie pondered about the slight feeling of nausea she had experienced the past couple of mornings. Was she pregnant? She turned to confide her thoughts to Paul but he stopped suddenly in his tracks and nudged her. Following the direction of his gaze she saw an old man sitting on one of the park benches.

'Ah, Maggie, look at him. Poor aul soul.'

The man's coat was threadbare and he had the collar pulled up around his bare scrawny neck. He was sitting, shoulders hunched up against the cold, staring blankly in front of him with red-rimmed eyes, and there was an air of despair and hopelessness about him.

'It's not right, Maggie, so it's not. That anyone should be in such need. Tut! Especially on Christmas mornin'. Wait here for me, love. I won't be a minute.'

Leaving her standing at the fountain, the holdall at her feet, he headed back up towards Waterford Street. Resigned, Maggie stood still, taking in the beauty of the scene around her. She was used to Paul's impulsive generosity. He was forever taking things into work to someone in need. Things that still had plenty of wear left in them. But she had not the heart to rebuke him. She wondered what he would bring down to give the old man – probably his second best coat, an ulster.

She was right: when he returned he had the coat over his arm and, approaching the old man, offered it to him. Tired old eyes looked at Paul blankly, then realising he was being given the coat, the man rose stiffly to his feet and without taking his eyes off Paul (perhaps afraid he and the coat would disappear), started to unbutton his coat. Watching Paul help him discard his own coat and don the warm ulster, Maggie's heart swelled with pride. And when Paul removed his muffler and wound it gently around the man's neck, she thought her heart would burst.

Embarrassed at the pride in Maggie's eyes when he rejoined her, Paul blushed fiercely, and when the old man shouted after him, 'May yer goodness be returned a hundredfold!' he laughed and jested, 'What would I do with a hundred coats, eh, Maggie?'

She reached up, eyes glowing with love, and pulled the collar of his coat up around his bare neck. 'No doubt you would soon find a worthy cause for them,' she chided, and her hands gently touched his face. 'But you could do with a muffler. Do you realise that was your only one?'

He pulled her close. 'He needs it more than me, Maggie.' His look became anxious as he held her gaze. 'You don't mind me givin' it to him, do ye?'

Smiling, she shook her head. 'No, no. But . . . let's not waste any more time. If we miss the early tram we might miss the train and I don't fancy waiting an hour in the cold, draughty station for the next one.'

Hearing the clatter of the tram approaching, Paul gripped her hand. Swinging the holdall high, he raced her down the park to arrive, breathless and laughing, at the corner of Sorella Street just in time to board it.

The Masons lived at Sydenham, some miles along the coast, and when the train drew into the station there, they found the twelve-year-old twins waiting for them. Different as chalk from cheese, the twins were dressed in what were obviously new clothes. Jean, tall and willowy, was dressed in a long skirt with a sailor top and a bonnet covering her dark brown curly hair. Sean, small and wiry, had on a bright red jumper which Maggie guessed had probably been knitted by their mother as Paul was always saying how gifted she was, and a pair of knickerbockers.

'This is a surprise!' Maggie greeted them. 'Have you been waiting long?'

'No, we reckoned you'd be on this train,' Jean answered. Her eyes were anxious as, nodding downwards, she asked. 'Do you like me new boots?'

Maggie examined the small black boots with the buttons along the sides and said gravely, 'They are beautiful. The latest thing in fashion. You're a very lucky girl.'

This brought a beam of delight to Jean's face. She had not been too sure about the boots, but if Maggie thought they were fashionable – well, if anybody would know, she would!

Sean was hanging on Paul's arm. Knowing that his brother longed to be tall, Paul lifted the cap from his mop of unruly curls. Ruffling them, he cried, 'My, but you've grown inches since I last saw you.'

Big blue eyes filled with delight as Sean beamed up at him. 'Really, Paul? Really? You mean that?'

Before he could reply Jean chirped in, 'Oh, don't be silly! He's just sayin' that to please ye. Ye can't grow inches in a couple of weeks, so you can't.'

Sean's face fell and his bottom lip trembled. Full of compassion, Maggie put her arm around his shoulders and drew him on ahead. 'You have plenty of time to grow,' she consoled him. 'Why, my brother is just starting to shoot up now and he's sixteen.' A pain ached inside of her as she wondered how tall William would have grown before she saw him again. Would she ever see him again?

'I'm only twelve,' Sean confided sadly. Sixteen seemed so far away.

Maggie hugged him. 'You've plenty of time and I think you'll be tall.' She quirked an eyebrow and smiled down at him. 'Do you know why I think that?'

He shook his head, his eyes hopeful.

'Because you have long legs.'

His eyes left her face and examined his own legs. 'They are long, aren't they?' he agreed in surprise, and was happy again.

Walking behind them, Paul was chastising Jean. 'That was an unkind thing to say.'

'Tut! He sickens me! He's always goin' on about his height. Who cares how tall he is?'

'He does! If you were small, madam, you'd probably be whingin' about your height, an' remember, you have heels on your boots,' Paul scolded her.

A scowl on her face, Jean walked in tight-lipped silence, head bent, examining her new button boots. 'I suppose you're right,' she muttered at last. 'I'm sorry.'

'Don't tell me, tell Sean,' Paul ordered.

'Sean!' she shouted after him and when he turned, she said humbly, 'I'm sorry.'

'It's all right,' Sean grinned back at her. His good humour restored by Maggie, he was forgiving.

Pushing the holdall into Jean's hands, Paul warned, 'Be careful with that, mind. It contains presents.'

A happy grin split her face in two as she hauled the magic bag up on to the crook of her arm, and it was a merry party that Anne opened the door to and ushered into the kitchen.

This kitchen was larger than the one in Waterford Street. The stairs were not in the kitchen itself but separated it from the scullery which was spacious enough to hold a table and six chairs. This was where the family dined.

'Isn't it awful cold, Maggie? Here, gimme yer coat.'

Anne hung Maggie's coat on a rack at the foot of the stairs and then turned to the dark, handsome young man seated by the side of the fire.

'Brendan! Let Maggie sit on that chair near the fire. Sure she's frozen, so she is!'

Brendan, second eldest of the family and best man at their wedding, rose obligingly, and with a smile of thanks Maggie sat down.

'Mary, make a cup of tea,' Anne ordered her eldest daughter. 'Emma! You help her. Brendan, fetch more coal in.' Her eyes landed on Jean who was rummaging in Maggie's bag and her voice rose shrilly. 'Jean! What on earth are ye doin'?'

Startled, she drew back, crying plaintively, 'It's presents, Mam.'

'Leave it 'till after dinner,' Anne ordered with a reproving look. 'An' then let Maggie unpack it,' she warned, before turning to her. 'You shouldn't have, Maggie. You savin' for your own house an' all.'

'I'm glad to be able to,' Maggie answered, smiling happily. She thought Paul's family were lovely. So friendly and unassuming.

'I'll just see what's keepin' the tea. Ye need something

47

to warm ye up, so ye do.' And with these words, Anne bustled into the scullery.

Bill, who had been watching his wife with a twinkle in his eye, leant forward, elbow on knee, towards Maggie, 'Now you know why I'm so quiet.' His head swayed from side to side. 'I never get a word in edgeways, so I don't. She talks from when she gets up in the mornin' 'til she goes t'bed at night. Mind you, I'm a good listener!' His hand rose and a finger patted the air. 'You mark my words! So if you ever need an ear to pour your troubles in, come t'me.'

His voice was full of love and affection for his wife and Maggie laughed softly, saying, 'I'll remember.'

Later, dinner was served in the other room and the table, which was decorated with candles and crackers, was weighed down with food.

Bill waved a hand at the table. 'All in your honour, Maggie. We'll be fed on the leavings for the rest of the week.'

'Don't heed him!' Anne cried in dismay. Then seeing the twinkle in his eye she wrinkled her nose and added, 'I hope I haven't overdone it, but we were flush this week. Ye see, Brendan got overtime . . . plucking turkeys, ye know! An' the boss gave him a turkey for me. Imagine! A twelve-pounder it was! Wasn't that kind of him? An' Emma was taken on at the shirt factory, so all in all we're rich. Different from last Christmas . . . then we hadn't tuppence t'rub together.'

The meal was delicious and Maggie solemnly conveyed her compliments to the chef, causing Anne to blush with pleasure. Then the three girls washed the dishes, declining Maggie's offer to help, shy Emma informing her, 'Mam would kill us if we let you help.'

And then the moment that Jean and Sean had been waiting for impatiently, arrived. It was time to open the presents.

Maggie was glad she had been able to buy good presents, they gave such pleasure. She in turn was delighted with the pale green shawl Anne had crocheted for her, fine as cobwebs, soft as silk.

'It's lovely.' Draping it around her shoulders, she dropped her cheek against its softness and repeated, 'Just lovely. Thank you very much. There must be hours of work here.'

'I'm glad you like it,' Anne replied, enjoying her pleasure; glad that Maggie appreciated just how much time had been spent on it.

With a deep chuckle, Paul held aloft for Maggie's inspection the muffler that Brendan had bought for him. 'I hope I don't get another ninety-nine,' he jested.

They smiled at each other, sharing their private joke. Maggie could see that Brendan was puzzled at their reaction to the muffler and hastened to reassure him. 'It's lovely, Brendan. Just what he needs.'

When his eyes fastened on hers, Brendan found himself unable to look away. Her eyes were a clear green now and he knew for a fact that they were usually grey because he admired her very much. Too much for his peace of mind. Since meeting her, he found himself often dwelling on thoughts of her beauty. She was the loveliest girl he had ever seen, and he envied Paul.

He stared so long that Maggie wriggled, uncomfortable under his scrutiny. Becoming aware of her unease, he was quick to apologise. 'I'm sorry for starin', Maggie, but your eyes have changed colour an' I'm fascinated,' he admitted with an admiring smile.

To her dismay, this brought everyone's attention to her and Anne exclaimed, 'Why, so they have! Well, I never. A minute ago they were grey an' now they're green.'

Paul grinned at Maggie's discomfiture but came to her rescue. 'Maggie's eyes can change to many colours. I think there's a bit of the witch in her,' he confided. 'How else do you think she snared me, eh?' His gaze too was admiring and he laughed aloud as her embarrassment deepened.

Although it was a dark afternoon, the sky laden with snow, they sat by firelight recalling former Christmases and making Maggie laugh. This warm, happy atmosphere was dispelled by a knock on the door. Brendan exchanged a worried look with Bill before going to open it and Anne threw Paul an apprehensive glance.

'Why, hello, Marie,' they heard Brendan say. 'Come on in.'

Hearing Anne mutter, 'Oh, my God,' under her breath, Maggie turned to Paul to ask who Marie was and why everyone was so concerned. She was disconcerted to find his raking away at the fire and studiously avoiding her eyes. Mentally alert, she watched the doorway.

The girl who entered the room, shrugging out of her coat, was tall and blonde. Her hair was done in the latest fashion of rolls and curls and she wore a skirt with a corselet waistband which showed off her small waist to advantage and brought attention to the full bust that strained at the buttons of the high-necked, lace-trimmed blouse she wore. The skirt had a peplum and this swelled out over her slim hips and then in at the thighs. Maggie had to admit that she certainly had a good figure. As she stretched to remove her hat, all eyes were on her and a pleased smile settled on her wide sensuous mouth. She took her time removing the hat and then stretched once more to place it on the very top of the dresser before turning her attention to the group around the fire.

'Come an' meet Paul's wife,' Anne greeted her and beckoned her forward. 'Maggie, this is Marie Collins, an old friend of the family.'

Rising to her feet, Maggie cordially extended her hand and said politely, as she had been taught to, 'How do you do?'

'Oh . . . very well, thank you.'

Limp fingers rested briefly in Maggie's hand then were quickly withdrawn, and pale blue eyes gazed into hers, causing her to blink in confusion at the venom she saw.

'How're you, Paul?' Marie's voice was sweet and coy when she addressed him, causing Maggie to frown. There was something not quite right here. Who was this girl, and why had Paul never mentioned her?

'I'm great, Marie. Never better.' He rose, offering the

girl his chair, but pushing him down again she perched on the arm, placing her hand familiarly on his shoulders and ruffling the hair on the nape of his neck.

Face ablaze with colour, Paul still avoided Maggie's eyes. He sensed Marie was in a mischievous mood and hoped she would not say anything incriminating. Maggie watched him, resentment mounting in her breast as still he avoided her eye. An awkward silence prevailed, no one seeming to know how to break it until Sean rushed in. He had been outside trying out the roller skates Maggie had bought him. When he entered the kitchen, Marie held out her arms and cried, 'How's my favourite boy?'

Running to her in all innocence he cried, 'Hello, Marie! I didn't think you'd come today, now our Paul's married.'

With a triumphant look at Maggie, she replied, 'Oh, but sure . . . Paul an' I are still good friends. Aren't we, Paul?'

Long slim fingers tipped with bright red nail polish ruffled his hair affectionately and Paul was forced to nod in reply. He was afraid to look in Maggie's direction; afraid to see her reaction. That was when the penny dropped and Maggie chided herself for not seeing the truth sooner. Obviously Paul and Marie had been close friends, that was why everyone was on tenterhooks. But how close had they been? She had guessed she was not the first woman Paul had taken, but to be in the same room as someone who had done that with him turned her stomach and filled her with unease. For the first time since they had met Paul was evasive, afraid to meet her eye. The easy, smiling harmony that had flowed between them all day had evaporated when this girl entered the room. Where was the simmering passion now? Where were the warm possessive glances? Had she cause for alarm?

Marie gave Sean a playful push towards the hall. 'Fetch my bag in. I have some presents in it.' Then she casually draped her arm around Paul's shoulders again, seeming pleased when he squirmed uncomfortably.

Hoping that no one would light the gas mantle and display her discomfort, Maggie sat wrapped in misery. The joy had gone out of the day for her and she was

51

desperately worried. It was obvious that this girl was very fond of Paul. Did he return the affection? How come he had never mentioned her? If he and this girl had been so close, why had he not married her? Unbidden, her father's words came to mind: 'Do you think for one minute he would bother with you if you were a poor Protestant from the Shankill Road?' Her mouth twisted cynically in the dim light. Well, if he had married her for money, he had been sadly disappointed. She had believed him when he vowed that he was not interested in her father's money. He had seemed sincere. Had love blinded her?

She was so deep in thought that she lost track of the conversation and with a start of surprise realised that they were all looking at her, expecting her to speak. 'I beg your pardon! I'm afraid I was wool gathering. Have I missed something?'

Speaking loudly, pronouncing her words roundly in obvious imitation of Maggie, Marie said, 'I was asking if you liked the nightshirt I have bought for Paul? If you do not, I can have it exchanged for something else.'

Maggie's stomach seemed to fall, sending a sick feeling all through her. She knew the neighbours in Waterford Street mocked her and it hurt, but this was the first time anyone had done so to her face. This girl was cruel. What had Maggie done for her to be so cutting? Suddenly, she realised what she had done. She had married Paul. At a loss for words, she tried to find something cutting to say in reply, but it was not in her nature to be deliberately rude, so she tried in vain.

'At the moment Paul doesn't wear anything in bed. Perhaps when he's older it will come in handy.'

She was just speaking the truth, but Bill quickly produced a handkerchief to hide a smile and Brendan gave her the thumbs up sign behind Marie's back. Somehow, she had given the right answer.

However, Marie Collins had come prepared for battle and this was too good a chance to miss. Paul would be annoyed with her. Well, let him be, she thought angrily; she did not owe him any consideration. He had let her down. Imagine sending her a letter! He deserved to be worried. Running her fingers caressingly down his cheek, she said coyly, 'Oh, how stupid of me to forget a thing like that.'

There was a ghastly silence and Maggie felt the colour leave her face as the implication of the words sank in. The silence dragged on, Paul biting on his lip as he tried to find something to say to fill the awful gap.

It was Anne who rescued him. Rising hastily to her feet, she broke the silence. 'I'll make some tea. Come help me, Maggie.'

Grateful to escape the charged atmosphere in the kitchen, and the pictures that would not be banished from her mind – pictures of Marie's and Paul's naked bodies entwined – Maggie followed her into the scullery. Silently, she prepared the cups while Anne cut up turkey and cheese, and buttered home-made griddled bread.

'He never told you about Marie.'

It was a statement but Maggie answered Anne sadly. 'No, just what should I know?'

'He should have told you hisself! It's not my place t'say,' Anne wailed.

'Well, he didn't! Please tell me, Anne, before I go back in there.'

'Well . . .' Anne's reluctance was obvious and Maggie pleaded.

'Well, all right. He went with Marie for about a year. We all expected them to get engaged but then . . .' she gestured vaguely in Maggie's direction. 'We all thought it would be a flash in the pan between you an' him, you being a Protestant an' all. But no! Next he astounded us by sayin' he was gettin' married. Marie was upset when she heard . . .' Anne's mouth twisted in a grimace as she recalled the scene enacted the previous year. 'Very upset. Bill an' I ranted on at him for wastin' her time, but he was adamant! Told us in no uncertain terms t'mind our own business. Said you two were meant for each other.' Her shoulders rose in a shrug. 'An' that was that.'

At these revelations, Maggie was so agitated her hands

shook. While she and Paul had been courting, all this had been going on in the background, and she had never guessed. Was there anything else she should know? Any more unsavoury secrets?

Reaching for Maggie's shaking hands, Anne gripped them tightly in hers. 'He should have told you, not let ye find out like this,' she whispered sympathetically. 'But . . . d'ye know something? He was right. Ye are meant for each other. I've never seen him so happy.'

'She's so lovely! How can he prefer me?' Maggie wailed, close to tears.

Anne shook her roughly. 'Lovely she may be, but *you* are beautiful an' don't you forget it.'

Maggie smiled wanly. She was not beautiful; Anne was being kind.

'Were you disappointed when he stopped seeing her?' she asked.

Looking sheepish, Anne admitted, 'To be truthful, yes, we were. She's a Catholic, ye see, an' your da bein' who he is – well, we thought our Paul was makin' a fool of his self. We thought he'd get hurt but we were wrong, I'm glad t'admit, an' I'm glad he married you.'

'Thank you, Anne.'

With an impulsive gesture, she pulled Maggie into her arms and hugged her fiercely. 'Don't let her upset ye, Maggie. That's why she's here! To upset you.' She pushed her back so that she could see into her eyes. 'Sure you won't let her get under your skin?'

When Maggie shook her head, Anne examined her face intently. Not quite satisfied with what she saw, she nevertheless nodded. 'Good! Come on, let's pour the tea or they'll be comin' lookin' for us. An' remember – chin up.'

Paul gave Maggie a rueful smile when she returned to the kitchen, but for the life of her she could not return it. If only she was sure of his love she could have laughed at the way this girl was fawning all over him, but Maggie's self-confidence was shaken. Paul himself was so uneasy, so evasive. He had never acted like this before. Marie still sat perched on the arm of his chair, her hip and breast touching his body, and Maggie felt resentful. He didn't have to sit there. He could get up, couldn't he? Of course he could! But if he was enjoying himself why move?

She retreated within herself, ignoring Marie's efforts to engage her in conversation. What did she want to know of the happy times Paul had shared with this girl? Paul watched her closely, but it was Maggie's turn to refuse to meet his eyes. He noted the closed face, the tight lips, and grew resentful. Marie was a family friend and Maggie had no right to ignore her like this. This was his mother's house. No matter how she might feel, Maggie should be civil to Marie under his parents' roof. What would his family think of her?

Maggie was beyond caring what anyone thought of her. She longed to be alone, to examine the thoughts that troubled her. Time dragged and as Marie droned on and on, Maggie felt like screaming. She was sure Paul was comparing them and finding her wanting. This girl had everything . . . looks and personality. Tears formed a hard lump in Maggie's throat as she listened to her teasing Paul. Surely the clock must have stopped? It must be later than half-three. How things had slowed down since this unpleasant girl had arrived.

Each of the family at different times tried to stop Marie's chatter, but in vain. She had come to make Maggie suffer and she intended to do just that. Hadn't Maggie stolen Paul away from her? At last, when Maggie thought she could bear it no longer, Marie rose and stretched and the three men eyed her figure avidly, bringing a satisfied smile to her lips. She kissed them all, even managing to plant a kiss on a reluctant Maggie's cheek. However, the relief Maggie was experiencing at her departure was short-lived, because when she was ready to go, turning to Paul, Marie asked sweetly, 'Will you walk me home?'

He saw Maggie's start of dismay, heard her indrawn breath, but hardened his heart. She had been behaving like a child, sitting there sulking! Marie had been so friendly towards her and she had been standoffish. Marie would think he had married a snob. Anyhow, he owed it to Marie to see her home. He owed her an apology. He had treated her shabbily and she was being very nice about his marriage and he wanted to make his peace with her.

Maggie anxiously awaited his reply. Her heart contracted when, avoiding her eyes, he agreed. 'Of course, Marie.'

Pulling on his coat, he avoided Maggie's look of entreaty and ushered a triumphant Marie out on to the street. An embarrassed hush fell on the room when the door closed on them. Maggie's eyes were full of tears that she was afraid would fall and she hated the pity that she could feel flowing like a wave from the Masons.

Unable to bear the pain, she mumbled, 'Excuse me,' and hurried through the scullery, out into the yard. Tears blurred her vision. When at last she sat in the wee house, hugging herself for comfort, the tears fell. What was she to do? Her tortured thoughts shifted about, seeking a way out of her dilemma. Did Paul love Marie? Had it been Maggie's father's money he was after? Oh surely not! They had been so happy. Correction, *she* had been so happy. Perhaps Paul had just been making the best of a bad job. After all, he could not change things now. Did seeing Marie make him realise how much he had lost? Did he still love her?

Maggie rocked back and forth, trying to stop the flow of her tears, knowing she must face the Masons again. At last anger took over from despair. Drying her face, she strove for control of her emotions. First she must go back inside and pretend that she did not care that Paul was away with Marie. Tears threatened to fall again at the very idea of it, but she fought them back. She dreaded facing the Masons and if there had been another way out she would have left by that way, even without a coat and with indoor shoes on her feet. But there was not. A high brick wall separated the houses from the back of those on the next street so there was no escape. Wiping still more offending tears from her face, she squared her shoulders and entered the scullery.

As she stood at the jawbox bathing her burning eyes, Mary came and placed a box of face powder beside her.

'Our Paul's a fool, so he is! He doesn't know when he's well off.' She gave Maggie a sympathetic pat on the shoulder. Gratefully, Maggie opened the powder box and with the puff, patted the powder around her eyes.

'How do I look?'

'You'll pass.' Mary smiled at her, but inwardly she was cursing her brother. 'They're still sittin' by firelight. We're an understandin' family, us Masons,' she jested. 'Come on in.' And with another encouraging smile, she led the way out of the scullery.

Brendan pushed a chair closer to the fire when Maggie entered the kitchen. 'Sit here, Maggie,' he said kindly, endeavouring to breach the awkwardness. 'You must be frozen.'

He was angry with his brother. Had Paul not been able to see how hurt Maggie was? It was so unlike him to be unkind. Surely he didn't still fancy Marie? Granted she was attractive in a common sort of way, and people were funny, wanting what they couldn't have. Paul had practically lived with Marie until Maggie came on the scene, but still he'd seemed so besotted with his wife.

'I suppose you thought I was away to Greencastle,' Maggie said dryly. Greencastle being on the far side of the lough from Sydenham, the tension was broken and they all laughed.

The crack was good as they kept Maggie regaled with scandal and gossip from the past, and it was with surprise that she noted it was now half-past seven. Paul had been away over two hours! Tears welled up again but she fought them back and reached for her boots, thanking Mary for the loan of her indoor shoes.

'What are you doin'?' Anne cried in dismay.

'I'm going home.'

'Ah, Maggie, ye can't go without Paul!' Agitated, Anne rose to her feet and offered her remedy for all ails. 'Have another cup of tea, Maggie. I was waitin' for Paul t'come before I made it.'

Smiling wanly, Maggie shook her head. Tea would choke her. Could they not see that her heart was breaking?

'Ye can't go home alone. Please wait for Paul,' Anne pleaded.

Brendan, furious at the way Paul was treating Maggie, came to a decision. 'She's not goin' alone. I'm goin' with her.'

Maggie shot him a startled glance. 'Oh, no! Really! I can't allow it. I'll be all right.'

Brendan bobbed up and down in front of her, fists in the air, trying to tease a smile from her. 'Come on now,' he jested. 'Try an' stop me . . . just try an' stop me.'

'Wait another wee while, Maggie.' Anne was wringing her hands in her anguish and sending pleading glances to Bill.

Trying to be of help, he joined in her pleas. 'He can't be much longer Maggie. Will ye not wait?'

Again she shook her head and, buttoning her coat, reached for her hat.

'She's waited long enough, Ma.' Brendan donned his coat and wound a muffler around his neck. 'Come on, Maggie, let's go.' And swinging the holdall over his shoulder, he led the way to the door.

Hugging her close, Bill whispered in her ear, 'Just wait 'til I see our Paul, I'll give him a piece of me mind, so I will. You're too good for him, so ye are.'

Anne was almost in tears, 'Are you sure you'll be all right, Maggie?'

'Of course she'll be all right,' Mary cried indignantly. 'Isn't Brendan goin' with her?'

Shy Emma hugged her sympathetically and the twins came tumbling down the stairs to bid her farewell. It was time to leave and still no sign of Paul. He must really be enjoying himself when he was willing to miss the eight-thirty train. The next was at eleven, meaning he would miss the last tram up the Grosvenor Road and have to walk from the station to Waterford Street.

Perhaps he won't come home tonight, Maggie fretted,

torturing herself with thoughts of Marie and Paul, alone somewhere, making love.

During the walk to the station, Brendan kept her occupied with tales about the customers who came into the butcher's shop where he worked, trying to chase the shadows from her eyes, but in vain.

Although she nodded and smiled, he noticed that her eyes were full of sorrow, and his anger against his brother grew. How could he treat a lovely girl like Maggie in this manner? He needed his head examined! Why, if she was his wife, he would look at no other.

They were sitting facing each other in the train, with just minutes to spare, when the carriage door burst open and Paul fell at their feet. With a look full of contempt, Brendan left him to struggle upright unaided. Bending he cupped Maggie's face in his hands and kissed her full on the lips. It was meant to be a brief kiss but in spite of himself it lingered on and on, his mouth leaving hers to return again and yet again. Mesmerised, Maggie sat wide-eyed and breathless with surprise until Paul's muttered, 'Hey . . . knock it off!' brought Brendan back to reality.

'That'll give him something to think about,' he whispered in her ear, and left the train without another glance in Paul's direction. Little did he know but it was to give him a lot to think about also and the memory of the kiss was to spoil him for any other girl.

Paul kept his eyes on Maggie's face during the short journey to Belfast, willing her to look at him; wishing the carriage was empty so that he could make his peace with her. She refused to look in his direction and gazed blindly out of the window. And noting the hurt, vulnerable look on her face, he was ashamed.

The short journey to Belfast seemed endless and when at last the train drew into Great Victoria Street station, Maggie hurried off, leaving Paul to collect the holdall from the rack. Trailing behind her to the tram stop at the bottom of the Grosvenor Road, he grew resentful. What had he done wrong? Nothing! Absolutely nothing! He had not had any choice. Surely Maggie should understand that? Marie was an old family friend and it would have been churlish to refuse to walk her home. Why, his da had been wrong to tick him off the way he had! As for Brendan, what on earth had gotten into him, kissing Maggie like that? And she hadn't objected. By God, no! Not one word of rebuff. In fact, she had seemed to enjoy it. He was the one who should be angry, and there was Maggie in the huff!

They travelled home, each locked in their own bitter thoughts and when they entered the house Maggie went straight up the stairs, grateful that Mollie was away from home. Pushing the poker into the centre of the banked down fire, Paul set it aglow. He pushed the already hot kettle from the side of the range onto the glowing embers to boil while he unpacked the holdall.

As he handled the presents he remembered the laughter and happiness they had all shared before the arrival of Marie, and the feeling of shame returned. He had to admit he could have asked Brendan to walk Marie home. What had got into him? First fear of what Marie might say had kept him by her side, then he had been flattered by all the attention she showered on him. God forgive him, he had even enjoyed the fact that Maggie was obviously jealous. Imagine showing off in front of her! What would he have done if the positions had been reversed and Maggie had played up to another man? He would have blown his top, that's what he would have done, he had to admit. Maggie had every right to be angry. Their first Christmas together and he had spoilt it. How could he have been so stupid?

Brewing a pot of tea, he set two cups on a tray with a plate of biscuits and headed for the stairs – to come to an abrupt halt. At the foot lay a pillow and some blankets. He stared in disbelief, then banged the tray down on the table with such force that the tea splashed all over. He took the stairs two at a time.

'There'll be none of this nonsense,' he vowed. 'No woman is goin' to keep me from my bed. By God, no!'

Outside the back bedroom door he paused, hand on the doorknob, his anger evaporating. What would he accomplish by breaking in? Probably a slanging match! And that would only make things worse. With a sigh, he swung on his heel. If Maggie didn't want him, so be it. He was not going to ask for any favours. By God, no! He had his rights and Maggie was lucky that it was against his nature to demand them. He descended the stairs grim-faced and after drinking a cup of tea, made up a bed on the settee and tried to sleep. However, Maggie's woebegone face kept flashing before his eyes and sleep eluded him. Dawn was breaking when at last he dozed off.

Shivering in the big double bed, Maggie heard the crash of the tray and the rush of footsteps on the stairs. She listened, ears straining, and the silence on the other side of the door puzzled her. When she heard him leave she could not believe it and almost cried aloud in anguish. Burying her face in the pillow, she muffled her sobs as the tears burst their banks, pouring from her nose and mouth as well as her eyes, all the pent-up misery of the day enveloping her, was Father right? she wondered. Is Paul about to show his true colours? She lay a long time, unable to quench the flow of her tears. Her nose was stuffed up and her throat ached from weeping. She could not remember crying so much in her life before and whispered bleakly in the darkness, 'And a happy Christmas to you too, Paul.'

Tossing and turning, she saw every hour on the clock and dawn was pushing weak, cold fingers across the patchwork quilt when at last she slept. It was full daylight when next she awoke and the light hurt her swollen eyes and made her head pound. Silence reigned. Had Paul overslept also? Surely he had not left her? Panic-stricken at the idea, and aware she must look a mess, she pulled on her dressing gown and descended the stairs. She had been wrong to keep him from her bed. If she had been more sensible they would probably have made up their differences last night. In the intimacy of the bed he would have explained and she would have forgiven him. She would not have had any other choice but to forgive him. Where could she go?

Paul was nowhere to be seen, but in front of the brightly

burning fire sat the tin bath. With Mollie away, Paul had promised her a bath today and in spite of the quarrel, he had kept his promise. Perhaps all was not lost.

Guessing he was at Mass, she bolted the outer door and filled the bath with water from the assorted pots and pans he had steaming way on the range. She wallowed in the luxury of hot soapy water. When she had dressed and camouflaged her blotched skin with face powder, there was a knock on the door. Sure it was Paul, she unbolted and opened the door and turned quickly away, aware she did not look her best. Then a voice brought her head sharply round in surprise.

'Are you not going to invite me in?'

William! Grabbing him by the arm, she pulled him into the kitchen. To her dismay, the tears fell again.

The parcel William held fell unheeded to the floor as he reached for her and rocked her gently in his arms.

'Margaret! What's wrong? Are you ill? Where's your husband?'

She pushed away from him, ashamed that he should see her in this state.

'I'm crying because I'm glad to see you!' she lied. 'Paul's at Mass. Come sit by the fireside.' Too late, she realised the bath of dirty water was still sitting in front of the range. More shame smote her. Why had William to find her like this?

'I've been bathing. Will you help me empty the bath?'

He tried, without success, to hid his distress as he gripped one handle of the bath. Maggie took the other and between them they manoeuvred it through the narrow scullery and outside to the yard. There she motioned him over to the drain and tipped up the bath to empty the water out. As she dried the bath, before hanging it on a nail on the wall, she was aware of William's horrified reaction to the yard.

His eyes roved all around and she heard the dismay in his voice when he exclaimed. 'How can you bear to live here, Margaret?' Before she could answer him, he hurried on, 'And don't tell me you're happy! You look awful.'

Then, reaching for her hands, he gripped them tightly and his voice took on a pleading note. 'Come home, Margaret. Come home before you have a child and I'm sure something can be arranged,' he urged her.

Convinced that she was already pregnant, she shook her head and surprised herself by saying, 'Catholics can't get a divorce.'

These words brought her up short. What was she saying? Divorce had not entered her head but now William would think she wanted to return home. 'I don't want to go home!' she cried. 'I love Paul, but we had a quarrel. Our first! But it will be all right, I know it will.'

His face twisted in disbelief. 'You sound as if you're trying to convince yourself instead of me,' he muttered, and added pompously, 'If he's not treating you right, Margaret, be honest with me, and I'll have a word with him.'

Even in her misery, Maggie had to hide a smile at the idea of William chastising Paul, but it was heartening to think that he cared what became of her. 'Thank you, William,' she said gratefully. 'Come sit by the fireside and tell me all the news.'

Lifting the parcel he had dropped when he arrived, he handed it to her. 'Sorry it's a bit late for Christmas.'

'Thank you, William.' She guessed by the feel of it that it contained a box of her favourite chocolates. 'How are Mother and Father?'

'They are both well. Very busy, now Father is back in office.'

'Do they ever speak of me?'

He thought of the bitterness with which their father reacted when her name was mentioned, the anger her mother often displayed when her absence disrupted their lives, but hearing the wistful note in her voice, he let her down gently.

'Not lately. I think they expected you home before now.'

The sound of Paul's step in the hall brought Maggie to her feet and she hastened to open the kitchen door.

Her look was beseeching. 'What do you think, Paul? We have a visitor. William is here.'

He nodded to let her know he understood. Their quarrel must be forgotten in front of William.

When Maggie introduced the man and the boy, they eyed each other. Paul saw a tall, fair haired lad with clear green eyes and William understood at once why Maggie was so besotted with Paul. He was a handsome devil, with his dark curly hair and intense blue eyes. Yes, he could see that Paul would be attractive to the opposite sex.

'I'm pleased to meet you at last,' he said, offering Paul his hand.

Paul did not think he looked in the least pleased, but noting Maggie's poor, tear-ravaged face, he did not blame the boy. He himself deserved to be shot for causing her such pain, especially on Christmas Day. God forgive him!

He gripped William's extended hand. 'I'm pleased to meet you an' all. Maggie speaks of you often.' This was not strictly true. She rarely mentioned her family.

'While you two get acquainted, I'll make some lunch.' Maggie rose and escaped into the scullery, closing the door.

A strained silence reigned in the kitchen, until Paul said ruefully, 'I don't mistreat her, ye know.'

'Don't you?' William sounded sceptical.

Paul shrugged, 'Believe it or not, it's our first quarrel. Or rather, misunderstanding.' He wondered why he was bothering to explain to this young lad. It was none of his business. He supposed he wanted him to have a good opinion of him.

'I should hope she doesn't always look like that! I happen to think my sister is a beautiful girl.'

'So do I!' Paul hastened to assure him. 'I agree with you wholeheartedly. To tell the truth, I'm ashamed of meself. It'll never happen again.'

'I hope you never hurt her again.'

Paul could not tell whether or not the words held a threat, but in his heart he was glad that the boy was standing up for his sister.

During lunch the tension eased and afterwards, quirking an eyebrow at William, Paul said, 'I'm goin' to a football match this afternoon. Would you care to join me?' Turning his glance to Maggie he saw the hurt closed look on her face, the shuttered eyes. He had intended asking her to join them too but refrained, afraid of a rebuff in front of William.

'I'd love to come.' William enjoyed football and in spite of himself was excited at the prospect. Then remembering Maggie's unhappiness, guilt made him add doubtfully, 'That is . . . if Margaret doesn't mind?'

'Of course I don't mind. Go and enjoy yourself.'

She started clearing the table – anything to keep her occupied until they left. At the door she smiled brightly as she waved them off, but once inside again she sat with hands clasped tightly in her lap, willing herself not to cry again. She would not have believed she could be such a cry baby.

This will have to stop! she warned herself. Paul must really regret marrying her or he would have taken her with them, in spite of the quarrel. He must still love Marie. What would she do? If she was pregnant, would he stay with her? No! She did not want to hold him that way.

Halfway down the street Paul stopped in his tracks. 'You walk on, William. Wait at the corner for me,' he ordered, and turning on his heel, retraced his steps. When he threw open the kitchen door, Maggie started up in surprise.

'Come on, woman! I'll not be able to enjoy the match without you.'

She remained motionless, unable to believe what was happening. Taking her coat from the banisters, Paul held it aloft. When she slipped her arms into the sleeves, he wrapped his arms around her, holding her close and nuzzling the back of her neck, making her go weak at the knees.

'Come on, William's waitin' for us.' He gave her a brief kiss and her spirits lifted. There was hope for them yet.

The afternoon spent at the football match was the most

enjoyable time Maggie had experienced in a long while and it was with sadness that they bade William farewell in the centre of town and caught the tram up Castle Street to the Falls Road. Both their throats were hoarse from cheering their team on and the journey home was conducted in silence. When they got off the tram at the top of Dunville Street, Paul nodded towards the fish and chip shop.

'I'll nip in and get some fish for the supper, Maggie. You go on ahead an' get the teapot on.'

As she set the table, Maggie realised that Paul thought the quarrel was over and done with, and she was in a quandary as to what to do. Should she just forget the incident or put Paul on the defensive again by bringing it up? It would be so easy to carry on as if nothing had happened.

No, it wouldn't! her conscience shouted. He let me down!

But did she want to spend another night alone, so cold in that big double bed? No! But neither could she ignore the misery he had caused her. He must explain, he must convince her that he loved her, not Marie, or she could never lie with him again.

Paul watched Maggie covertly as they ate and could see that she was still perturbed. When the dishes were washed and dried, to keep herself occupied, Maggie got out a bundle of clothes and started ironing, and Paul sat by the fireside trying to get interested in a newspaper and failing miserably. What was Maggie planning to do?

When the ironing was finished and bedtime could be put off no longer, Paul asked tentatively, 'Where am I sleepin' the night, Maggie?'

'That's up to you, Paul. I'm still waiting for an explanation.'

'Bah!' He turned away in disgust. 'There's nothing to explain! Good God . . . Marie's an old friend an' I saw her home! That's all there was to it.' How could he explain? How could he admit that he had been flattered? That he had enjoyed making her jealous? It sounded so childish, so immature.

Maggie expelled breath she had not realised she was holding in a long sigh. Her hand reached out to him appealingly and then fell limply to her side. He was the one in the wrong. He should be appealing to her. When he kept his head stubbornly away from her, she turned sadly to the stairs. Her foot was on the bottom step when he shouted, 'What about tomorrow night, eh? Mollie will be home. Where'll I sleep then?'

Patience exhausted, Maggie stamped her foot and punched the air with her fist. 'Damn you! Oh, damn you, Paul Mason! Why can't you explain? Do you still love her? Are you sorry you married me?'

Paul had never seen Maggie in such a temper before and, mesmerised, sat drinking in her fiery beauty. Angry colour highlighted her cheek bones and her eyes flashed green light. He felt passion rise in him at the beauty of her.

When he made no answer, she cried, 'Don't just sit there like an idiot, Paul. For heaven's sake, answer me! Was it my father's money you were after? Was . . .'

At the mention of her father's money he was out of the chair and had reached her in two strides. Fingers biting viciously into the soft flesh of her upper arms, he shook her so violently her head lolled on her shoulders and her teeth rattled.

'Don't you ever accuse me of bein' after your da's money again,' he growled through clenched teeth, and each word was accompanied by a vicious shake. Then he threw her from him in disgust. 'Good God, woman! You're actin' as if I've committed adultery!'

Maggie had grabbed the newel post to stop herself from falling. Still clinging to it for support, she whispered, 'Did you, Paul?'

She watched him. As if in slow motion his jaw dropped and his eyes widened in disbelief. He could not believe his ears. She could not think that! Surely she did not believe that he would do that? He bent towards her and his voice was hoarse and beseeching.

'Ah, Maggie . . . ye can't think that!'

'Can't you see?' she cried in bewilderment. 'I don't know what to think. I only know that I hurt. I hurt so much, deep in here.' A hand clutched her breast and pain filled her voice. She could see from the way he kept swallowing, as if a lump blocked his throat, that he was shaken.

At last he managed to speak. 'Maggie . . . surely you know how much I love you? Why, I could never touch another woman now I have you.'

'Then why did you do it, Paul?' She sounded so bewildered and lost that once again he silently cursed his own stupidity. 'Why did you go off and stay for hours? You left me sitting there, surrounded by pity, and now you act injured because I doubt you.'

He moved closer but made no attempt to touch her, afraid of rejection. How could he handle that, rejection from the woman he loved. But how could he have been so stupid as not to realise the extent of the misunderstanding? He felt appalled to think that Maggie could believe he would risk harming his marriage by touching another woman. Dear God, he wanted no other.

A silent prayer wended heavenwards. Dear God, help me convince her!

'Maggie, look . . . listen. So help me, I don't know why I behaved the way I did.' The words tumbled out on top of each other. He knew he was babbling but didn't care. He must make her understand. 'I suppose I was flattered,' he confessed. It sounded so naive. In despair he hurried on, 'But I wasn't alone with her. Lord, no! I went in to wish her parents a happy new year an' couldn't get away. An' that's the truth, love. I swear it!' He held her eyes, silently pleading for understanding. When she remained wary still, he hesitantly reached out for her.

Meeting no resistance he drew her close, saying humbly, 'I swear to God that's the truth, Maggie. I'm sorry, love. I'm really sorry my stupidity spoilt our first Christmas together but I'll make it up to you, that's a promise! Will ye gimme another chance, Maggie?'

The hurt still rankled and when he would have pressed her closer she held back, her eyes searching his, seeking reassurance. With her hands against his chest she strained away from him and each word was emphasised. 'Paul . . . I will not allow you to treat me like that.' His mouth opened to protest but, covering it with her hand, she continued, 'Just because I'm cut off from my family, don't think for one moment that I'll become a doormat.'

'No, Maggie, I promise that it'll never happen again. We have something wonderful between us. Don't let me spoil it by my carelessness.'

He was choked with emotion. He cupped her face with his hands and muttered brokenly, 'Sure, Maggie, without you the sun wouldn't shine for me. Forgive me, love . . . please.'

She relaxed against him. The ice that encased her heart started to melt. She could not doubt his sincerity. A question hovered on her lips but she swallowed it. Better not to know if he and Marie had been lovers.

When he started to remove the combs that held her hair in place, she whispered, 'Let's go to bed.'

CHAPTER THREE

Anne watched Paul prowling around the kitchen and warned herself to hold her tongue. Are we not all on edge? she reasoned. He had every right to be anxious. It was his first child. Maggie had gone into labour sixteen long hours ago and Paul was beside himself with worry. When he entered the scullery, Anne grimaced. She waited for the sound of the water running, the clink of the glass, but was aware he did not drink any water. He just could not stay still! He had been in and out of the scullery like a yo-yo for the past couple of hours and she felt like screaming at him.

On his return to the kitchen he sat down at the table, drumming away on its top with his fingers. Words of reproof rose to her lips. However, before she could utter them he went to the foot of the stairs and cocked his head in a listening attitude. He stood like this, tense and silent, for so long her nerves were stretched to breaking point. She cried out in exasperation, 'For heaven's sake, Paul, sit down. You're gettin' on me nerves, so ye are!'

Her son swung towards her, an angry retort on his lips, but noticing the lines of fatigue on her face, swallowed the words. He went to the armchair by the fireside and sat down, burying his head in his hands. His mother and Mollie must be ready to drop. They had been on their feet constantly since Maggie had gone into labour the night before. God, how he wished it was all over! What on earth was Doctor Hughes doing up there? He was glad he had insisted on fetching the doctor, in spite of assurances that Mollie was as good as any midwife. Maggie's muffled screams had been sending him crazy. What did it matter how much it cost, as long as Maggie was all right?

But was she? The doctor had been upstairs an hour now, and there was still no sign of the baby. He was beginning to think Maggie's muffled screams would be welcome again. At least then he would know that she was still alive. Poor Maggie, how she was suffering – and it was all his fault. Head bowed, he prayed as he had never done in his life before.

As if in answer to his prayers, a baby's cry broke the silence. A thin wail at first, but gathering momentum, bringing a weary grin to Paul's strained face.

His eyes locked with his mother's and simultaneously they cried, 'Thanks be to God!'

A few minutes later, when Mollie appeared on the stairs, a bundle in her arms, Paul rushed to meet her.

'You've a wee daughter,' she greeted him.

Barely glancing at the bundle, he asked tersely, 'Is Maggie all right?'

'She's fine,' Mollie assured him, but as he made to pass her, she blocked his way. 'Not yet, Paul! Ye can't go up yet. The doctor isn't finished with her.'

Fear like a tight, hard knot in his chest, he gripped her arm. 'Are you telling me the truth? Is Maggie all right?'

His mother took him by the arm and gently urged him towards the fireside where she had a basin of water ready to bathe the baby.

'Maggie's all right, son,' she stressed. 'It's just . . . well, there's things that have to be done. You can go up in a few minutes, when the doctor's finished with her. Come on now, let's have a look at yer wee daughter.'

Silently, Paul watched as she took the bundle from Mollie and gently unwrapped it. When she cried: 'Oh, . . . isn't she lovely!' he nodded his head in agreement, but he saw nothing lovely about the small red wrinkled face and the thatch of hair tinged with blood. Returning to the

71

stairs, he sat on the bottom step in a fever of impatience. What on earth was the doctor doing up there?

Upstairs, Maggie lay back on the pillows exhausted, soaked in sweat but satisfied at a job well done. Weary and sore, she closed her eyes, craving sleep, but it was not to be. Shaking her gently by the shoulder, Doctor Hughes said, 'Not yet, Maggie, you're not finished yet. I need another big push from you.' His hands were on her abdomen, pressing down, and he smiled encouragingly at her. 'Now, Maggie!' And at her feeble attempt to obey, he cried, 'Ah, now, Maggie . . . come on, you can do better than that.'

Summoning all her strength Maggie tried again, but nothing happened. Mollie, entering the room, met the doctor's worried eyes and hastened to her side.

'Here, Maggie, hang on t'me. Let's get this over an' done with. Paul's waitin' t' come up t' see ye.'

Once again Maggie gathered up all the strength she could muster and pushed. This time, she felt the afterbirth slide from her body and sighed with relief. Perhaps now they would leave her alone.

'Good girl! I knew you could do it. I'll leave now and give Mollie a chance to wash you down. I'll see you tomorrow morning.'

The doctor's praise was heartfelt, and a glance at Mollie showed that she had been aware of the danger. For a while it had been touch and go whether or not the afterbirth would come away, but to his relief it had. And no need for stitches. Maggie was indeed a lucky girl.

She was only half aware of his words, her mind and body relaxed. She remained in this dream-like state while Mollie washed her. Paul's voice, whispering anxiously in her ear, was the next thing she was fully aware of. When she opened her eyes, he was hovering at the bedside.

'Are you all right, Maggie?'

She nodded and a proud smile crossed her face. 'Have you seen our daughter?'

'Here she is,' Mollie cried, entering the room. 'An' a wee beauty she is an' all.' Placing the child in the crook of

72

Maggie's arm, she turned for Paul's verdict. 'Isn't she lovely?'

Still unable to find anything beautiful about the small wrinkled object, he gazed at Mollie's glowing face and was able to answer truthfully.

'Yes, she's lovely.'

'Hold her, Paul,' Maggie ordered.

With a worried frown on his brow, he did as he was bid. Lifting the child gingerly up in his arms, he cradled it against his breast, very much aware of the amusement in Maggie's eyes.

Tentatively touching the small hand, he exclaimed in amazement when the tiny fingers closed in a fist around one of his. 'Look, Maggie, look at her! She's as strong as a bull, so she is. Look at the grip she has.'

They had discussed names often, but failed to agree, Paul thinking the names Maggie favoured too fancy. Now, the last sixteen hours fresh in his mind, he though the choice should be hers. Hadn't she suffered all the pain?

'Have you decided on a name for her, Maggie?' he asked diffidently.

Mouth agape, she looked at him in surprise. Then a smile tugged at her lips and her eyes teased him. She could read him like a book and understood his reasoning. 'You choose a name for her, Paul.'

He looked deep into her eyes and his voice was humble. 'You really mean that, don't you, Maggie?'

When she nodded, he pursed his lips and sat in thought for some moments. 'Well, I would like her called Sarah Anne, after me grannie and me mam.' His grandmother had died three years earlier, but from the way he spoke of her, Maggie knew that he had been very fond of her. Once more she nodded her agreement.

'Are you sure, Maggie?' His eyes were still on her face, watching her reaction. 'If you want to call her Felicity or Valerie, ye can, love. I'll agree to anything you say.'

She laughed softly. 'No. Sarah Anne Mason is fine. I like it. It has a nice ring to it.'

A weak wail was emitted from the small rosebud mouth

and Paul hurriedly put the child back in Maggie's arms. Then, lifting one of her hands, he raised it to his lips. 'Thanks, Maggie. Thanks for giving me this lovely daughter.'

Eyes twinkling, she gazed up at him. In her dream-like state she had heard him say to the doctor, 'Never again! I could never go through that again.' Now she teased him. 'Next year it will be a son, Paul.'

He gaped at her in amazement, then seeing the twinkle in her eye, laughed wryly and confessed, 'I thought you were sleepin'.'

His hand caressed her cheek and throat and as her head moved in response to his touch, and her lips brushed his fingers, he knew that next year would probably see another child born. How could he resist such loveliness?

Surprised at the emotions he was arousing, that she could want him so soon after childbirth, after all the pain she had suffered, she muttered, 'You had better go. Mollie will be back up in a minute . . . besides, it's too soon.'

He laughed softly in triumph and kissed her chastely on the brow before he left the room.

The baby was Maggie's introduction to the young mothers of the district. When the weather was fine, they all gathered in the Dunville Park with their offspring and Maggie's heart beat fast the first day she pushed Sarah in her second-hand pram down to the park. It had taken her a while to come to terms with the idea of using someone else's pram, but new ones were so expensive, and Mollie had known the previous owner and had assured her it came from a clean home. Still, she had played with the idea of asking her parents for help – after all, it was their first grandchild and they could afford the money – but knowing how upset Paul would be, she had abandoned the idea and vowed to be content with her lot. As she walked, she was aware of all eyes on her. She knew that they called her Lady Muck but could no more change her way of speaking or her proud walk than she could stop breathing.

Observing all the other prams, she was glad that she had

not bought a new one; that would definitely have been out of place. As it was, she had walked twice around the park and was sadly heading for home, having been ignored by all, when one young girl took pity on her.

Raising a hand in greeting, she asked, 'What did ye get?' and with an inclination of the head, invited Maggie to share her bench. She thought her heart would burst with gratitude. They were never to become close friends, she and Meave Madden, but at least when she visited the park she had someone to talk to and compare notes with, and for this she was grateful.

Neighbours, being the same the world over, could not resist a baby and Maggie was, if not quite accepted, at least tolerated and so the days passed happily enough. She found that caring for the baby and looking after the small house kept her fully occupied.

It was a constant source of wonder to her how happy the people of the Falls were. Hardly a night passed that singing was not heard coming from the street corners where the young folk gathered. As for the weekends when they gathered at the main gates of the Dunville Park – then it was like holiday time. Often when the sound of soft refrains drifted up Waterford Street on the still air, Paul would lift one of Mollie's shawls and, gently wrapping it around his wife's shoulders, lead her from the house and down to the corner, where they could hear better. Sometimes as they sat on the windowsill of one of the shops, the barber, whose shop was next to the pub at the corner of Clonard Street, would come out and the sound of his violin would fill the air. Low, haunting melodies that brought a tear to the eye, or lively jigs that set feet tapping and couples twirling in the centre of the road. Remembering past visits to the Opera House and St Mary's Hall with her parents, to concerts and light operas, Maggie was astounded at the quality of the Falls Road singers and the way they could harmonise. Why, in another country they could become famous! How did they manage to be so carefree and happy, when they had so little going for them? Her respect for her neighbours grew and she assured Paul that she was quite content to stay in Waterford Street with Mollie. It made no difference; he was determined to move up the Falls Road and nothing she said could deter him.

As time passed, she began to regret her husband's generosity to the old man in the park. He had left himself only one workcoat and when the weather was bad, one was not enough. He still refused to wear his best ulster, saying he needed to look respectable at Mass on a Sunday. So Maggie worried and fretted. Some nights he arrived home from work soaked to the skin and as she watched his clothes steaming on the fender as they dried, she worried that perhaps they were still damp when he put them on the following morning. In vain she pleaded with him to buy a new coat, even a second-hand one, but he was scandalised at the idea. Were they not saving for a house of their own? He was adamant that they could not afford to waste money on clothes for him and so she was compelled to worry in silence.

When she discovered that she was pregnant again, Paul was overjoyed and vowed that she would have a home of her own before the birth of the second child. Every weekend they pushed Sarah in her pram up the Falls Road, looking for a suitable house. Up past St Paul's Church and St Catherine's School and the Dominican Convent, set in its magnificent gardens next to St Mary's Training College, and then some more streets of kitchen houses.

These houses, like the ones on the lower Falls, had been built by mill owners to entice cheap labour to the district, before the slump at the end of the previous century. On the left-hand side at Broadway the houses had been built for Protestant workers and on the right-hand side stood the Catholic homes. There was certainly no shortage of houses to rent or buy; the cost of food had risen so high that most of a man's wages was spent on it, not leaving enough for most families to better themselves – this in spite of the wage rise the unions had obtained by strike action.

Paul barely spared these mill houses a glance. When Maggie would have stopped he urged her on, up towards the Donegal Road district where new houses were being built, but each weekend they arrived back in Waterford Street dispirited. Even Paul's wage as a skilled worker was not enough to cover the deposit of sixty pounds and repayments of five shillings a week that was required for the new houses, and as time passed he grew more depressed. Then Mollie got the offer of the key to a house in Spinner Street, just across the Falls Road, almost facing Waterford Street. She was told that Paul had just to grease the palm of a certain rent collector, and he would see that the house was theirs. Excited and happy she informed Paul, but to her surprise he shook his head.

'Thanks, Mollie. I know you mean well . . . but I intend to take Maggie up the Falls. It's where she belongs. Ye know what I mean, don't ye?'

Sadly, Mollie nodded her head. She did understand. Paul had set himself a target and he intended to achieve it.

Grimly, no matter what the weather, Paul worked all the overtime he could get, determined to get the deposit gathered together. He had decided that if they could save the deposit, he would risk buying a new house, even at five shillings a week.

Then one Sunday as they passed Islandbawn Street, a short distance above the Training College, Maggie called his attention to a house for sale. Although it was one of the mill houses, it had obviously been well cared for. It had probably belonged to a manager at one of the mills who had bettered himself, Paul guessed. As he examined it back and front, in spite of himself, he grew interested. It was set in a cul-de-sac, with the River Clowney running along its back, and facing the street itself was Willowbank House, giving an air of grandeur to the road. Not as far up the Falls as Paul would have liked, but still a quiet, peaceful district, and close by was Willowbank Park with its sand-pits and paddling pool.

'There's room for an extension at the back, Maggie. I could build a bathroom,' he explained excitedly. 'It would only cost us the bricks and mortar and even those I'd get cheap. On Monday we'll get the keys and have a look inside.' He nodded his head. 'We should be able to afford this. Eh, Maggie? What do you think?'

Pleased to see him so excited, she nodded in agreement with him, and they hurried home to tell Mollie the good news.

The house lived up to their expectations. They had money to spare after paying the deposit, and the three shillings and sixpence a week they could afford comfortably. They decided that while working on the house they would stay with Mollie. It would be better to wait until after the birth and make sure Maggie was never alone. Sad to be losing this young family she loved, Mollie was delighted at this respite and set to, helping to make curtains, cushions and rag mats.

Discovering that he was quite handy with wood, having made a cot when Sarah was born, Paul set to work on a scullery cabinet and the time flew past. Happiness radiated from Maggie as she planned for the coming birth and her new home. William, a constant visitor now, had to admit that she was blooming, and he grew to like and respect Paul.

During the course of his visits, he met all the Mason family and he and shy Emma struck up a friendship. Aware that her brother would never risk hurting their parents, Maggie watched the friendship grow with trepidation. Emma was so shy and insecure, that Maggie worried about her. What if she fell in love with William?

One day when he had paid them a visit, walking to the corner with him as was her custom, Maggie asked a leading question. 'William, are you seeing Emma?'

'What do you mean?'

'You know fine well what I mean.'

Lifting Sarah into his arms, he gave her all his attention. Maggie could see that he was being evasive and her heart sank.

'Be careful, William. She's very shy.

'You're not shy, are you, Sarah?' he jested, swinging the chuckling child aloft.

'William! Nothing can come of it. You know that! Emma will get hurt.' Maggie was insistent. She was very fond of Emma and did not intend to stand by while William trifled with her affections.

Suddenly serious, he set Sarah down and the look he bestowed on his sister was bleak. 'I know . . . I'm getting too fond of her. I've decided to go over to England.'

'Oh, William. With Emma?'

'No. I wish I had the courage to take her with me but I could not do that to Father, he has so many plans for me.' He turned to her in despair. 'Plans I don't want or share, Margaret. If I get over to England, perhaps I'll be able to have a life of my own. Who'd want to be a councillor in this Godforsaken place? Certainly not I! And then there's Emma . . .'

'William, I'm so sorry for you.' It was such a waste. He and Emma seemed so suited. 'Poor girl, she'll miss you. So will I for that matter.' To hide the tears that threatened to fall, she bent over Sarah.

With a gesture, William stopped her. 'Let her walk . . . she's too heavy for you in your condition.'

Blinking back the tears, she faced him again. 'When are you going to England?'

'Soon. Father is getting me started in a friend's office. A solicitor's, no less. But that's not for me. I'll soon find something more suitable.'

'Father's helping you?'

At the amazement in her voice he grinned and nodded, but did not inform her that their father was only helping him escape to England to get him away from her influence. It was her obvious happiness that made him discontented with the plans his father had for him.

'He will be disappointed.'

'Mmm.' His shrug was indifferent and he quickened his stride to catch an approaching tram, saying over his shoulder, 'See you next week.'

Once things were set in motion time flew and it was

barely three weeks later that William said his goodbyes before sailing for England.

When next Emma visited them, Maggie could see that the news of William's departure came as a surprise to her. Anger rose in her breast at the cowardly way he had treated her sister-in-law, and tentatively she tried to comfort her. She was airily brushed off.

'Don't worry about me, Maggie. He never made any promises, so he didn't. And sure I knew in my heart it could never be. I was livin' in a fool's paradise.'

'Your turn will come, Emma,' Maggie consoled her. 'Just you wait and see. Mr Right is just around the corner.'

These words brought a wry twist to Emma's lips. 'You don't happen to know which corner, do ye, eh, Maggie?' Then, a brave smile hiding the pain, she continued, 'Enough about me! How are you? When is the baby due?' And it was many a day before William was mentioned again.

It was a damp murky day and fear was in Maggie's heart as she watched her husband's strong body bent low by a bout of coughing. It was obvious to her that he was a sick man but he would not miss a day off work. Almost in tears, she remonstrated with him. 'Paul, please stay at home today.'

'Maggie . . . now listen, love,' he reasoned with her. 'You know I can't stay off. We need so much for the new house.'

'We have all the necessary things. A bed, a cot, armchairs, a desk, a table. Why, we'll be better off than most people! A few days, Paul. Just stay at home a few days. Give yourself a chance to throw off this cough. We'll manage. We've a bit to spare.'

Shrugging into his workcoat, he tried to keep hold of his temper. Did she think he enjoyed standing in the wind and cold laying bricks? He'd love to return to bed and shut out reality for a while but he couldn't afford to be so foolish. The house in Islandbawn Street was not what he had hoped for. He had wanted a new house for Maggie, but he intended to make sure that she had at least a bathroom as soon as possible, and that cost money. He had plans for this house and it would take a lot of money to achieve them. A great deal of money . . . and the only way to get it was to work for it.

'Ach . . . give me head peace, woman. We need the money an' that's that! What about the new baby, eh? Eh? We'll need every penny we can get. I'll be all right. I'll go to bed as soon as I come home t'night.' And as the door closed on him, Maggie exchanged an anguished look with Mollie.

'I fear for his health, Mollie, but he won't listen to me.'

'I know, love. He's a proud, stubborn man. It breaks his heart that he can't give you the world. I'll get a half bottle of whiskey and t'night we'll try to sweat the cold out of him.' And with these words Mollie wrapped her shawl around her shoulders and left the house.

The whiskey did not work the required miracle and by the end of the week Paul was too weak to rise from his bed, and too sick to count the cost when Maggie announced that she was sending for the doctor.

Doctor Hughes's examination of him was thorough, and although Maggie watched him closely, his face gave no indication of what he thought.

'I'll leave you something to help you sleep,' he said, and squeezed Paul's shoulder in a reassuring manner before leaving the room.

Downstairs, Maggie faced him. 'Well, Doctor?' Her eyes sought his and he hesitated when he saw her worry.

'I want the truth, mind!'

With a slight shrug, he obeyed her. 'Your husband's a very sick man. His lungs are badly congested and, to tell the truth, I would like a second opinion.'

'What do you mean?'

'I want a specialist to have a look at him. However, he's too ill to move so I'll try to get Mr Ferguson to come over from the Royal to see him. He's the best man I know. I think he'll come.'

At the door she forced herself to ask, 'Will he be all right, doctor?'

'Let's see what the specialist says, Maggie. I'll try to bring him tomorrow morning. Is that all right?'

Unable to speak, she nodded wordlessly, but Doctor Hughes could find no words of comfort for her. In his opinion, Paul Mason was a very sick man.

Next day Maggie waited in a fever of impatience for the doctor to return, hovering nervously about until Paul cried out in despair for some peace. In her heart she knew that he was very ill, but reasoned that the sooner the specialist came, the sooner treatment could be started and her husband put on the road to recovery. It was late afternoon when at last Doctor Hughes arrived and ushered a tall, silver-haired man into the house.

'Maggie, this is Mr Ferguson,' he said in introduction.

She nodded in acknowledgement and led the way up the stairs, thinking, You spend years studying to win the title 'doctor' and then, when you become renowned, you are distinguished from your lesser doctors by becoming 'mister' again!

Paul was asleep but he awoke when the specialist gently opened his shirt to sound him. The examination he received was long and thorough and he lay silent throughout it.

When it was over, he asked bluntly, 'Well, just how serious is it?'

Deciding not to pull any punches, the specialist replied, 'You're a very sick man.'

'What's wrong with me?'

Maggie saw the specialist exchange a look with Doctor Hughes, then run an eye over her obvious pregnancy before replying, 'You have tuberculosis!'

Silence stretched as his words echoed round the room. At least that was how it seemed to Maggie, and someone was groaning as if in great agony. She discovered that the groans were coming from her own lips, when Paul caught hold of her hand.

'Steady on, love. Steady on,' he urged, and gripping her

hand tightly between his, addressed the doctors. 'Is there any chance of a cure?'

'There's always a chance of a cure. We're expecting a new discovery any day now,' Mr Ferguson assured him. 'Meanwhile, I'm prescribing some drugs and you must take them as directed. These are new drugs we're trying out and we have great hopes for them. I'll be back to see how you're reacting to them. Good day, Mr Mason.'

Once down the stairs he turned to Maggie. 'Mrs Mason, your husband would be better off in a sanatorium. He needs a room to himself.'

At these words, Mollie, who had been waiting anxiously for news, piped in, 'He can have my room, doctor.'

Gratefully, Maggie turned to her. 'Oh, Mollie, can he?'

'Of course he can!'

'Mollie, I must tell you the truth. Paul has TB.'

Mollie blanched visibly; even although she had suspected that Paul had the dread disease, it was a shock hearing it put into words, but her answer was swift. 'He can have my room.'

It was Doctor Hughes who intervened next. 'Maggie, you must think of Sarah and yourself and Mollie! This disease is very contagious. Paul would be better off in a sanatorium.'

She rounded on him angrily. 'Would you like to be in a sanatorium, cut off from your family and friends? How would I be able to visit him, eh? Tell me that! Where would I get the money to travel out of town every day? I'm not stupid. I'll be careful. He'll have his own towel and flannel. His own cutlery. I'll do all that has to be done.'

The idea of Paul being kept apart, treated as a leper, assailed her and her voice broke. Muttering excuses, she hurried into the scullery and closed the door, leaving Mollie to see the two men out.

Mollie left her to grieve in private, but when she returned to the kitchen she eyed her closely. Dry-eyed and composed, Maggie returned her look and Mollie's respect for her grew. This was no time for tears; Paul would need to be free from worry. She might have known that his wife would rise to the occasion.

The Masons were all devastated by Paul's illness but, united family that they were, they all rallied round and helped to ease Maggie's burden. Bill and Brendan changed the beds over and Paul was settled in the small room off the scullery while Mollie was moved up into the front bedroom.

This was better all round; it meant less running up and down stairs for Maggie, and Paul was able to sit in the kitchen for a few hours in the evening when his family visited. He was also able to make his way down to the wee house, a fact for which he was grateful. Maggie had enough on her plate without that to attend to.

The medicine seemed to work wonders for him and Maggie's spirits lifted as she watched him talking and laughing, looking as if nothing was wrong with him. Only when he was racked by a bout of coughing that left him like a limp rag, did her faith waver as she watched for the dreaded signs of blood. She never thought beyond today. Never dwelled on what would become of her should Paul die. No! She clung to the belief that he would get well, and prayed as she had never prayed in her life before, apologising to God for needing this great tribulation to make her aware of His presence.

The neighbours were kind, showing Maggie a side to them she had not believed existed. In spite of the contagiousness of the disease, they would knock on the door and inquire after Paul. They even brought fruit and second-hand books and, knowing that they could ill afford them, Maggie was overcome by their generosity. They always stressed that they did not want the books back, and when Paul was finished with them, Maggie burned them. She did not blame people for being careful. Did she not watch Sarah like a hawk? Making sure that she did not eat from her father's plate or use any of his things? Wasn't she always boiling and disinfecting things? However, there was one thing that she could not deny Paul and that was the company of his daughter, but she noticed that he did not encourage Sarah to come too close and was thankful for his understanding.

The rest of the family visited regularly but Brendan came every evening, in spite of the fact that he had to walk to and from the railway station no matter what the weather was like and the train fare was putting a big enough strain on his pocket. As soon as he had eaten his evening meal he would catch the train and come to sit with his brother, keeping him up to date on the local news, discussing at length with him the unrest in the country caused by England's proposing to pass yet another motion through Parliament for Home Rule in Ireland. It could lead to civil war! Down through the ages, the mention of Home Rule had caused trouble. Why should it be any different this time? Nothing had changed. The majority wanted home rule, but northern Protestants were against it and were marching in force to show their strength should England go against their wishes and impose Home Rule. All this added to Paul's worries. What would become of Maggie if he died in these troubled times?

One night he startled Brendan by asking him a question. 'Am I goin' to die?'

Taken unaware, Brendan blustered, seeking to find an answer that Paul would believe. Before he could gather his wits about him, Paul reached across and gripped his hand.

'I don't want to die, Brendan! It's not that I'm afraid of death. It's just that I have too many responsibilities, too much to live for. I can't leave Maggie to rear two children on her own. What will become of her if I die?' His eyes were bright, too bright as he confided in Brendan: 'This mornin' I coughed up blood, a lot of it. I didn't let Maggie see it, I burnt the rag, but it's made me realise that I'm fightin' a losin' battle.'

These words frightened Brendan. Maggie was so grateful that Paul was not spitting blood. So sure that the treatment was working and that in time he would get well.

'Ah, Paul, Paul!'

'Do ye know something, Brendan? I'm like an old man.

85

I can do nothin' without it half killin' me. An' Maggie, she looks awful. I'm killin' her too.'

'Ah, Paul, don't give up! For God's sake, don't give up.' In his anxiety, Brendan sat forward on the edge of his chair and the pressure of his hand on Paul's made him wince. 'Didn't the doctors say that they're expectin' a breakthrough any day now?'

Hearing the panic in his brother's voice, Paul decided not to burden him further. 'You're right, Brendan, you're right. There's always hope.'

He wondered why Brendan didn't tell him of his decision to try for the priesthood. His mother had confided in him but had sworn him to secrecy. But why? Why didn't Brendan tell him himself? Perhaps he was waiting until he was sure that he was going to be accepted before talking about it. That could be the reason. If only he had not decided to enter the seminary, Paul could have asked him to take care of Maggie. At least until she was able to manage on her own. But if he was going away, that put the lid on that idea. And now this unrest in the city. Blood would be shed if Home Rule was declared. Dear God . . . what would become of Maggie? Was anyone aware that her father was Clive Pierce, great upholder of the Orange Order? If only this terrible disease had not put in an appearance until Maggie was safely up in Islandbawn Street. He had been wrong to bring her to live on the Falls Road. Indeed, he had been wrong to marry her. But they had been happy until this curse had befallen him. Perhaps he was worrying unnecessarily; perhaps they would find a cure in time. In time to save him? He doubted it. There was a great fear in him that he was running out of time.

Brendan had not mentioned his intention of entering the seminary because he was having second thoughts about it. To his great shame, even though he tried not to see the wider implications of Paul's death, he was nevertheless very much aware that Maggie would then be a free woman. Not that he wanted Paul to die. Dear God, no! He would gladly change places with him if only he could, but although he urged Paul not to give up hope, he knew in his heart that his brother had not much time left. It looked ominous now that he was spitting blood, and shame besieged Brendan every time he thought of his own obsession with his brother's wife. Night and day her face haunted him and he longed to ease her burden, try to make her happy.

As Paul watched his wife prepare for bed that night, his heart ached. She was skin and bone and there was a sickly grey tinge to her face. She was so thin her stomach looked unnaturally big, even for pregnancy, a huge mound sitting in front of her. A horrified thought filled his mind. What if she was carrying twins? Twins ran in his family. But didn't they say that they missed a generation? Who said? Was it an old wives' tale? The thought of Maggie having twins brought a groan from his throat and instantly she was at his side, all concern.

He gripped her hand. 'Maggie ... what if you have twins?'

'The doctor says I won't,' she hastened to reassure him. 'I've asked him about that and he's sure there's only one child here.' She patted her stomach. 'So don't you start worrying about that. Just concentrate on getting well.'

He looked at her and dismay filled his heart. Huge, dark-ringed eyes swamped her small pinched face. She was so good! Dear God, what if she caught the disease from him? He was putting her at great risk letting her sleep with him. Doctor Hughes would be very angry if he ever found out. But how he needed her! Especially during the night when he was at his lowest ebb and plagued by worries and fears he could hold at bay during the day. Suddenly he came to a decision and spoke before he could change his mind.

'Maggie, I think you should start sleepin' upstairs.'

Startled, she gaped at him. 'Don't be silly, Paul. You need me!'

'No, I don't! I need room to breathe! This room's too small for both of us. It's stifling me. There's not enough air for two of us.'

87

Haunted eyes searched his face in disbelief, but when she opened her mouth to argue, he forestalled her.

'I mean it, Maggie. I need more room. You sleep with Mollie. I'm sure she won't mind.'

Her lips pressed tightly together then she said stubbornly, 'I'm staying down here. You need me. What if you need to go to the toilet during the night?'

Despair lent bitterness to his voice. 'For heaven's sake . . . I'm not quite incapable! Leave the bucket in an' I'll manage.'

Taken aback at his anger, she was at a loss what to do. Then she said decidedly, 'I'll sleep in the kitchen.'

'You will not! You'll sleep upstairs! You're smotherin' me, woman!'

A great ache, heavier than the child she carried, filled her. Silently she made sure that everything he might need during the night was close at hand. Then she turned to the door, only to pause. 'You're sure?'

Pleading eyes begged him to change his mind, but he nodded his head and turned aside in case he should weaken.

Choked with emotion, Maggie passed through the kitchen and climbed the stairs in despair. He did not want her! Oh, dear God, he did not want her. What would she do? She had heard of folk who, when they were sick, turned against those nearest and dearest to them, but that Paul should turn against her! How would she be able to bear it? Mollie was surprised when Maggie asked if she could share her bed but willingly made room for her. Questions hovered on her lips but she bit them back, knowing Maggie would explain in her own good time.

She was right. A few moments later, choking back sobs, Maggie wailed, 'He doesn't want me.'

Such a wealth of sorrow and despair came across on these words that Mollie felt tears in her own eyes. Fighting them back, she gathered Maggie's shaking form close and held her fiercely.

'Ye know he doesn't mean it,' she consoled. 'It's just because he's so ill.'

But Maggie was inconsolable and Mollie rocked her until at last she fell into a troubled sleep. The next day Mollie was determined to talk to Paul. Careful not to awaken Maggie, she arose early the following morning and descended the stairs. She got her opportunity to talk to Paul sooner than expected, because when she had cleared the ashes and lit the fire, he called her into the back room.

Grey and gaunt, he nodded to the floor beside the bed and she was not surprised to see rags stained with blood.

'So that's why you made Maggie sleep upstairs?'

He nodded. 'Will you burn them for me, Mollie?'

Hands on hips, she leant towards him. 'An' how long do ye think you'll be able to keep this from her, eh? Eh?'

'Ah, Mollie, it's not just this.' He wagged a limp hand towards the floor. 'It's her! She looks awful. I fear for her health.' A bitter grimace twisted his lips. 'Do you think I enjoyed staying down here on my own all night? I dread the nights, Mollie. I'm always afraid I won't see another day.'

'Now you listen t'me, Paul Mason! If you cut Maggie off from you, you're gonna send her over the edge. She has enough on her plate without rejection from you. You're her life. She needs to be with you.'

'I'm only thinkin' of her!' he protested hotly.

'Oh no you're not! You're salving your own conscience. You want t'feel noble.' She leant towards him beseechingly. 'Don't do this to her, Paul. You'll break her heart. Why, if anything had happened to you last night, an' her up the stairs, it would've killed her. Believe me, she needs your company as much as you need hers.'

'What about when I die, eh? What will become of her then?'

Realizing that he was testing her, she held his eye and answered solemnly, 'If you die.' She repeated the word to lay stress on them. 'If you die, well then ... we'll meet that hurdle when we come t'it. But for now, don't reject her, son,' she pleaded. She scooped up the cloths. 'I'll burn these rags before she comes down, but if you want my advice, you'll tell her you're spittin' blood. She has a right t'know!'

Hearing sounds from upstairs, and knowing that she had given him plenty to think about, she left the room and plunged the bloody rags deep into the heart of the fire, covering them with coal before Maggie descended the stairs.

Aware that her eyes would betray her bout of weeping, Maggie kept her head averted when she brought Paul a basin of water to bathe in.

'Maggie, look at me.'

Slowly she faced him and swollen eyes bravely met his. Despair filled him at the sight of her. He should keep away from her whenever possible, but Mollie spoke the truth: they needed each other. Or was he using her words as an excuse to keep Maggie near?

'I'm sorry, Maggie. I've been a fool,' he said softly.

Mixed and confused, she stared blankly at him. Why was he sorry?

'I need you, Maggie. I couldn't bear to spend another night like last night. Can you forgive me?'

'Ah, Paul . . .' she wailed. 'Ah, Paul, my love.' Her arms went around his neck and her faced pressed into the hollow of his shoulder. 'I thought you didn't want me. I thought you had turned against me.'

As he hugged her close, his mind ranted against God. Why are you doing this to us? Have we been such awful sinners? To her he said, 'I was thinkin' of you, Maggie. I'm terrified that you'll catch this awful thing that's killin' me.'

Amazed at his stupidity, she pushed back from him so that she could look into his eyes. 'Do you think I'd care if I did catch it?'

Tenderly, he pushed the damp hair back off her brow and planted a kiss there. 'Maggie, we must think of Sarah . . . and the baby.' His hand rested for a moment on her stomach and then he lowered his head to it. Meeting her eyes, a smile crossed his face. 'I can feel it kickin'. It seems strong, Maggie.'

'He *is* strong. Your son, Paul.'

'Oh, so it's a boy, is it? And just how do you know that?' he teased her, and his smile held a wealth of love.

'I just know it's a boy! And I'm going to call him Paul.'

As he held her close again, his cheek pressed against the softness of her hair, he doubted that he would live long enough to see this child and he fought back the tears that threatened to break loose. His wife had enough to worry about without him blubbering like a baby.

As if life wasn't hard enough, a heatwave engulfed the country. People were dying like flies, especially the very young, the elderly and the sick. Day after day the clammy heat slowly sapped what little strength Paul had left. Terror gripped Maggie's heart every time her husband coughed up blood and she decided to approach her parents for help. If Paul could get away to Switzerland to one of the special sanatoriums there, he might regain his health. But that cost money so she must swallow her pride, ignore the two letters returned unopened, and go to see her parents in person. Surely they would not refuse help if they knew the way she was situated?

However, the sight of her gaunt face in the mirror drove this idea from her mind. Her parents would not thank her for arriving in this state. She would phone! Yes, that was the best way. Why had she not thought of it sooner? Pulling one of Mollie's shawls around her shoulders, she assured Paul that she would not be long as she was just going down to the shops. With feet that dragged, she made her way down to the pub where she knew there was a pay phone. Paul would be angry ... well, that was something she would have to deal with. They needed help. Once in the small hallway she stood for some moments planning what she would say. Words jumbled about in her mind but she could not sort them out. She almost turned away in despair, but the thought of Paul forced her to lift the receiver. This was no time for pride; Paul's life was at stake.

It was a strange voice that answered her ring and she

thought she had rung the wrong number. But no, the voice was saying that this was the Pierce residence and could she help?

'Who are you?' Maggie asked in bewilderment.

'I am Mr Pierce's housekeeper. Who is calling, please?'

So they had missed her, after all. Missed the services she used to render. 'I am Mr Pierce's daughter. Can I speak to my mother, please?'

'I'm afraid you must have the wrong number, my employers do not have a daughter.'

And the phone went dead, leaving Maggie standing stunned. Slowly and carefully she returned the ear-piece. Feeling faint, she groped for the small bench that ran the length of one wall. Pressing her hands tightly together, she fought to still the tremors that were shaking her body. Her parents did not want to acknowledge her. She had been daft to think they would be willing to help. Paul's only chance was gone.

At last she urged herself to her feet. Paul would be worrying about her; she must go home. But first she must buy something to cover her excuse for being out. He must never find out what she had done. Never!

Aware that the end was near, the Masons whisked Sarah off to Sydenham but Maggie did not even notice her absence. All her efforts went into willing Paul to live. To outlast the heatwave. Every time he had a spasm of coughing, she held him close and murmured words of comfort until it passed, wiping away the blood, assuring him that the heat could not last much longer; but it lasted long enough.

Just one week later, Mollie knew as soon as she entered the house that Paul was dead. It was the silence that alerted her. No sounds of fighting for breath, no murmur of words from Maggie. With swift steps she hastened to the back room and paused in alarm at the sight that met her eyes. Paul lay still, the haggard lines smoothed from his face, at peace at last. Maggie pressed her body the length of his, arms around him, and she was so still herself that Mollie's heart missed a beat. Oh dear God! She hadn't done anything stupid, had she? Slowly, with a hand that shook, she touched Maggie's shoulder. Relief flooded through her when she whispered, 'He's gone, Mollie. He's gone.'

The following days were a blur of sounds and sensations to Maggie. She felt numb; it was as if she was far away, watching everything from a great distance; as if she was dreaming. Although Anne and Bill were devastated by the death of their first born, they tried to keep a tight rein on their emotions. Maggie had fallen to pieces; she needed them. Time enough for tears later, after the funeral.

With a tremendous effort, Anne and Mollie managed to make Maggie attend to her personal needs and Anne brushed her bright hair and caught it in a bun at the nape of her neck. Silently Maggie allowed them to minister to her, but once they were finished, returned to the back room where Paul was laid out and sat close beside the bed. No food passed her lips and not once did she inquire after Sarah. She was unaware she was keening softly as she rocked to and fro beside the corpse. Her eyes devoured Paul. He could not really be dead, her beloved. He looked so alive, so young, now that the strain and sorrow were gone from his face. Why, a smile seemed to hover around his mouth, and his lashes, so dark and thick, looked as if they were about to lift from his cheeks. Then he would smile at her and everything would be all right.

But she knew this could not be. She knew that he was dead. Hadn't she tried in vain to awaken him when no one was looking? It isn't fair! she thought wildly. He was too young to die. Placing a hand over his, in which rosary beads were clasped to his breast, she whispered, 'Don't leave me, Paul. Please, love, come back. I can't live without you.'

Paul had been well liked, and friends and workmates and neighbours came in a constant stream to pay their respects. They all offered Maggie their condolences, embarrassed in the face of her awful grief, but she had no

93

time to spare for them. She had so little time left with Paul, so little time to tell him of her love, her need.

She argued with God. Why take Paul? Did I do something wrong? Was it because I didn't become a Catholic? Guilt swamped her. Where had she gone wrong? She had promised God so much if only He would let Paul live, and He had not listened to her.

Leaning against the scullery cabinet, facing the door of the back room, Brendan watched Maggie, his heart wrung with pity. Even although he had known Paul was dying, he still could not believe he was gone. Paul had been so wise, so strong in Brendan's eyes, that he was having difficulty coming to terms with his death. He was also filled with great shame because of the love he bore for his brother's wife. He had not wanted to fall in love with her, but from the night he had kissed her on the train, she had held his heart. But I didn't wish you harm, Paul. Ah, no, I never wished you harm, he lamented silently.

Anne, entering the scullery, was brought up short when she saw the love and anguish in her son's eyes as he gazed at Maggie. She paused, hand to her lips to still the words. Oh, dear God, no. Not that! Isn't he goin' to enter the seminary? Tears blinding her, she turned away, almost knocking Bill down in her haste. Leading her gently to the settee, he sat beside her, holding her close.

Bewildered, she asked, 'You saw?' And when he nodded, she wailed, 'Oh, Bill, what's goin' to become of them?'

'Hush love, aren't you forgettin' something?'

Puzzled, she gazed at him. 'What do you mean?'

'I mean if God wants Brendan, he won't be able to resist the call. Who knows? Perhaps this is a test. Let's just leave it in God's hands. Eh, love?'

Anne tried to smile. Bill was right as usual. It was out of their hands. Giving her a final squeeze, he left her and went to say farewell to his son before they coffined him.

Brendan was brought back to reality by Mollie whispering in his ear, 'You'll have t'fetch Doctor Hughes.'

He looked at her in bewilderment and her voice was

rough as she explained, 'She'll never let them take him away an' the coffin'll be here in a half hour. The doctor'll give her a sedative.'

Mollie's nerves were stretched to breaking point. The last few days had been awful and she was dreading the night when she would be alone with Maggie. Understanding flickered across Brendan's face, and with one last anguished look at Maggie's rocking form, he left the house.

It was surgery hours and the doctor was busy. Brendan took his place in the waiting room, in a fever of impatience. At last his turn came. Entering the surgery, he explained why he was there.

'You should have explained to the housekeeper and she would have interrupted surgery,' Doctor Hughes cried in exasperation. 'How much time have we got?'

'About ten minutes.'

Wanting to relieve his pent-up emotions, Brendan longed to urge the doctor to hurry, but knowing he could go no faster, he held his tongue. At last Doctor Hughes snapped his bag shut. 'Let's go.'

The house was packed to the doors, the crowds spilling out on to the cobbled footpaths as they chorused with one voice the Hail Holy Queen. The rosary was over, they were just in time.

Brendan pushed his way through the crowd, making a path for the doctor, his heart aching when he heard Maggie pleading with the pall bearers not to put Paul in the coffin. Catching sight of him, she grabbed his arm.

'Brendan! Thank God you're here. Tell them they can't put Paul in that box.' She shook frantically at his arm. 'Go on, tell them. He'll be all alone down there.' When he just looked at her and sadly shook his head, she became frantic. 'Ah, please, Brendan. Please don't let them.'

Gently taking her in his arms, he said, 'Maggie, you must let him go.'

With an exclamation of anger, she pushed him away. 'You don't understand! He'll be all alone down there.' Wild-eyed, she looked from one face to another, seeking

95

help; a groan escaping her lips when none was forthcoming, the women weeping in sympathy with her, the men shuffling their feet in embarrassment.

Doctor Hughes took command. 'Please clear the room for a few minutes,' he ordered, and silently everyone filed out, leaving him alone with Maggie and Brendan.

'Maggie, you must let the doctor help you.'

Once again Brendan took her in his arms and this time she sagged against him, exhausted. Her best efforts had failed, she could do no more. She had no energy left. When Doctor Hughes bared her arm, she made no effort to deter him and soon slipped into merciful oblivion.

Quietness. Lovely peaceful silence. Maggie lay, eyes closed, grateful for the silence. All those Hail Marys being chanted at the top of people's voices had made her head pound. Did they think that God was deaf? she wondered. Turning on the bed, she reached out to Paul to ask his opinion. Seeing the smooth pillow and becoming aware that she was lying on top of the bedclothes, fully dressed, everything came rushing back to her. The awful empty void that was now her life.

'Oh, Paul . . . Paul, I don't want to live without you,' she moaned aloud, and swinging her legs off the bed, wrapped her arms around her swollen stomach. What was going to become of her and Sarah and this child that Paul would never see? Where could she go? How would she manage?

The bedroom door was opened softly and Anne peered into the room.

'I thought I heard movement,' she said, and sat on the bed beside Maggie. 'How do you feel, love?' Such a silly question, but what else could she say?

Tears coursed down Maggie's pale cheeks. 'I'll never feel well again.' And turning round, she pressed close to her mother-in-law. 'Oh, Anne, I wish I could die.'

Gripping her tight, Anne cried, 'Don't say that! You have Sarah and the baby to live for.'

For the first time in days, Maggie really looked at Anne, and the sight of her swollen eyes and pinched cheeks seared her with remorse. 'Anne, I'm sorry. I've been so selfish. He was your son. You had him longer than me! Your loss is greater than mine, and all I can think about is myself.'

They clung together, crying afresh, until Anne pushed her gently away. 'We'll help each other,' she vowed as she wiped her eyes. 'An' remember, we have Sarah an' the baby. An' God'll give us strength.' At these words Maggie grunted and threw her such a scornful glance that Anne continued, 'I know you'll find this hard to believe but He will! An' time really does heal all ills.' She could see by Maggie's expression that she didn't believe her so she changed the subject. 'Here . . . let me help you to undress an' get into bed properly.'

'Is it not near morning?' Dread of the night sent panic through Maggie.

'It's almost eleven, an' you need more rest. Don't worry, love. The doctor left you some tablets so you'll sleep all night. Look . . . while you put on your nightdress, I'll make ye a cup of tea. I won't be a minute.' At the door she turned, 'Do ye know something? That man's a saint. He wouldn't take any money for his services. Said it was his good deed for the day. That's one doctor who won't get rich in a hurry.'

Once Maggie was settled, tired and sorrowful, the Masons prepared to leave. Under the watchful eye of Mollie, Maggie had swallowed the tablets left by the doctor to ensure that she had a sound night's sleep. So, confident that she was in good hands, they bade Mollie goodnight and departed for Sydenham where Sarah was being looked after by the twins. All, that is, except Brendan. He had asked Mollie if she would like him to stay and she had nodded gratefully.

As they sat each side of the hearth, he saw the lines of fatigue on her face and voiced the thoughts that had entered his mind. 'Maggie's lucky to have a friend like you.'

'I love her, son. She's like me own flesh an' blood, but I despair for her now Paul's gone. What's to become of her? To be honest, she's never been accepted here. That's why Paul was so anxious to move further up the Falls. The people about here are good and kind, but ye see, they're jealous of Maggie. She's too beautiful, ye see, son.' Her head swung in a despairing arc. 'I don't know what'll become of her, so I don't.'

Nebulous ideas about Maggie's future were at the back of Brendan's mind but it was too soon to voice them. In fact, he might never be able to set them in motion. Why should Maggie ever turn to him in that way?

'We'll just have to wait an' see, Mollie. What about your job. Will they keep it for you?'

'I think so . . . in the circumstances. I'll take another day or two off an' see what happens.' She rose and headed for the stairs. 'I'll fetch some blankets and a pillow for you,' she said kindly. 'Sure, ye can hardly keep yer eyes open, son.'

'You're right, Mollie. I am tired. Won't ye make sure I'm up in time for work in the mornin'?'

'I will surely.'

When Mollie returned with the bedclothes, a worried frown puckered her brow. 'I've just had a look in on Maggie an' she's very restless so I'm goin' t'stay with her. You sleep on my bed, son. You'll be more comfortable there.'

'I could sleep on a thread, I'm so tired,' he confessed. 'But . . . will you be all right? You must be tired too.'

'Yes, I'll manage. If I need ye, I'll give ye a shout.'

'Thanks, Mollie, an' goodnight. See ye in the mornin'.'

'Brendan . . . Brendan! Wake up, son!'

Knowing how little sleep he'd had for the past three nights, Mollie hated having to disturb him, but Maggie was in labour and needs must. Opening his eyes he stared unseeingly at her and closed them again. She shook him roughly. 'Brendan, wake up! Come on now, son, wake up! The baby's coming an' we need the doctor.'

Shaking his head to clear it, he swung his legs off the bed and rose groggily to his feet.

With a firm hand, Mollie steadied him, saying urgently, 'Hurry son, an' fetch Doctor Hughes . . . he lives above the surgery.'

A scream brought Brendan's eyes to the ceiling and drove sleep from him. Without a word, he grabbed his ulster and pushed his feet into his boots as he left the house.

'I expected something like this,' Doctor Hughes confided in Brendan as they hurried back up Malcolmson Street. When he saw Maggie, he barked at Mollie, 'Boil plenty of water.' Then, removing his coat, he rolled up his shirt sleeves and bent over the writhing figure on the bed.

Huddled close to the fire, where pots and pans simmered, Brendan squirmed every time Maggie screamed. It was awful what women had to go through and some women suffered this torment every year. And poor Maggie was already so worn out . . . how could she survive? Impulsively, he sank to his knees but to his surprise it wasn't God he talked to, it was Paul. Beseeching him to help Maggie through the birth of his child. It was four hours later that the doctor called him upstairs and thrust a bundle into his arms.

'Baptise him! He's not long for this world. I only hope his mother doesn't follow him.'

Looking at the puny little infant, Brendan lamented inwardly, Is there no end to Maggie's troubles? He carried the child down the stairs into the scullery. At the jawbox he filled a cup with water and held the tiny head in the palm of his hand, steadying it over the jawbox and pouring water over it, saying at the same time, 'I baptise you, in the name of the Father and of the Son and of the Holy Ghost, amen.' Exactly as he had been taught in the catechism classes. When he returned to the kitchen, Mollie gently took the child from him and carried it to the fireside where a basin of water sat ready to bathe it.

'How is she?' His voice was full of fear and the tear-stained face Mollie turned to him did nothing to alleviate it.

'She's in God's hands. She hasn't the will t'live.'

When the baby was ready, Brendan took it in his arms and sat rocking it gently. It was such a puny wee thing, this son of Maggie's and Paul's. So quiet, hardly any sign of life. Time passed slowly and he was unaware when the small form stopped breathing, but gradually realised that the child was dead and knew what he must do. Placing the small corpse on the armchair, he sank to his knees in front of the Sacred Heart picture and prayed. Ignoring the great ache in his heart, he promised that if Maggie lived he would not forsake his vocation to the priesthood. For a short time he had been foolish enough to think he could take care of her and her children, but now he realised that it could never be. Maggie was not for him.

In a fever, Maggie tossed and turned for three long days. All the Masons took it in turn to sit with her, and once when Brendan sat by the bedside she grabbed his hand, a joyous smile illuminating her face.

'Paul! Is it really you?' Then, flinging his hand away, her eyes roamed the room, forever searching. In the early hours of the fourth day, Brendan was once again sitting with her when he must have dozed off because he had a dream. He dreamt that he was awakened by Maggie sitting upright in the bed; she who could hardly hold her head up, so wasted was she, was sitting gazing wide-eyed at something beyond him. Before he turned he sensed that no one would be there and at the sight of the empty doorway, he felt the gooseflesh rise on his arms and the hair at the back of his neck. A swift glance confirmed that the rest of the room was empty but Maggie was speaking and fear left him as he leant forward to listen.

'Please don't ask me to stay. Please . . .' Her head tilted as if she was listening and she whispered hoarsely, 'No! I won't stay!' Then, leaning forward, she clawed frantically at the bedclothes. 'Don't go. Don't leave me! Please, don't leave me . . .' Her voice trailed off and her body slumped forward in a faint.

With a start of surprise, Brendan saw Maggie really was slumped over in the bed. Glancing apprehensively over his shoulder, he rose slowly to his feet and approached the bed. As he laid Maggie gently back on the pillows, he noted that the fever had abated and her breathing was regular and normal. Bemused, he returned to the chair and went over in his mind what had happened. Had he dozed off? He must have! Hadn't he? Of course he had. He'd been dreaming. Next morning he awoke to find Maggie's big tragic eyes watching him. Rising stiffly from the chair, he took her hand in his and whispered, 'Welcome back, Maggie.'

Her eyes, huge in a small wasted face, travelled over the flat bedclothes. 'The baby?'

His grip on her hand tightened. 'You had a son, Maggie. We buried him with Paul.'

She squeezed her eyes shut and two tears welled over and ran down her cheeks. 'Then Paul isn't alone after all.'

With a deep sigh she turned her head aside and slept. Knowing that it was a healing sleep, Brendan went down on his knees and thanked God.

CHAPTER FOUR

Bleakness and despair was all Maggie was ever to remember of the following weeks. No matter what the weather was like, Saturdays and Sundays were spent in Milltown Cemetery attending to Paul's grave, and no one could persuade her that it was wrong to take Sarah to the graveyard, week after week.

Is it not her father's grave? she thought wildly, as she feverishly weeded and trimmed the grave, talking all the while to Paul and her young son, watched by a wide-eyed Sarah. Even when the weather was cold she failed to notice how chilled the child was; all she lamented about was the hardness of the soil as she endeavoured to turn it over. She thought it ironic that she had not seen her son's features. She had prayed that Paul would live to see his child, never doubting that she would not see him. Now they lay together, father and son, while she ... was left behind.

As she withdrew further and further from reality, Brendan decided to write to William. They had neglected to inform him about his brother-in-law's death. Only after the funeral, when Maggie lost the baby and Brendan realised she could never be his, did he think of William and hastened to write and let him know. To his surprise William wrote back expressing his deep regret, but did not mention coming home.

Well, he'll have to come home now, Brendan decided determinedly as his worry for Maggie's welfare increased.

He wrote and told William that his sister needed his assistance.

To his credit, William came home straight away and when he saw Maggie, confided to Brendan, 'She should go home.'

He nodded his agreement. With Maggie lost to him forever, it would be better all round if she returned to her parents' home. He was tormented by her availability, her need for comfort; but if he were to comfort her the way he wanted to, where would they end up? What would become of his promise to God?

'They did not know of Paul's death until I came home, you understand?' William excused his parents, a worried frown on his brow. 'If they had known, I'm sure they would have fetched her home,' he explained, adding lamely, 'I'll have a word with them.'

Feeling sure Maggie's father would be keeping tabs on her and would be aware of his brother's death, Brendan's nod was non-committal. It was up to William now to see to his sister.

A few days later, when Mollie answered a knock on the door, she knew at once that the woman on the doorstep was Maggie's mother. Who else, looking like royalty, would arrive in a horse-drawn carriage?

Tall and well-dressed, Ruth Pierce looked splendid in a dark green afternoon gown, the sleeves and skirt ornamented with heavy cream lace. The deep-brimmed straw hat that covered most of her chestnut hair was of the same shade of cream and around her shoulders was draped a fur stole.

Seeing the amused look in Ruth's eyes as she looked down her long arrogant nose at her, and noting the twitching net curtains across the street, Mollie became aware that she was gaping. Snapping her mouth closed, she curbed the urge to curtsey and asked politely, 'Can I help you?' being careful to pronounce her words properly.

Well-shaped eyebrows rose in her smooth white brow and nostrils flared in disdain. 'I am Ruth Pierce. I believe my daughter Margaret lives here?'

'Yes . . . won't you come in, please?'

Although the new skirt lengths swung to just above the shoes, Ruth swept her skirts high before passing through the small hall into the kitchen, as if afraid they might touch the walls and be soiled.

From the scullery, Maggie, hardly able to believe her eyes, uttered a pleased sound. However, she knew better than to give into the urge to rush and embrace her mother, knowing she hated any sign of emotion. Besides, her mother's rejection of her still rankled.

Nevertheless, she was pleased that her mother had come and her pleasure came through in her greeting. 'Oh, Mother, it's lovely to see you. Please sit down.'

With an inclination of her head she indicated the armchair, but a scornful glance dismissed this and Ruth chose a straight-backed chair at the table. Spreading her skirts carefully, she slowly examined the kitchen before turning her attention to Maggie.

With a twisted smile, Mollie watched Ruth examine and dismiss her home. Excusing herself, she went into the scullery and closed the door.

Once they were alone, Ruth eyed her daughter. 'We must talk, Margaret.'

Maggie smiled, she was glad her mother had come. Ever since William had visited her, she had been thinking longingly of home but had feared another rejection. Really she should be ashamed to see her mother, after the way she had treated Paul. But he was dead and she must think of Sarah. There was nothing here for her now that Paul was gone and Sarah would receive a better upbringing, a better education, if they lived with her parents. Yes, she must do what was best for Sarah. Although she was perturbed by the fact that not once did Ruth acknowledge, by so much as a glance, the chestnut-haired, green-eyed child who was her double.

'Thank you for coming, Mother,' Maggie said softly.

'I have a proposition for you, Margaret.'

She stood silent. From the tone of her mother's voice,

she guessed it was not a pleasant proposition, and was filled with misgiving.

Gazing at a spot somewhere above her daughter's head, Ruth said, 'Your father and I have examined your position from all angles and we have agreed that you can come home.'

A relieved sigh came softly from Maggie's parted lips and she visibly relaxed, but before she could speak, Ruth held up her hand for silence.

'Wait! I'm not finished.' She paused and for the first time looked at Sarah. Gazing into wide-spaced, clear green eyes, so like the eyes she saw each time she looked in the mirror, she paused for a moment, blinked in confusion, then tore her glance away. 'The child must stay with her father's family,' she finished unsteadily.

For a moment Maggie was rendered speechless, then she cried in astonishment, 'You can't mean that, Mother? Ah, no, no! Why . . . why . . .' For a moment, at a loss, she groped for words, then at last blurted out, 'She's your grandchild! Your only grandchild!'

Sarah looked a picture in her blue and white floral dress and clean white pinafore, her bright chestnut hair a profusion of curls. Gripping her by the arm, Maggie drew her forward. 'Look at her. Why, she's your double. How can you deny her her heritage? Why, you should be proud of her, so you should!'

Until then Sarah had been standing wide-eyed, gazing at this vision in beautiful clothes. But when her mother pulled her forward, overcome by shyness, she clung to her and buried her head in Maggie's skirt, starting to whimper.

This caused Ruth to throw her a disgusted look before saying to Maggie, 'Hush, Margaret. Control yourself, dear. You are twenty-five years old, past marriageable age. We think we can find you a suitable husband, but not if you have a child by your side. Why, that would be unthinkable.'

Face tight with anger, Maggie said, 'This might surprise you, Mother, but I have no inclination to marry again.' Then her voice took on a pleading note. 'Mam, all I want is what's best for Sarah.' Seeing no sign of softening in her mother's expression, Maggie found herself begging. This was Sarah's future she was fighting for. 'Please, Mam, you'll come to love her, I know you will. She's a lovely child . . . and so good. Why, you won't even be aware that she's in the house.'

'Margaret! Stop it! Please, stop it. The last time we tried to advise you, you would not listen to reason. You had to marry your Catholic and look where it's landed you. A widow at twenty-five . . .'

At this Maggie angrily interrupted her, 'Yes, it was awful inconsiderate of Paul to die, wasn't it? He just wanted to go and leave me here on my own. Good God, Mother, you're acting as if Paul had a choice!'

'You should never have married him! Didn't we warn you? You knew we were against your marriage but you would not allow it to be annulled. Oh, no, you were in *love.*'

There was such derision in these words that Maggie gasped in protest and once more interrupted her. 'Is that such a crime, Mother? To fall in love?'

'It would have been just as easy to love a Protestant. You didn't give yourself a chance. Think how different you life would have been if you had waited and married someone from your own class.' She leant forward and actually begged. 'Please, listen to reason this time. Be guided by us. Think of all we've done for you. The chances you threw away.'

Maggie heard the plea, but recalling her lonely childhood in the big empty house on the Malone Road, she wanted to accuse her mother of neglect, of having no time for her. Knowing that it would only make matters worse, she held her tongue.

'To be truthful, Margaret, after all the heartache and trouble you have caused us, I think we are being magnanimous taking you back, I really do,' Ruth continued, and looked at her daughter as if she was daft not to agree with her. Then she added, 'Questions will be asked. A lot of questions. There will be a lot of covering up to be done. And it can be done, it can be done,' she stressed. 'But not if a child is involved. Surely you can see that?' Her eyes rested briefly on Sarah. 'I'm sure her grandparents will be pleased to have her.' She was glad that the child had her face hidden against her mother's skirt. Looking into her eyes had startled Ruth, had taken the breath from her, but she had no intention of admitting it.

'You're her grandmother! She's your flesh and blood. Why, you should be ashamed of yourself for suggesting such a thing.' She realised that she was losing the battle. In spite of her effort to control it, Maggie's voice had risen shrilly. Ruth rose abruptly to her feet, head back in indignation.

'Please don't use that tone of voice with me, Margaret,' she cried. 'When you think it over, I'm sure you'll find that what we suggest is for the best.' She moved towards the door then turned and asked, 'Are you aware that there might be a civil war, or are the Catholics under the delusion that they can win? Ulster will never accept Home Rule.' She shook her head decisively. 'No, never! Why, there are rallies being held all over Ulster at the moment, and they're coming in their thousands to vow to fight for the right to remain part of Britain. Sir Edward is going to appeal to England and if they don't listen to him, you mark my words, Margaret, there will be civil war.' She scanned Maggie's stricken face and her tone softened, 'Come home, Margaret. Come home where you belong.' Once more her eyes swept scornfully around the kitchen, then came to rest questioningly on Maggie. 'Surely you can't really like living here?'

Ignoring this question, she pleaded, 'Let me bring Sarah, please, Mam?'

'Let me ask you something, Margaret. If we accept the child, can she be brought up in the Methodist faith?'

Maggie's voice was subdued when she answered; she was well aware that here was a stumbling block. How could she break the solemn vow she had made? 'I promised she would be brought up in the Catholic religion.' Would her mother convince her that she must do what was best for Sarah, vow or no vow? Would she allow herself to be convinced? Hopefully she waited. She need not have worried. She was not going to be put to the test; her vow was safe. Her mother was nodding her head in agreement with her.

'I know that, Margaret. I know that. Oh, yes indeed, we all know about the vow outsiders have to make when they marry a Catholic, but think how awkward it would be, your father being who he is, to raise the child a Catholic. It's unthinkable!' Her face grimaced at the very idea. 'She wouldn't be happy. She'll be happier with her other grandparents.'

'Ah, Mam, we could manage something. I'm sure we could,' Maggie implored, but in vain.

Ruth shook her head determinedly. 'It wouldn't work, Margaret. Be guided by me. Leave her! You are young. You'll have other children.' As if the matter was settled, she once more turned towards the door. 'Let me know when you are ready to come home and I'll send the carriage for you.'

Pushing past her, Maggie threw the door wide open. 'No, Mother, you'll never hear from me again. I'm not like you.' She choked back the tears that threatened, determined not to let her mother affect her so. To let her mother see her cry was unthinkable. 'I could never turn my back on my child the way you turned your back on me. Thanks for nothing!'

Ruth drew herself up to her full height and her green eyes glinted with anger. Her voice was hard when she retorted, 'I think one day you might eat those words, Margaret. The world is a cruel place for a woman on her own, especially in a place like Belfast.'

Maggie's face twisted scornfully and she waved at the door. 'Please go, Mother, go on . . . before I forget myself and tell you what I think of you.'

When Ruth, with a final disdainful glance around the kitchen, lifted her skirts and swept past her, Maggie slammed the door. Gathering a bewildered, whimpering

Sarah close to her, she whispered, 'Hush, love. It's all right. Everything's going to be all right.' But as she listened to the clatter of the carriage wheels roll down the street, she felt all hope for the future recede and blinked furiously to contain the tears. Would anything ever be all right again?

When Mollie closed the scullery door, she gripped the edge of the jawbox and shook with silent laughter. Imagine, almost curtseying to Maggie's mother! She looked more royal than royalty, that one, and not a sign of emotion towards her daughter. Unfeeling bitch! And Sarah was the spit of her, her double. Why, it was uncanny to see them together.

The shrill tones of Maggie's voice brought Mollie's head around and she stared at the door, ears straining, but after the first outburst the voices were low and she could not hear what was being said. When the outer door slammed, she left the plate she was washing to drain and, drying her hands on her apron, slowly entered the kitchen.

Maggie turned a white, stricken face towards her. 'She doesn't want Sarah,' she wailed. 'Can you believe it? She hardly looked at her. My beautiful Sarah. Her only grandchild.' She swallowed a sob. 'She wants me to leave her with Bill and Anne.'

Leading her to the fireside, Mollie gently pushed her into the armchair. 'Hush now, don't upset yourself. Sit there a minute an' I'll make us a cup of tea, an' we'll talk about it.'

However, when they were sipping their tea, Mollie found it difficult to start the conversation. She would have to choose her words carefully or Maggie might get the wrong idea. At last she started speaking haltingly. 'You know, Maggie . . . perhaps yer mother's right?'

When Maggie looked amazed and her mouth opened in protest, Mollie said placatingly, 'Hear me out! Hear me out!' Her face screwed up in concentration, she chose her words carefully.

'Listen t'me. There's nothin' here for you without Paul.

Ye know that! Just work an' drudgery. But if ye were t'go home ... well, that'd be a different kettle of fish altogether. One day you'll meet a young man of your own class an' marry again.' Seeing Maggie was about to interrupt her, she raised her voice. 'Let me finish!' Then, more quietly, 'You'll have other children, an' ye know Sarah'd be happy with the Masons. Sure they dote on her. An' who knows, eh, Maggie? Who knows? Maybe the man ye marry'll accept Sarah. Ye never know, Maggie. Ye never know. Ye must look ahead.'

White-faced and tight-lipped, Maggie heard her out. 'Are you quite finished?' Her voice dripped with sarcasm and Mollie knew she had offended her. 'Let me tell you something – I would go to hell before I would abandon Sarah.' Her lips tightened and her face hardened. 'I'm not afraid of hard work. I'll get a job ...' She paused and turned this idea over in her mind, nodding. 'Yes, somehow I'll get a job and ...' A look of alarm crossed her face as yet another thought struck her, and all her bravery left her at the idea that Mollie might forsake her. Gulping deep in her throat, a break in her voice, she wailed, 'Mollie? Ah, Mollie ... You won't put us out, sure you won't?'

Tears long contained rained down her face and sobs racked her slight frame at the very idea that Mollie might forsake her. Hastily, Mollie rose from her chair. Sitting on the arm of Maggie's, she clasped her tight against her breast.

'Never, me dear. Never in this whole wide world. Ye mean too much to me. More than me own sons, if the truth were told, but I had to point out to ye that you'd be better off at home.' She thrust Maggie back and looked earnestly into her face. 'Why, your mam's loss is my good fortune, so it is.'

Abandoning the milk and biscuit Mollie had given her, not understanding but wanting in on the scene, Sarah pressed close. Widening her arms to embrace her also, Mollie whispered, 'It'll all pan out. Just wait an' see, somehow it'll all pan out. It must. Dear God, it must.'

*

110

Although privately educated to a high standard, Maggie nevertheless had left school at fourteen to run the house for her parents as they pursued their work on the council. They did not think it necessary to further her education as a suitable marriage would be arranged in due course, so now work in a shop seemed the obvious solution to her problem. Determined to steer clear of the big stores in town, where she might meet her parents, Maggie tried to obtain work in one of the shops on the Falls Road. However, she was unsuccessful. If truth be told, the shopkeepers thought her too grand. Felt too uncomfortable in her company, were afraid she would find fault with their speech and manners.

Work in the library would have been ideal, but no full-time employment was available there so in despair she decided to try the mills, starting with the Blackstaff. The manager, who had not lifted his head when she entered his office to be interviewed, looked up in surprise when she said, 'Good morning.'

Rising slowly to his feet, his eyes roamed over her face and examined her figure which looked superb in a figure-hugging black velvet suit, bringing a flush to her cheeks. Seeing it, a perplexed frown furrowed his brow and he said quickly, 'I beg your pardon. I thought I was interviewing someone for a job in the weaving shop.'

'I *am* looking for work in the weaving shop,' Maggie answered politely, dismayed at his reaction. She should have listened to Mollie and borrowed her work shawl. Her endeavours to look well could cost her this job, then what would become of her and Sarah?

'Oh, I see . . .' At a loss for words he asked, 'Do you live nearby?'

'I live in Waterford Street.'

'Oh, I see.' But George Bowman did not see. Why was this obviously well-bred young woman living in Waterford Street? There was more here than met the eye. Why, she wouldn't last a crack in the weaving shop. 'Have you ever woven before?' he asked, trying to think of a way to let her down lightly. They would have to pay her while another weaver taught her how to weave, and it would be money thrown away if she did not stay.

'No,' Maggie admitted, and her expression beseeched him, 'but I'm a quick learner.'

She did not know what would become of her if she failed to get a job. The money Paul had saved, plus the deposit Brendan had managed to retrieve from the house in Islandbawn Street, together with the money collected by Paul's workmates when he died, was slowly dwindling away, and food prices had risen out of all proportion in the past few years. Mill workers' wages had risen hardly at all since the beginning of the century, but given a job she would at least be able to keep the wolf from the door. Visions of ending up in the workhouse caused her sleepless nights, even though Mollie assured her that while she could work, Maggie would never be homeless. Maggie loved her for her kindness, but she knew that if she was not there Mollie could rent her rooms and it would make life easier for her.

The anguish that radiated from her caught at George Bowman's heart and he decided to give her a try. 'Can you start on Monday?'

Relief flooding through her, Maggie's answer was heartfelt. 'Oh, yes, I can.'

'Report to the weaving shop on Monday morning at ten to eight and ask for Joe Wilson. He's the tenter you'll be working under. And, remember to bring your insurance cards.'

'I will . . . I will. Thank you. Thank you very much.'

'Good luck.' He dismissed her with a nod, but when the door closed on her he gazed at it thoughtfully for some moments, wondering what had brought her down in the world. Then with a shrug he returned to his paperwork. It was none of his business, but he doubted if she would last long in the weaving shop.

For it to be worth Maggie's while working, Mollie also sought and obtained work in the Blackstaff, on the shift that was known as the 'Granny shift' in the spinning department. It wasn't easy; work was scarce, but Mollie was a good spinner and she sang her own praises until the doff master decided to give her a try. This meant that when Maggie was coming out of work at six o'clock, Mollie was waiting with Sarah by the hand, to go into the Granny shift which was from six to ten, and Maggie took Sarah home with her. This way they were able to avoid paying for someone to look after Sarah and a routine was started that was to last until Maggie found more suitable employment.

She hated the weaving shop. The deafening clatter of the machinery made her head pound and the speed of the looms frightened her. The dust from the weft choked her, filling her lungs and clinging to her hair and clothes, giving them the smell that marked those who worked there, making her easily recognisable as a factory worker. Looking at her fellow workers, she wondered how these girls could appear so happy, working in such conditions. She voiced these thoughts to big rough and ready Nellie Matthew, who was teaching her how to weave. Nellie assured her that you soon got used to it, but Maggie doubted very much that she would ever get used to it. To add to her misery, she found Joe Wilson offensive.

The space between the looms was narrow and when Nellie had to ask him to tend her looms, he took every opportunity to press his plump body against Maggie. He eyed her lustfully, whispering obscene suggestions, knowing she would be afraid to complain in case she lost her job. Nellie was heartsore for her, knowing that she was out of her depth. Any of the other weavers would soon have put Joe in his place but Maggie's outraged response only egged him on. She did not know it but her proud haughty manner excited him, and as he became more attracted to her, he even had the audacity to suggest that if she was nice to him, he would make life easier for her. The very idea of his touching her made her flesh creep and her rejection of him was heartfelt, adding fuel to his anger.

This was to cause problems when she was put in charge of her own looms. The weekly pay was made up by each cut of cloth made from a loom. The beam of warp at the back of the loom contained a number of 'cuts', the number defined by the thickness of the material woven. The length of the cut was marked by a deep red dye mark that was woven into the cloth. When it was long enough to come round on the roller at the front of the loom, a cut was made across the centre of the red dye and it was pulled off the roller. That was a cut of cloth. The price a weaver earned was determined by the width and quality of the cloth. Now, if the mark could be seen on a Friday afternoon the tenter had the authority to initial the cloth in two places on the roller, enabling a weaver to cut between the two signatures and pull the cloth off early and thus receive full pay. But not once in all the time Maggie worked there did Joe Wilson sign her cloth for her, always making the excuse that the red mark was not near enough, even when it was almost ready to weave in. This filled her with resentment and frustration, but she did not waver in her resolve to keep him at arm's length.

Only the weekends spent with Brendan kept her sane. Regular as clockwork, he arrived every Saturday morning, and took Sarah and Maggie downtown window shopping, delighting the child by buying them tea and cones in one of the small cafes on Royal Avenue and making it the highlight of her week. Sometimes, if the weather was fine, they walked in the Botanic Gardens or caught the tram out the Antrim Road and climbed the Cave Hill on the outskirts of Belfast, where they looked across Belfast Lough to Sydenham and pretended that they could see Brendan's home. Maggie looked forward to the weekends, and grew to rely on him. This worried Brendan, but he could not tell her that he was entering the priesthood while she was working in the Blackstaff. That was unthinkable! Things were bad enough for her without him removing his support and company. Somehow, he did not think God would mind waiting. He just hoped his longing for Maggie could be kept at bay. The desire that was eating away at him was barely kept under control, and he prayed that God would help him in his dilemma.

Christmas passed quietly, Maggie refusing to leave the

house, and January brought heightened rumours of civil war. No one in the weaving shop ever mentioned the rumours to Maggie, and lost as she was in a world of her own, she failed to notice the whispering and the nudges as she was discussed.

However Mollie brought all the news home from the spinning room, and one night came home bursting with excitement. 'They say at least thirty thousand people gathered in Omagh at the weekend to hear Carson speak. Just imagine, Maggie, thirty thousand!'

Maggie was surprised. She knew of Sir Edward Carson; her father had a great respect for him.

At her surprised look, Mollie added, 'Aye!' Her white head wagged. 'Some arrived in charabancs and farmcarts, but the majority of them walked. God, but they must be keen to walk to Omagh!' she finished in awe.

'What do you think will happen, Mollie?'

'God only knows. Asquith is sendin' Winston Churchill over. He's the new First Lord of the Admiralty, no less, an' he's goin' to present the government's case for reform. Perhaps they'll work something out between them. I sincerely hope so.'

Mollie wished it was all settled. Home Rule had the approval of the majority in Ireland and the majority of elected representatives in Westminster. Had the Ulster Unionists the right to try to stop it being implemented? Had they the power to stop it going through? She was very much afraid that they did have the power to stop it. The grapevine was alive with rumours of thousands of loyalists meeting frequently to display their solidarity against Home Rule, and she knew fears ran deep because it could start civil war. Then what chance would the Catholics of the Falls Road stand? Sandwiched as they were between the Protestant Shankill and Sandy Row?

Maggie could also understand the Protestant side of the story. Most of the businessmen in Belfast were Protestants and they were proud to be part of the British Empire. They imported all their raw materials from the Empire and then sold manufactured goods back. Fear that Home Rule

115

would mean a Dublin parliament that might take Ireland out of the Empire made them bitterly opposed to it and willing to come out in force against it.

At the same time as all this was going on, the *Catholic Bulletin* announced that the time had come to bring into the bosom of the Holy Church the brethren that were separated from it. Maggie was amazed when Mollie showed her the *Bulletin*. Was the church daft? Did they not realize that this was what Protestants feared from a united Ireland? It was stupid at this time to air such views. Aware that anything she said might be misconstrued, she decided to keep her opinions to herself. After all, she was unlikely to change the course decided on.

Maggie was also aware that she was being watched and did not blame the men of the district for being careful; after all, she was an outsider and a politician's daughter. Her father was high in the Orange Order and his name was constantly in the newspapers. She was only too aware that the men of the district watched and discussed her although she feined ignorance to Mollie. Clive Pierce's name was often in the headlines as he supported Carson in his fight against Home Rule, and Maggie felt that she should try to get away from the Falls Road, but where could she go? With the exception of Brendan, Mollie was the only person in the world to whom she felt really close and she did not want to cut the ties that bound them. So she bore the whispers and the watching with great patience until the day Sarah arrived home in tears.

'Mam . . . is my granda an Orange man?'

Taking her gently in her arms, Maggie tenderly wiped away the tears and asked, 'Now who said that to you?'

'Ginny Hanna. She says my granda will be burning the Pope on the twelfth, so she did.' Big green eyes begged her to deny this as she asked, 'He won't burn the Pope, sure he won't, Mam?'

Rage rose in Maggie's breast, Ginny was only a child. She must have heard adults talking in the house to be able to repeat such hurtful things to Sarah. Waving aside Mollie's plea to her to ignore the episode, Maggie rolled

116

up her sleeves and stormed across the road. To her annoyance, Belle Hanna's front door was tightly closed and she would not open it to Maggie's knock. Not wanting to lower herself by shouting in public, she slowly retraced her steps and returned indoors. But she had shown that the worm had turned; she could be pushed just so far; thereafter Sarah was left in peace. And to Maggie's surprise, a grudging admiration was shown towards her by other neighbours. Many had suffered from the sharp edge of Belle's tongue and they admired Maggie's spirit.

These were bitter-sweet times for Brendan, watching Maggie grow strong, seeing her fill out, aching for her and knowing she could never be his. He felt great animosity against her parents. How could they refuse their grandchild a home? He had added his pleas to Mollie's that she leave Sarah with his family, but in vain. Maggie had bestowed on him a look of such scorn the words died on his lips and were mentioned no more. And so he watched her: beautiful, even in black mourning clothes, the black showing off the pure transparency of her skin and brightness of her hair, and he wanted her. How he wanted her.

His mother fretted as he became quiet and withdrawn, but Bill would not let her interfere. This was something Brendan had to work out for himself. Then to Maggie's delight Mr Weston, the head librarian, approached her with an offer of full-time employment. Maggie was so overjoyed that she hugged the frail, elderly man, bringing a blush to his sallow cheeks. The wages were slightly lower but the hours almost halved. She would have more time to spend with Sarah. Delighted, she thankfully said goodbye to the three looms she now attended in the Blackstaff, glad to be leaving fat oily Joe Wilson for good, and started work in the library. However, her happiness was to be dimmed because Brendan decided that he had delayed long enough. Now that Maggie was settled in a proper job, the time had come to enter the Seminary. Sore at heart, he waited his chance to tell her of his decision.

117

He was alone in the house with her, Mollie having taken Sarah to the corner shop for sweets, when he broached the subject. 'Maggie, I must talk to you.'

She looked at him in surprise. 'I thought we were conversing?' she said, a light laugh accompanying the words. However, the laughter died when she saw how serious he was. She stood silent, waiting, her eyes full of apprehension.

Drinking in her beauty, Brendan wondered, not for the first time, if he was doing the right thing. The longing to hold her and kiss her was so acute, it was a deep aching need in him. Sometimes he was quite ill with the worry of it, but he knew if once he held her, he would be lost.

What if God would prefer me to marry Maggie and take care of her and Sarah? he fretted inwardly. Who knew? Perhaps God meant for him to look after Maggie and Sarah. Surely he could get a dispensation and marry her? The Church had granted Doctor Keenan a dispensation to marry his dead wife's sister, so why not him? He was torn in two. He had prayed for guidance but no direct answer was forthcoming. Sometimes he was sure he was meant to marry Maggie, and other times was sure God was waiting for him to keep his promise.

Watching the different expressions flitting across his face, Maggie frowned. 'What is it, Brendan? Is something wrong?' she asked apprehensively.

'I have decided to enter a Seminary and try to become a priest.' The words came out in a rush, his fear of weakening acute.

Maggie's jaw dropped slightly and she gasped in disbelief. Her mouth opened and closed but no sound came. She turned away from him, trying to gather her wits about her. So that was why he wasn't interested in girls! And she, fool that she was, had thought he cared for her. He should have told her! He should have told her. He had no right to delude her. Dear God, what would she do? How could she weather another loss?

'I decided a long time ago, Maggie.' His voice broke through her despair, soft and apologetic.

'Why didn't you tell me? You should have told me!' She was unable to keep the anger from her voice, and he recoiled in dismay.

'I was waitin' till you were strong. Able to face life without Paul.'

Slowly she turned to face him, her emotions thinly under control. 'It was kind of you to think of me, but I wish you had told me.' Her lip trembled and she bit on it before continuing. 'I wish you every happiness and success, Brendan. Sarah and I will miss you.'

'You'll marry again, Maggie.' She swung her head slowly from side to side in a wide arc of denial, and he insisted. 'You will, Maggie. A beautiful girl like you'll have plenty of chances.'

Still shaking her head, she managed a weak smile and with her hand waved the very idea away. 'Don't worry about me, Brendan. I'll be all right. When do you go?'

'I'm not sure. In a couple of weeks' time, I should imagine.'

Wanting to appease her he moved closer, and then in spite of all his good intentions she was in his arms. Pressing the soft curves of her body against his, he sank his face into her hair. 'Ah, Maggie, Maggie.' A great shuddering sob shook his body. 'How I've dreamed of this, longed to hold you.'

Bewildered, she nevertheless pressed closer still. Had she misunderstood him? How could he want to become a priest if he felt like this about her? His lips sought hers and she surrendered willingly. Perhaps if she showed him that she cared, he would stay with her . . . she couldn't bear to let him go, but had she the right? She didn't love him! She cared . . . ah, but that wasn't love.

His lips trailed her face, her throat, and returned to the velvet sweetness of her lips. Then his hand cupped the softness of her breast. Only then did he become aware of his actions. Pushing her roughly away from him, he fought for self-control. 'I'm sorry. Ah, Maggie, I'm sorry. I had no right to do that . . . no right at all.'

Ashamed of her own actions, the encouragement she

119

had given him, Maggie turned aside. 'It's all right, Brendan. I understand,' she lied. How could she understand his decision to go away, if he loved her?

An uneasy silence stretched between them as they sought for words to cover the awkwardness, and their relief was apparent when Mollie and Sarah entered the kitchen, breaking the tension.

Maggie greeted her friend with obvious relief. 'What do you think, Mollie? Brendan is going to become a priest. Won't it be nice to know someone is praying for us?'

To say Mollie was surprised would be putting it mildly. She had been sure Brendan was in love with Maggie and it was just a matter of time before he set things in motion to get a dispensation so they could marry.

'Well I never!' she cried, at a loss for words. 'When did you decide this, Brendan?'

'A long time ago, Mollie. Long before Paul died.'

'Oh, I see.' Inane words, because she didn't see. Far from it. Perhaps before Paul had died, Brendan may have wanted to become a priest, but surely she was right in thinking that he loved Maggie?

Tea was a subdued meal, conversation coming in fits and starts, silences alive with things unsaid. When Brendan at last rose to go, they bade him goodnight with relief, glad to see him depart.

The dishes were washed in a silence at last broken by Mollie. 'That was a bolt from the blue. I wouldn't have thought Brendan would enter the Seminary.' Her tone was critical and Maggie, ignoring her own unhappiness and disappointment, rushed to his defence.

'He will make a wonderful priest. He has all the qualifications: compassion, generosity, and above all, selflessness.'

'I know, I know. I didn't mean to be critical. He's all you say. Aye, an' more. But . . .' Groping in her mind for the right words, she at last blurted out, 'Drat it, Maggie, I thought he was in love with you.'

'Well, Mollie, we were wrong and we must wish him well.'

Noting the use of the word 'we' Mollie felt like weeping, but she kept her mouth firmly closed and once more silence fell as they washed and dried.

Withdrawn and morose, Brendan made preparations to enter the Seminary, watched anxiously by his parents. At last Bill could bear it no longer and after tea one night, when he was alone with his son, asked haltingly 'Are you sure this is what you want?'

Brendan, who was reading a book, raised his head and gazed at him in surprise. 'What on earth do you mean?'

'Well, your mother an' I think perhaps you've grown too fond of Maggie.'

'Ah, Da.' Brendan laughed softly. 'If only it was as simple as that.' He shook his head, a woebegone gesture. 'It's not as easy as that. I only wish it were.' His sigh was from the heart. 'But when Jesus said to his disciples, "Come follow me", He didn't mean if you have no other commitments or you're at a loose end. Ah, no. He meant drop all an' come, an' I feel He wants me to try.' Seeing his father was not reassured, he added, 'I've been tempted . . . sorely tempted, but I made God a promise and I must try to fulfil it. Don't worry, Da. If I'm not meant for the priesthood, they'll soon let me know an' I'll be able to return with an easy conscience. If I don't go, I'll always wonder if I did the right thing.'

Bill nodded, satisfied. 'You're right, son. Time'll tell.'

With Brendan away, Maggie devoted herself to Sarah, work and sleep, in that order; although Mollie railed at her to go out and make friends, crying, 'You're only young once!', she fretted and worried about Maggie.

With the new respect that she had earned came tentative offers of friendship from the neighbours, especially the young single men, but Maggie kept her distance, knowing she was not really accepted, a Protestant in the heart of the Falls and one with no intentions of turning. Father Magee, the parish priest, had given up trying to interest her in the faith, having to be content that Mollie was seeing Sarah brought up a Catholic. Even Mollie had stopped trying to persuade her to accompany Sarah and her to church, being unable to answer her ever ready question, Why had Paul to die?

There had been spasmodic outbreaks of fighting, but so far civil war had been averted and no one bothered with Maggie. She rarely left Waterford Street so she was left in peace. To the dismay of the Ulster Catholics, Winston Churchill's visit was not a success. Feelings were running so high against Home Rule in Ulster, that the Liberals had been baulked at every turn in their endeavours to book a hall for the meeting, and Churchill's arrival in Belfast, on a cold wet day in February, was greeted by hostile crowds. They surged around his carriage, singing 'God Save the King', and using threatening behaviour. Being denied the use of the Ulster Hall, Churchill had to make do with a marquee set up in Celtic Park and here he spoke to a small Home Rule audience, with his voice loud to cover the sound of the pouring rain beating down on the canvas. He departed soon after, a very disappointed man, to report his failure to Asquith in England.

Determined to show their allegiance to the King and the strong wish to remain part of Britain, on Easter Tuesday a covenant was formed by the loyalists as a show of strength. It was estimated that over 100,000 Protestants marched at Balmoral in South Belfast, vowing to fight to the bitter end to keep Ulster part of the Empire should Home Rule be passed through parliament. As they marched they chorused aloud, 'No Surrender to Home Rule' and waved Union Jacks aloft, and tension was high.

However another tragedy was to push Home Rule from the headlines. The *Titanic*, the largest vessel in the world, built with pride by Harland and Wolff, a ship that some had said even God could not sink, hit an iceberg on her maiden journey and sank. Thousands of lives were lost and a great depression settled over the City of Belfast as they mourned the dead. It wasn't Harland and Wolff who had said that the ship was unsinkable but they would bear the brunt of the blame. Yet another thorn in the crown of sorrows that plagued Belfast.

Just a week earlier, on the 2 April, Mollie had persuaded Maggie to join her on an outing to see the *Titanic* sail for Southampton. The docks had been thronged and Maggie would never forget the majestic beauty of the ship as it gracefully sailed away. The newspapers had kept them up to date on her manoeuvres, and then on 15 April she sank.

Maggie buried herself in her job, living only for Sarah and for work. She loved her job and with Mr Weston's permission, organised a class twice a week when she helped to teach the old people to read. At last she felt her life held some meaning.

The months passed slowly, with just the odd outburst of fighting on the Falls Road, and if sometimes in the loneliness of the big double bed, Maggie wept at the empty years ahead of her, no one ever guessed. She was cool, calm, self-possessed and aloof. She had discovered that Anne was right. Time did deaden the pain of loss but it did not take away the loneliness.

Due to her background and manners, Maggie quickly acquired a prominent position in the library, second only to Mr Weston. When a vacancy occurred, it was she who interviewed Kathleen Rooney for a position in the library. Although Kathleen had not the required qualifications, Maggie liked her and recommended that Mr Weston give her a try. It was something she was to be grateful for in years to come because Kathleen was to be her salvation.

Plain, homely Kathleen was six years younger than Maggie and had started work in the library with trepidation. She had heard all about Maggie; had noted her haughty beauty when she'd had occasion to change her library book. Lady Muck she was known as, and to be truthful Kathleen had dreaded working with her. Only her love of books and her desire for a job away from the mills had made her apply when the opportunity to work in the library had become available. She had not been very hopeful about acquiring the position but to her surprise was offered the post and soon grew to like and respect

Maggie. As the friendship between them grew, she pestered Maggie to accompany her to the pictures until at last she wore her down.

Greatly tempted, Maggie hummed and hawed. She was lonely and craved friendship, and Kathleen was such a nice person . . . but would she fit in? Sensing that at last her friend was wavering, Kathleen urged her, 'Come on Maggie, come with me. You'll enjoy yourself, so you will.'

Maggie laughed but replied with reservations, 'I'll have to ask Mollie first. She has Sarah all week and may not want to be saddled with her on a Saturday evening.'

Kathleen laughed aloud at this. 'Ah, no sweat then. It's settled! Mollie dotes on that child, there's no way she'll refuse. Look, I'll meet you at the middle gate of the Dunville Park at half-seven tonight. All right?'

Pleased at having persuaded Maggie to accompany her to the pictures, Kathleen ran off in a happy state of mind. In the three months that she had worked alongside Maggie, she had grown very fond of her and, so far as she knew, Maggie went nowhere except to visit her in-laws once a month. It wasn't natural. All work and no play could make you eccentric. At first she had been in awe of Maggie, of her straight-backed posture, the proud tilt of her head, the way she rounded off her words. Then to her surprise she found herself copying her and wished that she could speak properly. She even toyed with the idea of going to elocution classes but they were costly, and aware that she would be ridiculed by the neighbours for trying to better herself, she decided against it.

When Maggie asked Mollie to look after Sarah while she went to the pictures she agreed readily, delighted that at last Maggie was showing an interest in things other than her daughter. Since Brendan had entered the Seminary, Maggie was living like a hermit and Mollie rejoiced to see her at last show an interest in going out.

Maggie paid particular attention to her appearance on Saturday night. When she came down the stairs, Mollie's eyes filled with tears. 'You look lovely, just lovely,' she whispered.

Maggie was hesitant. 'Mollie . . . is it too soon?' She nodded down at the clothes she wore.

Mollie was quick to assuage her fears. 'Not a bit of it! Paul would rejoice to see you out of those black clothes.' When Maggie still looked doubtful, she hurried on, 'You take my word for it, he would, Maggie!'

'The neighbours will talk.'

'Ha! When did you ever worry about the neighbours? Besides, those colours are semi-mourning. But . . .' her eyes twinkled. '. . . on you they look lovely.'

It was an old skirt Maggie wore but she had shortened it so that it no longer brushed the ground but swung around her slim ankles. Dark grey in colour, it had a corselet waist, clung to her hips and then flowed gently to her ankles. The blouse she wore with it was also grey, but very pale. Made of a soft silky material, with sleeves full to the elbow and tight to the wrist, it turned her eyes to silver and made her hair look brighter. To set the outfit off, a small straw hat was perched precariously on top of her auburn rolls and curls of hair. She looked beautiful and Mollie felt tears prick her eyes as she gazed at this girl who was like a daughter to her.

'You look lovely,' she repeated. 'Really lovely.'

'Thank you, Mollie.'

Pleased at the compliment, Maggie kissed Mollie on the cheek. Then she turned a stern look on Sarah who was a mischievous imp. 'Now you remember!' She wagged a finger at Sarah but was unable to keep a straight face when the little girl grinned back up at her. 'If you're naughty, no birthday party next month.'

'I'll be good Mam,' she promised, and wrapping her arms around Maggie's legs, beamed up at her. Regardless of the damage it might do to her skirt, Maggie hugged her close.

'Watch she doesn't crease your skirt, Maggie,' Mollie cried anxiously, and taking Sarah by the hand, winked at Maggie. 'Come on, Sarah! Let's you an' me go for some sweets, love.'

Without a backward glance Sarah set off with Mollie, leaving behind a relieved Maggie who had been afraid the child might cry to go with her. Kathleen was already waiting when Maggie arrived breathless at the middle gate of the Dunville Park, and arm in arm they dandered down the Falls Road to where Clonard picture house was situated. As they queued outside, waiting for the first show to be over, Maggie felt old, a misfit. All around her boys and girls flirted and laughed, so young and happy. Kathleen had been wrong. She was too old to enjoy all this young company. They made her feel about fifty.

Behind them in the queue a young man kept eyeing her and Kathleen introduced him as Sean Hanna, her next-door neighbour. Maggie blushed when she saw the admiration in his eyes, and when he teased her she was at a loss how to react and wished she was back home, safe with Mollie and Sarah. Never having flirted in her life, she felt awkward and uneasy, and aware that she was the centre of attention, squirmed uncomfortably. At last, to great relief, the first show was over and they filed slowly into the cinema.

Once inside she relaxed in the friendly darkness, and much to her surprise enjoyed the film, a Charlie Chaplin comedy that sent tears of mirth running down her cheeks. She also enjoyed the walk home with Kathleen, accompanied by Sean Hanna and his friend Jim Rafferty. As they walked, Sean drew her on ahead and soon had her talking easily. He was tall and handsome in a melancholy kind of way, with a long humorous face topped by a thatch of tight brown curls. Maggie liked him very much.

The Saturday night outings became a habit and Maggie, aware Sean was becoming fond of her, found great comfort in the fact that perhaps she might stand a chance of security for herself and Sarah. She did not mean to be mercenary, but she worried about the future and she knew that Sarah could do with a father.

Sean and Jim were two of the lucky few Falls Road men to have full-time employment. The sinking of the *Titanic* earlier that year had cast a shadow over the Harland and

Wolff shipyard, and Sean, who worked there, considered himself lucky still to do so. Jim was an apprentice shoemaker, having been given an apprenticeship by a family friend, and so both were in a position to marry. In spite of being an only child and spoilt by doting parents, Sean was a nice lad and Mollie also rejoiced that he was obviously fond of Maggie. She wasn't getting any younger and longed to see her friend settled before her time was up. It was something she prayed for daily.

As a special treat for Sarah's birthday, Sean took them all to the seaside at Helen's Bay for the day. Helen's Bay was just down the coast from Sydenham, and as they travelled down by train Maggie was besieged by memories of Paul. How often they had travelled this route. How happy they had been. Was he aware of how life was treating her now? Would he understand about Sean? She hoped so; hoped he would approve.

It was a beautiful day. The water was dark blue, calm, and warm enough to bathe in. The sun was hot, blazing down from a cloudless sky. They found a spot where some shade was cast by the harbour wall and soon Mollie was settled in the shadow and dozing off. As Maggie sunbathed, she watched Sean build sand castles for Sarah and saw how patient he was when he tried to teach her how to swim. She felt contented. She could see he was genuinely fond of children and the future looked less bleak. Indeed, it was taking on quite a rosy hue.

Brendan's absence had left a vast void in her life, but she knew from his letters that he was happy and that he was convinced he had done the right thing. She also realized she had imagined herself attracted to him because of his close proximity and her loneliness. Oh, yes, she loved him, but as a brother, and that was how it should be.

Sean became such a part of her life, she wondered how she had ever managed without him. They were seeing each other almost every day and although the feelings she had for him were tepid compared to her love for Paul, she did not expect lightning to strike twice, and he had her respect and admiration. Mentioning him in her letters to Brendan, she did not realise that she was unconsciously asking for his approval, but when he wrote back urging her to marry Sean and giving her his blessing, she was happy. She also felt she would be more secure married to Sean, because during the summer months meetings were held all over Ulster urging followers to show their loyalty to the Empire and Covenant day was set for 28 September.

Belfast came to a standstill on that day; the shipyards, mills and engineering works all stood idle as thousands queued outside the City Hall to sign the Covenant. Some were so keen they even signed in their own blood.

It was estimated that over 400,000 signed, and at the end of the day Carson's carriage was drawn by supporters to the docks where shipyard workers formed a guard of honour. Sean and Jim had gone down to see all the action and it was they who relayed the news to Maggie and Kathleen, painting vivid pictures of bonfires blazing on the hills and headlands around Belfast Lough, as Carson was ushered aboard the *Patriotic* and the ship set sail for England.

However, Asquith was not to be swayed by demonstrations and, undeterred by subtle threats, continued to try to get Home Rule through the Commons, fanning the anger of the loyalists.

As Christmas approached, Maggie was sure Sean would ask her to marry him, and she vowed that if he did she would spend the rest of her life trying to make him happy. Then one night the happy, secure future she saw ahead was shattered by, of all things, a single look.

They had been at the Clonard picture house with Kathleen and Jim, and at the end of the evening were standing at the corner of Leeson Street where Kathleen lived, discussing the film they had just seen. Maggie turned to say something to her friend but the words died on her lips when she saw the look on her face. Unaware that she was watched, Kathleen was gazing at Sean with such a yearning that Maggie's breath caught in her throat and she turned away in confusion. How had she not guessed? Oh, she was blind! Blind! This kind, affectionate girl, who had been so good to her, was in love with Sean, and Maggie, blinded by her own needs, had unwittingly come between them. What on earth could she do? She could stop seeing Sean, of course. But how? She needed him. Needed the security he could offer her and Sarah.

Sadly, however, she realised what she must do. If he asked her to marry him, she must say no. She did not love him . . . nothing had been said, no promises had been made, Kathleen must have her chance.

Life being contrary, Sean chose that night to ask Maggie to marry him. He was sure she cared and when they arrived at the bottom of Waterford Street took her gently in his arms.

Hiding her face against his chest, Maggie thought, Oh, no, no! Not now. Please Lord, not now! I need time to think.

Unaware of her agitation, and plucking up his courage, Sean cleared his throat nervously and said, 'Maggie, I know I'm not good enough for you, but if you marry me I'll take care of you and Sarah and do all in my power to make you happy.'

Eyes tightly closed, Maggie wished with all her heart that she had not seen Kathleen look at him. Then, in blissful ignorance, she could have agreed to marry him and obtain security for herself and Sarah. With a muffled groan she drew away from him.

'I'm sorry, Sean. I can never marry you.'

Mouth agape, he looked at her in bewilderment. He had been so sure she cared. Pulling her back into his arms, he found himself babbling, 'Maggie, I know you don't love me like you loved Paul, I realise that, but I'll be content with your affection.'

'Ah, Sean, forgive me. I care for you a lot, but not enough to build a marriage on.' It pained her to know that she was hurting him and she tried to soften the blow. 'I'm sorry, truly sorry. I didn't mean to hurt you. Please forgive me.' And, turning on her heel, she ran up the street.

Stunned, he stood as though turned to stone. Then anger flared through him. She had led him on! With her gestures and smiles she had led him to believe she cared. No! He could not believe she would do a thing like that. She was so kind, would not say a bad word about anyone. There must be some mistake. His brow furrowed. There was something not right here. Surely he was not mistaken in thinking she was fond of him?

He strode up the street, determined to have it out with her, but halfway up he stopped. He could not have a showdown tonight, not while he was angry. Tomorrow night he could meet her coming from work and if necessary beg her to marry him. She had spoilt him for anyone else. Only she would do. She must marry him. She must!

Next morning, after a sleepless night, Maggie was heavy-eyed and pale.

'Are you feelin' sick?' Kathleen asked, eyeing her solicitously when she arrived at the library.

Shaking her head, Maggie replied, 'Sean asked me to marry him last night and I refused, but I feel guilty about wasting so much of his time.'

'You refused?' Kathleen was astounded, her big blue eyes round with wonder. 'I thought you were fond of him,' she gasped.

'I am, but not enough for marriage.'

'Poor Sean. Ah, poor, poor Sean. Tut, tut. He must be in an awful state.' Kathleen shook her head, bewildered. 'I really thought you liked him,' she added accusingly, causing Maggie to round on her.

'He will soon find consolation,' she stated flatly, amazed at Kathleen's attitude.

'His parents'll be so disappointed. Mrs Hanna was just sayin' how much she likes you,' Kathleen lamented.

'Can we stop talking about it, please?' Maggie snapped. Heavens above, anyone would think Kathleen *wanted* her to marry Sean.

Cut to the bone, Kathleen shrugged and turned away. She had never known Maggie to snap at anyone before, and felt hurt.

130

That night when Maggie saw Sean waiting outside the library her step faltered.

One look at his face and Kathleen said, 'Oh, ho. I'm off. See ya.' And she ran across the road, leaving Maggie to face him alone.

Falling into step beside her, Sean did not speak until they reached the Dunville Park. Then, taking her by the arm, he said, 'We must talk.' When she would have demurred, he insisted, 'You at least owe me that. Come into the park, Maggie.'

So she allowed herself to be led across the road and into the park. Once seated on one of the benches, Sean gazed at her profile, admiring the way her thick lashes cast shadows on her cheeks, rosy from the frosty air, as she gazed fixedly at her hands clasped in her lap. How he loved her!

'Maggie, don't do this to me,' he begged. 'Have I offended you in some way?'

She shook her head.

Putting his hand over hers, he asked, 'You like me, don't you?'

This time she nodded, wishing she was anywhere but sitting beside him.

His voice warmed, became eager. 'Well then, that settles it! Forget I asked you to marry me. There's no big hurry.' He moved closer. 'Let's go on as we were. I'll teach you to love me, so I will.' His hand tightened on hers, his voice pleaded. 'Just gimme a chance, Maggie, don't take hope away from me.'

Looking into his kind face, seeing the appeal in his eyes, Maggie longed to go into his arms, feel the security of them around her; tell him that she did care for him. What if she had not become aware of how Kathleen felt? She would be in his arms now, happy and secure, planning for the future, and Kathleen would not hold it against her, she knew that. So why not? Kathleen wasn't encumbered with a child. One day she would meet someone else, so why not forget that look and agree to marry Sean?

Her thoughts swung this way and that, but her

conscience would not let her do that to Kathleen. Perhaps if she was madly in love with Sean or careless of her friendship with Kathleen, she would be unable to help herself, but she was not. All she wanted was security for herself and Sarah though she would have done all in her power to make him happy. But Kathleen was her best friend, indeed her only friend, and she must have her chance.

To her dismay, she heard herself say in a cold disdainful voice, 'Really, Sean, you must accept that I have made up my mind. I'm sorry, really sorry, but it is over.'

He went white with anger and his sensitive mouth set in a straight line. To her surprise, she felt passion rise in her. Passion such as she had never felt for him before. She wished with all her heart she had not seen Kathleen look at him. Taken unawares by the strong sensations racing through her, afraid of betraying her feelings, she rose abruptly to her feet.

'Please don't try to see me again,' she said, and head held high, quickly left the park, afraid he might see the tears in her eyes.

Sean sat for a long time on the bench, his shoulders slumped, his heart breaking. To his horror he became aware that he was crying and looked around him, shame-faced. Imagine crying in public! His step heavy, he walked down the length of the park and left by the side gate at Dunville Street. That way he could cut through the entry at Cairns Street and round into Leeson Street and avoid meeting any of his friends. He did not want anyone to see him making a spectacle of himself. He was never able to remember how he got home that night. All he could ever recall was Maggie's disdainful voice as she killed his dreams.

Maggie stopped her outings with Kathleen, wanting to stay out of Sean's way and give Kathleen a chance to win him. She was hurt at Maggie's apparent indifference. She had become very fond of her and could not understand why her friend was dropping her as well as Sean, but pride forbade her to ask. So all the old camaraderie was gone and they worked side by side, like polite strangers.

The weeks passed, long lonely weeks for Maggie.

Mollie, in the dark about Sean, watched and worried but held her tongue. Maggie knew her own feelings best and it was not for her to ask questions.

Christmas was a sad time and Maggie wondered if she would ever enjoy it again. Then, early in the new year, two things happened; Churchill managed to get the Home Rule bill passed in the House of Commons but when it went up to the House of Lords it was rejected by an overwhelming majority. They were back to square one.

The other occurrence of importance to Maggie was Kathleen's arriving at work one day and holding out her hand, shyly displaying an engagement ring for her to admire.

Impulsively, Maggie hugged her. 'Oh, I'm so happy for you and Sean.'

'Sean? Whatever gave you the idea I'm marryin' Sean? I'm marryin' Jim Rafferty,' Kathleen cried indignantly.

Wide-eyed, Maggie stared at her. 'I thought you were in love with Sean,' she said, wonder in her voice. Surely she had not been mistaken?

Kathleen sighed dramatically and gave a little shamed laugh. 'Oh, I've always been in love with Sean, but he never saw me in that light. Ah, no, I never stood a chance with Sean.' Her voice was sad then it brightened. 'We don't always get the one we want, but that's not to say we don't get the one best suited for us. Jim's the one for me. Not much on top,' she tapped her brow with a finger, 'but clever with his hands. He can make the most beautiful shoes, and I intend to see that one day he gets a shop of his own.'

Realising her sacrifice had been in vain, Maggie asked, 'How is Sean?'

'Don't you know?' Kathleen gasped, amazed. 'Honestly, Maggie, you may as well live on another planet. Sean hit the bottle after you dropped him. He's made a right mess of his life.'

133

'What do you mean?' Maggie whispered, a sinking sensation in her stomach.

'He got a girl into trouble an' had to marry her. A real slut she is. His ma's breakin' her heart watchin' him.'

Maggie felt a tremor start low in her. It spread through her until she was shaking uncontrollably.

'Maggie! What's wrong? Ah, now . . . here, sit down.' Pulling a stool forward, Kathleen pushed her down on to it. She was patting her comfortingly on the shoulder as she would to soothe a child. 'Listen! I thought you knew. Why, everybody was talkin' about it. Ah, Maggie, here . . . look, I'll get you a drink of water.'

Glad the library was empty, Maggie fought for self-control.

'Here!' A worried Kathleen pushed a glass of water into her hand. 'Drink this.'

After gulping at the water like a drowning woman, Maggie asked plaintively, 'Why didn't you tell me about Sean?'

Unable to understand why Maggie was so upset, Kathleen cried in exasperation, 'How could I? After you dropped him, you hardly spoke to me. How could I say Sean was breakin' his heart? You weren't interested!'

Maggie shook her head from side to side distractedly. 'Oh, I was. I *was* interested. I was very interested.' Looking at Kathleen in despair, she wailed, 'Ah, Kathleen, what have I done?'

'I don't understand Maggie. What *have* you done?' asked a bewildered Kathleen.

'I thought you were in love with Sean and I was coming between you.'

It was a while before the implication of these words dawned on Kathleen. Then she gasped in disbelief. 'You did that for me? You stopped dating Sean because you thought I was in love with him?'

When Maggie nodded, Kathleen slumped against the counter. 'Ah, Maggie, Maggie. An' I thought you'd gone off me!'

'You're the dearest friend I ever had, Kathleen,' Maggie

smiled wryly. 'And to be truthful, I missed you more than I missed Sean.'

'Ah, Maggie.' Kathleen was in tears, and as they clasped hands a friendship was sealed that was to last until the day Maggie died.

CHAPTER FIVE

It was when Sarah started school that Maggie determined to do all in her power to leave Waterford Street and move further up the Falls. It seemed to be the dream of all who lived in the identical terrace houses in these narrow cobbled streets, but alas few achieved it. She had been living in a vacuum since breaking with Sean but slowly became aware that she wanted something better for Sarah. She knew it would be a long hard struggle; the small amount of money she could afford to save each week would take many years to amass into the deposit for a house but it was something to plan for, something to look forward to. Besides, she was young and needed a dream to keep her going.

During the period that she had worked in the Blackstaff she had been aghast to note that small girls, some as young as twelve, worked as doffers in the spinning room. They were known as half-timers, meaning that they worked Monday, Tuesday and Wednesday and went to school Thursday and Friday one week and vice versa the following. These children worked long hours ankle deep in water in a damp steamy atmosphere. No wonder their skin was sallow and many died before they reached their teens.

At the beginning of the century a bishop had engineered the building of a school in Dunlewey Street and here, taught by the Sisters of Charity, the girls who were half-timers were educated, whilst around the corner in St

Finian's School the boys were taught. Some of these children would have avoided going to school at all but the parish priest was noted for his endeavours to see all received some kind of education. Daily he roamed the streets, ushering all truants he found along to school, angrily chastising the parents for their lack of interest.

Mollie explained to her that the children were those of parents who needed the money so badly, they defied the efforts of the clergy to stamp out child labour in the parish. Maggie spoke out angrily against the parents but her friend was quick to rebuff her, saying, 'There's no telling what can be necessary when your back's against the wall, and there's nowhere else to turn.'

Chastened, Maggie determined to hold her tongue in future. However, her resolve to make every effort to move further up the Falls was strengthened. William unwittingly came to her aid. Now a photographer working on the staff of a famous magazine, he was doing well in England and each time he wrote to her enclosed a ten shilling note. This money she salted away to help achieve her dream, which now didn't seem so unattainable. He didn't write often, but still, a ten shilling note!

On the grapevine, rumours were rife of paramilitary groups training all over the north and it was alleged that an army had been formed of 100,000 of the men who had signed the covenant. It was named the Ulster Volunteer Force. Soon guns and rifles were obtained, it was rumoured from Germany, and these men were armed and ready to defend Ulster should Asquith's government insist on Home Rule for Ireland. Of course the Nationalists were not sitting twiddling their thumbs while all this was happening and by early 1914 it became known that an army of volunteers had formed. This army was training down south but hundreds of Falls Road men rushed to join it. After all, who else would defend the Falls Road in time of need if not its own men? And the loyalists were unable to complain. Wasn't the Ulster Volunteer Force openly training and carrying arms? It was in Belfast where Unionists and Nationalists rubbed shoulders, as it were, that tension was highest and Civil War more likely to start . . . and there was the Falls district, sandwiched between the Protestant Shankill and Sandy Row.

King George V showed himself a kind and caring monarch in his efforts to help keep the peace. In an endeavour to avert civil war, he invited all leaders of the different Irish parties to a conference in Buckingham Palace. Hopes were high as news was awaited of the outcome of the conference, but alas in vain; agreement was not reached and civil war seemed unavoidable.

Other violence was also rife in early 1914: prominent buildings were attacked and burnt down, and these crimes were laid at the door of the suffragettes. It seemed these days even women were willing to resort to terrorism to make their views understood.

Reading the headlines from the *Irish News*, Mollie lamented to Maggie, 'It must be near the end of the world, there's so much goin' wrong. D'ye not agree with me?'

With an inclination of her head she sadly did so. The world was indeed in an awful state, with wars and troubles everywhere.

On 1 August Germany declared war on Russia, and three days later Britain was at war with Germany. This war succeeded where all else had failed. It brought Ireland back from the brink of civil war as Protestants and Catholics joined forces to fight the Germans. Some of the Ulster Catholics joined the Ulster Division, while others joined different Irish Regiments. For months training was carried out at army camps, and then on 8 May 1915 Maggie and Mollie joined the crowds that lined Royal Avenue as the Ulster (36th) Division marched through the centre of Belfast. The proud uniformed men, followed by horse-drawn wagons bearing the red cross sign, were cheered on by excited spectators as off they went to war.

For many of those left behind war brought prosperity as the shipyards, rope works, engineering firms and linen mills worked all out to produce necessary supplies to aid the fight against the Germans. Mackie's foundry, situated on the Springfield Road, obtained orders for the manufacture of ammunition and was working round the clock. This meant more work for the women of the Falls and Springfield Roads, as they were encouraged to do their bit for the Empire. It was heads down and hard toil for all concerned, but long hours of overtime were worked willingly to achieve a better standard of living. The difference this made to the families on the Falls Road was great. With wages coming regularly from the Ministry and plenty of work for the women, children were better fed and clothed and houses took on a new spruceness. Soon, however, there was a price to pay for all this prosperity. Nearly every family had someone away fighting and as news filtered through of the slaughter at the Somme, mothers and wives watched with dread for the yellow bicycles of the telegram boys, and one by one blinds were drawn as families mourned their dead. Very few returned and the few who did seemed ashamed to be alive when so many of their comrades had perished.

Any hope that Protestants and Catholics who had fought and died together during the war would achieve harmony at home was quickly dashed. With the end of the war in November 1918 animosity between Catholic and Protestant was renewed. During the war Catholic men had obtained jobs that they would not have stood a chance of beforehand and they had no intention of stepping down now. By sweat and toil, in their own way they had worked hard to serve the Empire and they intended staying put, whether the men back from the war were heroes or not! It was also alleged that Protestants were saying the Catholics had not played their part during the war. This was untrue and unjust. Thousands of young Catholic men had died at the Somme and this could have been proved. Mollie said the Protestants wanted the Catholics out, they did not want to know the truth, and again Maggie was forced to agree with her.

Since being elected as England's Prime Minister in 1916 when Asquith resigned, Lloyd George had done a lot to raise the standard of living in Ireland. During the war wages for manual labour were much higher, but now skilled workers were looking for pay rises to keep the pay differential between them and manual workers. When the Engineering & Shipbuilding Trades Federation negotiated a forty-seven hour week the shipyard workers were infuriated. They wanted a forty-four hour week. Aware that unlike the Clydeside shipyards their order books were full, and confident that they would win, they voted in favour of a strike. On 29 January 1919 all the shipyard workers downed tools.

This happened just when Maggie saw her goal in view. William was writing on a regular basis now and she had almost saved enough to afford to move further up the Falls Road where it was quieter. By scrimping and saving during the last six years, she had nearly enough money for the deposit on a house and although Mollie vowed that she would never leave Waterford Street, Maggie was confident that she could persuade her to change her mind. However, once more fate took a hand and to Maggie's dismay her plans had to be shelved. Fate had intervened once again in the form of the strike, soon to be known as the 'Forty-Four Hour Strike'. The shipyard workers were joined by the gas and electricity workers, and the city was quite literally brought to a standstill. The trams would not run, the cinemas were closed, and thousands of linen workers were put out of work. The ropeworks closed down as did the big engineering works, and those shops that would not shut their doors quickly changed their minds when their windows were smashed.

Although the pickets could not stop the steam-powered linen mills completely, they managed to cause great disruption and the strikers were confident that the corporation would listen to them and they would have a shorter working week. To add to the misery, by the end of the first week, bread – the mainstay of the poor people – was scarce as flour failed to reach the bakeries. The strike dragged on and as more workers were laid off, Mollie joined the unemployed. Then, in spite of fierce opposition from the Unionists, whom these same men had voted into power at the last election, the troops were brought in. As they manned the machinery in the gas works and the electricity station, the factories were soon working, the trams were set in motion and the town slowly came to life. The shipyards and engineering works remained idle for a further few days, then embittered and resentful against the corporation, the workers returned. The strike had been in vain.

The shock and worry of being out of work took its toll on Mollie and resulted in her being unable to return when the factories were open again. She was off work for many weeks, but Maggie was only too willing to keep the house going on her small earnings with help from her precious savings. She was indebted to her friend and could wait a little longer to move house.

Changes were also reported down south in the early months of 1919. On 21 January the seventy-three Sinn Fein MPs who had been elected the previous year had ignored Westminster and set up a parliament in Dublin, Dail Eireann, and declared an Irish Republic. On that same day the Anglo-Irish War started. The newspapers kept the north up to date on the state of affairs and in September they read that the British government had proclaimed the Dail illegal and the Irish Republican Army was engaged in guerrilla warfare with the security forces.

During the early months of 1920 the I.R.A. campaign extended to rural Ulster, but it was in July that riots errupted on the Falls Road. On the 'Twelfth Day' at Finaghy, where all the Orangemen amassed every year to celebrate the winning of the Battle of the Boyne, Sir Edward Carson delivered a very bitter speech. In it he expressed his fear that the loyalists of Ulster were in danger from Sinn Fein. He said that he was losing hope of the government defending them and that it was up to them to defend themselves. Nine days later, the Catholics were driven out of the shipyards. There had been outbursts of riots all over the north but on 29 July, the day the men were put out of the shipyards, all hell broke loose on the Falls Road. The district was in an uproar when the men arrived home in the middle of the afternoon, battered and bruised, with clothes in tatters on their backs. All were in a state of shock; some had blood running from wounds, many needed hospital treatment, and there were rumours that some had died. All were crying out in anger against their Protestant workmates, proclaiming that they had descended on the shipyards as if possessed by devils and driven all the Catholics out with hammers and spanners. Some men even had to jump in the lough amid a deluge of rivets and stones and swim for their life.

The following day angry workmen gathered at the junction of the Falls and Springfield Roads to await the trams that would bring the Protestant workers to Mackie's foundry. When the first tram arrived it was quickly disconnected from the overhead power line and stones were thrown at it. If the Springfield Barracks had not been so close at hand, just a matter of fifty yards away, things would have been much worse. The police were quickly on the scene. The crowd was baton charged and many ran down the Falls Road and up Waterford Street to escape down Malcomson or Springview Street, only to find that more police awaited them. They were sandwiched between two divisions.

Hearing the commotion outside, Maggie's first concern was for Sarah. Mollie had taken her to the shop at the corner of Malcomson Street for sweets. Heart thumping with fear, Maggie rushed to the door. As she opened it they arrived, just as crowds raced up the street. Gripping Sarah close, Maggie silently questioned Mollie over her head.

'Seems there's been ructions at the junction,' she responded. 'They derailed and stoned a tram. The police are chasing them.'

When Maggie made to close the outer door, Mollie stopped her. 'Take Sarah into the back room 'til this is all over,' she ordered, and to Maggie's surprise, kept the door open; half sheltering behind it to watch the angry scene going on across the road in Malcomson Street. Settling Sarah in the backroom and warning her not to leave it, Maggie joined her friend. To their amazement, in the midst of all the havoc, the parish priest appeared in the middle of Malcomson Street, brandishing the blackthorn stick he always carried. A small spare figure, he stood alone in the middle of the road and faced the policemen charging with batons drawn. To be heard above the noise of the crowd he shouted at the top of his voice, demanding that the chief constable recall his men to the barracks. A great hush fell as he and the police faced each other, but no one tried to pass him and soon the police were recalled to their quarters.

Mollie, who had been praying aloud throughout the confrontation, imploring God's help, cried out in relief. 'Oh, thanks be to God for that holy wee man!'

As the crowds dispersed Maggie entered the scullery to join her daughter, only to retrace her steps quickly when she heard Mollie say, 'Bring him in here, son.'

With consternation, she watched two men assist a third over the threshold while Mollie walked ahead, ushering them through the kitchen.

'In here, son. Put him on my bed. Sarah ... get you down, love.'

An excited Sarah quickly jumped down off the bed as the two men laid their companion gently on it. Then the older of the men, dark and sombre, touched his fingers respectfully to his forelock in acknowledgement of Mollie, but as he turned away his eyes locked with Maggie's and they gazed at each other for some seconds. Then he doffed his cap, and without saying a word, before Maggie's astounded gaze, went out of the back door and was over the yard wall in a bound.

With a slight shake of her head, Maggie brought herself back to reality. For a few seconds the man had seemed to mesmerise her and she hadn't liked it; it had been an uncanny feeling.

The man on the bed was unconscious. Blood seeped slowly from a gash along his hairline and caked about his nose, indicating that it too had been bleeding. His lips were swollen and bruised. Dragging her eyes away from him, and aware that the other man was watching her through narrowed lids, she turned to face him. This man

143

she recognised. His name was Danny, one of the unemployed who hung about the top of Dunville Street. He always greeted her respectfully when she had occasion to go to the nearby fish and chip shop. Now pale and gaunt he held her eye, then removed his cap and nodded in acknowledgement. Slowly she nodded back, then her attention returned to the man on the bed. She didn't recognise him. Still, it was hard to tell, his face was such a mess.

As if he could read her thoughts, Danny said, 'He's a stranger, an Englishman. He works on the boats with our Barry. They were on their way to the Bee Hive for a drink. They were just crossing the junction when the trouble started. He got caught up in the fight through no fault of his own. Our Barry's been taken to the hospital.' His look was pleading as he nodded at the figure on the bed. 'If ye could clean him up a bit I'll get him out of yer way.'

Mollie was already attending to the man's needs. She had poured water from the kettle that was always hissing at the side of the range and now she gently washed away the blood and applied disinfectant and salve.

'That gash needs a stitch,' she stated, looking askance at Danny.

'He works on the boats.' They could see he was perturbed. His hands were twisting away at his cap and crooked white teeth gnawed at his bottom lip. 'I don't know what to do, so I don't. He won't thank me if I take him to the hospital. Ye see . . . if they keep him in, he'll miss his ship.'

'His hair will cover the scar, so I suppose it'll be OK.' With a gentle hand, Mollie brushed the hair back from the man's forehead. 'He'll have a headache in the mornin',' she said with a grimace. 'He'll not thank us for that either.'

As she rinsed the bowl at the jawbox, she glanced over her shoulder at Maggie. 'Can I sleep with Sarah t'night, Maggie?'

'Yes, yes . . .' Maggie sounded doubtful. Did Mollie mean that the two men would stay all night?

Sensing her unease, Danny assured her, 'We'll be away

144

first thing in the mornin', missus.' And shot a grateful glance at Mollie.

Taking her consent for granted, Mollie started to get things organised. 'I'll throw a blanket over him.' She nodded at the still figure laying on top of the bedclothes. 'An' you, Danny . . . you take a nap in the armchair. Sure yer out on yer feet, so ye are.'

The hours until bed-time passed slowly with Danny, after eating a bowl of Mollie's broth and some home-made bread, dozing most of the time and the other man remaining unconscious. Before retiring for the night, Maggie hovered anxiously over him to reassure herself that he was still alive. What if he was in a coma? What if he died? Then they would be in trouble. She was bent low over him, assuring herself that he was still breathing, when suddenly he opened his eyes. A look of wonder crossed over his face and bright blue eyes examined her.

Relieved to see him awake, Maggie promptly told him to go back to sleep. Gently patting his hand, she whispered, 'You need all the rest you can get.'

His hand lifted from the bed clothes and before she could draw back his fingers trailed her face. 'You're . . . real?'

Before she could reply, heavy lids fringed with thick gold lashes concealed the blue of his eyes as he drifted off to sleep again. Contented that he was on the mend Maggie climbed the stairs to bed. She tossed and turned all night; memories of the first time she had met Danny keeping her brain active, preventing sleep from claiming her. It was back in the old days, when Paul and she had sat at the corner and listened to the singers. One night he had beckoned a young lad over. 'Hows about singin' a song for Maggie? Eh, son?'

Danny had been about fourteen; dark and handsome, with twinkling blue eyes. He bestowed on her a smile of pure delight and began to sing 'Danny Boy', his voice sweet and clear on the still air. It was hard to believe that the pale, gaunt young man with the bitter eyes was the same lad. But then . . . he had been inside since, lifted for nothing other than that he was a Catholic and, with no job, had nothing better to do than loiter at street corners.

If the rumours of what happened to these lads when they were inside was true, it was no wonder that Danny looked like an old man. The cruelties reported were atrocious and Maggie's blood ran cold at the very idea. It strengthened her resolve to renew her efforts to leave Waterford Street. Get Sarah away before she became interested in the opposite sex. She didn't want her marrying someone caught up in the fight for the 'Cause'. Most of those young men died young. Perhaps she had set her sights too high. She would keep an eye out for a house near Broadway; they would not be so expensive there. That house in Islandbawn Street had been nice. She would watch for one on sale there. But would it really be any different up there? Was it all a pipe dream? She could only hope it would be better; where else could she go? On this thought she drifted asleep and when she descended the stairs next morning the two men had departed.

'Was the stranger all right?' she questioned Mollie who had made them breakfast.

'He was, yes . . . very quiet but nice. Very nice! I liked him, so I did. Maggie . . . you'd have sworn he was Irish! Ye should've heard him. I asked him if his parents were Irish. It seems his da was, but he died young so he didn't pick up his brogue from him. He said he picked it up on the boats, there were so many Irishmen workin' with him. They left at half-five. He'd a boat t'catch. He works with Barry Monaghan . . . but *he* won't catch the boat. He's a broken leg.' A twinkle appeared in Mollie's eye as she added, 'He asked after you.'

'Me?'

'Yes, you. Seems you made an impression on him. He inquired if anyone else lived here and when I said yes, he sighed and said he thought he'd been dreamin'. He said he was sorry he couldn't stay to meet you . . . asked me to thank you for all your kindness to him.'

'What was his name?'

Mollie stopped her task of brushing the hearth and,

sinking back on her heels, gaped up at Maggie. 'Do ye know something? I never asked!'

'And the other man . . . the one who went over the wall . . . do you know him?'

Mollie's look was keen; she had noted the interest shown in Maggie the night before. Now her voice held a warning. 'Aye, I know him all right. His name's Kevin McCrory. He's not from about here. He's organisin' groups to protect the houses, but I personally think he's dangerous. And . . . I've a feelin' he'll be back to see you.'

'Oh, you think so?'

'I think so . . . and, Maggie, take my advice, chase him if he comes.'

'Of course I will! I'm not interested in him.'

Mollie eyed her with raised brows and Maggie blushed when she realised her reasoning. Why ask about him, then? And in her mind she answered the unspoken question: Why indeed?

The episode at the junction had repercussions and at different engineering works more Catholics were attacked and put out. The Protestant workers from Mackie's were shot at as they left the premises and some were wounded. Fear hung like a cloud over the district as retaliations were awaited.

They were not long in coming: the next horror to hit the parish was crowds sweeping down from the Shankill Road in the dead of night and setting fire to houses in Clonard District. Women and children fled down to the Falls Road but the men stayed to try to save their homes. Maggie and Mollie became aware of these awful events when a workmate of Mollie's knocked them up, seeking sanctuary for her daughter and grandchild. During August, they were to shelter many more children and old people as more families were burnt out of their homes on the streets running out on to Cupar Street.

They were also, during the following weeks, to nurse a few wounded men. There being no males in their house, the military neglected to search it when seeking men wounded in the riots that were now completely out of hand. Seven were reported dead and there were hundreds wounded.

Although afraid of being found out, Maggie pulled her weight and helped all she could. She worried that if the military caught them sheltering wounded men, it might become known that she was Clive Pierce's daughter. She feared her father's reaction to the scandal that would surely follow. She could imagine his wrath and consequently lived in a state of terror.

During the course of these operations she often came in contact with Kevin McCrory and always he seemed to mesmerise her, just for a few seconds, but it was always he who broke eye contact. He never made any attempt to get to know her, but somehow she felt it was just a matter of time and vowed to have nothing to do with him when he did.

The following weeks were a time of persecution. Houses were plundered and set alight. In all, one hundred and eight fires were reported in Belfast and over three hundred people, mostly Catholics, were driven from their homes. But the Protestants on the edge of Catholic estates were also vulnerable and many of them lost their homes too. When Maggie and Mollie thought it could get no worse, to their horror on 29 August the military knocked on doors and warned residents in the streets near the Shankill (the Clonard district and the streets running off Cupar Street and Conway Street) to be prepared for an attack as crowds were amassing on the Shankill Road. They later learnt that the other side of the Falls Road had also been warned of an attack from Sandy Row.

Word spread to Waterford Street and without weapons the people felt naked and vulnerable. Stones were gathered and laid at different points and any heavy objects that would suit as weapons were left at hand as the people prepared to defend their homes. But what use would stones be against petrol bombs and guns?

Aware of raised brows and nudges, Maggie helped to gather possible weapons. Why were they surprised? she thought resentfully. Wasn't it her home also that was under threat? The assault started off at the bottom of the Falls Road in Townsend Street and Albert Street and spread up the road. In spite of the warning and care taken, two more Catholics were shot dead and many were wounded and more left homeless.

'Is there no end to it, Mollie?' Maggie asked, as yet again they sheltered three young children as their parents awaited the corporation finding them shelter.

'I can't see an end to it. Nobody cares about us, Maggie.'

And she agreed. It appeared that the Catholics had been abandoned. The main roads were open and business went on as usual, but from the streets running off the Falls Road shots could be heard regularly as gunfire was exchanged, and the report of machine-gun fire showed that the military were also involved in the battles. It wasn't just the Falls Road that suffered. They heard that Ardoyne, the Market, the Loney and other Catholic districts were also under siege and the number of homeless grew. The trams were running for those who dared to travel on them, journeys downtown were available, but it was no good risking your life going to town – especially with empty pockets. Maggie found it hard to believe that rich people and those who lived outside Catholic areas were living life normally, going out and about, with full bellies and plenty of money, while thousands of Catholics were near starvation.

On 30 August the army enforced a curfew on Belfast. On the Falls Road they erected and sand-bagged emplacements, and an empty building at the corner of Waterford Street and the Bee Hive Bar up at Broadway were taken over and turned into barracks. Places of entertainment were to close at nine-thirty and trams were also to stop running at this hour while everybody was to remain indoors between ten-thirty and five. In spite of the curfew, violence continued all over Belfast. On 25 September, on the Falls Road at Broadway, two constables were shot dead. In a state of terror the district awaited repercussions.

Retaliation came swiftly. On the lower Falls, near the Public Baths, a barber was shot dead, and on the Springfield Road two more men were murdered. In all, during the following two weeks, another twenty-three deaths occurred. To help enforce the curfew, eight hundred Military Police were drafted over from England. These men, nicknamed the Black and Tans because of the colour of their uniforms, soon came to be hated and were later reinforced by a Special Police Force especially sworn in to assist them. This force was made up of the very men who had helped drive the Catholics from their places of work and from their homes. They learnt from the newspapers that even over in England there was an outcry when Westminster paid the wages of these men. Soon the 'B Specials' were feared and hated even more than the Black and Tans, especially on the Falls Road.

Under cover of the curfew, the Military Police and the 'B Specials' took to raiding houses. Secure in the knowledge that no one but military and police were allowed on the streets, they would swoop down on a particular house and tear it apart, ruining the contents and threatening the occupants. During these raids it was alleged murder sometimes took place.

The men of the district called a meeting and it was agreed that to ward off these attacks sentries must be posted at chosen locations each night, and when uniformed parties were seen approaching whistles would be blown in warning. This was put into practice and when a sentry's whistle was heard windows were raised and a barrage of noise made with pots and pans. This noise and shouts of 'Murder! Murder!' quickly brought the men of the district out in large numbers and resulted in the Black and Tans and 'B Specials' stealing off into the darkness.

This method was so successful it was practised in all Catholic districts and there was less murder and looting. Kevin McCrory got the credit for thinking up this ruse and was praised and looked up to.

150

One night shortly before curfew time, he and Barry Monaghan arrived at Mollie's door. Barry had never returned to sea and once he was mobile again had turned all his attention to protecting the Falls from attack. Warily, Mollie invited them in. She admired Kevin. To give credit where it was due he was an inspiration to the district. But she was uneasy about Maggie. Kevin was handsome and Mollie sensed that in spite of herself Maggie found him attractive.

They stood in the centre of the kitchen and Mollie was dismayed when Barry spoke. 'Kevin needs to be put up for a week or so. I thought maybe you . . .?' His voice held a question and Mollie became flustered.

'I'm sorry, but all my rooms are occupied.'

Slowly, Maggie left the scullery where she had been listening to the conversation. 'Is it necessary?' she asked, her eyes on Kevin.

He nodded gravely and once again she had difficulty escaping his gaze. Yet again, he was the first to look away. She turned to Mollie. 'He can have Sarah's room if you like. She can sleep with me.'

Mollie didn't like it . . . she didn't like it at all. But what could she say? She found herself nodding.

'Thank you very much.' Kevin's voice was soft and his dark eyes roved Maggie's face. 'I'll be back in ten minutes.'

Barry added his thanks and they left the house. Ten minutes later Kevin returned alone, a holdall over his shoulder, to find Mollie had relegated him to the room off the scullery. He grinned at her to let her know that he knew the reason why. As it turned out, Mollie need not have worried about her lodger's influence on Maggie. They saw little of him; he left early each morning, and in spite of the curfew arrived home late each night. On the rare occasions that he was present in the evenings, he spent his time in the back room writing letters and Mollie was glad of it.

It was estimated that during these months ten thousand Catholic men and over a thousand Catholic women were put out of work. The riots intensified and seven more Catholics and six Protestants were reported dead.

As November passed in comparative quietness, though, Maggie and Mollie shared their neighbours' hopes that perhaps peace was at hand. Their hopes were heightened with the news that Westminster was to try yet another solution to the Irish Question. It intended giving Belfast a new role in its own affairs. Since fear of being drawn into a Dublin government appeared to be at the root of the troubles, it was decided that as well as giving Dublin Home Rule, Ulster would also be given Home Rule with their own parliament in Belfast. So in spite of fighting long and hard against Home Rule, the six north-eastern counties of Ireland were elected, with Belfast the capital, as the only part of Ireland to accept Home Rule.

On 23 December 1920 royal assent was given and the constitution of Northern Ireland was set up. Early in 1921 things settled down a bit but April was another month of terror for the Falls district and Maggie received first-hand knowledge of the start of it. She had taken Sarah downtown for material for a skirt for school and after purchasing a remnant in Smithfield Market was heading for home when all hell broke loose. She was just about to cross the road to board the tram when, at the corner of Fountain Lane, from amongst a crowd of people, gunmen emerged and opened fire. Their targets were a party of Police Auxiliaries from County Sligo who were passing through Belfast. Two of the cadets were shot dead. There was pandemonium when people panicked.

Sarah was swept away from her mother's side as the crowd stampeded and Maggie screamed when she saw her fall. Like a wild animal she clawed her way to where she had last seen her daughter, sobbing with relief when she found her cowering in the doorway of a shop. Taking her in her arms, she protected her with her body as people milled to and fro. After what seemed liked hours, but was really only a few minutes, military and police arrived. As the crowds dispersed, Maggie led her shaking daughter along Castle Street and eventually caught a tram up to

Waterford Street. When she arrived home she found Mollie in an awful state.

'Oh, thank God you're all right! We heard that some civilian bystanders were wounded. I was worried about you, so I was.' Taking Sarah in her arms she rocked her gently. 'It's all right, love,' she soothed her and offered her remedy for all ills. 'You're safe now. Look, sit down. I'll make a cup of tea.'

It was the following morning when Mollie was returning from Mass in Clonard Monastery that she learned of the shootings that had occurred in Clonard Gardens, murder in the early hours of that morning. Murder that was to shock the nation. Two brothers had been shot dead in their own home during curfew time. It was alleged they were shot by men in trench coats.

'Maggie, imagine ... it happened about midnight, and their relatives had to stay with their bodies 'til the curfew was over before they could venture out and get help.' As she relayed the grim news, she confided, 'The murderers left a dog behind them ... so they should soon be able to find out who they are. Hah! Chance would be a fine thing! It'll come to an untimely end, you mark my words!'

She was right. The dog was 'accidentally' shot dead.

The brothers were from a well-respected family and as word of the tragedy spread, crowds gathered to pay their respects. On the evening that their remains were removed to church, thousands thronged the streets. The two great oak coffins were borne on the shoulders of volunteers and the hearse, covered with wreaths and floral tributes, was grasped by the shafts and pulled to St Paul's Church by willing hands, horses having been dispensed with as a mark of respect. During the funeral procession, an armoured car and two lorries full of armed military were in attendance, but once the bodies were carried into the church the military withdrew from the scene and family and friends mourned together until curfew time. After Mass the next morning the funeral procession started its long journey to the family burial grounds at Glenravel on the Antrim Road. The coffins, draped with the Sinn Fein colours, were carried by relays of volunteers and the footpaths along the way thronged with mourners. All Belfast mourned the deaths.

An inquiry was held into the murder of the brothers and the District Inspector of the Springfield Road Barracks called to tell the parish priest the results. Later, as the Inspector left the parochial house, he was shot at and wounded. He was carried back into the parochial house and a doctor who lived nearby attended to his wounds until the ambulance arrived. That night fear hung over the parish as retaliations were awaited but the new day dawned without any more shooting.

On 3 May 1921 Belfast officially became the capital of Northern Ireland. This brought little comfort to the Catholics. Didn't it mean that Protestants would be in charge?

Sinn Fein, representing the majority of all Ireland, had rejected Home Rule out of hand, and in the southern counties war raged between the Irish Republican Army and the British army. Nevertheless, in Belfast things were quieter, although there were still tit-for-tat killings. Through ill-health, Sir Edward Carson stepped down and Sir James Craig was persuaded by loyalists to resign his seat at Westminster and become head of the Unionist Party in Belfast. He immediately called for a general election on 24 May.

This was the first parliamentary election since proportional representation had been introduced by the English Parliament and Belfast was divided into four constituencies, each returning four members. As well as Labour, the Nationalists decided to contest the constituencies but would decline to sit in the Orange Parliament. The election was bitter, with blatant intimidation keeping people away from the polling stations. The three Labour candidates booked the Ulster Hall for their final rally, only to find when they arrived that they were unable to enter. The loyalist shipyard workers had barricaded the hall against them.

On the Falls Road excitement was high as one and all turned out to vote for Nationalist Joe Devlin. The results were awaited with bated breath and when Joe, who had been born and reared in Hamill Street, was elected with over ten thousand six hundred votes, excitement ran high. But when it was also announced that he had secured almost nine and a half thousand votes in Co. Antrim, meaning he was also certain of election as the first Catholic representative of the stronghold of Carsonism outside Belfast, excitement broke all bounds and bonfires were lit as celebrations got underway. Quickly, by word of mouth, the news reached Waterford Street and houses emptied as everyone surged down to the Falls Road to await the triumphant procession that was sure to arrive in celebration.

They were right; soon St Peter's Brass and Reed Band could be heard in the distance and when it reached and then turned up Clonard Street, Mollie gripped Sarah's hand and nodded to Maggie to do likewise and they joined the thousands that thronged behind Joe Devlin and added their voices to the cheers. Thirty thousand were estimated to have amassed when at last the procession arrived back at Hamill Square. Joe Devlin made a speech and thanked all his supporters amid resounding cheers. When the excitement had died down and the bonfires had burned low, Maggie assisted a tired Sarah home. As she undressed her, she wondered just what difference the Catholics thought one wee man would make. As in the Bible, his would be a lone voice crying in the wilderness. But still, as Mollie had pointed out, one was better than none.

When she returned to the kitchen she found Kevin sitting at the fireside, and as usual when in his company she felt ill at ease. Why did he have this effect on her? It was late but Mollie made a cup of tea and, tired though she was, out-sat Kevin. At last, with bad grace, he retired to the back room and Maggie accompanied Mollie up the stairs.

At first she had been glad when her friend foiled the odd attempts Kevin made to get her alone, but now? Well, she did wonder about him. They knew no more about him now than when he first arrived, and if they were alone she might learn more. And she had to admit that he did interest her . . . aye, and half the district! She was aware that he did not have to seek out female company. The women were throwing themselves at him. Even some of the married women showed willing.

Restless, she was unable to sleep. As she tossed and turned she envied Mollie snoring away in the next room and at last rose from the bed. Perhaps a drink of cocoa would help her to sleep. Shrugging into her dressing gown she quietly left the room and descended the stairs. She was very quiet as she heated the milk but was not in the least surprised when Kevin came out of the back room to stand watching her. He was naked to the waist and she found his presence overpowering.

'Would you like a drink of cocoa?'

He nodded and she added more milk to the pan. In spite of the care she took, her hand shook when she lifted it to fill the cups. With a slight smile curving his mouth, he relieved her of the pan and his body brushed hers as he leant round her in the confined space to pour the milk. Covertly she eyed the muscles rippling under the dark hair on his arms, and her awareness of him was so acute she had to fight an overwhelming desire to relax against him. Annoyed with herself, she took the cup he handed her and bade him a curt goodnight.

Alarmed at her obvious intention of returning to bed, he caught hold of her arm. 'Please stay and talk a while. Your friend may as well be your chastity belt, she never leaves us alone.'

The touch of his hand on her arm was sending tremors through her body. His face was so close she could see the little yellow flecks in the brown of his eyes, the dark shadow of stubble on his jaw. Although uneasy, she nodded her consent and was relieved when he released her arm. In the kitchen she sat in the armchair and he sat at the table.

'Tell me about yourself, Maggie.'

The look she bestowed on him was mocking. 'I'm sure you know all about me.'

A smile acknowledged this. 'I know the basics . . . but what makes you tick? Why is there no man in your life?'

'Because I choose not to have a man.'

'What about sex?'

When she recoiled in distaste at his bluntness, he laughed softly and whispered, 'What have we here . . . a prude?'

Abruptly she rose from the chair and, not wanting to have to pass him, left her cup on the mantelpiece and headed for the stairs.

He was right behind her. 'I'm sorry . . . really I am! That was uncalled for.'

She was very aware of his hand on her arm, the husky passion of his voice. The blood raced in her veins. Warily, she turned to face him. His eyes were waiting to mesmerise and she stood enthralled. Slowly, caressingly, he drew her into his arms and pressed her gently against him, brushing her lips with his. Soft as a feather they trailed her face and throat before returning to her hungry mouth. As the kiss deepened her arms crept up around his neck and all the pent-up loneliness poured forth as she returned his caress. They strained together, passion mounting, and he edged her towards his room. They had almost reached the bed before she became aware of her actions. What was she doing? Had she no self-respect? She was acting like a trollop. Angrily, she pushed him away, wiping her mouth with the back of her hand.

He gripped her by the arms and barred her escape. 'Hey . . . come on now. Don't play around with me. This is what you came down for, isn't it? Come on, be honest, admit it. It took you longer than I thought it would, but I never doubted that you would come. Ah no, Maggie . . . you've wanted me from the beginning. And I want you. How I want you! So why not?'

Once more he drew her into his arms. Almost weeping with shame, she nevertheless pressed close. Throwing caution to the winds, she raised her face for his kisses and

157

allowed herself to be lowered to the bed. As his hands explored her body and passion mounted, she cried out aloud.

She awoke in bed and started up in alarm, heart thumping against her ribs. A dream! She had been dreaming, but it had seemed so real. She still tingled from the feel of his lips, the pressure of his body, and an insane longing filled her. It took all her will power to remain in bed. A cup of cocoa would be welcome. Would he be awake? Burrowing her head in the pillow she wept long and sore. Was she doomed to spend the rest of her life alone?

As the weeks passed and most of the Catholic community was denied the right to earn their livelihood it fell to the bishop to come to their aid. He was in despair at the plight of his flock. Thousands were out of work with no prospect of employment. Houses needed to be rebuilt for the homeless and there was no money to do so. In desperation he called on the people of the rest of Ireland to come to their aid, and in spite of the war that was raging in the south against the Black and Tans, the response was generous beyond words. One hundred and fifty thousand pounds was collected and sent north.

However, the bishop realised that even that amount was not enough and turned his attention to America. Once again he did not plead in vain. As always the Americans were generous. An organisation named the White Cross Fund was set up and every week five to seven thousand pounds was sent to Belfast alone, to help feed and clothe the poor. The organisation also donated grants towards the cost of building new houses for the homeless. Ireland was profoundly grateful to its American friends in this time of need.

When Mollie arrived home from work one night in a state of collapse, Maggie put her to bed and sent for the doctor. Confident that it was a bad cold, she was shocked to the core when, after examining Mollie, he returned to the kitchen sadly shaking his head.

'Is it bad, doctor?'

'I'm afraid so.'

'But she will get better?'

He didn't reply, just kept shaking his head. Dismayed, Maggie sank on to a chair and waited for him to explain.

'She's worn out and her heart is showing the strain she has been under.'

'I'll nurse her back to health.'

'I'm sorry, Maggie. There's nothing we can do. I give her a week.' And he pressed her shoulder in a comforting gesture before leaving the house.

Maggie sat stunned for a long time as she tried to come to terms with the knowledge that her dear friend could be dead within a week. The thought of life without her dismayed Maggie and fear filled her heart.

Since the night of her dream (or nightmare) she had studiously avoided Kevin. She was aware that he was perplexed and that Mollie, before her illness, had also given her puzzled looks but the dream had frightened her; made her aware of the great void in her life. Kevin was not the one to fill it, she knew.

However, during the days that followed as Mollie hovered between life and death, she was glad of his company, and surprised at the compassion he showed her friend. Mollie lasted two weeks, praying constantly for the safe return of the king and queen to England. It was on 22 June that King George V opened the new parliament in Belfast. In spite of fear for his safety, accompanied by his wife he had travelled to Northern Ireland. The plight of the king seemed to keep Mollie alive. Again and again she lamented to Maggie the awful stigma that would befall Belfast if anything should happen to a good, caring man like the king.

On 23 June Mollie died with Maggie and Kevin kneeling by her bed, he reciting the rosary. That night Maggie asked him to leave the house. He said he understood that the neighbours would talk if he stayed, but he would keep in touch with her.

She knew better than to tell him the truth, that his

presence was too much a strain on her self-restraint. It might have put ideas into his head and she had no intention of taking chances, not with Sarah in the house.

CHAPTER SIX

Opening the door Maggie stood to one side. With a curt nod Bob Grahame passed her and entered the kitchen. Tall, handsome Bob, the apple of Mollie's eye and breaker of her heart. The old resentment Maggie bore him rose to the fore when she thought how rarely he had visited his mother. Even during the worst of the troubles he had been conspicuous by his absence. She gave a tight smile in answer to his nod.

He was followed by his wife, May. Small and bird-like, she passed Maggie without a greeting, her pointed nose raised in disdain. Next came Agnes, their eldest daughter, plump, easy-going and pleasant. She smiled at Maggie, eyes taking in her smooth skin and shining hair.

Why, she could pass for a girl in her early twenties, she thought. There must be something wrong with her, for her to still be unattached. A woman with her looks? Her husband must be dead about ten years now. Yes, it would be near enough ten years since he died. There must be something wrong with her. Perhaps she's too stuck-up to acknowledge the men about here. Ah, but then, her first husband was a bricklayer. Ah well! Not for me to wonder why.

Agnes sighed at the idea of such a waste. Now, if she looked anything like Maggie ... well, for a start she would not be marrying Frank Crossin. Indeed, no. Her sights would be set much higher. Maggie bore Agnes's

161

appraising stare with a resigned smile; she was used to being stared at and talked about.

Last came Margaret, the picture of her mother. She also smiled, and returning the smile, Maggie was glad that this slim young girl had not inherited her mother's sourness as well as her looks.

Closing the door, which was adorned by a big black bow, as was the custom when someone died on the Falls Road, Maggie followed them into the kitchen.

When she saw that they were all seated, she asked in a mildly reproving voice, 'Are you not going to pay your respects to your mother, Bob?'

Face ablaze with colour, he rose and went through the scullery into the back room where Mollie lay coffined, the rest of his family trailing sheepishly behind him. He was annoyed with himself for giving Maggie an opening to reprove him. She was too high and mighty for her own good, that one, and given the chance he'd soon take her down a peg or two.

As they trooped back into the kitchen, Maggie answered another knock on the door and this time admitted Brian and his family. She did not bear Brian the same animosity she directed at Bob. Brian lived in Warrenpoint so it was expensive and, during the riots, difficult for him to visit. Bob lived a short distance away on the upper Springfield Road, outside the troubled area, but had not bothered to visit his mother.

Maggie greeted Brian in a friendly manner and was pleased when, without any prompting from her, he headed for the back room.

After greeting Maggie courteously, Evelyn, Brian's wife, blonde and pretty, gazed around the kitchen in obvious surprise and, catching May's waiting eye, raised her brows and pursed her lips before following her husband and two young sons through the scullery and into the back room.

Silence reigned in the kitchen. Watching May avidly eyeing the good pieces of furniture and the black and grey kitchenette grate that now replaced the old black range,

162

Maggie thought, You may well look, Madam. A lot of changes have occurred in the last couple of years.

At first Mollie had been loath to part with the range: 'That thing will never cook a proper meal,' she had lamented when Maggie had taken her to town and shown her the grey gas stove she intended to buy for cooking, but no one was happier than she when proved wrong.

Kathleen Rooney, now the very happy wife of Jim Rafferty, loved going around the countryside to auctions. Jim had taught her how to drive, and when he could spare the van she and Maggie delighted in touring about looking for bargains. During this time Maggie discovered that she had an eye for antiques and Mollie and she spent many happy hours restoring the old pieces of furniture that she bought to their former beauty. It had started during the worst of the troubles. Confined to the house for days on end, with nothing better to do, they had renovated an old chest of drawers bought by Mollie down in Smithfield Market the previous year. Seeing the transformation that took place as they sanded and waxed and polished Maggie was amazed and caught the antique bug when she accompanied Kathleen to auctions. Mindful of the old chest of drawers, she had picked up some bargains and the hours of curfew had been well spent working on them.

With Mollie's health causing concern, Maggie had shelved her plans for moving and spent some of her savings on antiques and renovating the house. The kitchen showed just how successful they had been.

Under the stairs, where the coalhole used to be (the coal having been relegated to the yard and the wall knocked down by Kevin, to leave an alcove), stood a rosewood chest whose satin sheen threw back the reflection of the fire. Two shillings was all she had paid for it, but she knew it was now worth a lot of money. It had taken Mollie and her many weeks to restore it but their efforts were well rewarded. Against the wall, between the kitchenette grate and the window, a chiffonier housed Maggie's few precious pieces of china; one and sixpence was all she had paid for that. If only people realised the value of what they were throwing away, but as Mollie had been fond of saying, 'Never look a gift horse in the mouth, girl. Let's just be thankful for small mercies and the chance to own some nice things.' Tears filled Maggie's eyes as she thought of how proud Mollie had been of their home.

'The nicest in the district!' she was fond of saying, and had daily thanked God for sending Maggie to her. How empty their lives would be now she was gone.

Brian, Evelyn and the boys returned to the kitchen and brought Maggie back to reality. She waited quietly while they settled themselves. When at last they were all seated, after a nod of approval from May, Bob cleared his throat and addressed Maggie. 'We're surprised to see Mother has such lovely pieces of furniture.' His words brought a murmur of assent as the rest agreed with him.

Running her hand caressingly along a highly polished table, Maggie waited for silence. 'Yes, they are lovely,' she agreed, 'but then if you had visited your mother in the last few years you would have seen all these.' She raised her brows inquiringly. 'Surely your mother mentioned them when she visited you?'

'Well, yes, she did, but we thought it was old second-hand furniture,' Bob replied, and laughed lightly at the idea. Again the others nodded their heads and chorused agreement, and Maggie's lips tightened angrily.

'It is old second-hand furniture, Bob,' she stressed. 'If you had visited your mother, you would have seen how good she was at restoring it.' She enjoyed pointing out that he had been neglectful.

'I didn't know me mother was so ill.' His voice was terse in answer to the implied criticism, his eyes angry. 'If I had, I'd have visited her!'

Lip curling with scorn and eyes flashing in anger, Maggie lashed out at him. 'She ailed a long time, Bob, but thank God she went quick at the end. It was what she was praying for. She would have hated to linger.'

With another scornful glance she left the kitchen and went to say farewell to her friend. Gazing down at the woman who had been like a mother to her, she was choked with emotion. She remembered the time Paul had died, and how she had wanted to follow him. The weeks when she had not cared whether she lived or died. It was Mollie who had forced her to face up to life and look after her daughter. She remembered the feel of Mollie's arms around her when her mother had made her choose between a new life or staying with Sarah, and how she had assured her it would all pan out. When Brendan had gone away, that other bereavement in her life, it was Mollie again who had comforted her. She had felt so alone, so unwanted and unloved. The past years had not been easy, indeed no, but without her friend they would have been intolerable.

Ah, Mollie, Mollie ... who will look after me now you're gone? she lamented inwardly.

Feeling a small hand being pushed into hers, she clasped it and drew her daughter close to her side.

'We'll miss her, Mam.'

'Yes, Sarah, we'll miss her,' Maggie agreed. How they would miss her!

'Do you think she's in heaven yet?' Big green eyes searched Maggie's imploringly. Sarah was at that age when everything had to be explained to her satisfaction, and Maggie was at a loss how to answer her question. She herself did not believe in life after death, but her friend had made sure Sarah had been instructed fully in the Catholic faith, and Maggie knew she was picturing Mollie burning in Purgatory.

She thought for a moment then chose her words carefully. 'Mollie was a good, holy woman. I don't think she'll be in Purgatory long.'

With a relieved sigh, Sarah nodded her head, satisfied. Silence reigned for some minutes as they gazed sorrowfully at the corpse. Then Sarah craned her neck to gaze up into her mother's face.

'Mam?'

'Hmm?'

'Will Agnes be coming to live with us?'

Maggie's brows drew together, marring the unlined smoothness of her brow. 'Agnes?'

'Her in there.' Sarah jerked her head in the direction of the kitchen.

The frown on Maggie's face deepened and her eyes widened. 'Agnes Grahame? Whatever gave you that idea?'

Sarah's shoulders lifted in a shrug. 'Her mam asked her if she would like to live here after she got married, and she said yes.'

Putting an arm around her daughter's shoulders, Maggie drew her closer still. Her eyes were blazing in a face now white with rage, but she managed to control her voice. 'No, Sarah, I can assure you, Agnes will not be coming to live with us.' With her free hand she covered her friend's where they lay joined on her breast. 'Wise Mollie, you were right. They will try to take the house from me,' she whispered, and her voice broke, 'Oh, Mollie, what will become of us?'

All speculation came to an end with the arrival of Father Magee who arrived at the same time as the hearse. Mollie had expressed the wish to spend the night before she was buried in church, so after the rosary was said, the lid was put on the coffin and it was carried from the house and placed in the hearse. Bob, Brian and their families climbed into the two carriages, and these followed the hearse slowly down the street. No one asked Maggie if she would like to go, so taking Sarah by the arm, she decided to take the short cut over to the church. She hurried down Malcomson Street, across the Springfield Road and down Crocus Street, arriving breathless at the corner of Cavendish Street to await the funeral cortege.

Kathleen and Jim were already outside St Paul's Church, talking in hushed tones to Anne and Bill, and she was aware that Kevin and Barry waited in the porch with some of the neighbours. She was glad that they had come as a sign of respect. The twins were also there with their respective partners. Sean had gotten his wish; he stood six foot tall and resembled Paul so much that Maggie's breath caught in her throat each time she saw him. Jean had married the ginger-haired lad who had carried her books all through school. She had married young and was now the mother of two girls.

Just as the hearse drew up at the church, Mary and Emma arrived. Mary had the two eldest of her children with her. She never went anywhere without at least one of her children, even though she was teased unmercifully about them. She just said with a smile that she felt undressed unless one of them accompanied her. Emma was still a spinster and Maggie wondered if she still carried a torch for William though she never mentioned him and Maggie respected her privacy. All her efforts had been directed towards carving out a career for herself and she was now a buyer for a small, select shop in the centre of town – the kind that had one gown in the window and a price tag that took your breath away. She travelled abroad a lot, and Maggie had watched her grow into an attractive, poised young woman. As they gathered around her Maggie relaxed, glad these friends had come. With their support she would be able to handle the Grahames.

After the short service Maggie avoided Mollie's family. Quickly leaving the church, she hurried down the Falls Road with her friends. To her surprise Bob hurried after her and called her to one side. Excusing herself, she fell back to join him.

'Can we come to see you tomorrow after the funeral?' he asked politely.

'Why?' Worry made her voice sound imperious.

'We must talk.' His answer was abrupt; her tone of voice offended him. Snooty bitch, he thought, but kept his face impassive.

Drawing herself to her full height, Maggie raised her eyebrows. 'What do we have to talk about now that your mother is dead, Bob?'

The unctuous expression left his face and his nostrils flared. Then thrusting his head towards her, he growled. 'We have me mother's personal belongings to discuss, among other things.'

Annoyed at herself for letting him get the better of her, Maggie inwardly reproved herself. She should have been

167

prepared for this. Of course they would want to discuss Mollie's belongings. She nodded her head. 'Yes, come after the funeral.' Then, leaving him abruptly, she hurried across to join Kathleen and Jim who had paused to wait for her at the bottom of the Springfield Road. A slight smile appeared on her face when she observed the way Jim was glaring across the road at Bob. It was nice to know he was ready to defend her should the need arise.

'He wants to come to the house to see me, after the funeral tomorrow,' she explained.

'Does he indeed? Well, I hope you told him where he can go,' Kathleen cried indignantly.

She was worried because she was aware Bob could put young Agnes in her grannie's house and there was nothing Maggie could do about it. It was unfair but that was the way it worked. Whoever's name was in the rent book had priority, and Agnes still bore her grannie's name. Once she was married it would be easy to have her name changed. Normally, Agnes would not dream of living in Waterford Street, having lived the last few years in a house with a bathroom, bought when her father was promoted. However, Maggie had her house so nice, any young girl would be glad to start married life there. There were plenty of houses on the market at the present time in mixed districts that were going cheap. Houses that people had fled from in terror, after watching their neighbours being burnt out, but no one was willing to risk living there. So Maggie's house, relatively safe in the midst of the Falls, would be a god-send for the like of Agnes. With the cost of living so high unskilled workers like her future husband could not afford high rent for houses available up the Falls Road. Yes, indeed . . . Agnes would be in her glory living in Waterford Street on Frank's small wage.

About to speak, Kathleen caught a warning look from Jim and the words died on her lips. As usual, he had read her mind and she realised that he was right. Maggie would know soon enough. Let her live in ignorance for another day.

Helped by Sarah, Anne was preparing sandwiches when

168

at last the trio arrived at the house. Maggie flashed them a grateful smile. 'Thanks, Anne. Thanks, Sarah. We were talking to Bob,' she explained. 'He wants to come and see me tomorrow after the funeral.'

Anne drew back, a look of chagrin on her face. 'Whatever for? He never bothered when Mollie was alive, so why come now?'

'I suppose he will want Mollie's personal belongings. I think he will also want some of the furniture.'

Across the room Maggie caught Bill's eye. 'There's some of the hard stuff in the bottom of the bureau. Will you get it out for the men, Bill?' Giving her the thumbs up sign he went to the bureau and Maggie turned her attention back to Anne.

'Surely he's not entitled to any of your lovely furniture?' her mother-in-law said.

'I'm afraid he is.' Maggie's long fingers caressed the rosewood chest. 'You see, Mollie and I bought everything between us, so I suppose her sons really are entitled to her share.'

'Mollie'll turn in her grave if May or Evelyn get their hands on her things,' Anne cried aghast, then sighed deeply. 'Tut! Life's so unfair, so it is.'

'I just wish it was all over. I dread them coming.' She smiled at her friend. 'But Kathleen has offered to come and give me moral support.'

'Shall I come too?' her mother-in-law quickly volunteered.

'No, Anne. Thanks all the same but Kathleen is enough. I just don't want to be alone with them.'

'Them?' Anne gasped in dismay. 'Ye think they'll all come?'

With a wry smile Maggie replied, 'Oh, yes, I think they'll come in force. Evelyn won't want May to put one over on her.'

'Don't you be puttin' on a feed for them, mind,' Anne warned.

'No, Anne, I've made up my mind. Tea and biscuits will be their lot.'

She stayed downstairs late that night, drinking numerous cups of cocoa, but at last sadly climbed the stairs to bed. She hadn't really expected Kevin to come . . . not really. Then why was she so disappointed?

To their credit, Bob and Brian had done their mother proud. It was Mollie's own money, saved religiously by her for her funeral, but they had not scrimped and for this Maggie was grateful. She hoped her friend knew she was going out in style; she would be so proud.

Today, instead of the plain old work horses of the night before, the hearse, highly polished and brasses aglitter, was drawn by two fine well-groomed horses and followed by two splendid horse drawn carriages. After the Requiem Mass, Mollie's family climbed into the carriages, accompanied by Father Magee, and the crowds fell into line and the funeral cortege moved slowly up the Falls Road.

Once again, Maggie was not invited to go in one of the carriages so watched until the long procession that followed the hearse had disappeared around the corner at Broadway Village. Then, putting a comforting arm around Sarah's trembling figure, she headed home. Alarmed at how white and shaken her daughter was, she exchanged a worried glance with Kathleen who hurried along beside them.

As soon as they entered the house, Sarah rushed into the scullery and retched and retched at the sink until dry shudders tore at her slight frame. Then pulling free from Maggie's supporting arm she fled up the stairs, completely ignoring Kathleen's offer of sympathy.

With an apologetic look at Kathleen, Maggie followed her. Curled up on the bed lay her daughter, sobbing as though her heart would break. Maggie knelt by the side of the bed and gathered her close to her breast. 'Hush, love. Don't cry. You know Mollie hated to see you cry.'

'I loved her, Mam. Ah, Mam . . . I really loved her, so I did!' The words came out on a hiccup and sobs choked her as she wiped at her nose with the back of her hand.

'I know you did, love, and Mollie knew you loved her

170

and it made her very happy.' Maggie dabbed at her face with a handkerchief. Taking it from her, Sarah blew into it.

'I wasn't always good. Sometimes I was awful to her.'

Sadness enveloped Maggie. Was everybody plagued with regrets when someone they loved died? 'Listen, Sarah! Mollie knew you were no angel, but she would not have changed one hair of your head.'

From swollen eyes, Sarah watched her intently, hope fighting despair. Maggie repeated, 'Not one hair would she have changed.'

'Really, Mam? You're sure?'

'Really, Sarah. I know.'

For some time Sarah continued to gulp back sobs, but soon fatigue overcame her and she had difficulty keeping her eyes open. Making soothing noises, Maggie held her close until she was sure she was asleep. Then, rising stiffly from her cramped position by the bed, she covered Sarah with a blanket before descending the stairs.

From the scullery, Kathleen watched her anxiously. 'Is she all right?'

Receiving a weary nod in reply, she pulled a chair closer to the fire. 'Come an' sit down. I've a pot of tea ready, so I have.'

When Maggie shrugged out of her coat, her attention was caught by the crackle of paper. Mystified, she extracted a brown envelope from her coat pocket. Her face cleared when she remembered how, after the Requiem Mass, Father Magee had quietly taken her to one side and given her the envelope. Ripping it open, she slowly withdrew a smaller white envelope with her name scrawled across it. Her eyes filled with tears when she recognised Mollie's handwriting.

Full of concern, Kathleen moved closer and put a comforting hand on her shoulder as Maggie took a single sheet of notepaper from the envelope and read aloud:

'To whom it may concern, I the undersigned make this, my will, in the presence of Father Magee and Doctor Hughes. I leave all my personal belongings

171

and anything else I may be entitled to when I die, to Maggie Mason who has always been like a daughter to me.

> Mollie Grahame
> Witnesses: Father T. Magee (Parish Priest.)
> G. Hughes (General Practitioner)

While tears coursed down Maggie's cheeks, Kathleen soundlessly thanked God. These were the first tears her friend had shed and Kathleen was glad to see them. It was unnatural the way Maggie was bottling up her grief.

'Oh, Kathleen. Even when she was dying she was worrying about me. I don't deserve such kindness.'

The comforting hand on her shoulder ceased patting immediately, and now both her shoulders were gripped as Kathleen shook her. 'Don't you dare say that! Do you hear me? You were like a daughter to her. You made her life worth livin', so ye did!' Her voice softened as she finished, 'Go wash your face while I pour you a cup of tea. The Grahames will be here soon.'

All signs of tears camouflaged, Maggie was composed and calm when she opened the door to the Grahames and ushered them into the kitchen. The younger members of the family were not with their parents and Maggie saw May's face drop when her eyes scanned the table and she saw that there was only tea and biscuits for their consumption.

Bob had obviously been elected spokesman. When he finished his tea, he set his empty cup on the table, looking important, and squared his shoulders. Receiving the usual smile and nod of approval from his wife, he cast a sidelong glance in Kathleen's direction and began, 'Could we have a word with you alone, Maggie?'

'Anything you have to say can be said in front of Kathleen. She is my best friend,' Maggie assured him gravely.

With an indifferent shrug and a wry twist of the mouth, Bob cleared his throat and continued. 'Well now, the family had a meetin' last night to decide what to do with Mother's belongin's.'

Tilting her head to one side, Maggie raised her brows inquiringly but did not speak. Once more Bob cleared his throat.

'We understand of course that some of the furniture belongs to you, but . . .' The jovial laugh he gave was forced and Maggie's lids veiled her eyes to hide the contempt in them. 'I'm sure we can come to an amicable agreement,' he finished. He shifted about in his seat uncomfortably, wishing he had stood up to speak. From his position in the armchair he felt at a disadvantage as he had to look up at Maggie where she stood, relaxed and easy, in front of the fireplace. 'I don't know if you are aware that Agnes is getting married in September?' His look was inquiring and when Maggie nodded in reply he continued, 'Well, she has expressed the wish to start married life here, in her grannie's house.'

Maggie's lips pursed into a silent 'oh' and he rushed on.

'Of course we realise we're not giving you much notice, so May,' he nodded in his wife's direction, 'an' I have agreed that she can live with us 'til you find other accommodation.'

Maggie had been staring fixedly at Bob whilst he spoke, but now she slowly moved her head and allowed her eyes to rest on May.

'That's very kind of you.'

May's face went scarlet. Maggie's demeanour was affable, but for the life of her May could not decide whether or not she was being sarcastic. She examined Maggie's face intently then gave a condescending nod.

'Will there be anything else?' Maggie inquired politely.

Relieved, because he had expected some opposition, but convinced Maggie was going quietly, Bob rose and faced her, a smile on his lips. 'No. Well, that is . . . perhaps you would like to choose which pieces of furniture you'd like to keep?' He decided they could be generous and let her have whichever pieces she wanted. Within reason, of course!

Inwardly thanking Mollie for her thoughtfulness, Maggie took the sheet of paper on which her friend had written her will from her pocket and handed it to Bob. 'I don't think that will be necessary. I think you had better read this.' And to her great satisfaction she saw the colour drain from his face as he scanned the paper.

Concerned, May was on her feet. 'What is it, Bob? What does it say?'

With a malevolent glare at Maggie, Bob thrust the paper at his wife. She quickly scanned it and gasped in disbelief, then passed it to Brian who smiled faintly when he read it. He was glad Bob was being thwarted; he had thought he was being too high-handed.

'We'll contest it,' May hissed.

'That is your privilege.' Maggie bowed her head in acknowledgement, knowing full well that no one would doubt the word of a priest and doctor.

Bob, realising this, shushed his wife to silence. Glaring balefully at Maggie, he said, 'I must ask you to give me me mother's rent book. An' we'll be requiring the house as soon as possible,' he finished with a triumphant sneer.

All through this discourse, Kathleen had sat listening, proud of the way Maggie was conducting herself, but at Bob's spiteful words, worry for her friend returned. It was not right that a person could live in a house for thirteen years and then be put out because their name was not in the rent book, but that was the way it worked. Unfair it might be, but it happened regularly. It looked like this spiteful man would win after all. If only Jim and she had a house of their own, instead of living in rooms above the shop.

True to her word, Kathleen had not stopped or stayed until Jim had acquired his own shoe repairing business. They considered themselves lucky; even during the war business had flourished. With the shortage of new shoes and boots people had to make do and get their old footwear mended, but all the money he made was ploughed back into the business. Just when they planned to buy a house, the troubles had broken out. Now, with so many out of work, business was bleak except for the military having their boots mended. Still, they had managed to save enough for a deposit on a house, but that was not going to help Maggie. She would need somewhere to go immediately.

Bewildered, she watched Maggie calmly walk to the bureau which stood below the window. Opening the flap, she withdrew a small blue book from one of the pigeon holes and handed it to Bob. An unpleasant smirk creased his face as he made to place it in the inside pocket of his jacket, but with a gesture Maggie stopped him.

'Please look at the name on the inside cover,' she directed.

Apprehensively, Bob slowly opened the book and glanced inside the front cover. Then the book sailed through the air to hit Maggie on the shoulder and fall at her feet. 'By God, you've done your work well,' he sneered. 'You must've brain-washed me mother . . . played on her sympathy, to make her ignore her own flesh n' blood.'

On her feet again, May cried, 'What's wrong, Bob? For heaven's sake, what's wrong?'

Flinging a hand in Maggie's direction, he yelled, 'Her name's in the rent book, so it is! That's what's wrong. She's a crafty bitch, so she is. Standin' there, lookin' as if butter wouldn't melt in her mouth.' Wagging a finger in Maggie's face he threatened, 'I'll have more to say about this. You mark my words! I'll be at the rent office first thing in the mornin'.'

With one final wrathful glance he stormed out of the house, slamming the door as he went. Unfortunately, May was on his heels and as the door almost caught her in the face, she reared back like a frightened rabbit and an oath escaped her lips. This brought forth a deep chuckle from Evelyn, quickly concealed by a cough. She was glad to see May and Bob brought down. They had been grabbing everything without so much as a by your leave to Brian, and their downfall pleased her.

As he passed Maggie on his way to the door, Brian

paused. 'You'll never believe this, but I'm glad mother left you everything. You were good to her . . . I only wish I'd been a better son.' He struggled to find words to express his regret but failed. With a rueful lift of his shoulders, he left the house, closing the door quietly, even reverently, behind him.

Grinning from ear to ear, Kathleen pounded the arm of the chair with excitement. 'By! But you gave it to him that time,' she chortled. 'I'm so glad your name's in the rent book . . .'cause believe me, Maggie, your kind neighbours too will be tryin' to get this house for their offspring.' Her affection was apparent when she added, with a glint of tears in her eyes, 'Ah, Maggie, I'm proud of you.'

Maggie's smile was wan. 'I didn't believe Mollie when she said, given the chance, they would try to put me out.' She frowned, and bewilderment clouded her eyes. 'How could Mollie, who was so good, produce sons like those two? Brian is just weak, but Bob is obnoxious.'

'I agree with you there. Yes, I agree with you there. That habit he has of clearin' his throat. Phew! I don't know how May sticks it. It would put me away in the head, so it would. I felt like sayin' to him: "Cough it up, for heaven's sake, Bob, an' put us all out of our misery!"' She lifted her coat from a hook at the foot of the stairs and slipped her arms into it. 'I'll have to go now, Maggie. Me ma'll think I'm lost. Those two girls of mine are a handful.'

'Thanks for coming, Kathleen,' Maggie said gratefully.

'Any time, Maggie. Any time.' With an admiring glance around the kitchen, she added, 'Mind you, I don't blame Agnes for wantin' to live here. It's like a wee palace, so it is.'

'Away with you!' Maggie blushed with embarrassment. 'It's just comfortable.'

Throwing her head back, Kathleen laughed aloud. 'Well now, there's comfort an' there's comfort, but let me tell you something, Maggie Mason – Mollie was a wise woman . . . gettin' your name put in the rent book.'

'Yes. Mollie was wise and kind and good.' Maggie's

voice broke on the words. 'I don't know how I'll manage without her.'

'You'll be all right, so ye will.' Kathleen gripped her by the shoulders and gave her an affectionate shake. 'Do you hear me? You'll be all right. Just remember! When God closes a door, He opens a window.'

With these words of wisdom, Kathleen hugged her friend close and then hurried from the house.

Kathleen was right: the neighbours got up a petition to get Maggie put out of the house. The rent collector, an elderly man, told her that they had collected forty signatures. It saddened her that so many people, people she had worked alongside during the worst of the troubles, whom she thought regarded her as a good neighbour, could want to be rid of her.

Sensing her dismay, the rent man was quick to assure her that most of the names were probably people who did not even know her. He winked and nodded knowingly. 'Ye know what I mean? People obliging a friend of a friend!' He also assured her that Joe McGuinness (the owner) was a fair man and since her name was in the rent book that would be the end of it. She never found out if Bob did go to the rent office, as he had threatened to do, but she knew that if he did so, he got no joy out of Joe McGuinness because he had sent her word, via the rent man, not to worry. Nevertheless she did worry! How could she do otherwise? How could she be sure which neighbours were for her and which against? With a few exceptions she could not, so kept her distance and was left alone.

In spite of King George's plea for peace, July was another terrible month with continuous gun battles. For days Maggie and Sarah were confined to the house as armoured cars toured the streets, sometimes firing indiscriminately as they searched for snipers. Innocent people were shot dead when they ventured outside their homes. Some even died inside, killed by ricocheting bullets. She learnt that the Grosvenor Road as well as the Falls was under siege and by the end of the 'twelfth weekend', twelve had died, over a hundred were wounded and a vast number of homes destroyed. In the midst of all this a truce was declared between the I.R.A. and the British government. It made no difference; the riots continued but were not as severe. Maggie had never known such loneliness. Unable to leave the house for some time, she was cut off from those she trusted. Everyone was in the same boat, afraid to venture outside their homes.

Into this loneliness, Kevin arrived. Before the current siege she had expected him, but as time passed and he failed to put in an appearance, the expectancy had dimmed. Now, as she sat at the fireside darning the elbow of a cardigan of Sarah's, a noise bought her to her feet in alarm. Someone was in the scullery.

'Don't be frightened . . . it's only me.' As he entered the kitchen, he chided her, 'You should keep the back door barred.' And he waved a key in front of her astounded face.

Regaining her composure, the look she gave him was full of wrath. 'I didn't expect anyone to come over the wall. How dare you enter my home unasked? How dare you come over the wall like a thief in the night? I suppose Mollie gave you that key . . . well, I want it back!'

'I know, I know, easy on. I apologise. I had to see you and didn't want the neighbours talkin'. What we do is none of their business,' he said meaningfully, and ignoring her outstretched hand, returned the key to his pocket. 'No, Mollie didn't give me the key. I got it cut.'

Fear niggled at her mind. 'What do you want?'

"I just called to make sure you were all right. I heard about the petition and I was worried about you.' His eyes held hers and there it was again, that look, bringing a blush to her cheeks, a weakness to her knees.

With a great effort of will she dragged her gaze away from his. 'That was kind of you. I'm all right, thank you.'

'A cup of tea would be very welcome . . . if you don't mind?'

She dithered, then headed for the scullery. After all, he had been kind when Mollie was ill. It would be churlish to deny him a cup of tea. 'You can't stay, mind! I'll make you a cup of tea but as soon as you drink it, you go.'

'Whatever you say, Maggie. I just wanted to make sure you're all right. I know you'll be missin' your friend. It can't be pleasant, here alone with the child.'

When she handed him the cup of tea, he frowned. 'You're not joinin' me?'

'No. I've already had a cup.'

'Well, at least sit down. Lord God, I'm not going to eat ye.'

Slowly, she made her way to the armchair and sat down, aware that she must be careful; if she gave him an inch he'd want a mile.

As he drank, his eyes examined her. Roaming familiarly over her body, making her feel naked.

She squirmed uneasily. 'Are you finished? Will you please hurry? It's late.'

A smile tugged at his mouth. 'Why are you so nervous, Maggie? I'm not goin' to hurt you.'

'I know you're not! As soon as you finish that tea you're on your way.'

'What if I refuse to go? What then, Maggie, eh? Will you call the military? Would you do that, Maggie?' He sounded aggressive as he taunted her. Then his look and tone changed, became rueful. 'Look, Maggie, I'm handlin' this all wrong. I came here because I need a favour. I need to be able to come an' go without the B&Ts knowin'. Just for a couple of days.'

'You're up to no good, Kevin McCrory, and I want nothing to do with you. I've Sarah to think about ... I can't afford to take chances. Besides, you're not fooling me. There are plenty of women about here who would put you up.'

He had risen slowly to his feet while she ranted at him. Now he stood gazing down at her, his eyes trying to seduce her. 'Ah, but then, none of them excite me like you do, Maggie,' he teased her. As a blush darkened on her face and rose to meet her hairline, deepening her beauty, his voice became husky with passion. 'You know, from the

179

first night I set eyes on you, I've wanted you. But you do know that because it's mutual . . . isn't it?'

When her mouth opened to deny this accusation, he forestalled her. 'Don't worry. I'm not goin' to try anything. At least not t'night. I've business to attend to and I need access to this house . . . at least to the yard. Ye see, Maggie, there's stuff in the yard that must be moved. If the military find it there you'll be in trouble. I really am thinkin' of you. I didn't want you wakin' up screamin' in the night and alertin' the army.'

Seeing the fear in her eyes, with one swift movement he had her out of the chair and in his arms. 'Don't worry. It'll be moved t'night . . . I'll see t'that. But I'll be back t'morrow night.'

When he claimed her lips his kiss was urgent and to her shame she responded hungrily. At last, with a sigh of regret, he released her, his eyes glowing with triumph. 'I wish I didn't have to go, but I'll see you tomorrow night. That's a promise!'

And before she could evade him, he planted a quick kiss on her brow before leaving the house, via the back door.

Unable to sleep, she lay with ears straining for sounds from the yard but she heard nothing. What was out there? Had Mollie been aware that the yard was being used? No . . . no! She would never have given her consent to anything underhand. One thing was sure: tomorrow night the back door would be barred and there was no way Kevin would be able to persuade her to open it.

She laughed ruefully at this idea. Not let him in? Wasn't she aching for him? He had awakened the need in her. But where would it lead? She was too lonely, too in need of love, but she didn't trust Kevin, not one bit! She would have to be very careful. If she let him, he would love and leave her, and that would never do.

All her own troubles faded into the background when, the following morning, Kathleen arrived in tears. Full of concern, Maggie led her friend inside and gently pushed her into the armchair.

'What's wrong, Kathleen?'

'We were petrol bombed last night.'

Sinking to her knees beside her, Maggie gathered her hands between her own. However, before she could speak, Kathleen continued.

'We've been warned, but I never really believed they'd do it. Bomb their own? I mean ... Jim has been so generous to our lot. Mendin' their boots for next t'nothin'. An' that's the thanks we gets ...' She sat stunned at the thought of it.

'But why? Why did they do it?'

'Jim was repairin' boots for the army.'

Dismayed, Maggie gripped Kathleen's hands tighter still. She knew only too well how people who catered for the army were treated. 'Ah, Kathleen ... Kathleen!'

'I know ... I know you'll think we deserved it.' At Maggie's swift denial she continued, 'We did ... I know we did. But we needed the money and Jim thought if we refused the army, the other side would object, and they were more likely to harm us than our own. We were wrong.'

'Are Jim and the children all right?'

'Oh, yes, they gave us time to get a few things together.'

'That was unusual, surely?'

'Well, I think it was because *he* was there.'

'He?'

'You know who I mean ... it's as much as my life's worth to mention his name.'

'You mean ...?'

'Yes ... him!'

Maggie gaped at her in amazement for some seconds, then shook her head; she must be picking her up wrong. 'We've crossed wires here.' She laughed ruefully. 'You can't possibly mean Kevin?'

'Oh, but I do! Indeed I do!'

'Oh, my God! I can't take it in. Where will you live?'

'Jim's with his mother ... an' me an' the two kids are at me mam's. But she's no room. Our Nora and her three have been there since they were burnt out of Bombay Street. I don't know what we're gonna do.'

181

'You can stay here.'

'Ah, Maggie, it's kind of you, but I don't want to meet him. Does . . . does he still come to see you?'

As if on cue, with a tap on the kitchen door Kevin entered the room, to come slowly to a halt at the sight of Kathleen.

Obviously agitated, she rose quickly to her feet. 'I'll have to be goin', Maggie. I'll see you later.'

'No need to run away because of me.' With a raised hand he stopped her. 'As a matter of fact I came here to leave a message for you. There's an empty shop down the Falls at the corner of Alma Street, and if your husband applies for it, I guarantee he'll get it.'

'That shop's for sale . . . we can't afford to buy. After all these years of hard work we've just managed to get the deposit gathered together for a house.'

'I've arranged for you to rent it, but tell your husband not to delay or he'll miss his chance.'

With one last bewildered look at Maggie, Kathleen lifted her bag and headed for the door. 'Goodbye.'

When the door closed on her, Kevin moved towards Maggie. Eyes full of anger she stood her ground, daring him to touch her.

Slowly he came to a halt and his voice was defensive. 'They deserved it, ye know. If I hadn't been there, they'd have been worse off. At least they had time to gather their personal bits and pieces.'

'Are you trying to tell me they were the first you've bombed out? What about the people you didn't know, eh? Did it not matter about them? Don't you care that people are homeless because of you?'

'Hey, hold on a minute . . . what about all our ones? Thousands thrown out of work! Thousands more homeless!'

'Two wrongs don't make a right,' she interrupted him, but he shouted her down.

'Oh, don't they? You tell that to the people sleeping in the brickworks an' in the fields. Tell that to those queuing up for handouts through no fault of their own! Do ye know

182

something, Maggie? Folk like you sicken me! You're all right . . . a cosy home an' a safe job.' At the stricken look on her face, his voice trailed off.

'I do my best to help . . .'

'I know that.' He had the grace to look ashamed. 'Ah, Maggie. I know that. I'm sorry.'

She turned aside, tears blinding her. Why did she feel such a sense of loss? Had she really wanted him to come back? Did he mean that much to her? 'Please go.'

'I'll see you tonight.'

'No, you won't! Kathleen and her children are coming to live here.' The look she turned on him was bleak. 'You see, she has nowhere to stay.'

A wry grimace twisted his mouth. 'Fate, eh, Maggie? Well, I think we make our own fate an' I intend to see you again. You can depend on that!' At the door he turned. 'The yard's clear so don't be worryin'.'

When the door closed, she sank down at the table and buried her head in her arms. She hated his kind, meting out punishment as he thought fit, but he had awakened a great aching need in her; a need that longed to be assuaged. Would she be able to resist him?

At last she squared her shoulders. She entered the scullery and washed and powered her face. Before Sarah came home from school, she must go and assure Kathleen that she was welcome to share her home. And while her friend lived with her, she would be safe from Kevin.

Jim Rafferty got the shop at the corner of Alma Street facing the Public Baths. He got it at a reasonable rent, just like Kevin had predicted, and also discovered that the shop in Donegal Street was not too badly damaged. Most of his equipment was salvaged and in no time he was back in business. Although not as profitable as the shop in the town centre, the new one kept the wolf from the door and for this Jim was grateful. A deposit was put down on a house in St James Park and soon Kathleen and the children moved from Waterford Street and once again Maggie and Sarah were alone.

Kevin proved to be elusive and in spite of herself

Maggie was intrigued. By asking a question here and there, she learnt that he was on the run from the military. What had he done now? Killed someone? She did not dare to criticise him. He was a hero, looked up to and followed by the youth of the district. And didn't she long to see him?

The riots continued in spite of the truce. The south still boycotted goods from the north, helped by the I.R.A. raiding freight trains and destroying goods from the north that found their way into southern shops. In October a delegation from Dail Eireann travelled to Downing Street to negotiate terms with the British government. Sir James Craig was not invited to attend and Ulster waited with bated breath for the results of the negotiations. It was 6 December when the Anglo-Irish Treaty was signed in Downing Street. The results were sent post haste to Sir James in Belfast and he was devastated. The south was to become an Irish Free State and a boundary was to be placed between it and the north. A boundary that could mean parts of the north being given to the south. Perhaps even the Mourne Mountains, the source of Belfast's water.

On the Falls Road, rumour had it that Sir James wrote many bitter letters to Lloyd George, threatening that Northern Ireland might find it necessary to retaliate by calling for help from the members of the Royal Orange Institution, to supply money for arms and ammunition. It was alleged that the loyalists might declare independence and seize the government departments and the customs offices. Then in November control of law and order was passed to the Northern Ireland government, and at once more 'B Specials' were recruited. In the Catholic districts you could almost taste the fear in the air. Once again the riots intensified and by the end of November another twenty-seven people had died.

It was two days before Christmas when Maggie next saw Kevin. He came over the yard wall and was in the scullery before she was aware of him.

'I told you to bar the door at night,' he gently chided her. She knew she should upbraid him, tell him to get out, but her tongue would not obey her. When, overcome by the look in her eyes, he reached for her, she went willingly into his arms. He held her close for some time, rubbing his cheek against the softness of her hair, his hands caressing her back. When he at last pushed her away from him, to look at her, there was awe in his eyes.

'Maggie . . . ah, Maggie. You care?'

These words brought her back to reality. Pushing away from him, she shook her head in bewilderment. 'I . . . I don't know. I just know that I was worried about you.'

His grin was wide. 'That's a start.' But when he reached for her again, she was suddenly overcome by shyness.

'Are you hungry?' she asked, her eyes begging him to be. 'Will I make you something to eat?'

He eyed her through narrowed lids, then nodded. After all, she was his for the taking. A half hour wouldn't make any difference.

She watched him eat the sandwiches she had prepared, and all the while her mind tortured her. This was wrong! What if Sarah awoke and came downstairs? He watched her covertly and could see that she was having second thoughts. Draining the cup, he left it and the plate on the hearth and held out his hand to her.

She cowered back in the armchair. 'Kevin, I've been thinking . . . this is wrong.'

Swiftly he left his chair, kneeling beside her to grip her hands. 'Listen, Maggie. Listen t'me. These are bad times . . . we have to take our pleasure while we've got the chance. Don't deny me your comfort.'

Tentatively, her hand touched his face, and after that there was no turning back. He undressed her slowly, savouring every moment. He had waited a long time for this, had pictured it often, and now at last she was to belong to him.

She was beautiful lying there, the fire casting the only light, setting her hair aglow, giving her skin the gleam of pearls. At last he was free of his clothes and joined her on the rug.

Maggie's heart was thumping. This wasn't how she had

imagined it would be. She couldn't forget that Sarah slept upstairs; that she was about to commit a sin. Why, she didn't even know whether or not he was married!

The question hovered on her lips and she forced it out. 'Kevin . . . are you married?'

Raising himself on one elbow, he stared at her in amazement. But seeing the fear in her eyes, cautioned himself to be careful.

'You're a bit late askin' that.'

'Well, are you?'

'Does it matter?'

'Of course it matters!'

'It doesn't, ye know, Maggie. All that matters is that I'll take care of you.'

Obviously he was married! Roughly she pushed at him and tried to rise, but he forced her back.

'You've gone too far this time to draw back, so just enjoy yourself, Maggie.'

She opened her mouth to scream, but remembered Sarah in the room above and closed it again. Then it really was too late as his hands aroused hungry emotions and she gripped him close. However, she was to be saved in spite of herself. Loud voices outside the kitchen window brought Kevin to his feet in an instant.

'Some bastard must have seen me come in and reported me!'

He was hurriedly dressing as he spoke, and when he stuffed his feet into his boots, hauled her roughly to her feet.

'You'd better get dressed. They'll not come directly here, but they will come, so be prepared. I'll be back . . . some night soon.'

Fear making her hands tremble, Maggie dressed. She heard the military arouse the household next door and then it was her turn. The loud knock on the door brought Sarah down the stairs to join her in the hall as she opened the door. The soldier on the doorstep brushed past them and climbed the stairs; another one took his place.

'Is any one else here?'

'No! What are you searching for?'

'This will only take a minute.'

The first soldier to arrive descended the stairs and made his way through the scullery and out into the yard. When he returned he shook his head and his companion said, 'Thank you for your co-operation. Sorry we disturbed you.'

Thankfully, Maggie closed and barred the door. Would Kevin escape? Who had betrayed him?

It was Barry who brought her the news of his death. At tea-time on Christmas Eve he arrived. She knew when she opened the door that he was the bearer of bad news and motioned him inside.

'So they caught him?'

'No!' When her jaw dropped, he continued, 'He's dead.'

'But . . . but you said they couldn't catch him?'

'Oh, no. The military tried to *help* him escape. That's why they set up such a racket outside your window last night, then searched other houses before they searched here. It was to give him a chance to get away.'

'I don't understand . . .'

'Don't you?'

He sounded sceptical and she frowned. 'Should I?'

'He was an informer.'

Maggie swayed from the shock that rocketed through her body. With an arm around her, Barry assisted her to the armchair. But once she was seated he stepped back and there was contempt in his eyes as he gazed down at her.

'I didn't know. Honestly . . . I didn't know. I . . . I actually thought he was high up in the I.R.A., so I did.'

Her sincerity was so apparent that the doubts Barry had harboured faded. Sinking down on to the chair facing her, he sighed. 'It seems he fooled everybody. I couldn't believe it when it became obvious to me that the military was receiving information known only to him and me. Of course no one else would believe me. I had a hard job persuading them to set a trap for him . . . an' he fell right into it!'

'How did he die?'

'He was shot. You'll read about it in the papers. It will say he died while being chased by the military . . . but it wasn't them that shot him. He'll be buried as a hero. After all, we can't let the youth of the Falls know that he was a traitor. No, that would never do. And his wife and children will be safer, poor blighters.'

At her start of dismay, he sighed again. 'He didn't tell you he was married?'

'No . . . no!'

Rising to his feet, he squeezed her shoulder sympathetically. 'It could have been worse . . . he could have left you with a child. There's a couple about here with full bellies because of that bastard.' And with these words he quietly let himself out of the house.

Maggie sat for some time going over in her mind the horror of what might have befallen her. How could she have been so foolish? That was her finished with men. She was obviously meant to spend the rest of her life alone so may as well resign herself to the fact. But her heart was a lead weight in her breast as she went about her duties, and when she saw Kevin's wife and two sons at the funeral it was tears of shame she wept.

Fate had not finished with Maggie. Some months later life was to deal her yet another blow. One night Sarah burst into the kitchen agog with excitement.

'Mam! Mam! The library's on fire.'

'Again?'

The I.R.A. had declared war on all government buildings and this was the third time the library had been set alight in about twelve hours.

'This time it's really burnin'! It's bad, Mam, come and see.'

Grabbing her coat, Maggie followed on her daughter's heels. Near the library she came to a halt, aghast at the scene before her. Sarah was right. It was bad. The other two attempts had been easily doused but now, while the military protected them from attack, the firemen were

188

working all out. It looked like they were fighting a losing battle.

As she watched children running off with arms full of smoke-damaged books, fear made Maggie's bowels churn and she turned away, in a turmoil. It was obvious to her that the library would be closed for some considerable time. It would practically need to be rebuilt. How could they be so stupid? Did they not realise that it was the people of the Falls that would suffer through the loss of the library, not the government?

What would become of her? The last time she was out of work, Mollie's money had kept them going until she got started in the Blackstaff. Was that to be her fate again, three looms under Joe Wilson? She went cold at the very idea of it. Indeed she would be lucky to get started at all, there were so many out of work. The prosperous years during and after the Great War had come to an end and about a quarter of Belfast was unemployed. What would she do? How would they manage?

Her life was lived in a cocoon. She worked and returned to her home, and that was all. All hope of moving further up the Falls had died a slow death. Now every penny was saved for a rainy day. But her savings would not stretch far once she started using them. The only time she was in town was when Sarah needed new clothes; there were so many killings, so many bombings, that she preferred to stay on the Falls Road. She felt safe there. It seemed strange for her to admit that she felt safe on the Falls, but she did! Dear God, what would become of them now she was out of a job?

When he heard of her plight, William, who was making quite a name for himself in England as a freelance photographer, much to the disgust of their parents wrote urging her to join him. He described his flat and the area where he lived outside London in glowing colours and Maggie was tempted. After all, what had she here? A rented house in an area that was like a time bomb. Some good furniture, and a lonely old age to look forward to. However, would it be fair to take Sarah across the water?

No! She belonged here with her friends and the only grandparents she knew. Besides, old habits die hard and the idea of living in London petrified her. Better the devil you know than the devil you don't.

Brendan in his letters urged her to remarry. This brought a wry smile to her lips: Brendan must still have the idea in his head that she was beautiful, and could pick and choose. Even if she *was* beautiful, whom would she marry? There was a shortage of men. Very few had returned from the war and many had been killed and maimed during the riots. Even if someone suitable came along, she would be afraid of ruining their lives, as she had ruined Sean Hanna's. Sean, who had not returned from the Somme.

Fear of the workhouse drove her up the Springfield Road to the Blackstaff. She reasoned that if she was to be employed, she stood a better chance there where her work record was good. Luck was with her because she was interviewed by the foreman over the weaving shop, and when she had worked there before he had noted her good work record. He promised to send for her if a vacancy occurred. Maggie was not very hopeful; work was scarce and no one was leaving their job. She would be waiting for dead men's (or in this case women's) shoes – and that was exactly what she got! An elderly woman died of a heart attack and the foreman sent for Maggie.

However, she was unfortunate enough to be put on looms tentered by Joe Wilson. Glad to be employed, she determined not to let him annoy her. She would do her work, expect no favours, and with a bit of luck everything would pan out, as Mollie would have said. The first week she was lucky; the looms went smoothly and she did not have to ask Joe Wilson to tend them. Monday of the second week, the beam emptied and as the cloth at the end of a beam had to be signed by the tenter, it was with trepidation that she asked Joe to sign her cloth.

To her relief he signed it and was quite affable without being familiar, and she breathed a sigh of relief. On Tuesday morning he wheeled a new beam of warp to the back of the loom and commenced to tie it in. As he lay under the loom she managed to keep the other two looms going and stay out of reach of his hands. Then, to her dismay, a thread broke right in the centre of the cloth facing the loom he was tying the new beam in. As the loom dwindled to a halt, Maggie considered leaving it off until Joe was finished but could not afford to have two looms standing idle. So, keeping as far away from him as possible, she leant over the loom to tie in the broken thread.

Her eyes were off him for just a few seconds but he must have been waiting his chance. When his hand ran slowly, suggestively, up her leg, she stood transfixed with horror. Encouraged by her stillness, he ran his hand further still and when it touched the bare flesh where her stocking ended, rage and disgust filled Maggie. Without thinking, she reached for the spare shuttle and all her weight was behind it as she brought it down on his head. He saw the blow coming and moved quickly aside; but not quickly enough. The steel point of the shuttle caught him on the temple, and to her horror Maggie saw blood spurt from a gash and run down his face. The next thing she knew, she was in the foreman's office.

'Really, Mrs Mason, I'm surprised at you!'

'I'm . . . I'm sorry.'

'I should think so!'

'He put his hand up my clothes,' Maggie whispered, and a shiver of loathing ran through her at the remembered touch.

'It was an accident. I accidentally touched her ankle,' Joe Wilson cried indignantly, and Maggie gaped at him in dismay.

The foreman looked from one to the other of them. Was Maggie being prudish or had Joe really gone too far? Weavers were plentiful but a good tenter was hard to find. And Joe was that.

'Let's have a look at that wound.'

Looking pained, Joe removed the cloth he was holding to his temple and the foreman examined the gash.

'It'll need a stitch or two . . . I trust you don't want the police involved?'

Joe had no intention of involving the police, his wife might not find it so hard to believe Maggie, but he said diffidently, 'Well now, I don't know . . .'

Picturing the scandal of the police coming for her, and maybe believing Joe's story, Maggie interrupted him. 'Please don't send for the police.'

'Well, now . . .' The foreman turned to her. 'I'll have to give ye yer cards, Mrs Mason. Ye realise that?'

Maggie nodded. She would not be able to work under Joe Wilson again anyhow, so her cards were better than the police coming and charging her with assault. Ten minutes later she was outside the gates of the Blackstaff, tears in her eyes and her insurance cards clasped in her hand. She would have to call back on Friday to collect money owed to her as they worked a week in hand. As she made her way down the Springfield Road she felt weak and was aware it was due to the shock she had just received and to lack of food. She grinned grimly to herself. There would be even less food now she was out of work. Dear God, what would become of them? The houses between the Blackstaff and Malcomson Street had steps leading up to them and Maggie forced her legs towards them. She needed to sit down to regain her strength.

She never reached the steps. The next thing she knew she was lying on the couch in Doctor Hughes's waiting room and he was taking her pulse. She tried to sit up, but he put a restraining hand on her shoulder.

'How did I get here?'

'That gentleman,' he nodded towards the door, 'saw you faint and carried you in here.'

Maggie looked at the young man hovering near the doorway and whispered, 'Thank you. Thank you very much.'

He just nodded and smiled at her and said to the doctor, 'I'll run on now or I'll be late for my appointment.' And with another nod at Maggie he left the room.

'You know why you fainted, don't you?'

192

'Yes.' She was only too aware why she had fainted.

'You'll have to start eating properly, you know.'

She smiled wryly and started to rise to her feet. 'Thank you very much doctor. I'm afraid I'll have to owe you the money. You see, I've just lost my job.' To her dismay tears started to fall and she groped for a handkerchief. Doctor Hughes thrust one into her hand and gently pushed her back down on to the chair.

'Sit there. I'll get Mrs Black to make you a cup of tea and something to eat while you tell me all about it.'

Responding to his kindness, Maggie poured out all her worries, and when she was finished thanked him once again. 'I feel much better now that I've talked about it.'

'You know, I doubt if the police would have been called. That type of man usually has a bad reputation. He would not have risked calling the police.'

'I couldn't take the chance. Besides, I could not have worked under him again. He would have tortured me.'

'You could have demanded a change of position. Would you like me to phone the foreman and have a word with him?'

'Oh, no! No, but thank you all the same. I'll try and get started in Clonard Factory.'

The conversation was brought to an end with Mrs Black arriving with a cup of tea and a plate of sandwiches. Maggie devoured the food, watched by a perturbed doctor, and when she rose to leave, Mrs Black silently wrapped the remaining sandwiches in a napkin and handed them to her. Embarrassed, Maggie nevertheless gratefully accepted the parcel; it would do for Sarah's tea. One thing less for her to worry about.

The next morning, as she prepared to go and seek employment in Clonard Factory, there was a knock on the door. When she answered it she was surprised to see Doctor Hughes on the doorstep, but cordially invited him inside.

He stood in front of the fireplace, hands laced behind his back, teetering back and forth on the balls of his feet. He peered at her over the top of his spectacles. 'I'll not beat

193

about the bush, Maggie. Mrs Black is coming up seventy and she had been trying to retire for the past few years, but I hate change and have always managed to talk her out of it. With the boys at school now, my wife doesn't need help with the flat. Yesterday Mrs Black and I became aware at the same time that you would be an excellent receptionist. So how's about it? I need a receptionist and you need a job. Would you fancy working for me?'

Emotion welled up inside Maggie, a huge ball of it, that brought tears to her eyes. Unable to believe it, she stared speechlessly at him.

She was silent so long he said tentatively, 'Perhaps you would prefer to work in a factory?'

Unable to speak, she mutely shook her head. Imagine him thinking she would prefer to work in the factory to working in his beautiful surgery.

Puzzled at her reaction he asked, 'Is it the money? I'll give you at least as much as you were getting in the library.'

'No! No, it's not the money.' She stopped as tears threatened to fall, and blinked furiously. 'I'm just so grateful to you for thinking of me.'

Her gratitude embarrassed him and he said gruffly, 'Great! That's great. That's settled then. When can you start?'

'Any time . . . any time you say.'

'Well then, I'll see you tomorrow morning at eight sharp. Mrs Black will stay on for a couple of weeks to show you the ropes, so don't worry about anything.' As he turned to the door, she made to follow him but he stopped her. 'Don't come to the door,' he said mischievously. 'Let's give Belle Hanna something to wonder about, shall we?'

When he left the house, Maggie sank down on a chair, breathless with relief. She had a job! Then why was she crying? Oh, that dear, dear man. Words once spoken by Anne about him entered her mind. 'That man's a saint, so he is.' Now Maggie agreed with her. 'You are right, Anne. Yes, you are so right. He is a saint.'

She soon got into the routine required and enjoyed working for Doctor Hughes in the big house on the Springfield Road. The months passed quickly and as Sarah approached her fourteenth birthday, full of plans for the future, Maggie realised she had left it too late. Her daughter was strong-willed and Maggie knew she would not now be able to persuade her to leave Belfast. So it seemed she was doomed to end her days in Waterford Street.

She was even more grateful to Doctor Hughes some months later when the library was at last ready for occupation. Instead of opening, it was sand-bagged and turned over to the Black and Tans for barracks. It was obvious that the Falls Road would be without access to books for some time to come.

CHAPTER SEVEN

The prospect of Sarah's fourteenth birthday filled Maggie with apprehension. Was her daughter doomed to enter one of the mills when she left school? Determined that she would not work in one of the mills that flanked the Falls Road, Maggie watched the job vacancies in the *Irish News*. At last she saw what she was looking for, Robinson Cleavers, one of the big department stores in town, were advertising for a trainee saleswoman. To Sarah's disgust and dismay, Maggie arranged for an interview.

Under the watchful eye of her mother, Sarah dressed in her best clothes and they set forth. Seeing the long queue of girls waiting to be interviewed, Sarah breathed a sigh of relief. The chances of her getting the job were slim, especially when she said that she lived on the Falls Road. She was glad. These big stores were supposed to be unbiased against Catholics now, but she found that hard to believe. Besides, she didn't want to work in a shop. She wanted to work in the Blackstaff with Alice Smith. Alice was her best friend and now in charge of three looms in the Blackstaff, although she had only started there three months ago. To be truthful, she worked long hours and very hard, but Sarah wanted to join her, wanted to be one of the girls.

When it was their turn, squaring her shoulders, Maggie entered the inner office, leaving Sarah to follow. The woman seated behind the desk looked up to greet them and Maggie was dismayed. It was Irene Carson, the daughter of a friend of her mother's – a girl much younger than herself.

'Why, hello, Margaret!' Irene smiled warmly at her. She had always admired Maggie, thought her beautiful, although she had been very young when Maggie had been married, she remembered her mother and father discussing the harsh treatment meted out to her by her parents. They had thought Maggie was badly done by.

'Hello . . . Mrs Gray?' There was a query in Maggie's voice as she read from the sheet of paper in her hand. Irene answered it.

'Yes, that's my married name.'

'I'm sorry. I didn't know you were married.' Maggie's voice was low; she was embarrassed. How could she ask this young woman for a job for Sarah?

Sensing her discomforture, Irene took pity on her and tried to set her at ease. 'Sit down, Margaret,' she said kindly and looked askance at Sarah. 'This must be your daughter?'

Maggie sat down and motioned Sarah to do likewise. 'Yes, it is. Sarah, this is a friend of my family.'

Irene examined Sarah's features, noted the bright green eyes and small straight nose, the soft cloud of chestnut hair. She exclaimed in surprise, 'Why, she's the picture of your mother!'

Sarah sat all ears. Her mother refused to talk about her parents but perhaps today she would learn something. Maggie nodded her agreement and Sarah's eyes widened in surprise. Imagine! She was the picture of her grannie and her mother had never once said.

'How is my mother?' Maggie asked politely.

Irene eyed her in surprise, head tilted, one eyebrow raised. 'Surely you know she has remarried and gone to live in New Zealand?'

It was obvious that Maggie didn't know. The colour drained from her face, leaving her ashen.

'You mean to say she didn't let you know?' Irene was dismayed. How could a woman leave the country without informing her only daughter? But then, she had always thought Ruth Pierce a cold woman.

Mutely, Maggie shook her head then cried in distress. 'Father has been dead such a short time . . . and they were so close. How could she?'

'Six months was all she waited,' Irene agreed dryly. 'But Margaret, please understand, she was a lonely woman. Your father's death left a vast emptiness in her life and Ben Sherman, the man she married, is very like your father in looks and manner. It was often commented on.'

Aware that Irene was trying to soften the blow, Maggie was grateful to her. She had attended her father's funeral, hoping her mother would relent in her attitude towards Sarah. But no, although she had thanked her for coming, Ruth had made it perfectly clear that she no longer considered Maggie her daughter. Indeed, she had implied that the stress and strain of having a daughter living on the Falls Road, even although they had disowned her, had hastened her husband's death. She also stated that she held Maggie partly responsible, together with William's gallivanting about the world instead of taking his place beside his father, for driving him to an early grave.

This had added to the guilt Maggie was already feeling, and she was glad she had not allowed Sarah to accompany her to the funeral; she would probably have been ignored and scorned. William was not at the funeral; being on assignment in America he had arrived home too late, thus further incurring his mother's wrath and widening the rift between them. Was he aware that their mother had remarried? No! He would have told her had he known.

'Are there many waiting outside?' Irene directed the question at Sarah to give Maggie a chance to gain control of her emotions.

'No. We're the last.'

'Good! Then we shall have a cup of tea while I ask you some questions.'

Going to a corner of the room, she filled a kettle and put it on a small primus stove to boil. Maggie found herself unable to concentrate, and answered Irene's questions mechanically. She could only hope that Sarah was making a better impression. It was with relief that she saw Irene rise to her feet, signalling that the interview was at an end. Thanking her for her trouble and for the cup of tea, Maggie quickly left the room, and the building. In great agitation she hastened to the tram stop with a disgruntled Sarah trailing behind. Sarah was unhappy; from nuances picked up from Irene, she had a feeling she would get the job in Robinson Cleavers. She did not want it, but she did not dare mention it to her mother. Did not dare to voice the questions that hovered on her lips, because she could see that her mother was in an awful state.

Maggie was indeed in a state. She was devastated! No matter how great the differences between her and her mother, she could not believe she would be so cruel as to leave Ireland without so much as a goodbye. How could she do such a thing? Always, at the back of her mind, she had been sure that if anything happened to her, her mother would make herself responsible for Sarah. Now she was living on the other side of the world. How could she just go off like that? Now she had no one to turn to should she fall seriously ill or be in need of help. Mollie dead, Brendan a priest, with a parish down south, and William running all over the world. Everyone she had ever felt close to was either dead or out of reach. The Masons were there, and they were good and kind, but they had their own problems.

She was alone. How her mother must have turned against her, to have left without so much as a goodbye. Or had she ever cared? In her heart she knew her mother was wrong to blame her children for their father's death. You could not expect your children to live their lives to please you. You had to let them spread their wings; learn by their own mistakes. But then, was she not forcing Sarah into a job she did not want?

It's for her own good! she lamented inwardly, not understanding how anyone could want to work in the weaving factory. Was that what her parents had thought when they wanted to get her marriage annulled? It's for her own good! Oh, dear God! She was all mixed up and she had no one to talk to. Even Kathleen seemed out of reach. Now that she lived in St James Park, with three young children and a fourth on the way, Maggie hardly ever saw her. Well, that was her own fault. Her friend was tied to the house with the children but there was no excuse for Maggie. She was always made welcome when she visited them. She would visit them more often, she vowed silently, keep in touch. Her thoughts swung back to the interview. What kind of an impression had Sarah made on Irene? She had no idea; she had been too upset to give the interview the attention it deserved. Only time would tell. They must wait and see.

Much to her regret, but Maggie's delight, Sarah did get the job in Robinson Cleavers. She hated it, but Maggie was proud to see her go off every morning in her neat grey dress with its white collar and cuffs. She compared her with the mill girls in their scarfs and hair curlers and could not help feeling proud and happy. Sarah was getting a chance to make something of herself. If she worked hard and put her mind to it, she could become a buyer or window dresser; there were all kinds of possibilities open to her. However, it soon became obvious to her that her daughter was unhappy. She never talked about work and all her spare time was spent with Alice Smith, leaving Maggie alone. Realising that she was being played upon, she decided to have it out with Sarah.

'Why do you not like working in Robinson Cleavers?' she asked plaintively. 'Why, you should be proud to have landed such a good position.'

Sarah just shrugged her shoulders and turned away. Trust her mother to say 'position'. It was just a job, like any other job, and she hated it.

Pulling her round to face her, Maggie cried, 'You're not giving yourself a chance to like it. You made up your mind right from the start that you wouldn't stay there, isn't that right, eh?' Getting no response from an impassive Sarah, Maggie shook her roughly and cried, 'Answer me!'

'All right!' Taking up a stance, hands on hips, and

leaning forward aggressively, Sarah cried defiantly: 'Do you want the truth?' And not waiting for an answer, she continued. 'I'm not like you. I don't speak properly. I'm a Falls Road girl and proud of it! I don't look down my nose at people who work in the mill. They're the salt of the earth an' I want to work with them, so there!' And lips pressed tightly together, she glared at her mother.

Maggie stood speechless, aghast at what she was hearing. 'Sarah! How can you say that? I have never looked down on anyone in my life. Why, Mollie was the most honest, caring person I ever knew, and Kathleen is my best friend.'

Sarah was sorry that her mother was upset, but she was telling the truth as she saw it. All her life her mother had nagged at her to speak properly. Correcting her in public, humiliating her. But it had not worked. No! She had been determined to speak like Alice and all her friends. She did not want people to laugh at her behind her back, saying she spoke as if she had a marble in her mouth, the way they ridiculed her mother. Oh, no! She didn't want that!

In an effort to make amends she said pleadingly, 'Look, if I try, really try, to like Robinson Cleavers, will you agree to let me leave at the end of six months if I still hate it?'

Seeing no other solution to their problem, Maggie quietly agreed, hoping against hope that Sarah would change her mind. After a few weeks, during which Sarah seemed cheerful enough, Maggie dared to hope that she was settling down, but alas it was not to be. At the end of six months she arrived home with two weeks' pay and her insurance cards.

'I'm sorry, Mam. I did try, honestly I did, but it was no good. I just couldn't tell people they suited the kind of clothes they picked, if they didn't. No, Mam, I'm sorry, but I wasn't cut out to be a sales woman.'

'Ah, Sarah, Sarah . . .' Saddened, Maggie turned away. Were all her efforts in vain? Sarah was no better off than she would have been if Maggie had left her with Anne and Bill all those years ago.

Tentatively, Sarah asked, 'Mam, can I start in the

Blackstaff? Alice is asking Bill Cartney if she can teach me to weave.'

Maggie nodded in resignation. Then, remembering her own experiences with Joe Wilson, and afraid that Sarah might be led astray, she haltingly tried to warn her of the fate that might await her.

To her amazement her daughter shrugged it off with a laugh. 'Ah, Mam! I know how to look after meself. I'll soon put a stop to anything like that.'

Maggie gazed at her in wonder. Her little girl was growing up, and she was bemused and uneasy at the idea. Still, she hoped Bill Cartney would not be as lewd as Joe, because surely her daughter could not be all that worldly wise, could she?

Soon Sarah was in charge of three looms and apparently very happy, and the weeks flew past. When her fifteenth birthday drew near, she asked if she could invite Alice and another friend called Annie round to tea. Maggie agreed.

On the day of her birthday, a Friday, Maggie was putting the finishing touches to the table when there was a knock on the door. Surprised, she glanced at the clock and saw that it was half-past five. A frown furrowed her brow. None of her friends would come at this time as they, like herself, would be busy preparing tea. Perhaps someone had run out of something and had come to borrow. Although this would be unusual because she still kept herself to herself. Drying her hands on her apron, she entered the small hall and opened the outer door.

She gazed up at the man who stood outside. He was no taller than Paul had been, but whereas Paul still had the look of a youth about him when he died, this was a man; a broad-shouldered, handsome man. The late evening sun turned his hair to gold, and vivid blue eyes regarded her from under sun-bleached eyebrows. Maggie was aware that the earth couldn't really have moved, that it must be an illusion or her imagination. Realising she was staring rudely at him, she blinked a few times to break the spell he seemed to have cast on her and asked politely, 'Can I help you?'

Barney Grahame's eyes devoured the vision in front of him; she was every bit as beautiful as she had been in his dreams. He smiled, a slow sensuous smile, and Maggie's heart raced.

'You don't remember me?'

Bewildered, her eyes travelled over his face; there was something familiar about him but surely she would know him right away? Had they met before? A man as handsome as he she'd remember, surely? Doubtfully, she shook her head. 'I'm afraid not.'

His brows quirked and he tried to jolt her memory. 'Four years ago?'

Slowly comprehension dawned and a smile appeared. 'The young man who was wounded? The English man? Hah! Mollie said you didn't sound English.'

His grin widened and he nodded. 'I never got a chance to thank you. That's one of the reasons I'm here.'

Standing to one side, Maggie motioned him in. 'Come on in . . . come on.'

'Thank you.'

When she closed the door and followed him into the kitchen, she found him eyeing the table.

He turned a look of awe on her. 'You're psychic, you knew I was coming.'

'I'm afraid not,' she protested laughingly. 'It's my daughter's birthday.'

The way he seemed to fill the small kitchen overwhelmed her and she was surprised at the effect he was having on her. She would never have recognised him. The man whose wounds Mollie had bathed had appeared very young – about eighteen, she had judged him – but this man was about twenty-six, so he would have been twenty-two when wounded.

The disappointment Barney Grahame felt at her words was out of all proportion. This girl's face had haunted his dreams for four years. Why had he never imagined her with a husband? He had just met her – why did it matter to him that she had a husband? His eyelids fell, hiding the dismay he knew he must be showing, and giving his face a shuttered look.

'Please sit down.'

He remained standing. 'I don't want to take up too much of your time. Won't your husband be arriving home?'

'You're welcome to join us for tea. My husband is dead and my daughter and her friends won't mind.'

Her husband was dead! He was dizzy with relief. 'Thank you. I would enjoy that,' he said, and was amazed to find himself breathless. 'Let me introduce myself. I'm Barney Grahame.'

'That's strange . . .'

He watched her brow pucker and interrupted her. 'I know what you're going to say. I just discovered that the other woman who lives here is probably my grannie. I'm dying to see her . . . is she at home?'

For a moment Maggie gaped at him speechlessly. 'Ah, no.'

It was his turn to frown. 'What do you mean?'

'She's dead! Mollie's dead! If only you had known that day. She longed for news of your father. Why did he not write?' Her voice was accusing and he rushed to explain.

'He died young . . . very young.'

'And your mother? Couldn't she have let Mollie know that her son was dead?'

'She was delicate and died shortly after my father. I was reared by my grandparents.'

'And they never told you about Mollie?'

'I'm afraid not.'

The clock chiming made Maggie aware of the time. 'Well . . . look, we can talk later. I'm Maggie Mason and I'm pleased to meet you. Hang your coat at the foot of the stairs and take a seat. The girls will be here soon. I'll put the kettle on to boil.'

Maggie thankfully escaped into the scullery where, hands pressed to burning cheeks, she warned her thumping heart to behave. But it didn't pay any attention to her. She must control herself or this stranger would think her a fool. Stranger? Somehow he didn't seem like a stranger. The feeling she had experienced at the door was one of welcoming someone home, as though she had been biding her time waiting for him.

Oh, don't be silly, girl, she told herself. Of course he's a stranger. If only Mollie had lived to see him. She would have been so proud!

Opening the door, Sarah stopped abruptly when she saw the man sitting at the fireside. This caused Alice to bump into her and she sent up a howl of protest. 'For heaven's sake, Sarah! What are you doin'? What's wrong?'

Alice entered the kitchen rubbing her shin which she had grazed on the heel of Sarah's shoe in the collision. She too stopped dead when she saw the man, her hand covering her mouth in confusion.

Coming from the scullery, Maggie made the introductions. 'Sarah, this is Mollie's grandson. He was one of the young men she assisted during the troubles. Do you remember him?'

Sarah examined his face and slowly shook her head. 'No . . . I don't.'

'Well now, I can't remember you, either.' There was a frown on his brow as he pondered.

Maggie explained. 'Sarah saw you, but she was very young at the time. You didn't see her . . . you were unconscious. These are her best friends, Alice and Annie. The terrible three they're called. Girls . . . this is Barney.'

He had risen to his feet when the girls entered the room. Now he extended his hand to each in turn, saying gallantly, 'I don't know about terrible, but they are all certainly very pretty.'

This brought a smile to their faces, and Alice, who had a riot of bright red curls, big blue eyes, and a button of a nose above a wide sensuous mouth, cried, 'Wait 'til you see us in all our finery. We're a sight for sore eyes!'

This caused Barney to throw back his head and his deep laughter filled the room, making them all smile. Maggie's heart warmed even more towards him. Annie was a complete contrast to Alice: tall, pale-skinned and dark-haired, she was the kind of girl poets write about, but she was also very shy. She just nodded in Barney's direction

205

without looking at him and followed the other two into the scullery to wash her hands.

The tea party went with a swing, Sarah and Alice vying with each other for Barney's attention while Annie shyly looked on, big doe eyes stealing furtive glances at him and going bright red when he caught her eye.

Dishes washed, the girls took it in turns in the scullery, before going upstairs to change into their good clothes, Alice and Annie having called in at lunch time to leave their best in Maggie's house in preparation for their night out. They were going to a gig down Divis Street.

Lying back in the armchair, legs stretched out in front of him, Barney marvelled at how much at home he felt here. His eyes took in the well looked after kitchen, roamed over the antique furniture, and came to rest on Maggie. She sat in the chair facing him, eyes demurely downcast, and he examined her under lowered lids. She really was a beauty. Big, pale, dark-lashed eyes, high cheek bones, full sensual mouth – she was exquisite. His eyes travelled the length of her body. Full bust, slim waist, long legs. He wondered if there was a special man in her life. Surely there must be? If not, the men on the Falls Road needed their eyes examined. But at least she wasn't married. He stood a chance. Uncomfortable under his scrutiny, Maggie moved restlessly.

He said quickly, 'I'm sorry.' His warm admiring glance showed not the least bit of remorse and brought a hot flush to her cheeks. 'Tell me about my grannie.'

'She was a wonderful woman. If only she had asked your name that morning.' She sighed then assured him, 'She liked you. She told me so.'

'I'm sorry to hear she's dead. I liked her too, but I didn't know I had a grannie living in Belfast at that time.'

'But don't you see? If she had asked you your name, all might have been revealed. At least she would have had you questioning your other grandparents.'

'You're right, of course. Tell me about her.'

'What do you want to know?'

'Anything that comes to mind.' A startled expression crossed his face, and he asked quickly, 'Are we related?'

Slowly shaking her head from side to side, Maggie frowned. 'No. What made you ask that?'

'It just suddenly dawned on me that we might be related. You living here and all.' He sighed, and the relief on his voice was apparent.

Her eyes laughed at him. 'No, we're not related. You have two uncles, two aunts, and four cousins.' Her mouth twisted into a wry smile. 'Now, that's a treat in store for you!'

'You make it sound ominous,' he said apprehensively.

'I'm sorry, I shouldn't have said that. They are your relatives and you will probably think they're great.' She grimaced slightly, adding, 'I'm afraid I'm prejudiced.'

With a clatter Sarah descended the stairs and twirled in front of Maggie.

'Mam! Is this dress all right?' she asked anxiously.

She wore the new dress Maggie had bought her for her birthday, styled from many layers of chiffon, draped softly around shoulders and bust and swirling just below her knees. Maggie had been dubious about the new short length but had to admit that it showed Sarah's long slim legs off to advantage. Pale green in colour, the dress enhanced the colour of her eyes and contrasted with the chestnut hair, cut in a shingle and hugging her small head like a silk cap. Maggie had been aghast when she had arrived home one Saturday minus her long locks, but today she had to admit that her daughter's looks suited the new cut. Maggie's breath caught in her throat, Sarah looked so lovely.

'It's just right. You look beautiful,' she whispered huskily.

'You're sure, Mam?' Sarah was smiling openly at the appreciation in Barney's eyes as they examined her legs. She felt quite daring in the new short look.

'I'm sure.' Maggie was bemused; just yesterday Sarah had been all elbows and knees. It seemed that overnight she had turned into a beautiful swan.

All the girls looked lovely, Alice in blue and Annie in pink. They awakened in Maggie memories of when she was fifteen. How lonely her life had been, confined to the house, looking after her young brother. When they had said goodbye and departed, to Maggie's dismay Barney rose to his feet. He stretched, seeming to fill the kitchen. Eyeing his fine physique, she was startled to feel stirrings of long forgotten passion.

'I must be off! I'm meeting Barrie Monaghan to go for a drink. Would you care to join us?' He was annoyed with himself when he made the suggestion. This girl would not be a frequenter of bars.

None of the disappointment Maggie felt showed on her face. It was better that he should go; better for her peace of mind. God knows what Barrie would tell him about her. 'No . . . no thank you. I don't drink.' Going to the bureau, she wrote on a piece of paper and handed it to him.

'Those are the names and addresses of your uncles. I'm sure you'll want to visit them.'

He took his coat from the hook and shrugged into it, surprised at how nervous he felt. He was behaving like a callow youth instead of a man of twenty-seven, a man who had been around the world numerous times, but he was going to ask this woman out and he was afraid she would refuse. Drawing a deep breath, he took the plunge.

'Would you show me around Belfast Castle tomorrow, Maggie? I hear it's worth seeing.' After all, she can only say no, he thought. Nevertheless, he found himself holding his breath while he awaited her reply. He saw her hesitate, but to his relief she was nodding and smiling, and they gazed raptly at each other. At last he forced himself into the hall, out on to the street, before the urge to kiss her became uncontrollable. She might not take kindly to that. He must not take any chances. Somehow this woman was very important to him. Perhaps tomorrow she would seem ordinary, but tonight she was special. He had met plenty of women, all kinds, all races, working on the boats as he did, but never before had he felt so at home with another person. Outside he turned and faced her. Now that he was leaving, the urge to linger held him. 'Do you think Sarah would like to accompany us?'

With a shake of her head Maggie replied, 'I don't think she would be interested.' This was one time she did not want her daughter with her.

'What time shall I pick you up?'

'I stop work at one on a Saturday. Shall we say two?'

'Two it shall be.'

With a smile and a wave of his hand he strode down the street. Maggie would love to have watched him out of sight, but noticed Belle Hanna's net curtains move and knew she was being watched. Regretfully, she closed the door and for a moment leant against it and tried to still her racing heart. Would Barrie put him off? Would it matter all that much if he did? Why, I'm behaving like a teenager on her first date, she thought. Oh, I'll have to stop acting so foolish. He's only being polite. Besides, had she not vowed to have nothing more to do with men?

However, the next day she hurried home from work and dressed with great care for her date with him, watched by an amused Sarah who was glad to see her mother going out.

'He's very handsome, Mam, so he is.'

'Mmm! Yes, I suppose he is.'

'Do you fancy him?'

'Don't be so crude, Sarah. He just wants to find out all about his grannie.'

'Here he is now.' Sarah jumped to her feet. Going to the kitchen door, she swung it open. 'Come on in,' she cried, accompanying the words with a sweep of her hand and a deep bow.

He smiled at her. 'Hello Sarah.' Then his eyes came to rest on Maggie.

At the admiration in them, she felt her cheeks go pink and shyness overcome her. 'Hello.'

'You look lovely.' His voice was low and husky. Nothing had changed: she still looked exquisite. His pulse raced and his heart filled with happiness.

She was wearing a pale grey suit and a white blouse that

was ruffled at the throat. Below the fitted cuff of the jacket more ruffles showed. Her eyes were a clear silvery grey and her translucent skin glowed as if lit from within. This made her hair, under the small grey cloche hat pushed forward around her face, look more coppery still. Barney had never, in all of his travels, seen anyone lovelier.

As they walked down the street he gallantly offered her his arm and self-consciously she took it, aware that all eyes would be on them. They caught the tram at the corner of Clonard Street and travelled to the outskirts of the town where they climbed the path that meandered up the side of the Cave Hill to the Castle. Built in the late-nineteenth century, the castle was a fine example of Gothic architecture, and surrounded by beautiful gardens, a truly magnificent sight. Because of its height, panoramic views of the surrounding country could be seen, one of these being a breathtaking vista of Belfast Lough stretching away to the left.

In complete rapport Maggie and Barney chatted like old friends as they strolled in the castle grounds. The sun shone high in a clear blue sky but a slight breeze kept the heat from becoming too unbearable. When he took her hand in his she did not demur. He smiled, a slow intimate smile that made her legs tremble. Surprised at the turmoil of her emotions, and to gain control of herself, she questioned him.

'Tell me about your parents, Barney. How come you didn't know about your grannie?'

'Well Maggie, as I said before, my father died when I was three years old. It seems a young lad fell in the river and Dad jumped in after him, although he couldn't swim. He was caught in the current and drowned. The irony of it was, the youngster caught hold of a branch and was eventually rescued. After his death my mother returned to live with her parents. I can't remember her very well. She died before I was five.'

Remembering how she had wanted to die when Paul left her, Maggie whispered. 'Perhaps she didn't want to live without your father.'

'Perhaps.' His ears picked up at the sad tone in her voice and he examined her face intently. Was her husband recently dead?

'Poor Barney, how lonely you must have been.'

Throwing back his head he laughed aloud, causing people to turn and smile in their direction. 'Not a bit of it! My grandfather was a wonderful man. He took me fishing and to football matches, hunting and climbing. You name it, I've done it! I missed out on nothing. He taught me everything I needed to know, and I'm grateful to him. My grandmother spoilt me too. In fact, I was a spoilt brat. Got my own way in everything. I even talked them into letting me work on the boats. They had other plans for me, but I wanted to see the world.'

'How come they never told you about your Grannie Grahame?'

'I don't know.' He paused, deep in thought, and Maggie took the opportunity to gaze at him. To admire the strong jaw and straight nose; the bright blond hair, the cleft chin. He was so handsome, all the other men she knew paled in comparison with him. Aware of her scrutiny he slowly turned his head and smiled at her, once more throwing her emotions into turmoil.

'Perhaps they were afraid of losing me,' he said, taking her hand and caressing it between his own. 'You see, Mother was their only child. When Grandfather died last year I wasn't surprised when my grandmother followed him a month later, they were so close. Then I found a package addressed to me. Among other things it contained letters, some to Dad from his mother. It's a shame really. I have been in Belfast so often and could have visited her.'

'She would have been so pleased. She often spoke about your father, wondered why he didn't write.' She tried to remove her hand but he just smiled at her efforts and held on tightly. 'You know something, Barney? She was a wonderful woman. You would have loved her. I could not have survived without her. When my husband died, I wanted to die too, but she cared for me and made me live. I loved her very much.'

Her voice was music to his ears and he encouraged her to keep talking. 'Tell me about yourself, Maggie. How a girl like you comes to be living on the Falls Road.'

She told him about her lonely, sheltered childhood. How she had met and married Paul. How he had died at twenty-five.

'Why didn't you go back to your parents when Paul died?'

'They didn't want Sarah.' Even after all this time the hurt still came through in these words and his heart ached for her, but she smiled and continued. 'Mollie . . . your grannie . . . was my salvation. She was wonderful to me. I couldn't have managed without her. I only wish she had lived to meet you. She would have been so proud.'

'If only I had known about her years ago.' Looking at Maggie's glowing beauty, he thought, If I had, we might have been married by now and had a couple of kids. The thought startled him. He had never before contemplated marriage – but then, he had never felt like this before. 'There must have been other men, Maggie?'

With a quick shake of the head she denied this. She did not want to talk about Sean Hanna. She was too ashamed of how she had treated him. As for Kevin . . . well, that had been all physical and luckily had never amounted to anything. Had Barrie said anything to Barney?

Deciding she was being modest, Barney did not question her further. Instead he changed the subject. 'Come over here, Maggie, and see the lough. With a bit of luck, you might see my ship.'

When they were standing gazing out over the water, she slanted a sideways glance at him. 'I thought this was your first time up at the castle?'

Colour flooded his face and ears, and she was glad it was his turn to be embarrassed. Seeing the teasing look in her eyes, he laughed ruefully. 'I couldn't think of anywhere else on the spur of the moment.'

Her eyes were warm, her smile happy, and she said softly, 'I'm glad.'

Every spare minute of his leave they spent together and

212

the night before he was due to sail, she invited him to tea. Sarah greeted him quietly when he arrived and made no effort at conversation when Maggie was in the scullery making the tea. She resented him. Resented the time he spent with her mother. She had hardly seen Maggie since he arrived and her nose was out of joint. She didn't like it. No! She didn't like it one wee bit.

Eyeing her covertly as she sat pretending to read a book, Barney decided he was going to have to make a friend of her if he wanted to make headway with Maggie. He was aware that she was Maggie's life and knew she would probably always come first, so he set out to charm her. In no time he had her laughing and talking. He had not travelled the world without learning how to charm a woman, and a young girl like Sarah was putty in his hands.

Thus Maggie found them: bright chestnut curls and crisp blond locks, close together, talking earnestly, and her heart sank. She recalled the appreciation in his eyes when he saw Sarah in her green dress. Was it her young daughter he was really interested in? Did he see her as a prospective mother-in-law? He was so much younger than she, eight years at least. Maybe as much as ten. He was closer to Sarah's age. It did not matter how much older a man was than a woman, but when the woman was older than the man ... that caused all kinds of complications. She had been foolish to imagine he was attracted to her.

Barney could not understand the change in Maggie. She was polite and friendly, but something was missing. Had he offended her in some way? Surely not? He had been so careful. He had already decided to make her his wife, if possible, and was treating her with the respect she deserved.

When the time came to say goodbye, Maggie envied Sarah the way she could throw her arms around his neck and kiss him. If only she could do that. She formally offered him her hand. 'It's been a pleasure meeting you.'

She tried to remove her hand from his clasp, but holding it firmly, he held her gaze and asked, 'Will you answer my letters if I write to you?'

Relaxing a little, she smiled and answered, 'Of course I will, and please feel free to call any time you're in Belfast.'

'Thank you, I will.' And, leaning forward, he kissed her on the cheek.

This time, Sarah by her side, Maggie watched until he reached the corner and turned down the Falls Road. From the corner he waved and they waved back, before returning to the kitchen.

'He's nice, Mam.' Sarah had decided that he was too young for her mother and that her fears were groundless.

'Yes.' Maggie's reply was non-committal, and a great ache filled her breast. She was dismayed at her reaction to him and Sarah laughing together. What if he fancied Sarah but thought her too young and was was waiting to show his interest when she was older? Dear God, she could not bear to have him for a son-in-law. Oh no, no! It was unthinkable!

Would he come back? Was it Sarah he had his sights set on? Because she was so enthralled with him, Maggie couldn't think straight. But one thing she was sure of – she didn't want him for a son-in-law. Ah, no! That she could not bear.

That night she fell asleep, her hand cupping the cheek he had kissed, recalling the feel of his lips. She found herself praying – not that she believed in God, but just in case there was one – 'Dear God, please don't let him want Sarah.'

CHAPTER EIGHT

Setting the iron down on the hearth, Maggie leaned on the card table on which she was ironing and gaped at Sarah. Pale and wretched-looking, she stood just inside the doorway. She had just dropped a bombshell, as far as Maggie was concerned. Surely she had heard her wrong?

'What did you say?' she queried, anxiety already puckering her face, making her voice shrill.

'I said I wanted to get married to Mick Ross as soon as possible.'

'Ah, don't be silly, Sarah. Good heavens, you're only seventeen! Don't tie yourself down. Enjoy yourself first. I wish I'd had the chance to enjoy myself when I was seventeen. You don't know you're alive. The world's your oyster.'

Sarah's lips tightened and her face became mutinous as she listened to her mother. Then: 'Ah, Mam! Stop treating me like a child,' she whined. 'Why, I've been working three years. I'm grown up, so I am.'

'That doesn't mean you're ready for marriage,' Maggie argued reasonably. Then, deciding to meet her halfway, added, 'Look, get engaged by all means, but wait for a couple of years. Get to know each other better. Why, you've only been going out with Mick about four months. Save up! Try to have the deposit to put down on a house. Surely you don't want to start married life in rooms?'

Sarah heard her out in silence but instead of answering

215

her question, she cried, 'Mam! Stop it! I have to get married. Do you understand? I *have* to get married!'

Feeling the blood leave her face, Maggie groped for a chair and sat down. 'Ah, no, Sarah! Ah, no. Not you! Surely not you?'

Shame made Sarah's voice strident when she answered. 'Yes, me!' Then seeing Maggie's face crumble in disbelief, she wailed, 'Ah, Mam, don't look like that. I'm not the first and I won't be the last.'

Anger brought Maggie to her feet and there was a resounding smack when she slapped Sarah's face. Emotions high, she actually hissed, 'You slut! You dirty little slut!' causing Sarah to cover her face and cringe in dismay. Then, seizing her coat, Maggie stormed from the house as if the devil was on her back. Her fury propelled her down Malcomson Street and up the Springfield Road. Passing the Blackstaff factory, she cast a resentful glance over its bland facade and fumed, 'I should never have let her work there. I should have made her stay in Robinson Cleavers. Why, she hardly knows Mick Ross. Just a few short months . . . a few months. How could she? Oh the shame!' The awful shame of it. Filling the neighbour's mouths, no doubt. Maggie knew only too well how glad they would be to see her brought low. She could imagine the talk, the sly nudges, the sniggers.

'All those walks down Dan O'Neil's Loney, that's how it happened! I should have put my foot down. Forbidden her to go there. But I trusted her.'

Becoming aware that she was muttering aloud, Maggie shook her head in despair and tried to get a grip of her emotions. After all, you did not get pregnant just walking in the Loney, and all who walked there were not carrying on. It was a beautiful place, especially in summer when the trees were laden with hawthorn and the scent of fresh cut grass permeated the air. She had walked there herself many an afternoon, but never in the twilight. No, Sean Hanna had never brought her there in the twilight, but she could imagine how romantic it would be to stroll in the Loney at dusk. And just what had she against Mick Ross?

Eh? Nothing! He was a good lad. Better than Spud Murray. She had been glad to see the back of him. He knocked about with the wrong people. It was all right being patriotic, but it didn't make for happy marriages and she had been glad when Sarah had finished with him. Since the withdrawal of the Black and Tans from the Falls Road, there had been peace; uneasy, but peace nevertheless, and everybody should be trying to keep it that way. Not standing on the corners talking about a united Ireland. There had been enough deaths; enough pain. So she should be glad that it was Mick Ross that Sarah wanted to marry. Wanted to marry? *Had* to marry! There. That was what she had against Mick Ross. He brought Sarah down! her mind shouted. Brought her low! But wait. Wait now. Hold on a second, girl. It takes two to tango. Be fair. It's not right to put all the blame on Mick. Nevertheless, she did. He was twenty-three, six years older than Sarah. He should have known better.

In her mad dash she had turned down Oranmore Street and when she reached the corner where it joined Clonard Street she saw the monastery looming in front of her. When the Redemptorist Fathers chose to build their monastery on the site where the old tin church once stood, the people of the Falls Road were jubilant. Both Brendan and Mollie had tried to persuade her to go and see the monastery when it opened, but she was not interested in the Catholic religion. What good had all her praying done when Paul died? So she had stubbornly refused to accompany them. Now she hesitated. She needed to think; somewhere quiet. Aware that the doors of the church stayed open until eleven every night, she decided to go inside. She had half an hour before it closed; it was just half-past ten. The doors were heavy and it took all her strength to push them open. It was dark in the porch and she paused for a few seconds to get her bearings, then entered more doors into the church itself, to stand in awe, gaping about her.

'Why, it's beautiful!' she whispered aloud in surprise.

Well, hadn't Mollie told her it was beautiful? Hadn't

Brendan told her she would love the peace and quiet of it? Except for one man kneeling in front of the high altar, the church was empty. Down the right-hand side she could see the shrine to the Immaculate Conception glowing in the candle light. Mollie had described this shrine to her but it was more beautiful than she had imagined it. They came from near and far to pray in front of this shrine. Oh, yes, she knew all about it. Mollie had been forever singing its praises. As if drawn by an invisible hand, she made her way down the side aisle, her heels sounding loud in the hush and stillness, in spite of her efforts to tip-toe. Once in front of the altar she stood and gazed up at a statue of a young girl dressed in blue and white, her foot on a serpent's head.

Just a statue. She sighed, turning away, disappointed. Only a statue. How can people get all het up about a piece of plaster? It must be indoctrinated into them, she decided.

Wearily, she sat down in the first pew and closed her eyes. She found herself thinking about the young girl portrayed in the statue. Had she not been in the same position as Sarah all those years ago? Had her mother ranted and raved at her? Had she slapped her face and called her a slut?

God forgive me, Maggie lamented. What right have I, to sit in judgement? Her eyes went back to the statue and she found herself arguing. But it was different for her. She was carrying the Infant Jesus. Ah! But did her mother believe her?

She was Sarah's mother, not her judge. God would not turn His back on her so what right had Maggie to condemn her? Why was she suddenly so sure that there was a God? She had managed without one all these years, so why now did one figure in her thoughts? She found herself praying for guidance and was surprised to find a hand shaking her gently by the arm, bringing her back to reality.

'I'm sorry, my child, but I must lock up the church. It's a quarter past eleven.'

How the time had flown! Once more her eyes sought the statue. Just plaster . . . but she had felt a presence such as

218

she had never known before. She could not deny it; did not want to; she had felt a presence and she had been comforted.

Following the priest down the now empty church, she paused at the door and surprised herself again by saying tentatively, 'Father, I would like to learn more about the Catholic Faith.'

He showed no surprise. Did they not come from all denominations to find sanctuary here? Smiling kindly at her, he said, 'Come and see me any afternoon and we shall talk. My name is O'Conner.'

Thanking him, she left the church and hurried home, smiling ruefully to herself as she thought, This will be something else for the neighbours to talk about. They'll be having a field day.

When the door closed on her mother, Sarah stood gazing at it, stricken with shame, tears flowing freely. Why had she played up to Mick? Because he was much sought after and she had wanted to make sure of him, that's why! And it had been only the once and not very nice at that. It had certainly put her off, but she had learnt her lesson too late. Now she was pregnant and afraid. Afraid to think she was carrying a baby, and that in spite of his offer of marriage, Mick would never respect her. If only she had waited. How she regretted her actions. She was lucky that Mick still wanted her, and to give him credit he hadn't hesitated. When she admitted her predicament to him, he hadn't paused to reflect. Right away he had said, 'Let's get married.'

Entering the scullery, she washed her face at the sink. As she patted it dry she saw reflected in the mirror the red mark on her cheek, and once more tears started to fall. To think that her mother had hit her! Never before had she lifted her hand to her daughter, and Sarah was the first to admit that at times she must have been sorely tried. It was the neighbours that her mother worried about. She was so proud, held her head so high, and now the neighbours would have something to gossip about. And it was all her fault.

Maggie found Sarah curled up on the settee asleep when she arrived home. Seeing her tear-stained cheeks she was contrite and shook her gently by the shoulder to awaken her. Immediately the big green eyes filled with tears.

'I'm sorry, Mam. I know I've been stupid, but Mick loves me, he'll stand by me, so he will,' she wailed, tears flowing anew.

'It's all right, love. You just took me unawares, knocked the wind out of me as it were. Now . . . are you sure you want to marry him?'

Sarah rubbed her eyes with her knuckles and nodded. Maggie thought how childlike she was, she who thought herself a woman of the world. Poor Sarah, she was in for a rude awakening.

'I love him, Mam. Can you forgive for me lettin' ye down?'

Pulling her close, Maggie stroked the damp hair back from her brow. 'It's all right. We'll manage. We'll have to see the priest and make all the arrangements. I'll write to Brendan. Perhaps he'll be allowed to perform the ceremony. Wouldn't that be nice?' she asked, trying to make amends. For the first time, Barney entered her mind. How would this affect him? Would he be disappointed? Would his visits cease? Was she about to lose his friendship?

She wrote to both men and in due course received answers to her letters. Brendan had received permission to say Nuptial Mass and Barney wrote to say he would do all in his power to be at Sarah's wedding. Had he been waiting for her to grow up? Was he angry that he had not acted sooner? Questions, questions. And she had no answers. She had no idea how Barney felt. In the two years she had known him, he had not committed himself in any way. He was courteous and kind, and generous to a fault, but she still did not know where his interest really lay. He treated them both with kindness and affection, but the odd kiss he gave her was friendly, no more. In fact, he seemed content to keep her at arm's length and his warmth and care embraced them both. They were friends. Did he just want to learn all about his grannie, the woman he regretted not knowing? He was forever talking about Mollie. Forever lamenting how fate had kept them apart.

But she, God help her, was besotted by him, although she did all in her power to hide the fact. She had learnt her lesson where Kevin was concerned. Barney never mentioned a wife, or girl friends for that matter, and she was afraid to ask. Could a handsome man like him be free? In the two years since they had met, he had been in Belfast a total of just five weeks, but she was not getting any younger and she loved him so much, so very much. Should she show her feelings?

The sun shone for Sarah on her wedding day; it was Easter Saturday and she made a beautiful bride. She looked radiant in the cream voile dress. Maggie had spent long hours hand-sewing the dress but it had been worth the effort. It had saved a lot of money and she was pleased with the results. The neck was modestly high and the sleeves came to a point on the back of the hand while a satin sash spanned the waist and flowed behind Sarah when she walked. The skirt was full and covered a taffeta underskirt, swirling around her slim ankles above the latest high-heeled court shoe, which Jim Rafferty had dyed the same cream shade as the dress. On her head she wore a wide-brimmed picture hat and carried a spray of yellow roses. Alice and Annie were her bridesmaids and were dressed in identical pink dresses and carried small posies.

As she ran her eyes critically over her daughter's slim figure, Maggie was relieved that her pregnancy did not show. No sign of a bump at all, she was relieved to note. Time enough later for the sniggers and the tongue wagging. That Sarah would be watched and the months counted, Maggie did not for one minute doubt. The

221

neighbours would be saying, 'Why else the haste?' and in her heart she did not blame them.

Mick was handsome in a pale grey suit, and a workmate dressed in a dark suit was best man. In spite of herself Maggie wept as she knelt in the front pew beside Anne and Bill. She wept for all the hopes and dreams that would never be fulfilled. Now she realised how disappointed her own parents must have been when she had arrived home and said she was married. Especially to a Catholic! She had thought them hard and unfeeling, thought they did not understand. They had understood only too well. But her short time with Paul had been worth the hardships, and she would help Sarah all she could. She would not forsake her, as she had been forsaken.

'Are you all right, Maggie?' Anne gave her a sharp dig in the ribs with her elbow.

'Yes! Yes, I'm all right.' Maggie wiped her eyes surreptitiously.

'Ah, don't cry, Maggie.' Anne whispered 'Sure you're not losin' a daughter, you're gainin' a son. An' a fine one at that.'

Gritting her teeth, Maggie thought, If anyone else says that to me, I'll scream.

She looked towards the altar, meeting Brendan's worried eyes, smiled reassuringly at him. She was glad he had been able to say the Nuptial Mass, glad of his comforting presence. When the bride and groom returned from signing the register, she went forward to meet them.

Hugging her close, Sarah whispered, 'Ah, Mam, don't look like that. Be happy for me.'

Maggie was dismayed. She had not meant to be a wet blanket. Now she exclaimed, 'I am love, I am. Just give me time.'

Mick enveloped her in a bear hug. He was ashamed, knowing he had hurt her, bringing her daughter down. But it takes two! He had not forced Sarah. Ah, no, he had not forced her.

'I promise I'll do all in me power to make her happy, Maggie,' he whispered in her ear.

'I know you will, son,' she replied, but sadly she doubted it he could.

William was taking the wedding photographs. He had arrived the night before with his wife and child. Dressed in a smart suit and weighed down with cameras, he looked the part. As he made everybody pose this way, and that, Maggie thought how beautiful Sarah looked, her face framed by the picture hat, eyes glittering like emeralds.

All the Masons had turned out for the wedding, the first time they had been together in a long while. Now that they were all married, they were spread all over Northern Ireland and today was a big occasion for them; an excuse to get together. Dressed in their finest clothes, their hats were a riot of colour, nearly every colour of the rainbow being portrayed and shining in the bright sunlight. As they exclaimed over each other's offspring, Maggie noticed Emma, who alone was unwed, standing back from the crowd gazing in bewilderment at William's wife. Maggie herself had been surprised at her brother's choice of a wife, knowing his liking for glamour girls. Perhaps he got enough glamour from his job because Elsie was homely – that was the nicest compliment anyone could pay her. She had a warm, friendly personality and plenty of self-assurance, but good looks she had not. In her arms she clutched a squirming, chuckling baby boy, and Maggie saw the longing in Emma's eyes as she examined the child.

In contrast to Elsie, Emma was striking. Tall, slim and pretty, she wore her clothes with the air of a mannequin. Her suit was a deep emerald green and her hat and accessories were black, the hat relieved with an emerald feather. They were the latest fashion from Paris, acquired on one of her many journeys abroad for the firm she did business for. Over the years she had achieved a veneer of confidence on her travels abroad, but Maggie knew her old shyness still plagued her. Her father had been heard to remark that Emma was born an old maid, her lack of interest in men being very apparent. However, Maggie guessed she had given her heart to William a long time ago and had yet to recover. In her early-thirties, she was a great businesswoman, but every year found her more withdrawn, more cynical. As she watched, Maggie saw William meet Emma's gaze, saw the renewed interest brighten the green of his eyes as they swept over her sister-in-law's figure, noted the slow intimate smile he bestowed on her, and her heart sank. She was surprised to hear Brendan speak.

By her side, he eyed her anxiously. 'Sarah's looking lovely, Maggie, but what about you? Are you all right?'

She nodded reassuringly, and smiled. 'I'm fine. Yes, she is lovely,' she agreed with him. 'But so young. So very young.'

'Don't worry about her, Maggie. Mick's a good lad.'

'I know.' she was silent for a moment then admitted wryly, 'It's only now I realise what a shock my parents must have received when I landed home and said I was married. Especially to a Catholic. No wonder my father struck me.'

'Do you regret marrying Paul?'

His look was understanding and she admitted, 'Sometimes.' She looked shame-faced, felt like a traitor, but he just nodded and gave her arm a comforting pat. Then William came and bore them away to be photographed with the bride. Once her brother was finished with them, Maggie took Emma by the arm and drew her away from the crowd.

'Will you come with me, Emma? I want to make sure everything is ready for the reception.'

They walked in silence along Cavendish Street towards Hawthorn Street where the parish hall was situated. Then, with a sidelong look at Maggie, Emma blurted out, 'She's so plain! I pictured her often, you know.' She grimaced 'I pictured her beautiful and glamorous.' She paused then wailed, 'Why, Maggie? Why did he choose her?' She swallowed deeply and her expression was appealing. 'I know he loved me.' A finger prodded her chest to emphasise her point. 'I just know he did. But he married her! Why didn't he marry me?'

Her bewilderment was so acute, Maggie hastened to assure her. 'I think he would have married you if you had not been a Catholic, but my parents were still recovering from the shock of my marrying a Catholic. William was afraid Father would have a heart attack,' she explained, deeply sorry for Emma's obvious pain.

'Hah! If he had only known! He'd just to ask. Do you know something, Maggie? All those years ago I was willin' to give up my religion for him. God forgive me, but I was. Imagine! All he had to do was ask and I'd have run away with him. Married him in the Register Office. I loved him so much . . . so much. When your father died, I was sure he would come for me, so I waited and waited.' She fell silent a moment then continued, 'When I heard he was married . . .' Her eyes were wild at the memory. 'I nearly went out of my mind. Ah, Maggie, it was awful! Awful . . .' Her voice broke as memories plagued her.

At a loss as to how to console her, Maggie remained quiet and they walked in silence for some minutes. Then, as if to torture herself further, Emma continued, 'When I saw her today, I couldn't believe it. She's so plain. I feel cheated, so I do. That child she has should be mine. He should be my son.' Then her face cleared and she turned to Maggie and cried in triumph, 'An' I'll tell you something else, Maggie. He still likes me. I can feel it. I know he does!'

As she listened to her, Maggie became more and more worried. Why, she was obsessed. What would become of her? 'Emma, don't do anything foolish,' she begged. 'He can only bring you unhappiness.'

Looking her straight in the eye, Emma cried triumphantly, 'You saw it too! You know he's still attracted to me.'

'Any man would be attracted to you, Emma. You're a lovely girl, but he's married. Forget him! Don't let him hurt you again.'

Arriving at the door of the hall, Emma gripped Maggie's arm and squeezed it. 'Don't look so worried. I feel much better for gettin' it off me chest. Thanks for listenin' to me. An' ... I'm unlikely to get the chance to do anything foolish. He's only here for the week-end, and chance would be a fine thing.'

Maggie was relieved and said earnestly, 'Any time ... any time at all you need company, or any kind of help, remember I'm here and I'm very fond of you.'

Inside the hall, she was glad to note that each long narrow window had a vase of flowers on its sill and the tables, pushed together along one wall, were covered with snow white cloths and decorated with candles and flowers. Walking the length of them, Maggie inspected them critically. She was pleased with what she saw. Legs of chicken, roast pork, boiled ham and savoury pies were all laid out amidst dishes of tomatoes, eggs, beetroot and everything needed to complement the meats. A feast fit for a king. A woman waited at the bottom of the hall and Maggie walked slowly towards her. Seeing her smile, the woman visibly relaxed.

'Thank you, Mrs Divine, everything is lovely.'

Maggie handed over an envelope containing most of her life's savings. Thanking her, Mrs Divine put it in her pocket and shrugged on her coat, preparing to leave. 'Remember, Mrs Mason, just stack all the dirty dishes in yon room.' She nodded towards a door at the side of the stage. 'Me an' my clan'll come back t'night an' wash them an' take them away.'

'Thank goodness for that,' Maggie answered with a mock shudder. 'I don't envy you your task.'

'All in a day's work. We're grateful for your custom, so we are.'

'I will recommend you any time,' Maggie said, and meant it.

When this woman approached her and offered to do a buffet lunch for Sarah's wedding reception, Maggie had been dubious. The price was reasonable, but what if the spread was awful? It would be too late to do anything about it. Mrs Divine and two other women, all widows of men killed on the Somme, had grown tired of slaving in the mills, earning barely enough money to raise their children. A year earlier they had united and now ran quite a profitable catering business. It was Father Magee who had assured Maggie that she could leave everything in their capable hands and she was glad now that she had done so.

Emma had disappeared into the cloakroom, and knowing she needed time to compose herself, Maggie refrained from joining her. Satisfied that everything was ready, she stood by the door to await the arrival of Sarah, Mick and the guests. When they at last arrived, the 'Ohs!' and 'Ahs!' were music to her ears as they eyed the tables, and she was contented. Kathleen and Jim were the last to arrive. One of their daughters had been flower girl and they had brought the rest of their children to the church to see their sister in her lovely long dress. Then after the Mass they had taken them to Kathleen's mother, down in Leeson Street, who was having them for the day.

Eyeing the tables, Jim said to Kathleen, 'You may forget your diet for the day, love.' And Kathleen, about fourteen stone in weight, solemnly agreed with him, much to Maggie's amusement.

Looking around the crowded hall, her friend exclaimed, 'Heavens, Maggie, you'd think half the Blackstaff was here.'

'Half the Blackstaff *is* here, Kathleen,' she replied dryly.

The buffet was a high success, to judge from how little remained when everybody had eaten their fill, and when William had taken photographs from every angle imaginable, the floor was cleared for dancing and Bill and his friend got out their fiddles.

When Maggie saw them take up position in a corner, she hurried to them. 'Go up on the stage, Bill, you'll have more room up there.'

His jaw dropped in surprise and he laughed nervously. 'Us up on the stage?' he gasped. 'Ah, Lord no, Maggie. We'll be all right here. Just so long as they can hear us, that's all that matters.' And he chuckled at the idea of him up on stage. So Maggie left them to it and soon music filled the air.

Sarah and Mick leading off to the strains of a waltz, were soon joined by all the young guests and the dance was under way. Sitting at a table with Brendan and Anne, Maggie was restless. Barney had failed to put in an appearance and she was disappointed. Watching her from beneath lowered lids, Brendan wondered what was wrong. Why, she's like a cat on hot bricks, he thought.

Suddenly Maggie's brow was smooth again and her face lit with joy. Following the direction of her gaze to see what had wrought such a change in her, Brendan saw a tall, fair-haired man at the door. He gazed about him until he caught Maggie's gaze; their eyes remained locked as he made his way through the dancers until at last he stood at their table.

From the expression on his mother's face, Brendan guessed that she was as much in the dark as he was and waited patiently to be introduced. Face ablaze with hot colour, Maggie dragged her eyes off the man and sheepishly turned to them. 'Brendan ... Anne, this is Barney Grahame ... Mollie's grandson. Barney, this is my mother-in-law Anne, and brother-in-law Brendan.'

Shaking hands first with Anne, Barney then greeted Brendan saying, 'I'm pleased to meet you at last, I've heard so much about you.'

'You're one up on me then. I've never heard tell of you,' he said dryly, and lifted an inquiring eyebrow at Maggie.

Looking at Maggie in surprise, Barney saw her go redder still. She was dismayed; she had never mentioned him in her letters to Brendan because right from the start he had been very dear to her and she had felt that nothing could come of it. He was so much younger than she ... ten whole years. Even younger than she had at first thought! It seemed a lifetime and yet she had dared to hope. Probably in vain. Why would a handsome young man like Barney be interested in a woman ten years his senior? Her distress was evident to Barney who came to her rescue. Placing the box he carried on the table with a 'That's for Sarah,' to no one in particular, he bowed courteously to Maggie.

'Would the mother of the bride be so kind as to dance with me?'

Silently she entered his arms and they danced off, watched by a bemused Brendan who turned to his mother, 'Have you ever heard of Barney?'

Anne looked perplexed. 'I remember Maggie mentionin' him one time. Seems he was caught up in the troubles . . . oh, years ago. The time the Catholics were put out of the shipyard. Young Danny Monaghan brought him to Mollie's to get a wound attended to. Then a couple of years ago when he was in Belfast he called to thank them. Mollie was dead, of course . . . an' if I remember rightly, it was just by chance he discovered he was related to her.'

'Mmmm.' Brendan watched them as they danced across the floor and thought what a handsome couple they made. He so tall and fair, she reaching just to his chin. She had removed her hat and her burnished copper hair gleamed, while her creamy skin was shown off to perfection by the peach-coloured dress she wore. Brendan thought she had never looked lovelier.

Unknown to him, Barney was agreeing with him. 'You look lovely,' he was whispering in her ear.

'Thank you.'

Drawing her closer, he bent his head so that his cheek rested on her hair. 'Maggie, you know I love you. Will you marry me?'

Silence. He drew back and looked down askance. To his dismay great tears were slowly running down her cheeks. Embarrassed, he hastily guided her to a corner and sat her down on a chair, shielding her from view. Immediately, Sarah was at her mother's side, a protective arm around her shoulders.

Green eyes flashing, she glared at Barney. 'What's wrong? What have you done to her?'

'I only asked her to marry me,' he answered defensively.

Slowly, Sarah straightened up, the colour draining from

her face. 'Marry you? Don't be daft! She's too old for you.'

Keeping her head lowered, Maggie silently agreed with her. She was too old. 'I haven't said I will,' she muttered.

Winded, Barney dropped like a brick on to the chair by her side and stared down blindly at his shoes. He was stunned! She did not care. He had been so sure that she did. He had been patient, never giving in to his longing to seduce her. And in her lonely frustrated state, he was aware that it would have been easy. But he had refrained, giving her the respect she deserved as his future wife. Not wanting to rush her. Nevertheless, he had been so sure she felt the same as he did.

Giving Sarah a none too gentle push, Maggie cried, 'People are staring, go back to your guests.' And when she hesitated, 'Go on. I'm all right, I tell you.'

At a loss, Barney sat silent. He had spoilt everything. Although they had met over two years ago, they had spent so little time together. He should have known Maggie was only taking pity on him because his gran had been her best friend. Now she might tell him not to come back. If only he could take back his words, go on as they were before!

Maggie's hand on his arm brought him back to reality. 'Come back to me, Barney, you're far away,' she beseeched softly. Once she had his attention, she added, 'Sarah is right, you know. I am too old for you.'

She was letting him down lightly. She felt sorry for him. Keeping his head averted so that he would not see the pity in her eyes, he apologised. 'I'm sorry, Maggie, I seem to have spoken out of turn. I thought you felt the same way as me.'

'I do.'

It took a few seconds for her words to penetrate his misery. Then his head jerked up as he dared to hope. 'Then why did you cry?' he asked huskily.

'Sheer relief. I thought you looked on me as a friend. Just someone to visit when you were in Belfast. You never said anything to make me think otherwise.' Her hand rested on his arm and her eyes reproached him. 'Why, for all I know you could have a girl in every port.'

He rose swiftly to his feet and, taking her hands in his, pulled her up into his arms. 'Let's dance. I need to hold you.' And they danced across the floor, bodies entwined, unaware that they were the focus of many eyes.

As they passed Sarah and Mick on the floor, she snorted, 'Look at them! Acting like a couple of kids. It's disgustin', so it is!'

Following the direction of her gaze, Mick smiled, 'They're in love.'

'Humph! She's almost forty! Too old to be carryin' on like that.'

'Sarah!' Mick's voice held a reprimand. 'Love has no age barrier. I for one, wish them well.'

'Do ye know something, Mick Ross? You sicken me, so ye do. What'll happen to us if they get married? Eh? Where'll we live? Tell me that!'

Mick looked nonplussed, then shrugged. 'We'll find a couple of rooms, like most young ones do,' he said, drawing her closer. 'I don't care where we live as long as I'm with you.'

She was saved from answering him by the music coming to an end and they made their way over to Brendan's table.

'That's your present, Sarah.' Barney nodded towards the box on the table. 'I hope you like it.'

When Sarah opened the box and disclosed a radio, her thanks were sincere. 'It's what I've been longin' for, Barney. Thank you.'

Lifting the box and the radio, Mick said, 'Thanks, Barney. It's decent of you. Let's put it with the rest of the presents, Sarah.'

He was glad he had made this suggestion because as they moved away, they heard Barney say, 'Anne, Brendan, I want you to know, Maggie has agreed to marry me.'

When Mick glanced at Sarah to see her reaction, he was disconcerted to see tears pouring down her face.

231

Glad they were alone, he said, 'Ah, love, don't take it so badly.'

'This is my big day and she's spoilin' it,' Sarah wailed.

'Now, Sarah! Nothin' can spoil it. Come on now, love, pull yourself together. We must congratulate them.'

He shielded her from view while she wiped her eyes and when they congratulated the happy couple, if the smile on Sarah's lips did not reach her eyes, it was apparent only to Maggie and Mick.

Maggie's happiness was dimmed, but before going off on her honeymoon, three days in Dublin at Maggie's expense, Sarah hugged her close.

'Mam, everything was lovely. It must have cost you a bomb. Thanks, love. And about Barney . . . well, it's your turn to give me a little time to get used to the idea.' She looked at Maggie, head tilted to one side, eyebrows raised appealingly.

Relieved, Maggie nodded and smiled. 'It must have come as a shock to you. Don't worry about anything, love. It will all pan out, as Mollie would have said!'

Next day, Easter Sunday, was another glorious day. The sun shining high in a bright blue sky lightened the heart and lent a festive air to the dull dingy streets. Barney arrived early from the Stella Maris hostel where he was staying and Maggie suggested that they go up to the Falls Park. When he agreed, she packed a picnic lunch and they set off. They took the tram to the depot and entered the park at the top gate. This was Maggie's favourite spot. To their left lush green grassy banks dotted with bluebells and daisies rose steeply to meet gnarled old oak trees and high hedges, and to their right the river babbled and gurgled along over age-worn stones. As they strolled along the river bank, arms entwined, Maggie was contented. Here she had often walked with Paul. She felt that now she was introducing Barney to him, and was sure that he approved.

'Have you told Sarah we're getting married on my next leave, Maggie?'

Grimacing, she shook her head. 'I decided to let her

enjoy her honeymoon first.'

He was dismayed. 'I thought she liked me? You think she won't approve?'

'I know she won't.' She giggled lightly. 'Mind you, I can see her point of view. They will be living with me, and when we get married they'll have to find rooms elsewhere.' Suddenly she stopped, a finger to her lips, hand raised commandingly in the air when he would have spoken. She tilted her head. 'Listen! It's the band. Can you hear it?'

He nodded, smiling at her excitement; admiring the smooth pallor of her throat, the bright light of the sun reflected from her hair. Tugging at his arm, she pulled him along.

'Come on, let's go to the bandstand.'

Crossing the small wooden bridge that spanned the river, they headed for the centre of the park where members of the orchestra could be heard tuning their instruments. They cut dashing figures in their bright red, brass-buttoned coats and black trousers with the wide satin stripe down the leg. Soon they were ready to play and the strains of 'Easter Bonnet' filled the air.

'How handsome they look,' Maggie cried, and would have sat on one of the chairs that surrounded the bandstand. However, Barney had other ideas. Taking her by the arm, he guided her further up the park to a spot under the trees, a place dappled in sunshine.

'Let's sit here,' he argued. 'We can still hear the band, but more important still, woman, we can eat. I'm starving!'

He dropped the haversack he carried over his shoulder and threw himself down on the grass beside it. With a deep chuckle, Maggie dropped to her knees. Opening the haversack, she spread a cloth on the ground and unpacked the food. It was the remains of the wedding buffet. Barney nodded his approval as his eye noted the chicken and ham and crusty bread. He set to with gusto and Maggie watched him, her heart overflowing with happiness. She thought him the handsomest man she had ever seen and smiled every time his eyes met hers.

'You're not eating, Maggie,' he chided.

'You're eating enough for both of us!'

Suddenly serious, he held her gaze. 'Maggie, I can't believe someone like you can love me. You must have had so many chances to marry?'

There was a question in the words and Maggie shook her head in denial. 'That's exactly how I feel. That I don't deserve your love.' She neatly turned the conversation, not wanting to discuss her past.

Contented, he returned to the food and Maggie lay back on the grass and gazed up at the heavens. She watched fluffy white clouds chase each other against the deep blue curtain of the sky. Just like lambs gambolling, she thought. Then laughed inwardly at herself. It must be love that was making her so poetic, so aware of the beauty around her. Never before had the trees looked so stately, the grass so lush and green.

'How lucky we are to get such good weather,' she said. 'Why, last Easter the weather was foul.' Her fingers plucked at the grass. Not wanting to whine she added wistfully, 'If only you could stay another day, we could go to the Cave Hill and watch the children trundle their Easter eggs.'

Washing the food down with a drink of lemonade, Barry wiped his mouth and held out his hand to her. 'Come here, Maggie. We must talk.'

She moved over beside him, snuggling close when he put his arm around her, breathing in the wonderful masculine smell of him.

'Maggie, I know you have made a lovely, comfortable home for yourself and Sarah, but tell me, would you mind leaving it?'

Puzzled, she shook her head, then as a thought struck her, cried in dismay, 'I could never live in England, Barney. I'm too old . . . and you would be at sea. I'd be alone.'

He hastened to reassure her. 'No, love, no. I would

never ask you to leave Ireland. Let me explain. I've always been a careful chap and have quite a tidy sum saved. I also have the terraced house my grandparents left me and that will fetch a few hundred. Now here's what I suggest. You buy us a house. I'll let you know how high I can afford to go and make arrangements for you to have access to my money. What do you think?'

'It sounds wonderful,' she replied. Then in a dubious tone, 'But what if you don't like the house I choose?'

He lifted her hand and kissed the palm of it, sending tremors racing through her and bringing rosy colour to her cheeks.

He smiled at her blushes. 'As long as you're my wife, I don't care where we live. But this way, Sarah won't need to look for rooms.'

His hands gently caressed her shoulders and once more she whispered, 'I wish you could stay longer.'

'So do I, but if I don't leave tonight, I won't get back to my ship on time. I was lucky we were docked in Scotland and I was able to get over for a couple of days.'

'I know.' She sighed deeply. 'I'm being greedy.'

They sat listening to the music and making plans until the band packed up and left and people started drifting home. Watching young couples with children pass by, Maggie turned a worried face to him.

'You realise, don't you, that I may not be able to have children? I'm thirty-nine, so much older than you.'

He cupped her face with his hands and looked earnestly into her eyes. 'It doesn't matter. All I need is you. If we have a child it will be a bonus.' His voice was earnest as he stressed, 'Believe me, Maggie, it really doesn't matter. All I need is you.'

Then he was kissing her, soft tender kisses at first, becoming passionate and soul-searing force. He was full of the months of frustration and restraint, touching an echoing response in Maggie that filled him with joy. She pressed closer still, eager, submissive, and was affronted when he put her firmly from him and pulled her to her feet.

'Come on, it's time we were going home,' he said and

started to pack the haversack. Peeved, she assisted him in silence.

Becoming aware of it, he asked anxiously, 'Is something wrong, love?'

He sounded so worried, her bad humour left her. Laughing, she replied, 'I'm wondering what to give you for your tea.'

Arm in arm they made their way down the park to the depot and caught the tram home, sitting close, feeling as one, contented and happy. The evening air was chilly and when they arrived home Barney lit the fire, while Maggie made supper. They ate bacon, eggs and soda farls (Barney's favourite Irish meal) from a table placed in front of the fire, and afterwards sat wrapped in each other's arms, making plans for their wedding.

'I shall arrange a month's leave, and if you've found a house we'll decorate it while I'm home. That is, unless you want a week or two in Dublin first?' He hugged her, whispering, 'I don't mean to be selfish. All I need is to be with you, so whatever you say goes.'

'I would prefer to decorate our home. I only hope I find a nice house.'

'There's plenty on the market and not much money about, so I don't think you'll have any bother finding somewhere suitable, Maggie.'

'Kathleen and Jim live in a big house up in St James Park with gardens back and front. I love visiting them.'

'Soon you'll have a house with a garden if that's what you want. Remember, although I'm not rich, I am quite well to do. I think we could afford a house near Kathleen. Would you like that?'

Maggie nodded, her eyes bright at the idea. She waved a hand around the comfortable kitchen. 'Sarah will be pleased to have this house.'

'I should think so. I hope she realises how lucky she is to have you for a mother,' he answered. Privately, he thought Sarah spoilt and selfish, but he knew Maggie could see no fault in her, so kept his opinions to himself.

'She's so young. Too young to be married.'

Hearing the anxious note in her voice, he tried to reassure her. 'Mick's a good lad. She'll be all right, love.'

She met and held his gaze and then he was kissing her, lifting her on to a plane she had thought she would never experience again. He explored the column of her throat with his lips, seeking out the pulses, bringing tremor after tremor of excitement. And when his lips touched her bare breast, a shaft of pure joy ran through her, and her lips and hands urged him on. It was almost fifteen years since she had felt like this. Indeed, had she ever felt quite like this? The long interval since Paul's death had heightened the feelings racing through her and a woman's urgent passion was rising to meet this man she loved so much. She was so hungry, aching for satisfaction. Wanting nothing between them, her hands fumbled with Barney's clothes – tearing at his shirt, pulling at his belt. Consternation filled her when he pushed her roughly to one side and abruptly left the kitchen, leaving her bewildered and afraid. Cowed, not knowing what had wrought the change in him, she sat with ears strained. She heard him dunking his head under the water tap and shame filled her. He did not want her! Her cheeks blazed with hot colour which quickly receded, leaving her deathly pale.

With hands that shook she tried to button up her blouse, to hide her shame, but she was trembling so much this simple task was beyond her. Gathering the two sides of the blouse together, she clutched them in her fist to cover her nakedness and wished that she was dead. Barney would not want her for his wife now. His kisses had released the wanton spirit that Paul had loved, but Barney must think her a loose woman. And no wonder! A few kisses and she had been willing to give her all. Perhaps he thought she made a habit of it. At this thought her mind baulked. Oh, dear God, no, surely not? Surely not! He could not think that. What would she do? How could she live without him?

Barney, drying his hair in the scullery, was angry with himself. Was he trying to spoil everything? Letting himself get carried away like that. Maggie would think he

237

had no respect for her. But he was hungry. He had not had a woman since meeting her and two years was a long time. When he returned to the kitchen, apologies hovering on his lips, he was astounded to see her stricken face. Falling on his knees beside her, he gently released her blouse from her clenched fist and buttoned it up to her throat. When she refused to meet his eyes, he cupped her face with his hands, saying imploringly, 'Maggie, don't look like that. I love you. I couldn't take a chance, love. What if you became pregnant and something happened to me?'

Her eyelashes fluttered and rose, revealing eyes dark with despair. Pulling her into his arms, he held her fiercely. 'Listen, Maggie, I want everything to be right between us. If we have a child, I want it to be born in wedlock.'

She buried her face in his neck, whispering, 'I thought you didn't want me. I thought you found me too easy and didn't want me for your wife.'

'Maggie ... Ah, Maggie. You'll never know how hard it is for me to leave you tonight. The next six months will be the longest of my life, but we have so much to look forward to.' With his hand under her chin, he tilted her face up. 'Come on now, love. I want a smile. I want to remember you smiling.'

She managed a trembling smile and he said, 'That's my girl. That's much better.' He kissed her again and as he felt renewed desire, said, 'Look ... I'd better go now, before all my good intentions fly out the window.' And once more he put her gently from him, rising to his feet and reaching for his coat.

Full of sadness, she watched him stride down the street. At the corner he turned and waved and she waved back, not caring that Belle Hanna was making no effort to hide the fact that she was watching her. Thumbing her nose in Belle's direction, she closed the door, then shame smote her. She was being unkind. She should not let Belle annoy her like that. Only a lonely woman would get her pleasure out of watching other people.

She sat on the settee, eyes closed, feeling cheated. Six months was a long time. It stretched in front of her, unending. Then she was struck by a thought. A thought that brought her to her feet. What if anything happened to him and he did not return? The sea could be treacherous. Standing in front of the picture of the Sacred Heart that Mollie had always kept in the kitchen, she prayed long and earnestly, begging God to bring him safely back to her. She was attending Clonard Monastery every week and receiving instruction into the Catholic Faith. Father O'Conner assured her it would not take long as she had already picked up so much information from Brendan and Mollie. She was glad she was being instructed in the Catholic Doctrine. Barney would be so pleased when she told him. She did not intend doing so until she was received into the church; when it was an accomplished fact. It would be nice to be married in St Paul's, and perhaps Brendan would be allowed to say the Nuptial Mass?

With these happy thoughts she prepared for bed and quickly fell into a deep sleep.

CHAPTER NINE

'Oh, drat it!' This was the nearest Maggie ever came to swearing. She had decided to let Sarah and Mick have the two upstairs rooms when they returned from Dublin, and was in the process of dismantling the bed in which she slept. All to no avail! The bolts of the iron frame had been tightened by Brendan when, after Paul's death, she had moved back upstairs. They defied all her attempts to loosen them. Hearing the kitchen door open, she went to the top of the stairs and peered down.

'Hello! Anyone at home?'

Brendan! 'I'm up here, and I could do with some help,' she called.

Hanging his coat on the banisters, he took the stairs two at a time. He laughed aloud when he saw Maggie, hair dishevelled, a smudge on her cheek, standing with a spanner in her hand.

'You certainly do need help. Here, gimme that spanner.'

Soon he had the spring released from the ends of the bed and turned to her. 'You weren't thinkin' of tryin' to bring this down the stairs yourself, I hope?' he said accusingly, and when guilt turned Maggie's face bright red, he scolded her. 'Ah, Maggie! Have a bit of sense. Are you tryin' to wreck yer back?'

When, between them, they got the bed downstairs and into the back room, she agreed with him. 'You were right, I would never have managed on my own,' she confessed, as she watched him put the bed up in the confined space.

Tightening the last bolt, he straightened up and his eyes scanned the cramped quarters. 'Will you have enough room here, Maggie?'

Remembering the months she had shared the room with Paul, she smiled faintly and nodded. 'It's only for a short time. Barney and I are getting married on his next leave.' She watched Brendan closely for his reaction to these words, wanting his approval. She need not have worried.

Grabbing her hands in his, he squeezed them tight. 'That's the best news I've heard in a long time, Maggie. You need a man to look after you,' he said, his voice and eyes warm.

She smiled at him. 'I think you deserve a cup of tea after all that hard work, Brendan. Are you hungry?'

He shook his head. 'A cup of tea will be fine, Maggie.'

As she filled the kettle, he stood and watched, his eyes noting the bloom of love on her face, the contentment in her eyes. He felt sad. If only things had been different, she could so easily have been his.

Voice soft and low, she confided in him, 'I love him, Brendan, but people will talk. I know they will! He's so much younger than I.'

He pushed all self-pity from him and chided her. 'I'm surprised at you, Maggie, worryin' about other people. It's not like you.' At these words he was pleased to see her chin rise and her shoulders square determinedly.

'I know. You're right, of course.' She laughed softly. 'I'm going daft in my old age. He's buying me a house,' she confided. Their eyes locked and each knew the other was thinking of the house Paul had been buying for her when he died. 'Do you think he would mind, Brendan?' she asked piteously, her eyes anxious.

'Never!' He was adamant. 'Put that idea from your head. He'd be happy for you.'

Relaxing, she lifted the tray she had prepared while they talked and motioned him into the kitchen. Taking the tray from her, he carried it in and placed it on the table.

'I have another bit of news for you, Brendan.'

His head dipped and his brows raised inquiringly.

'I'm being instructed in the faith.'

Surprise and joy lit up his eyes. Placing his hands on her shoulders, he gazed down into her face. 'Ah, Maggie, you'll never know how much this means to me. I've prayed for this to happen, and I've prayed you'd meet someone you could love. You deserve some happiness.'

Her large silvery eyes, framed in thick, dark lashes, gazed up at him, full of happiness and trust, and the soft contours of her mouth were parted in a slight smile. Suddenly he remembered the day he had kissed her on the train. The day he had fallen in love with her. Remembered how, after that kiss, other girls had paled into insignificance compared to her. After Paul had died, when he could have kissed her, he had been afraid to do so. Afraid he would renege on his promise to God. His promise to enter the priesthood. Had he been a fool?

Now, her perfume filling his nostrils, her body so near yet not touching his, it was as if it was yesterday and he longed to feel the velvety touch of her lips under his once more. Dismayed at the strength of the feelings surging through him, unable to stop himself, he drew her into the circle of his arms. With a tender smile he brushed the dust from her cheek and whispered, 'Maggie! Maggie!'

She stood passive and at peace, her thoughts full of Barney. The longing to kiss her became irresistible and to resist temptation, with a strangled sob, he pressed his face into the soft mass of her hair. Becoming aware of his agitation uneasiness filled her and she remembered the last time he had held her. Remembered the passion she had encouraged. When she tried to ease herself gently from his hold he clung tighter still and in a panic she pushed frantically at his chest. Abruptly, he released her, consternation in his eyes. They faced each other, Maggie dismayed and Brendan angry at himself. Before he could speak, with a perfunctory knock on the door, May Murphy entered the kitchen. May was Maggie's next-door neighbour and to say that she looked surprised was an understatement. Her jaw dropped and she gaped in horror at the scene before her.

Aware of their guilty expressions, Maggie's face blazed with hot colour. She could imagine what May must be thinking. And May was indeed thinking the worst. If ever a pair looked guilty, they did. She had never seen Maggie with a hair out of place in her life and look at it now! As for him – he looked as if he could not see her far enough. Why on earth didn't they shut the big door? she thought.

Maggie opened her mouth twice and no sound would come. At her third attempt she managed to croak, 'Can I help you, May?' her hands going instinctively to her hair, catching the stray locks and securing them as May's eyes swept over her.

Thrusting a cup at her, May squeaked, 'Could ye lend me a cup of sugar?' She wished the ground would open up and swallow her. She was horrified yet excited at what she had just witnessed. Imagine, Maggie carrying on with a priest! Maggie Mason of all people!

Just wait 'til Belle Hanna hears about this, she thought with glee; only to crush the thought at birth. No! She mustn't mention this to anyone, that would be wrong. But in her heart she knew she would be unable to keep this to herself. It was too juicy a bit of scandal to mull over alone.

In the scullery, Maggie filled the cup with sugar and tried to compose herself. She was shaking like a leaf and sugar spilled all over the place as she tried to fill the cup. About once a year May would ask to borrow something – and it had to be at that particular moment, when they must have looked as guilty as hell. What could she say to try and save the situation? Nothing! Anything she said would sound like an excuse.

May wished Maggie would hurry back with the sugar. She could not bring herself to look at the priest. She recognised him as a regular visitor to Maggie's house. Remembered vaguely hearing that his brother had been Maggie's first husband. He had died before she had come to live in Waterford Street, but Belle Hanna had brought her up to date on everyone's history. Now, shuffling her feet, she stared at the floor, unable to think of anything to say.

Drawing a deep breath, Brendan broke the uneasy silence. 'I've just been congratulating Maggie on her engagement.'

'Oh!' May's head was up and her bright blue eyes examined his face. Could she have been mistaken?

Entering the kitchen, a relieved Maggie backed him up. 'Yes, I'm marrying Mollie's grandson Barney in October or November.'

'Well now, that's great news, so it is. Sure he's a lovely man. Wouldn't pass without biddin' ye the time of day. May I offer my good wishes an' all?' May was all smiles and Maggie breathed a sigh of relief.

'Thank you, May.'

Taking the cup of sugar from her, she said, 'I'll return this tomorrow.' And with a nod at Brendan. 'Goodbye, Father.' She left the house, closing the big hall door as she went.

With a flush on her face, Maggie went into the hall and opened the big outer door. Somehow she felt compelled to do this, and when she returned to the kitchen, eyed Brendan in silence. 'She'll tell Belle Hanna,' she muttered at last, worry making her voice gruff.

'It can't be helped.' Brendan knew Belle was the muck raker of the Falls.

'But we're innocent!' Maggie cried in vexation.

Privately, Brendan thought May had been sent to prevent him making a grave mistake, and in doing so losing Maggie's respect. It was indeed true that God worked in mysterious ways.

'Well, what can't be cured must be endured,' he said lightly. 'Come, pour the tea and tell me who's giving you instruction.'

They sat either side of the table and Maggie spoke in glowing tones of Father O'Conner. Was he not the nearest thing to a saint she was likely to meet? Brendan listened, nodding and smiling, letting her ramble on. He knew Father O'Conner and Maggie could not be in better hands.

He promised that he would try to be at her baptism, and when she asked if he would say Nuptial Mass at her wedding, assured her that he would do his best to obtain permission to do so.

Later, when he left Maggie and was making his way up Waterford Street, to cut through O'Niell Street on his way to Clonard Monastery, he met Belle Hanna. He wished her 'Good day', and when she answered with a knowing smile, guessed she had been talking to May Murphy. Well, May certainly hadn't wasted any time. Any feeling of well-being left him. He was angry with himself. They had been warned often enough never to put themselves in compromising situations, but he had always treated Maggie like a sister. Until today!

What on earth possessed him? Acting like a callow youth. For desire to have been awakened after all this time, shocked him. Hopefully, Maggie had not noticed his overwhelming desire to kiss her. Or had she? He hoped not. He could not bear to lose her respect. He could only hope that Belle Hanna wouldn't cause any mischief. Bowing his head, he prayed earnestly as he climbed Clonard Street to the monastery.

On their return from Dublin Mick remonstrated with Maggie when he discovered that she had given up her room for them. 'Sure we'd have been all right in the back room, Maggie. You've done enough for us already.'

Throwing him a surprised look, Sarah casually thanked Maggie, causing her to fume inwardly although she smiled in reply. Only now was she beginning to see how selfish her daughter was, taking everything as her due. Poor Mick! He was going to have his hands full with her. Deciding to break the news and get it over with, she blurted out, 'You will soon have the house to yourselves. Barney and I are getting married on his next leave and we're buying a house.'

'So you're goin' through with it?' Sarah asked.

Maggie sensed rather than heard the contempt in her

245

voice. Then, with a slight sneer on her face, Sarah finished, 'Do you not think you're a bit old for him?'

Maggie erupted. Jumping to her feet, she thrust her face close to Sarah's and cried, 'No! I don't think I'm too old for him, and thank you very much for your good wishes. You've just made my day!'

With these words, she grabbed her coat from the banisters and with tears blinding her, literally ran from the house, giving into a rare display of temper by banging the door behind her.

Mick turned to reprimand Sarah, but the words died on his lips when he saw she was crying. 'Ah, be happy for her, love. She deserves some happiness. She's always been good to you,' he said softly, gathering her close.

'I know.' She sniffed against his chest and he thrust a handkerchief into her hand. 'It's just . . . I've never had to share her before an' I'll need her when the baby comes.'

'But sure now . . . is that what's worrying ye? Did you not hear her? She's not goin' to England or anything like that. Didn't ye hear her say they're buyin' a house?'

'It won't be the same. I won't come first with her any more.'

'Well, you'll always come first with me, love,' he assured her fondly.

Personally, he was happy for Maggie and glad they would have the house to themselves. Nevertheless, Sarah's tears tugged at his heartstrings and he nuzzled her neck whilst edging her towards the stairs.

'Oh, for heaven's sake! Is that all you can think about? The answer to all ailments,' she cried in exasperation, pushing him roughly away.

There was a hurt look on his face as he turned aside. 'I thought you needed comfortin', but obviously I was wrong,' he muttered, and he too left the house, his lips a tight line in his face. He closed the door with exaggerated care, his anger carefully controlled. The honeymoon had been a bit disappointing; not what he had expected. Sarah was a bit frigid and he did not know what to do about it. Still . . . it was early days and she was pregnant.

Standing in front of the white sink that now replaced the brown jawbox, Sarah's tears mingled with the dishwater. She felt mean. Why couldn't she be generous and kind like her mother? She liked Barney, but not as a stepfather. Her mother had obviously been hurt by her reaction and although she would apologise, the damage was done, her mother now knew how she really felt. If only she had held her tongue!

Relations were strained for the next few days. Sarah apologised and Maggie politely received the olive branch. As for Mick he hardly opened his mouth, afraid of saying the wrong thing.

It was a week later when Maggie awoke in the night, to lie wondering what had disturbed her. Some noise: she was sure of that. Fearfully she eyed the window. Is someone in the yard? she thought apprehensively. Then she heard it again, a long drawn out moan. In an instant she was out of bed, through the kitchen and on the stairs, bumping into Mick on his way down to fetch her.

'Thank God you're awake, Maggie. Sarah's in awful pain,' he cried, and turned to lead the way back up the stairs.

Sarah was sitting on the edge of the bed, clutching her stomach. Her eyes dark with fear, she turned to Maggie. 'Mam! Oh, Mam!' A pain gripped her. Biting hard on her lip, she moaned deep in her throat.

'Lie down, Sarah.' Pushing her gently, Maggie made her stretch out on the bed, shouting over her shoulder at Mick, 'Heat a water jar. Listen, Sarah, are you bleeding?'

At her nod, Maggie asked, 'Bad?'

Again Sarah nodded.

Maggie pushed her nightdress up and saw that she had placed a pillowcase between her legs to staunch the flow of blood. Easing it gently away she saw that Sarah had miscarried.

'Sarah, love . . . you've lost the baby.'

'Ah, Mam!' The words came out on a sob and Sarah turned her head away, staring blindly at the wall. What would Mick think? He had married her because of the baby. Being an orphan, he had been sought after. He brought out the mother in girls and many a one had chased him. At first he had treated her as a child, but she had soon changed all that and had made sure that she got him. Now there would be no baby. Would he regret marrying her?

Fetching a clean pillowcase, Maggie rolled the soiled cloth up and put it to one side. She helped Sarah change her nightdress and changed the sheets, glad to see that Sarah was not haemorrhaging. With a bit of luck they would not need a doctor. When Mick brought the stone jar filled with hot water, she said to him. 'Mick son, Sarah has miscarried.'

'Is she all right?' He looked as if he was about to weep, and her heart went out to him.

'I think so. We will know in the morning whether or not we need the doctor.'

Mick took Sarah's hand in his and gripped it tight in sympathy, but she refused to look at him.

Putting the hot jar at her feet, Maggie pulled the bedclothes up and tucked them tightly around her. 'We must keep her warm. I'll stay with her, Mick. You need your sleep, having to be up at six.'

When he would have demurred, she insisted. 'Go on, son. Sleep in my bed.'

He leaned over the bed, 'Sarah, love?' he pleaded, but still she would not look at him, and sad at heart he turned to Maggie.

'Goodnight, Maggie. Thanks for everything.'

'Goodnight, son.'

Lying in Maggie's bed, Mick wondered what difference this would make to their marriage. He had taken Sarah down and the baby was the only reason she had married him. He blamed himself for the pregnancy: he should have been able to control himself better. He was a mature man and Sarah was only seventeen. But then, young as she was, she had seduced him with her fresh loveliness. Still, he should have known better. He was aware that she did not love him as he loved her, but the baby would have held them together. Would he be able to hold her now? She was so young, six years his junior, and so lovely. He was ready to settle down, but was she? He tossed and turned and was still awake when dawn, pushing weak, pale, light into the room, told him it was time to rise for work.

Maggie soaked the blood-stained clothes in the tin bath, and adding plenty of salt, covered the bath with a board. No need for anyone to know about the miscarriage. Sarah would be up and about in a day or two, before she was missed. No one need be any the wiser. She was glad now that she had resisted the impulse to confide in Kathleen or Anne. Before Mick left for work that morning, she had said to him, 'No one need know Sarah was pregnant.'

He understood at once and agreed earnestly, 'Not from my lips they won't, Maggie. I don't want anyone pointin' the finger at her.'

She relaxed. Belle Hanna could watch and count all she wanted, but she would be disappointed. To her surprise, she mourned the loss of the child's soul. Six months ago she would not have even thought of that, but Father O'Conner had explained to her that once a child was conceived it had a soul and she knew that soul would now be in a place called Limbo. However, she would not have been human if she had not been glad that no one need know Sarah was not a virgin when she married. It was true what they said, every cloud did have a silver lining.

On a dark, wet day at the end of October, Maggie was received into the Catholic Church. Anne and Bill were her sponsors and her only regret was Brendan's inability to be there. Since Sarah's wedding she had received only one letter from him, to inform her he could not attend her baptism, but the hurt cut deep when he was unable to perform the Nuptial Mass when she married Barney. He did not even come to the wedding although she knew for a fact that he was home on leave, Emma having unwittingly let the cat out of the bag. She could therefore only assume that he objected to her marriage, although he had said otherwise, and her heart was sad. It was the only cloud on an otherwise perfect day.

For her wedding outfit, she had chosen a pale green dress of finest wool with a matching jacket, and Emma, her bridesmaid, was in pink. The outfits were the very latest fashion, brought from Paris by Emma, and Maggie knew she looked her best. Kathleen had been her first choice for a matron of honour, but big with child, had sadly declined. Tim Neely, Barney's best friend who worked on the boats with him, was best man, and Maggie was to rejoice that she had asked Emma to be bridesmaid because it was soon obvious to all that Tim was smitten with her.

William was unable to come over for the wedding, his wife being in hospital awaiting the arrival of her second child, and Maggie was glad. Without William there to distract her attention, perhaps Emma would give Tim a chance. She seemed to like him.

The wedding reception was in the Royal Avenue Hotel, a treat paid for by Kathleen and Jim as their wedding present, and Jim took them down in relays in his new car. Not a brand new car, but new enough to be the envy of many. He still made quality shoes for the well-to-do and the shoe repairing side of the business was thriving. With money in the city tight, people were unable to afford new shoes and he reaped the benefits. As he confided in Maggie, he had to make it work with five children to feed and clothe and another one on the way.

It was a small but merry wedding party: Sarah and Mick, Anne and Bill, Emma and Tim, Kathleen and Jim, and of course the bride and groom. The rest of the family and their friends, who had been at the church to see them wed, were invited to a party later that evening. This party was to be in Maggie's new house, up in St James Park, close to Kathleen's. At last Maggie had moved up the Falls Road!

After a lovely breakfast, the ladies retired to the cloakroom to powder their noses. Catching Maggie's eye in the mirror, Anne smiled.

'You make a lovely bride, Maggie. I wish Brendan

could have been here to see you,' she said wistfully. 'He'll be heartsore to have missed yer big day.'

Maggie snorted, causing Anne to draw back, blinking in surprise.

'Why isn't he here then? Eh? Ah, Anne, I know he's home on leave, so why isn't he here? Does he disapprove?'

'Oh, no! No! You've got it all wrong,' Anne said in a rush. 'He's very happy about your marriage.'

'Then where is he? Why didn't he come?'

Maggie's disbelief was obvious, and drawing herself to her full height, Anne cried, 'I'll tell you why he didn't come!'

Maggie watched mesmerised as Emma plucked distractedly at her mother's sleeve, saying urgently, 'No, Mam, please don't.'

Shrugging off her hand, Anne said, 'She has the right t'know. I always said she should be told, so I did.'

Resignedly, Emma drew back. 'Brendan won't thank you for tellin' her.'

'Telling me what?' cried Maggie.

Sarah, who was five months pregnant and comparing notes with the more experienced Kathleen, drew closer, and Anne blushed when she discovered all eyes were on her.

'Tell me what?' Maggie repeated.

Unsure now, Anne looked to Emma for guidance, but she stared at the floor and refused to come to her mother's assistance.

'She has the right to know,' Anne repeated, but she was not so confident now.

'Well, for heaven's sake, tell us then, Anne,' Kathleen cried in exasperation.

Anne's head swung from side to side, as if she was looking for inspiration. Then, coming to a decision, she blurted out, 'All right! Brendan'll be angry . . . but anyhow . . . well, he's been forbidden to have any contact with you, Maggie.'

251

Maggie's face went slack with surprise and her eyes started from her head.

'It seems one of your neighbours wrote ... to the Bishop, no less.' Anne's lips pressed tightly together at the idea. 'That Brendan was seein' too much of you and that you were seen embracin'.' Her gaze wavered. Could there be any truth in it? Of course not! God forgive her for thinking such a thing. But Brendan had been very fond of Maggie.

'Oh, no. No!' Maggie looked so white and shaken that both Kathleen and Emma moved to her side to support her.

'Oh, yes, I'm afraid. That's why Brendan isn't here today. I'm sorry for upsettin' ye, Maggie, but I couldn't bear to hear Brendan being blamed in the wrong.'

'You were right to tell me.' Maggie looked around at the faces of her friends and her gaze came to rest on Anne; she had sensed her doubt. 'You don't believe it, do you?'

They all answered her at once, reassuring her in different ways of their good faith, Anne loudest of all. Her doubts were laid to rest at Maggie's obvious anguish.

'It must have been Belle Hanna. Only she would go to such lengths to cause trouble,' Maggie fumed. 'She has never forgiven me for staying on in the house after Mollie died. She wanted it for her Mary. Oh, but she's wicked, real wicked!'

She was almost in tears and Anne implored, 'Don't upset yourself, Maggie. I'll never forgive meself if your weddin' day is spoilt, but I couldn't bear to hear Brendan put in the wrong. He was so worried about you. So glad you were marrying Barney. Ye understand, don't ye?' Her look was appealing and Maggie hastened to reassure her.

'Yes, Anne, I understand, and I'm glad you told me. I thought Brendan disapproved of my marriage and that hurt me, but now I know he's still my friend. Yes,' she nodded, 'I'm glad you told me.'

Taking Maggie by the arm, Kathleen said, 'Come on, the men'll think we're lost.' And leaving the cloakroom, they made their way back to the lounge.

Maggie resolved not to tell Barney about the incident.

She was recalling, how much she had talked about Brendan when first they met, and a remark he had jokingly made when he at last met him: 'I'm glad Brendan is a priest, or I wouldn't stand a chance with you.' No, better let sleeping dogs lie. She was afraid she would see doubt in Barney's eyes and she would not be able to bear that. After all, she was innocent!

St James Park was a wide, tree-lined street, within walking distance of the Falls Park, built around 1912 for middle-class workers, who at that time could afford the £80 deposit and weekly repayments of eight or ten shillings. Due to the current depression and the difficulty in selling houses, Barney had managed to get a bargain for cash and Maggie loved her new semi-detached house. She was not sorry to leave Waterford Street, glad to be free of the uneasy feeling of living sandwiched between the Shankill Road and Sandy Row.

Although the house was not nearly as big as the one she had been reared in on the Malone Road, it was nevertheless much bigger than the house in Waterford Street. The hall was wide and spacious, with doors leading to a sitting room, a living room and a kitchen, which filled Maggie with delight. Upstairs there was three bedrooms and a bathroom.

'Imagine! A bathroom, Barney. No more washing myself in the cold, draughty scullery.' A blissful sigh left her lips. 'I can't believe this is all happening.'

The house was at the end of the row, and at the front the garden was pocket-sized, but out the back there was a good lawn at the bottom of which, in all its splendour, stood an apple tree. Her immediate neighbours were professional people, a solicitor, his teacher wife, and their son who attended Queen's University and lived in a flat near the college. To complete Maggie's happiness, Kathleen and her brood lived in a four-bedroomed house at the top of the street.

If Barney could just find a job and stay at home, Maggie knew she would be as near to heaven as one could expect in this world. However, with thousands of men on Outdoor Relief this was unlikely to happen and she knew she should be glad that he had a job, even if it took him away for months at a time.

Another thing she liked about St James Park was the fact that the neighbours kept themselves to themselves. That was not to say that they were unfriendly, just reticent. To her delight, the only time she heard of the troubles was on the radio or what she read in the newspapers, and for this she was thankful. In any case, poverty had pushed the political troubles into the background. Meetings held nowadays were concerned with fighting for a chance to get work or for a better method of Relief for the unemployed, and both Catholic and Protestant working class were united as they fought for a livelihood.

The Outdoor Relief was not granted until all other avenues were explored and exhausted. Savings must be used sparingly and anything considered a luxury item must be sold. Then and only then was Outdoor Relief granted. It was handed out in the form of chits for food, no allowances were made for clothing or rent or heating, while the names of those who received it was posted up on notice boards all over town, making the proud cringe with shame. This was unlike England, where it was paid out in money for the families to spend where it was most needed. Able-bodied men, although unable to find work, found it hard to persuade the powers that be that they were in need, and without the help of charitable organisations many would certainly have starved. Resentment and unrest were rife, like a bomb waiting to be detonated.

Maggie thanked God daily for sending Barney into her life and for her beautiful home, but she could not help being afraid that it was too good to last . . .

Sarah's first child, a girl, was born on 5 March and Mick asked if she could be named Elizabeth after his mother. Knowing that this was about all he knew about his mother, Sarah readily agreed and, to her amusement, Mick promptly shortened it to Beth.

During the summer months, she put Beth in her pram and pushed her up the Falls Road to St James Park where envy of Maggie's house made her discontented with her lot.

In her heart she knew she was lucky. Against all the odds Mick was still employed in the shipyard and he was devoted to her and Beth. Being clever with his hands, he constantly renovated their home, and compared to other houses on the Falls, hers was really lovely. But when she saw Maggie's bathroom and sunbathed out the back on the lawn, she longed for a house like it. She was forever urging Mick to move house, to be adventurous, but although he gave in to her on most issues, on this he remained firm. He could not be sure of his job. What if he was laid off? Where would the money come from to pay for a house like that? Better to stay in Waterford Street; at least they would have more chance of finding the rent for there. In her heart Sarah knew he was right, but resentment put a discontented droop to her mouth.

Their second child, another girl, Eileen, was born when Beth was fifteen months old, and if Sarah envied Maggie her house, Maggie envied her her two beautiful children. Her heart ached when she watched Barney play with her grandchildren, and she yearned to be able to give him a child of his own. He was a young man, he deserved to have children, she fretted, but when she mentioned it to Barney he assured her he was contented with his lot. 'Sure, have I not your two fine grandaughters to spoil?' he argued, and he would lovingly kiss her and touch her, and show her just how much he loved her.

Sunlight streaming in through the window awakened Gerry Docherty. Lying unable to sleep, he thought of the summer months ahead with gloom. What on earth had possessed him, promising to spend the summer vacation at home before he started work in September? He could have gone down south and toured the Ring of Kerry with some other students, but no, wanting to please his parents he had agreed to stay with them. After all, without their help and support, he would not be a solicitor today, with great prospects in front of him. This he realised and he was grateful to them. It would have been all right if they were at home, but they were out working all day and he was bored.

Children's laughter brought him out of bed and over to the window to stand gazing down into the garden next door. Two children were playing on a rug at the bottom of the garden, but it was not they who caught his eye. On another rug lay a young woman, skirts hitched high, displaying long slender legs to the sun. It was the beauty of her that caught his attention. Her arms were stretched above her head, hands loosely linked, and he could see that she had a good figure. Thick lashes rested on cheeks the colour of honey and a riot of chestnut curls caught the sun. Gerry's pulse quickened. He had never seen anyone as lovely, and in his years at university he had met plenty of lovely girls.

As if sensing someone was watching her, Sarah slowly sat up and looked around her. Gerry gazed fixedly at her, willing her to look at him. When at last her eyes met his, he grinned in triumph.

Blushing, Sarah pulled her skirt down over her knees and tossed her head angrily. How dare he spy on her? He must be Gerry Docherty. Well, it looked like her sunbathing days were over and just when she was getting a nice tan.

Hurriedly bathing and dressing, Gerry ate a light breakfast and then presented himself at Maggie's door. When she answered his knock he said, 'Hello, I'm Gerry Docherty. I thought I would introduce myself as I shall be here all summer. Perhaps I'll be able to do odd jobs for you as I hear your husband's at sea?'

Maggie had seen Gerry before, rushing in and out when he came home some week-ends, but this was his first sight of her and his gaze was admiring.

'Oh . . . well now, I'm pleased to meet you, but I'm not going to put you to work. Come in and meet my daughter and grandchildren.' She ushered him through the house and out into the back garden where Sarah gave him a defiant stare.

'Sarah, this is Mrs Docherty's son Gerry. Gerry, this is Sarah and my name is Maggie. And this,' she lifted plump, smiling Eileen up in her arms, 'is Eileen. The quiet one is Beth.'

Sarah gave him a curt nod and Maggie flashed her a surprised look, at a loss to explain her bad manners. Rising from the grass her daughter sat on the garden bench and started to leaf through a magazine. Maggie frowned. Unaware of her mother's displeasure, Sarah thought if she ignored this cheeky young man he would go away.

Smiling inwardly, Gerry set out to charm her. He had not spent years at University without learning the art of small talk and soon the book was forgotten as he kept them enthralled with tales of life at college.

As she listened, Sarah became even more disenchanted with her lot when she thought of all she had missed out on. Here she was, twenty years old, tied down with two young children, and Gerry, about the same age, had the world at his feet. It was not the first time she had chafed at her ties. Quite often lately she found herself day dreaming, wishing she was single again. Wishing she had listened to her mother and enjoyed herself before she got married. She blamed Mick for getting her pregnant; he should have known better. She had been only seventeen, but he had been twenty-three.

Gerry became a regular visitor to Maggie's who, finding the sun taxed her strength, stayed indoors a lot, glad Sarah had someone young to keep her company. She could not understand why she felt so tired. Probably it was the change. As Kathleen kept reminding her, she was not getting any younger. She would have to go to the doctor and get a tonic.

After an afternoon nap one Saturday, Maggie rose. Going to her bedroom window she looked down into the garden and fear gripped her heart. Beth and Eileen were playing at the bottom, but it was not they who caused her apprehension. It was Sarah: she lay on the grass with

Gerry lying beside her, propped up on his elbow, and they were gazing at each other with such longing that Maggie's breath caught in her throat.

Dear God! How had she not noticed which way the wind was blowing? She must have been blind. In future she would have to stay with them. She would have to put a stop to Gerry coming in. But how? What reason could she give? Later that evening, as was her habit, she poured all her worries into Kathleen's sympathetic ear, and they decided they would try to get Mick to accompany Sarah when she visited on a Saturday.

With this idea in mind they called into Sarah's house after Mass the next day. Every Sunday they travelled down the Falls Road to Clonard Monastery to early Mass. They usually came straight home, as Kathleen's brood all went to ten o'clock Mass in St John's Church and Jim needed help to get them ready. This particular Sunday, however, they went to twelve o'clock Mass in Clonard and surprised Sarah by calling to visit her.

'Mam! Come in, come in. This is a surprise. Hello, Kathleen, how are you?'

'Very well, thank you. Hello there Mick. My, but you're a stranger.'

'Sit over here, Maggie.' He nodded towards the settee. 'You too, Mrs Rafferty.'

'Oh, for heaven's sake, Mick, call me Kathleen. You make me feel ancient,' she admonished him.

Laughing, Sarah headed for the scullery. 'I'll put the kettle on. Beth, don't touch your grannie's coat. Mam, take your coat off, these two were eating chocolate and it gets everywhere. Mick, hang their coats up for them.'

As he hung their coats at the foot of the stairs, Maggie said, 'Kathleen's right, Mick, you are a stranger. Have you gone off me?'

'Ach, no, Maggie, never that. I know when I'm well off.' His grin was infectious and she grinned back at him.

'Then why don't you come up on a Saturday with Sarah to visit me?'

'Most Saturdays I work 'til twelve, Maggie. You know

that! It's the only overtime I get nowadays and I can't afford t'miss it. I have to keep my three girls in style, ye know.'

'Well, you know what they say ... all work, no play, makes Mick a dull boy.'

Backing her up, Kathleen cried, 'She's right, ye know. You should come up with Sarah on a Saturday.'

Brows drawn together, Mick looked from one to the other of them. Something was wrong. Why ... they were embarrassed! Quickly, he made up his mind. 'Since you're so anxious to see me, I'll come up next Saturday after I finish work an' get cleaned up. All right?'

Coming from the scullery, Sarah asked, 'Where are you goin' next Saturday?'

'Up to visit Maggie.'

Colour flooded his wife's face and she turned quickly away, but not before he had seen it.

'I'm always askin' him to come up, but he doesn't like sunbathin',' she cried, obviously flustered.

Watching her, Mick recalled it was a long time since she had asked him to accompany her and was more perturbed than ever.

On the tram going home, Maggie was anxious. 'I sincerely hope I've done the right thing, Kathleen.'

'Of course you have. Mick'll soon put a stop to Sarah's flirtin', you mark my words!'

'I hope you're right. Oh, I do hope you're right.'

Kathleen patted her arm consolingly and assured her, 'You did the right thing!'

But when Maggie looked at Gerry the following Saturday, her heart quailed. Dear God he's only a boy, she lamented inwardly. What if Mick hits him?

One stroke from Mick's big fist could kill him; murder could be done and it would be her fault. In her distress she cried out at Gerry: 'Surely a young man like you has a girl friend to go walking with, eh? This good weather won't last for ever.'

'Mam!' Sarah cried in surprise, but Gerry just laughed.

'I haven't got a proper girlfriend,' he assured her, and was glad to note Sarah's relief.

'Well, you won't find one sitting here with two married women,' Maggie retorted.

'Mam!' Sarah's eyes were round with wonder at her mother's attitude and she cried indignantly, 'What's got into you? Gerry will think he's not welcome.'

When Maggie made no effort to deny this, Gerry, at a loss, rose slowly to his feet.

'I seem to have outstayed my welcome,' he said, heading slowly for the trellis at the side of the house that opened on to the drive.

'Oh, sit down, Gerry,' Maggie cried. 'Come on, sit down. I don't know what's wrong with me.' She patted her face with a handkerchief. 'Blame the heat, it saps all the strength out of me.'

Gerry remained at the trellis, unsure what to do, and she insisted, 'Come on, son, sit down.'

Later, when she suggested making the lunch, Sarah rose quickly to her feet.

'No, Mam, you stay there. I'll make the lunch.'

'I'm too hot, Sarah, I'll make the lunch and you can wash the dishes.'

'OK, Mam.'

'Are you staying for lunch, Gerry?'

'No, thank you, Maggie. I'm expected home.' He hesitated. 'Is it all right if I come back later ... after lunch?'

'By all means,' she said resignedly. 'It's time you met my son-in-law. He's coming this afternoon.'

Squeals of delight greeted Mick when he arrived just as they were finishing lunch.

'Look at them. You would think they hadn't seen him for a fortnight, instead of a few short hours,' Maggie cried fondly. 'Sarah, pour a cup of tea for Mick and give him those sandwiches I've left ready.'

While Sarah was indoors pouring the tea, Gerry arrived and Maggie introduced him. 'Gerry, this is Sarah's

260

husband. Mick, this is my next-door neighbour, Gerry Docherty.'

The two men eyed each other: one tall, broad, and deeply tanned from working out of doors. The other slightly built and pale complexioned, in spite of much sunbathing.

Maggie compared them and wondered, How can Sarah admire a callow youth like Gerry when she has a husband like Mick?

Mick nodded at Gerry but did not offer him his hand and Maggie thought, He knows. He senses something's wrong.

And he did: it was in the air all around them and he found himself watchful. After he had eaten the sandwiches and drunk the cup of tea, Sarah jumped up and, taking his cup and plate she went in to wash the dishes, followed by Gerry. Mick gazed thoughtfully after them, a frown on his brow. So this was why Maggie and Kathleen were worried.

Sure he's just a bid of a lad, he thought. But then, Sarah is not yet twenty-one, he reminded himself.

Laughter rang out in the kitchen and he grew resentful. It was a long time since his wife had laughed like that at home. He could do nothing right; she was always finding fault with him. Becoming aware of Maggie's gaze, he met her eyes and shrugged.

'What can I do? Hit him? I'd be the laughing stock of the Falls Road.' When Maggie made no answer, he cried, 'It'll blow over.'

However, when Sarah and Gerry returned to the garden, he found he could not bear to watch them together. He had to admit that Sarah was worth looking at; she had blossomed into a beautiful woman. The sun teased copper highlights from her hair and her eyes flashed like emeralds. Catching Mick's eye Sarah blushed guiltily and the resentful look she usually regarded him with returned to her face. She was angry with herself for blushing. She had nothing to feel guilty about. Gerry made her feel attractive with his compliments and warm glances. Mick now! He took her for granted, treated her like a skivvy, made her feel old and drab.

Annoyed at her expression, he turned angrily, rising abruptly to his feet. 'Who'd like to come to the shops with me for sweets?' he cried. And even to his own ears, his voice sounded too bright.

'Oh, Dad. Me, me!'

Beth grabbed his hand and pulled him towards the trellis. Allowing himself to be pulled, he laughed and said, 'What about Eileen?'

'She's too wee, Dad.' Face screwed up, Beth explained, 'I want to climb the Giant's Foot.'

'Ah, Beth love, we can't leave Eileen.'

Eileen not really understanding what it was all about, nevertheless thought tears were called for and started to wail.

'Come on, love. Take my other hand.' Without a backward glance, Mick left the garden with the two children clinging to his hands, and Maggie watched him go, an ache in her heart. Seeing Gerry exchange a warm intimate look with Sarah, her lips tightened and she vowed never to leave them alone again. If their romance was ever going to get off the ground, it would have to be somewhere else; not on her home ground.

After buying them some sweets Mick took the children for a walk up the Giant's Foot, so named because in the past a stream had tumbled down the hill from the Black Mountains beyond and the constant pressure had hollowed out the impression of a huge foot. It was a hill that led to Dan O'Neil's Loney, a favourite walk for courting couples as he well knew. It was a big name for a little hill but Beth loved to climb it, and heaven knows it was big enough for her short legs. Eileen soon tired and lifted her arms up to him. 'Up, Daddy, up!'

She was asleep over his shoulder when he returned to Maggie's and Beth's footsteps dragged as she clung to his hand.

'Put her up on my bed, Mick,' Maggie ordered, and rose

to lead the way into the house, but Sarah's voice stopped her.

'No! Keep her here or she won't sleep the night. Give her to me, Mick.'

Silently, Mick lowered the sleeping child on to the grass beside Sarah and she cajoled her awake, but the two children were tired and quarrelsome and at last Mick cried in exasperation, 'Let's go home, Sarah. The kids are out on their feet.'

'It's too early to go home,' she answered sullenly. 'Trust you to spoil my day! Imagine taking them up the Giant's Foot! They're too little to climb that hill. If you hadn't have come they'd have been contented to play in the garden.'

She was almost in tears. How she wished he had stayed at home. She had not been alone with Gerry all afternoon. Even when Mick was away with the kids her mother had not left the garden. Not that they ever did anything, just looked, but it made her feel warm and admired. Mick never made her feel like that.

Mick could see that his wife was disappointed, but he could also see that her mother was tired.

'Your mam's tired. Come on, Sarah, let's go home.'

Maggie shot him a grateful glance. 'I am tired,' she confessed. 'I feel rundown, but first thing on Monday morning I'm going to see the doctor and get a tonic. Otherwise Barney will think he's married to an old woman.'

Mick commenced to tidy the children's toys away and Sarah had no choice but to follow suit. Gerry helped and when the garden was clear of toys, gave Sarah a long lingering look before bidding them all good day and leaving.

Going home on the tram Beth wanted to go up on the top deck, but Sarah hustled her inside and when she demurred, slapped her legs. Mick was grim-faced, anger only just held in control. The mark on Beth's leg hurt him more than it was hurting her. Once home, he silently heated water to bathe the girls, while Sarah gave them bread and ham and a glass of milk to wash it down.

Usually, this was a happy laughing hour. When Sarah returned home on a Saturday evening, Mick would have the tea ready and the water heating, and she was always in a mellow mood. Now he knew why. It was because she had been basking in Gerry's admiration all day. This thought made him more grim-faced than ever and he decided to have it out with her. That was the finish of it. He would put his foot down. No more Saturdays spent up in St James Park. Not until Gerry got a job and, hopefully, moved away. And the further away the better.

That night both Mick and Sarah were angry and silent and Beth and Eileen must have sensed something was wrong. They were both docile and quiet as Sarah washed them in the big tin bath and passed them to Mick to be dried. Soon they were dressed in clean pyjamas, hair brushed until it shone, and tucked up in bed.

Tea was a silent meal. After helping wash the dishes, Mick sat down. He had made up his mind to talk to Sarah, clear the air. She, on the other hand, was determined to give him the silent treatment for spoiling her day. She set up the card table on which she ironed and fetched a bundle of clothes from the back room and commenced to iron them.

'For heaven's sake, Sarah, leave that, an' sit down,' he growled.

'Oh! An' what good samaritan is goin' to do it for me, eh? Tell me that!'

'If you spent less time up in St James Park, you could have your work all squared up, and maybe we'd have time to talk to each other.'

Ignoring the signs of anger – after all, two could play at that game – Sarah said sweetly, 'Oh ... so you want to talk? Well, I can iron an' talk at the same time. Clever I am.' She leant across the table smiling coyly. 'What would you like to talk about? The weather? The kids? Or just for a change shall we talk about the opera or the ballet?'

Her voice dripped with sarcasm and Mick rose from his

chair and took a threatening step towards her, face flushed with anger. Sarah's bright green eyes dared him to lift his hand. With fists tightly clenched at his sides, he turned away, fighting for control.

Muttering through clenched teeth, 'I'm away down for a pint,' he lifted his coat and left the house. The echoing slam of the door resounding on the still evening air, brought a startled May Murphy to her door to stare after him in amazement.

Sarah glared angrily at the closed door and her stabs at the clothes with the iron were vicious. Some life she had! Her one day a week out and he had to spoil it. Then she thought of Gerry and his open admiration, the yearning in his eyes. He would never treat her like that! No, he was a gentleman. Her expression softened and she grew mellow as her thoughts dwelt on him.

CHAPTER TEN

Doctor Hughes smiled across his desk at Maggie, gave a wag of his head, and said, 'Maggie, you never cease to amaze me. You never look any older.'

'At the moment I feel about ninety,' she replied, smiling at the compliment.

He linked his hands together in front of him on the desk and enquired gravely, 'Tell me what's bothering you?' During the years that she had worked for him, he had watched Maggie struggle to give Sarah a decent home. Had watched her do without that Sarah might have the best, and he admired her very much. He knew she would not be sitting in his surgery today unless she was really worried.

'Tiredness, Doctor. I go to bed tired, and I get up in the morning tired, even after a good night's sleep. I just can't understand it. I keep remembering when Paul was ill ... how tired he was.'

'Hmmm.' Nodding towards a screen, he said, 'Nip in there and get undressed. I want to examine you.'

When, after a very thorough examination, she was once again sitting across from him, he said reassuringly, 'I can't find anything wrong with you. Your lungs are perfectly clear so don't worry about T.B. And your heart and your blood pressure are all right. Perhaps you're anaemic. We'll know when I get this tested.' He held up the small phial of blood he had taken from Maggie's arm. 'Meanwhile, bring me a urine sample and I'll have it analysed as well.'

Smiling, she reached into her shopping bag and produced a small bottle. 'I thought you would never ask.'

He chuckled as he took it from her. 'Ah, Maggie, I wish more of my patients were like you. Can you come back on Friday morning?'

'Any time, Doctor.'

Gentleman that he was, he rose and opened the door for her. 'Until Friday then.'

The week passed slowly for Maggie. She felt no better and was apprehensive when she entered the surgery on Friday morning. She found Doctor Hughes looking very solemn.

'Is . . . is it something serious then, Doctor?'

'Sit down, Maggie.' He waited until she was seated. 'Maggie, you are a bit anaemic and you are going to have to be very careful.' She remained silent, worried eyes never leaving his face and he continued, 'If you don't do everything I tell you, the child you're carrying will be a puny wee thing.'

Relaxing back in his chair, he grinned across the desk at her.

Maggie stared blankly at him. He couldn't mean . . .

Doctor Hughes was puzzled. He had expected her to be overjoyed. Leaning forward again, he asked, 'Don't you want a baby, Maggie?'

'You mean I'm really pregnant?' Her eyes were starting from her head and her voice was shrill.

'Yes, Maggie, you're really pregnant.' He was smiling again. 'I thought as much on Monday, but I wanted to be sure before I raised your hopes.'

She swallowed, then her fist went to her mouth and she pressed hard on it to try and stop the sobs that were threatening to burst from her lips.

On his feet at once, Doctor Hughes hurried around his desk and patted her consolingly on the shoulder. 'There now, Maggie. There now. This will never do. Think of the baby,' he advised, thrusting a handkerchief into her hand.

'Doctor Hughes, you will never know how much this means to me. To be able to give Barney a child. I can't believe it! It's so unexpected. I thought I was going through the change,' she confided. Blowing her nose, she peered at him over the top of her hands. 'I'm not dreaming, am I?'

'No, Maggie, you're not dreaming,' he assured her.

An anxious expression crossed her face and she clutched at his arm. 'Will it be all right?'

'There is always a risk, Maggie, at your age. It's in God's hands. Meantime, you'll have to look after yourself. Eat plenty of vegetables and fruit . . . and you must rest. That's important, plenty of rest. OK?'

'I'll be very careful, Doctor.' Still she clutched his arm, her eyes seeking his, needing reassurance. 'You think it will be all right?'

'I don't see why not. You're healthy and I know you'll be careful. I think you're going to be fine, Maggie.'

She breathed a sigh of relief. 'Thank you, Doctor. Thank you very much.'

His eyes twinkled at her. 'Well now, Maggie, I really hadn't much to do with it.' His smile was roguish and, bright pink with embarrassment, she laughed and wished him goodday.

She couldn't wait to tell Sarah the good news. Oh, but she was happy! Her step was so light she felt as if she was walking on air as she crossed the Springfield Road, down Malcomson Street and over to Sarah's house. When they were first married, she had waited anxiously every month for evidence that she might be pregnant and each month had brought disappointment. With the passing of time she had given up hope and reconciled herself to the fact that it was not to be. And now this! The wonder of it took her breath away.

When Sarah opened the door, she drew back and eyed Maggie from under drawn brows. 'You look like the cat that swallowed the canary.'

'And well I may. You are looking at a pregnant woman!' her mother announced proudly.

'Mam! Ah, Mam! Well, I never!' Sarah reached out and

pulled her close. She knew how much this meant to her mother. 'I'm so pleased for you.'

'I can't believe it. I just can't take it in. Barney will be thrilled.' Maggie, still bemused, kept repeating, 'I just can't believe it.'

'He will indeed. No, Mam, don't lift her.' Sarah stopped Maggie as she was about to swing Eileen up into her arms. 'No more of that! She's too heavy. You'll have to be very careful from now on, so ye will.'

Lifting Eileen up into her own arms, she said, 'Come an' sit down, Mam. I've just baked some scones. Let's have a cup of tea.'

So excited she was unable to sit, Maggie followed Sarah into the scullery, getting in her way in the confined space. Sarah was very patient; she nodded and smiled and let her ramble on. It was a long time since she had heard her mother talk so much and it took Sarah's mind off her own problems.

'When I felt so tired all the time, I thought it was the change. My periods kept coming and going and Kathleen kept reminding me that I wasn't getting any younger. *She'll* be surprised, so she will.' Maggie laughed at the idea and hugged herself. 'Oh, Sarah, just think, in about seven months time, Barney will be a father.'

Smiling fondly at her excitement, Sarah said, 'He won't half be pleased.'

Her mother nodded happily. 'I can't wait to tell him.'

'Which would you prefer, Mam, a boy or a girl?'

'I don't mind in the slightest. All I ask is that it's normal. Do you think it will be all right, Sarah? I'm so old.'

Worry hung in the air between them and Sarah said sharply, 'Now don't you start talkin' like that. It'll be all right, Mam. It'll be all right.'

Mick, who had been quiet and withdrawn all week, chuckled when his wife relayed the news to him that night.

'Well ... what do ye know? Old Barney will be pleased,' he said, and as they discussed the coming birth

269

they were closer than they had been in a long time, but sadly Mick realised she would continue to go up to her mother's house. Perhaps more often. He had intended forbidding her to go there while Gerry was on vacation, but now Maggie would need her and he would appear churlish if he stopped her going. Fate was working against him. Of course, there was the chance she might have defied him anyhow, but now he would never know.

Fear gripped his heart when he remembered how Sarah had looked at young Gerry. She was in his company so often and Gerry did not try to hide the fact that he was attracted to her. Indeed, no; he was seducing her with his eyes, the young bastard! It had been painful to watch. She had married him because she was pregnant, was he about to lose her to this young lad? Dear God . . . it didn't bear thinking about. How could he exist without her?

There was an unspoken agreement between them that there would be no more children until Sarah thought Eileen was old enough, but she was almost fourteen months now and still Sarah kept her back firmly to him in bed. Should he force himself on her? After all, he had his rights! Perhaps she would become pregnant, then she would not have time to fawn over Gerry. But was that the answer? No! That would never do. That wouldn't solve anything. It would probably turn her against him. Things would just have to take their course. Hopefully, when Gerry started work, he would live away from home. Far away.

When Maggie was five months pregnant, instead of waiting at the gate for Barney as she usually did when he arrived home on leave, she stayed indoors. She heard his key in the lock and stood to attention in the living room, waiting patiently for him to enter the door. Then she turned slowly around and let him see her from all angles, proud of her protruding stomach.

'Now do you believe . . . doubting Thomas?' she teased.

With a contented sigh, he took her into his arms. 'Yes, I believe. I just couldn't take it in when you wrote. I thought

I must be dreaming.' Scanning her face anxiously, he asked, 'Are you well?'

'I never felt better. I just tire easily.'

'Well now, for two weeks you are going to do absolutely nothing. I am going to lift you, and lay you, and spoil you rotten.'

'Mmm . . . sounds lovely.'

The love she felt for him was written all over her and he drew her closer still. His kisses were the kisses of a hungry man but as his passion rose, he put her resolutely away from him. 'Forgive me, love! I know we must be careful.'

Determinedly, she pulled his arms around her again. 'I asked the doctor about that. It's all right. We can't cause any harm.'

'You're sure?'

She nodded, her eyes shining. 'I'm sure.'

'Ah, Maggie . . . Maggie.' And he kissed her and touched her and proceeded to show how much he had missed her.

True to his word, for the next two weeks Barney spoilt his wife and Maggie lapped it all up, knowing she was about to make his dream come true by giving him a child. Two nights before he was due to return to his ship, he insisted Maggie should go with him for a short walk. It certainly was a short walk; at the corner of the street, he stopped. Pointing across the road, he said, 'Do you see that empty shop at the corner of Rockmore Road?'

Looking at the shop that had previously been a newsagent's but which had stood empty for many months, she nodded, mystified.

'Jim Rafferty and I are going to rent it and open it as a greengrocer's.' He drew away from her to watch her reaction. 'What do you think of that?'

Mouth agape, Maggie managed to cry, 'I don't understand! Jim and you?'

He patted her stomach. 'I have no intentions of leaving you to rear our child on your own. Jim and I are going to be partners. He wants to branch out. He will look after the legal side, since he has the experience, and I'll manage the

271

shop. There must be a radius of a mile here without a greengrocer's. I think it should pay off.'

Now she knew why Jim had been popping in to see them nearly every day and why Barney had stood at the gate talking to him for ages.

'You mean, you'll be at home all the time?'

'Well now, I might go out now and again,' he teased.

She shook his arm. 'Be serious! You know what I mean.'

'Yes, love. I know what you mean. I'll be living at home. Mind you, Maggie, money will be tight for a while and it might not work out. But I think it's worth a try, don't you?'

She nodded her head vigorously in agreement. Her eyes shone, then clouded over. 'I'm afraid, Barney. So afraid. No one should be this happy,' she whispered.

'You deserve happiness, Maggie, and I'll spend the rest of my life keeping you happy. That's a promise!'

Arm in arm, they retraced their steps down the street, Barney humming a happy tune. However, Maggie distrusted such happiness, and out of sight her fingers were tightly crossed.

Stabbing the iron viciously at Mick's shirt, Sarah wished it was his neck. They were drifting further and further apart. Well, see if she cared. Let him go down to the pub, if that was what he wanted. Things had changed drastically in the past few months. No more coming home on a Saturday night to find the tea ready and the water heated to bathe the girls. No more unopened pay packets. Oh no, Mick helped himself now. He still gave her plenty, so she couldn't complain, but she was aware he kept at least half of his overtime. What did he spend it on? If she had not Gerry's company to look forward to every Saturday, life would be dull indeed. Her face softened when she thought of Gerry, with his compliments and unspoken passion. She shivered, wondering what it would be like to feel Gerry's hands on her body. This is the way a woman should feel, she thought. Her mother had been right; she had married too young and now it was too late.

Or was it? Tomorrow she would talk to Mick. They must decide what was best for the children. She nodded her head. Yes, tomorrow she would talk to him. Get things sorted out. Then she frowned. What if Gerry didn't want a ready made family? There would be obstacles! Her mother for one . . . and Gerry's parents would hit the roof. Would he be man enough to stand up to them? To face excommunication from the church? Oh, she would worry about that when it happened, but tomorrow she would talk to Mick. That was the first step to take.

Hurrying home from nine o'clock Mass next morning, she paused on the edge of the kerb at the Springfield Road to allow a tram to pass. Puffing and panting, Belle Hanna stopped beside her.

'How's yer mam, Sarah?' she gasped breathlessly.

'Very well, thank you.' Sarah was abrupt. She found it hard to be civil to Belle. They had never found out who had written to the Bishop about Brendan and her mother, but Sarah was convinced it was Belle and kept her at a distance.

When they had crossed the road she was about to excuse herself and hurry on but Belle, with a sly sidelong glance, said, 'That was a nasty accident at the shipyard, wasn't it? Such a young man. Taken before he'd lived, ye could say.'

Matching her step to suit Belle's, Sarah cast about in her mind. Vaguely, she remembered Mick mentioning someone falling down the side of the ship and being killed. She remembered he had seemed very upset about it. 'Oh, yes, I remember. What was his name?' She was feeling her way because she was aware Belle was about to tell her something and did not want to show her ignorance.

'Sean Simpson. He leaves a young widow and child. They live in one of those old houses at Beechmount. But then, you'll have met them I'm sure, what with Mick being so good to them.' Again that sly glance from the corner of her eye.

Completely in the dark, Sarah agreed with her. 'Yes,

273

he's very good to anyone in need. He's very kind-hearted.'
She was wondering what on earth Belle meant, but she left
her in no doubt.

'Aye, it's not many men who would take a widow and
child down town every Saturday. Still ... I suppose you
don't mind, since you be up in yer mam's.' With a derisive
laugh and a nod of dismissal, Belle headed for her house,
leaving a bewildered Sarah to hurry home to her husband.

'I'll have to run or I'll be late,' he cried in exasperation.
He was surprised at Sarah, dallying down Malcomson
Street with Belle Hanna. He knew she did not like the
woman, and now because of her he would be late for
Mass.

Once inside the house, the rage bubbling up inside
Sarah erupted. How dare he! How dare he! 'Takes a
widow and child down town. Takes a widow and child
down town. Takes a widow and child down town.' She was
hissing the words and each was accompanied by a thump
on the back of the armchair with her fist, until Beth and
Eileen came into the room to stand and watch her, amazed.

'Takes a wid ...' Catching sight of the children, and
seeing fear in their eyes, she stopped chanting. With a
sickly smile, she held wide her arms to them and when
they ran to her, clasped them close and fought back the
tears. Now she knew why her husband needed extra
money. He had a fancy woman!

Mick was mystified. For two days Sarah had hardly looked
him in the face. At night she clung to her side of the bed
as if, should she accidentally touch him, she would get the
plague. Things had been bad before but this was awful.
Fear clouded his reasoning, making him unable to think
straight. Was she planning to leave him? She had spent
Sunday night and last night in the scullery, from the time
the children went to bed until it was time to retire for the
night. Then she lay on the edge of the bed, stiff as a board.
Now, tonight, she had been in there an hour. Surely there
was nothing left to clean? Perhaps if he went out for an
hour or two she would come into the kitchen and take a

rest. Reaching for his jacket, he pulled it on and opened the scullery door.

'Sarah, I'm goin' out for a while, I won't be late.'

Her lips tightened. He never told her where he was going now. That way he didn't have to tell her any lies. She conveniently forgot that it was a long time since she had shown any interest in where her husband went. She had been too absorbed in her own budding romance. Elbow deep in suds at the sink, she turned her head and looked him full in the face. The first time she had done so since Sunday morning.

'Are you goin' to see the Widow Simpson?' she asked quietly.

Any hope she'd harboured that Belle Hanna might be wrong, was quickly dashed. Mick's face blazed with colour and guilt was written all over it.

'What do you know about Maisie?' he gasped.

Maisie! Throwing back her head, a sound that was supposed to be a laugh escaped her lips. 'Well now, everyone else knows you take her down town every Saturday, so why not me, eh? Why not me? Did ye think no one would tell me?'

'Now listen, Sarah! You listen t'me. I can explain!' His voice was placating and he stepped towards her, hand held out beseechingly.

Backing away from him until she was against the yard door and could go no further, she cried shrilly, 'Don't . . . touch . . . me!'

Anger coursed through him. Gripping her roughly by the upper arms, he shook her and growled, 'I bet you don't say that t'Gerry.'

Her head came up and seeing contempt in her eyes, his hands fell limply to his sides. 'Ah, Sarah, what's to become of us? We can't go on like this. What are we goin' to do?' he cried despairingly.

Stabbing a finger into her chest, she replied, '*I* know what *I'm* goin' to do . . . I'm stayin' here with my kids. But I want you to get out.' The words were out of her mouth before she could stop them. Dear God, what had she done? Fingers pressed tightly to her lips she gazed at him, eyes huge in a face the colour of flour.

Mick actually reeled back, he was so shocked at her words. 'You can't mean that!'

Her heart wept but pride forbade her to back down. 'I do mean it. I suggest you pack you bags an' go now, while the kids are asleep. That way they won't be so upset.'

'Sarah, please, hear me out. I can explain.' His voice was thick with emotion, but for two days she had tortured herself with thoughts of the neighbours gossiping. She pictured them sniggering behind her back and her pride was hurt. There was no place for pity in her. Weary and sick at heart, she turned back to the sink. 'Get out. Go on! I don't care if I never see you again.'

When, reluctantly, he turned and left the scullery, she sagged against the sink. What had happened? Things had got out of control. How would she manage without him? What way would Gerry react? Tears of self-pity filled her eyes, but she fought them back. Time enough for tears when he was gone.

He descended the stairs carrying a bag and paused, undecided. She stood at the fireplace, gripping the mantelpiece so hard her knuckles showed white. In a broken voice, he said, 'Sarah . . . please let me explain.' Her back stiffened but she made no reply. Heavy at heart, he quietly left the house.

When the hall door closed on him, she sank down on to a chair at the table and, cradling her head in her arms, cried long and sore. Then, wiping her eyes, she berated herself. Isn't this what you wanted? Aren't you in love with Gerry? You should be glad he's gone. Now there's nothing to stop you and Gerry getting together. Why then did she feel as if her heart was breaking? She did not know . . . could not understand why she was so hurt, so stricken, when she was getting what she wanted – freedom to go to Gerry. But was he strong enough to face all the opposition that going off with a married woman would mean? His parents would object. Strongly. Very strongly. And the church . . . what about the church? It would be on their backs, trying to save their souls. Had she ever really believed that Gerry loved her? No! Lusted after her, yes, but love her . . .?

It was six weeks before Maggie found out about the separation. Six long miserable weeks for Sarah. Every Tuesday, Thursday and Saturday afternoons she spent at her mother's house, and how Maggie never guessed from things the children said, Sarah would never know. Probably because she was so wrapped up in thoughts of the coming baby. Every Saturday Mick had the two girls for the day, returning them at tea time, and although he did not know it, he was pushing Sarah closer and closer to Gerry. He visited her every afternoon when Maggie was taking her nap, and now there were no children to chaperone them on a Saturday.

It was Kathleen who unwittingly broke the bad news. Calling in to see her friend one afternoon, as was her custom, she asked, 'Has Mick left the shipyard, Sarah?'

Shaking her head, Sarah hoped she would not pursue the matter, but with a puzzled frown, Kathleen continued, 'I've seen him so often lately over Beechmount, I thought perhaps he was working on the building site there. You know, those new houses?'

Sarah sat on the arm of her mother's chair and put her arm around her. She realised the truth was about to come out and decided to break the news herself. 'Mam, I've a bit of bad news to tell you an' I don't want ye upsettin' yourself, 'cause I'm managin' all right.'

'What's wrong, Sarah? Is Mick ill?'

'No, no, nothing like that. It's just that . . . well . . . Mick an' I have separated.'

Maggie's heart sank but she wasn't surprised. Hadn't she seen this coming? 'Separated? Ah, Sarah. When did this happen?'

'Six weeks ago.'

'Six weeks?' Maggie's voice rose shrilly. 'And you never said?' Gazing wildly around the room, she cried,

'Where's the children?' As if they must be hiding somewhere.

'Mick takes them out every Saturday.'

'It's because of Gerry, isn't it?' Maggie's voice was accusing. 'Do you love him? His parents will be furious. And . . . they'll blame me. They'll think that I encouraged it.'

'I don't know, Mam. I'm all mixed up.' Sarah successfully hid the annoyance she felt. All her mother was worried about was what the Dochertys would think. What about her? Didn't she deserve some happiness?

During all this, Kathleen sat in stunned surprise. Now she wailed, 'I'm sorry, Sarah. Every time I open my mouth I put my big foot in it.'

'It's all right, Kathleen. She had to know sometime and she's better hearin' it from me.'

'Oh, you and Mick'll be back together again in no time. He's just jealous,' Kathleen assured her.

A flicker of a smile crossed Sarah's face. 'I'm afraid it's more serious than that, Kathleen. You see, Mick has met another woman. She lives in one of the old houses at Beechmount . . . that's why you see him so often. He's lodging with her.' She was glad her voice did not betray how much that hurt her. Admitting that Mick was living with another woman.

'Mick Ross with another woman!' Kathleen was scandalised at the very idea. 'I don't believe it! Why, he worships you.'

Shrugging, Sarah turned away. Ignorance was bliss. Kathleen was not aware that he had been forced to marry her or she would not have said that. Mick worship her? That was a laugh. He had been glad of the excuse to leave, couldn't get away quick enough, and in her heart she did not blame him. She had treated him abominably.

Maggie looked pale and drawn and Sarah said, 'Mam, please don't let this upset you. Remember what the doctor said. I'm sorry this had to happen just now, when you're not supposed to be worried.'

'I'm all right.' As Sarah hovered anxiously over her,

Maggie repeated, 'I'm all right. But if Kathleen doesn't mind me leaving her, I'll go up for my nap now.'

At once Kathleen rose to her feet. 'Not at all, Maggie. Not at all! I'll come over tomorrow an' see how ye are. Away ye go an' have a nice wee rest.'

When Maggie left the room, seeing Sarah was abstracted, Kathleen made her excuses and went off to town, leaving her sad and depressed.

In the coolness of her room Maggie lay on the bed. She had been ordered to rest every afternoon and she obeyed the doctor religiously. Oh, how she longed to hold this baby in her arms. It would be wonderful to feel strong again. Although her body was resting, her mind was in turmoil. Poor Mick. Separated from the three people he loved best in the world. Not for one minute did she believe he was in love with another woman and her heart cried for him. Her ears pricked up when she heard the back door open and close, steathily. There was the cause of the trouble, creeping in like a thief in the night. Why, for two pins she would go down and confront them. Half rising from the bed she started to swing her legs to the floor, then sank back again. She could not take the chance, not with her blood pressure causing concern. Wearily she closed her eyes and soon fell into an uneasy doze.

Quiet though he was, Sarah heard Gerry enter the kitchen, but remained at the sink. Standing behind her, he put his arms around her and cupped her breasts in his hands. With her eyes closed, she tried to work up some emotion, some passion for him, but in vain. It surprised her how little he affected her. Before they had touched, the very idea of it had sent shivers down her spine, but now he left her cold. Nevertheless, she turned in his arms and raised her face hungrily for his kisses. She needed to be wanted, needed comfort. Lately Gerry was hinting at more than kisses, but having trapped one man that way she kept him at a distance. Somehow she did not trust Gerry to make an honest woman of her if she should fall pregnant. In her heart she knew he was just using her to pass the time, so when he reminded her that you never missed a slice of a cut loaf, she remained firm. Even though he knew Mick was out of the house, he never referred to it. Nor did he make any promises concerning the future and she was too proud to prompt him. She knew she should chase him off, tell him to get out of her life, but then she would have no one. So she allowed him to kiss her while trying to keep at bay thoughts of her husband with another woman. Why did it hurt so much thinking of Mick with another woman, when she did not love him? It must be her pride. That's what was wrong, her pride was hurt!

Holding her away from him, Gerry looked at her askance. 'You're miles away,' he chided.

'I'm sorry,' she apologised, and slipping from his arms turned back to the sink. 'I'm tired.'

Taking her gently by the arm, he led her towards the hall. 'Come into the sitting room and rest for a while,' he coaxed.

She pulled herself free and once again returned to the sink. 'No, I've a lot to do before I go home.'

He watched her through narrowed eyes. 'Sarah?' His voice was soft.

'Yes?' Turning her head, she met his gaze.

'We can't go on like this.'

'What do you mean?' Her lips tightened and her eyes flashed dangerously.

'You know what I mean.' He ignored the warning signs, he was too angry; time was passing and he was getting nowhere with Sarah.

'Spell it out for me, Gerry,' she spat at him.

'All right, I will. You've kept me on a string all summer and I'm getting tired of waiting.'

'Waiting for what, Gerry?'

'For you to make up your mind about me.'

Not a word of reassurance. No! Just that he was tired of waiting. Waiting for what? Sex? Disappointment swept over her, but she pushed it away and asked, 'Is this an ultimatum, Gerry?'

With an exaggerated sigh, he answered regretfully, 'Yes, I think it is.'

Drying her hands very deliberately on her apron, she went to the back door and opened it. 'Goodbye, Gerry.'

For some moments he stood in silence, looking at her. She had lost weight, but this just emphasised her high cheek bones, making her more beautiful. He felt desire rise in his loins and was tempted to offer her security. Then he thought of her children and hesitated, not wanting a ready-made family. Would Mick let her take the girls? He had heard that there was another woman involved, but it was too risky; he was too young to rear another man's children. With a shrug he passed her and she closed the door with a sigh.

To her surprise, she was relieved it was over. No more shame and recriminations. She would be able to go to confession and make her peace with God, and what a relief that would be. She missed having the security of her religion behind her. Mick and she had always received the sacraments together, had tried to live up to their religion, but she had spoilt all that, with her infatuation for Gerry.

Shame filled her when she thought how long and patiently her husband had waited for her to turn to him. It couldn't have been easy for him ... no wonder he had found another woman. It was all her fault. What had possessed her? It must have been the sun. They were not used to so much sun. It had been such a long, hot summer. It must have been summer madness.

Every Saturday when Mick returned with the children, he was torn in two. He sent Sarah money every week in an envelope pinned to the inside of Beth's coat, and when he pinned it on the child always started to cry. She knew he was about to leave them and when Eileen cried in sympathy with her it nearly broke his heart. Sometimes he decided he would have to stop seeing them, they were so upset, but the day spent with them was the highlight of his week and he found that he could not give it up. Since he had left the house, he had seen Sarah on two occasions, but she had been unaware of him. Her appearance troubled him: the hollow cheeks, the dark-ringed eyes. She was losing too much weight, her clothes hung on her. What had happened to all the joy and laughter Gerry used to bring her?

Given the chance again, he knew he would not leave the house. That was something he regretted deeply. She had taken him unawares. He should have stayed and put the onus on her. Let her decide what to do about Gerry. But no, fool that he was he had let her put him out. Another thing he regretted was not making her listen to the tale of how he became involved with Maisie. She meant nothing to him except as a friend, but he had to admit to himself it was her companionship that had kept him sane. Without her and her young son, Donald, he would have hit the bottle.

As usual when he entered the house a meal was ready for him. He smiled gratefully at Maisie, but she detected the sorrow in his eyes. She marvelled how anyone could be so stupid as to put a man like Mick out. This Sarah must be a fool, or else Gerry must be quite a man. When her husband had been killed, it was Mick who had organised a collection for her and brought the money to her. When he saw the poor circumstances she and her son lived in, he had returned again and again to help her. Maisie knew he never thought of her as a woman, she was just a friend, a comrade, someone in need of help.

Although Maisie did not know it, Sarah and she had started off married life in the same way. Swept off their feet and wed when just seventeen, but there the likeness ended. The apple of her father's eye, Maisie had been deeply ashamed of her own behaviour and he had never forgiven her. Sean had bitterly resented being pushed into marriage at eighteen and had taken out his frustrations on his young pregnant wife. He had ill-treated her so badly she had left him and returned to her parents' home. Her mother would have allowed her to stay but her father had still been bitter and had shown her the door. He had never gotten over the shock of his only daughter having to get married and, although usually a compassionate man, had told her, 'You've made your bed, now lie on it.'

It was Sean's mother, a widow, who had taken pity on her and Maisie had lived with her until the baby was born. Then she had made her second mistake. She had let Sean sweet talk her into giving him a second chance. Soon the beatings had started again, and this time she had a child to protect and worry about. Although she would have denied it, she was relieved at Sean's death. Drink had been his weakness. Sober he was gentle, but even a couple of pints turned him into a mean aggressive brute. The morning he had fallen to his death, he was still half drunk from the night before and this was why Mick felt so guilty. If he had not felt sorry for the young lad and covered for him, he would have surely been sacked but would have been alive today. At least that was how Mick saw it and he felt obliged to help Maisie and young Donald all he could.

Since Sean's death Maisie had blossomed. Gone was the haunted look and the air of despair. Her slightly protuberant blue eyes were clear and contented, and her short blonde hair curled close to her head and shone like spun gold when the light caught it. The only cloud on her horizon was her love for Mick because she knew he loved his wife and that she did not stand a chance with him. Unless, of course, Sarah was stupid enough really to let him go.

Pushing his plate to one side, Mick cried, 'Ah, Maisie, I'm sorry, but it sticks in me throat.'

She knew he did not mean that there was something wrong with the food and asked, 'Did something happen?'

'Ah, no more than usual, but today Beth asked me if I still loved her. How can you convince a child ye love her when ye leave her in tears every week?' He sat with bowed head and she longed to go to him, offer him comfort, but was afraid of betraying her feelings.

Rising from the table, he moved to the fireside to sit gazing blankly into the fire. With an involuntary movement Maisie stepped towards him, hand outstretched, but stopped herself in time and started to clear the table. Knowing he liked her, she was aware that in his present dejected state she could probably seduce him, but she did not want him to feel obligated to her. Once Sarah was out of the picture, that would be a different matter. Then she would make him realise that second best could be all right. Not for the first time she wondered what Sarah looked like.

She was to find out the next morning. Usually an early riser, she went to eight o'clock Mass every Sunday morning but this particular Sunday she slept in. Mick always went to ten o'clock Mass in St Pauls, so she walked down there with him.

Every Sunday saw Sarah at ten o'clock Mass in Clonard Monastery, but this particular Sunday Eileen was poorly, so leaving her next-door with May Murphy, she nipped over to St Paul's Church, with Beth by the hand. She did not like going upstairs to the balcony that surrounded St Paul's but to humour Beth she climbed the stairs. She was kneeling, elbows on the pew in front of her, head in hands, when Beth let out an excited yell.

'There's Daddy, Mam. There's my daddy.'

'Hush, Beth.' Sarah's face was scarlet as heads turned in surprise. The priest coming out to the altar saved her from further embarrassment as the congregation rose and Mass began.

Casting surreptitious glances across the church towards where Beth had pointed, Sarah at last saw Mick, staring fixedly at her. She half smiled before realising the blonde girl by his side might be the young widow, Maisie. Never had a Mass seemed so long; she could not pray and in spite of herself her eyes kept straying in her husband's direction. He appeared to have forgotten she existed because after the first look he kept his head bowed in prayer.

Mick was in fact very much aware of Sarah, but was worrying about Eileen. Was she ill? Why had Sarah left her? Was she in the house on her own?

When the Mass ended, Sarah hurried Beth down the stairs, hoping to avoid Mick, but quick though she was, he was quicker. He was waiting outside and she had obviously guessed correctly; the blonde and a young boy stood with him. She would have hurried past with a nod but Beth ran to her father and he swung her up in his arms.

'Where's Eileen? Is she sick?' he asked anxiously.

'No, she has a slight cold. May Murphy's lookin' after her.'

Forced to stop, Sarah looked pointedly at Maisie and Mick remembered his manners. 'Sarah, this is Maisie Simpson. Maisie, this is my wife, Sarah.'

The two women eyed each other. Sarah saw a pert, pretty face, with large cornflower blue eyes, and noted that she was a natural blonde. And Maisie knew now why Mick never noticed her as a woman. Sarah was beautiful! Even with shadows under her eyes and a sad droop to her lips, she was beautiful. Mick glanced uneasily from one to the other of them. Why did they not speak? He relaxed when Sarah nodded her head and Maisie nodded back.

'I'll go on home, Mick.' Grabbing a reluctant Donald by the hand, Maisie dragged him away and hurried up Cavendish Street. Tears blinded her. She would never stand a chance with Mick! Never! Sarah was beautiful.

Mick did not even see her go. He was too aware of the closeness of Sarah. If she had not been conscious of the covert glances being cast in their direction, she might have seen the longing in his eyes, but catching sight of Belle Hanna in a huddle with other women, she was mortified. How dare he flaunt his fancy-woman in front of her? It just showed how little he cared. Reaching for her daughter, she tried to remove her forcibly from his arms. Beth's arms tightened around her father's neck and Sarah felt tears of frustration fill her eyes.

'Why can't you leave me alone?' she cried.

Seeing her distress, he loosened Beth's hold on him. 'Go home with your mam, love, an' I'll bring you a surprise next Saturday.'

Beth's lip trembled, but at the mention of a surprise, she asked, 'What, Dad? What will ye bring me?'

He chucked her under the chin and chided, 'It won't be a surprise if I tell you. Wait an' see, love.'

285

Without another word Sarah took Beth's hand and hurried down the Falls Road, stumbling in her haste, aware that he was standing looking after her. He watched until they were out of sight, barely acknowledging people who spoke to him, and when he could no longer see his wife and daughter, he turned and walked up the Falls Road. He did not consciously head for Maggie's house, but when he arrived at her door she was not surprised. Opening the door to his knock, Maggie reached for his hands in silent sympathy. She drew him along the hall into the living room. Then, pushing him down on to a chair, she clasped him to her bosom and rocked him as she would a hurt child.

'There, son. There now.'

Only then did he realise he was crying. 'I love her, Maggie. I know she never loved me, but she cared.'

'Oh, yes, she cares all right,' Maggie consoled him. 'She just can't see the forest for the trees.'

'Does he still come in?' He jerked his head towards Dochertys' house.

Thinking of Gerry creeping into the house the day before, Maggie sadly nodded her head.

Digging into his trouser pocket, Mick produced a handkerchief, wiped his eyes and blew his nose. 'I'm sorry, Maggie. I'm ashamed of meself. I don't know what came over me.'

'Never be ashamed of true emotion, son,' she replied. 'I'll make us a cup of tea.' And she left him alone, so that he could pull himself together.

As she waited for the kettle to boil, she made a pact with herself. First she must find out where the widow fitted into things and then she would have it out with Sarah. Bad enough her risking her own soul, but to drive Mick into another woman's arms! Why, she was pulling him, the widow, and Gerry down with her. Yes. She would have to make Sarah see sense. But first she must talk to Mick. They drank the tea in silence, Mick ashamed of his outburst and Maggie sorting out her thoughts.

At last she said, 'I must ask you a question. Now, I don't

want you to think I'm being nosy, because I'm not.' She paused then said, 'Would you be willing to take Sarah back or are you committed to this young widow?'

He looked stunned. 'Committed to Maisie? Heavens no, Maggie, I just lodge in her house. Listen, let me explain. Maisie's husband Sean was foolish where drink was concerned. Sober he was the nicest bloke ye could hope t'meet, but a few pints and he was a different person. A few months before he died, he started comin' t'work still half drunk from the night before, an' I covered for him.' He looked at her piteously. 'I didn't think I was doin' any harm, Maggie. I didn't want him to lose his job. But when he fell t'his death, I was weighed down with guilt. Ye see, I felt if I hadn't covered for him he would have gotten the sack and would still be alive.'

Sighing deeply, he paused for thought before continuing, 'I lifted a collection for his widow an' went to see her. Normally I would have confided in Sarah, but she was so wrapped up in Gerry, she didn't want to know. So I went up to Beechmount an' met Maisie for the first time.' Again he met her eyes, asking for understanding. 'Ah, Maggie! You should have seen the conditions her an' the child were livin' in. The house was practically empty. It seems Sean was pawnin' things t'get money for drink. As for Maisie . . . she was skin and bone. The lad was all right. He obviously got whatever food was goin'. She was so glad of the money, Maggie. "The first thing I'm goin' to do is buy Donald clothes," she said, and she looked so frail I offered to go down town with her. I kept goin' back . . . but only 'cause she needed help. But I swear that was the only reason! Honest to God, Maggie.' He raised his brow at her. 'You understand?'

She nodded. 'Carry on, son.'

'Well, when Sarah asked me to leave the house . . .'

Maggie interrupted him. 'Sarah asked you to leave the house?'

Frowning, he nodded, his eyes questioning her.

'I thought you left because of the widow.' She sounded puzzled.

'Well, in a way ... it was because of Maisie. Ye see, someone told Sarah about me taking Maisie down town every Saturday ... when she was up here with you, an' she wouldn't give me a chance to explain.'

'Who told her?'

'I'm not sure ... but I think it was Belle Hanna.'

Maggie nodded: she could understand how Sarah would react. Her proud Sarah. The neighbours talking behind her back would infuriate her, cause her to hit out blindly. She probably regretted asking him to leave, but she would never admit it. No, she would never admit it.

'Continue, son.'

'I went down to the Salvation Army Hostel, but it was awful. So when Maisie offered me her spare room, I was glad to move in. Mind you, I pay for my keep an' she's glad of the money.' Draining his cup, he placed it on the table and rose to his feet. 'Thanks for listenin' to me, Maggie. I feel better for gettin' it off me chest. I'll be on me way.'

She walked to the door with him. 'I'll have a word with Sarah. Mind you, you are not without blame, so try and meet her halfway.'

'Halfway? Maggie, if she gives me a sign, I'll crawl back on my hands an' knees.'

Maggie wanted to warn him, say: 'No! Sarah would not admire you for that.' But she decided he was upset enough without her adding to his pain.

He tried to smile in farewell, but only managed a sickly grimace. At the gate he lifted his hand in salute, then squaring his shoulders he strode up the street.

May Murphy was worried when Sarah arrived back from Mass and she saw how white and shaken she was. `What's wrong? Are you feelin' sick, Sarah?' she inquired anxiously.

'Just a headache, May.' Headache? Heartache would be more like it! 'I'll be all right when I get a cup of tea.'

'Come on in an' I'll make you a cuppa,' May offered, opening the door wide and motioning her inside.

Sarah shook her head. Friendly as May and she had become, she did not trust her to keep a secret. What if in her depressed state she confided any of her feelings to May, and May told Belle Hanna? She shuddered at the very idea of it and May cried, 'You're shiverin'! Come on in, Sarah.'

'No, thanks all the same, May. I'll be OK. Thanks for mindin' Eileen for me. I hope I can return the favour sometime.'

'I'll mind them any time, Sarah. Any time. You know that.'

May watched until Sarah entered her own house then went indoors. She was sad that Mick and Sarah were separated, and was always glad to help Sarah in any way she could. She and her husband were very fond of their next-door neighbours and looked on the children as the grandchildren they would never have. Bitterly regretting the day she had told Belle about seeing Maggie in the young priest's arms, May was forever trying to make amends. Imagine Belle having the cheek to write to the Bishop! How she'd had the nerve May would never know. Because if you dipped a spider in ink and let it run over a sheet of notepaper, it would look better than Belle's writing. But write she did and received an answer telling her the matter would be looked into. To May's shame the priest was never seen in Waterford Street again. Not even when Maggie was married.

Guilt had driven May up Clonard Street to the monastery to confession. She choose Father O'Conner to confess to; him being old and saintly, she thought he would go easy on her. After hearing her out in silence, he gave her absolution. Then for her penance, he told her to take a feather pillow up to the Falls Park one morning and shake all the feathers out. She was to return and tell him when she had done it. Mystified, May did as she was bid. Catching the tram early one morning, she went to the park and walked until she was sure none of the early morning walkers could see her. Then she took an old pillow from her bag (she had decided there was no sense in destroying a good pillow) and shook all the feathers free from the side she had cut open. She watched as the wind lifted them, sending them in all directions. Who would have thought a pillow could hold so many feathers? Why, it's like a snow storm, she thought, bemused. She was well pleased with herself, having figured out that the reason Father O'Conner had given her such a penance was because of the shame of being seen. Yet she had accomplished the deed without one spectator! Proud of herself, she returned to confession the following Saturday and told Father O'Conner what she had done.

'Good girl!'

Surprised at his praise, she smiled smugly, although she could not see anything wonderful about her actions. Her surprise turned to dismay when next he spoke. 'Now, this week I want you to go up and gather each and every feather up again.'

On the other side of the grille, May's mouth gaped open. 'But Father . . . that's impossible.'

'I know it is, child. And that's what happens when you spread a wee bit of scandal. Whether it's true or not doesn't matter. It causes pain and has ruined many a decent person's life. Because, you see, the spoken word can never be recalled.'

'Oh, Father, I'm sorry.' May's tears were genuine, she was truly sorry.

'Have you learnt a lesson from all this?' he asked sternly.

'I have, Father! Oh, indeed I have.'

'Go in peace, child.'

Trying hard to turn over a new leaf, May avoided Belle whenever she could and when she found herself dying to pass on a tit-bit of scandal, thought of the feather pillow and bit on her tongue.

*

Sarah's hands were shaking as she made herself a cup of tea. The children were whining for her attention, but she did not even hear them, so deep was her misery. How could Mick do this to her? She would not have believed he could be so cruel. How he must hate her! The thing she found hardest to bear was the fact that it was all her own fault. She had brought it all on herself.

A scream from Eileen sent her rushing from the scullery. Beth stood in the middle of the kitchen clutching a rag doll her father had bought her and Eileen was trying to pull it from her arms.

'Mammy . . . it's my doll! Daddy bought it for me,' Beth screamed, hitting out at Eileen.

Lifting Eileen up in her arms, Sarah shushed her. 'Where's your doll, pet? Beth, where's Eileen's doll?'

'Don't know.'

'Try an' find it for her, love.' And when Beth made no movement, she pleaded, 'Please, love?'

With a mutinous look on her face, Beth went into the back room and returned with the doll. Sitting on the settee, Sarah gathered both children close and rocked them gently. Poor little mites! They did not know what was wrong and she was to blame. To think she had imagined herself in love with Gerry. How could she have been so foolish? To have lost Mick's respect all because of Gerry. Not his love, no, he had never loved her, but he would have been faithful to her, she knew. Until she had seen Mick and the widow, side by side, she had not realised how, unconsciously, she was taking it for granted they would somehow come together again. After all, they were Catholics! There could be no divorce. And Mick was such a devout Catholic. But she had pushed him too far. By bringing the widow to church with him, he was showing where his interest lay. Now it was up to her to get a job so that he did not have to send her so much money. He was generous. Too generous. It wasn't fair, everything was her fault, so she must get a job.

If she had listened to her mother, she would be a saleslady today. Short hours, light work – better than working in the weaving shop from eight to six. She could not leave the children all day. No, she must get a part-time job in the Blackstaff, from eight to one or one to six. Tomorrow she would ask May if she would look after the children while she worked. She nodded her head. Yes, tomorrow she would have a chat with May, and if she was willing to mind the children then Sarah would go to the Blackstaff and see if she could get started. It wouldn't be easy working and bringing the kids up on her own but at least it would keep her occupied.

Slowly, the realisation that she was pulling her young son off his feet seeped through the misery that engulfed Maisie. Drawing to a halt, she drew the bewildered, whimpering child close.

'It's all right, love. It's all right.'

'I want to stay with Uncle Mick,' he wailed.

'Later, love . . . he'll follow us home later.'

But would he? Surely that fool of a wife of his would see the yearning in his eyes and take him home. How could she resist him? If only he would give *her* a chance. She'd soon show him. The jealousy that had swamped her when Mick introduced her to his wife had taken her unawares. Beautiful, haughty and cold she'd labelled her, but the yearning that emanated from Mick had caught Maisie in the raw. Had anyone noticed her anguish? No . . . Sarah was too busy trying to untangle her young daughter from her husband's arms to notice and Mick had only eyes for his wife. She'd have to be careful; if he became aware how she felt about him, he'd be off back to the Salvation Army Hostel. It would never dawn on him to use her. He was too decent, too kind, and a very devout Catholic.

Had she really thought that he would turn to her? What a fool she was. Why, he hadn't even noticed when she had made her excuses and walked away. He had been too wrapped up in the antics of his wife. And *she*, the cold bitch, couldn't get away from him quick enough! Still . . . there was always hope. Sarah might decide to live in sin with the great Gerry and then it would be up to her to win Mick over. It would not be easy; he was so devout. Sin would seem an insurmountable barrier to him, but she was no stranger to men's needs and would certainly do her best to win him.

As she stuffed the chicken for the mid-day meal, her ears strained for the sound of his footsteps. At last she heard them and breathed a sigh of relief. Slow, dragging, not his usual measured tread. But at least he was here. She watched him covertly as he removed his coat, but with just a nod of greeting, he tousled Donald's hair and climbed the stairs to his bedroom, closing the door.

Well, obviously there had been no great reunion. He looked miserable. Maisie's mind was working overtime as she chopped cabbage and peeled potatoes. Should she approach him? Would he be affronted and leave the house? She turned the idea over in her mind. It was worth a try. If he was shocked she would laugh it off, pretend she was bluffing. Who knows? This could be her big day.

Every Sunday afternoon Donald went to her friend Mary's house to play with her children, so after dinner she would try her luck. With this in mind, while the dinner was cooking, she locked herself in the scullery and washed herself down. Next, she retired to her bedroom, powdering and perfuming herself and dressing in her best underwear; not very fancy, but clean. The only other alternative would be to approach Mick in the nude and that would never do, although she had a good enough body to face any man. She laughed softly at the idea. Why, the shock would probably kill him. Once Donald left the house, she would discard her old jumper and skirt, put on her best frock and . . . do what comes naturally.

At dinner, the way Mick played with his food brought home to Maisie just how miserable he was. Never before had anything affected his appetite to this extent. At last he pushed the plate away from him.

'I'm sorry, Maisie. I'm not hungry. Put the leg to one side an' I'll eat it later.'

When he rose and reached for his coat she almost cried

aloud. All her plans were in vain. If he went out now, he would be gone all afternoon.

Her son came to her rescue. 'Uncle Mick . . . can I come too?'

'Aren't you goin' to visit young Patrick?'

'I want to come with you!'

Mick looked at her with raised eyebrows. In a quandary, she groped about for a reason to delay him.

'Donald . . . young Pat's expectin' you,' she reminded her son, and then turned a wan look on Mick. 'I don't feel very well . . . could you take Donald round to Mary's an' while you're there ask her for a stomach powder for me? Would that be too much trouble?'

At once he was all concern, just as she had known he would be. 'No trouble at all, Maisie. Are you very bad? Was it something you ate?'

'I'm not sure . . . I just feel queasy.'

'Will May have a powder?'

'May is always prepared . . . she'll have a powder.'

'You go on t'bed, I'll be back as quickly as I can.'

When the door closed on them Maisie jumped to her feet. He would be back in about fifteen minutes. She must be ready for him. At least now she did not have to worry about approaching him. When he returned she would be in bed, clasping a hand to her brow, and from then on she'd play it by ear.

The house was dark and quiet when Mick returned some half hour later. Contrary to what Maisie had said, Mary had not had the required powder and he had walked to a shop that he knew would be open to obtain it. Had Maisie fallen asleep without it? Tip-toeing up the stairs, he tapped lightly on the bedroom door.

'Maisie . . . are you awake?' he whispered.

'Come on in, Mick.' Her voice, low with a hint of pain in it, reached him and he entered the room. She lay with bedclothes modestly up to her chin, a hand to her brow.

'Did you get the powder?'

'Yes . . . Mary hadn't any, so I went down to the

294

Springfield Road for it. That's what kept me. Are you no better?'

A slight shake of the head answered his question and he moved closer and hovered beside the bed, brandishing the small sachet of powder in the air. 'What do you take with this? Water? Milk?'

'Just mix it in a little water, please.'

When he returned with the mixture, she was sitting up in bed and he noticed that her shoulders were bare except for shoelace straps and the material of her nightdress was very fine. He averted his eyes as he became aware how full her bust was, how white her skin.

'Thank you, Mick.'

When he handed her the glass, their fingers touched and he pulled his hand quickly away at the contact. What on earth was he thinking of? Maisie was ill and here he was acting like a fool.

'Oh . . .' As she doubled over in pain he moved closer and self-consciously placed an arm around her shoulders.

'It is very bad? Will I go for the doctor?' He trembled at the feel of her skin, soft as silk under his rough hand; her hair brushing his cheek.

'No . . . no, that won't be necessary. Just hold me 'til the powder works.' Sitting on the edge of the bed, he gathered her close. She did not have to feign dizziness, his nearness sent her blood racing. She whispered shakily, 'Mick . . . does my stomach feel swelled to you?'

Gently his hand travelled across her nightdress, feeling the contours of her stomach. She heard him gulp and his breathing quicken.

'Mick . . .'

Feeling dazed, he raised unfocused eyes to her face. Her lips trembled close to his. Without further thought he kissed her and when Maisie's arms crept up around his neck, he was lost.

That night as he lay in bed he was very aware of Maisie on the other side of the wall. In spite of the shame he felt at the betrayal of his marriage vows, excitement kept sleep at bay as he recalled Maisie's reaction to his kiss.

295

Completely uninhibited, she had taken him to heights of passion such as he had never known before; so different from Sarah. Still, it mustn't happen again. Would they be able to put it behind them, go on as before? Perhaps he should move out. The very thought of moving back to the Salvation Army Hostel filled him with dismay. Was it really necessary? He groaned . . . he'd sleep on it. That's if he was able to sleep.

Next morning when Maisie descended the stairs he was gone. The evening before had been spent in uneasy harmony, with Mick avoiding any contact with her and Donald receiving all his attention. She could see that he regretted his actions. What would he do? She spent a miserable day as she pictured him moving out of the house. She was aware that Mick had enjoyed himself but knew that he would now be wrapped in guilt at the sin he had committed. Had he enjoyed it enough to come back for more?

The day dragged for Mick; his mind was in turmoil. He would have to go back to the Salvation Army Hostel. How could he live under the same roof as Maisie after his actions the day before? She had been ill and vulnerable and he had taken advantage of her. He was ashamed of himself. Ashamed of the fact that he had enjoyed committing sin . . . and had been the cause of her sinning also. How could he face her?

It was with dread that he entered the house that night. However, Maisie was her usual self; no reproachful looks, no recriminations. Recounting the day's happenings as if yesterday afternoon had never happened. He ate his meal in silence, all the while arguing with himself. Surely he must leave the house? If there was a chance that his marriage could be saved he must leave Maisie's home. He now knew what was wrong with his marriage. He wasn't satisfying Sarah. No wonder she had turned to Gerry.

Before the evening meal he had tried to apologise but Maisie covered his mouth with her hand. 'It takes two, Mick. Don't have any regrets. I haven't . . . I'm glad it happened.' Taking the blame on her own shoulders, she assured him, 'I needed comfort and you gave it to me and that's the end of it. It was just one of those unforeseen things!'

Relieved, he agreed with her . . . it had been an accident and mustn't happen again. However, this was easier said than done. During the meal his eyes kept straying to the close-fitting sweater that she wore, and remembering the soft silky feel of her breasts, excitement tightened his loins. In order to resist temptation, as soon as he had finished eating he excused himself. 'I think I'll go to the pictures.'

He went to the second house at the Broadway Cinema. The film was boring and his thoughts kept straying to Maisie. Would she be in bed when he got home? He hoped so! Otherwise he might not be able to curb the need within him. She had opened a door for him and he wanted more. The realisation that he must move out of the house filled him with misery. If he didn't leave the house temptation might prove too much for him. He'd have to go. It was unthinkable that he and Maisie should have an affair. What about his marriage vows? But then . . . what if Sarah went off with Gerry?

Long after midnight Maisie heard him enter the house and was not fooled. She knew that he was fighting temptation; staying out until she was safely in bed. When he paused outside her bedroom door she held her breath, willing him to enter the room, but after a few seconds he entered his own, closing the door gently. Aware that he would not repulse her, she rose from the bed and pulled on her old worn dressing-gown, smiling wryly to herself. Not exactly the gown to cause excitement. The tuffted lines of the candlewick material were worn almost flat and it was washed colourless, but it was all she had.

However, once out on the small landing she hesitated. Would he think her a trollop? How could he think anything else, the way she was tricking him? With these thoughts she proceeded down the stairs; she couldn't risk driving him from the house. The next move must come from him.

She was sitting huddled over the remains of the fire, a

cup of tea clasped in her hand, when she heard him on the stairs. His voice reached her in a whisper.

'Are you all right, Maisie? I heard you come downstairs an' . . .'

'I'm all right, Mick. I just fancied a cup of tea. Will I pour you one?'

'I'll get it, Maisie. You sit there.'

Soon he was sitting facing her. Placing the mug of tea on the hearth, he leant forward, his gaze earnest. 'Maisie . . . please understand . . . I must move out.'

'I know . . . I'm sorry.' Her voice was sad.

'Not as sorry as I am! I'll miss you and Donald.'

'Well then, don't go. We can forget yesterday afternoon. Please, Mick, stay.'

'Maisie, honestly . . . I never meant to take advantage of you.'

'Ah, Mick I know that,' she assured him. 'We're two lonely people, but it needn't happen again. I'll keep out of your way. Please don't leave.'

'Maisie . . . you don't understand how it is with men.'

Oh, didn't she? Didn't she just!

He continued, 'Much as I love Sarah, I'd find it hard to live under the same roof and stay away from ye. It took all my will power to pass your door tonight.'

Her heart was thumping so violently against her ribs, she was sure he must hear it. What was he saying? Did he mean . . .

'So ye see, Maisie, I must move out.'

She was out of the chair and on her knees beside him. He tensed, fists clenched on his thighs, and she covered them with her hands.

'Don't go, Mick. We're adults and we won't be hurtin' anyone.'

'Maisie, I have nothing to offer you. If Sarah says the word I'll go back. I've the kids t'think about.'

'There'll be no ties, Mick. I understand the situation an' I'll take what comes.'

Rising to her feet she removed the dressing gown and he sat gazing up at her. At the short nightdress that hid

298

nothing. This was wrong, this was a sin his conscience was telling him, but his flesh was becoming excited. When he rose and reached for her, his conscience lost the battle. She turned to lead the way upstairs and he eagerly followed her.

CHAPTER ELEVEN

Before Maggie had a chance to talk to Sarah, something happened. On Monday morning she awoke with a cramped sensation in her stomach; sharp tight pains that made her grimace. Rising, she dressed slowly and was halfway down the stairs when a sharp pain doubled her in two by its severity. She clung to the banister until it passed and the dizziness left her, then made her way down the remainder of the stairs into the hall. It was half-past seven, a wet miserable morning, and she was afraid, very afraid. Should she wait until Kathleen made her daily morning call? Indeed, dare she wait? No! She must not take chances. The doctors thought she had another four weeks to go but they could be wrong or the baby could decide to come early. That was no ordinary pain she had just experienced. If she recalled correctly, she had started labour and although she knew it might take a long time for the baby to arrive, she wanted assurance that everything was all right.

Mrs Docherty had told her to bang on the wall if she ever needed help and this she proceeded to do. She needed to catch them before they left the house at eight o'clock to go to work. It was Annie herself who came to the door and Maggie admitted her with apologies which her neighbour waved away. As they walked down the hall another pain gripped Maggie and, putting an arm around her, Annie supported her until it passed and then assisted her into the sitting room. Settling her on the settee, she pressed her hand reassuringly.

'I'll phone the doctor,' she said gently, 'and send Gerry over for Kathleen. Doctor Hughes is your doctor, isn't he?'

When Maggie nodded, Annie squeezed her shoulder sympathetically. 'I won't be long. You're going to be all right.' And she hurried out, grateful that she had a phone. Maggie was in labour!

Sitting beside the bed, Kathleen gripped her friend's hand tightly every time she had a contraction. 'Poor dear,' she sympathised, 'It'll be like havin' a first baby, after all these years. You'll be glad to get it over with.'

'I only hope it's normal,' Maggie whispered. 'I've worried, you know, with me being so old. How I've worried! Do you think Barney will accept it if it's deformed?' Her eyes clung to her friends, seeking reassurance.

'Don't talk like that!' Kathleen admonished her. 'It'll be all right! Just wait ... this time t'marra you'll wonder what all the fuss was about.'

'I don't care how long it takes or how much I suffer. I just pray the baby is normal ... Ahhh ...' Maggie clamped her lips tightly together as a pain gripped her and she clung fiercely to Kathleen's hand.

After what seemed an eternity Doctor Hughes arrived and Kathleen hurried to let him in. He smiled reassuringly when he was examining Maggie, but once finished he beckoned Kathleen out into the hall.

'I want to know if anything's wrong, doctor,' Maggie shouted indignantly. 'I'm not a child!'

With a wry smile he entered the room again and said resignedly, 'All right, Maggie! I'm sending for the ambulance. The baby isn't lying right and the hospital is the best place for you.'

'Will the baby live?' Maggie was remembering the son she had not seen and was filled with foreboding; he, too, had come early.

He heard the fear in her voice and reassured her. 'The

baby's heart is as strong as a sledge hammer, Maggie. I'll go now and phone the ambulance.' He only hoped she herself would be up to the strain because he could see a long hard fight ahead.

Kathleen accompanied him to the door. 'Will Maggie be all right?'

'It's in God's hands, Mrs Rafferty. It's in God's hands,' he confided. And at his words Kathleen's blood ran cold and goose bumps rose on her arms.

The ambulance came quickly, and before accompanying Maggie to the hospital, Kathleen gave her oldest son a message to deliver to Sarah. He attended St Finian's School which was down the Falls Road near Waterford Street and could call into Sarah's on the way to school. In the note Kathleen just said the baby was coming early and her mother was in the hospital. Not wanting to worry Sarah unnecessarily, she did not mention anything unusual. So Sarah took her time: she went to the shops and tidied the house, before leaving the children with May and heading for the hospital. From experience she knew babies took their time coming into the world and felt her mam could not be in a better place than the Royal Victoria Hospital. Her mother would be glad the baby was coming early. Her longing to hold this child in her arms was very apparent. Both Beth and Eileen had been delivered at home by Nurse Morgan, the local midwife, but with the infant mortality rate so high in Belfast, hospital was the best place for Maggie on account of her age.

Inside the hospital, Sarah paused to get her bearings and the first person she saw was her Uncle Brendan, deep in conversation with another priest who looked familiar. Catching sight of her, Brendan said something to his companion. He turned and glanced in her direction, and she recognised Father O'Conner. With a brief nod of acknowledgement at her, Father O'Conner strode off down the corridor and Brendan approached Sarah.

'I didn't know you were home, Uncle Brendan,' she greeted him warmly.

A faint smile touched his lips in reply, but did not reach

his eyes. 'Just for a week, Sarah. I arrived last night.' He wished with all his heart he was still in his parish in Cork, unaware of what was happening here. He dreaded telling Sarah the bad news; guessed what her reaction would be. Taking her by the arm, he led her to the waiting room and was thankful to find it empty. 'Sarah, I've some bad news.'

A puzzled frown gathered on her brow as she digested the words. Then her face crumpled with alarm. 'Ah, no, Uncle Brendan. Don't tell me the baby's deformed?'

With a shake of the head, he replied, 'The baby isn't born yet.'

'Isn't born yet? Then what's wrong?' she asked, bewildered, then clutched his arm as fear gripped her. 'Is Mam all right?'

'Sarah, this is one of those occasions we hope will never happen to us.' He paused and drew a deep breath before continuing, 'The chances are . . . the doctors can only save one life.'

Absorbing this information, Sarah felt as if everything was moving in slow motion. There was a strange feeling in the air. A feeling of unreality. Was she dreaming? What was he talking about? Then she gasped as the implication of the words struck her.

'Ah, Uncle Brendan.' She backed away from him, her hands raised as if warding off a blow. 'Ah, no! Dear God, no! You can't let Mam die. You can't!' Surging forward she lashed out at his chest with her fists. 'Do you hear me? You can't let Mam die.'

He gripped her fists tightly in his hands and looked sternly down at her. 'That's for Maggie to decide.' He gave her hands a shake. Did she think it was easy for him? 'That's why I sent for Father O'Conner. God forgive me, but I couldn't put it to her meself.'

As if on cue Father O'Conner entered the room and Sarah glared wrathfully at him.

'Your mother wishes to see you Sarah,' he said gently. 'She's in the room at the end of the corridor, the one on the left-hand side.'

Pushing roughly past him, Sarah ran down the corridor

but paused outside the door to try to compose herself before entering the room. Taking deep breaths and blinking furiously, she at last regained some semblance of calm and entered the room. Maggie's eyes were fastened on the doorway, waiting. When Sarah entered, she held out her hand. Grabbing it Sarah held it against her cheek. Then she threw herself on her knees and buried her face against her mother's breast.

'Mam! Ah, Mam,' she wailed. 'Mam . . .'

'Hush, love. Don't cry.' Maggie pressed her close for a moment then gripping her hair, pulled Sarah's head and forced her to look up. 'Listen! I want you to promise me something.'

'Anything, Mam.' Had they not told her mother after all? Sarah wondered. How could she know and remain so calm? However, it was soon obvious that she did know.

'I want you to look after the baby for me. I know Barney will be all mixed up, but one day he will want his child.' Her eyes beseeched Sarah. 'If he rejects it at first, will you take care of it? Even if it's not normal?'

'Ah, Mam! Please let them save you!'

'Sarah!' Maggie's voice was sharp. 'Listen to me. I haven't much time.' She gripped her daughter's hand tighter still in her anguish, wanting her to understand. 'I want to give Barney a child. There's no way I could let this baby die.'

'What about you, Mam? Don't you count?' Sarah was frantic. She just had to convince her mother that her sacrifice would be in vain. 'Barney'll never accept the baby if you die havin' it. You know he won't! Your sacrifice'll be in vain.'

'That's why I need you to promise to look after the baby. It's understandable that he'll be upset at first, that's only natural, but I know Barney and one day he will want his child. Please, love, promise to care for it? Please?'

Sarah's slight frame shook as she fought for control and Maggie's eyes misted over.

'Don't cry, love. God fits the back to the burden. I'm resigned. There's a reason for this to happen.' She had been dumbstruck when Father O'Conner had explained the situation to her. Her first reaction: 'Why me? What have I done to deserve this?' was quickly followed by: 'Why *not* me?'

'I wish you hadn't become a Catholic. Then we wouldn't be facin' this problem,' Sarah cried.

These words made Maggie lose her temper and she shook Sarah roughly. 'Do you honestly think I'm giving my life away because I'm a Catholic? Ah, Sarah . . . how little you know me. Why, I couldn't let this baby die even if I didn't believe in God. Surely you understand? This is Barney's child, it must have its chance. Besides, it's not just Catholics who give their lives that their child may live. You know that!' As pain gripped her she stiffened and a nurse motioned Sarah to the door, but Maggie clung fiercely to her hand. 'Please, Sarah. Promise?'

'I promise, Mam. I promise ye I'll look after the baby.'

Still Maggie clung to her. 'Even if it's abnormal?'

Choked with emotion, Sarah nodded her head and bent over to kiss her mother's cheek. 'Don't worry, Mam. I'll look after it, no matter what.' Then, tottering like an old woman, she allowed herself to be led from the room.

Back in the waiting room, the first person she saw was Mick. She flew into his arms. Gazing up at him, face awash with tears, she asked, 'Mick, can't we get Barney here? He'd change her mind, I know he would!'

Mick had been brought up to date on the state of affairs by Brendan, who had sent for him much earlier. Now he said consolingly, 'Hush, love . . . hush. I've set things in motion to contact Barney.'

However, when she cried, 'Will he be here soon?' he had to admit it would be days, perhaps a week, before Barney could possibly arrive.

She clung to him and he savoured the sweetness of holding her close, the softness of her hair under his cheek, thinking, It's an ill wind that doesn't blow some good.

Across the room, he met Brendan's eyes, and seeing the sorrow there wondered not for the first time, Why? Why Maggie?

305

As if his thoughts had been transferred to her, Sarah drew away from him. Swinging round, she shouted at Brendan, 'Why, Uncle Brendan? Tell me why? Mam has had so little happiness in her life, an' the world's full of bad people . . . people who don't deserve to live! So why is God takin' Mam?'

Brendan looked defeated. 'I don't know, Sarah,' he said with a sad shake of the head. 'Perhaps because your mother is ready to meet God an' the others aren't. It's not for us to question His will.'

With a snort, Sarah again buried her head against her husband's chest. With steps that dragged, Brendan quietly left the room. He wanted to be alone for a while to pray. He would be asking for a miracle.

Two hours later they were informed that Maggie had a son, a fine healthy child. Time dragged as they waited until at last the doctor entered the room. He looked exhausted and it was to Brendan he spoke.

'I think you would be as well giving her the Last Rites.'

Sarah stood with hands clasped in front of her as if in supplication and when Brendan left the room the doctor faced her.

'I don't want to raise your hopes but your mother's a fighter . . . she just might pull through.'

'Oh, thanks be to God!'

The doctor lifted his hand. 'Now, she's not out of the wood yet . . . but I am hopeful. I have to admit, I'm hopeful.'

'Oh, God! Oh, dear God!' Sarah pressed a fist to her mouth and squeezed her eyes shut tight as she fought for control. 'Please let Mam live . . . please, God.' Then to the doctor, 'Can I see her?'

He nodded. 'Soon. When Father Mason is finished, you may see her for two minutes . . . no longer.'

Half an hour later they were allowed to see Maggie. The baby lay in the crook of her arm and Sarah thought her mother had never looked more beautiful. Her skin clear and shining, her eyes aglow. And so peaceful! She could not imagine herself taking things so calmly. No! She would be ranting and raving at the unfairness of it all.

'He's perfect, Sarah. Thank God,' Maggie said softly, as she spread the little fingers, examined the tiny toes.

'He's beautiful, Mam,' Sarah agreed, reaching out gently to touch the baby's head.

'I want him named Bernard.'

Sarah nodded mutely.

'Ah, Sarah, don't. Don't upset yourself, love.' Maggie beseeched her. 'I'm prepared.' And she was. Brendan had promised that if the worst came to the worst he would stay with her until the end. 'Sure it'll be like leaving one friend to go to another,' he had promised, and she believed him. She was not afraid. Besides ... with both Brendan and Father O'Conner praying for her, she thought her chances of pulling through were good. The blood was seeping from her body but the doctor was hopeful that it would stop. Feeling her strength ebbing and her eyes dimming, she said, 'Sarah, take the baby.' And when her son-in-law entered the room and came up behind Sarah, she whispered, 'Take care of them, Mick.'

Swallowing the lump in his throat, he vowed, 'I will, Maggie. I will.' And taking his wife by the arm, he led her from the room.

After much persuasion, Mick got his wife to return to Waterford Street to await further news of Maggie. Earlier he had arranged for his daughters to be taken to stay with their great-grandparents at Sydenham and the house was cold and empty when they arrived home from the hospital. They had been warned it would be a couple of days before they knew the outcome, so he had persuaded Sarah that there was no point sitting in the hospital waiting room, arguing, 'Aren't we just a few minutes away?'

Once in the house he built up the fire and made her sit near it. She was white and shaking. 'I'll make ye a bite to eat ... a cup of tea will soon warm ye up.'

'No ... I'm not hungry.'

She clung to him. Gathering her close, he murmured

307

words of comfort. 'Don't worry, Sarah. God's good. Let's put our trust in him, eh, love? Would you like me to stay the night? If ye like I'll sleep on the settee,' he offered.

Shaking her head she turned away and the tears that were so near the surface fell once more. Relieved to see them, Mick drew her close again and she relaxed against him. 'There, love, cry it all up. It'll do ye good.'

'I was such a selfish daughter,' she sobbed against his chest. 'Always thinking of meself.'

'Hush, now, love. We all have regrets when someone we love's in danger. It's only natural. Here.' He thrust a handkerchief into her hand.

'I was jealous of her beauty. Imagine, being jealous of your own mother! I envied her her lovely home. It was so wrong of me. I had so many blessings, an' still I begrudged her her happiness. How will I ever come to terms with that, eh? Oh, Mick!' she sobbed in despair, 'I wish I could turn back the clock.'

Her husband floundered about in his mind for words of comfort and said haltingly, 'Sarah . . . Maggie loves you dearly, you can do no wrong in her eyes.' To his dismay, these words only made her feel worse.

'I know! I know she loves me dearly. But I didn't love her enough! Can't you see? I should have let her know I loved her instead of always whingin' in her ear. Worryin' her when she should have had peace an' quiet. If she dies, I'll never get the chance to make amends.'

At a loss for words, Mick sat with her on his knee, rocking her gently, until the shuddering sobs became hiccups and she fell into an exhausted sleep. As he carried her up the stairs, he was very much aware of the swell of her breast against his hand and warned himself to be careful. Sarah was weak and vulnerable at the moment and he must be careful not to take advantage of her. He removed her dress and shoes, fretting at how thin she was. Covering her with the bedclothes, he was turning away when she grabbed his hand. 'Stay with me, Mick! Please, stay.'

'Don't worry about a thing, Sarah. I'll stay downstairs. You try an' get a good night's sleep.'

Still clinging to his hand, she pleaded, 'I didn't mean that.'

He looked at her and was sorely tempted. How he wanted her! His need for her was like a great ache in him, but he had caused Sarah trouble once that way and had vowed never again. No! He had made up his mind he would only come back if he was sure she really wanted him, and in her present state she probably only thought she did.

So, resisting the temptation, he said consolingly, 'You'll be all right, love. Just you get a good night's rest.' Gerry was still very much in the picture as far as he was concerned. First they must see if Maggie recovered, then he and Sarah must decide what to do about their marriage.

Mortified, she lay regretting her moment of weakness. Now she knew for sure that he did not want her. And it hurt! How it hurt! She would have to stop whining and being so weak. She must pull herself together. Be independent. If her mother recovered she would talk to May, find out if she would be willing to look after the children. If her mother died . . . there'd be three children to mind. Perhaps that would be too much for May, especially a young baby. What if May couldn't mind the children while she worked? Well, she would just have to find someone else. But she trusted May. Would she be able to trust someone else? Perhaps a complete stranger?

One thing was sure: she would have to pull herself together. Mick must have his chance of happiness with the young widow. There was no point in everybody being miserable. He had been so unselfish, staying off work, giving up all his spare time to help her. Gerry had not even called in to inquire about her mother. She bit hard on her lip when she thought of him. How foolish she had been Well, now she must pay the price.

Wearily, she closed her smarting eyes, sure she would be unable to sleep, and was surprised when she slept right through until seven the next morning. Downstairs she found the fire lit and a pot of porridge on the stove, but Mick had already left for work. After a visit to the hospital, where she found her mother weak and ashen but holding her own, Sarah decided to visit St James Park and make sure the house was ready should her mother recover . . . *when* her mother recovered. She must think positive! Wandering around the house, Sarah looked at things with blind eyes. All these belongings she had begrudged her mother were nothing if she should die.

Tears of self-pity filled her eyes. Sinking to her knees she buried her head in her arms on the seat of her mother's favourite chair and prayed as she had never prayed in her life before. If only God would let her mother live she would turn over a new leaf, become a model daughter.

A knock at the door brought her slowly to her feet. From behind the window nets she saw Gerry on the doorstep. He must have seen her arrive. Well, let him go away. She didn't want to talk to him. He knocked again, louder this time, and resignedly she entered the hall. When she opened the door and he saw how grief had ravaged her face, he thought the worst.

'Ah, Sarah . . . is she dead?'

'A lot you care!'

He reached for her but she eluded him and turned back into the house. Quietly, he followed her into the sitting room and she stood silent, waiting for him to speak.

'I'm sorry about your mother, Sarah. She was a fine woman,' he said diffidently.

'My mother is still alive.'

'But . . . but . . . I thought you said she was dead?'

'No . . . I said a lot you care.'

She turned away in disgust. Moving closer, he said pleadingly, 'I've learnt one thing, Sarah. I can't live without you.'

This was so unexpected that she spun round and gazed at him in amazement.

He nodded eagerly. 'Yes, that's right. I love you,' he stressed and drew her into his arms. She stood passive, a wary look on her face. This was the first time he had said those words. As if sensing her doubt, he repeated, 'I love you very much. I've been a blind fool. Listen ... I've obtained a position in a law firm down in Dublin and I want you to come with me.' He drew back to see what effect his words would have on her.

Hope rose in her breast. Was she going to have someone after all? 'What about the children?' she asked. 'If Mam dies I'll have three to look after.'

Face slack with surprise, he cried, 'Three?'

'Yes.' She nodded. 'I've promised Mother I'll look after the baby when Barney's at sea.'

'Ah, Sarah!' His head swung slowly from side to side as he gazed at her in wonder. 'You're a glutton for punishment, so you are ... but you know Mick won't let you take the girls out of Belfast. By all means bring the baby, if it will make you happy.' He drew her close again. 'And one day we'll have children of our own. You'll like that, won't you?'

He crushed her against him, his kisses hungry, his hands urgent. At last he was admitting the depth of his feelings for her. No other girl could arouse him like she did. A couple of weeks had passed since he had last seen her and the enforced separation had made him aware of how much he wanted her. He had decided he would face his parents' wrath, take on the two children, if necessary, rather than lose Sarah. Anything, so long as she was his.

Feverishly returning his kisses, she pressed closer and closer, thinking, 'Why not? It was a way out of her dilemma. A new life. She could fight Mick for the girls. Surely a mother would be first choice? A mother who was living in sin? No ... but she could try! At least she would not have to see the widow and Mick together. And she was very fond of Gerry.

Suddenly, she knew why not. She didn't love him. Fondness was not enough. She could not bear the thought of not seeing Mick again. Twisting out of his arms, she cried, 'It's no use, Gerry, I don't love you.'

His jaw dropped and he gaped at her. 'You could have fooled me. That was no act just now,' he hissed angrily.

311

'I know! I know! I'm hungry for love ... for affection ... but not from you. Do ye hear me? I don't love you.'

He eyed her through narrowed lids and could see from her expression that she was speaking the truth. White-lipped with anger, he walked to the door, only to turn, anguish washing away the anger. 'If you should change your mind, I'm open to offers,' he muttered. 'You have two weeks to make up your mind. I leave at the end of the month.'

Barney arrived home the day Maggie was declared out of danger. He dashed straight to Waterford Street and Sarah got a shock when he plunged into the kitchen without knocking. She could see that he was at the end of his tether. His hair stood on end and his eyes were bloodshot for want of sleep. He looked demented, had aged ten years, and when he clumsily reached for her, she gripped him close.

'Am I too late, Sarah?'

Smiling through her tears, she hastened to assure him: 'No, Barney! No! Mam's goin' to get better, so she is. She's goin' to get better. Isn't that the best news?'

His relief was so great he sagged in her arms and with an effort she lowered him on to the settee. Once he allowed his eyes to close he was out for the count. Removing his shoes, Sarah lifted his feet on to the settee and covered him with a blanket, leaving him to sleep his fill. He was just what her mother needed; the final sip from the healing cup. Now he was home her recovery should be complete.

Although Maggie was on the road to recovery, she was too weak to handle her young son and it was agreed that Sarah would take him home until her mother was well enough to leave the hospital, thus leaving Barney free to help nurse his wife back to health.

Mick was a tower of strength and each evening on his way home from work called to see if he could be of any assistance. The evening before Maggie was due to leave the hospital he offered to mind the children while Sarah paid a visit to St James Park to make sure all was ready for her mother's homecoming. When she returned Beth and Eileen were in bed and Mick was nursing Bernard by the fireside.

'Would you like a cup of tea?' she asked as she removed her coat.

'Yes, please,' he nodded eagerly, and neglected to tell her that he had just finished a cup of tea, glad of the excuse to stay a while longer in her company.

When the tea was ready she placed a mug of it and a plate of sandwiches close to his chair, and taking Bernard from him she cradled him in her arms. As long as he was fed and dry, he was such a good baby. Holding him over her shoulder to burp him, she rocked gently to and fro. The electric light, recently installed, shone down, turning her hair into a burnished mass of light and shadow. Thinking that perhaps she had just come from Gerry, Mick was consumed with jealousy. She was his wife! That should be his child she was nursing. If he had acted like a man and given her another child, she would have been too busy to notice Gerry. Torn with jealousy, unable to stop himself, he blurted out: 'Have you seen Gerry lately?'

Silently she nodded. Now was her chance to set him free, then he could go to the widow without guilt. 'He has obtained a job down in Dublin. He wants me to go with him.'

White with anger, he was on his feet instantly. Towering over her, he bawled, 'An' you'd go? After the way he's treated ye . . . you'd go? Are ye daft? Well, let me tell ye something, girl. Go with Gerry if you must, but don't you dare try to take the girls out of Belfast! Do you hear me? Do ye hear?' Shaking with wrath he grabbed his coat and stormed from the house as if old Nick himself was after him.

Sarah looked at the untouched tea and sandwiches, and sinking her face into the baby's shoulder, wept bitterly, 'Oh, don't be daft, girl. It's only a couple of sandwiches,' she lamented, but still the tears fell.

Maggie's release from hospital left Sarah free to

approach May and when her neighbour readily agreed to look after the children every weekday morning, Sarah sought and obtained work. She started part-time in the Blackstaff, on three looms.

On Saturday morning two weeks later, having received her first pay packet the day before, she pinned a note to Beth's coat when she was going down to meet her father. In it she explained to Mick that she had started work and would require only half the money that he sent her each week.

She had not seen him since the night he had stormed out of the house two weeks earlier, and picturing him happy and contented with the widow, she was unprepared for his reaction. He slammed open the kitchen door, causing her to start up in surprise.

Waving the note under her nose, he bawled, 'What's the meanin' of this, eh?'

Chin thrust out aggressively, she cried, 'You can read, can't ye?'

'Who minds the kids while you work?'

'May! And she looks after them well.'

'Why are you workin'?' He sounded and looked bewildered. 'Am I not givin' ye enough money?'

'Ah, don't be daft! Of course ye are, but I can't keep takin' money from you forever. You've a life of you own t'live.'

'Look . . . I never told ye, but I got promoted a few months back. I can afford to support my kids, so I'll decide when to stop givin' you money. So don't you dare go back to work.'

Hurt held her silence for a moment. Hurt for him and hurt for herself. He had been promoted and he had never told her. She pictured how, if things had been right between them, they would have planned how best to use the extra money. The excitement, the pride! And she had denied him all this; he who deserved someone to share his good news with. Then she thought of Maisie. Was she daft? Of course he would have shared the excitement and joy with the widow. Unused to working long hours, Sarah was tired and irritable. Her days were long and full of hard work. To think she had imagined Mick treated her like a skivvy! She hadn't known how well off she was. But now she was dropping with tiredness. All she wanted was for him to take Beth and Eileen out for the day. Then she would fill the tin bath and take a long leisurely bath and a nap. In her fatigue, she lashed out at him.

'Don't you dare tell me what to do! I'm me own boss and I'll do what I like. Now get out. Go on, get out, an' give me head peace.'

He opened his mouth to argue, then catching sight of Beth and Eileen, standing in the hall on the verge of tears, thought, God forgive us. Lowering his voice, he said, 'I'll never willingly enter this house again.' He took the children by the hand and stormed down the street, almost pulling them off their little feet, so great was his anger.

Shaking like a leaf, Sarah sank down on a chair. I don't blame you. No, I don't blame you one wee bit, she thought. There's no happiness here, just misery. Stay with the widow. See if I care. All I want is a bit of peace. I don't need anyone else.

And in her misery she actually believed this.

As she walked up Waterford Street, Maisie berated herself. You're a fool Maisie Simpson. She doesn't deserve a chance. You could make him happy, ye know ye could. So what are ye doin' here?

In her heart she knew why she was going to see Sarah. She loved Mick too much to take advantage of his misery. In spite of the comfort she gave him, he was still breaking his heart and she could not bear to watch him any longer. Now if Sarah did not want him . . . well, that would be a different kettle of fish. Once she was sure there was no hope of a reconciliation she would tell Mick about the baby and force his hand. But only if she was sure that there was no chance of a reconciliation, only then would he learn about the baby.

At times she was terrified when she thought of the consequences of her actions. To have Mick's child would be wonderful . . . but not if she had to rear it on her own. She had set out to get him. Now, if Sarah took him back, she quite literally would be left holding the baby. Unless her period was just late. Oh, if only it was. If only.

Sarah opened the door to her knock and stared at her in surprise.

After a prolonged pause, Maisie asked irritably, 'Can I come in a minute?'

Without a word, Sarah turned back into the kitchen and Maisie entered and closed the door behind her. Looking around the well-furnished kitchen and noting the electric light, Sarah being one of the first to obtain such luxury, Maisie said, 'Do ye know what's wrong with you? Ye don't know when you're well off.'

Head high and spots of angry colour in her cheeks, Sarah retorted, 'I'm sure you didn't come here to admire my kitchen, so why have you come?'

'I'm here because I need me head examined,' Maisie bawled across the kitchen at her, wondering to herself just why she was there. She should have left this bitch to stew in her own mess. 'Because I'm daft, that's why! I want to know just what you're playin' at! Just why Mick can't see you for the cold bitch ye are I'll never know . . . but tell me, are ye goin' to take him back?'

Sarah gaped at her in amazement. 'You came here to ask me that? What business is it of yours whether or not I take him back, eh? What's it got to do with you?'

The colour in Maisie's cheeks matched Sarah's. 'Plenty! It's got plenty to do with me. Ye see, if you don't make up your mind soon, I'll take him from ye. An' I can, ye know. He's lonely and miserable . . . but I know given the chance, I can make him happy.'

Sarah stood silent. She had been sure that Maisie had already won Mick over, sure that they were . . . Well, it looked like she was wrong. Would he come back if she sent for him?

The silence stretched until at last Maisie cried in exasperation, 'Well, do ye love him? Are ye goin' to take him back?'

Still Sarah stood silent; she did not want to discuss her affairs with this stranger. How much had Mick told her? Did she know about Gerry?

As if reading her thoughts, Maisie said, 'Look, I've never seen this Gerry fella . . . but he'd have to be great to come up to Mick's standards. But to be truthful, I hope ye run off with him. I know I can make Mick happy an' I'm fed up waitin' for you to make up your mind. If ye haven't sent for him by Saturday I'll take him from ye! An' I can! You mark my words . . . I can!'

Overcome with emotion, Maisie turned and grasped the door handle. 'Remember! Ye have 'til Saturday night. No longer.' Pulling the door open, she stumbled in her haste to leave the house. She had a feeling that she had just burnt her boats.

When the door closed, Sarah gave herself a little shake to make sure she was not dreaming, and then her thoughts were busy, planning ahead. There was no way this common little tart was going to get her husband. No way!

On Saturday morning she sent Mick a letter pinned to Beth's coat. He had said he would never willingly enter the house again. Would he come? She was relieved when she heard him in the hall, and opening the door motioned him inside. When Beth would have followed him, she whispered in her ear, 'Take Eileen into May's and stay there 'til your dad comes for you.'

When Beth hesitated, preparing to argue, Sarah gave her a little push. 'Go on. May's got sweets for you.'

That magic word worked, and taking Eileen by the hand Beth dragged her towards May's house. Once they were safely inside, Sarah closed the big outer door and entered the kitchen. Mick stood just inside the kitchen door, a wary look on his face. He had an idea why Sarah had sent for him and no way was he going to agree to her proposal! No way!

Stealing a glance at him, Sarah's heart quailed when she saw how stern and cold he looked. He was much thinner and she saw that his hair was threaded with silver. Had she put those threads there? Unable to find words to begin, she moved in front of the fireplace. Becoming aware that she was actually wringing her hands, she clasped them tightly together while trying to form words in her mind. Mick could see his wife was agitated but he hardened his heart against her. She had sent for him. Let her speak first.

Sarah felt sick; nerves had gathered her stomach into a hard ball and she wanted to retch. What if he didn't want her back? The idea of him rejecting her threw her into a state of panic. Her pride made her want to let the chance pass; ask him something stupid, send him on his way. That way she could escape with her pride intact, but pride would be cold comfort on a winter's night. She stole another glance at him and met the cold hard contempt in his dark blue eyes. Eyes that were usually warm and kind. It wasn't working out the way she had planned. She could not go through with it.

Unable to bear the silence any longer he asked sarcastically, 'Has the cat got your tongue?' Even his voice had a cruel tinge to it and she winced. As she groped for words, he added, 'Look, I know why you sent for me, an' the answer is . . . no!'

Mortified colour washed over her face, then faded, leaving her ghastly white. How could he know? If he guessed her reasons, why had he come? To humiliate her? How could he? How could he humiliate her like this? She turned away from him, fighting tears, striving for composure. Determined not to let him see her weep.

'There's no way I'll let you take Beth an' Eileen down south . . . so if ye go with Gerry, ye go alone.'

Swinging back to face him, her face slack with surprise, she cried, 'I don't want to take the kids down south.'

It was obvious that he was taken aback. Confusion blanked all other expression from his face. 'Then why did you want to see me?' he asked in bewilderment.

But Sarah had had enough. It was clear he didn't love her. If he loved her, he would be begging her to stay. He would not be saying, 'Go, as long as you don't take the girls.'

There was no point raking through the ashes.

'I'm sorry. I've been stupid. I seem to have made a mistake, please go.' Her voice sounded calm enough to her ears and for this she was grateful, but tears clung to the ends of her lashes. Afraid they would fall and betray her, she turned abruptly away.

As always, her tears tugged at his heartstrings and he moved closer. 'Ah, Sarah, don't cry.'

He was so close his breath fanned the hair on the back of her neck, and the familiar smell of him wafted around her. But he did not touch her. Angrily dashing the betraying tears away with the back of her hand, she proudly threw her head high and turned to face him.

'I'm not cryin' . . .' Seeing the naked yearning in his eyes, the words died on her lips and she gazed at him in wonder. Then, slowly, she lifted her hand and drew her finger in a caressing gesture down his hollow cheek. 'You're too thin,' she chided.

He remained motionless, not daring to believe what he read in her eyes. Was it his imagination, was he seeing what he wanted to see, rather than the truth?

'I sent for you . . . because I . . . I've been tryin' to tell ye that I love ye,' she whispered.

His eyes, questioning, searching, probed hers. She stood silent, head high, and it was as if he could see into her very soul. Slowly, joy permeated his being. Reaching for her, he pulled her close – all the frustration and longing of the past months apparent in the tender way he held her. They clung together; not kissing, just savouring holding each other. At last he drew back and looked down into her face.

'What about Gerry?'

'That was over a long time ago.' Her voice was low and ashamed.

'An' ye didn't tell me?' he cried, astounded.

'I thought you loved Maisie, an' I was tryin' to be noble an' make it easy for you to be with her.'

'Ah Lord, Sarah! Maisie's just a good friend.' These words brought him up short and he sank his face in her hair to hide the guilt that swamped him. A good friend? Was that what adultery did to you? Was that how you

319

squared your conscience? But Maisie would understand. Hadn't she said there'd be no ties, that she would take whatever came? Hadn't he told her that if Sarah called he would return to her. Ah, yes ... Maisie would surely understand. Then why did he feel such a cad?

Sarah was nodding in agreement with him. 'Ah, but I didn't know that. I was sure that you an' she were ... ye know.'

Ignoring the question in her eyes, he slowly manoeuvred her towards the stairs. 'How long will May keep the kids?'

''Til you go for them.'

At that he hustled her up the stairs in front of him. 'What are we waitin' for then?'

He undressed her slowly, savouring every moment. It had been a long time. When her breasts were free of her cotton camisole, he could wait no longer and delayed the undressing while he paid their beauty homage. At last she lay naked on the bed and as his eyes adored her she felt shy. She had never been naked in front of him before; all their couplings had been conducted under bedclothes or in the dark. Pulsing with excitement, she watched as he hastily removed his own clothes, thrilled by the sight of the muscles rippling across his shoulders and down his arms; his strong, tanned muscular body. Her eyes shyly travelled the length of his body and a blush stained her cheeks. He smiled at her embarrassment.

When he lay down beside her she turned eagerly to him, but he pressed her back. He intended that this time he would call the tune. Maisie had taught him a lot and he intended putting it to good use. He was aware that Sarah did not get all the pleasure she should out of their love making. He had wanted it to be different, had always wanted to kiss every inch of her, but it hadn't seemed manly and she had been so off-hand and embarrassed when he tried that he had not persisted. Now he intended to change all that. He was going to do all in his power to arouse her, really arouse her.

Gently, he set his ideas in motion. His lips barely

touched her face as he sought out the pulse at her temple, then at her throat. Bright green eyes watched him raptly, and when he reached her mouth he smiled when he saw her lick her lips in anticipation. Each time she reached for him, he pressed her back and she watched him, fascinated. His hands were doing such wonderful things to her body, sending thrill upon thrill to the very core of her being. A heat spread through her until she writhed and panted in great need, and still he kept her waiting, holding her on the raw edge until at last she begged, 'Please, Mick. Ah, please don't tease.'

Only then did he draw her close, sending her senses spinning, and the world fell away as they were lifted on a wave of passion such as she had never known existed.

Sarah was incapable of coherent thought. All she knew was that she didn't want this magic to end. Locking her limbs around him she arched herself against him and her mouth hungrily savaged his, seeking more and more pleasure. Afterwards she didn't want to open her eyes. Didn't want anything to intrude into her satiated world. When at last she did, Mick was watching her with a triumphant smile on his face. She had read many love stories but had not believed it could really be as described. That it should happen to her took her breath away. She gazed at him in awe.

'Why did it never happen like that before?'

'Because I was too inhibited. Too afraid of failin', an' you laughin' at me.' He tapped the tip of her nose with his finger. 'An' you, my love, were always in a hurry. As if ye had a tram t'catch.'

Guilt bowed her head. She knew he spoke the truth. She had derived so little pleasure from their union that it was a case of getting it over with as soon as possible. Just so long as he enjoyed it, she had been content. Hell, she hadn't known what she was missing, and obviously he had not been getting all the satisfaction that he should.

He tilted her face up so that he could see into her eyes. 'From now on, we do things my way.'

'Yes, please,' she dimpled up at him, her smile wide, her eyes happy. That suited her fine.

'An' what I say goes,' he warned as he cupped her breast in his hand.

Again she agreed, saying humbly, 'Yes, Mick.'

Pulling her closer still, he placed his chin on the top of her head so that she would be unable to see the grin on his face. His Sarah humble? Never! In a couple of days she would be her old fiery self again, and he would not want her any other way. But for now? Well . . .

'Kiss me, wench,' he cried, and she eagerly lifted her face for his kisses. She was so happy, but like her mother before her, distrusted such happiness.

Voicing her thoughts, she said, 'Mick, I'm afraid. No one should be this happy. I don't deserve happiness after the way I treated you.'

He kissed her long and hard, then said earnestly, 'Sarah, let's not spoil our happiness by misunderstandings. I was at fault too! I knew you weren't getting satisfaction, but you were a bit of a prude . . . like, for instance, always wanting to make love in the dark. So I did it your way, and almost lost you.' Once more he kissed her long and hard, thinking just how close he had come to losing her. 'We must remember that sometimes things are not as they appear, and when things go wrong – an' sure they're bound to go wrong sometimes – we must always talk it out. An' we must always be honest with each other and thankful that we got a second chance. There's so much we can learn together.'

She looked at him, eyes teasing and lips pouting. 'You mean, there's more?'

He threw back his head and laughed aloud. 'Much more!'

Her finger outlined the planes of his face. How good he was. How she loved him. She was ashamed when she thought of the time and effort she had wasted on Gerry. Never again! Never again would she look to left or right.

Hesitantly, she said, 'Mick, about Gerry . . .'

322

With a hand over her mouth he interrupted her, 'I don't want to know. It's over, finished.'

And he didn't want to know. He didn't want her comparing them, and perhaps finding him wanting. Sarah had been so pliable in his hands that the thought had crossed his mind that perhaps she had already been down this road with Gerry. And who was he to cast stones? Had he not been with Maisie? Still . . . he didn't want to know. So long as he didn't know, he could bear it.

Tenderly kissing his hand, she removed it from her lips and gently shook her head. 'Remember what you said just now?' She wagged her finger back and forth in front of his face. 'How we must always be honest with each other?'

'Yes, I know what I said, but that's over, I don't want to hear about it. Ye see, if we had been honest with each other, it would never have happened. Let's just start afresh.'

She guessed what he dreaded hearing and smiled tenderly at him. 'I disagree with you. I think you have to know the truth so that we can start afresh.'

He closed his eyes to hide the fear in them.

'Nothin' ever happened. Just a few kisses,' she said softly.

Joy spread through him and tears were close. 'Ah, Sarah. Sarah, my love.' And he held her fiercely, as if he would never let her go. Thoughts of Maisie were pushed aside. He could never confide in Sarah about his affair. He knew her too well; she might at this moment willingly forgive him, but she was not the type to forget. It would be dragged out of the cupboard every disagreement they had. No, she must never know. Maisie was good. She was his friend. Yes, Maisie would understand.

The radio was leading the listeners through the last few minutes of 1929 and as they awaited the sound of Big Ben ringing in 1930, Maggie regarded her family with affection. Having beaten death, Christmas had been a bonus for her. A happier Christmas she had never known, with Barney constantly at her side and a beautiful son to fuss over. As for Sarah! Covertly she eyed her daughter and son-in-law where they sat on the settee. When she had left hospital, Maggie had intended giving Sarah a good talking to. Make sure she was aware of the havoc she would cause should she run off with Gerry. But there had been no need. Sarah and Mick had been like newly weds and now Sarah was expecting her third child. Gerry had left for Dublin without seeking her out again and everything in the garden appeared to be rosy. What had wrought such a change? Sarah had not confided in her mother and, glad to see her so happy, Maggie had not pried. God had been good to her. Despite a high mortality rate in new babies she had delivered a healthy child and, against the odds, lived to enjoy him. The fact that her daughter's marriage appeared on course was the icing on the cake.

The 1920s in Belfast had not been an easy era: first the riots raging out of control, causing death and destruction, then when the I.R.A. were at last driven south, unemployment had brought thousands on to the streets to march against poverty and homelessness, to fight against the pittance they were expected to live on and the slums they were expected to live in. Just a few months ago the corporation had come up with a scheme to ease unemployment. They had decided to concrete the roads. Now hundreds of men were employed digging up the cobblestones and crushing them with a huge machine. The stone was mixed with sand and cement and the roads concreted. However, the workers were not paid a conventional wage, but were paid with grocery chits. For the time being, the men were willing to put up with this, glad to be able to feed their families. What would happen when clothes and household commodities were needed, God only knew, but for now they were glad to eat. This scheme was a great help to Barney and Jim. Their small greengrocer's shop was reaping the reward of these chits. The men knew they could depend on getting value at The Green Haven, as the shop was called, and brought their custom there. Meanwhile the Wall Street collapse in

America had wrought havoc worldwide and businesses big and small were going bust. Without the workers' custom the Green Haven would have joined them. Indeed, God was watching over them.

Sarah caught her mother's eye and winked. She could imagine the trend of her thoughts. Since her close encounter with death, her mother was constantly counting her blessings. However, Sarah did not agree with her that she should be thankful to have a rented house. Indeed, no. If the child she was carrying was a boy, it would be another bargaining point in her endeavours to get Mick to move house. Staying with her mother over the past few days, so that they could see the new year in together, had made Sarah even more determined to have a house with a bathroom and a garden. Now she moved closer to Mick and was delighted at his quick response as his arm embraced her. He was putty in her hands at present; 1930 would see them in a new house, this she was sure of. Perhaps one of the houses built recently on the Whiterock Road. The corporation was having trouble selling those houses. They were priced beyond people's pockets. In the new year they might have to lower their prices and then she would bring pressure to bear on Mick.

As he held her close his thoughts were with Maisie. Unknown to Sarah he had called to see her and young Donald before Christmas. He felt guilty where she was concerned. When he had acquainted her with the news that he and Sarah were to give their marriage another try, she had been cool but pleasant enough about it. When he tried to apologise she had interrupted him, assured him that she understood; had gone into their affair with her eyes open. Still, he had worried. Only the fear of Sarah finding out and getting the wrong impression had prevented him from returning again to make sure that Maisie was all right.

But he could not let Christmas pass without a sign that he cared about her welfare. So, clutching a toy for Donald and perfume for her, he had presented himself at their door. He had been pleased to find her in the company of another man. She had looked well, had even put on a bit of weight. He was glad that he had gone to see her. The presents that he had brought had salved his conscience and meeting her new friend had eased his mind. He could now look forward to 1930 without guilt.

The chimes of Big Ben filled the room and he rose and drew Sarah to her feet. Any second now the knocker would sound and Jim and Kathleen would first-foot them, bringing gifts of silver and coal. The state the country was in, prospects didn't look bright for the new year but at this time every year hope for a better future brought families and friends together to ring in the new. A loud knock heralded the arrival of the Raffertys and as Barney went to admit them Mick started to pour the drinks. Roll on 1930!

The Wasted Years

Author's Note

The Falls Road and St Paul's parish portrayed in *The Wasted Years* actually exist, and historic events referred to in the story are authentic. However, I would like to make it clear that the story is fictional, and all characters are purely a figment of my imagination and not based on anyone alive or dead, and any similarity is purely coincidental.

The author would like to thank the following:

My husband and two youngest sons for bearing with
me when meals were late and their patience must have
been sorely tried. My oldest son and daughter-in-law
Debbie for their help and encouragement. My mother
for letting me pick her brains about the past and my
sister Sue who first suggested that I could and should
write a book, and who was with me every step of the
way. And last, but not least, my friend Margaret
Russell who was always there with words of encouragement when I despaired of ever getting it
published. My grateful thanks to them all.

I would also like to thank the staff of the Irish and
Local Studies Department of the Belfast Library for
their help in my research and the staff of the
Darlington Library for obtaining reference books I
needed for authenticity.

Chapter 1

Belfast, 1938

The power went off, and as the looms ground to a halt the weavers changed their old, comfortable shoes for more serviceable ones, donned their coats and headed for the door. In spite of the glass roof lights being whitewashed against the glare of the sun, stifling heat still built up inside the factory and they were relieved to escape out into the fresh air. One of the many mills that provided work for the people of the Falls and the Shankhill Roads, the Falls Flax Factory was situated in Cupar Street; right in the centre, at the 'T' junction where it curved sharply to the right and continued on up to the Shankhill Road to the Protestant districts, while the left-hand turn became the Kashmir Road and ran on to the Springfield Road and the Catholic districts.

Arm in arm with Rosaleen Magee, May Brady felt the tension ripple through her friend as they walked out of the gates on to Cupar Street. She knew what was causing Rosaleen such concern, or rather who, and sure enough, there he stood, about six feet tall, jet-black hair and eyes as blue as a summer sky. This was the third night he had been waiting outside the factory. But for whom was he waiting? Mr Blair's secretary?

1

Yes, it must be Miss Maynard he was waiting for. She was the only one May could picture him with, although May had seen and been dismayed by the look that had passed between Rosaleen and the handsome stranger on Monday night, the first he had been there. She was also aware that Rosaleen had her old work coat lying open, disclosing the fact that she had taken the time to remove the overall she wore to protect her clothes when working, and May could see that she was wearing one of her better skirts and a cream-coloured blouse that was just a few weeks old; a blouse that enhanced the fairness of her skin and lightened the green of her eyes. This was unusual, very unusual, because dust from the weft in the weaving shop got embedded into everything, causing a fusty smell, and it was customary to wear old clothes to work.

Why on earth is Rosaleen wearing her new blouse? May mused. Surely she did not fancy the handsome stranger? A small frown puckered her brow as she pondered. All the same, she must. Why else risk ruining the new blouse? Oh, don't be ridiculous! she admonished herself, but was unconvinced. Isn't she engaged to be married?

Rosaleen's thoughts were running along similar lines to May's. Why was she so aware of this man? In four months' time she would be married to Joe Smith. Big, kind, handsome Joe. She loved Joe. So how come a single glance from a pair of blue eyes could floor her? She kept her own eyes demurely downcast, but she was very much aware that the man's eyes never left her face, bringing a bright blush to her cheeks, and that when they passed him, he turned to look after them.

'I wonder who the big hunk's waiting for?' May muttered, with a sidelong glance, covertly watching Rosaleen's reaction to her words. 'Probably Miss Maynard,' she continued, and jerked her head back towards the factory. 'She's the only one in there I can

2

picture him with. I can't see *him* with a weaver or a winder.'

'Who are you talking about?' Rosaleen asked, trying to appear disinterested and failing miserably.

'Oh, that big, tall, handsome stranger that you never noticed,' May answered crossly. She was annoyed with Rosaleen and showed it. Why couldn't she be honest and admit that she found him attractive? Unless . . . surely she couldn't find him *that* attractive? Oh dear God no, that would never do. 'All the men around here wear Crombie overcoats and patent leather shoes that you could see yourself in,' she continued scornfully. 'So of course you wouldn't notice him.'

Hot colour brightly burned in Rosaleen's cheeks. She could not understand why, but she did not want to discuss the man with May. Perhaps because he affected her so deeply. On Monday night she had been laughing when he had caught her eye and an electric current seemed to run like a live wire between them. Time hung suspended as they gazed in awe at each other. Just a few seconds, but it had filled her with rapture, and she had recaptured the feeling often in the past few days and hugged it to her.

Joe did not have this effect on her and she felt guilty and uneasy at her reaction to this stranger. Last night and tonight she had avoided looking directly at him, scared of the effect he had on her, but she had been very much aware of his scrutiny.

Now she muttered, 'No, you're wrong. Miss Maynard stops work at half-five so she'll be long gone. It's not her he's waiting for.'

May shot her a sharp glance and saw the heightened colour. So, she *had* been giving him some thought and wondering who he was waiting for.

'Who do *you* think he's waiting for?' she asked, slyly.

But Rosaleen was no fool. She knew May's curiosity was aroused and did not want to continue the conversation, afraid of betraying the emotions the stranger had aroused. She wanted to put all thoughts of him from her mind; his obvious interest in her made her feel uncomfortable.

Shrugging her shoulders, she cried gaily, 'Oh, who cares?' And to change the subject, she asked, 'Are you going out tonight?'

She and May had been friends since their first day at primary school and only the arrival of Joe on the scene had come between them. They still had one night a week out together, a Friday night, and this they spent at the Club Orchid Ballroom. Joe did not like dancing but Rosaleen loved to dance and this way everybody was happy.

May was not hoodwinked. She knew Rosaleen was deliberately changing the subject, but decided to let her get away with it.

She gave a deep sigh. 'No, I'm washing my hair tonight and I've some clothes to launder.'

Being the eldest child of a family of six, she preferred to launder her own clothes than have them done with the family wash. Her mother was inclined to boil everything together in an old tin bucket and many a jumper and cardigan had been ruined, hence her desire to do her own laundry. She envied Rosaleen, who had only one sister and who was lifted and laid by her mother.

'Well, see you tomorrow.' She squeezed Rosaleen's arm before letting it go. 'Don't do anything I wouldn't do.'

'That gives me plenty of scope,' Rosaleen retorted, with a toss of her head that sent the blonde hair swinging about her face, making May wish, not for the first time, that she was blonde and beautiful, instead of plain and mousy.

With a deep chuckle, she turned down Clonard Gardens which joined Clonard Street and ran down on

4

to the Falls Road where she lived, while Rosaleen continued on up the Kashmir Road.

As she hurried along, her thoughts returned to the dark stranger. Why did he affect her so much? Chemistry, that's what it was! If they were to meet and talk they would probably bore each other to tears. With this observation she relaxed and turned her thoughts to Joe. Kind, handsome Joe. Nothing must interfere with her plans to marry him.

Her first and only serious boy friend, he was a wonderful person who idolised her. He had put down a deposit on a house in Iris Drive, off Springfield Avenue, and was in the process of decorating it, for them to return to after their honeymoon in Bray. No greasing someone's palm with a tenner for the key to a rented house; no, not for them! Not every girl was lucky enough to marry a man with his own business. Just a small business, dealing in wrought-iron gates and railings, but there was room for expansion, and Joe was full of plans for the future. No, she would be foolish to let anything interfere with their plans. Why, it was wrong even to think of another man.

Nevertheless, in spite of her good intentions, the minute the alarm clock shattered the silence on Thursday morning, her thoughts returned to the stranger and she jumped out of bed. Dampening her hair, she rolled the long blonde strands in curlers and left it to set while she quickly washed herself down in the draughty scullery and then ate the breakfast her father prepared for her every morning. Her father was a good man; there were not many like him. Every morning he was downstairs first, and after lighting the fire he prepared breakfast. Then, without fail, he carried a cup of tea and a round of toast upstairs to her mother, before departing for Greeves Mill where he worked in the flax store.

Once ready for work, with her hair swept up at the sides and hanging to her shoulders in the current page-

5

boy style, she gave into the temption to use a little make-up. Just a little. A light touch of Pan-stick and a hint of rouge. She did not want May to notice and comment on it.

But alas, she may as well not have bothered. There was no sign of the tall, handsome, stranger outside the factory gates that night and she did not know whether to be glad or disappointed.

On Friday morning she was pushing away at her looms, lost in thought, when Betty Devlin came and stood beside her. She did not know Betty very well; a non-smoker, she did not therefore gather in the toilets where one met all the newcomers and was kept up to date on all the gossip. Knocking off the handle of the loom, Rosaleen gripped the comb and helped the loom to stop more quickly. Then, with a smooth, fluid movement, she exchanged the empty shuttle for a full one and set the loom in motion again, before turning to Betty, an eyebrow raised inquiringly. At the same time she removed the empty bobbin from the shuttle and put a new one in from the cage of weft that sat above the loom. Looms had to be kept constantly on the move or they left marks in the cloth, bringing the wrath of the examiners down on the culprit's head. So keeping an eye on the three looms, she gave half of her attention to Betty. She guessed the girl was probably collecting for something; someone getting married or maybe someone retiring.

While Rosaleen changed the shuttles, Betty eyed her closely. She had known right away who her brother was talking about when he had described her. There were not many girls as lovely as Rosaleen and she could understand why her brother was attracted to her.

Leaning close to make herself heard above the clatter of the looms, she cried, 'Did you notice a tall guy standing outside the factory a couple of nights this week?'

6

To her amusement, colour flooded Rosaleen's face and neck. Even her ears went a bright pink, causing Betty to laugh outright.

'Obviously you did! You and half the factory! Well, he was waiting for me. He's my brother Sean and he wants a word in with you.'

Rosaleen found herself smiling in return. It was a long time since she had heard that expression: 'Wants a word in with you'. Not since she was about fifteen. Still, Betty was barely sixteen, so that would account for her using the term. Then the girl's words sank in and she went redder still. He wanted a date with her!

She shook her head and said, 'I can't. I'm engaged to be married.'

Betty eyed her bare left hand in disbelief and Rosaleen quickly explained, 'I don't wear my ring in here, the stone's too big.'

That sounded like boasting, but it was the truth. Joe had invested a lot of money in her engagement ring, a huge solitaire. She had demurred but he had said, 'May as well, while I can afford it. It's an investment, so it is. A ring like that can only grow in value and . . . God forbid . . . if we're ever stuck for money . . . well, it'll be there.'

However, she was nervous when wearing the ring, it was an awful responsibility, and she would not dream of wearing it in the factory.

Betty shrugged and gave a rueful smile. 'Oh, well.' She forced an exaggerated sigh from deep in her chest. 'Our Sean will be disappointed, but still I did my best.'

Deep blue eyes, just like his, laughed into Rosaleen's. Then, giving Rosaleen a wink and a nod, Betty turned and made her way down the shop floor, weaving in and out of the fast-moving machinery with graceful steps and a seductive sway to her small, neat bottom. Very much aware that her progress was watched avidly

7

by two fitters who were maintaining a loom. Rosaleen watched her for some seconds, amusement in her eyes, then turned her attention back to her work, but her actions were automatic, her mind full of thoughts of 'Sean'. Imagine him wanting a word in with her. He had a cheek all the same. Sending word in like that, instead of asking her himself. This thought sent dismay flooding through her. What if he was outside tonight and spoke to her? The very idea of it made her tremble and she chastised herself: Stop acting like a fool! He means nothing to you.

One of the looms dwindled to a halt and when Rosaleen saw the flaw that had been caused by a broken thread, she muttered to herself as she let out the web and started to rip out the flaw. That's what you get for daydreaming. Get your mind back on your work, you silly girl!

That night, keeping her head down, she gripped May's arm and hustled her quickly through the gate and past the corner where he usually stood. Not even trying to catch a glimpse of his well-polished brogues, should he be there.

May allowed herself to be propelled along Kashmir Road in silence, a resigned look on her face, but when they reached Clonard Gardens she said, with a gentle shake of her head, 'He wasn't there.'

'What?' Trying to look indifferent, Rosaleen tossed her head and added, 'I don't know what you mean.'

'Ah, Rosaleen, be honest!'

Shame-faced, Rosaleen muttered, 'He's Betty Devlin's brother. He wants a word in with me.'

May gaped at her and Rosaleen laughed softly before repeating with a smile and a nod: 'He wants a word in with me.' She chuckled aloud at the idea. 'Imagine! I felt about fifteen when Betty said that to me.'

'He actually wants a date with you?'

Rosaleen's smile deepened at May's amazement and once more her head dipped and her lips pressed tightly together to contain her mirth.

'And what did you say to that?' May asked, tentatively.

'Now what could I say? Eh?' Rosaleen's brows rose in surprise at the question. 'Me engaged to Joe?' A wistful look passed over her face and she added, with a deep sigh, 'Perhaps if he had come along sooner I might have been tempted. Oh, my, but he's a handsome brute, so he is.'

Alarmed at these revelations, May gripped her by the shoulders and shook her fiercely.

'Don't be daft! You'll never get anyone as good as Joe Smith,' she warned.

As far as she was concerned, the sun rose and shone on Joe Smith. If only he had fallen for her, life would have been marvellous.

'I know! I know when I'm well off. I won't do anything silly,' Rosaleen promised, and hit May playfully on the shoulder. 'Never fear. I've no intention of spoiling things.'

Relieved, May relaxed and laughed. 'Now, why couldn't he have picked me?' she jested. 'Eh? Twenty-one and fancy free.' But she knew why – the same reason that Joe had picked Rosaleen. Rosaleen was beautiful. She was mediocre.

Glad that he had not put in an appearance, Rosaleen heaved a sigh of relief and hurried home to prepare for her night out with May. This was the highlight of her week, Friday night at the Club Orchid. Not for the world would she admit it, but she felt as if she was already a staid married woman. Joe was wonderful but a bit dull, and their relationship lacked sparkle. They were both staunch Catholics and lived up to the rules of the church. No long kissing or close embracing; no walking in dark lonely places that were an occasion of sin.

9

Still, sometimes she found it hard to bear when Joe put her firmly away from him, telling her that they must wait. He was able to control his emotions so much easier that she, and she felt frustrated and wicked because she longed to be held close and cuddled. Nothing serious, just a few kisses.

It will be different once we're married, she assured herself, not for the first time, and tried to picture Joe sweeping her off to bed on a wave of passion, but the man in her imagination had dark hair and deep blue eyes, and she blushed with shame as her thoughts ran on.

The Club Orchid was situated above a pub, on the corner where Castle Street met King Street, down near the town centre. As usual, Rosaleen met May at the bottom of Clonard Street and in high spirits they caught the tram down the Falls Road.

They felt very daring going to the dance at the present time, because since De Valera, the Prime Minister of Southern Ireland, had drawn up a constitution laying claim to the six counties, there had been trouble. The Protestants did not want a united Ireland, and Lord Craigavon had challenged De Valera, by calling a general election a few months earlier. The campaign was low key in most places but in Belfast it was bitterly fought and the troubles which had been dormant for a time were rekindled. The country had gone to the polls on February 9th and it was a day of bitter violence. Cars were wrecked and burned, and windows broken. Republican and Nationalist women had fought each other in the street and the hated 'B' Specials were on full alert, their guns prominently displayed.

To the delight of the Protestants, Craigavon won the election and the riots eased off a bit, but resentment still simmered, with the Catholics very much aware that

10

the majority of those out of work were of their faith, and that any jobs going would be given to Protestants. However, Rosaleen and May thought it was worth the risk of going to the dance, in spite of recriminations from their families and Joe, because they knew the crowd, and Catholics and Protestants mixed quite amicably together in the Club Orchid.

The ballroom was packed, as was usual on a Friday night, and as usual Bill Murray (Joe's young cousin) lifted Rosaleen in the first dance. She often wondered if Bill kept an eye on her and reported back to Joe, but she did not misbehave so she had nothing to worry about.

It was a slow foxtrot and Bill was a good dancer so she gave herself up to the sheer joy of dancing. Then, suddenly, an awareness came over her and as surely as if he had hailed her, she knew *he* was there. She could feel his presence, and eagerly her eyes roamed around the dancers until they locked with his and a thrill coursed through her body, making her tremble.

'Are you cold, Rosaleen?' Bill drew back and gazed down at her in concern.

'No, no, somebody must've walked over my grave,' she assured him, and over Bill's shoulder she looked at *his* partner. It was Betty, who raised a hand in greeting, and chiding herself for feeling relieved, Rosaleen nodded in their direction before giving all her attention to Bill. When the dance ended she went to the side of the dance floor where all the girls gathered, and joined May, tugging anxiously at her sleeve.

'May! He's here. What am I gonna do?' she whispered urgently.

'Eh?' May's glance was blank. Her attention on the lad with whom she had just danced, and who was waiting for the next. 'Who's here?'

'Oh! Ye know! Him!' moaned Rosaleen, in anguish. 'Oh, here he comes.'

'Can I have this dance please?'

11

Worried by the effect he was having on her, she determined to refuse him, but one look up into his intensely blue eyes and she was lost.

With a slight nod of her head, she silently entered his arms and was drawn close. Their steps matched perfectly, and lost in a bubble of joy, Rosaleen let his remarks on the music go over her head.

The dance was half over before he spoke again. Drawing back, he mouthed the words down at her. 'I'm sorry, please forgive me, I didn't realise you are dumb. How stupid of me.'

Her head reared back and she gaped up at him, her mouth opening in protest. Then she saw the twinkle in his eye and laughed ruefully.

'I suppose you can be forgiven for thinking so,' she agreed, and quirking an eyebrow at him asked, 'What would you like to talk about?'

'Well, let's start from scratch, shall we? Do you come here often?'

His face was alive with suppressed laughter and she dimpled back up at him. 'Every Friday night.' Both brows arched high, inquiringly. 'And you?'

'First time here. You see I'm in the Merchant Navy and I'm away from home a lot.'

'Oh.' Rosaleen wondered why she was so disappointed. Why she felt such a sense of loss. After all, he meant nothing to her.

'I have another week's leave,' he said, and drew her closer. 'Come out with me. Please!' His deep voice was low, pleading.

She shook her head. 'I can't, I'm engaged.'

He glanced at her left hand, at the large diamond sparkling there, and pretended to shade his eyes from the dazzle.

'Ooops, that's a whopper. Where's he tonight?'

'He's plastering walls of the house we've just bought.' She gave a little laugh and added proudly, 'This is my night out alone.'

He pulled her closer still and his eyes scanned her face intently, marvelling at the purity of her skin and the beauty of her eyes.

'He's a fool! If you were mine I wouldn't let you out of me sight.'

She drew away from him, pleased but embarrassed, and with a toss of her head replied tartly, 'Well then, thank God I'm not yours. I need some time to myself or I would feel smothered.'

'When are you getting married?'

'The beginning of August, all being well. That's if the troubles don't get too out of hand.'

'So soon?' he cried, dismayed. He had so little time to make her change her mind. 'Look, surely you can come out with me on one date?'

Seeing she was about to refuse again, he rushed on. 'Just once! One date.'

'No . . . I'm sorry, but I can't.'

She did not realise how regretful she sounded, but he did and asked softly, 'Are you afraid?'

Once more her head reared back, her small chin jutted forward, her eyes flashed green fire, and he fell more in love with her.

'Of course I'm not afraid! Why should I be?' she exclaimed.

'Why not come out with me then? Eh? Just once. We'll probably hate each other and I'll be able to go away with an easy mind. Come on, put me out of my misery.'

She looked up at him, a slight frown ruffling her smooth, wide brow as she digested his words.

Why not? Why not indeed? One date would not hurt her, and Joe need never know.

He could see that she was weakening and again pleaded: 'Please, Rosaleen, just one date.'

'All right.' Guilt and shame made her add urgently,

13

'But don't dance with me too often. Joe's cousin is here.'

He nodded in understanding.

'When?'

'Tuesday night. Does that suit you?'

Every Tuesday night Joe went to the confraternity in Clonard Monastery. He usually called to see her afterwards but she would make up some excuse to put him off.

Aware that the next three days would drag, Sean, grateful for small mercies, nodded in agreement. 'Where shall I meet you?'

'Outside the London Mantle Warehouse.'

'At the corner of Chapel Lane?'

'Yes, that's right. And please ... don't tell Betty we're meeting.'

Her eyes pleaded with him and he guessed, rightly, that she was having second thoughts.

'I won't tell anyone,' he promised, and after another dance he left the ballroom. He did not want Joe's cousin reporting anything amiss in case she did not show up on Tuesday night. Having accomplished what he had set out to do, he was contented. She was meeting him; it was up to him now.

Having told Joe not to call to see her on Tuesday night as she would be going out with May to visit a sick aunt, Rosaleen prepared carefully for her date with Sean.

Watched by her young sister Annie, she brushed her thick hair until it glowed like dull, pale gold, and highlighted her cheekbones with blusher. Her eyes needed no help to enhance them. Thick dark lashes framed clear green irises edged with a dark ring, and well-shaped dark brows arched above them as if in approval.

'Are you sure you're going out to visit May's sick aunt?' Annie queried, from where she lay sprawled on the bed eyeing Rosaleen. 'Are you telling wee porky pies, eh, Rosaleen?'

Her sister threw her a look of rebuff and did not deign to answer. Inspecting her clothes in the wardrobe, she chose to wear a white suit, knowing it would show off the translucency of her skin and the green of the blouse she wore under the jacket, darkening the green of her eyes.

Examining herself in the mirror she was aware that she looked lovely, all aglow! How come she did not look like this when she went out with Joe? It must be the secrecy; the idea of doing something naughty. That must be what added the sparkle.

Annie showed that she was aware of the difference also.

'Hey, our Rosaleen. Have you a date with someone else?' she asked, her face agog with excitement. Even as she said the words, her mind rejected them. Rosaleen would never do anything underhand. Dismayed at the question, Rosaleen gaped at her, but as she groped about in her mind for a suitable answer, she saw the doubt die in Annie's eyes.

It was with relief that she hugged Annie, who whispered wistfully, 'You look lovely.'

'Thank you, love. See you later.'

And bracing herself to pass her mother's scrutiny, she descended the stairs.

Her mother looked at her askance. 'Where are you goin'?'

'I'm going with May to visit her aunt, she's not very well,' she lied, and knew by the way her mother's face creased in disbelief that she was not fooled.

Rosaleen was consumed with guilt and shame. Why was she doing this? Usually honest, she found it hard to lie, but tonight she felt a person apart. Tonight she wanted to be different. Just this one time. One date with an exciting stranger, before she got married.

15

'See you later, Mam.'

'What about Joe? What will I say to him when he comes in with your da, after the confraternity?' Thelma Magee was worried and it was apparent in her attitude. 'He always calls. Ye know he does.'

'He won't be calling tonight, I've told him I'm going out.'

And before any more embarrassing questions could be asked, Rosaleen closed the door firmly and hurried down the street. Just one date she had promised herself, but she was determined to enjoy every minute of it.

Sean Devlin was growing worried when at last he saw Rosaleen step off the tram at the bottom of Castle Street. He had begun to think that she had changed her mind. As she walked towards him, blonde hair bobbing on her shoulders, he noticed how many heads turned to watch her and wondered how this Joe fellow could bear to let her out of his sight. The suit she wore was close-fitting, the skirt below the box jacket hugging her slim hips and swinging gently to below the calf of her legs, and his breath caught in his throat at the beauty of her.

'Hello.' Her voice was shy, uncertain, and her even white teeth nipped at her bottom lip.

'Hello.' He smiled warmly down at her. 'Would you like to go anywhere in particular?'

She shook her head, her cheeks bright pink at the admiration in his eyes.

'Shall we go to the Imperial then? I hear the film's good.'

This time she nodded her head, feeling tongue-tied. She was annoyed at her shyness. He would think her a fool.

With one accord they turned and walked down Castle Street towards the town centre and when he reached for her hand and pulled her arm through his,

16

hugging it close to his side, she did not demur. Tonight was her last night out alone with a man, before she wed. A kind of hen night. She did not worry that someone might see them and tell Joe. No! She felt that they were invisible, alone on a cloud, and as they queued up outside the Imperial Picture House in Cornmarket, she was enclosed in a bubble of contentment and happiness.

During the film he held her hand, and every now and again he lifted it and brushed his lips across her palm. The emotions this aroused frightened her and she had to keep reminding herself that it was only a date. The film was a sad love story, and she was unable to stop the tears from falling. Surreptitiously, she wiped at her cheeks with her free hand. She did not want him to think her a fool. Joe often chided her for being soft-hearted, but to her surprise Sean squeezed her hand in sympathy and presented her with a handkerchief. As the film drew to a close, she was sad that their night out was nearly over and when he asked her if she would like a coffee, she nodded eagerly, glad of the chance to spend more time with him.

They sat either side of the table in a dimly lit cafe and when he had ordered the coffee, he reached across the table and gripped her hands in his.

'It can't end like this.'

'It must! You promised! One date you said,' she cried in dismay.

His eyes held hers and his head swayed slowly from side to side as he denied this.

'No. I said we would probably hate each other if we were to go out together. Remember?'

'You did promise. You said one date,' she whispered, greatly agitated, and dragged her eyes away from the magic in his.

The warmth of his look embraced her. 'Ah, Rosaleen, I didn't promise. But even if I had promised,

17

I would gladly break it . . . because I know now that I love you. We were meant for each other. Can't you feel it?'

His hands tightened on hers. 'Look at me, Rosaleen.'

The thick dark lashes that fanned her cheeks slowly lifted and their eyes met, and there it was again, that lovely, warm feeling of belonging.

'There now, you feel it too,' he chided her. 'Don't deny it.'

The arrival of the waitress with the coffee caused him to let go of her hands, and grateful to be free of his overpowering touch, she leant back in her seat out of his reach. There could be no more dates; it was too dangerous. She must make him understand that nothing had changed, that she was marrying Joe.

They argued the whole way home, but she was adamant and at the corner of Colinward Street, where she lived, offered him her hand.

Ignoring the outstretched hand he took her by the shoulders and drew her into the shadows where he kissed her; his lips persuasive, compelling. She stood for some moments, cold and passive, but then her body betrayed her and her lips moved hungrily under his and her arms crept up around his neck. They strained together for many moments and then he drew back and looked at her, a puzzled frown on his brow.

'Does this Joe fellow not satisfy you?'

Pulling angrily away from him, she cried, 'Don't talk like that! That was a sin! I shouldn't have let you kiss me like that.' There was a break in her voice as she lamented, 'Joe and I are saving ourselves for our wedding night.'

'Listen, love.' His voice was gentle, soothing. 'I'm not talking about heavy petting, but surely he shows his love like this . . .' he pulled her close again and to her shame she let him, wanting to recapture the joy of the first kiss '. . . and this.'

18

His hands caressed the back of her neck and trailed down her back, before gently gripping her buttocks and fitting her body to suit his. Sending thrill upon thrill coursing through her, awakening emotions that she had not known existed; making her feel weak at the knees. Butterfly kisses covered her face, her eyes, then her nose, then gently, so gently, her mouth. She stood in a trance, unable to break the spell he was weaving around her, until his hand cupped her breast. Then sanity returned and she reacted in anger, pushing him roughly away, hissing: 'Don't! That's a sin! Oh, I never want to see you again. Never again!'

Her voice broke on a sob. Turning, she ran down the street, her cheeks hot with shame. Joe had been courting her for eighteen months and not once had he been disrespectful. Not once had he touched her breast. He respected her too much. And tonight she had let a stranger, an exciting, wonderful stranger, but a stranger nonetheless, touch her . . . and, worse still, had wanted more. Much more, she realised, and shame engulfed her. She must never meet him again. It was too dangerous.

The rest of the week passed in a daze and she clung to Joe like a drowning person, feeling safe only in his company.

Sean was outside the factory on Wednesday and Thursday nights, but she refused to talk to him. In despair, he called May aside.

'Look, I go away tomorrow and I won't be back until the end of July. Talk to her. Please, talk to her,' he begged in a ragged voice. 'She doesn't love this Joe fellow. I just know she doesn't. She'll be unhappy married to him.'

Watching Rosaleen scurry ahead like a scared rabbit, May cried. 'I suppose you think she loves you?

She was angry with him. Rosaleen had been unhappy and jumpy since her date with him and May placed the blame squarely at his door. However, Sean was sadly shaking his head. He had thought he would be able to make Rosaleen talk to him, listen to his pleas, convince her that they were meant for each other, but he had failed miserably. She was strong-willed, much stronger than he, and he had to admit defeat. If only he was not due back on his ship. If only he had more time to wear her down.

'No, she doesn't love me,' he said sadly. 'Or at least she won't admit she loves me, but she doesn't love Joe.'

He was so earnest that in spite of herself May was impressed and asked, 'What do you mean, she doesn't love Joe? Who are you to say?'

'So help me, I don't know. I only fear she will be unhappy with him.'

'You're wrong. Joe's a good man, and they're hard to come by. He has his own wee business, so he does. He'll provide well for her. She'll never want for anything.'

He looked astounded. 'An' you think that's all that matters? A meal ticket?'

'Yes, I do!' May was adamant. 'I wish I was marrying a man like Joe. I'd look to neither left nor right, I can tell you.'

He swung away from her in anger and then swung back again to bawl, 'In the name of God, are you all thick? Do you think money's everything?'

Stung, May put her hands on her hips, threw her head high and bawled back at him. 'No, but it helps to get everything.'

The look he bestowed on her was full of pity. 'You poor fool. You poor, poor fool.'

Without another word he turned on his heel and strode down the street, leaving her standing gaping after him.

The weeks flew past and Rosaleen, caught up in preparations for her wedding, managed to push all thoughts of Sean to the back of her mind. She would not fancy marrying a Merchant Navy man, she convinced herself. Her Aunt Margaret was married to a sailor and half her life was spent waiting for him to come home on leave. No, that was not for her. She wanted a man who was always there, someone to hold her close in the night. If, when Joe kept her at arm's length, she longed for the rapture she had experienced with Sean's kisses, she assured herself that it was worth waiting for. Just a matter of a few months, and then they would be married and Joe could show his love for her. Meantime, there was plenty to keep her occupied. What with decorating the house and attending fittings for her wedding dress and all the other things attached to preparing for a wedding.

A week before the wedding, her last day at work until after her honeymoon, she came through the factory gates laughing and happy. She was covered in confetti and in her arms carried a large box, her present from the girls in work. The laughter died on her lips and her step faltered when she saw him standing there, magnificent in his Merchant Navy uniform; the target of many admiring eyes. Then she was past him, almost running in her haste, her stupid heart thumping against her ribs, panic gripping her. Dear God, why was this happening to her? She did not want to feel like this. Why couldn't he have stayed away another week and then she would be safely married to Joe?

His long strides quickly caught up with her and, gripping her by the elbow, he forced her to slow down, at the same time throwing May a look which she rightly interpreted as, 'Get lost.'

Seeing May scurry out of sight, Rosaleen turned and faced him.

'You shouldn't have come. I have nothing to say to you.'

'Why didn't you answer my letters?'

21

'I've already told you why – I have nothing to say to you, Sean Devlin. Don't you understand? I'm marrying Joe next week and that's that!'

'Is that box heavy? Here, let me carry it.'

'No!' She resisted his efforts to take the box from her. 'No . . . I can manage it myself, thank you.'

'Are you going to the Club Orchid tonight?'

'Listen you!' she cried in exasperation. 'I'm going to the dance with the girls out of work tonight and I don't want you coming and spoiling it for me. Do you hear me? Leave me alone!'

With these words she stormed ahead and he let her go. She would be at the dance tonight and whether she liked it or not, so would he. Grimly, he nodded his head. Oh, yes, he would be at the Club Orchid tonight. Just let anyone try to keep him away!'

That night, he was the first person she saw when she entered the ballroom. He was dancing with a tall, attractive girl, whom, to her shame, she found herself avidly examining.

The evening was nearly over and although he had danced with May, Sean did not ask Rosaleen to dance with him. Annoyed for feeling peeved, Rosaleen reminded herself that she had warned him not to annoy her, had told him to leave her alone. Had she not chased him? And even if he had asked her to dance, she would have refused him. Wouldn't she? Still, she felt slighted and covertly watched him, annoyed with herself for caring that he did not dance with any one girl in particular.

It was the last dance and she was moving sadly on to the dance floor with a partner when Sean appeared. Taking her firmly by the arm, he said, 'Sorry, but she promised me the last dance.'

Before she could object, he swept her into his arms and on to the dance floor.

Her heart was racing and she held herself stiff in his

arms.

'You had no right to do that!' she stormed up at him, annoyed yet excited at the effect he was having on her.

'Would you have danced with me if I had asked you to?'

'No!'

Her shake of the head was definite and he said, 'That's why I did what I did.' He gave her a little shake. 'Relax, for heaven's sake. I'm not going to bite you.'

He was a terrific dancer, long smooth strides covering the floor expertly, and in spite of herself, she relaxed against him and they twirled around the floor as one. They danced in silence, each aware of the magic bond that held them, and as the music came to an end, he steered her over to the cloakroom door.

'I'm seeing you home, so tell your friends to go on.' She opened her mouth to protest and he growled, 'Do you want me to make a scene?'

When she hesitated, he insisted, 'I will, you know. I intend talking to you, whether you listen or not.'

'It won't make any difference,' she muttered. 'You're wasting your time. My mind's made up.'

'Then you have nothing to worry about,' he assured her, and abruptly turned away, saying over his shoulder, 'I'll see you outside.'

When she told May that Sean was walking her home, her friend eyed her with concern.

'Do you want me to tag along?' she asked anxiously.

'No, no . . . it's all right. I can look after myself. You go home with the rest of the girls and I'll see you sometime tomorrow.'

It was a beautiful, moonlit night and they dandered up Castle Street in silence. At Victor's Ice Cream Parlour in Divis Street, famous for its Italian ice cream, he stopped and bought two ice-cream cones.

She had to smile when he handed her a cone with a flourish, as if he was giving her the crown jewels.

He's very handsome, she admitted to herself, as she

23

observed his straight nose and strong jaw. But then, so is Joe, she reminded herself. Once Joe and she were married and her frustration was at an end, she would not be attracted to another man. She would be fulfilled and need no other.

It came as a surprise to her when they arrived at Colinward Street. They had so much in common, so many shared interests to talk about, that the time had flown. It was with regret that she offered him her hand, but instead of shaking it, he pulled it through his arm and drew her on up the Springfield Road.

When she tried to break away from him, he begged, 'Please, Rosaleen. I may never see you again, please walk with me for a while.'

Against her better judgement she did as he asked. When they arrived at the Dam, that dark lonely place frequented by lovers, he steered her off the road and down a grassy bank.

She felt uneasy. She never liked being near the Dam, even in daylight. Too many people had drowned in it. Some accidentally, some by choice. Nevertheless, it was a favourite spot for courting couples, full of shadows and corners. Of course Joe would never dream of taking here here, he respected her too much, yet here she was with a stranger. But she did not really feel that Sean was a stranger. She felt as if she had known him all her life. It was not him she was afraid of, it was her own emotions. Feeling panic rise, she realised that this was an occasion of sin. Did the priests not warn them to stay away from lonely places when out with boys?

'I must go home,' she cried, and twisting out of Sean's hold, she started back up the grassy bank, but he grabbed hold of her arm and pulled her down again, into his arms. Her heart was racing and he was aware of her agitation.

'Don't be afraid, Rosaleen,' he whispered softly. 'I won't harm you.'

24

His hands caressed her back, sending sensual tremors shivering along the edge of her nerves, and in spite of her misgivings she sank against him, excitement a tight knot in her groin. In the moonlight her eyes were pale and glittered like diamonds, and her hair was like silvered silk. The moon's light was ghostly and as she cast apprehensive glances around in the eerie light, she shivered. Sean opened his jacket and drew her against the warmth of his body.

'Are you cold?' he asked, wrapping his jacket around her. She shook her head, her hair swaying like a silver bell. He put his lips against its perfumed softness and his pulse quickened. Excitement sent the blood pounding through his veins. He groaned, feeling real pain at the very thought that she was to wed another. He had to stop her. Aware of his anguish she drew back, looking up at him askance.

'You can't marry Joe,' he cried. 'I won't let you. Do you hear me? I won't let you.'

'Tut! Of course I'm marrying Joe. Don't you realise my parents have spent all their savings on this wedding? Haven't I told you Joe has bought and decorated a house?' she cried, annoyed at his persistence.

His grip on her tightened. 'You wouldn't be the first girl to realise she had made a mistake.'

This really riled her. 'Oh, but I haven't made a mistake! I love Joe,' she cried in exasperation. 'And next Saturday I'm marrying him.'

'Then why are you here with me?' he asked quickly. 'Eh? Tell me why.'

'Because I felt sorry for you, that's why,' she hissed, and once more turned to leave him.

He pulled her roughly back against him. 'Sorry for me? Sorry for me?' His voice was hoarse. 'Well now, let's see a little more of your pity.' His grip on her tightened and his lips savaged hers.

She stood rigid, fear a tight knot in her stomach, as his lips angrily bruised hers, crushing them against her teeth; making her wince.

Coming to his senses, he turned aside, apologising.

'I'm sorry . . . I'm sorry . . . forgive me. I had no right to do that.'

He sounded so upset, compassion overcame her fear. Pulling him around towards her, her hands tenderly brushed his face.

'Hush . . . hush. It's all right . . . it's all right,' she soothed him.

Gently now, he pressed her close and his lips touched her face. She lapped it up, enjoying the sensual tremors that were rippling through her body; the mounting excitement. Why couldn't Joe kiss her like this, instead of constantly pushing her away and telling her they must wait? Surely kisses like this were not a sin?

Unconsciously, her face moved restlessly until his lips found hers, and as his kisses became more insistent, her arms crept up around his neck, and she returned kiss for kiss, caress for caress; pressing urgently against the hard lines of his body. When his hands gently explored her, seeking out the forbidden places, she knew why Joe did not take chances. This was wrong, one part of her mind insisted. Very wrong! She knew she should push him away, stop him, but her body would not obey her mind as his hands brought her to the edge of ecstasy, and over, and soon it was too late. There in the shadows they came together as naturally as night follows day. It was the easiest thing in the world. Not awful, as she had been led to believe, and she lost all track of time as he made her his own. Lost in a well of passion that carried them above all reason, senses alive to nothing but each other, they were as one.

They clung together for a long time, at peace with

the world, but at last he pushed her gently away, until he could see into her eyes.

'Now do you know why you can't marry Joe? You're mine! All mine! We were meant for each other. I knew it the minute I saw you.'

His voice was gentle and confident, and smug.

It was the smugness that came across to Rosaleen as sanity returned and she realised just what she had done. She stood aghast, panic setting in. Was she mad? A week before her wedding and she had given herself to another man. She was a whore. A tart. A sinner. Dear God . . . how could she have been so stupid? How could she have done this terrible thing?

Appalled, she hurriedly adjusted her clothing and groped about on the grass for her handbag. Without looking at him, she started to clamber up the grassy bank. Sean took her arm to assist her, aware that all was far from well, but not knowing why. Surely she understood? Hadn't he proved to her that they were meant for each other? Angrily, Rosaleen shook him off, hitting out at him with her handbag, deep sobs choking her.

Once up the slope she almost ran down the Springfield Road, the tears blinding her, and when he followed close behind, she rounded on him and hissed, 'Leave me alone! Leave me alone! Go away. I never want to see you again.'

'You're being a fool, Rosaleen. You can't possibly marry Joe after what happened back there.' His voice became pleading. 'Ah, Rosaleen, I love you. I love you so much. Surely you know that? Don't you feel the same?'

Stopping in her tracks she rounded on him. 'Love? You call what happened back there love? That was lust! We were like two animals. Now I know why Joe insists that we don't pet. That's what happens when you pet. You lose control and act like animals.' Her

27

voice broke and she swallowed deeply before continuing. 'Let me tell you something, Sean Devlin. Joe wouldn't have lost control. In fact, he respects me too much to take me to a place like that. That's the difference between you and him. He respects me.'

Stunned at her words, he grabbed her and pushed her roughly against the wall.

'I love you! That's why that happened. Believe me, if I hadn't loved you, it wouldn't have. I'm no fool, I know the difference between lust and love . . . and you wanted it too, so don't act innocent with me,' he growled.

She stood, head averted, lips tightly pressed together, and he cried, 'Ah, Rosaleen, you wanted it too. Come on now, love, don't deny it. Don't put all the blame on me,' he begged, wanting to reach her, but he pleaded in vain.

'If you're quite finished, I'd like to go home.'

Her voice was cold, lifeless, and he knew he had lost her. He had not meant to take her. Not like that! No, he had wanted to woo her with flowers and gifts, but time was against him and he had let himself get carried away. He bitterly regretted his actions, but it was too late. At the contempt in her eyes, his arms fell limply to his sides and without another glance, she left him.

He watched until she turned the corner of Colinward Street and then he went to the corner and watched until she entered her own doorway. It was late and he wanted to be sure she got home safely. Then, with steps that dragged, he continued down the Springfield Road, his heart a heavy lump in his breast.

Inside the small hall, Rosaleen wiped her face and tried to compose herself. She knew her mother would still be downstairs; she never retired until Rosaleen and Annie were indoors. Sure enough, the light was on in the kitchen. Opening the door, she stayed in its shadow and said, 'Goodnight, Mam.' But she was not going to be let off the hook.

'Come in here a minnit!' Her mother ordered, and slowly Rosaleen entered the room.

'You're late t'night! Were you with Joe?'

Her mother sounded suspicious and seeing her nose twitch, Rosaleen's heart missed a beat, feeling sure she could smell the sex on her; she felt she stank of it.

She lied abruptly. 'Yes, I was. I'm tired, Mam, I'm going to bed.'

And before her mother could ask any more questions, she withdrew into the hall. Climbing the stairs, she entered the room she shared with her young sister Annie, wishing they had a bathroom. She felt so dirty; wicked and dirty.

It was easy running away from her mother, but not so easy to escape her conscience. If only she had come home with May. Would Joe guess that she was not a virgin when they spent their first night together? Only one more week and she would have experienced that wonderful pleasure with Joe. Oh, why hadn't she come straight home? How could she have been so stupid?

Oh, dear God, please forgive me. Please don't let Joe guess and help me make him a good wife, she prayed earnestly on her knees, before crawling into bed beside Annie.

As she tossed and turned, causing Annie to twitch irritably at the bedclothes, she realised that at least now she would not be afraid on her wedding night. Some girls said that it was awful the first time, and a lot said that it didn't get much better but once the kids came they compensated for everything. Well, she shouldn't have listened to gossip. She had thought it wonderful. The most natural thing in the world. It had just been the wrong man. One thing she was sure of, she was going to enjoy married life.

May was surprised when, leaving the factory on Monday night, she saw Sean waiting at the corner of

29

Cupar Street. He approached her. She was horrified at his appearance. He looked as if he had not slept for a week. When he humbly asked her if he could have a word with her she silently nodded her agreement. He walked the full length of Clonard Street with her. Right down to the Falls Road and over to the corner of Spinner Street where she lived, speaking all the while of how much he loved Rosaleen.

He was in such a state that she took pity on him and promised to try to persuade her friend to meet him once more. And, that night, calling to see Rosaleen, she did try. Pleading his case until she was blue in the face, but to no avail.

Rosaleen was adamant. Eyeing May reproachfully, she chided, 'You've changed your tune. I thought you didn't want me to have anything to do with him?'

'I know, Rosaleen, but to tell the truth, I feel sorry for him. He looks awful. Will you not see him just once, and put him out of his misery?'

'No, May. You don't understand. I like him, I like him a lot, too much . . . but I'm marrying Joe.'

May nodded. She did understand. Once more she lamented the fact that Sean had fallen for Rosaleen. Why could he not have picked her? Rosaleen was lucky to have two handsome men in love with her, but she had made the right choice. Joe would make a better husband and father than a sailor would. There was no doubt whatsoever in May's mind that Rosaleen had made the right choice.

Saturday dawned with clear blue skies and Rosaleen made a beautiful bride. Her dress was made of soft, ivory-coloured satin and swirled around her ankles above matching satin shoes, and she carried a bouquet of lilies and freesia. Annie had been horrified at her choice of flowers, saying lilies were for funerals and were considered unlucky. However, Rosaleen loved the waxed, pure beauty of lilies and she was not in the least superstitious. She had two bridesmaids; Annie was in pink, and May in blue, and each carried a small posy of mixed flowers. Oh, yes, her mother had been determined to splash out and Rosaleen felt indebted to her. Both her parents too looked splendid in new outfits. The pale blue of her mother's matching coat and dress made her look younger and her father was very handsome in his new grey lounge suit. It had all cost a fortune, and there was no way she could have changed her mind. No way! Her parents had scrimped and saved to make her day perfect and she could not have backed out. Not that she had wanted to, she reminded heself. She would soon forget Sean Devlin, now that she was married. All week she had been plagued by doubts, overcome every now and again by memories of the rapture she had felt in his arms, but when she saw the tears of pride in her mother's eyes, she knew she had done the right thing. Joe was the man for her. Everybody thought so ... and surely everybody could not be wrong? She was sorry she had hurt Sean but a handsome man like him would soon find someone else.

Then she saw him. He was standing on the far side of the Falls Road, facing the church, against the wall that used to house the old asylum. She gave a gasp of dismay when she saw how haggard and ill he looked. Immediately Joe was all concern. 'Are you all right, love?'

'Yes!' her answer was so abrupt, he drew back to get a better look at her face, and she hastened to assure him, 'Yes, I'm fine, fine. Just nervous.'

She moved closer to him and gripped his arm tightly. Would Sean approach them? Would he say anything that would betray her? While the photographer took the wedding photos, she kept her eyes averted, and when she next dared to look, Sean was

31

gone and she breathed a sigh of relief. She only hoped that she had not ruined the wedding photographs by her own stupidity.

Chapter 2

With a mumbled excuse, Rosaleen pushed her chair away from the table and hurried from the room. A slight frown gathered on Joe's brow as he gazed thoughtfully after her. This was the third morning she had rushed from the table, out to the bathroom that he had built on to the back of the house. It was almost as if she was . . . but then, she couldn't be . . . Could she? His mind boggled at the idea. Could she possibly be pregnant?

In the bathroom, on her knees at the toilet bowl, Rosaleen retched and retched, her whole body contracting in an effort to bring up food from an empty, exhausted stomach. At last, flushing the toilet, she pushed herself wearily to her feet and turned to the wash-hand basin, despair in her heart. Whilst she washed her hands and splashed her face with cold water she examined her reflection in the mirror. She looked awful! There wasn't a vestige of colour in her face and her eyes were like saucers; saucers with great dark rims round them. A sigh left her lips, a great, deep sigh from the heart. She would have to tell Joe. There was no alternative. A shiver coursed through her body at the idea. In the short time that they were married, she had discovered that Joe was very strict where morals were concerned. Black was black and white was white. There was no grey as far as he was concerned. You were either good or you were bad, mistakes ought not to happen. What would he do when he discovered that she was pregnant? Would he put her out? Where would she go? Back to her parents' home? Would they let her return.

In a state of terror, she pictured the horror on her parents' faces when she told them that she was pregnant and that Joe wasn't the father. The recriminations, the questions. Fearfully, she looked around her. What was that noise? To her dismay, she realised the strangled sounds were coming from her own mouth. A sob rose in her throat and burst from her lips, and she pressed the towel to her mouth to stifle the sounds as she fought for control.

This was all Sean Devlin's fault! What if she had not been getting married? She was in a state as it was, but what if she was single?

Her mind baulked at the very idea, filling her with panic. Imagine her pregnant and him away in the middle of the ocean. Not that it would be much better once she admitted to Joe that she was pregnant, but at least she had a wedding ring on her finger, Mrs in front of her name, and she could hope that Joe would not broadcast her shame to all and sundry.

O, dear God, help me, she begged. But how could she expect God to help her? Hadn't she been wicked? Even if God in all His mercy had forgiven her, how could she expect Him to make Joe understand?

With steps that dragged, she returned to the kitchen; she may as well get it over with.

Joe watched her sit down, watched her clasp the mug of tea with both hands, as if seeking warmth, and asked gently, 'Are you not feeling well, Rosaleen?'

Lost in thought, trying to find words to confess her guilt, she jerked upright, sending tea dripping down her fingers on to the table.

Immediately Joe was on his feet and around the

table, bending over her full of concern. Taking the mug from her shaking hands, he gently dried them on a tea towel.

'Is it something you ate, do you think?' he asked, solicitously rubbing warmth into her cold hands; his eyes taking note of her lack of colour.

Closing her eyes, Rosaleen forced the words into her mouth and out. 'I'm pregnant.'

She sat still, waiting for words of condemnation, perhaps a blow. God knows she deserved it. At last, unable to bear the silence any longer, she glanced up and her mouth dropped open in amazement. Instead of the look of horror she expected to see on Joe's face, there was a look of bemused wonder.

Even as she gaped at him, he reached for her, drawing her up into his arms, muttering, 'Ah, Rosaleen, Rosaleen my love, you have just made me the happiest man in the world.'

He sank his face into her hair, and she felt his tears soak through and wet her scalp. 'I thought I wasn't able . . . you know what I mean . . .' His voice trailed off, then filled with awe. 'And to discover that I am . . . why, it's an answer to my prayers.'

Bewildered, Rosaleen clung to him, trying to sort out her jumbled thoughts. Surely Joe did not believe that his few futile attempts at making love had resulted in a pregnancy? He could not be so naive. Could he? Another stealthy glance at him showed her that he did indeed believe.

It seemed *her* prayers were being answered too.

Leading her into the living room, he made her sit down on the settee. 'Put your feet up, love. There'll be no work for you today. In fact, perhaps it would be better if you left work.' He brushed the hair back from her brow and planted a tender kiss there. 'What do you think?'

Still in a daze, she answered him mechanically. 'I

would like to work on for a while. We could do with the money.'

When she was settled with a rug over her legs and a cup of warm milk in her hand, he returned to the kitchen. Shouting in excitedly to her, making plans, as he washed the dishes. At last, after much fussing over her, he left for work.

Glad to see him go, Rosaleen relaxed and set her mind to work on her problem. Should she tell Joe the truth? She must! Surely she must? She owed it to him. To let him rear another man's child as his own would be a sin. One thing was sure: if she let him believe he was the father, her lips must be sealed forever.

What if she was found out? But then, she couldn't be found out. Only she, and she alone, knew the truth. No one would be able to blow the whistle on her; not even Sean. And, really, she would be doing Joe a good turn, wouldn't she? Because it looked as if he would never father a child. But had she the right to make such a decision?

Her thoughts whirled, making her head ache, and at last she could bear it no longer. Pushing the rug irritably away, she rose to her feet. For some moments she stood undecided; then she entered the bathroom and set the taps running in the bath, a determined look on her face. Her mind was made up. From now on, as far as she was concerned, this child she was carrying was Joe's. As soon as she had bathed she would go up and break the news to her mother and then make an appointment to see the doctor. Thoughts of a laughing face with dark blue eyes flitted across her mind, but she pushed them resolutely away. These thoughts she was beginning to dwell on so often lately must stop.

All of a sudden, against her will, she was blinded by tears as the memory of the night up at the Dam returned to haunt her. She could feel his arms around her, hear his declaration of love, and self-pity filled her. Lying in the bath, she wept long and hard for what might have been. Her only consolation was that she need never see Sean again. Need never know who he married or where he lived, and for this she was grateful.

Thelma Magee eyed her daughter closely when, after a light tap on the kitchen door, she entered the room. The signs of weeping were well camouflaged but she saw them and her heart sank. It dismayed her to feel Rosaleen's unrest, but what could she do? It would be wrong to interfere between husband and wife. Rosaleen had made her bed, now she must lie on it. Who would have thought that Joe would be found wanting? A big man like Joe? It was hard to believe.

'This is a surprise,' she cried. 'Why are you not at work?'

'I've some news for you, Mam. What do you think? I'm pregnant!'

Relief flooded through Thelma at her words. Everything must be all right; things must have sorted themselves out.

Rosaleen felt the relief that radiated from her mother and smiled wryly. Her mother would be sure to think that pregnancy solved all her problems. How wrong she was. It only added to them.

'Oh, that's wonderful, Rosaleen. Just wonderful. Wait 'til your da hears, it'll be another excuse for a drink. As if he needs one.'

'Ah, Mam, don't. Me dad's not that bad. Why, he only drinks at set times. In fact, I can't remember seeing him really drunk, just happy.'

'Humph!' Thelma turned away, a cynical look on her face.

Rosaleen couldn't understand her mother's attitude towards her father. Heaven knows he was always bending over backwards to please her, he lifted and laid her, but she never gave him credit for anything. He was such a quiet, inoffensive man, and was devoted to her mother, but still she was forever finding fault with him.

Rosaleen eyed her mother covertly. Why, she was absolutely beaming. She was certainly pleased about the baby. She remembered the day she had plucked up the courage to ask her mother's advice about her matrimonial problems. To her surprise, her mother had been more embarrassed than she. Bright red, she had refused to meet Rosaleen's eye and had pleated her apron, pulled it apart and pleated it again, and again, making Rosaleen want to scream, and sorry that she had broached the subject at all. At last her mother had muttered, 'That's between you and him. It's something you must work out between you. Because . . . well . . . ye see, I . . . really . . . I . . . I'll make a cup of tea.' And had sought refuge in the scullery. The conversation was never resumed.

'When's the baby due?'

'I'm not sure. I've to see the doctor yet, but I imagine . . .' Rosaleen paused, remembering in time that her mother knew that she and Joe were having trouble.

'I think about June,' she finished, adding on an extra month. Was this the beginning of a life of deceit?

'Oh, that's a lovely time. You'll have the whole summer to get out and about. A summer baby gets a better start in life than a winter child, so it does. Ye know what I mean. It gets out in the sun an' all. Our Annie'll be glad. She dotes on kids, so she does.'

'How's her romance going?'

'Oh, it's still on. I've warned her, mind. He'll never cross over this doorstep, I told her, but she's stubborn, so she is. You'd think she could find herself a good Catholic boy. The Falls Road's full of them. Somebody like Joe. That's one thing about you, Rosaleen, you never give me any sleepless nights. You never ran around with Protestants.'

'George seems a nice lad, Mam.'

'You've met him?'

Her mother sounded so scandalised, Rosaleen laughed aloud.

'Yes! And he didn't bite me, and he didn't have horns.'

'Really, Rosaleen, I'm surprised at you, condonin' her behaviour. You're as bad as your da.'

'Oh? Does me da not object?'

'Hah! He keeps throwing every convert he knows in my face. A fat lot he knows. You're better with your own sort, I told him. But then, of course, he would be prejudiced.'

'Why? Why would he be prejudiced?' Rosaleen asked, her look intent.

Her mother grew flustered. 'Well, ye know what I mean. He's worked with Protestants all his life. He can see no harm in them.'

'Mam . . .'

It was on the tip of Rosaleen's tongue to ask her mother why she had married her father, but when Thelma quirked a brow inquiringly at her, the words died.

'Oh, nothing, just . . . about our Annie – don't push her. If you leave her alone, I bet you she'll stop dating George, but as sure as you nag her, George will seem more wonderful. We all go through these phases.'

'You didn't!'

'I know . . . I know . . . but times change. The young ones are more independent nowadays. Annie's no fool. She'll be all right!'

The door was pushed open. Annie's eyebrows raised at seeing Rosaleen. 'Who's taking my name in vain?' she cried.

'Nobody! What are you doin' home?'

With a discreet wink at Rosaleen, Annie solemnly

39

answered her mother, 'I'm meeting George. We're going down to pick out an engagement ring.'

'In the name of God, are you mad?' Thelma rose from her chair in panic. 'You'll get out of this house, mind. Ye can pack your bags if you get engaged to that Prod.'

'Mam! She's only joking.'

Rosaleen gave Annie a disapproving look. Fond as she was of her young sister, there were times when she wished that she would date Catholic boys. Her mother was right; there were plenty of young men on the Falls Road, but so far Annie had dated only Protestants.

Now Annie grinned wickedly, and continued, 'Did you hear that, Rosaleen? She'd put me out and I'd have to go and live on the Shankhill Road – in sin.'

Seeing her mother's face blanch, Rosaleen sought to change the conversation.

'Stop acting the fool, Annie. I've some good news. What do you think? I'm pregnant.'

Annie's mouth gaped slightly open and she gazed in wonder at Rosaleen. Then, nodding her head, she said: 'I'm glad for you. Surprised, but glad.'

Rosaleen gaped in amazement and cried, 'What do you mean, surprised?'

'Well, perhaps I shouldn't say this . . . but I didn't think Joe had it in him. I always thought he was a bit of a wimp.'

Open-mouthed, Rosaleen sat in stunned silence, surprised at how perceptive this young sister of hers was. Just past seventeen and she was more worldly than Rosaleen would ever be.

'Oh, listen to knowall. From the mouths of babes comes rubbish,' Thelma cried in dismay. Annie was too forthright for her own good. What if Rosaleen took offence? 'Why are you home?' she asked again, to change the subject.

'We're on strike! We all walked out because Jean Morgan was given the sack for bad time-keeping.'

'An' you think they'll take her back? You think ye can blackmail the firm?' Thelma's face fell in disbelief. 'Sure, they could fill the factory ten times over, there's so many stitchers out of work. You'd never get another job. You're even dafter than I thought ye were, girl.'

'Mam, you can't let them get away with everything. Next time it might be me.'

Hands on hips, Thelma challenged, 'Why you? Eh? Tell me, why you? You're not a bad time-keeper. You're never off work. Why would they sack you?'

'They would find some excuse. My face doesn't fit.'

'That's because you can't keep your big mouth shut!' Thelma bawled. 'Ye fight everybody's battles, so ye do. You should mind your own business.'

'Tut!' Annie turned aside in disgust. It was no use telling her mother that Mr Benson didn't like Catholics. 'Anyhow, we're going back in tomorrow. I think Benson will give her another chance. He's too many orders in to do otherwise, but meanwhile we'll have made our point. He'll know that he can't push us around.'

Thelma opened her mouth to argue, but with a slight shake of her head, Rosaleen stopped her. In this mood Annie would only humour her mother so long, then there would be a blazing row.

'Will Jean go back?' she asked, seeking to ease the tension.

'Oh, yes, I think so. Mind you, she's been warned to pull up her socks, 'cause next time we won't back her. She'll be out for good.'

With an apologetic smile, she placed a hand on Rosaleen's shoulder and squeezed it. 'I'm sorry about what I said just now about Joe. You know me. Speak first . . . think later. He's a fine guy and I'm very fond of him. You know that, don't you?'

Rosaleen patted her hand and smiled, graciously receiving the olive branch.

41

Later, when Rosaleen had departed, Thelma rounded on Annie.

'Are you daft. Eh? That was a terrible thing to say. Joe's a fine figure of a man, so he is. Imagine saying to someone's face that their husband's a wimp . . .' For some seconds words failed her. Then: 'Rosaleen could've easily taken offence, girl.'

'I know, I know.' Annie made placatory gestures with her hands. She sorely regretted her remarks. Would she ever learn to control her tongue? And now her mother was on her hobby horse . . . keeping her in line. 'It was stupid of me, I admit! But luckily enough Rosaleen didn't take umbrage, so there's no harm done.'

'Your big mouth will get ye into trouble one of these days, so it will. Even in work ye can't keep it shut.' Thelma glared at her. 'What if you get the sack? Eh? If Benson gives you the push, don't come t'me for sympathy. Do ye hear me? An' if he doesn't give you the push . . . keep yer big mouth shut in future!'

With a grimace, Annie turned away and headed for the scullery; afraid to retaliate; afraid of starting a full-scale row. Her father would be home soon, and although a kindly man, he always sided with her mother. She hadn't realized how much Rosaleen had shielded her from her mother's sharp tongue until her sister had married and her comforting presence was withdrawn.

Her mother's voice followed her. 'As for that Prod yer dating, don't you ever dare bring him near this door . . .'

To escape further recriminations, Annie carried on through the scullery and out into the yard, closing the door with a sharp decisive click. Drawing deep breaths of air into her lungs, she fought for control. If only her mother would try to understand her. She couldn't help that she was different from Rosaleen, and the way her mother kept comparing them made her blood boil. All right, so she wasn't as good-living as her sister. Could not get interested in a Catholic boy. It wasn't from choice. Catholic boys just didn't ask her out, whereas Protestants did. One thing she was sure of: she certainly didn't want anyone like Joe for a husband! To her, he appeared a cold fish. Oh, he was kind, generous to a fault . . . Rosaleen wanted for nothing. Still, he never showed her any affection in public; no wee spontaneous kisses or hugs. No warm 'I'm glad you're mine' looks. But perhaps he was different in private.

Or perhaps, as her mother was always pointing out, she read too many romantic novels. The man Annie dreamed of meeting would be loving and passionate; sweep her off her feet. Kiss her and hug her whenever the notion took him. She sighed as her thoughts ran on. Even the thought of how things could be made her feel all mellow. Her mother was right all the same . . . she would have to learn to control her tongue or, awful thought, she might even scare Mr Right away. With these thoughts she entered the house, prepared to eat humble pie to keep the peace.

That night, as she sat on the opposite side of the hearth from Joe, Rosaleen found her self examining him but could not agree with Annie. As far as appearance went, Joe was all man: tall, broad-shouldered and handsome. Were his good looks a bit too pretty, though? No, not really. With his fair hair and thick-lashed pale grey eyes, he wasn't as rugged as Sean, but neither was he soppy-looking. Annie, not being aware of his problem, was doing him an injustice.

As the weeks passed and Rosaleen started to get bigger, Joe, released from the pressure of having to perform his duty now that she was pregnant, suggested moving into the spare room.

43

'You need a bed to yourself, love,' he explained with a tender smile. 'I don't want to crush you now you're getting bigger.' And he gave her stomach a patronising pat.

Annoyed, the look Rosaleen gave him was so long and appraising that he blushed bright red. He became so flustered she felt pity replace the annoyance, and thanked him bleakly for his thoughtfulness. She had not married him to sleep alone, but, she reminded herself, it would be better on her own than having to put up with Joe starting something he could not finish. Perhaps she would not feel so frustrated. Sometimes she was angry with Sean for making her aware just what she was missing out on. She had not expected to enjoy that side of married life and she would not have known any better, but then, she reminded herself, she would probably have ended up childless; this way she would at least become a mother.

Rosaleen worked up until six weeks before the baby was due, to help pay for the bathroom. Joe didn't want her to, because with the threat of war all the big engineering firms were making parts for planes and ships and his small business was doing well on smaller home jobs, but she preferred to be active and the money would come in handy. She knew how lucky she was; not many young married couples were able to afford their own house. And she got on very well with her mother-in-law, which was another blessing; none of the married girls in work could abide their mothers-in-law.

Joe's father had died when he was very young and he had left money in trust for Joe and that was how he had been able to start up on his own. He was an only child, so Rosaleen had been afraid his mother might be over possessive. But no, if anything, she clung more to Rosaleen than she did to Joe, and since she lived just around the corner in Cavendish Street, this was a blessing.

Annie's romance with George had died a natural

death once her mother stopped talking about him and a delighted Thelma confided in Rosaleen that Annie had a new boy friend, a Catholic!

Every Tuesday night, when Joe went to the confraternity in Clonard Monastery, Rosaleen accompanied him as far as Dunmore Street. There they parted company, Joe going down Dunmore Street towards the monastery and Rosaleen going on up the Springfield Road to visit her mother; to be collected later by Joe.

A smile curved her lips as she walked up the Springfield Road this particular night. Tonight she was meeting Annie's boy friend. A paragon of virtues as far as her mother was concerned (although he had been on the scene just a few short weeks).

When she opened the kitchen door and saw Sean sitting at the fireside, she almost fainted. Why had she not asked the name of Annie's boy friend? Clinging to the door for support, she drew long gasping breaths into her lungs, fighting the dark cloud that threatened to engulf her.

Sean was on his feet instantly, and putting an arm around her. He half carried her to the settee and made her sit down. He was dismayed; he had not meant to take her unawares. How come she did not know about him? Annie was a chatter-box, so how could Rosaleen be unaware that he was dating her sister?

'What's wrong, Rosaleen? Have you started? Do you think the baby's comin'?' Her mother's voice was shrill with panic. 'Will I send for the nurse? Eh? Will I? Some first babies come early.'

Pushing his arm away from her, Rosaleen turned thankfully to her distracted mother.

'I'm all right, Mam. Just a bit faint. Could I have some water, please?' She was playing for time, trying to still her racing heart.

Sipping the water, she smiled weakly at her mother.

45

'I think I had better go straight home again, Mam. Just in case.'

She wanted to get away from Sean's disturbing presence, but to her dismay he immediately said, 'I'll see her home.'

'Oh, would you, Sean? And will you stay with her 'til Joe comes home from the confraternity? I'll chase him home the minnit he comes.'

'Of course I will.'

'No! No . . . what about Annie?' Rosaleen wailed. She could not bear to be alone with him.

'Sure she'll not be ready for another half hour. Ye know what she's like. She can go down with Joe when he comes. Sean won't mind. Sure you won't, Sean?'

'No, no, I'll be glad to see her home.'

'By the way, Rosaleen . . .' Her mother bestowed a fond smile on Sean. 'I suppose you've already guessed that this is Annie's new boy friend?'

Rosaleen nodded mutely and rose to her feet. She needed to get home, to be alone to sort out how Sean dating Annie would affect her life.

At last they were out on the street, away from her mother's fussing. Sean examined her from the corner of his eye. He saw the bloom of her skin, the thick lashes that he knew concealed the vivid green of her eyes. Here she was, full of another man's child, and still he wanted her; craved for her touch.

Rosaleen plodded along beside him, feeling fat and ungainly. Wishing that she had worn her green swagger coat. What on earth was she saving it for? She was aware that her ankles and hands were swollen and that her hair needed washing. Why hadn't she paid more attention to her appearance before she came out?

Dear God, what was she thinking of? What did it matter how she looked? She was another man's wife! Aghast at her thoughts, she quickened her step and

46

Sean lengthened his stride to suit hers.

'Take your time, I'm not going to bite you.'

'Seems to me I heard those assurances from you once before. To my cost,' she cried bitterly.

His lips tightened, but he bit back the angry retort that sprang to them. He had thought that if he saw her again, especially as Annie had mentioned that her sister was expecting a baby, he would be able to lay her ghost. But, no, every pore of his body still ached for her.

At the door of her home, Rosaleen turned to him with a relieved sigh. 'Thank you for seeing me home. I'll be all right now.'

She made no attempt to open the door. She did not want to see him in her home; he would fill it with ghosts.

But Sean had other ideas. 'If you won't invite me in, I'll wait here until your . . . your husband comes.' He found his tongue stumbled over the word 'husband', and this made him more angry still. He glared down at her and growled, 'I promised to stay with you until your . . . until he comes, and I intend to do just that.'

Resigned, she silently opened the door and he followed her inside. 'Would you like a cup of tea?' she asked sullenly.

He was no bigger than Joe but seemed to fill the room. She felt an insane longing to fall into his arms and weep, which terrified her.

'No, thank you. Here . . . gimme your coat.' He gently helped her off with it. 'Now sit down and rest.'

She obeyed him and watched him hang her coat at the foot of the stairs, her eyes wide with fear.

Seeing the expression, he cried in exasperation: 'For heaven's sake, stop looking at me like that. I'm not going to tell anyone we went out together.'

'May knows.'

Alarm flared in his eyes, and his jaw dropped slightly. He did not want to cause her any trouble.

'She doesn't know about . . .' His hands made motions

in the air and hot, vivid colour rushed to her face when she realised what he meant.

'Oh, no! No!'

He smiled slightly at her indignation. 'Well, then, you can warn her off, can't you? Isn't she trustworthy?'

Dear God . . . it sounded as if he intended being around for a long time.

'Are you serious about our Annie?' she asked, her look beseeching him to deny it.

'Why not?' he asked reasonably.

'You're doing this for badness, aren't you? You're getting your own back on me.'

'Don't flatter yourself.' His nostrils widened in disdain. 'I admit I first danced with Annie because she was your sister, but don't underestimate her. She's a lovely girl, warm and kind, and I find her charming.' His shoulders rose slightly. 'One thing led to another and . . . why shouldn't we date? We're both free.'

He refrained from telling her that she was often the topic of conversation; that he milked Annie dry obtaining information about her. He was surprised that Annie had not twigged on, but she was very fond of Rosaleen and enjoyed talking about her.

'She's too young for you, so she is!' Rosaleen cried indignantly. 'She's only seventeen.'

He smiled wryly. 'Well now, she says she's almost eighteen.'

'Oh, she's only a child, so she is!'

He watched her through narrowed eyes. 'Do you know something? Annie is more worldly than you. She has no strong beliefs about kissing and hugging.'

He saw her go pale and sinking to his haunches beside her, gripped her hands. 'Don't look like that,' he begged. 'Please . . . I was having you on. I assure you I've never taken advantage of Annie. As you say, she's very young. I'll never harm her.'

She looked at him, and although her eyes swam with

tears, he could see the pain there.

'I wish you'd repected me, like that.'

Her voice was sad and he gripped her hands tighter still.

'Ah, Rosaleen . . . I did respect you,' he cried in dismay. Her lips pressed tightly together and she shook her head in disbelief.

Cupping her face in his hands, he pleaded, 'Believe me, Rosaleen, please. I did respect you . . . but I loved you, too, and one got in the way of the other.'

'Well then, please don't do this,' she begged. 'Leave our Annie alone.'

'Ah now, Rosaleen. That's not fair,' he countered. 'I'm a young man, and I intend to marry and have children, and I really am very fond of Annie.'

The child in her womb chose that moment to turn over and she thought wildly, It knows. It knows he's its father.

And soon everybody would know of her shame if she produced a dark-haired boy the picture of him. How would she be able to hide the truth if he was there for all to compare them?

The closeness of her, the soft trembling lips were his downfall. Unable to help himself, he kissed her. A kiss full of hunger and need. How she got the strength to pull her mouth away from his she would never know, because her whole body cried out for want of him, but with a vicious shove she sent him flying. Crouched on his haunches as he was, her push took him unawares and he found himself sprawled on the carpet.

'Don't you dare touch me again, do you hear me? Don't ever touch me again,' she cried, her voice rising hysterically. 'You're evil, and I hate you. I hate you. I hate you . . .'

The sound of Joe's key in the lock halted her tirade. Gulping deep in her throat for control, she cried, 'Get up, you fool. Get up. It's Joe and Annie.'

49

When Joe entered the room, she was lying back on the settee and Sean was coming from the kitchen with a glass of water in his hand.

'How are you, love?' Joe asked, hovering anxiously over her.

'I'm fine, Joe, fine.'

Sipping from the glass of water, dismay filled her when, over Joe's shoulder, she saw the anxious faces of her parents as well as Annie. They mustn't stay. They must go and take Sean with them.

Since she had left work, she had become very close to her father; him being on the sick this past four months and at home all day, and her mother doing home help to a neighbour, meant she saw more of him than she did of her mother. Now her eyes pleaded with him and he did not let her down.

'I think she should go to bed,' he said.

Then, as if in answer to her plea, he added, 'It's rest ye need, love, being so near yer time. Away t'bed. I'll come down tomorrow and see how ye are.'

'Thanks, Da.'

'Maybe I should stay off work tomorrow, eh, Rosaleen? Just in case,' her mother asked anxiously.

'No, Mam, that won't be necessary. Old Mrs Grant needs you. I'll be all right. If I need you, me da'll go for you. O.K.?'

'All right, love, we'll go now and let you get t'bed.'

To her relief, Annie and Sean left with them, Annie promising to bring Sean back when Rosaleen was feeling better. This caused Joe to insist that they come back on Saturday night, all being well, and Rosaleen thought she would die when Sean quickly took him up on the offer. How was she going to bear seeing Sean and Annie together, watching Annie fawn all over him?

Joe was working late the following night and Rosaleen

decided to meet May coming out of work, to ask for her silence about the fact that Sean had once fancied her. She had worried all day about the coming Saturday night visit and felt the walk out in the air would do her good. It was some time since she had seen May and had come to the conclusion that she must be courting.

From where she stood waiting on the corner where the Kashmir Road met Cupar Street, Rosaleen saw May come through the gates of the factory deep in conversation with Billy Mercer, foreman over the fitters who maintained the looms. To her surprise, she saw Billy bend and kiss May before they parted, he heading for the Shankhill Road and May walking towards Rosaleen. Her jaw dropped slightly and bright colour stained her cheeks when she saw Rosaleen, but her arms reached out and she greeted her warmly.

'Rosaleen! Oh, you're a sight for sore eyes. What brings you here?' Returning her hug, Rosaleen jerked her head after Billy's retreating figure.

'What's all that about?'

'Oh, I've been out with him a few times.'

May's voice was airy and Rosaleen eyed her closely.

'Well, what brings you here?' May repeated.

'I want to talk to you about something. Can you come up to the house for a while after you get your tea and we'll have a natter? It's been ages since I saw you.'

'Ah, Rosaleen, I'm sorry, but I'm going out with Billy.'

All Rosaleen's problems receded when she thought of the implications of May going out with Billy.

'May!' she gasped. 'He's a divorced man. You da will kill you if he finds out.'

John Brady was a violent man, a real bully, and May had many a time arrived at work with a black eye when she had been unfortunate enough to incure his wrath.

She shivered now and retorted, 'Do you think I don't

know that? I've nightmares about him finding out.'

Bewildered, Rosaleen cried, 'Then why take chances?'

With a resigned sigh, May stopped in the middle of the pavement and faced her. 'Look, Rosaleen, it's all right for you to talk. With your looks you could pick and choose and you got the most eligible bachelor around here. You don't know what it's like to be an onlooker. You've never sat a dance out in your life, but me ...' Her finger poked her own chest to demonstrate her point. 'I'm twenty-two and I've never had a guy serious about me. Until now.'

Her gaze wavered and fell before Rosaleen's steady look.

'Billy wants to marry me,' she finished flatly, with a defiant tilt of the head.

'But you can't marry him! He's old ... and he's divorced. The church won't let you marry him.'

The horror Rosaleen felt at the very idea of her friend wanting to marry Billy came across in her words, and May clasped her hand to her head and laughed. Then, with a deep sigh, she once more looked at Rosaleen. 'You're so innocent. He doesn't want to marry me in church, and he isn't all that old – only ten years older than me.'

Aghast, Rosaleen thought, this can't be happening. Why, May was too good-living to contemplate marrying anywhere but in church.

They had reached the corner of Dunmore Street. This would take Rosaleen out on to the Springfield Road near Iris Street and thus to Iris Drive.

As she paused, she sensed relief in May's voice when she said, 'Look, Rosaleen, I'll have to run now. I'm meeting Billy at seven and I've loads to do. I'll come up next Tuesday night when Joe's at Clonard and tell you all about it. O.K.?'

'O.K. Don't forget now, I'll be waiting for you.'

'No, I promise. See ya.'

Rosaleen turned away, but May caught her attention again with a shout. 'Hey! What did you want to see me about?'

'Good Lord, I forgot about that.'

Rosaleen moved closer again and May said with a wry twist of her lips, 'It can't be very important.'

'Well, it seemed important until I heard about your romance,' Rosaleen cried indignantly. 'You knocked the wind out me, so you did.' She rolled her eyes at May. 'It's just – well, our Annie is going out with Sean Devlin. You remember Sean, don't you?'

May laughed. 'Tall, dark and handsome? How could I forget?'

'Well, I just want to make sure you don't let the cat out of the bag if you happen to meet them. Remember, I was engaged to Joe when I went out with Sean and it could cause all kinds of complications.'

May gaped at her. 'Ah, Rosaleen . . . do you think I'm daft? I would've known better than to say anything.'

'I just wanted to be sure, May. Didn't want you taken unawares. See you next Tuesday night, all being well.'

The week seemed to drag, but suddenly it was Saturday. Annie and Sean were coming at eight o'clock and Rosaleen had prepared a light supper for later on. As she dressed, she was angry at herself for wishing she was slim and attractive again. She felt huge and ungainly even though her new maternity dress had flattering panels that hid most of the bulk of her, and she suited the pale primrose colour. Joe had remarked at her use of make-up and she had been quite abrupt with him. If he had his way she would never use make-up. She had not worn any for a long time, but she vowed that in future she would take care of her appearance. She was not going to let herself go.

Even though she was prepared for the sight of him, she still felt winded when Sean entered the room. What on earth was going to happen to her if he married Annie? She could not exist in a state of panic like this.

The conversation was stilted, as was usual when a stranger entered a family group for the first time, but then Joe suggested having a game of cards and everyone relaxed.

As the evening wore on, Annie said, 'I'd better warn you, we won't be staying late. So if that spread you've out in the kitchen is for us, you'd better serve it now, Rosaleen, I don't think I mentioned it, but Sean's in the Merchant Navy and he's due back tomorrow.'

Rosaleen expelled a soft sigh of relief and rose from the table. He would be gone tomorrow.

'I'll make the tea.'

Annie followed her into the kitchen and said, 'Isn't it funny? In our street this is the scullery, and down here it's the kitchen.'

'It is a bit bigger, you have to admit,' Rosaleen retorted, pride in her home apparent.

'Well, I suppose so.' Annie's nose wrinkled in disdain and then she leant closer and whispered, 'What do you think of him?'

'Mmmm . . . who?'

'Huh!' Annie eyed her in amazement. 'Sean, of course! Who else?'

'Oh, he seems very nice, so he does.'

'Oh, he is . . . he is. And so different from the boys I've known.' Annie hugged herself. 'They all seem so childish compared to him. And he's so kind and respectful. I honestly don't know what he sees in me, why he singled me out, but *I* love him, Rosaleen,' she confided. 'I love him very much.'

'He singled you out because you're lovely! There'll be plenty of boys interested in you before you meet Mr

Right,' Rosaleen retorted. 'He's a bit old for you, don't you think? Remember, not so long ago you thought anyone over twenty-one was an old man?' Seeing Annie's lips twitch with mirth at the memory, she added, 'So just watch you don't get hurt, won't you, Annie?'

'I know I used to think like that,' she agreed with a grin. 'But I've grown up. And I'm well aware that he's older than me, but I don't care. As for getting hurt . . . well, ye know what they say. Better to have loved and lost, than never to have loved at all. I love him and I can only hope he doesn't tire of me. You're lucky, Rosaleen. You've always been admired. You're everybody's favourite. But me . . . I've always been second best.'

'What on earth do you mean?'

'Oh, you know what I mean. You're the only one I've ever felt close to. Me mam thinks I'm too flighty, and me da . . . well he thinks the sun rises and shines on you.'

'You're wrong, Annie. Me da has always treated us equally. As for me mam . . . well, she worries about you.'

'I know, I know. But still, you're a hard act to follow. You never bothered with Protestants. You fell in love with the right man and gave no cause for concern. Anyhow, I hope Sean falls in love with me because I love him.'

Dreading the answer to her next question, Rosaleen asked it anyhow. 'Does he not commit himself?'

'Not so far,' Annie answered sadly. Then straightening to attention she vowed, 'But he will, he will, I'll make him love me. I'll make him want to marry me. Just you wait and see.'

And knowing that Annie usually accomplished anything she set out to do, Rosaleen believed her and her spirits sank.

It was with relief that she closed the door on that night. She had been jittery with nerves all evening. She had noticed Joe watching her, a concerned look in his eyes, and fear had gripped her heart in case he guessed how she felt about Sean. She was glad when she heard that he would be away for six months. Surely by the time he returned, she would be able to control the emotions that he aroused in her? It was just because she was pregnant that he affected her so. Didn't they say pregnant women were unstable emotionally?

'Sean's a nice bloke, isn't he? Annie could do a lot worse than marry him.'

Joe's words brought her back to earth with a bang.

'He's a bit old for her, don't you think?'

'That makes him more responsible, and it's plain to see that he dotes on her. He'll be able to keep her in line. She's a bit of a rebel, is Annie. Likes to get her own way.'

Was it obvious that Sean doted on Annie? 'Well, six months is a long time. It will probably peter out.'

Joe drew her down on to the settee and sat with his arm around her. She squirmed uneasily. He was in one of his sloppy moods. He would be easily pleased; a bit of a cuddle, a few kisses and a lot of excuses for not disturbing her, but these episodes left Rosaleen frustrated and unhappy. Tonight she could not bear it! Unhappiness was already a deep pain in her chest.

Rising abruptly to her feet she said, 'I'm tired, Joe. I'm going on up to bed. Goodnight.'

She stole a glance at his face and saw chagrin there. Serves him right! she thought. He wouldn't be so ready for a cuddle once the child was born. No, he would be afraid to start what he couldn't finish.

The next morning she was up early, preparing for the midwife's weekly visit. Now that she was so near her time, Nurse Morgan came once a week. Rosaleen answered the door with a smile on her face which quickly slipped when she saw Sean standing on the pavement. She closed her eyes. She must be seeing things, the result of lying awake half the night thinking of him. But no, he was still there when she opened them again.

'I lost a glove last night and I wondered if perhaps it's here?'

Silently, she turned back into the house and he followed her.

'I never noticed any glove when I was clearing up,' she assured him. Well, she couldn't very well call him a liar, could she?

Going to the settee, he looked down between it and the wall, and then reached down and produced a black leather glove.

'You left that there,' she accused him, wide-eyed. When he nodded gravely in reply, she cried. 'Why? What did you hope to gain? I don't understand.'

'I just wanted to see you for a few minutes alone, Rosaleen. I'll be away for six months this time.'

'Ah, Sean . . . Sean . . . what am I going to do about you. Can't you see? If you keep this up you'll ruin all our lives. I'm married to Joe and . . .'

Quickly, he interrupted her. 'But you regret it, don't you? Tell the truth, Rosaleen. You regret it. I could see last night that you don't love him.'

'No, you're wrong.' She shook her head. 'I don't regret marrying Joe.' Her gaze held his steadily. She must convince him that she was happy with Joe or he would never leave her alone.

'You're wasting your time. And Sean . . . ?' Her look was beseeching. 'Annie and I are very close, please don't hurt her.'

He stepped nearer to her, a sceptical look on his face, but what he would have said she was never to know, because Nurse Morgan arrived. Tight-lipped,

Sean wished Rosaleen goodbye and left the house.

Her daughter was born two weeks later, and Rosaleen sighed in relief when she saw that she was so blonde she appeared bald. Her eyes were blue but the nurse assured her they would probably change colour; that all babies were born with blue eyes. She was right. They did change colour – to green like Rosaleen's own. There was nothing about her in the least like Sean, and Rosaleen thanked God for letting her off the hook.

Her mother was in her glory helping to look after the baby. She came every day to see her, and one day, when the baby was two weeks old, arrived bursting with excitement.

'Who do you think called up to see me today?'

Not waiting for an answer, she rushed on: 'Kate Brady. What do ye think of that?'

Rosaleen's heart sank. She sensed that she was about to hear bad news. May had not paid the promised Tuesday night visit and when she had also neglected to come to see the baby, Rosaleen had guessed something was amiss.

She sat silent and her mother gaped at her. 'Don't tell me you knew all about it?'

'All about what, Mam? I don't know what you're talking about. I haven't set eyes on May for weeks.'

'She's gone! Took off a month ago. My, but they kept that quiet. I suppose they hoped she would get disillusioned and come back, before she was missed. But, no, she got married in the register office. I felt heartsore for Kate. She's worried stiff. It seems the big fellow waited ouside the Falls Flax yesterday and nearly killed the guy May married. It's as well May doesn't work there any more. He'd have swung for her.'

'Oh, poor May . . . poor May.'

'Poor May my foot! She should know better. It'll

cause trouble ye know! Once the boyos hear about it, big John's life won't be worth living. I suppose that's why he beat the guy up. He was proclaiming his disapproval of May's actions.'

'Ah, Ma! She probably fell in love,' Rosaleen cried. 'Why can't we do as we please. As for the boyos . . . who are these faceless guys that everyone's afraid of?'

'Hush . . . don't talk like that.' Thelma glanced over her shoulder as if they might be overheard even though they were in Rosaleen's living room. This action brought home to her just how awful it must have been during the troubles in the twenties, when you were afraid to speak your mind. 'As for May . . . well, she should've known better. She should've fell in love with a Catholic, so she should,' Thelma continued, then sighed and added gruffly, 'I suppose you're right. Ye can't help who you love. Ah, no, love makes fools of us all.'

Thelma's face reddened when she caught Rosaleen's appraising look, and she quickly changed the subject.

'Your da says there's goin' to be a war.'

Rosaleen just nodded, she knew her mother was changing the subject; the fact that her father was talking about the war was nothing new. He was always talking about the war. He ranted on about the government not making enough preparations to protect the people of Belfast. He kept explaining to anyone who would listen that Belfast was now a prime target, since it was turning out planes and ammunition for England, but no one listened to him. What did he know, working in Greeves Mill all his life? Hadn't the powers that be over in England assured the Stormont government that Hitler would not travel across England to bomb Ireland? Nevertheless, her father continued to point out that Belfast stuck out like a sore thumb, situated as it was on the edge of the lough, and that, mark his words, the Germans would come.

But there had been rumours of war for a long time now. Indeed, a new aircraft factory, Short and Harlands, had been opened two years ago, bringing work to thousands. It had just completed its first Bengal Bombay last month and was working all out building more. Surely if the English government thought Belfast would be bombed, it would protect its assets? Rosaleen remembered the flurry of activity last summer when war had seemed imminent. Trenches had been dug around the harbour and in the parks, and sandbags had been distributed to all important buildings, shops and offices to protect against blast damage. But then all activity came to a halt as fear of war had apparently receded. The rumours had lingered too long now to cause Rosaleen immediate concern and it was May her thoughts dwelled on. Would Billy be good to her? Oh, she hoped so, she hoped so. May deserved a bit of kindness.

It was a month later that she received a letter from May, asking to meet her in the Dunville Park. Wrapping the child up warmly, she put her in her pram and near the stated time made her way down to the park.

May was already sitting on a bench near the fountain when Rosaleen arrived. She rose swiftly to her feet and embraced her friend fiercely.

'Oh, it's so good to see you.'

They clung together for some moments and then May turned her attention to the child in the pram.

'It's obviously a girl,' she stated laughingly, noting that everything was pink. Pulling back the blankets, she peered in at the sleeping child. 'She's lovely, Rosaleen. Just lovely. What did you call her?'

'Laura. Laura Marie. How are you, May?'

'I'm great, Rosaleen, never better. Billy lifts and lays me.' She winked, her tongue poking cheekily from between her teeth, causing Rosaleen to laugh outright.

'You certainly look great. Why, you're absolutely blooming.'

'Don't sound so surprised.' May gave her a playful push. 'Here, let's sit down and have a natter.'

Rosaleen's eyes ran over May's attire. She was dressed in a quality wool coat, dark green in colour, on her feet a pair of soft brown kid shoes, and she carried a matching kid handbag.

'Looks like you fell on your feet,' she exclaimed.

Somehow she had expected May to be sad and cowed. After all, she had acted foolishly, but instead she looked defiant. That was the only word Rosaleen could think of to explain how May looked.

'Well, Billy isn't short of a bob or two, and he's an only child. His parents dote on him.'

'How do they feel about you?'

'They love me.'

Seeing Rosaleen's look of disbelief, she nodded her head vigorously.

'They do! Honestly!' Her head bobbed up and down to lay stress on her words. 'Now if Billy had married me in the Catholic Church that would have been another matter. They would have disowned him, only child or not. They didn't like his first wife, so I consider myself lucky that they've taken to me.'

'Had he any children, May?'

'No. No children. And it was her fault the marriage broke up. She ran off with someone else.'

'Well, her poor taste was your good fortune, but your ma's breaking her heart, May.'

May's retort was quick.

'Not because of me, she's not. She's breaking her heart because I've left the church. She doesn't care whether I'm happy or not.' She tossed her head defiantly. 'I suppose you heard how me da beat Billy up?' When Rosaleen nodded, May cried, 'I bet you didn't hear that he had two of his pals with him?' At

Rosaleen's look of surprise, she cried, 'I thought not. If he had been alone Billy would have been able for him. But big and all as me da is, he needed help. The big bully! You should have seen the state Billy was in.' She gulped deep in her throat before continuing. 'His face was like a bit of liver. His mates wanted to retaliate, but he wouldn't hear tell of it. He said he felt he deserved the hiding for running off with me, and I was worth every last blow.'

Although tears were running down her face, she smiled wryly at Rosaleen. 'I never thought I'd hear a man say that about me. And, Rosaleen, he does love me.'

Rosaleen gripped her hand tightly.

'You underestimate yourself, May. You're worthy of any man's love.'

In her heart she could not help but wish that May had waited for a Catholic. Surely she must feel uneasy living on the Shankhill Road? She found herself voicing her thoughts.

'Are you not scared living on the Shankhill?'

May paused in wiping her face and giggled.

'Not a bit of it,' she declared. 'They're just like us. Honest to goodness, Rosaleen. Listening to them is just like listening to the ones on the Falls Road.

Rosaleen found this hard to believe. She remembered the few times she had gone shopping on the Shankhill Road. She had imagined everyone knew she was a Catholic. Hadn't she been led to believe that they could smell Catholics? Certainly she had been glad to hurry back down Conway Street to the Falls Road. Now she could not hide her disbelief.

'Honestly, Rosaleen,' May assured her again. 'Do you know something? Billy and his parents go to church every Sunday. They're a lovely couple, and the neigbours are friendly. Everyone talks to me.'

'You don't go to church?'

Rosaleen was scandalised at the idea of May attending a service in a Protestant church.

'No, I don't. But why shouldn't I? We all pray to the same God. *He* doesn't ask if you're a Catholic or Protestant.'

She couldn't bring herself to admit that she had gone to church one Sunday with Billy but had found the church cold and bare. Not in the least like Clonard Monastry, with its shrines and altars.

'Listen, Rosaleen, besides wanting to see you and your new baby, I asked you to meet me because I want to ask a favour of you.'

Wide-eyed, Rosaleen remained silent.

'I'm worried about me ma. With me da and our Colin not working, I know she depended on my money every week.'

She delved into her handbag and produced an envelope.

'Will you give this to her for me? Tell her I'll get money to you once a month for her.' Her look was entreating. 'That's if you don't mind . . . Please?'

Aware that Joe would object to her being a go-between, Rosaleen hesitated.

'It's all right. I'm sorry I asked. I had no right to put you on the spot.' May opened her handbag to return the envelope, but with an abrupt movement Rosaleen stopped her.

'Here, give it to me. At least this way you will have to stay in touch.'

'Thanks, Rosaleen. You're a true friend. And I have another bit of news . . . I'm pregnant!'

Rosaleen forced herself to smile; to act pleased. However, inside she was worried. The child would be brought up a Protestant. How will May be able to live with that? she wondered. And another thing, what would big John do when he heard about it?

To her amazement, May eyed her keenly and asked,

'Are you happy, Rosaleen?'

'Of course I am. What made you ask that?'

'Oh, I don't know.' May gave a little laugh. 'You'd have a cheek not to be happy. Married to Joe . . . a beautiful home . . . and now a lovely baby.'

May's reply was appeasing; Rosaleen's answer had been too quick, too emphatic, and May wasn't fooled. Remembering Sean had come back on the scene, she inquired after him.

'Is Sean Devlin still going out with Annie?'

She was dismayed to see hot colour stain Rosaleen's cheeks.

Aware that she was blushing, Rosaleen answered abruptly. 'He's at sea at the moment, but yes, he is dating Annie.'

'Oh . . . I see.'

'What do you mean, you see? What do you see?' Rosaleen asked sharply.

'I . . . I . . . ah, now, Rosaleen, I just asked.'

Rosaleen managed to get control of her voice before she replied. May was no doser, she must never guess that Sean was still interested in her. 'I'm sorry, May. I'm just worried in case Annie finds out about me going out with him.'

'Rosaleen, it was just a couple of dates . . . Oh, I see. You're afraid of Joe's reaction, is that it?'

Rosaleen nodded, relieved that May was being diverted.

'Well, he'll never hear from my lips, so he won't. Not that I'm likely to be talking to him.'

She sighed. 'I miss you, Rosaleen. I have to admit, I'm a bit lonely.'

Rosaleen squeezed her hand. 'Why not come and visit me every Tuesday night when Joe's at the confraternity?' she asked.

'Oh no, I don't think that would be a good idea.' May turned the thought over in her mind and repeated sadly, 'No, me da might find out. I'm not just anxious about myself. I just don't want you involved. I'll have to be satisfied seeing you once a month.' She reached for a parcel that was lying on the bench beside her, and thrust it at Rosaleen. 'Here! Just a wee present for Laura.' She peered once more into the pram at the sleeping child. 'She's lovely, so she is. I wish she had awakened . . . but perhaps next time.'

'Thanks, May, thanks a lot. She sleeps most of the day and night at the moment, but I've been warned that that state of affairs won't last long. Next time she'll winge and gairn and you'll be glad to get away from her.' For a moment they both gazed in wonder at the sleeping child, then Rosaleen said, 'I'll be here waiting, this day four weeks. If it's raining, I'll be in the summer-house. O.K.?'

May rose to go. 'That'll be great, Rosaleen. I'll look forward to seeing you.' She reached for her friend's hand and clasped it warmly. 'So long for now, and thanks for coming.'

Rosaleen watched her walk across the park towards the side gate that led out on to the Grosvenor Road. At the gate she paused and waved, before heading for the tram stop. Rosaleen waved back.

Lost in thought, she sat on until a hungry cry from Laura brought her back to reality. A glance at the face of the clock on the wall of the hospital opposite brought her hurriedly to her feet. If she didn't get a move on Joe would be home before her and that would lead to a lot of questions. She had no intention of mentioning her arrangement with May, so haste lent wings to her heels as she pushed the pram up Cavendish Street.

Chapter 3

Kept busy with the baby and the running of the house, Rosaleen looked forward to her monthly meeting with May in the Dunville Park. The park was a sanctuary where young mothers, after leaving their older children at St Vincent's girls' school in Dunlewey Street or St Finian's boys' school on the Falls Road, pushed their prams and, when weather permitted, spread rugs on the grass to sunbathe whilst their babies slept in the warm air protected from insects by pram-nets. When the weather was fine, Rosaleen often walked down and sat in the park to give Laura the benefit of fresh air, but the days she met May were special. On those days she wore her best clothes and carefully made-up her face, knowing a new, splendid May would arrive in the latest maternity wear. She was happy that things were working out for May, although she could not understand how she could be happy living among 'Them' on the Shankhill Road.

As she sat waiting, Laura blissfully asleep in her pram, the sun warm on her plump, bare limbs, Rosaleen examined the park and took delight in its layout. She was sitting on a bench with her back to the hospital, so she had a view that seemed like countryside. This was deceptive as the park was completely surrounded by a built-up area. The Royal Victoria Hospital loomed high on the far side of the

Grosvenor Road behind her, and to her left the busy Falls Road was hidden from view by high hedges and bushes, the other two sides flanked by rows of terraced houses. However, the houses were blocked from view by thick bushes and it was easy to forget that they were there.

The park had been given to the people of the Falls at the end of the nineteenth century by William Dunville, owner of the whiskey distillery which, at that time, had premises off the Grosvenor Road. A family man, he had felt sorry for the people uprooting themselves from the countryside to come and work in the mills, their young children playing barefoot on the then cobbled streets. He had arranged for the building of the park, complete with washrooms, and had set up a trust to maintain it, for the enjoyment of the public and as a lasting memorial of his sister Sarah. His gift was appreciated by all and Rosaleen liked to believe that it was kindness that prompted his actions. Her grandmother had thought otherwise because of the comment 'Perhaps now the people of the Falls will manage to keep themselves clean' allegedly made by Mrs Dunville, and spoken in the hearing of the newspaper reporters. It caused an uproar when blazoned across the newspapers the next day and had made the older generation very bitter in their attitude towards the gift. But whatever the reason for the building of the park, it was a favourite spot for the younger generation.

The middle of the park was dominated by a huge fountain, once brilliant white, now weathered to a pale grey and at the moment out of order. Around the top were carved gargoyle heads and Rosaleen remembered the fear with which she had once regarded them. Were they not there to guard the fountain? To prevent naughty children from defacing it? Oh, yes, she remembered well the day Marie Brannigan, the school hero who feared nothing and no one, had carved her initials into the stone work with a nail. For days the rest of the girls in the gang had waited with bated breath for something terrible to befall her, but they waited in vain. If anything, Marie thrived.

No more did water tumble down from the mouths of the gargoyles, to be recycled in a continuous circle. She could well remember how breathtaking it was, remember paddling in the shallow water at its base, and in the winter, the naughty excitement of sliding about on the frozen ice. This was forbidden, for although not deep, many pairs of boots were destroyed when it cracked and feet occasionally went through. She sighed for times past, and continued her perusal of the park. To her left, in the far corner, the old weigh house still stood. Here, in the not too distant past, at the beginning of the century, the farmers had stopped to have their livestock weighed on their way down to the market – but that had been before her time, in the days of the horse-drawn trams, the days of mucky roads. Now the house was occupied by the caretaker and his family, the trams were electric and the roads concreted. Nearer the centre, to the left of the fountain, stood one of a pair of summer-houses, the other hidden from view by the fountain. These were where the older men of the parish played chess and dominoes or read their newspapers while having a quiet smoke or even forty winks.

Flowerbeds dotted the park as if thrown by a careless hand. Great big mounds of turned earth, a riot of colour at the moment, with sweet williams, stock, dahlias and pinks permeating the warm air with their heavy perfume. Four lawns of dark, lush green grass flanked the fountain, sloping gently down from a raised height, and in the centre of each lawn was yet another large flower bed; each one a different shape. Some distance to her right, at the very bottom of the park, was the play area, where there was an assortment of amusements to entertain the older children. Some slides, swings, swinging boats, a witch's hat, and in the centre, in pride of place, the maypole! Rosaleen recalled how, when she was younger, looping a rope around the handle of the maypole she had sat and swung for many a long hour. Oh, yes, the park was indeed appreciated by the people of the Falls, no matter what their age.

The thud of someone sitting on the bench brought Rosaleen back to reality with a start. She turned, and her mouth gaped in surprise when she saw it was Kate Brady.

'Sorry to startle you . . . I just want to see May,' Kate explained apologetically. 'See for meself that she's all right, ye know? She'll not mind, will she?'

Wondering how Kate had known just when she and May met, and not knowing how May would react to seeing her mother, Rosaleen confined her answer to an abrupt shake of the head. She hoped that there would be no unpleasantness, and made inane conversation as time passed with no sign of May.

She was aware that her friend took the tram to the stop at the bottom of the park to avoid meeting any neighbours at the busy junction where all the roads met. This was where the post office, home bakery and other shops were situated, and was always busy with shoppers. Rosaleen wondered if May had seen her mother as she passed by in the tram, and declined to meet her. However, the thought had just entered her mind when she saw her friend hurrying up the park, dressed to kill. From the corner of her eye, Rosaleen watched Kate's reaction to the new, stylish May. She saw her face twist with amazement and her mouth agape.

And no wonder! May was a sight for sore eyes. Dressed in a long pleated maternity skirt with a

69

matching loose hip-length jacket, she looked every inch the grand lady. Made of slub rayon material, and blue in colour, the suit brightened the colour of May's eyes and Rosaleen noted that she had lightened her mousy fair hair to a pale ash blonde.

When she saw her mother, her arms stretched wide. 'Ma! Ah, Ma! It's good to see you.'

Rising slowly to her feet, Kate tentatively embraced her, all the while examining this stranger.

'Ye look well,' she muttered. Then, noticing the slight bump, she wailed, 'Are you expectin'?'

Some of the joy faded from May's face as she nodded confirmation to her mother's question.

Her face crumbling in distress, Kate wailed, 'Oh, my God. Wait 'til your da hears.'

'It's none of his business,' May retorted, tight-lipped. 'He won't be asked to rear it.'

'I should bloody well think I won't be asked to rear the bastard!'

The blast of these words brought Rosaleen to her feet to join the others, and all three turned to face big John Brady where he stood in the shadow of a tree. He must have entered the park by the gate near the weigh house and crept down to hide behind the tree. Rosaleen's lips curled and she bestowed a look of scorn on him at the very idea.

Kate moved until she was between husband and daughter, but blind with rage, he pushed her roughly to one side. Rosaleen could see spittle foam at the corners of his mouth as he fought to find words low enough to degrade May. She pushed the pram with her precious child in it to one side, out of harm's way.

'You dirty wee bitch!' he hissed, as he advanced towards them. 'You dirty . . . friggin' . . . wee friggin' bitch!' His words were sliding into each other and he gulped for control. 'T'think of a daughter of mine, lyin' in the arms of a bloody orange man . . . It gnaws at

70

me guts, so it does. Turns me stomach.' His mouth gaped and words failed him at the very thought of it. He hovered over May with clenched fists. 'An' an ugly bugger he is too. Surely even a plain Jane like you could have done better,' he sneered.

May flinched at these words. She was aware that Billy was no oil painting, and that neither was she, but it hurt to have it thrown in her face. After all, not everybody could be beautiful. Bravely she stood her ground, head high, lips pressed tightly together. Aware of people gathering to watch, colour burned in her cheeks and tears glistened in her eyes, but still she stood her ground.

Father and daughter glared at each other and then, seeing that May would not be cowed, with an angry oath, John's hand (as big as a shovel) rose in the air. May saw it coming and stepped back as it swung her way, but she did not move quickly enough and it caught her on the side of the head. The weight of the blow sent her staggering and she ended up sprawled on the gravel path, a look of outrage on her face.

As she lay stunned, Rosaleen hovered anxiously over her, glaring fiercely up at big John, daring him to strike again; protecting May from another blow.

This defiance caused him to turn his wrath on her.

'Why don't you mind your own bloody business, eh? Stay out of it! There'll be no more go-betweens. She's made her friggin' bed, now let her lie on it. We don't want any Prod's charity!' His glare swung back to May. 'Do ye hear me? We want no charity from a friggin' Prod. Our bloody windows have been put in . . . twice.' At May's wail of dismay, he repeated, 'Yes, twice! Ye didn't know that now, did ye? An' it's all your bloody fault!'

With these words, and another glare of wrath, he gripped his wife's arm and pulled her roughly towards the gate at the far side of the park, leading out on to

71

Dunville Street, at the same time shooing the embarrassed crowds away with threats of what he would do if they didn't shift.

Stumbling along beside him, Kate tried to shake off his hand but he was adamant. Throwing Rosaleen an apologetic look, she mouthed the words: 'Will you look after her?'

Rosaleen gave her a reassuring nod and, bending, assisted a bewildered, weeping May to her feet. When May saw that the rough path had scored through the elbow of her new jacket she started to howl. Great harsh sobs, from deep down in her chest, not caring who saw or heard her.

'The bastard! Oh, how I hate him, Rosaleen. How I hate the friggin' bastard! Hate him! Hate him! Hate him! The unfeeling brute!' Then her eyes fell on the few stragglers still hovering about, all eyes and ears, and leaning forward she bawled, 'Well? What are ye waiting for?' And flapping her hand at them: 'Go on . . . go on now. The show's over.'

'Hush, now. Never mind them,' Rosaleen said consolingly. 'Do you feel all right?' She nodded down at May's stomach, and her friend's eyes stretched wide with alarm as she patted her bump.

'I . . . think so. I haven't any pain,' she assured Rosaleen, anxiety dampening the flames of her wrath.

Pushing her gently down on the bench, Rosaleen said, 'Just take it easy for a while, 'til we see how you are.'

May buried her face in her hands, muttering, 'I'm sorry, Rosaleen. It's awful that you had to be involved in all this.'

'Don't be silly. It wasn't your fault.'

May's head jerked up and down as she disagreed with Rosaleen.

'It was. Oh, yes, it was. If I hadn't asked you to be go-between, all this would never have happened.'

72

'But you weren't to know that your mam would come round and that your da would follow her, so don't be so silly.' Rosaleen sighed and added, 'With hindsight, I suppose it was stupid us meeting here, so close to Spinner Street. It was obvious some of your good neighbours would see us and tell your da.'

'Did you know our windows had been put in?' May's brow was furrowed with worry.

At Rosaleen's shake of the head, she continued, 'It mightn't have had anything to do with me, ye know. Maybe me da or one of the boys have done something wrong. I'd hate to bring trouble to them . . . me mam has enough to put up with. Do you think it was because of me?'

Rosaleen thought it was more than likely that May was the reason for the broken windows. Really, she should stay away from the Falls Road. Coming in all her grandeur like she did was like thumbing her nose and saying, 'Look, see how well I'm doing on the Shankhill?' Rosaleen realised that she should not have encouraged her back by agreeing to meet her, but they were best friends and she had wanted to keep in touch.

Not wanting to distress her more than she was already, she muttered, 'I don't know, May. I really don't.'

'I feel so guilty, Rosaleen. I wanted to send money, but it was guilt money. I was salvin' me conscience, giving money every month. I felt awful deserting me ma. With him not working she needs my money, and I didn't even get giving her any today. Him and his bloody pride! It's me ma that'll suffer most. An' our poor wee Jenny . . . I bet she's suffering an' all. With me not there for him to vent his temper on, me da will turn it on our Jenny.' Tears flowed afresh. 'Poor wee mite, she's terrified of him.'

Not knowing what to say, Rosaleen remained silent. She had guessed that big John was a bully, but it dismayed her to hear it put into words. Obviously, May had suffered more than the odd blow.

Picturing May's brother Colin, twenty years old and not very tall, but no scrawny wee thing either, and the next one down, thin, lanky Daniel, eighteen years of age, she ventured to say, 'Surely Colin and Dan will be able to stand up to your da, and look after Jenny?'

'They'll be getting picked on an' all. Because of me.' May smiled wryly. 'You don't understand, Rosaleen. You live a very sheltered life. He never touches the boys, not since they left school. Even our wee Kevin's left school now. Oh, he picks on them, but he knows better than to lift his hand to them. They'd all gang up on him.' She sighed and nodded. 'Yes, they'd hit back. It'll be Jenny he'll pick on most. Her being the youngest. An' he's a crafty aul bugger, he'll pick on her when nobody else is about.'

She turned to watch Rosaleen's expression when she asked the next question. 'Does your da ever beat your ma?'

When Rosaleen's face showed surprise, she laughed bitterly. 'No! I can see he doesn't. You don't know how lucky you are. Everything handed to you on a plate. You've always had it easy.' She gave a long heartfelt sigh. 'Ah, it's different in our house. My da can't get a job . . . and to be honest, he does try . . . but he just can't get a job, so he tortures me ma for the wee bit of money she has coming in.' She shot Rosaleen a derisive glance. 'Do you know something? When me ma pays all the bills – or I should say all the bills she can afford to pay, she has to decide every week whose turn it is to be paid – the little she has left to see her through the week she has to hide. She's running out of places to hide it. You should see me da hunting for it. He wrecks the house . . . It would be laughable if it wasn't so bloody serious.'

She fell silent, then taking a compact from her

handbag, tried to repair her make-up. Watching her, Rosaleen noticed that a bruise was already appearing on her cheek.

'How will you explain that?' she asked, dismay in her voice. 'What will Billy say?' She could understand letting big John away with his attack on him, but May was a different matter. He obviously loved her, so there could me more trouble.

May examined her cheek in the small mirror of the compact. 'I'll put some Pan-stick on it . . . that should hide it.'

'It's very close to the eye. What if you've a black eye in the morning?'

A smile twisted May's lips. 'I'll accidentally fall and hit my face when I'm in the bathroom tonight.' Seeing Rosaleen's start of surprise, she added proudly, 'Oh, yes, I've a bathroom.' Then, squeezing Rosaleen's arm, she added, 'Don't look so worried. Remember I'm used to explaining bruises away. Do you remember at school? Miss Watson thought that I was accident prone. If she had only known . . . I hardly ever fell.'

Rosaleen sat aghast at these revelations. She remembered how, apparently, May was always falling down the stairs or getting hit on the face with a swing in the park, but she had been so bright and cheerful when she explained her wounds that no one had ever doubted her.

Unable to think of any words of comfort, Rosaleen sat silent and was relieved when Laura chose that moment to let out a wail. Lifting her from the pram, she hushed her, rocking her gently over her shoulder.

'Can I hold her, Rosaleen?'

With a smile, she handed over the sweet-smelling bundle, and May stretched the child out on her knee, playing with the tiny hands and little bare feet, all the while exclaiming at her loveliness.

'God knows when I'll see her again,' she said sadly.

'Now listen, May. We're not going to let this stop us from meeting. We'll meet somewhere else.'

'Where, Rosaleen? Tell me where?'

'Would you not consider coming to my house, May?'

'And have me da put a brick through your window?'

At these words, Rosaleen drew back in disbelief. 'Surely he wouldn't dare?'

'Oh, he'd dare all right. You don't know him. Not that you'd ever be able to prove he did it. He's a cute aul bugger.' May watched Rosaleen from the corner of her eye when she asked the next question. 'I don't suppose you'd come to visit me?'

She saw the look of horror spread over Rosaleen's face and cried bitterly, 'For goodness' sake, Rosaleen, don't look like that! Nobody'll bite you. They're not a lot of savages, ye know.'

Shamefaced, Rosaleen smiled wryly as she replied, 'I know, I know. I believe you.'

May had never felt less like laughing in her life, but when she saw Rosaleen square her shoulders before declaring, 'All right!' as if preparing for battle, she laughed aloud.

'Good for you!' she cried, her eyes teasing, 'I'll write and tell you the easiest way to get to our street. I'll draw a wee map, and send it to you, so I will. Then next month, you can visit me.'

They smiled at each other and the time flew as they exchanged ideas and advised each other.

It was Laura starting to whinge and nuzzle about, looking for something to eat, that brought Rosaleen to her feet in alarm. A glance at her watch told her it was a quarter to five and she gasped in dismay.

'If I don't hurry Joe'll be in on my heels and there'll be no dinner ready for him,' she cried, settling Laura in her pram, and turning to May for a last farewell.

She was surprised to find her friend gaping at her. 'Surely Joe won't mind?'

'No, not really,' she lied, because Joe did mind, he minded very much. He expected his dinner to be on the table when he came home from work. 'It's just that, with me not working, I like to have a meal ready for him when he comes home.'

'Well, just let him wait today. Don't you kill yourself pushing the pram up that hill in a hurry . . . especially in this heat,' May admonished her.

'I won't. But, look, I'll run on now. Don't forget to write.' And with a final hug and wave Rosaleen set off at a trot, leaving a bemused May staring after her.

When Sean came home on leave, he always, weather permitting, caught an open-deck tram up the Falls Road to Beechmount, the estate where he lived. Today was no exception and as he sprawled on the seat looking about him, Rosaleen was not very far from his thoughts. As the tram trundled across the junction where the Falls divided the Springfield and the Grosvenor Roads, he sat up in delight, because there she was, waiting to cross the road, a brand-new pram in front of her, and looking young and sweet in a spotted cotton dress; the sun catching her hair and turning it to silver. On his feet instantly, he rang the bell for the tram to stop at the next stop and descended the stairs two at a time.

A short distance up the Springfield Road, he caught up with her and put a restraining hand on the handle of the pram.

'Why the big rush?'

Alarm brought her to a halt when his hand descended on the pram but when she saw who it was, taken unawares, joy lit up her face as she stared up at him in amazement.

'I thought you weren't due home for another couple of months!' she gasped.

His eyes twinkled down at her as he tried to steady

the thumping of his heart. She would probably deny it but she was pleased to see him. It was in her eyes and the warmth of her greeting.

'Oh, have you been counting the weeks? Eh, Rosaleen?' he teased.

'Oh, don't be silly.' Her hand flapped at him, but a smile tugged at her lips and crinkled her eyes. 'I'm fed up listening to our Annie counting the days.' Her brows lifted slightly. 'Does she know you're home?'

'Not yet.' He shook his head, and peering into the pram, at the little red, screwed-up face, declared, 'My, but she has a fine pair of lungs.'

'She's hungry,' Rosaleen cried defensively. 'She's usually very good.'

'Here!' He thrust his holdall at her, and before she could demur, lifted Laura from the pram. The little rascal stopped crying immediately.

'She's spoilt rotten, so she is,' Rosaleen admitted, with a wry smile.

'Put the bag on the pram and I'll carry her home for you,' he ordered. And without waiting for her agreement, he started walking up the Springfield Road, leaving her to follow.

Noting the way he supported Laura's back and head, Rosaleen asked. 'How come you know so much about babies?'

'I'm an uncle four times over. Three nephews and one niece.' He tickled Laura under the chin and when she rewarded him with a big, toothless smile, he added, 'I must confess I've a weakness for girls. She's lovely, Rosaleen.' His eyes scanned her face and his voice caressed her. 'Just like you.'

Colour stained her cheeks at the compliment and she was glad it was one of her days for meeting May and that she was looking her best, in her new cotton dress with the squared neckline and puffed elbow-length sleeves. Seeing her blush, he had a great urge to hug her and kiss her. If only he was coming home to her and this was his daughter. Why, it would be like heaven on earth.

With the past events still fresh in her mind, Rosaleen found herself telling him about May and her father. He let her ramble on, just giving her an encouraging nod now and again. When her voice trailed off, he glanced at her, and seeing her nip in her lips and an apprehensive look pass over her face, knew at once what was wrong.

'It's all right, Rosaleen. I won't say a word.'

She flashed him a grateful smile and wrinkled her nose at him. 'I did go on a bit, didn't I? It's not like me. Usually I can keep a secret . . . not that it was a secret, mind. I wasn't sworn to secrecy.' She hastened to explain. 'But, well, really I shouldn't have mentioned it.' She held his eye. 'You won't say anything to our Annie, sure you won't?'

'I won't say anything to anyone,' he assured her gravely, lost in the green wells that said far more than she realised.

'Thanks . . . I got carried away. You're so easy to talk to, so you are and . . . I trust you,' she added shyly.

Often he had recalled their last meeting but one, when she had called him evil, treated him with scorn. Her words had stung him, hurt him to the very core, and he had lost sleep over them. Now he took these words and tucked them away in his heart. She trusted him.

A frown puckered the smoothness of her brow. 'I'd better hurry. Joe will be home soon.'

With these words she walked faster and as he lengthened his stride to suit hers, it was his turn to frown.

When they arrived at the corner of Iris Drive, she turned to him.

'Put her back in the pram now, Sean. I'll take over

from here, and you can go on home.'

She nodded along Oakman Street that ran down on to Beechmount Avenue.

'No, I'll carry her in for you. And I'll tell you what. Since you're behind time, I'll give her a bottle while you make Joe's tea. How's that?'

To his delight, colour again stained her cheeks, deeper this time as she confessed, with lowered eyes, 'I breast feed her.'

His eyes teased her again, bringing an answering sparkle to her face. 'I'm glad to hear that. If she was my daughter, I'd want her to be breast fed.'

She was glad that they had arrived at the small forecourt at the front of the house. Glad that she could bend down to open the gate, and that her hair swung forward to hide the dark blush that suffused her face and neck as guilt assailed her.

To think that he was holding his own daughter in his arms and didn't know it.

If he should ever find out . . . why, it didn't bear thinking about. Once more she tried to send him off, but he was adamant.

'While you feed the baby, I'll start Joe's dinner.'

'I can't ask you to stay, mind,' she lamented. 'I've only one chop.'

'I've already eaten,' he lied, and she knew he lied and was grateful to him. He was so kind, so understanding.

'But what about you? Are you not eating?' he asked, his glance keen. Surely she could afford to eat properly?

'I'm on a diet. I've another few pounds to get rid of. I'll have salad later.'

Having witnessed his sisters starving themselves to lose weight after the birth of each child, this reassured him and he relaxed.

Heading for the kitchen, she said, 'Since you insist . . .' and pulled open the door of a cupboard. 'The pots and pans are in there, the chop, a couple of sausages and cooking fat are on the top shelf in the larder, and the potatoes are under the sink. Now I had better get this wee girl upstairs before she turns blue.'

As she fed Laura, she thought how wonderful it would be if he was coming home to her. If only she had listened to him! With a sad smile on her face, she pictured how things would go. She would finish feeding Laura and then make him his tea, and they would talk for a while . . . She found herself laughing softly at the very idea. Who did she think she was kidding? The way he was looking at her, if she was his wife they would be at it hammer and tongs right away and she would not object. Oh no, she would not object . . . not one wee bit. Sadness settled like a mantle on her shoulders. If only she had met him sooner . . .

After she had changed Laura's nappy, she combed her hair and powdered her nose. Descending the stairs, she entered the kitchen.

He was turning the chop in the pan and the potatoes were bubbling away on the back ring. He had removed his jacket and donned one of her aprons but still managed to look all man.

'What about veg?'

Dismay filled her, and her face crumpled. 'Oh! I completely forgot about vegetables.' She ran her fingers through her hair, undoing all the careful combing and leaving it standing on end. At last she muttered, 'Tut! Joe hates tinned peas, but it's too late to do anything else.'

'If he's hungry, he'll eat anything.'

He was eyeing her intently and she grimaced, but did not reply. 'I'll take over now, Sean. Thanks very much.'

He was about to demur, but one glance at her face and he knew she did not want Joe to see him in the kitchen, so he whisked off the apron, gently took

Laura from her arms, and with a wink at her, went and sat in the living room.

Joe must be a right sod. It was obvious that she had to be home before him, to have his meal ready. His heart ached for her. With hindsight, he realised that he should have phoned in sick last year and made her listen to him. But would she have done? He doubted it. Anyhow, now it was too late. Not that Joe was mean. No, far from it. As his eyes examined the room in which he sat, Sean was aware that money had been spent, and spent to advantage. The settee on which he sat was new, no second-hand things here, and made of a moquette velvet in deep rich autumn colours. Matching armchairs graced each side of the grey and black kitchenette grate, and curtains that toned exactly hung at the window, separated by fine nets. And setting all these off to a treat, a square carpet, thick-piled and dark rust in colour, covered most of the floor. Rosaleen was obviously being denied nothing, so why did sadness lurk in her eyes? Because it did; when her face was in repose, sadness was apparent. But then, perhaps he had caught her on a bad day . . . perhaps Joe and she had had words this morning?

When Joe arrived, he paused just inside the door, his eyebrows rising in surprise when he saw Sean.

'I met Rosaleen on the Falls Road and walked home with her,' he explained, and thrust his hand at Joe in greeting.

Clasping his hand, Joe said, 'I thought you weren't due home for another month or two.' His eyes were very intent as he examined Sean's face. Somehow he looked too at home, too comfortable, sitting here in *his* living room, young Laura on his knee.

'Well, it seems we're likely to be at war soon, so we're getting our leave early.'

'Oh?' Joe reached down and tickled Laura on the

tummy. 'So we're going to war at last?'

'It looks like it.'

'I thought something was going to happen when they sandbagged the City Hall last week and ordered a complete blackout, but when everything slackened off, I imagined it was another false alarm.'

Sean shook his head, and his voice was grave. 'No, I think that this time we'll be going to war.'

Rosaleen's voice came from the kitchen. 'Your dinner's ready, Joe. Come eat it.'

Excusing himself, he entered the kitchen and when he saw the table was set for one, enquired in surprise, 'Did you not make Sean some?'

'He has eaten already, and his mother will be expecting him home soon,' she explained, and raising her voice called, 'Sean, will you have time for a cup of tea?'

'For tea, I'll make time,' he called back, glad of the opportunity to stay in her company for a while longer.

As he drank the tea, she watched him, watched his hands as he played with Laura, bringing squeals of delight from her small, rosebud mouth. In spite of the tight rein she had on her feelings, Rosaleen was remembering the excitement his hands had brought to her, and she wriggled uncomfortably in her chair. If only she had met him sooner!

Feeling his eyes on her face, she refused to meet them, afraid of what he might see. She was relieved when, tea finished, he rose to leave.

Placing Laura on her knee, he went to the door of the kitchen. 'I'm away now, Joe.'

Joe rose from the table, but with a motion of his hand, Sean stayed him. 'Finish your dinner, I'll see you before I go away again.'

'Come round on Saturday night with Annie, Sean. We'll be glad to see you.'

'Ah, well . . .' His eyes sought and caught Rosaleen's

83

at last, and teased her once again. 'I'll have to see about that. Annie might not want to share me with anyone else.'

She grinned back at him. 'Oh, listen to the conceit of that! I'm sure she'll be glad of a break away from your brand of humour,' she retorted, but in her heart she thought that Annie would be daft if she didn't keep him to herself, and really it would be better for her if she didn't see him again. Still, she found herself hoping that they would come. At the door she mouthed the words, 'Thanks for everything.'

His eyes held hers, deep and soul-searching, and she stood entranced. At last he whispered, 'The pleasure was all mine.' And leaning closer he assured her with a nod of his head. 'And it was a pleasure, Rosaleen.'

As he strode along Beechmount Avenue, his thoughts were busy. He had seen the scepticism in Joe's eyes. He was no fool, and Sean was aware that if he wasn't careful, he could place Rosaleen in a compromising position. Joe must never guess that he was interested in his wife, or Rosaleen was the one who would suffer. Yes, he would have to be very careful. Joe must never guess. The best thing would be for him to break with Annie. He had used her to see Rosaleen, to find out how she still affected him, how, after months at sea, he would react to her presence. Now he knew the answer to that. He loved Rosaleen with a deep abiding love, but he would have to get out of her life before he ruined it. There was no way, no way at all, that she would be lured into an affair with him. She was too good-living and her conscience wouldn't let her. Even if by some chance he managed to play on her feelings for him, because he knew that physically she was very attracted to him, and they started an affair, what would happen? Why, the guilt and worry of it would kill her. Besides, he didn't want an affair; he wanted a wife and children. No, he must get out of her life. Joe was providing a comfortable lifestyle for her and it was up to him to leave her in peace.

That evening when he called at Colinward Street to visit Annie, all Sean's good intentions were forgotten. Annie's delight at seeing him, her warm, eager embrace, touched his heart. She was lovely and they got on well together, so why not court her? Because she was Rosaleen's sister . . . that was why not! If only she wasn't. But then, he would never have met her otherwise. He would never have danced with her, asked her out. Oh no! He would have considered her too young.

Annie rushed upstairs to get ready to go out with him, wrapped in a bubble of happiness. When her mother had answered his knock on the door and ushered him into the kitchen, she had been unable to believe her eyes. Even when she was in the scullery making him a cup of tea, she had found herself going to glance into the kitchen to make sure that he was really there.

Since meeting him, her thoughts had been full of him; he even managed to invade her dreams at night, where she was forever chasing him, only to see him fade away as she approached. However, his letters to her had been friendly . . . no more . . . the kind of letters that he would write to his young sister. Even she, in her bemused state, had been unable to read anything serious into them. Now, as if in answer to her fervent prayers, here he was! He had just arrived home today. Surely this would not have been his first port of call, unless he cared for her.

To make things even more perfect, her mother doted on him and she could see that her father respected him. It would be lovely to do something that had her parents' blessing for a change. If only . . . Oh, if only he would fall in love with her, she would spend the rest of her life making him happy. But, according to

Sean, her father had been right in his prophecy of war. If it happened, Sean would be plunged straight into it. What if he was killed? This thought dampened her happiness and brought her to her knees beside the bed. Please . . . please God, don't let anything happen to him, and bring him safely home to me. He's the best thing that ever happened to me, and if You do, I promise . . .'

Her muttered prayer trailed off and aghast she chastised herself. What was she thinking of? You didn't try to blackmail God. God was good! You trusted him. His will be done! And with a muttered excuse, she rose to her feet and finished her preparations.

Annie called in on her way home from work the next night to inform them that, bar word from the Navy, she and Sean would be down on Saturday night, and when Rosaleen saw the happiness that spilled from her, she envied her. A man should be able to excite you and make you happy like that. Not dampen your spirits by making everything seem sinful.

As she prepared for their visit on Saturday night, there was a quiet happiness in her heart but she was aware that she had better be careful. Neither Annie nor Joe was a fool, and she did not want them to become suspicious.

These thoughts startled her, brought her to a standstill, to examine her thoughts with dismay. Suspicious of what?

She was acting as if she and Sean were lovers. If only they were! Oh, if only they were! Shame made her cheeks burn at the longing in her, and she wept as she begged God's forgiveness for her sinful thoughts. What on earth was she coming to?

On Saturday night, she remained in the kitchen when Joe went to answer the knock on the door. She was so worked up that she was afraid to greet Sean under Joe's watchful gaze. Afraid of blushing and stammering like a schoolgirl. That was what she felt like – a teenager in love.

Annie joined her in the kitchen and Rosaleen was pleased when she exclaimed at the assorted dishes that had been prepared.

'You're becoming a proper wee housewife, aren't you?' she teased.

'It helps pass the time. I find the days long, even with Laura to look after. She's such a good baby.'

'Dad would mind her for a few hours a day, Joe's mother even would take her,' Annie exclaimed. 'Either of them would be glad to earn a wee bit of money. Why don't you go back to work, part-time? It would give you a bit of independence, so it would.'

'Joe would never hear tell of me leaving Laura. Oh, no. Not that I would anyhow. She's far too young to leave,' Rosaleen cried, surprised at Annie for suggesting such a thing.

Aware of many friends who had no choice but to leave their children, and had to work to keep the wolf from the door, Annie grimaced at Rosaleen's indignation and holding a hand up in protest, retorted, 'It was just a thought. No offence meant.'

'Sorry, Annie,' Rosaleen apologised. 'I'm awful edgy lately. I must be run down.'

'Perhaps you're pregnant again?'

'No, no . . .' Rosaleen could not help smiling faintly at this idea. Chance would be a fine thing. Joe had yet to offer to share her bed again, and she had vowed that she would not invite him. The first move must come from him.

'What's so funny?' Annie asked huffily. She hated to be treated like a child, and she thought Rosaleen was being patronising.

'Ah, Annie, I didn't mean to offend you. Let's not squabble. Let's enjoy ourselves, eh?'

87

With a smile, Annie acknowledged the logic of what Rosaleen said and in good spirits they entered the living room.

At first, Rosaleen thought she was imagining that Sean was slighting her. Not that 'slighting' was the right word, but considering all that they had been through together, he was treating her like a casual acquaintance. As the evening wore on, she became more and more depressed. What had she done wrong? Did he think it was all right to tease and flirt with her, as long as Annie wasn't present? Was he serious about her? Could she bear to have him as a brother-in-law? Her thoughts swung this way and that, and dismay filled her when she realised that he was in the right and she was wrong. She was a married woman, and he was making it plain to her that he was interested in Annie, and only Annie.

Well . . . she didn't want him to be interested in her. Had she implied that she did? Had she been too forward? Red blazed in her cheeks at the very idea, and she found herself sitting closer to Joe, hurt and bewildered.

Since he could read her like a book, Sean knew that she was confused and hurt. He wanted to get her alone, to explain why he was acting so strangely, but the opportunity did not arise. Anyhow, he knew that to explain would only undo all his careful work. He knew without a doubt that Joe was suspicious, had seen it in his eyes as he watched them together. Sean's lips tightened when he saw Joe put his arm around Rosaleen and draw her close in a possessive manner, and he in turn placed his arm around Annie's shoulders. With a pleased smile she moved closer. Too late, Sean realised that he had made a mistake. He was acting like a callow youth instead of a mature man. Joe had every right to put his arm around Rosaleen, after all, she was the man's wife, and the sooner he accepted that fact the better. With war about to be announced, he should be thinking of getting married. He was the only son in a family of five, and it was up to him to keep the family name going.

The evening dragged a bit, and it was with relief that he agreed with Annie when she suggested that it was time they were getting a move on. At the door he took Rosaleen's hand in his, a cold limp hand that did not return the pressure of his fingers. And when he bent to kiss her cheek she drew away from him, and the hurt, reproachful look she gave him cut him to the heart. It also made all his efforts appear to be in vain because he saw Joe's eyes narrow at Rosaleen's action, and guessed that Joe probably thought that he and Rosaleen had disagreed in some way or other. And now he would be wondering how and when they'd had the opportunity to disagree.

He was making a mess of everything. With a curt farewell, he left the house, a happy Annie hanging on his arm.

As she brushed her hair before retiring for the night, Rosaleen went over the entire evening, word for word. No, she had not been mistaken. Sean had kept her at arm's length. How dare he! HOW DARE HE! To come into her home and treat her like that. Remembering the wonderful rapport of Tuesday afternoon, her heart sank. Had she made a fool of herself? Did he think that she was trying to charm him? Was this his way of warning her off? Her lips tightened angrily at the thought. Well, he would never get the chance to humiliate her again. From now on, as far as she was concerned, he just did not exist. She would show him! With this thought, in despair, she threw herself on top of the bedclothes. This would never do. She was a married woman. In future she must act like one.

Joe's hand on her shoulder startled her.

'Are you all right, Rosaleen?'

Glad that she had not given in to the desire to weep, she assured him. 'Yes. Why shouldn't I be all right? What would be wrong?'

She was surprised to see him in her bedroom; he usually avoided the intimacy of that setting. Now he sat down on the edge of the bed and his eyes roamed over her face, then down the soft curves of her body. She was lovely . . . desirable and sweet. He did not blame Sean for fancying her, but she should know better than to encourage him.

'Have you and Sean had a disagreement?' he asked casually.

She gaped at him in amazement, 'Of course not. Whatever gave you that idea? Why, I haven't seen Sean since he left here on Tuesday afternoon, so I haven't.'

Her surprise was obviously genuine, and he began to doubt the evidence of his own eyes. Was it jealousy that had made him think that there was something going on between her and Sean? His eyes searched her face, but she held his gaze steadily and his eyes were the first to fall away.

'Was that what brought you into the lion's den, eh?' she hissed. 'Did you come in to make accusations? Are you not afraid to be alone with me?'

To her surprise, he rose and slowly drawing her into his arms, sank his face into the softness of her hair. She stood stiff as he hugged her close, feeling the desire mount in him. She did not want this . . . could not bear, tonight of all nights, to be left frustrated. Unhappiness was sharp within her breast.

'Rosaleen . . . please be kind. Please?' He gulped deep in his throat, 'I can't help myself. Do you think I like being the way I am? Do you think I don't want . . . to . . . to . . . oh, you know what I mean.' His voice trailed off miserably and compassion smote her.

'You could see a doctor.' She drew back and gazed

up at him beseechingly. 'I'd go with you,' she offered.

'No.' His voice was stubborn. 'No, I won't see a doctor.' He swallowed deeply and continued haltingly. 'Rosaleen, I don't think . . . that you understand.'

Wide-eyed, she returned his look. 'Don't understand what?'

'Well, you see, the physical act of love . . .'

She interrupted him angrily. 'You mean intercourse?'

His eyes narrowed and his lips tightened. 'Don't be so crude.'

'Oh, but I'm not being crude,' she assured him, adding with a knowing nod of the head, 'That's the name for it.'

'Well, whether you believe it or not, the act is not all that important. It's for procreation, not for pleasure or lust.'

Again she interrupted him. 'What about love, eh? Aren't you forgetting about love? Do you love me, Joe?'

'Of course I love you!' he cried in amazement. 'How can you doubt it?'

'Huh! With little difficulty.' Her voice became coaxing, 'Joe, if you love me . . . go to the doctor. Find out what's wrong with you.'

His look remained mutinous and he drew her close again. 'Perhaps if we try again . . . Eh, love?' he pleaded, and as his hands began their exploration of her body, she cringed inside. Now she knew why he always made her feel so dirty. He believed he was committing a sin, and unconsciously the message came across to her. Closing her eyes, she prayed that this time it would be different; that this time he would succeed, but she was not really hopeful . . .

Sean was also angry with himself. All he had succeeded in doing was hurting Rosaleen and making Joe more suspicious than ever. And another thing . . . Annie was getting more serious about him. It was not fair leading her on, just because he wanted to be in Rosaleen's company. Since he did not intend to marry her, he must break it off and leave her free to meet someone else. Yes, he would break it off, but not until the end of his leave. He wanted to see Rosaleen one more time . . . just one more time.

He sighed. He was kidding himself. There would always be one more time, and he was using Annie while she was falling in love with him. Would it be so wrong to marry her? He was very fond of her, and he knew that he could make her happy, and he had enough money saved for a deposit on a house. They could buy one far away. Up the Glen Road, or even on the other side of town – Glengormley, for instance. It was a nice village, and he would still see Rosaleen now and again.

His thoughts were in a turmoil when they arrived at Annie's front door, and to his surprise she did not invite him in for coffee as she usually did. Instead, she stopped in the hall and when he followed her in, closed the hall door. In the intimacy of the enclosed space, she leant against the wall and eyed him expectantly. In a dilemma, he returned her gaze; dark blue eyes locked on green, so like Rosaleen's. Contrary to what Rosaleen might think, he had never touched Annie. Just a chaste kiss on the cheek or brow, in spite of much encouragement. Now he was tempted . . . he would be going back to sea soon and, who knew, he might not return.

He knew Annie well enough to ask her to marry him and on his next leave, if God spared him, they could get married. It would be nice to know that he had a wife waiting for him and perhaps, in time, a child. If war was declared, and there didn't seem any doubt about it now, it would be no picnic, and Annie was lovely and sweet and in love with him. Slowly, he reached for her and when her arms crept up around

92

his neck, and the soft curves of her body pressed close to his, felt passion rise. His lips sought hers and he kissed her long and hard, but try though he did to dispel it, Rosaleen's face, swimming behind his closed eyelids, kept him from going any further. With a sigh of regret, he put Annie firmly away from him. Her mouth opened to protest, but he was saved by her mother's voice, coming from the kitchen, inquiring suspiciously what was keeping Annie.

With a grimace, she gave him a reproachful look and asked, 'Well, will I be seeing you again?'

As though she had said it, he realised that she was going out on a limb; that she was giving him an ultimatum.

After some thought, he found himself nodding. 'Tomorrow night? Shall I pick you up at seven?'

With a relieved sigh, she nodded, planted a quick kiss on his lips, and bade him goodnight. She was happy; without speaking, she had managed to inquire whether or not his intentions were honourable. He, much to her delight, had indicated that they were, and now all was well with her world.

Rosaleen stayed away from her mother's house while Sean was on leave, afraid of meeting him. Afraid of betraying how he affected her. Although she longed to see him in case war was declared.

If it was, she might never see him again. She saw Annie, and in a happy confiding mood her sister told her that Sean had committed himself, that his intentions were serious. The future stretched before Rosaleen, long and painful, as she pictured him as her brother-in-law.

The declaration of war came as a surprise to the people of the Falls Road. First the general election and then the riots had hogged the headlines of the newspapers, and although everybody was aware that

Hitler was taking all in front of him, they had their own troubles and strife, and had not expected England to declare war on Germany.

Rosaleen heard the announcement as she stood at the kitchen sink peeling potatoes.

'Today, England has declared war on Germany.' The rest of Mr Chamberlain's words coming over the radio were lost on Rosaleen as she stood aghast. With sinking heart, she wished she had not been so proud and foolish. Sean would be called back at once, and what if he did not return? What if he was killed? She might never see him again. Panic gripped her. She just had to see him again. She must see him somehow! Joe visited his mother every Sunday night, so tonight when he was round in Cavendish Street she would nip up and see her parents. Annie had remarked that her mam was inquiring if anything was wrong, it was so long since she had visited them, so tonight she would keep Laura up late, and go up to Colinward Street and, with a bit of luck, see Sean.

Fate was against her, however. Sean had taken Annie out for a meal, to celebrate their engagement. As soon as he had heard the announcement of war, he had proposed to her with a ring ready – a ring that had belonged to his grandmother. For an hour and a half Rosaleen listened to her mother rave about the virtues of Sean. Describing how big the stone in Annie's ring was. 'Every bit as big as yours Rosaleen,' she gushed. Just when Rosaleen thought she could bear it no longer, Joe arrived from his mother's. After a quick cup of tea, a relieved Rosaleen wrapped Laura's blanket around her, settled her in her pram and prepared to go home.

As they said their farewells at the door, her father casually let drop that Sean had been called back to his ship, and that he was leaving first thing in the morning. Tears stung Rosaleen's eyes at this news. To think he was leaving without saying goodbye to her and Joe and Laura. She would never forgive him, she vowed. Never.

On the way home, she only half listened to Joe moaning on about taking Laura out in the cold night air.

'Your mother looked all right to me,' he fumed. 'What was wrong with her?'

To cover the lie she had told him as an excuse to visit so late at night, Rosaleen assured him that her mother had been unwell but was recovering. Still, he lamented, she wasn't bad enough to justify taking Laura out at night; it could be the death of her. And on and on he went. As usual, when Joe kept lamenting about something, she began to worry in case the cold night air did affect Laura. What if she caught a cold and one thing led to another and she died? It would be her fault, and Joe would not let her forget it. She wished he would, now and again, be a comfort to her, instead of always making her feel in the wrong. Even when she was in the right and he was in the wrong, he was able to twist things about until she was the one who ended up feeling guilty and miserable.

He made her feel so inadequate, her life was becoming one big well of guilt and remorse. Arriving home she bade him an abrupt goodnight and carried Laura straight up the stairs, away from his recriminations, vowing to bathe her in the morning.

Each in their own room, they were about to retire for the night when a knock on the door brought a frown to Joe's brow.

Putting his head around the door of Rosaleen's room, he asked, 'Are you expecting Annie to call?'

'No . . . no, she never mentioned anything to me.'

His eyes flicked over her in her negligee set, and he warned, 'You stay here,' before descending the stairs.

Rosaleen examined herself in the full-length mirror.

Joe would not agree with her but her negligee set was quite modest, hinting rather than revealing, and when she heard Sean's voice in the hall, she descended the stairs without hesitation.

Sean felt a lump rise in his throat as he gazed at the beauty of her. Face free of make-up and hair loose around her face, she looked about seventeen. Frowning fiercely, Joe turned to her. 'Sean has called to say goodbye,' he said unnecessarily.

'So you're off tomorrow, then, Sean?' she said softly.

He nodded, and when Annie proudly thrust her left hand forward, displaying the solitaire diamond ring, watched Rosaleen closely.

Glad that she had been forewarned, Rosaleen exclaimed in admiration and hugged Annie warmly, before offering Sean her hand in congratulation.

He sighed. He did not know whether to be glad or sorry; Rosaleen obviously did not care one way or the other whether or not he married Annie.

'Look . . . why are we all standing around?' Rosaleen cried. 'Sit down, sit down, and I'll make a cup of tea.'

At this suggestion, Joe interrupted her. 'I'll make the tea. You had better put on something warm or you'll catch cold,' he admonished her. And with another disapproving look at her night attire, headed for the kitchen.

'I'll have to use the bathroom. Excuse me, please. Too much wine . . . ye know what it's like.' With these words, Annie followed Joe, to go through the kitchen into the bathroom, and Sean and Rosaleen were left alone in the living room.

Aware of Joe in the kitchen, she whispered, 'I thought you were going to leave without saying goodbye.'

'Never, Rosaleen. I could never do that,' he whispered back.

Not another word was uttered, but his eyes spoke

volumes. Rosaleen lapped it all up, and wept inwardly for the loss of him.

As they drank their tea, it was Joe who asked the question that Rosaleen desperately wanted to know and did not dare to frame.

'When's the big day then?'

It was Annie who answered him.

'I'm going to set things in motion. You know . . . see about letters of freedom and the like, and get the banns read. With us both belonging to St Paul's parish, it should be all right. Then the first chance Sean has of a pass, no matter how short, we're going to be married. Isn't that right, love?'

Sean answered her question with a nod, and avoided looking at Rosaleen. Knowing full well that without a word he had just been telling her how much he loved her. He felt ashamed; he had no right to exploit Annie like this. Why did life have to be so mixed up? he thought in anguish. Annie was lovely . . . why wasn't it her he desired?

At the door, when they were about to leave, Sean said to Rosaleen, 'Give Laura a big kiss for me.'

'Would you like to see her before you go?' she asked quickly, and when he nodded in delight, turned and led the way upstairs.

Glad that Annie did not accompany them, and good manners forbade Joe to leave her, Rosaleen entered her bedroom, followed by Sean. The big double bed and large cot took up most of the floor space, and there was not much room for manoeuvre. Laura was stretched out in the cot, the clothes kicked away from her body, her chubby arms and legs spreadcagled, her cheeks flushed with sleep.

'Ah, Rosaleen, she must be a delight to you and Joe.' Sean's voice was sad. If only Laura was his child.

Close beside him in the confined space, Rosaleen nodded, her eyes hungrily devouring his profile as he gazed down at the sleeping child. Etching it on to her memory.

'Are you not training her to sleep alone?' he asked in surprise, knowing that his sisters swore that the earlier you started, the easier it was to train babies.

To his amazement, Rosaleen blushed crimson and muttered, 'It's time enough. We haven't the back room ready for her yet.'

She doubted very much that Laura would ever have a room to herself; Joe's problem was no better, and he was adamant about not seeing a doctor, saying there could not be much wrong with him for: 'Haven't I given you a daughter?'

And what answer could she find to that?

Becoming aware that the other bedroom door was open and that he was bound to see the bed with the clothes turned down ready for occupation, she added quickly, 'We're going to space our family.'

Sean felt a great surge of resentment against Joe rise in his breast. Was the man a fool? Did he not know that Rosaleen needed to be loved? Such a well of sensuality going to waste. Did Joe not know that children could be spaced out without the withdrawal of warmth and comfort from the matrimonial bed?

Then he remembered how good-living Joe was. Still, how could the man stay away from the beauty of Rosaleen? If only he was her husband . . . there'd be no separate beds. What's more, he would take full responsibility for their actions. He would be the one to confess to birth control. Rosaleen would be free from worry.

Now he questioned her. 'Is that what you want, Rosaleen?'

'Of course. Especially now that we're going to war.'

He smiled slightly at this. 'I don't think Hitler will be too bothered about Ireland. It's too far from Germany. No,' he shook his head and smiled reassuringly at her, 'he'll be concentrating his wrath on England for daring to stand up to him. They didn't come near Ireland during the '14-'18 war, so I can't see the Germans bothering this time.'

'Me da disagrees with you. He says that this time we're building far more planes and ships for England, and that Hitler's no doser and is sure to try to bomb Short and Harlands and the shipyard.'

Sean pursed his lips and a frown puckered his brow. 'He could be right . . . yes, he could be right at that,' he agreed.

The urge to hug her one last time became overpowering and he turned away. Her hand on his arm, long slender fingers tipped with pale pink nails, stopped him.

'You'll take care, won't you, Sean?' she whispered softly.

Placing his hand over hers, he fought the desire to raise it to his lips. 'I'll take care,' he promised.

When they had departed, she sadly climbed the stairs again, Joe on her heels.

'I hope you realise that you were an occasion of sin in that negligee,' he grunted, his lips a hard, tight line in his face.

On the small landing, mouth agape, Rosaleen turned to face him.

'I was no such thing!' she cried, but already her conscience was beginning to plague her. Had she deliberately set out to make Sean desire her?

'Of course you were. Look at it. It shows more than it hides.'

For a moment she was at a loss for words, then she lashed out at him in retaliation. 'Well, it doesn't turn you on. So how was I to know, eh? Tell me that. How was I to know?'

And with these words she entered her room and only the thought of the late hour and her sleeping neighbours prevented her from slamming the door.

Burying her face in the pillow, she wept long and sore for chances lost. To think that she had not wanted a seaman for a husband because she had wanted someone to hold her close in the night! Chance would be a fine thing. Well, she had made her bed and now she must lie on it. And – miserable thought – Sean was to be her brother-in-law.

Chapter 4

At first the war made no difference to Rosaleen. Life went on as before, and remembering that Sean had said Hitler would not be worried about Ireland, she was inclined to agree with him. Then she became aware that Joe was worried and waited anxiously, knowing that he would confide in her when he was ready and not before. And sure enough, one night after they had finished tea, he confessed to her that work was drying up.

'It's a bad business I'm in at the present time, Rosaleen. Wrought-iron railings and gates.' He grimaced. 'Trust me! I couldn't have been in a worse one. Iron's like gold dust at the moment. It's all being channelied into munitions factories.'

'Why not concentrate on the brick building side of the business?' she asked, thinking about the small sheds and garages he had been building lately.

He shook his head and a rueful smile twisted his lips. 'No one in their right mind is building anything at the moment . . . they're afraid that Hitler will come and bomb it.'

'There's not much chance of him bombing here, is there?' she asked fearfully.

He shrugged. 'It's hardly likely. His troops are in the North of France now, and I can't see them travelling a thousand miles across England and back again.' With lips pursed, he shook his head. 'No, I can't see Hitler sending bombers all that distance . . . but who knows just what that madman will do? After all, we are supplying planes, ships and ammunition, and . . . God forbid! . . . if they take England, we're sitting ducks. Still, I can't see England falling to them. Churchill's a great man . . . he knows what he's doing. Ah, well,' He sighed deeply. 'Who knows? Maybe everyone will have the same idea and business will pick up,' he finished on a more cheerful note, and Rosaleen breathed a sigh of relief.

The war did make a difference to her father. He was in his glory. On the sick for months with a bad chest, he had despaired of ever getting work. The doctors in the Royal Victoria Hospital had forbidden him to return to Greeves Mill, where he had worked for thirty odd years in the flax store, and where he had picked up the linen dust that was the cause of his congested lungs. They had issued him with a blue card, stating that he was only fit for light work, so that he was compelled to obey their orders. However, light work was hard to come by and Rosaleen had watched him grow quieter and more depressed. Her heart ached for him, a young man of forty-five, on the dust heap. Her mother, pushing the *Irish News* open at the vacancies column at him every morning, had not helped any. It was as if she thought he wasn't trying to get work, as if he was lazy.

This wasn't true. The vaguest possibility of a job that was suitable had him away, trying to get an interview. It had been no use telling her mother that he hadn't a snowball's chance in hell of most of the jobs advertised. Not with a blue card and the added stigma of being a Catholic.

Now, at last, he had obtained employment. He had been started as gatehouse man in the Blackstaff Linen Factory. This was another one of the mills that flanked the Falls Road, whose books were full with orders for heavy duck material for tents and rucksacks, and other less heavy material for uniforms for the forces. Not great money, but being just down the Springfield Road a bit, within walking distance from Colinward Street as it were, there were no tram fares to worry about. No wonder his step was lighter, his mouth more ready to smile. At last, he could feel independent. It was indeed true that it was an ill wind that didn't blow some good. If war had not been declared, resulting in a mad rush of young men to enlist, her father would never have got this job, and Rosaleen was happy for him.

Her visits to May had become fortnightly instead of monthly as May drew near the end of her pregnancy. The first time Rosaleen had visited May, her heart had been quite literally in her mouth, and her knees had knocked hell out of each other as she nervously pushed the pram up the street where her friend lived. But, to her surprise, she noticed that the rows of terraced houses looked like any street on the Falls Road, with the same mixture of houseproud and couldn't-care-less occupants. There was only one difference; some of the footpaths had the kerb edge painted red, white and blue. It looked ugly, took away from the quiet nature of the streets, and Rosaleen was glad that none of the street kerbs on the Falls Road were painted green, white and gold.

May's house was one of the houseproud: windows shining, net curtains snow white, and a well-scrubbed half circle around the spotless doorstep. It was with a mixture of pride and diffidence that she ushered Rosaleen in and, before settling down for a cup of tea and a gossip, took her on a tour of the house. It was a parlour house with three bedrooms, and in the smallest of these Billy had installed a bathroom suite, while the second bedroom was all decorated, ready for the arrival of the baby. Lovely nursery wallpaper and curtains made Rosaleen jealous as she pictured her own spare room crammed with Joe's belongings.

'It's lovely, May. You must be proud of it,' she said graciously, and smiled. May smiled in return.

'It is nice, isn't it, Rosaleen?' she agreed shyly. 'I never dreamed I would ever own a house like this. Billy's a lovely man.' She leant closer and her eyes begged Rosaleen to believe. 'Honestly, Rosaleen, he really is.' Her head nodded to emphasise her point. 'Ye know, you don't have to be a Catholic to be good.'

Mouth agape, Rosaleen cried aghast, 'Have I ever said otherwise?'

May smiled faintly as she shook her head. 'No, of course you haven't. Still . . .' her head tilted slightly and an eyebrow rose '. . . I get the feeling that you don't approve of him.'

'Ah, May, that's not fair,' Rosaleen cried in despair. 'I think he's a lovely man. It's just . . . well, ye see . . . I worry about your soul,' she finished lamely.

At that, May laughed aloud. 'Well now, how's about you letting me do the worrying, eh?'

'Willingly! Willingly! I'll say no more.' Rosaleen held up her hand, palm facing outwards, as if to ward off the reproach in May's voice, and then gave her friend a sly glance from under lowered lids. 'Does this mean that you want me to start being nice to Billy? You know, the odd wee embrace and the odd wee kiss? Just to show how much I like him.'

'No fear. You keep all that for Joe,' May warned her with a laugh, and Rosaleen turned away to hide her pain. Her joke had backfired. She had been caught on the raw. Joe did not want . . . all that.

May's son was born in February and all hell broke loose when big John heard about it. Rosaleen was kept up to date on all the happenings by Annie, who, when the stitching factory closed down due to lack of material for ladies underwear, had found herself a job in Mackie's Foundry.

During the First World War Mackie's had played a prominent role, producing bullets and components for planes, so it was no surprise when they were roped in by the ministry to supply ammunition. Now they were working round the clock. Annie worked alongside Colin Brady (that was another thing about the war, it supplied employment for many on outdoor relief), and brought all the news home to Rosaleen.

It seemed that for a solid week big John was drunk and eventually ended up in jail for being drunk and disorderly. When he was released, Kate and the lads would not let him back into the house and got a court order to stop him molesting her and the family. Of course big John heaped all the blame on May's head, calling down vengeance on her. Vowing to get even with her for ruining his life. Not wanting to worry May, Rosaleen never repeated a word to her. She could only hope that big John's threats to get his own back were idle ones.

It was August of 1940 before work was started on the first air-raid shelter in the parish, but nobody worried about this. After all, during the First War, the Germans never came near Ireland and why should this time be any different? The shelter was built behind St Paul's Parochial House and was large and fitted out with padded seats. It was much more comfortable than the other air-raid shelters that followed it along Cavendish Road. It was said that this was because it would have to accommodate the policemen from the barracks on the Springfield Road.

August 24th was the day they started to build. Rosaleen was always to remember that date – it was the day Sean and Annie got married.

Rosaleen was matron of honour, and with Sean being an only son and all his close friends at sea, he asked Joe to be best man. For her wedding dress. Annie had chosen cream chiffon, shot with a tiny pink flower pattern. The dress was long and swirled around her slim ankles and clung to the curves of her slim body. To her mother's dismay, she shunned the conventional veil, saying that picture hats were in fashion, and wore one of these on her dark chestnut hair. She was breathtaking: her eyes glinting like emeralds, her skin clear and pure, and happiness radiating from her.

Seeing the adoration in her eyes as they followed Sean about, Rosaleen could understand his wanting to marry her, in spite of the complications that might arise. She only hoped that he would make her happy, but not for one minute did she doubt that he could satisfy her. Annie was a very lucky girl.

One thing was sure: as effectively as if he had used bricks and mortar, he had put up a wall between them, because by marrying Annie he had placed himself even further beyond her reach.

Although Rosaleen was not aware of it, she was every bit as beautiful as Annie. Her dress was pale blue chiffon, and her picture hat was caught under the chin with a swathe of white chiffon, throwing into relief the pure oval of her face and turning her eyes to silver. Since the birth of Laura she was heavier, but this just added a seductive curve to her bust and hips and did not detract from her beauty.

Much to Thelma's annoyance, the reception was held at home in Colinward Street, but with not knowing just when Sean would obtain leave, this was unavoidable. Also to her annoyance, there was not enough clothing coupons for both Tommy and she to get new outfits, and he had to make do with the lounge suit purchased for Rosaleen's wedding. Not that he was annoyed. Far from it! He hated breaking in new clothes and was happiest when wearing clothes that

106

had matured. However, Thelma wanted Annie's big day to resemble Rosaleen's as closely as possible. They were both her daughters and she meant to do her best for them. To her delight, although rationing was beginning to be felt, she had managed to get caterers in at short notice, and the spread was lovely.

To Rosaleen's relief, Betty Devlin, having joined the WRENS, was not at the reception. She had been worrying about meeting Betty, but when she had inquired after her, Sean had smiled and told her to stop worrying, that everything was going to be all right. She did not agree with him, but then, how was he to know that things would never be all right with her again? Annie and Sean were having a few days in Dublin for their honeymoon and lying alone in the big double bed that night, Rosaleen tried to block the picture of them together from her mind, but fought a losing battle in which tears were shed. She awoke heavy-eyed the next morning and descended the stairs to find Joe still in the kitchen.

Normally he was away to work before she descended the stairs and she greeted him with surprise.

'Did you sleep in?'

'No, I want to talk to you. You were too tired last night. Too preoccupied . . .' His eyes scanned her pale face, noting her heavy eyes, and he frowned. 'Are you all right?'

'Huh? Oh, yes, I'm fine. What do you want to talk to me about?'

He grimaced before saying, 'I don't know how to say this . . . you'll think I'm daft . . . but, well, I've joined up.'

Bewildered, she asked blankly, 'Joined up what?'

'I've enlisted. You know . . . joined the army.'

'But why?' Rosaleen was dumbfounded. Everybody was thanking God that there was no conscription here in Ireland; that there was no need for married men to worry about having to leave their wives and children, and here was Joe saying he had joined up. 'You're right. I do think you're daft. You don't have to go.'

'It's like this, Rosaleen. There is just not enough work for me and Owen.' Seeing that she was still bewildered, and guessing what she was thinking, he reached over and took her hand in his.

'I know what you're going to say. I'm the boss. Let Owen Black go. But, Rosaleen, he's in his forties, he's got four kids, and besides, he's too old and won't be able to get another job. Especially now the big foundries are all closing down for lack of material to carry out repairs. Rosaleen, things are in a bad way . . . hundreds are being thrown out of work every week. I think it's a ruse to get more young men to join up, but whatever the reason, it's up to the young men to join. Leave what jobs there are for the older men.'

Realising that what he said was true and not wanting to whinge, she remained silent. He continued, 'With me away, Owen will keep the business going. Even if he only gets the odd wee building contract, it will keep it running until the war's over, and I can trust him to put something away every week, no matter how small. It'll be waiting for me coming home . . . but it'll be in a joint account, so that if you should need any money, you have just to go to the bank. I doubt if he'll get any iron. In fact, they're talking about taking the railings off the parks. That's how bad it it. But he should get enough work to keep one man going.' He chucked her under the chin. 'At least one thing's sure – there should be plenty of work for me after the war.'

'You could concentrate on building garages or sheds,' she cried. 'Expand a bit.'

'I've already explained that to you, Rosaleen. People are just not building anything at the moment.'

'You could at least try to get a job,' she interrupted him indignantly. 'What about me and Laura?'

108

'Ah Rosaleen . . . I couldn't work for anybody else, not after being me own boss all these years. Besides, you know there aren't any jobs. Why do you think so many are enlisting? And you and Laura will be all right. I've money put away. If anything happens to me, you'll be comfortably off.'

'I don't want to be comfortably off. I want you here with me and Laura.'

The idea of being in the house alone with her baby when the sirens went off did not appeal to Rosaleen. Joe might not share a room with her, but at least he was there. He often fetched his mother round to sit in the cubby-hole under the stairs with them. She couldn't picture herself and Laura sitting alone under the stairs when the sirens went off. So far they had all been false alarms, but what if the Germans did decide to come over? They heard daily on the radio how badly England was being blitzed. What if the Germans came over here? What if it was their turn next?

'That's another thing . . . I want you to go with the rest of the women and children, out into the country. I want to go away with an easy mind.'

'Hah! Be evacuated?' Her face screwed up at the very idea. 'No way! If you go . . . if you decide you must fight for Britain . . . I'll do my bit. I'll get a job in Mackie's.'

'I'm not fighting for Britain.' The anger he felt came across in his voice. 'I'm fighting for a safe future for my wife and child. That's why I've joined up. And I want you away from Mackie's. It's like a big bomb sitting up there, in the midst of all the houses.'

She knew what he said was true.

'I'm sorry . . . but you took the wind out of my sails,' she said appeasingly, then asked, 'When do you go?'

'In two weeks' time.'

'Oh my God!'

The strength left her legs and she groped for a

chair. With an arm around her he led her to the settee and sat beside her, drawing her close. As she cuddled against him for comfort, she was beseiged by doubts. Was he going just to get away from her? She had started to repulse him; hating the way he always ended up crying in her arms. It had been driving her insane.

Now she regreted her actions. Joe crying in her arms would be better than being on her own.

'Joe . . . are you going because of . . . you know?' Her shoulders lifted in a despairing gesture and she swallowed deep before finishing the sentence. 'How things are between us?'

'No. No, Rosaleen, I'm not,' he consoled her. He smiled slightly and squeezed her closer still. He didn't blame her for her actions; the fault was all his. Now he tilted her face up so that he could look into her eyes. 'That's not the reason I'm going. I'm going because I think Hitler is a madman and must be stopped. I really don't think the war will last long. Maybe another year. And although I hate you being so near Mackie's, I don't really think that Hitler will come. He hasn't bothered with Ireland so far, has he?'

He held her gaze, and she shook her head as she agreed with him. 'No, he hasn't.'

'Are you feeling all right, now you're over the shock?'

When she nodded sadly, he said, 'I'm going round now to break the news to Mother. You'll keep an eye on her for me, won't you?'

'Of course I will.' Her eyes lit up and she nudged him excitedly. 'Now there's an idea! She can stay here with me while you're away. We'll be company for each other.'

His faced closed up and his nod was non-committal. Rosaleen turned away, annoyed. She could not understand Joe's attitude to his mother. She got on very well with Mrs Smith, but Joe did not encourage their friendship; he kept his mother at arm's length. Not that he wasn't good to her. He was. She wanted for nothing. But still, he did not encourage her to visit them. Did not make her at home in their house, saying that he did not want her popping in and out all the time, and he was not pleased if Rosaleen called in too often to visit her. Well, if he chose to go to war, she would be her own boss and would ask Mrs Smith to live with her in spite of his attitude. It would solve a lot of problems.

Two weeks later, Joe, handsome in his new uniform, left for England. Rosaleen, his mother, and the delight of his heart, Laura, accompanied him to the docks. They stood amidst the crowds and he crushed Rosaleen and Laura together in a fierce embrace.

'When I come back . . . when the war's over . . . I promise to go and see a doctor. All right, Rosaleen?'

Wet-eyed, she gazed up at him in amazement and nodded mutely. The kiss he gave her was full of promise.

Planting a more sedate farewell kiss on his mother's lips, he climbed the gangway and, with a final wave, disappeared from view. He had warned them not to hang about in the cold with Laura, and sadly they made their way through the crowd waiting to wave farewell to their loved ones. Leaving the quayside, they made their way to the tram stop.

Sure that Mrs Smith would be delighted to move in with her, Rosaleen put the suggestion to her, and was surprised when she regretfully declined the invitation.

'It's very kind of you, Rosaleen, but I don't think Joe would approve.'

'But why? You needn't give up your house. We can keep an eye on it. It's just 'til he comes back.'

Mrs Smith laughed softly. 'I'm not worried about the house. No, it's just . . . look, I can't explain. Someday I will, but not now. Besides, I don't want to be a

111

nuisance. And Rosaleen? Do you think you could ever get used to calling me Amy?'

'Amy . . . that's a lovely name. But don't change the subject! What about when the sirens go off? What will you do? I'll be worried sick about you, so I will.'

'I'll be all right! I'll go in next door. Besides, it won't take them long building the shelters. But never mind me, what will *you* do?'

Determined that in time she would be able to make Amy change her mind, Rosaleen's answer was airy.

'Oh, I'll manage . . . I'll manage. Me da's an air-raid warden, he'll look after me. Don't you worry about me.'

In the following weeks, try though she did to persuade Amy to change her mind, she did not succeed, but they became close friends.

When Amy offered to look after Laura, now a mischievous eighteen months old, while Rosaleen took a part-time job, she at first demurred.

'She's too boisterous for you, so she is, Amy. You'd never be able to handle her.'

'Look, if you got started in the Blackstaff on the afternoon shift, she'd be asleep most of the time. You know rightly she sleeps for at least two hours every afternoon, and it would do you good to get away from her for a few hours every day. Go on, Rosaleen. I'm sure the money would come in handy.'

This argument helped to sway her. Joe had been gone six weeks, and so far no money had come from the ministry for her. Whenever he could afford to, Owen was depositing some money straight into an account for her but she knew that it would not be much and had vowed not to touch it unless she had to. But, with Joe's money being held up, she would soon have to dip into their savings. Therefore Amy's offer tempted her. She was aware that it sometimes took months for the army wages to get through, and Amy was right, the extra money would come in handy.

'Are you sure?' she asked diffidently.

Seeing that she was weakening, Amy hastened to assure her, 'Of course I'm sure. I wouldn't have offered otherwise.'

So Rosaleen sought and obtained employment in the Blackstaff, just five minutes' walk away from Iris Drive.

She was in charge of three looms, weaving heavy black duck and drill material which would be used for making tents, and life became so busy she did not feel so frustrated. Her only regret was that it put a stop to her visits to see May, as she did not want to leave Laura in the evenings and felt that she was too young to keep out in the evening air. Besides (to May's disgust), she did not fancy being caught on the Shankhill Road if the sirens went off. She wanted to be amongst her own kind.

May wanted her to visit at the week-ends, but Rosaleen had so much shopping and cleaning to do then that it was impossible to trek away across to the Shankhill Road, and anyhow she did not want to intrude when Billy was at home with his wife and child.

She began to dread her mother's daily visits. Every time she came she lamented in her ear about Annie's behaviour. After the disappointment of not being pregnant, Annie had started going to dances with the girls out of work. Bringing home men from the forces to meet her parents. Going to the pictures with them and entertaining them generally. Seeing the furrow of worry on her mother's brow, Rosaleen sought to console her.

'Listen, Mam, she's not doing anything wrong. If she was she wouldn't be bringing them home, now would she?'

'How do we know what she's doing, eh? She's not like you. You know your place.'

Rosaleen felt hot colour blaze her face and turned

113

aside to hide it, fussing over Laura; hoping her mother would not notice. Why did everybody assume that she was a good girl? She could not picture Annie having it off up at the Dam. Yet here *she* was, considered a goody-goody, and Annie who was forthright and open about her actions was considered fast. It was true what they said, quiet ones were the worst.

'She'll go too far, so she will. What will Sean do if he hears about her actions?' her mother continued, too preoccupied to notice Rosaleen's manoeuvres. 'That one doesn't know when she's well off, so she doesn't.'

'I don't think Sean will mind ... who knows? Perhaps some girl somewhere is being nice to him. I'm inclined to think that you're worrying unnecessarily. Annie won't do anything to jeopardise her marriage.'

'Will you have a word with her, Rosaleen? Eh? She'll listen to you, so she will. Go on, love ... have a wee word in her ear.'

Against her will, Rosaleen promised to have a word with Annie. It certainly wasn't her place to criticise anybody, especially Annie, but having promised, she waited her chance. It came sooner than she expected; the following evening her sister called down from work for a chat.

'This is a pleasant surprise,' Rosaleen greeted her, a happy smile on her face. 'My, but you don't half suit that boilersuit,' she added enviously, her eyes roaming over Annie's slim figure.

And the boilersuit did indeed become Annie. Not so long ago it had been considered a scandal for a woman to wear trousers, but the war had changed all that, and the long slim lines of Annie's body and legs were emphasised by the navy boilersuit which all Mackie's workers wore.

'You look lovely, Annie. Really nice.' Her look turned reproachful and she childed, 'Long time no see.'

'I know.' Annie lifted Laura up in her arms. 'How I've missed you, love,' she cried, hugging the child close and covering her face with kisses. 'You're a wee bundle of joy, so you are,' she added, as Laura squirmed and giggled in her arms.

'Well, what kept you away then? It must be two weeks since you've been down,' Rosaleen chastised her.

'Longer,' Annie agreed with her. 'Too long, but I've been very busy.'

'So I hear . . .'

At that, Annie sat Laura down on the settee with a plop. 'You sit there a wee minute, pet, and be a good girl. I've something nice for you,' she promised, and turned to face Rosaleen.

'You've been talking to me mam,' she said resignedly as she removed the turban that bound her hair, and ran her fingers through her long, chestnut tresses. 'Gosh, but these turbans are warm. I wish we didn't have to wear them.' She moved to the mirror above the fireplace and fluffed her hair out, pouting at the attractive picture she made, before asking, 'And just what has Mam been saying about me?'

'She's worried about you. And from what I hear, I don't blame her.'

Anger flared in Annie's eyes and she turned on Rosaleen and growled, 'Just what did you hear, eh? What? That I'm carrying on with soldiers and sailors? Is that what you heard?'

At the look of guilt on Rosaleen's face, she grunted.

'Huh! I can see I'm right. Well, let me tell you something. I hope some girl, somewhere, is being nice to Sean. You can be nice and entertain a man without doing "that", ye know, and I'm not doing anything wrong. Would I bring them home if I was carrying on? Eh? Tell me . . . would I? No. I'd bring them where some of the girls bring them. Up to the Dam, or over Daisy Hill. That's where I'd bring them, and no

115

one need be the wiser.'

The anger left her and a wry smile crossed her face. 'Honestly, Rosaleen, most of them just want company. Someone to talk to about their wives and girl friends. And I supply that company. So the neighbours can gossip all they want! That's all Mam's worried about . . . what the neighbours'll think.'

At the mention of the Dam, Rosaleen felt the colour leave her face. Did Annie know? Had Sean confessed to her? She made herself look Annie in the face but her sister's attention was back with Laura. Giving her a small bar of chocolate, Annie once more lifted the child up in her arms and hugged her close.

Close to tears, she muttered, 'I wish I was pregnant. If only I was pregnant . . . If Sean's killed, I have nothing . . . nothing.' She broke off on a sob, burying her head in a silent, wide-eyed Laura's neck.

Going to her, Rosaleen gathered her close to her breast. 'Ah, Annie, don't talk like that. Sean will come back. I just know he will.'

Clinging to her, Annie sobbed for some seconds, at the same time trying to smile to please Laura who was wiping at her tears with a chubby fist, muttering. 'There now, Auntie Annie . . . hush now . . . it'll be better soon, so it will.' Repeating like an old woman the words that Rosaleen used to comfort her when she wept.

'I hope you're right, Rosaleen. I hope you're right. You're lucky. If anything happens to Joe, you've got Laura.'

They drew apart when Amy, after a tap on the door, entered the room.

'Oh, I'm so sorry . . . I didn't know you'd company. I'll come back later . . .'

Seeing Annie's tear-streaked face, her voice trailed off in embarrassment and she made to back out again but Laura wriggled from Annie's arms, slid down and ran to Amy, tugging her skirt for attention.

116

'You're all right, Amy,' Rosaleen assured her kindly. 'Come on in. I was just going to make Annie a wee cup of tea. Do you fancy one?'

Amy's eyes searched both their faces and when Annie said graciously, 'Sit down, Amy. I'm just feeling sorry for meself, it's nice to see you,' she accepted the offer of a cup of tea.

'Well, if you're sure. A cup of tea would be lovely, thank you.'

They talked and laughed for a couple of hours, and when Annie left, at the door she confided to Rosaleen.

'Sean might be home for a couple of days. His ship's in port in England, for repairs and he's going to try to get over for a while. Who knows? I might get pregnant yet. Here . . .' she extracted a small packet from her pocket and thrust it into Rosaleen's hand '. . . a wee present for you.'

'What is it?' Rosaleen asked, feeling the parcel with inquisitive fingers.

'A couple of pairs of silk stockings. With seams!'

'Oh, really?'

'Really,' Annie said smugly. 'And they really are pure silk. Save them 'til Joe comes home and give him a treat.' Her head tilted back and her brows rose. 'What's this they say about an ill wind?' she jested. Then, observing the worried look on Rosaleen's face and guessing the reason for it, she bawled, 'Oh, for heaven's sake, Rosaleen . . . I didn't do anything wrong to get them. You can take them with a clear conscience, so you can!'

Rosaleen grimaced, guiltily. 'I'm sorry, Annie. Thanks very much.'

Appeased, Annie grinned at her. 'You're welcome. And there's more where they came from, so keep your fingers crossed that I see that particular sailor again.' She backed away from the door. 'See you soon.'

'Don't wait so long next time,' Rosaleen warned her.

Grinning wickedly, Annie retorted, 'Now I'll not know whether you want to see me or are hoping for more stockings.'

'Oh, you! See you soon.' And with a flap of her hand, Rosaleen waved her on her way.

Sean did manage to get three days' leave but this time Rosaleen only saw him in passing; a hello and goodbye, as it were. When he returned to sea, Annie counted the days, jubilant when her period was late, inconsolable when it arrived.

Christmas came and went practically unnoticed except for the religious ceremonies, more profound and beautiful than ever because of the war. The priests said that was how it should be, and they were right of course. Still, it would have been nice to have been able to splash out a bit, but rationing and shortage of clothes and sweet coupons put paid to that.

Early in 1941 the sirens were going off more regularly; still false alarms as the planes continued to blitz England and returned to base without approaching Ireland at all, but nevertheless disrupting lives and causing worry.

When Billy, accompanied by May, visited her and urged her to seek refuge out in the country, Rosaleen was tempted. The bombings on the west coast of England were too close for peace of mind and she felt guilty leaving Laura with Amy and going off to work every afternoon. Felt that she should be taking Laura to apparent safety, especially now Joe's money was getting through.

So when Billy pleaded, 'Think of Laura, Rosaleen,' she was tempted, although she had to laugh at his reasoning.

Realising the trend of her thoughts, Billy reddened, and giving a shamed laugh, confessed: 'I suppose you're thinking I'm only worried about Laura because

May won't go away without you? And in a way you're right. I *am* worried about May and Ian . . . but I really do believe that you should take Laura away too.'

She smiled kindly at him. 'I know how you feel, Billy.' She turned to May. 'But suppose we're sent to different parts of the country?'

'That's what I said to him.' May sniffed and tossed her head defiantly. She had no intention of going anywhere without Rosaleen, danger or no danger. 'I said you can't pick and choose. I told him you've to go wherever they send you.'

'Tell you what, I'll have a word with me da. He might be able to fix something up for us. He'll certainly be glad of the chance. He's at me every week to take Laura away.' She looked at Billy. 'So will you leave it in my hands? I'll see what can be done and I'll get in touch with you.'

Happy to have set things in motion, Billy agreed to leave it in her hands, warning her not to delay too long.

Glad that Rosaleen was at last consenting to be evacuated, Tommy Magee did all in his power to find them accommodation together. It was during lent, three weeks before Easter, that he at last succeeded. When he called in to tell Rosaleen of his success, she was far from pleased.

'It's too near Easter, Da!' she exclaimed. 'Can we wait 'til after it?'

'No, ye can't wait. Look, I've knocked me arse out of joint getting you and May on the same farm, so you'd better not let me down.'

'A farm?' Rosaleen interrupted him, her face alarmed. 'A farm? We don't want a farm. I thought we'd be in some wee town or village.'

At these words Tommy blew his top.

'Now you look here, madam, you're goin', like it or not. You're goin'. You're not goin' to make a fool out of me. There's no bloody vacancies left in wee towns or villages. Do ye think that they were just waitin' for you to make up your mind to go? Eh? Do ye?'

His anger startled Rosaleen; in all her life she had only seen him give vent to it on a couple of occasions, and with just cause. Now she found herself meekly agreeing to get in touch with May.

After that, once Billy heard, there was no turning back and Saturday found them in Great Victoria Street Station, waiting for the train that was to take them to Dungannon, in County Tyrone.

Rosaleen hugged her father tightly, glad that her mother and Annie had consented to say their goodbyes at home; this was heartbreaking.

'You'll come for me if I hate it, won't you, Da?' she asked anxiously.

'Of course I will love . . . ye know I will. But now give yourself a chance to get used to it, won't ye?'

She nodded and pushed him away. 'Go on . . . go on home before I change me mind,' she cried, thinking that perhaps it was not such a good idea leaving Belfast.

With a brief glance inside the coach at the closely entwined figures of Billy and May, her father rolled his eyes and pursed his lips.

'I'll wait outside for Billy. Goodbye, love.'

One more hug and kiss for his beloved grandchild, who was taking everything in, wide-eyed, and he left the platform.

Rosaleen chatted and played with Laura and hovered in front of the door to the carriage, preventing other people from entering, giving May and Billy a few precious extra minutes alone. She tried to keep her eyes away from them but did not succeed, envying them their closeness. How wonderful, after two years of marriage still to desire each other with such intensity. May did not know how lucky she was.

When at last the train roared into life, and its great

frame shuddered and puffed, Billy pushed May away from him, patted his young son on the head, and hugging Rosaleen, whispered, 'Look after her for me.' He rushed from the train, cheeks wet with tears.

Hanging from the carriage, May watched him out of sight and then wiped the tears from her own cheeks before lifting Ian from the seat. Hugging the child tight, she sat down on the seat facing Rosaleen, at the window. Glad that they had a compartment to themselves and could talk freely, she said wryly, 'I'm sure you think I'm a fool, Rosaleen. You'd think I was going to war instead of safety.' She gave an embarrassed laugh. 'It's just not being able to finish what we started that frustrates me.' She wrinkled her nose. 'You know what I mean.'

Oh yes, Rosaleen knew exactly what she meant. She knew all about the frustration of starting what couldn't be finished. Now she just nodded her head in agreement. How she envied May; to be loved like that must be heaven.

Observing the sad droop of her mouth, May reached across and squeezed her hand sympathetically.

'It must be awful for you . . . Joe away fighting. You must miss him something awful, and here's me, rambling on about Billy.'

Embarrassed, Rosaleen nodded her head again. She did miss Joe; read and re-read his letters, longed for the comfort of his presence about the house, but she did not miss him in the way that May meant.

At Dungannon they were met at the station by a tall, thin, young man in a small, open-backed lorry. Into the back of this, the surly owner loaded their cases, prams and gas masks. Then, barely glancing at them, he hoisted Rosaleen and Laura, followed by May and Ian, up into the cabin. The nearest he came to an apology for the tight squeeze was a muttered, 'It won't be for long. Just fifteen minutes,' as he swung up in beside Rosaleen.

The journey was conducted in silence, and after

121

thirty minutes Rosaleen was just about to ask sarcastically if time stretched longer in the country when the lorry turned off the road and bounced and trundled up a rutted track and around the back of a low, sprawling, one-storeyed building. The big, sturdy, oak door was pulled open immediately and a small, plump woman bustled out. Reaching up with great difficulty, she wrenched open the door of the lorry and assisted May to the ground, at the same time introducing herself.

'Hello, hello . . . I'm Mrs Magill, Maggie . . . call me Maggie. An' you must be . . .?' Her eyes noted the young child in May's arms and she finished, 'Mrs Mercer. I'm pleased to meet ye. You too, missus,' she shouted up at Rosaleen, and turning to the young man, exclaimed testily, 'Well, don't just stand there, Vince. Help her down.'

Reaching up, the man lifted Rosaleen bodily from the cabin and set her on her feet. When he lifted Laura down and placed her in her mother's arms, Rosaleen thanked him.

He shot her a swift glance. Only then did Vince Magill realise that Rosaleen was attractive, very attractive indeed.

Head back, he looked down the length of his long thin nose and examined her face. Noted the bright pale gold hair escaping from the headsquare that covered it, and interest kindled in his eyes, bringing a blush to her cheeks. Then he startled her by smiling, something she had not thought him capable of, and the smile changed his face completely. It exposed even white teeth against the dark, rugged tan of his skin, and made her aware of bright blue, mocking eyes. It was with relief that she turned at his mother's direction and followed her as she led the way into the house and through a big, spotlessly clean kitchen. Rosaleen was pleased to note this: the big wooden table was scrubbed white, and the long range that ran the length of one wall was well black leaded, no mean feat, as Rosaleen well knew. It took her hours to keep her own small kitchenette grate in apple pie order. A quick glance around also showed copperware gleaming on the wall above the range, a well-scrubbed redstone floor, a big brown jawbox in the corner, and brasses on the wide stone hearth, shining in the firelight.

After showing May into a room, Mrs Magill led the way to the front of the house, and stopping outside a door, explained, 'I've put you in the parlour, Mrs Smith. I only had one spare room but when we heard you an' your friend wanted t'be t'gether, I offered t'put a bed in the parlour. I think you'll find it comfortable.' With these words, she opened the door and ushered Rosaleen in. 'Vince, that's me son, will bring in the pram and yer gas masks, and then he'll fetch ye some hot water, so that ye can refresh yerself and the chile b'fore tea. I've made the tea early 'cause I'm sure you're hungry. The laverty's at the bottom of the yard, so it is.'

Rosaleen stood and took stock before she answered her. It was an attractive room, with a deep bay window that looked out over open countryside. The bed was double, with a bright, clean, patchwork quilt. She noted that there was no sign of a cot.

'Thank you very much, Mrs . . .'

'Don't be formal . . . please call me Maggie. An' I know that you're Mrs Smith.'

Rosaleen acknowledged the introduction with an inclination of her head.

'I think I shall be comfortable here, thank you.'

When the door closed on her, Rosaleen pulled back the bedclothes and felt the mattress. It was dry; no sign of dampness, and the bedclothes were freshly laundered. Perhaps it wouldn't be too bad staying here after all. Maybe it would be just like a holiday.

'I trust it meets with your approval?'

123

Rosaleen swung around, embarrassed colour staining her cheeks. She had not heard Vince enter the room.

'And I trust that in future you knock on the door before you enter my room,' she retorted angrily.

'I did knock . . . but you were too preoccupied to hear me.'

He accompanied the words with a derisive smile, and wheeled the pram into the corner. Rosaleen longed to call him a liar, but bit on her tongue. She did not want to antagonise anyone, not when she was going to have to live here. He swung the gas masks in her direction and with a deft movement she caught them.

'Ye might be interested to know that we were worried about you too,' he informed her. 'We've been hearing all kind of reports about very dirty refugees. Ye know, lousy heads an' all.' His eyes took stock of the soft shining cloud of hair, now released from its headsquare, and her clean, tidy appearance. 'But you look clean enough.'

Before Rosaleen could think of a suitable reply to his accusations – which she knew to be true, from reports she had read in the *Irish News* – he added, 'I'll fetch ye some hot water now, but this is no hotel. In future you'll fetch your own. And tea will be ready in fifteen minutes.'

Another derisive glance was thrown her way, and then, lifting a big jug from a basin on the dresser, he left the room. While she waited for him to return with the water, Rosaleen decided to find the toilet. Laura was starting to squirm, any minute now she would be whimpering. 'Wee wee, Mammy,' and as she usually left it to the last moment to inform Rosaleen, it would be as well to find out just where it was.

Taking Laura by the hand, she made her way out to the back of the farm, bumping into May, in like mind.

'Well . . . what's your room like?' she asked.

'Not bad. Not bad at all. Will you be all right in the parlour?'

'It seems comfortable, but there's no lock on the door.' Rosaleen eyed May anxiously. 'Perhaps it'll be all right here. Eh? What do you think?' she asked, seeking reassurance.

'I hope so.' May snorted. 'Huh . . . I've often heard tell of the arse hole of nowhere, and now I know where it is.' She smiled wryly at Rosaleen's outraged expression. 'I'm sorry to be so crude, but you have to admit I'm right. How on earth will we pass the time?'

'At least the children will be safe,' Rosaleen said consolingly, but as they approached the toilet, her nose wrinkled in distaste. For one horrible moment, she thought it was a dry toilet. Her eyes met May's in distress.

'It's all right. That's the piggery you smell, so it is. On a farm like this one, they're bound to be civilised enough to have toilets that flush,' May assured her, and a relieved Rosaleen was glad to discover that she was right.

The toilet was clean, with whitewashed walls and a well-scrubbed wooden seat, and on the wall, hanging from a nail, were neatly cut squares of newspaper threaded on a piece of thick string. This brought a smile to her lips; not so long ago, that had been a fixture on her parents' toilet. Back when money was scarce, before she and Annie had started work and added to the family budget. This was something she could tolerate. The smile broadened as she imagined Laura's reaction when she had to use the newspaper squares; she was a fussy young madam.

Tea was an uncomfortable meal. Rosaleen was dismayed to find that what she had assumed was butter was instead margarine; she had lavished it on the scones and home-made bread before her discovery. She thought she would choke trying to force it down her throat. She sensed May's amusement at her predicament and smiled grimly at her. May smiled demurely back. Margarine was all right when you were used to it, and May never ate anything else. Halfway through the meal another big, surly man entered the room. Built like a bull, he had a thatch of bright red hair and bushy eyebrows that curled upwards, giving him a demonic look. Rosaleen was not surprised when Laura, without removing her eyes from the man, left her chair and stretched her arms up to her mother to be lifted, aware that if she had met him herself in the dark, she also would be frightened. When Mrs Magill introduced him as her husband, Rosaleen and May greeted him politely, but he just acknowledged them with a grunt and Rosaleen felt her temper rise. How were they going to manage to live with these surly people? You would think that they were taking in refugees out of the goodness of their hearts, instead of receiving a tidy sum from the ministry for their trouble. Well, she would see that she and Laura got their money's worth, Rosaleen vowed. Tomorrow she would ask for butter; she had never eaten magarine in her life before and she did not intend to start now. She was also very much aware that Vince watched her covertly and this dismayed her. Life would be bad enough here without any other complications and she determined to keep him at arms' length.

After tea they decided to go for a walk while there was still daylight. Both children had slept fitfully during the day and on the journey down, and were now wide awake. So deciding the country air would help them to sleep, they set off down the lane, pushing their prams in the direction of Dungannon. A lane that Mrs Magill assured them would cut their journey in half. They walked quickly, hoping to make it to town and back before dusk; they wanted to get their bearings and see what treats the future had in store for

126

them. An hour later they arrived on the outskirts of Dungannon and pushed the prams with arms that ached up a long narrow street, arriving at last in the heart of the town. Bigger than they had anticipated, Dungannon was prosperous-looking and they stood in the great market square and looked around them with interest. It was now late afternoon and most of the shops were closing but Rosaleen noted that the Belfast Bank and Post Office were up in the right-hand corner, beside the Police Barracks. She pointed these out to May, knowing that they would be needing to draw money during their stay in Dungannon.

'Well, what do you think?' she asked.

'Looks all right . . . bigger than I thought it would be. Pity all the shops are closing, but we can come back in on Monday and browse around.'

Failing light and rising winds decided them to return to the farm but the size of the town had raised their spirits and they were in a happier frame of mind as they retraced their steps.

Mrs Magill met them in the hall. 'You're welcome to sit in the kitchen with me and Vince t'night, if ye feel like it. We listen to the radio.'

Before May could open her mouth, Rosaleen answered for them both.,

'Thank you very much, but we've very tired . . . and Mrs Magill? Since there is no cot for Laura, I wonder if I could have a rubber sheet? She rarely wets the bed, but her routine has been upset today and I'd prefer to be safe than sorry.'

Immediately, Mrs Magill was all apologies. 'Oh, that was a mistake, so it was. Not on our part, mind ye. Vince has already put a cot up in the parlour, Mrs Smith. We just didn't realise that your child was so young. We were told a four-year-old would be comin'. Obviously there has been some mix up. An', remember, you're welcome in the kitchen any night.

There's not much to do about here, once the light goes . . . except tomorrow night. Every Sunday night there's a dance in the town. I'm sure Vince would be glad to give you a lift in, he goes every week.'

This time May forestalled Rosaleen. 'That would be very nice, thank you, Mrs . . . Maggie.'

When Rosaleen had settled Laura for the night, she made her way down the hall to the back of the house, to where May's room was situated. To her surprise Ian was soundly asleep in his cot but of May there was no sight. Puzzled, she slowly entered the kitchen.

'Oh, so you've changed yer mind, have ye?' Mrs Magill greeted her. 'Come over here and sit down near the fire.' She reached across and poked the turf in the grate, sending a warm welcoming glow around the room. 'It's quite chilly t'night. Come on, come over to the fireside.'

Only when she saw May up to her elbows in suds at the big brown jawbox did Rosaleen realise that she would have nappies to wash out each night.

'Were you looking for me, Rosaleen?' May asked. 'I'm almost finished. Is there anything you want me to rinse out for you while I'm at it?'

'I'll do me own, thank you, May.' She turned to Mrs Magill and asked politely, 'Is that all right, Mrs Magill?'

'Of course! Of course! We've always plenty of hot water, and don't be so formal . . . call me Maggie.'

'Thank you, Maggie. I haven't much . . . just a few wee things . . . I'll fetch them.'

They did stay in the kitchen after all, bringing Mrs Magill up to date on things in Belfast and discovering that twice a week, Tuesdays and Saturdays, a bus passed close to the farm, should they want to go into Dungannon. At eleven o'clock, after a cup of hot cocoa, they retired for the night. A relieved Rosaleen was glad that Vince had not put in an appearance.

Awakening early next morning, she rose and thrust

the curtains wide open, raising the blackout blinds. Back home in Belfast, she had often wondered what it would be like to awaken to a beautiful view, to see the sun rise and set. Now she would find out. To her dismay, everything was shrouded in mist. All she could see was the hedge that surrounded the house and barns. Everything else was grey and dreary. Disappointed, she closed the curtains again, remembering that she would be in full view as she washed herself down.

At breakfast, when she asked if she could have butter for her toast, Mrs Magill informed her that although they made butter, it was all for the market and if she wanted any she would have to pay extra for it. Annoyed, Rosaleen agreed to do so. She was more annoyed still when she discovered that if she wanted one of the big brown eggs that were abundant for Laura each morning, this would also have to be paid for.

As she spoon fed a soft boiled egg to Laura, she asked, 'How far is it to the Catholic church?'

'Ah . . . I was wonderin' about that. Did ye not notice it in town yesterday? But never worry, Vince goes t'church every Sunday. Not the Catholic Church, mind, the Church of Ireland, but he'll give ye a lift in, so he will. You can leave the bairns with me, if ye like.'

'Why, that's very kind of you, Maggie,' May gushed, seeing a refusal hover on Rosaleen's lips. 'What time have we to be ready for?'

'Half-past ten.'

A glance at the clock made May cry, 'Oh . . . then we'd better get a move on, hadn't we? Come on, Rosaleen, come on.'

She gathered Ian up in her arms, leaving Rosaleen to shovel the last spoonful of egg into Laura's mouth and follow suit. Entering May's room, Rosaleen rounded on her.

'You're not going to leave Ian with her?'

'Why not?' May asked, reasonably.

129

'We didn't come here to palm the kids off on to someone else. That's why! We'll take them with us.'

'Look, Rosaleen, I'm going to mass to please you . . . remember, I don't go to church any more. So if you want me to stay at home and look after the kids, that's all right with me.'

'Of course I want you to come to mass, but . . .'

'But, nothing,' May interrupted her. 'The church will probably be tiny, and the kids won't like it, so they'll probably play up and cause everyone to look at us. We don't want that, do we?' When Rosaleen's head swung slowly from side to side, May added, 'We'll stick out like a sore thumb as it is, so let's be grateful to Maggie for offering to mind them. Not everyone would offer, you know.' And a disgruntled Rosaleen had to agree with her.

May was wrong: the church was big, old and beautiful, and after mass they took a walk along the market square, window-shopping. The shops contained the usual regulation coats and dresses, but there were some smaller stores packed with bits and pieces from the year one and Rosaleen nudged May with delight. They beamed at each other, thinking of the hours of pleasure they would spend in these shops, a bit like browsing around Smithfield Market, only on a much smaller scale. On the lower corner of the square they saw a poster stating that tonight the local band would provide music for dancing. One look at the hall and Rosaleen sneered, 'You won't find me going to any dances there.'

Tight-lipped, May retorted, 'Well then, perhaps you'll look after Ian for me, 'cause if I get the chance I'll go.'

'You'd go to the dance?' Rosaleen turned a horrified look on her.

With an exaggerated sigh, May exlaimed: 'Honestly, Rosaleen, you astound me! You sound as if you were about fifty, instead of twenty-four. I didn't think you were such a stick in the mud. I, for one, will be glad to get to the dance. Do you realise that there's nothing else to do in this Godforsaken hole?'

Hurt at May's attitude, Rosaleen replied huffily, 'We didn't come here to enjoy ourselves. We came to protect our children, so we did.' Her look was reproachful. 'I don't understand you, May. I thought you loved Billy.'

'What on earth has my love for Billy got to do with going to a dance? Eh? Come on . . . tell me. I'm all ears.' And then the absurdity of their quarrel struck May, and slipping her arm through Rosaleen's, she apologised. 'Look, I'm sorry. You're right, of course. We should be respectable, staid, married women. We'll just sit in every night and talk to Maggie,' she said appeasingly. 'All right?'

Her apology only served to make Rosaleen feel guilty, just as May had known it would, and Rosaleen found herself compromising.

'Look . . . if Maggie will keep an eye on the kids, let's try the dance tonight. It will probably be awful and we won't want to go back, all right?'

And a relieved May agreed with her, happy to have won her over.

Maggie good-naturedly did consent to keep an eye on the children, and it was with trepidation that, once Laura was settled, Rosaleen left her bedroom and entered the kitchen. Not realising that there might be a bit of a social life, she had just brought a selection of skirts and jumpers with her, and now she wore a pale green skirt and a cream twinset. She was dismayed to see that May had come prepared, and looked lovely in a dress of floral colours, with a full flowing skirt, a white cardigan draped around her shoulders.

'You both look lovely, so ye do. Now away ye go!' Maggie urged. 'Go on, Vince is waitin' outside for ye, an' ye better hurry up. He's very impatient, so he is.'

'Laura's asleep, but she's a bit restless . . . you will listen for her, won't you?' Rosaleen asked anxiously.

'Never ye worry. I've reared six of me own.' Maggie laughed at the surprised reaction these words provoked. 'Yes, six, and they're all married except Vince. So I know how to take care of babies.'

Once outside, Rosaleen motioned May up into the cabin of the lorry first, then climbed in beside her, receiving a mocking smile from Vince. May gave her a puzzled look but remained silent, and only when they were in the cloakroom of the dance hall did she query it.

'Have you anything against Vince, Rosaleen? He hasn't been too handy . . . ye know what I mean?'

At this, Rosaleen drew back and laughed aloud. 'No, of course he hasn't. Do you think I'd hold me tongue if he had?'

'Perhaps.' At Rosaleen's surprised look, May sighed and added, 'I keep forgetting you led a sheltered life. If you knew the things I've had to pretend never happened, just to keep the peace, you'd swoon away.'

'Ah, May . . .' There was a wealth of sadness in Rosaleen's voice and May laughed.

'Oh, it hasn't done any lasting damage, so it hasn't,' she declared. 'I mean, it wasn't anything serious . . . you know what I mean.' When Rosaleen still looked concerned, May became flustered and with a final look at her reflection, tossed her ash-blonde hair and said, 'Come on . . . let's go in and see what the local talent is like.'

In spite of herself, Rosaleen enjoyed the dance. The last time she had danced had been at her own wedding reception. The sound of the music set her feet tapping and soon she was twirling around the big wooden floor, to quick-steps and slow foxtrots, and even enjoyed the Gay Gordons, a dance she usually avoided.

It was after the Gay Gordons, as they stood flushed

and breathless, that Vince approached them and offered to buy them a drink. As they waited for him to return, May confided in Rosaleen.

'I often wondered what it would be like to be lifted in every dance, and now I know. It's heaven.' She hugged herself, then gazed beseechingly at Rosaleen. 'You will come back next week, won't you, Rosaleen?'

'Of course. It will be the highlight of our week by the looks of it . . . and Joe and Billy won't mind if we enjoy ourselves, sure they won't?'

'No! Of course they won't mind. For heaven's sake, relax, Rosaleen. Anyone would think it was a sin to dance,' May admonished her, then leant forward confidentially. 'Did you notice the big horsey girl that Vince dances most with?' When Rosaleen nodded, May whispered, 'Well, that's his future wife.'

'Really?' Surprise made Rosaleen's voice shrill, and she covered her mouth with her hand to try to contain her astonishment. '*Really?*'

'Yes, really.' They fell against each other and giggled at the idea. 'So you needn't worry about not having a lock on your door. He's "promised", and by the look of yon one, he'll be afraid to look sideways at anyone else.'

When Vince returned with two orange juices, he was accompanied by the big horsey girl whom he introduced to them as Mavis Cartwright. Avoiding each other's eyes, Rosaleen and May politely shook hands with her. Still afraid to look at each other, for fear a single glance would make them start to giggle, they made inane conversation and were relieved when the music started up again. Then, to Rosaleen's amazement, Vince turned to her.

'May I have this dance, please?'

Flustered, she looked at May for guidance but, relieving her of her glass, May gazed somewhere above her head, looking as if butter would not melt in her mouth.

A glance at Mavis showed tight-lipped disapproval, and Rosaleen was just about to refuse to dance with him when Vince put his arm around her waist and drew her on to the dance floor.

Once out of earshot, she looked up at him. 'Won't your friend be angry?'

'Who cares?' His shoulders lifted in a shrug of indifference and his narrowed eyes examined her face. 'Every time I tried to dance with you I was beaten to it, so I took the opportunity when it was offered.'

'Are you engaged to Mavis?'

He nodded and his face closed up and Rosaleen knew he was warning her not to trespass.

Most of the farm helpers and country lads plodded around the floor, but Rosaleen had to admit that Vince had class. His steps were light and his long strides covered the floor expertly. She gave herself up to the joy of dancing with a good partner.

They danced in silence and when the music trailed off, Vince looked down at her flushed, happy face and whispered, 'I thoroughly enjoyed that.' And Rosaleen could only nod her head in agreement, knowing that he was aware that she had enjoyed it also.

'Will you save me the last dance?' he asked softly.

Uneasy again, Rosaleen countered, 'No . . . I don't think that would be right. Won't Mavis object?'

'No. Mavis and I have an agreement. She won't object.'

Against her better judgement, Rosaleen nodded her consent. 'All right.'

Somehow or other, she thought that Vince meant that Mavis did not dare to object and she felt sorry for her.

After the last dance Rosaleen had to admit to herself that the priests really did know what they were talking about when they preached from the pulpit about close dancing. An uneasy bond had been formed between

Vince and herself, a bond that would never have shown itself had they not danced, and Rosaleen was apprehensive and quiet on the drive home.

Not so May; she eyed Vince and asked demurely, 'Are you and Mavis engaged?'

He nodded, and to Rosaleen's surprise volunteered information.

'She's an only child and will inherit the farm adjoining ours. It should be a good match.'

And that explained everything. Obviously, Mavis wanted Vince and Vince wanted the farm, and there would probably be a lot of strings attached . . . like him doing as he pleased when it suited him. Poor Mavis. It seemed like she would get the thin edge of the wedge.

When they arrived at the farm, Rosaleen was relieved when May whispered, 'Are you going down to the loo?'

She nodded, and bidding Vince goodnight, they made their way down the yard. She was glad of May's company, had been afraid of meeting Vince in the dark, feeling that somehow she had given him the wrong impression by enjoying her dances with him. And in spite of what May had said, she was more worried than ever that her door did not have a lock. Much more worried. She had seen the desire in his eyes.

Once back in her room, Rosaleen looked around for some means of securing her door. Something that would make a noise and awaken her should anyone try it during the night. The only chair in the room was too low and the back did not reach the door handle, so she abandoned that. At her wit's end, she at last tied a belt to the door handle and then secured it to the pram. Next she piled the pram high with objects and at last crept into bed.

Should Vince try to enter her room during the night, she should be forewarned, and consoled by this

135

thought she drifted off to sleep.

The clatter that brought her from the bed in confusion and panic, to stand shivering on the cold oil cloth, resounded through the quiet household. The room was pitch black because the dark blinds and heavy curtains that prevented any light from showing outside also prevented natural light from entering the room. She heard a muffled oath outside the door, then voices.

'What on earth's wrong, Vince?'

She heard Mrs Magill approach her door and Vince answer her.

'I don't know, Ma. I heard this awful noise . . . I think it came from Mrs Smith's room.'

Quietly, Rosaleen removed the belt from the doorknob and opened the door slightly.

'I'm sorry,' she apologised. 'I'm afraid I had a nightmare and accidentally knocked over the pram.'

'Oh? The pram?'

Rosaleen sensed Mrs Magill's doubt and added appeasingly, 'I really am sorry to have disturbed you.'

'Rosaleen . . . are you all right?'

Glad to hear May's voice, Rosaleen opened the door wide and entered the hall, forgetting that she was in her nightdress until Vince's eyes scanned her body, making her feel naked. Crossing her arms over her chest, she sank her chin on to them and answered May.

'I had one of my nightmares, you know how it is? I forgot where I was, and in the dark knocked the pram over. I'm sorry to have awakened everybody.'

May frowned. She had not been aware that Rosaleen suffered from nightmares . . . then she saw the chagrin on Vince's face and the penny dropped.

Why, the cheeky bugger! Giving him a look of venom, she backed Rosaleen up. 'Oh, you poor dear. Will I stay with you the rest of the night?' The look she bestowed on Vince was derisive. 'Just in case your nightmare returns?'

136

'No, no, I'll be all right now. You go back to Ian. Goodnight, everybody.'

With these words, Rosaleen entered her room and closed the door, glad that Laura had slept through all the noise. She did not think that Vince would risk trying her door again but to be on the safe side, she secured the door as before and fell into a sound sleep the minute her head hit the pillow.

The next morning it rained, and on Tuesday they awakened to more rain. Bored, they decided to brave the elements and catch the bus into town. And when Mrs Magill offered to mind the children, Rosaleen did not hesitate to take her up on her offer, having come to the conclusion that she was fond of children. She was also aware that farmer's wife though she may be, Mrs Magill had time on her hands. It was the woman and two young girls who came to 'do' every day who scrubbed and polished and black leaded, while the men attended to all the outside work, leaving Mrs Magill free to attend to the cooking.

In Dungannon, they spent some hours browsing in the small shops full of old second-hand stuff, Rosaleen bought some ornaments, which she was convinced would grow in value, and May bought a shawl made with silk threads and shot with all the colours of the rainbow. Pleased with their purchases, they had tea and scones in a small cafe and returned to the farm in a more settled frame of mind.

On Wednesday they awoke to more rain and were glad to break the monotony by lending a helping hand in the dairy.

They churned butter and helped to make cheese and then assisted Mrs Magill in baking bread. Then donning wellingtons, amidst squeals of laughter, they collected the free range eggs, letting a delighted, giggling Laura help them. The week passed slowly, but at last Sunday dawned, bright and dry, and Rosaleen had her first experience of watching the sun rise. When she opened the curtains, she knelt on the window seat and gazed in awe at the scene before her. A huge red ball of flame slowly rose and swelled, its rays colouring everything it touched, setting the sky on fire and awakening birds and wildlife as it spread its glow. As she gazed in wonder, her breath caught in her throat at the beauty of it, and her belief in God was strengthened. It was an experience she knew she would never forget.

As before Vince, who had been gone before they entered the kitchen for breakfast each morning, and had been absent each night, gave them a lift into church. On the way home, he casually asked, 'Will ye be wantin' a lift into the dance t'night?'

May remained silent; it was up to Rosaleen, it was she Vince fancied. Rosaleen was in a dilemma. All week she had silently vowed that she would not dance with Vince again. It was too dangerous! However, she knew that May longed to go to the dance, and to be truthful, so did she. It would ease the boredom. So she found herself nodding her head.

'Yes, thank you.'

And May's happy smile was her reward.

As she prepared for the dance that evening, Rosaleen found herself taking care with her make-up and brushing her freshly washed hair until it seemed to have a life of its own and sprang from her head, full of electricity. Becoming aware of her actions, knowing in her heart that she was making herself attractive so that Vince would admire her, she was aghast.

With a damp flannel she wiped the make-up from her face, leaving it clean and shining, but there was nothing she could do about her hair, it framed her face in a soft silver cloud, and none of her efforts to make it lie down were successful.

She chose her most dowdy sweater and skirt, a dark

138

grey that did nothing for her, and entered the kitchen feeling virtuous; she had done her best. May gaped at her, her eyes roaming over Rosaleen's old skirt and jumper in amazement. Then she twigged on. Rosaleen was playing down her good looks. She would be afraid of feeling that she was encouraging Vince, afraid of being an occasion of sin to him. May had yet to meet anyone as scrupulous as Rosaleen; she simply let her conscience torture her.

May sighed and smiled wryly at her. Little did she know that she could never look plain. The drab grey of her sweater only emphasised the silver of her hair, and her skin did not really need make-up to enhance it, while the dark grey deepened the green of her eyes, making them dark and mysterious-looking. She simply glowed, and May could see by the look in Vince's eyes that he agreed with her.

The minute they entered the hall they were rushed for dances and as the night wore on and Vince ignored her, Rosaleen heaved a sigh of relief. He had learned his lesson; he was going to leave her alone.

She was wrong. Toward the end of the evening, Vince approached her and asked for a dance. She assured him that she had promised the next dance, but when the music started, his arm circled her waist and without a word she allowed herself to be led on to the dance floor.

Hadn't she been waiting all evening for this? And didn't Vince know it? They danced in silence, their bodies twisting and turning to the steps of the tango. She had heard the tango called the dance of seduction and she could well believe it true, as their bodies moved as one to its suggestive steps. When the dance was over, he drew her to one side.

'I want to talk to you.'

Her eyes sought May. She did not want her to be left standing alone, but May was talking to a partner, and resignedly Rosaleen sat down on the chair away from the crowds that Vince ushered her to. He sat beside her, one arm along the back of the chair, and she squirmed uneasily.

'Ye made a right fool of me last Sunday night, didn't ye?'

'You shouldn't have tried to enter my room,' she retorted angrily.

'You led me on. I thought ye wanted me t'come,' he growled.

'I did not!' she cried in dismay. 'You're a good dancer and I enjoy dancing with you, but that's all.'

'Come off it!' His voice and eyes mocked her. 'Hey! Where do ye think you're goin'?'

She had risen swiftly from the chair and was making her way down the hall. He caught up with her in three strides, just as the band started to play. Expertly, he swung her into the quickstep.

'All right, you win. We just dance.'

'Promise?'

'I promise . . . Unless you decide otherwise.'

Her head reared back and she gave him a startled look. 'Don't bank on it.'

Vince eyed her from under lowered lids. He couldn't understand her. She wanted him. He had not lived all his life on a farm without learning the signs of arousal, and he was sure that she wanted him. It was in her eyes, in her awareness of him. The way she coloured when he eyed her. And what harm would it do? She was a married woman and you never missed a slice of a cut loaf. No one need ever know. Well, time would tell; he would try to wear her down. In fact . . . he was confident that he could wear her down. He danced the last two dances with her and then informed her that he had arranged a lift back to the farm for her and May, as he was seeing Mavis home.

That night, as she lay unable to sleep, Rosaleen kept seeing the look in Vince's eyes when he had promised – unless she decided otherwise – and she was more confused than ever. He had sounded as if it was just a matter of time, and this frightened her. Why was her body reacting to Vince even though she didn't like him? Was she a bad woman? One part of her mind assured her that it was because she did not have a proper marriage, and she latched on to this belief. That must be the reason . . . it must . . . otherwise, she would make a first-class whore.

Once more Monday dawned dull and wet. March had been a miserable month – at least this past week in Dungannon had been awful. Hail, rain, winds, everything but snow. Was it only dry on Sundays in Dungannon? Rosaleen wondered as she made her way down the mucky yard to the toilet, a whinging Laura by the hand. The child hated it here, whinged all the time to go home, and Rosaleen did not blame her. How long were they doomed to stay? Would the war last much longer? Joe's letters always came in bunches and she had received three that morning, forwarded by her father.

He tried to sound happy and assured her he was well, but she sensed his loneliness and her heart ached for him. He admitted that there was no sign of the war ending in the foreseeable future and no hope of leave.

The week dragged past, with Rosaleen and May putting on a happy face when in the presence of each other, but secretly longing for home.

Vince had not put in an appearance since Sunday night, so on Thursday night, when the need to use the toilet drove Rosaleen out into the dark yard, he was far from her thoughts.

There was a moon, but it was obscured by clouds. By

the faint light, Rosaleen retraced her steps back up the yard. A hand on her arm brought a squeal of terror from her lips but this was quickly stifled as another hand covered her mouth. She was lifted bodily into the barn and the door closed. For one horrible moment, in the darkness, she thought it was Mr Magill and panic set her heart thumping within her breast. Then, as her eyes became accustomed to the dark, she saw that it was Vince and breathed a sigh of relief.

She could handle him. He had promised.

To her dismay, she saw that he stood with his back against the door, blocking her escape.

'Just what do you think you're doing?' she asked, trying to appear calm.

'I think we should have a wee talk, Rosaleen. Rosaleen . . . now that's a lovely name. It rolls off the tongue. Ros . . . a . . . leen.'

His voice was caressing and slurred. Dismayed, she realised that he had been drinking. He moved slowly towards her. She backed away until she could go no further, and when her back was to the wall, he placed a hand on either side of her head and gazed down at her. She could smell the sweat of him and instead of filling her with distaste, to her dismay it just emphasised the maleness of him.

'Now, my teasin' Rosaleen, how's about a kiss. Mmmmmm . . . come on now, ye know ye want me. Ye know ye do.' One hand left the wall and as she stood unable to move, it trailed down her face. Surprised that he was receiving no opposition, he cradled the nape of her neck, and tilted her face up to his. Even in the dim light, she could see the hot passion in his eyes, and as his breath quickened, panic gripped her.

Thick with passion, his voice muttered her name over and over. As his face slowly bent toward hers, she came to life and jerked her head aside. His lips landed on her ear. To her amazement, this appeared to excite him.

'Ah! What have we here? Do ye like it rough? Eh? Do ye like it rough, me lovely Rosaleen?'

His pleasure at the idea was unmistakable. Terrified, she tried to break from his hold, but his arms bound her fast against him.

As he trust his body at hers, probing, seeking, to her horror and dismay she felt excitement shiver through her and fill her loins, and she relaxed against him, her body craving fulfilment.

At his soft laugh of triumph, sanity returned. Only once before had she known and given into desire, and look what it had cost her. At this thought, anger and bitterness swept through her, lending strength, and her sudden surge to life caught him unawares. Remembering stories from long ago of how to defend oneself, her knee rose in the air and viciously landed where it hurt most, desperation making her aim accurate. Gasping for air, he doubled in two, and she broke free and leapt for the door. But she was not going to get away so easily. In pain though he was, he managed to grip her ankle and she crashed to the floor, rattling every bone in her body.

Aware that he was moving towards her, she ignored the pain that throbbed through her and on all fours scrabbled towards the door. Obviously still in pain, he managed to throw himself on top of her and his fingers were vicious on the soft flesh of her arms. Realising that if he regained his full strength, nothing would save her, she sank her teeth into his hand and bit as hard as she could; pleased to taste that she had drawn blood. With a howl, he relaxed his hold on her and before he could regain control, with a mighty thrust, she got to her knees again, throwing him off her back and to one side. Rolling away from him, she managed to get to her knees again. Then she was up and at the door, sobbing as she pulled it open and staggered outside.

His voice, full of venom, followed her. 'I'll get ye for

this, ye damned wee temptress. You mark my words. I'll get ye.'

And not for one minute did she doubt him. She would have to get away from this farm. Belfast with all its dangers beckoned like heaven and she resolved to return there as soon as possible. In her mad scramble back up the yard in the dark, she fell, scraping her knee and the palms of her hands as she tried to save herself. Thankful to escape to her room unnoticed, the tears ran down her face as she removed her soiled, mucky skirt and jumper. She looked as though she had been through the wars. Her hands and knee were bleeding and bruises were already appearing on her upper arms. Why did she have to get into these predicaments?

She should have entered a convent, so she should. At least there she would have been free from this kind of temptation, because in her heart she knew that Vince was right. Her body had wanted him, and only the fact that her heart hadn't agreed had saved her.

Next morning, as she and May worked side by side making butter, she tried to form words to explain why she must leave the farm. May, suddenly gripping her hand and exclaiming at the raw scratches on her palm, gave her an opening.

'How on earth did you do that?'

Haltingly, Rosaleen recounted the events of the night before, bringing cries of pity and concern from May's lips.

When she had finished, her friend gasped. 'You actually kneed him?' At Rosaleen's nod, May cried in approval, 'Good for you! Good for you! I hope he can't use it for a week.'

These words brought a reluctant smile to Rosaleen's lips and her reply was heartfelt. 'So do I! But, May . . . I can't stay here. To tell you the truth, I'm scared of him.'

'Of course you can't stay. Look, tomorrow morning we'll catch that bus into town and order a taxi . . .'

'Wait, May!' Frantically, Rosaleen interrupted her. 'There's no need for you to come. Billy'll go daft if you arrive home.'

May smiled smugly. 'No, he won't. I can tell by his letters that he's missing me something awful, and only Ian is preventing him from asking me to come home.' She smiled shyly, making Rosaleen aware of just how much Billy had changed her life. 'I want to go home, Rosaleen. I just didn't like to say . . . after all the bother your da went to, to get us fixed up.'

'Ah, May. We've both been suffering in silence.'

May grinned, a great beam of happiness. 'Looks like it. Listen, we'll pack our things tonight, go to town in the morning, find out the time of the train, and order a taxi to collect us in time to catch it. How does that sound?'

'Heaven.' Rosaleen's smile reflected the joy in May's. 'You've forgotten just one thing.'

May frowned, and thought deeply, 'What's that?' she asked, at last.

'We'll have to send wires to Billy and me da, so that they can meet us at the station.'

'Imagine me forgetting that. But once we get to Belfast, there'll be no holding us. We can walk home if necessary. And another thing . . . you come for me if you need to go to the loo tonight. O.K.?'

'O.K.' Rosaleen agreed gratefully.

The price of the taxi to the station took their breath away. Luckily, they had inquired first, and by promising a tight-lipped, angry Maggie to forward the money owed for butter and eggs, they managed the fare between them. Rosaleen felt sorry for Maggie, whom she had grown to like. She was bewildered, poor soul, saying that she had thought they were settling in nicely. But how can you tell a woman that you are afraid of her son?

The train arrived in Great Victoria Street Station at eleven o'clock, and tired and weary they stood on the platform, surrounded by their belongings as the crowds thinned out, until they were alone in the station.

'What do you think happened, May?'

May bit her lip and shook her head, a puzzled frown on her brow.

'They can't have received our telegrams.'

They had deliberately caught the last train because they had been warned that the telegrams would not be delivered until about six o'clock. Now here they were, stranded. They could have managed the tram fares, but the last tram was away.

'Well, it looks like we'll have to walk, Rosaleen.' May sighed. Somehow it didn't sound so inspiring as it had done when they had planned their return. 'Here . . . gimme the cases, they can go on top of my pram – it's bigger. You tie the gas masks to the handle of yours, and let's get a move on. I only hope the sirens don't go off.'

The long climb up the Grosvenor Road seemed endless, but at last they were at the Falls Road junction. They had long ago stopped trying to cheer each other up, and started across the Falls Road in silence, knowing that the road still ahead of them was as long as the one they had just climbed. Then, miraculously it seemed, Tommy Magee was in front of them. Peering at them in the darkness, crying, 'What on earth are you two doing out at this time of night?' Then, eyes getting accustomed to the gloom, 'Good God! It's our Rosaleen.'

Next thing they knew, they were inside the pub at the corner of the Springfield Road, sipping cups of tea, after assuring the pyjama-clad landlord that they did not want anything stronger.

'Why on earth didn't you order a taxi, Rosaleen?'

'We had no money, Da. We're broke,' Rosaleen reproached him. She had already explained their predicament to him.

'Good God, do ye think we'd have turned you away from the door?'

May and Rosaleen looked at each other and started to laugh. It had never occurred to them to get a taxi and someone would pay at the other end. Wiping tears of mirth and relief from their faces, they shared a happy smile. They were home, and that was all that mattered.

Chapter 5

The relief and joy of being at home was short-lived. On Monday, the start of Holy Week, Rosaleen was preparing for bed when, shortly before midnight, the siren sounded. Rosaleen actually smiled to herself as she got Laura ready. It was great to be home, even with broken nights. Unruffled, she took her time: dressing the child in warm clothes, cushioning the pram with pillows, and filling a bottle with juice, before setting off to enter one of the new air-raid shelters. There was no great urgency. The planes never reached this far. It would be a false alarm as usual. After breathing a prayer for the poor people in England who were being blitzed, she debated whether or not to bring the gas masks with her. They were a nuisance to carry about, and the rattlers that would signify they might be needed had yet to sound. As she stood undecided she remembered the meeting she had attended in the Broadway Picture House when they had been shown how to use the masks. They had also been shown a newsreel portraying the effects of the mustard gas on humans, and recalling the horrific sights, she decided not to take any chances and tied them to the handle of the pram, just in case! It would be silly to take chances.

To her amazement, when she reached the corner, chatting away to her next-door neighbour, her father descended on her. Gripping her pram with one hand and her neighbour's with the other hand, he urged them down Oakman Street, away from the air-raid shelters, begging them to hurry. Quickening their step, Rosaleen and her bewildered neighbour obeyed him, wondering why he was so agitated.

'They're comin', love,' he gasped, in answer to their unspoken question. 'They're comin'. *Now!* There was no bloody early warnin'. Listen! They're right above us.'

Another tortured breath escaped from his poor, weak lungs before he could continue, 'Can't ye hear them? They'll be after Mackie's.'

Only then did Rosaleen become aware of the drone of the planes which was getting louder every second. Her legs turned to jelly, causing her to stumble. Dear God, the Germans were coming . . . it was their turn to be bombed. Her father hauled her roughly upright and pulled her along, past dalliers, shouting for them to get a move on.

'Lift your feet! Lift your feet! Can't ye hear the planes?' he scolded. And to Rosaleen, 'Come on, love . . . come on – if they hit Mackie's the district will go up an' we'll all be goners.'

Never had Oakman Street seemed so long, but at last they left it and hurried along Beechmount Avenue towards Daisy Hill and open fields.

Once they were safely away from buildings, without wasting breath on words Tommy turned on his heel and headed back the way they had come, just as the first bomb fell. It was some distance away, in the direction of the docks, but they heard the great 'BOOM!', saw in the distance the sky redden from its glow.

'Da! Da, don't go back. Stay here,' Rosaleen beseeched him.

But he didn't pause, just gasped over his shoulder, 'I must go back. I'll be needed . . . if there are fires . . . in the parish.'

149

It was a bright moonlit night, and the fields were crowded, everyone coping in their own way with the fear that gripped them. Some seemed too stunned to do anything, just sat gazing in front of them, cringing closer to the ground at every shot, every blast. Some actually sang between bombs falling, causing others to laugh and jest that if they sang loud enough the planes would certainly go away, to escape the awful din. Someone else started the rosary and as others joined in, Rosaleen added her voice to theirs and prayed. She prayed that somehow or other the Germans would not see Mackie's, in spite of the clear moonlight. If they did, she would have no home to go back to. As her father had stated, the district would go up if Mackie's was bombed. She prayed that her mother and Annie were safely away from the houses, away in the fields further up the Springfield Road, and prayed for the brave men, like her father, who were putting out the flares that the Germans dropped to help to identify their chosen targets.

Their prayers were answered. It was a long night, with bombs and incendiary devices falling constantly, causing fires and doing God knows what other damage. Dawn was breaking when at last the all clear sounded but, as everyone started the weary journey home from the parks and countryside, Mackie's still stood!

Although as raids went it was deemed a small one, it caused a lot of damage. On Tuesday morning Rosaleen heard on the radio that the fuselage factory attached to Harland and Wolff the ship builders had been completely demolished, and that the docks had also suffered severe damage. Fear gripped her bowels, sending her running to the bathroom every time she thought of Mackie's Foundry, just a short distance away, surrounded by houses; a huge bomb in itself, so easily detonated. The raid brought home to her how

150

vulnerable Belfast was, and she regretted bringing Laura back from Dungannon. Prayed that if her baby was killed she would be taken also, because she would never be able to forgive herself, never!

How come her father, a mill worker, had been aware of the danger they were in, while the brains of the country had not? Or had they? Had they known and thought Belfast not important enough to worry about?

Some of the fear abated when the morning newspapers stated that the planes were just a half dozen strays that had lost their way while on a raid over Clydeside on the west coast of England, and would probably not return.

However, her father disagreed with the newspapers. 'They'll be back . . . you mark my words. Now they know how few defences we have, they'll be back,' he predicted.

'Huh! How do you know what kind of defences we have, and you working in the mill, Da!' Rosaleen ridiculed him.

'I'm an air-raid warden, ampt I? And I hear a lot of criticism of the government,' he retaliated. 'You mark my words! I know what I'm talkin' about and we've very few defences.'

'What do you mean, Da, few defences?' she asked fearfully.

'I mean the government has neglected to provide us with enough planes and machine guns to retaliate. We've some Hurricanes at Aldergrove and some anti-aircraft guns, and that's about it.'

And hearing this, Rosaleen was inclined to agree with her father that if the Germans were now aware of their vulnerability, they would return. The final casualty figure for that night was thirteen dead and eighty-one injured, twenty-three of them seriously, but the Falls Road had escaped without a scratch and everyone went about their business as usual.

151

The rest of Holy Week passed uneasily. Each night Rosaleen prepared for a hurried departure from the house should the dreaded sirens sound, which they did frequently, but, thankfully, they were all false alarms. Although enemy planes were heard, and sometimes seen high in the sky, no bombs were dropped and each morning she thanked God for a night free from terror.

All the Holy Week ceremonies were well attended; the crowds spilling out into the church yards at each mass and each Way of the Cross, and the queues for confession hit an all-time record.

At mass on Easter Sunday, Rosaleen noted that she was not the only one to have splashed out on new clothes, as she had for herself and Laura. Indeed, no. Clonard Monastery was full of women and children in new dresses and hats, determined to use some of their precious savings while they had the chance, and not to be outdone the men were sporting new jackets and, once outside, new caps. Not that there was anything really fashionable in the shops. Annie and she had travelled the length and breadth of Belfast before managing to buy two dresses. One was green, the other blue, but in style they were much alike, the regulations being that as little material as was reasonable must be used in all clothes, and nothing was to be wasted in fancy work or pockets. Being slim, they both suited the square-shouldered, belted-waist design; not like the plump girls who it did nothing for. The only concession that was given to femininity, was the slightly flared skirt with pleat back and front.

Easter Monday morning brought a knock on Rosaleen's door and when she answered it, who should be standing on the doorstep but Billy Mercer looking very dapper in a smart sports jacket and grey flannel trousers. His dark hair was slicked down with Brylcreem, and he carried a holdall slung over one shoulder.

'Billy! This is a surpise.' Her eyes darted beyond him. 'Where's May?'

'She's down in Spinner Street visiting her mother.'

Her hands reached out and she drew him into the living room.

'Come in . . . come in. It's good to see you.'

'I'm ashamed, Rosaleen.' He hung his head, eyed her from under dark brows and looked embarrassed. 'I'm afraid I'm using you, as usual. You'll be saying the only time ye see me is when I need something. I've an hour to waste before I meet May at the corner of the Springfield Road and she said you'd gimme a cuppa, to pass the time.' He raised an eyebrow inquiringly at her, and when she smiled and nodded, swung the holdall to the floor and added, 'In fact, I've been ordered to persuade you and Laura to accompany me down. We're going to Bellevue, to the zoo.'

'Is it safe to go so far from home, Billy? I mean . . . well . . . after that raid on Tuesday?'

'Ye wouldn't think there'd been a raid!' he exclaimed. 'Why, the trams are packed, and there's crowds going into the railway station. There's an offer on "To Bangor and back for a bob", and it looks like it'll be a sell out. And you should see the queues outside the picture houses! Honestly, Rosaleen, it's hard to believe that we were bombed on Tuesday.'

'Me da says they'll be back. Do you think they'll come back, Billy?'

'To be truthful, Rosaleen, I don't know. Maybe they were just strays, like the papers say, and Hitler isn't going to bother about Ireland. But anyhow . . . I can't see them bombing during daylight. So come on, get yourself ready and come to the zoo with me and May. She'll be disappointed if I land down on me own. You wouldn't want her to be scrowling at me all afternoon, would ye now?'

'No, Billy, that would never do,' she assured him

with a chuckle, and glad of the opportunity to get away for the day, she quickly changed Laura's clothes. By the time Billy had finished his fresh Hughes bap and mug of tea, she was dressed and ready for the road.

'What about eats, Billy?'

He pointed at the holdall, a wry smile on his face. 'May's enough in the bag to feed an army, Rosaleen. No need for you to bring any,' he assured her, with a wink and a nod.

First, Rosaleen called into Amy's house and informed her where she was going. Her father called regularly to check that she was all right and he would worry if no one knew where she was. Then, excitement mounting, she accompanied Billy down to meet May.

Rosaleen and May had not seen each other since their arrival home from Dungannon and once on the upper deck of the tram they chatted and laughed, bringing each other up to date with gossip, all the way to Bellevue, watched by an amused Billy.

The Cave Hill, on the outskirts of Belfast, was the favourite spot at Easter for trundling eggs, and right on the side of the hill was Bellevue Zoo. It looked down over Belfast Lough and today, in spite of the fear of air-raids, it was packed. They joined the crowds that thronged the animal pens and caves, delighting in the joy and happiness of the two excited children. It was after their tour of the zoo, as they made their way along the Cave Hill to watch older children trundle their brightly painted eggs, as was the custom, and to eat the picnic lunch May had packed, that the mournful sound of the sirens filled the air.

The crowds scattered in all directions and Billy, who had often climbed the Cave Hill as a boy and remembered its terrain, quickly guided them some distance down the hill into a cave where they sheltered. To their amazement, although the planes were high they could clearly see them. They made no effort to hide; it was as if the pilots knew that there was no danger and were thumbing their noses at them. It was awesome to see them, as well as hear their drone and some people, in spite of the danger, actually stood out in the open, shading their eyes and gazing up at them in wonder. Luckily, no shots were fired, no bombs dropped, and soon the planes were but specks in the distance. When the all clear sounded the crowds carried on in their pursuit of pleasure.

From their picnic spot on the top of the Cave Hill they discovered that looking across Belfast Lough, they could see where the bombs had demolished part of Harland and Wolff on Tuesday, and the desolation of it put a damper on their spirits and fear in their hearts. Had they just been stray planes that came over on Tuesday?

What about the planes that were spotted during the week? They had been spotted a few times. Why had those planes flown over today . . . in broad daylight? What was their game? Were they lulling the people of Belfast into a false sense of security? Would they attack when they were least expected? Questions . . . questions that no one could answer.

After a day that was quite enjoyable in spite of the ever constant fear of an attack, they parted in town in good spirits. May and Billy to catch a tram up North Street on to the Shankhill Road and Rosaleen to make her way around to Castle Street and from there, take a tram up the Falls Road. They vowed to keep in touch, come what may, and Rosaleen arrived home in a happy frame of mind. However, this did not last long. Her neighbours were agog with talk of the lunchtime alarm, and of course gossip had it that the Germans were sizing up Mackie's and would return that night. Alone in the house with Laura, having refused to go and stay at her mother's, it struck terror to the very heart of Rosaleen and she was apprehensive as she prepared for bed.

The planes did return later that night. In the early hours of Easter Tuesday morning to be exact, and the sirens wailed warning of their approach at about ten-thirty. After all the false alarms during the week, Rosaleen was tempted to ignore them. Weary and sore after climbing the Cave Hill, she had retired early and longed to remain snug in bed. However, the thought of Mackie's, but a stone's throw away, made her swing her aching legs out of bed and prepare for another night in the fields.

They were lucky that the weather was mild, she consoled herself. It would be awful if it was bitter cold or pouring down rain. One had to be grateful for small mercies. After all, it wasn't usually so mild in April. The planes passed over the city for over two hours, their drone deafening. Sitting on the grass in a corner of one of the fields beyond Daily Hill, trying to pacify a whinging child, Rosaleen's nerves were stretched to breaking point. She actually got to the stage where she wished that they would drop their bombs and get it over with, but to the surprise and relief of all, once again no shots were fired, no bombs dropped.

Next morning her father voiced his opinion to all who would listen. He said the Germans were probably surprised at just how little opposition they were encountering and had come back on Tuesday to see if any changes had been made.

Few had; after all, no one had expected German planes to come right across England. Not even those in higher places, so Belfast was unprepared, complacent, and few extra resources were forthcoming.

'They'll be back!' Her father prophesied. 'You mark my words. They'll be back. They'll make use of the full moon, and we're stuck out on the edge of the lough like a sore thumb.'

And once again he was right. On Tuesday night, when the moon was almost full, the planes came in force. They approached between the Divis and the Black Mountains and were very low. There seemed to be hundreds of them, and their drone was deafening. The sirens gave warning of their approach at about ten o'clock and five minutes later the streets were thronged. No one dallied now. They feared that the Germans were out to get Mackie's and terror lent speed to their feet.

Some, mostly the elderly, sought refuge in the shelters, but these were soon full. Of course this was something else to lament; something else that the government had neglected to do. They had not built enough shelters, so those able to run and those with young children headed for open country. Laura was teething and Rosaleen was glad that she had managed to get her to drink some water laced with whiskey and sugar, because tucked snugly in the pram, she slept like a log. At the corner of the street Rosaleen found Amy waiting for her.

'Can I come with you, Rosaleen? I could have gotten into our shelter but it stinks. Youngsters, an some aul lads too, use the shelters if they're caught short . . . and then we're expected to stay in them when the siren goes. It's a disgrace, so it is. I can't bear to be in them.'

'Of course you can come with me, Amy. Here, hang on to the pram.' And slackening her pace to suit Amy, Rosaleen assured her, 'I'm glad of your company, so I am.'

After a wet start to the day, the evening was mild with a light south-westerly wind and they picked their way across the fields by the light of the three-quarter moon, seeking a sheltered place to sit down. As they walked in the bright moonlight. Rosaleen was aware that the same moon would show the German planes just where Mackie's was and she kept heading as far away from this danger as she could.

However, she soon discovered that the Germans had

157

no need for moonlight. The first planes over dropped huge flares. They fell from the sky like giant torchlights, hundreds of them, and as they hung over the town, suspended from parachutes, everyone stood in the fields and gaped at them. The sound of anti-aircraft guns thundered as they endeavoured to put out the flares, but more and more fell, and soon the sky became as bright and clear as daylight, making the moon look pale and insignificant. Belfast was shown in detail, as if under a huge spotlight. Huddled together on an old raincoat, Amy and Rosaleen prayed as the next lot of planes dropped a constant barrage of bombs, incendiaries, and parachute mines. Anti-aircraft guns woof-woofed in retaliation, and the ground beneath them shook, even though the bombs were falling in the city.

There was no singing now. Everyone was sure it was to be their last night on earth and each, in their own way, was begging God's forgiveness for past sins. The night dragged on; they saw flares fall in the vicinity of Mackie's and thought the bombs would surely not miss, but Mackie's fire watchers were diligent in their labours, and as dawn broke and the all clear sounded, Mackie's still stood.

St Paul's parish had only one serious casualty, and that was a house at the corner of Springfield Drive (better known as Mackie's Height), a row of posh houses, with three bedrooms and a bathroom, built just a few years earlier on an elevated sight facing Mackie's Foundry.

So close, so very close. Enough to make the blood run cold. The house had been hit by an incendiary device and was badly burnt, in spite of prompt action by the air-raid wardens, but it was empty at the time and there were no casualties.

The rest of the town was not so lucky, with the docks again suffering devastation, and at Shorts and Harland four Stirling aircraft that were almost finished were ignited by explosions and burnt to a cinder.

York Street spinning factory, said to be the largest of its kind in Europe, was hit, and brought down houses in Sussex Street and Vere Street in its wake, killing thirty people instantly. They also learnt that a bomb falling near a shelter in Percy Street had taken another sixty lives, and tram lines were wrecked and water and gas mains fractured.

In despair, firemen worked trying to keep the fires that raged all over the city from spreading. With the pipes having been cracked, the water pressure was low, and realizing that they were fighting a losing battle, help was sought from the south. And the south did not fail Ulster in its hour of need. Indeed, no. In spite of the obvious danger, in spite of being a neutral country, fire engines from Dublin, DunLaoghaire, Drogheda and Dundalk rushed to their fellow countrymen's aid. With the Lord Mayor of Dublin himself riding up front in one of his city's engines, they fought the flames side by side with the Ulster brigades, until the fires were extinguished, leaving half of Belfast a smouldering mass.

Next day on the radio, Rosaleen learnt that five hundred were dead and this number was expected to rise steeply. Over a thousand were injured, thousands more homeless, and there was an exodus to the countryside as Belfast's inhabitants sought refuge with friends who lived outside the city.

Food kitchens were set up and the schools, closed for the Easter holidays, were reopened to house the homeless. These were mostly from Protestant areas, and everybody was urged to give all they could in the way of bedding, clothes and food to held the needy.

As Rosaleen piled blankets, clothes and tins of food ready to be collected, her mother arrived.

'Have you heard the latest?' she asked.

'Well, it all depends on what the latest is. I've heard so much today my mind boggles.'

Her mother smiled faintly as she asked, 'About the Pope leading the German planes in?'

Rosaleen's mouth dropped open. 'Ah – ' she waved her hand in disbelief '. . . you're having me on!'

'No. No, I'm not, the rumour's goin' around that the Pope must be leading the planes in. Ye see, a lot of Protestant churches were hit last night and not one single Catholic church was touched.'

'Tut! I never heard the like of it.'

'Aye, I agree with you.' Thelma had to smile at Rosaleen's outraged dignity. 'Are you goin' down to help out in one of the schools?'

'Yes, St Paul's. Are you?' When Thelma nodded in confirmation, Rosaleen added, 'I'm waiting for someone to collect these things.'

'We've a pile of stuff ready too. Your da has the key, he's calling to collect it.' Thelma's face puckered and there was a catch in her voice. 'It must be awful to lose your home . . . all your belongings.'

'And so many dead. We were lucky last night, but tonight we might not be. I'm not waiting for the sirens to go off. I'm going to take Laura up to the Falls Park the minute we get our dinner. As far away from Mackie's as I can. I learnt one thing last night: those fields beyond Daisy Hill aren't far enough away. If Mackie's got hit, there'd be pieces flying everywhere.'

'We'll come with ye, so we will. Where's Laura now?' Thelma's head went back as she looked reproachfully down the length of her nose at Rosaleen. 'Ye know, you should've kept the child in the country, so ye should.' Her voice was accusing and Rosaleen turned angrily on her.

'Do you think I don't know that? I'll never forgive myself if anything happens to her.' She blinked furiously to contain the tears before adding, 'Amy

160

has her at the moment.'

Thelma had the grace to look ashamed. Rosaleen was bound to be feeling guilty without her piling on the agony.

Suddenly they both leapt to their feet and Thelma screamed, 'Jesus, Mary and Joseph . . . what's that?' as a huge explosion rent the air and the house shook.

They bumped into each other in their effort to get out of the door to see what was wrong, and over and over again in Rosaleen's mind ran the plea: Laura . . . Laura . . . Oh, please let Laura be all right. Please . . . please!

Once out on the street Rosaleen saw from the direction of the thick smoke that the explosion was round behind Iris Drive, further up Springfield Avenue. She was also relieved to see Amy turn the opposite corner, an excited Laura by the hand.

'Thank God you're all right.' Rosaleen hugged Laura tight, and eyeing Amy over her head asked, 'What happened?'

Amy mutely shook her head. It was a passerby who answered Rosaleen.

'A delayed bomb went off at the corner where Springfield Avenue meets Cavendish Street. It has demolished some houses, but thank God nobody's hurt.'

Thank God indeed, Rosaleen agreed with him, and her mind was full of the thought that it could just as easily have been her home.

As they worked side by side with Protestant women, making up camp beds and sorting out groceries, Rosaleen was close to tears. There were three hundred refugees here in St Paul's school and her father said as many again were in St Gall's and some further up the Falls Road in St Mary's Training School. And that was just this end of town; there must be thousands

161

homeless. It was heartbreaking watching people wandering about in a daze. Some of them didn't even know whether or not the rest of their families were still alive, and each policeman, each air-raid warden that appeared was besieged with questions.

To add to their problems, as a result of fractured pipes, water was not reaching the houses and everybody had to queue up at water stands in the street to fill their kettles and buckets, and some houses were also without electricity.

Their duty done for the day, after a rushed scanty meal, Thelma offered to look after Laura, when Rosaleen and Annie voiced their desire to take a walk and see what damage had been done the night before. The radio had requested that sightseers stay away from the bombed areas, as they were hampering rescue work, but Rosaleen and Annie did not intend going too near. They just wanted to see for themselves what the town was like.

The sights that met their eyes as they walked down Divis Street, past Percy Street, where a bomb had taken sixty lives, were awful. They could see that complete rows of houses were demolished and piles of rubble were all that was left of what used to be prominent buildings. In some streets, pathetic heaps of furniture which had been salvaged from houses stood on the corner, as though rejected, furniture that had probably been someone's pride and joy.

Most of the bombs had fallen on civilian targets and soldiers still toiled digging bodies from the ruins, laying them side by side until such time as they were delivered to the morgue.

To their surprise the town centre appeared to be all right, although as they walked along Royal Avenue they could see that the Public Library was pitted all over and every window in the big Co-op Stores in York Street was broken. Even as they watched, looting was going on, furtive figures darting from buildings with stolen goods in their arms. They also observed that the nurses' home in Frederick Street was completely demolished, and wondered how many lives had been lost there.

It was soon obvious to them that it was the poor districts that had suffered most, and as they made their way home they pondered how lucky they on the Falls and Springfield Roads had been.

'I can't stand it,' Annie cried. 'We were very lucky last night, but that could be our street tomorrow. I know one thing – never again will I feel guilty about making bits of planes and bullets.' She thrust her face towards Rosaleen. 'I did, ye know. I felt awful when I thought that maybe the bullets I was helping to make would kill someone. But not any more . . . Oh no, not any more. I just hope the Germans are suffering like we are.'

They arrived home in Iris Drive to find their father on the doorstep. He was dropping with fatigue and didn't need any coaxing to stretch out on the settee.

'I came to warn you t'get away up the Falls Road early t'night. Don't wait for the siren t'go off. As soon as ye get your tea, start out.'

'Yes, Da, we're not stupid . . . that's what we intend to do,' Annie informed him. 'Are you coming home with me now for your tea?'

'Aye, I am Annie. And I hope to get a couple of hours sleep.'

'You'd need to. You're out on your feet, Da. Come on, the sooner we go, the longer you'll be able to sleep.'

Still he lay prone, too tired to move, his mind full of the horror of the night and the long day.

'It's been awful. They couldn't find anywhere big enough to store all the bodies. The City Morgue's stacked high with coffins, and there's a hundred and fifty more in St James's Market. So they came to the

Falls Road. The Fall's Baths are piled high with coffins, they're everywhere. They arrived in hearses, lorries, coalcarts . . . even the bin lorries brought some. And when they ran out . . . do ye know what we had to do?'

When Rosaleen and Annie could only shake their heads mutely, he continued, 'They let the water out of the pools and we wrapped the bodies in blankets and laid them on the tiled floors. There was just limbs . . . legs, arms . . . awful, I even saw a head lyin' on its own . . . it was awful.'

His voice trailed off and they sat some moments in silence, minds alive with horrible pictures of the scene he described, waiting for him to continue his narrative, until eventually it dawned on them that nature had taken its course and he had fallen asleep.

When Annie would have wakened him, Rosaleen stopped her.

'Don't. Let him be. I'll waken him at about seven and give him a bite to eat. That should be early enough, shouldn't it?'

'Yes, about seven . . . or even eight. That'll give him four hours sleep. Thank God I'm on the dayshift. It'll be awful on the night shift in Mackie's after last night . . . it was bad enough before. Me mam and I'll bring Laura down for you to get ready, at about half-eight and we'll go up to the Falls Park. All right?'

Rosaleen nodded, 'Yes, I'll have all Laura's things ready and we can call for Amy on our way out.'

The nightly journeys up the Falls Road to the park and countryside became a monotonous, boring habit and if it hadn't been for Laura, Rosaleen would have taken her chances and stayed at home, in spite of being so close to Mackie's Foundry. Thousands made the journey every night, and some didn't bother coming down again, staking claim to old barns and shacks. They had no home to go to and the Corporation was finding it hard to find accommodation for all the homeless.

The Corporation had ordered buses to be kept ready at the depot at the bottom of the Glen Road, to take those who preferred to be further afield out into the countryside when the siren sounded. The first to arrive every night settled in the buses and a party atmosphere reigned as stories were told and songs sung, and the dreaded siren was awaited.

Days passed without any further raids and it was decided that the bodies that weren't identified would have to be buried. There was a notice in the newspapers, and for those who were homeless and unable to buy them, posters were pasted up all over town advising those with relatives still missing that they had two days left to try to find them.

The stench of the decomposing flesh and the risk of infection was too great to risk keeping them any longer, and arrangements were made for a communal burial. As she listened to her father, who had volunteered to help out in the Baths, recount tales of men and women hunting for their lost partners or members of their family, and then having to be sprayed with disinfectant as they left to lessen the chance of infection, Rosaleen's mind baulked at the horror of it all. Imagine not knowing whether or not one of those horribly mutilated bodies that were rotting away was a husband or a wife or one of the family. The stench would stay in your nose forever. No wonder so many people were wandering about in a daze, not caring what happened to them.

The funeral of the unclaimed dead was held on Monday, April 21st. There had been so many private funerals that people were used to seeing hearses go up the Falls Road and would bow their heads, say a prayer and then go on about their business, but for the communal funeral it was different. Thousands lined the road, and both men and women cried openly. The authorities had ordered the bodies to be examined, and any with crucifixes or rosary beads or prayer leaflets were deemed Catholics and the others taken to be Protestants. After separate religious services, by a Catholic priest and a Protestant minister, the bodies were taken in military vehicles to the City Cemetery where the Protestants were to be buried and then continued on up the Falls Road to Milltown Cemetery for the burial of the Catholics. Those with relatives and friends still missing formed a procession behind the vehicles and followed them up the road, stunned and despairing. It was a scene that would stay with those who observed it until the day they died.

Due to the demolition of the shipyard and aircraft factory, thousands of people were out of work and others had neither the energy nor the inclination to spend the night in the fields and parks and then go into work. So, according to the newspapers, production was down a quarter of what it was before the awful blitz on April 15th, and the government urged all hands to help get production going again in case of another raid. Mackie's, having received only a few minor hits, all taken care of quickly, was working all out, taking over some orders that Shorts' aircraft factory was unable to fulfil and employing more staff as a result.

One good thing emerged from all this desolation and trouble. A new affinity was created between Catholic and Protestant. As they gathered together night after night and listened to each others' tales of woe and sometimes even joy, like when a child was born or a beloved relative thought dead was discovered alive, they realised that they were all the same under the skin. They had the same aspirations for their children – better homes and jobs, a better start in life than they themselves had known – and many firm friendships were made that were to stand the test of time.

Rosaleen discovered that the people of the Shankhill, were just the same as the people of the Falls, encumbered with the same lesser paid jobs and slum areas that were a breeding ground for the dreaded disease T.B., which was becoming very common among the working classes. How come she had thought that the Shankhill Road people were better off? Just because they were Protestants? She thought it was only the Catholics that were the underdog. Now it looked like she was wrong.

Disenchantment with the government and fear of Hitler brought to Catholics and Protestants a closeness they had never achieved before. They were also united in their resentment of the Corporation. Never was the prestige of the Belfast Corporation so low, and bitterness against it was rife as the homeless queued up for food.

'Other big cities were prepared. So why wasn't Belfast?' they asked angrily.

Other problems also gave cause for grave concern. The people on the Antrim Road and surrounding district were worried about what would happen if the zoo at Bellevue was bombed. Wild animals would be free to roam the countryside, so it was decided that all the dangerous animals must be put down. These included the beautiful lions, tigers, and wolves Rosaleen had been admiring at Easter, as well as a giant rat she hadn't liked the look of. The thought of their fate brought tears to her eyes, and she was not surprised when it was reported in the newspapers that the head gamekeeper had cried when his lovely animals had been slaughtered.

After many false alarms, Sunday, May 4th dawned bright and frosty, and as the day wore on Rosaleen was filled with hope. There was been no bombing since April 15th; perhaps Hitler was finished with Belfast! The afternoon was hot and sunny and it was the first day of the new scheme thought up by the government to save fuel by lengthening the hours of daylight. That morning the clocks had been put forward an hour, meaning dusk would be one hour late. Encouraged by the hot weather and the extra hour of daylight, Rosaleen decided to wash some bedclothes. For boiling bed linen and whites, she had a small boiler which was kept in a shed in the yard. Now she pulled this out into the warm sunlight and, filling it with water, stripped the beds and gathered together towels and whites. May as well make hay while the sun shines, she thought happily as she set the water to boil, and later, when Amy popped in on a visit, they sat out in the yard, lapping up the sunshine and watching the washing sway in the light breeze.

But the hope that lifted Rosaleen's spirits was soon dashed. The Germans chose that night to launch their second major bomb attack on Belfast and it was another night of horror.

This time the moonlight was so bright in a sky free from clouds that the planes didn't need flares to see their targets and their aim was accurate as they devastated the shipyards, destroying three corvettes that were nearing completion. They also managed to inflict more damage to Shorts' aircraft factory and hit the Harbour Power Station. York Street Railway Station was reduced to rubble.

It was on this night that St Paul's parish suffered its worst damage. At dawn, as Rosaleen and company trailed wearily home from their night in the Falls Park, they saw as they neared Beechmount Avenue that a bomb must have fallen nearby. Smoke hung in a dense cloud over Our Lady's Hospital on the Falls Road just above Beechmount Avenue and wafted down on to the road, catching their breaths. Horrified, they deduced that one of the streets that ran off Beechmount Avenue must have been hit. Crowds were milling to and fro and Annie grabbed a man by the arm.

'Where did the bomb hit, mister?'

'The top of Beechmount Street, and it's demolished about eight houses,' he informed her.

Dazed, Annie stood as if turned to stone, and Rosaleen clutched her. They were thinking of Sean's family who lived at the top of Beechmount Street.

It was Thelma who took control. 'Rosaleen, you go with Annie and see about Sean's family. I'll see Amy home and then bring Laura to my house until you come back. We'll go down the Falls Road way, it's too smoky for Laura over there.' She nodded in the direction of Beechmount Avenue. 'Take your time. Stay as long as you have to, but don't leave until you know how Sean's family are. O.K.?'

'Yes, Mam. O.K.' With a kiss on the brow for the sleeping child and a nod of farewell to Amy, Rosaleen slipped her arm through Annie's and led her down Beechmount Avenue. 'Come on, Annie, let's go and see what we can find out.'

At the bottom of Beechmount Street, air-raid wardens tried to turn them back but when Annie explained that her in-laws lived at the top of the street, they were allowed through. It was with apprehension that they climbed the street, to stand aghast at the sight that met their eyes. The houses at the top were completely demolished and covering their mouths and noses with handkerchiefs against the thick dust and grime, they watched fearfully as bodies were carried from the ruins. It was with relief that Annie hailed one of the stretcher bearers.

'Mr Devlin . . . Mr Devlin!'

When the grime-covered figure turned at her call, she threw herself into his arms and sobbed against his breast.

'I'm so glad you're all right . . . is the rest of the family all right?'

Jim Devlin nodded his head. 'Yes, love . . . yes, we're all right. But that complete family has been wiped out.' He nodded to where bodies lay, but Annie kept her head down and refused to look.

'Why were they in the house?' she cried. 'I would've thought that anybody with sense would make for the open country.'

'I know, Annie . . . I know. And normally they would've been away in the fields, but ye see, the man of the house was in a wheelchair and he was poorly, so his wife and son stayed to keep him company.'

'Oh, dear God . . . how awful . . . awful!'

'Ah.' He sighed and shrugged his shoulders. 'Who know? Perhaps they would have preferred it that way. All to go together. They were a very close family. But look here, Annie . . .' he glanced down at her kindly '. . . you must be tired. You can do nothing here, so away home. But thanks for coming to see how we've fared.'

With a gentle push, he sent her in the direction of Rosaleen. 'Take her home, love.'

Before he could turn away, Rosaleen caught his eye. 'Is your house all right?' she asked, and was relieved when he nodded. Then taking Annie by the arm, she pulled her away and down the street.

'Oh, thank God Sean's family is safe. Those poor, poor people.'

Rosaleen let Annie ramble on, knowing it would help relieve the tension, but when they passed Iris Drive, on their way to pick up Laura, and she saw Bobby Mackay leave her doorway and, seeing them at the corner, come towards them, she felt a shiver run down her spine. Bobby and her father were both wardens and had been partnered off. Somehow she was aware that he was the bearer of bad news. How,

170

she didn't know, but she felt fear squeeze her heart.

Bobby stopped in front of them, bringing Annie's lamentations to an end, and they both gazed speechlessly at him.

Rosaleen had met him just once before, on the night she had returned from Dungannon, and he had reminded her of a great St Bernard dog with his long sad face and heavily lidded eyes. It was obvious from Annie's blank expression that he was a stranger to her.

The great hangdog face topped by a mop of untidy thick brown hair swung slowly from side to side, the slack jowls quivering with emotion.

'What's wrong, Bobby?'

Rosaleen didn't recognise her own voice and she was aware that neither did Annie because she turned on her with a look of amazement.

'He wouldn't listen to me, so he wouldn't. I warned him . . . tried to keep him down on the main road, but he wouldn't listen. Insisted on going to check on those people.'

'Who on earth's he talking . . .' Annie's voice trailed off when Rosaleen gripped her arm and shook it.

'Is he badly hurt, Bobby?' she asked fearfully.

The heavy lids lifted and big brown eyes full of sorrow looked from one to the other of them, begging their forgiveness. Why couldn't it have been him, a widower without child or chick? he lamented inwardly.

'I'm sorry, girls . . . I couldn't face your mother, just couldn't . . . they were so close.'

Rosaleen's mind was saying over and over again. Me da's dead. Me da's dead. Oh, sweet Jesus . . . let me be wrong. Please let me be wrong.

But no, she was right, Bobby was continuing, 'He knew that there was a family in one of the top houses in Beechmount Street . . . and he had just started off in the direction of the house to check that they were all right, when the bomb fell. I was at the bottom of the

171

street and was lifted off me feet. He was thrown a great distance and when I saw him lying still . . . well, I thought that he was just stunned. I never dreamed . . . Ah, Rosaleen, it was an awful shock to find he was dead.'

Turning on her heel she quickly started to retrace her steps. One of the bodies at the top of Beechmount Street must be her father's. She had to go to him. Annie was whimpering and caught at Rosaleen's arm.

'Does he mean me da's dead?'

Rosaleen could only nod mutely and Bobby cried, 'Rosaleen . . . he's not over there.' He nodded back towards Beechmount Avenue. 'He wasn't buried . . . just caught by the blast . . . they've taken him away. Look, you come with me and we'll find out where they've taken him. And you, love . . .' he turned his gaze on Annie '. . . will you tell your mother?'

'Oh, Rosaleen . . . Rosaleen!' The horror of it made Annie sway and she clutched her sister by the arm.

'Hush, Annie love. Look, you go and keep me mam company and I'll go with Bobby.' Seeing the tremor in Annie's face, Rosaleen asked gently, 'Will you be all right?'

'Yes . . . yes . . . you go find me da.' And Annie staggered away, her mind full of dread. How was she going to break this awful news to her mother?

In a daze, Rosaleen allowed herself to be led towards Cavendish Street. Her legs felt like lead weights and she was so weary, she was afraid she would pass out. With a great effort of will, she moved when Bobby moved, paused when he paused, and soon they were outside the Royal Victoria Hospital.

'We'll try here first, Rosaleen, and if he's not here we'll have to go down to the City Morgue.'

Once inside the hospital, Bobby left her standing and went to the crowd milling around the reception desk to ask directions. Weariness was like a great weight sitting on her shoulders and a bench in the corner seemed to beckon her over. With dragging steps she made her way to it, and with a sigh of relief gratefully sat down. However, she had barely touched the seat when Bobby was in front of her again, urging her up, leading her down long corridors and down flights of stairs, until at last they were in the morgue.

It was very cold and she shivered as she looked around. It was like a giant locker room, with great drawers lining the walls on either side. Once more Bobby left her, and followed an attendant along one wall, shaking his head as he examined each corpse. This time there was no friendly bench nearby and Rosaleen drooped as she watched the men, hoping they would not have to go downtown to the City Morgue, yet dreading seeing Bobby nod his head to confirm that her father was there. Even as she watched, more coffins were brought and stacked along the corridor, and Bobby had to inspect these.

When she thought that her legs would no longer bear her weight and she would collapse, Bobby shook his head for the last time and approached her.

'He's not here Rosaleen. We'll have to go to the City Morgue.'

Becoming aware of her fatigue, he exclaimed, 'Ah, Rosaleen, what on earth am I thinking of? Sure, you're out on your feet!' Putting a supporting arm around her, he led her forward. 'Come on, love. Let's get you a cup of tea.'

This was easier said than done. Each nurse he approached looked at him as if he was an idiot, asking for tea at a time like this, shaking their heads abruptly and then hurrying on about their business. At last, in despair, he led Rosaleen into a small office that was at the entrance to a ward. They found tea-making facilities and he put the kettle on to boil. Helping himself to some sugar and milk he prepared a cup.

'Just what on earth do you think you're doing?'

'I . . . oh . . . look, I'm sorry, but this young woman's in a state of shock. Her father was killed tonight and we're looking for his body.'

The harassed young doctor framed in the doorway looked at Bobby blankly for some seconds. Then, as if the words had just registered, he turned his tired gaze on Rosaleen.

'I'm just making her a wee cup of tea before we go down to the City Morgue. She's out on her feet, so she is, an' I want to waken her up a bit,' Bobby explained, his voice pleading. He knew he was in the wrong; had no right to be in the office, no matter making tea.

A long drawn-out sigh left the doctor's lips and he rummaged in his pockets. Producing a phial, he shook two small tablets into the palm of his hand. 'Here . . . give her these . . . They'll waken her up. You'd better hurry up, and not let Sister catch you in here.' And dismissing Bobby's thanks with a wave of his hand, he left the office.

'Here, take these with your tea . . . the doctor says they'll waken you up,' Bobby said kindly, and waited until Rosaleen put the tablets in her mouth before pressing the cup of tea into her unsteady hands.

Rosaleen didn't think anything could waken her up; she just ached with tiredness, longed to close her eyes and sleep. Guilt added to her fatigue. What must people think of her, searching for her father's body and unable to keep her eyes open? She felt so ashamed. They must think her uncaring. But to her surprise the tablets did waken her up and by the time Bobby was ready to move on, she was wide awake and clear-headed.

They had just come through the gates of the hospital and were making their way down the Grosvenor Road when a car pulled up on the other side of the road and an arm waved them over.

'You wait here, Rosaleen,' Bobby said, before warily crossing the road, but after conversing with the occupants of the car, he beckoned her over. 'We're getting a lift down to the City Morgue,' he informed her. 'These young doctors have been sent to help out down there.'

And Rosaleen recognised the driver of the car as the doctor who had given Bobby the tablets.

The journey to the morgue, although a short distance by car, seemed endless. As they approached the city centre, they could see fires blazing. With a smothered oath, the doctor reversed the car and approached the morgue via Sandy Row and then across the back streets to the Donegal Road. On their journey, they could see streets demolished and smoking desolation.

Once at their destination, the procedure was the same as before. Corridors, stairs, more corridors, and then the morgue itself. There were coffins everywhere, the lids removed and resting against them for each viewing, and there was a long queue waiting to examine the bodies. They joined the queue and Rosaleen felt dazed and shocked as she viewed horrible corpses, all twisted out of shape, staring eyes, faces and hair thickly matted with dust. Young people, old people, some with the clothes blown off their bodies, one woman still clutching a child to her breast. And to add to the horror of it all, the smell of excrement permeated the air, causing the bile to rise in her throat. It took a great effort of will to choke it down again. Unknown to herself, she was whimpering. Taking her gently by the arm, Bobby led her outside and to a bench where other people were waiting.

'You wait here, Rosaleen. As you have seen, some of these bodies are not a pretty sight. If your father's here, I'll call you.'

She sat, full of dread. What if her father was

disfigured? How would her mother react? She remembered the night of April 15th. Remembered her father talk about laying bodies on the floors of the swimming pools in the Falls Road Baths, and her heart sank. Is that what was happening tonight? Would she have to climb down into the swimming pool to identify her father? Dread made her mouth dry up and a great lump gathered in her throat, causing her to gulp as she tried to swallow it. If only Joe was here . . . or Sean. They would know what to do. There would have to be a funeral. What did she and Annie know about funerals?

At last Bobby came and beckoned her forward.

'He's here, Rosaleen,' he said softly, and put a comforting arm across her shoulders. 'Come on love. He's in the morgue itself . . . it's not so gruesome.'

With dread she entered the room and, eyes downcast, approached the big drawer that the assistant held open. There was a big ball of fear where her heart should be. What if he was badly disfigured and she fainted?

As if realising the trend of her thoughts, Bobby whispered in her ear, 'It's all right, Rosaleen. It's all right. He isn't marked. And remember . . . I was with him. I closed his eyes, straightened his limbs. You'd think he was just sleeping.'

He was right; except for a discolouration at the right side of his brow, her father looked as if he was just taking a nap. Unconsciously, she reached out her hand and gently touched his face. It was cold, firm and waxy. Tears blinded her as she turned away. He was dead all right.

'It's him,' she said, for the benefit of the attendant who was watching her gravely, and who now nodded and pushed the great drawer shut. 'I'll need you to sign a form and then I'll get the doctor to give you the death certificate,' he said softly, as he led the way out of the room, glad that another body had been identified.

176

The minute Rosaleen entered her mother's kitchen she knew Annie had not told her the bad news and her heart filled with bitterness. Why did she have to do everything? Annie should bear her part of the burden.

'Make Rosaleen a cup of tea, Annie. She looks foundered.'

At her mother's words, with a pleading, apologetic look, Annie disappeared into the scullery. Rising to her feet, Thelma greeted her daughter brightly. 'My, but you were a long time. Laura's asleep. I've put her up in my bed.'

'Mam . . . Mam, please sit down, I've something to tell you.'

Thelma made no effort to obey Rosaleen. Instead she moved away from her outstretched hand and over to the fireplace. Here she stood warming her hands at the blaze and continued in the same bright voice, as if Rosaleen had not spoken: 'You can leave Laura here. When she wakens, I'll bring her down.'

With a sinking heart, Rosaleen realised that her mother guessed the truth and was afraid to face it.

Going to her, she put an arm gently across her mother's shoulders and tried to lead her to the settee, but with an angry thrust, Thelma pushed her away.

'He's dead, isn't he?' she cried, and great tears welled up and ran down her stark, white face. 'Do you think I don't know?' Her hand clutched at the regions of her heart. 'Part of me died with him. I knew something was wrong . . . I just knew it. I couldn't understand why I felt so bereft. Couldn't understand . . . It was as if I had lost something, but didn't know what. Just a feelin' that I'd lost something.' She fell silent for some moments and allowed the awful feeling to swamp her. 'Then, when Annie said that you were away somewhere with Bobby Mackay, I knew . . . I knew . . .' a sob gathered in her throat, almost choking her, and she gulped before she could finish '. . . just how much I'd lost.'

Full of compassion, Rosaleen tried to urge her mother towards the settee. 'Come on, love, sit down. Can I get you anything?'

Resisting her efforts to make her sit down, Thelma cried, 'Yes! Yes, ye can! Ye can get me your da.' She clutched at Rosaleen's arm, and eyes full of dread, asked, 'Where is he? Is he in the swimming pool?'

When Rosaleen shook her head, Thelma bowed hers.

'Thank God for that. He would have hated that. He thought it degrading.' Her eyes swung to the picture of the Sacred Heart that hung on the wall. 'Why are you doing this to me?' she cried. 'Eh? Eh? I didn't do anything wrong.' Then, bowing her head, she pleaded. 'Oh, sweet Jesus help me . . . help me to bear this.'

Wiping the tears from her own cheeks with the back of her hand, Rosaleen once more tried to comfort her mother.

'He was a good man, Mam, he'll have been prepared.'

Another thrust sent her staggering and she plunged down on the arm of the settee and grabbed the back of it to save herself from toppling over.

'Prepared? Oh, he'll have been prepared, all right. I'm not worried about him. He'll have made his peace with God long ago, but what about me? What am I gonna do?' She wrung her hands in despair. 'Oh . . . you don't understand, you don't understand.' She turned away, then swung back again, crying in anguish. 'Why couldn't he have stayed at home with his wife like other men? Eh? No . . . no . . . he had to be out saving strangers. It didn't matter about me.' She thumped her breast with her fist and bawled, 'If he had stayed at home, he might have died in his own bed and I'd have had some warnin'. Do you hear me? I'd have had some warnin', so I would.'

Stung on behalf of her father, Rosaleen cried, 'Mam, that's not fair! He was doing what had to be done.'

'Oh, I know, I know. Don't pay any attention to me. Ye see . . . well . . . Oh, you don't understand!'

Frustrated, Rosaleen felt like shouting, 'Well then, tell me. Explain.' But her mother was actually pulling at her hair . . . yanking at it . . . pulling it down with both hands, her eyes wild, her mouth trembling, and Rosaleen was afraid to question her. Then suddenly, just like air leaving a balloon, her mother's body sagged, her legs buckled, and with a great howl she collapsed. On her knees, at the settee, she buried her head in her arms and wept, great sobs tearing at her slight frame.

In the face of such grief, Rosaleen was at a loss what to do. Who would have dreamt that her mother had cared so deeply for her father? Was she being a hypocrite? If not, she had certainly hidden her true feelings all these years. Because of her offhand attitude towards her father, Rosaleen had in her own mind concluded that her mother had married him as a last resort. Of course she had cared for him, but not enough to warrant this breakdown, surely?

During her mother's tirade, Annie had come to the door of the scullery and was standing, her clenched fist pressed against her mouth, panic in her eyes. Now, catching her eye, Rosaleen mouthed the words: 'Get Doctor Hughes.'

Without a word, Annie lifted her coat and fled from the house, glad to escape from the sight of her mother's mindless grief. Stumbling down the Springfield Road, she felt ashamed. She was aware that she should have broken the news to her mother. Rosaleen had every right to be angry with her. When her mother had descended the stairs after settling Laura in bed, she had tried to tell her, but Thelma would not listen to her. She had rambled on and on, not letting her get a word in edgeways and, to her shame, she had been so tired she had drifted off into a doze as she listened to her mother's voice droning on and on.

As she entered the hall of the doctor's surgery, she whispered a quiet prayer that Doctor Hughes would be present. What would they do if he wasn't in?

He was not there. His housekeeper informed her that he was down at the Royal Hospital, lending a helping hand.

As she turned away, despair in her heart, the housekeeper said, tentatively, 'His father's here . . . I'll see how he is this morning.'

Annie knew that she was referring to old Doctor Hughes, who must be about seventy and who had retired some years ago, and who sometimes, if he felt well enough, came out in an emergency.

To her relief he shuffled into the waiting room, and agreed to come and see her mother. Soon they were out on the Springfield Road, she slowing her step to suit his and he plying her with questions about her mother's condition.

When they entered the kitchen, they found Rosaleen sitting on the settee, her face buried in her hands. Of their mother there was no sign.

Going to Rosaleen, Doctor Hughes gently took her hands away from her face and asked, 'Where is your mother?'

'She's up cleaning the rooms.'

Her voice was bitter, scornful. After a quarter hour of mindless grief and belittling Rosaleen's attempts to comfort her, Thelma had calmly dried her face and risen to her feet. Watched by a bewildered Rosaleen, she had fetched her brush and dust pan, duster and polish.

'You'll have to excuse me now – I must clean the rooms for them bringing him home.' And without another glance in Rosaleen's direction, she had mounted the stairs, her back straight, her step firm. Imagine! Her husband was dead and she was worried about what the neighbours would think if the rooms were dusty.

Taking Rosaleen's wrist between his fingers, Doctor Hughes examined her face intently as he took her pulse. He felt heartsore for these two girls whom he had brought into the world.

'Rosaleen, you must not judge your mother by her actions. She's coping in the only way she can. You need to rest,' he said, with a gentle tap of reprimand on the back of her hand. 'I'll go up to your mother.'

Sitting down beside her on the settee, Annie tried to explain. 'I tried to tell her, Rosaleen. Honestly, I did, but she wouldn't listen to me.'

'I know, Annie. I know. She was the same with me. Listen . . .' the look she turned on Annie was full of dread '. . . what are we going to do? I wish Joe was here. How I wish he was here.'

'And Sean,' Annie fervently agreed. 'They'll get compassionate leave, won't they?'

'Huh! It depends on where they are and what they're doing,' Rosaleen cried in despair. 'Don't count on them getting home. We'll probably have to manage on our own.'

They fell silent when they heard Doctor Hughes on the stairs.

'I've given your mother a sedative. She'll sleep for about six hours and I'll leave some tablets . . .' He opened his bag and took a small bottle from it. 'Make sure she takes two of these every six hours. They'll keep her calm.'

He placed the bottle on the mantelpiece and eyed the girls.

'Now . . . what are we going to do about you two? You look dead beat.' His teeth gnawed away at his bottom lip as he stood deep in thought. 'Have you an uncle or male cousin? Someone to see to the funeral arrangements?'

'We'll send for Sean and Joe ... our husbands,' Annie informed him.

'That will take too long. Is there no one else?'

Before they could reply the door was thrust open and Amy entered the room, followed by Bobby Mackay.

'Oh, you poor, poor girls.'

Kneeling in front of them, Amy put an arm around each of them as she explained, 'Mr Mackay came for me. Wasn't that good of him?'

Clutching her, Rosaleen wailed, 'Oh, Amy, what are we gonna do? Do you know anything about funerals?'

'You leave all that to me, Rosaleen,' Bobby interrupted her. 'I'll make all the arrangements.'

Relieved that someone was in charge, Doctor Hughes produced more tablets from his bag, and pouring some into the palm of his hand he proffered them to Amy.

'Here, see they take two each ... it will make them sleep.'

As she listened to his words, Rosaleen felt hysterical laughter well up inside her and pressed her lips tightly together to contain it. Tablets to waken her up ... tablets to make her sleep. She'd feel like a pill bottle before this was all over.

'Thank you, Doctor. I'll see that they take them,' Amy assured him, and duty performed, Doctor Hughes bade them good day and left the house.

'Rosaleen?' Bobby hovered in front of her awkwardly. 'Before you take the tablets, can I have the death certificate? I'll need it to make the funeral arrangements.'

Rosaleen, who was still sitting with her outdoor coat

on, searched the pockets. When she failed to find the sheet of paper, she panicked and began feverishly to search them again.

Gently, Bobby stilled her frantic hands. 'Rosaleen, I think you put it in your cardigan pocket for safety. Remember? Eh, love?'

With a relieved sigh, she unbuttoned her coat, extracted the certificate from her cardigan pocket and gave it to him.

'Will you need me here, Mrs Smith?' he asked Amy, and when she shook her head, said, 'Then I'll away down and set things in motion.'

When the door closed on him, Amy turned to the girls.

'Where's Laura?'

'Upstairs.'

'Well . . . here's what I suggest. Rosaleen, you and I will take Laura and go to my house. That way I can look after her for the next few days and leave you free to support your mother.' With an apologetic look she turned to Annie. 'Will you be all right here, near your mother, in case she awakens?'

'Oh, yes . . . yes. Don't worry about me. I'll look after Mam. But, what about Sean and Joe? Shouldn't we let someone know, so that they can be sent for?'

'Mr Mackay is seeing to all that, so he is. My, but he's a good man.'

'Do you know Bobby, Amy?' Annie questioned her.

'No . . . no, Annie. I didn't know him from Adam when I opened the door to him an hour ago. He stood on the doorstep, big and sorrowful-looking, and informed me that he was Bobby Mackay, your father's warden partner. He said that your father had been killed and he thought I might be needed.'

'Oh, thank God for that,' Rosaleen exclaimed. 'That was kind of him. We were worried about the funeral arrangements. It's a relief to know Bobby's helping us.'

'Amy, do you think Sean and Joe will get home?'

Annie was eyeing her beseechingly, and Amy was sorry to have to disillusion her.

She shook her head. 'I'm afraid not. I can't see them getting home in time for the funeral.' But when both their faces dropped, she hastily added, 'But ye never know . . . ye never can tell.'

Joe did get home; he arrived the day before the funeral and when Rosaleen opened the door and saw him, she fell into his arms and wept. She wept for joy at seeing him, and she wept because she was horrified at how thin and gaunt he was. Just like a bag of bones in her arms. She thought her heart would break as she hugged him close.

Her mother had refused to allow her father to be taken to spend his last night in the church. She said she wanted to keep him at home with her as long as she could; and near eleven, when everybody had departed at the sound of the sirens, she settled down in the chair she had occupied constantly since they had brought him home, near the trestles on which the coffin rested.

When the sirens had started their mournful wail, they had ignored them. Just as they had the previous night when a few planes had passed over the city and dropped bombs. Somehow, nothing seemed to matter any more. There was no way they were going to leave Tommy on his own, no way. They had been outraged when a neighbour had the effrontery to remark that they were daft and should get themselves away up into the fields, saying, 'Sure, ye can't kill a dead man. What about the child?'

Annie had rounded angrily on him. 'She's safe. She'll already be up in the fields, but we're staying with me da.' And she had bestowed such a look of wrath on him, he had said no more.

When Rosaleen retired to the scullery to make a cup

184

of tea, Joe followed her in. This was the first time they had been alone since he had arrived that morning, and coming up behind her he put his arms around her waist and sank his face into her hair.

'How I've missed you, love . . . you'll never know how much I've missed you.'

She sank back against him, and closing her eyes pulled his hands over her breasts and revelled in the comfort of his arms. As she felt his passion rise, her heart soared. Surely this time it would work? It was different, she could feel the difference as he gripped her tighter still against his body.

Swiftly she turned in his arms and lifted her face for his kisses. Gripping her arms tight around him, she moved her body sensuously against his, her long months of frustration making her act like a wanton woman. Aware of her mother in the kitchen and Annie upstairs, she urged him so that his back was against the scullery door and no one could take them unawares.

Such was her great need to be held and loved, it was a minute or so before she realised that Joe was not responding to her frantic actions. He was actually squirming in her arms, and hot with shame she pushed her body away from his and turned away from him.

Her knuckles showed white as she gripped the edge of the stove, and wrapped in misery, fought for self-control. She was a fool! Why should it be any different? He was still the same man.

Sean's face surfaced in her mind but she pushed it away. She had no right to think how differently he would have responded to her actions. No right at all!

'I'm sorry . . . I'm sorry, Rosaleen. I'm . . . I'm very tired.'

Joe's voice, soft and apologetic, invaded her misery, and thinking grimly that it may as well be a headache, she avoided his outstretched hand and busied herself at the stove.

'It's all right. Never worry.'

Keeping her attention fixed firmly on what she was doing, she set a tray and when she had poured the tea, motioned for him to carry it into the kitchen. She was amazed at her own stupidity. Had she really believed that Joe would get carried away enough to make love to her, and her mother sitting in the kitchen? No, she had been daft . . . but he could have held her and kissed her and suggested that they wait until they were alone. He could have softened the blow. After all, he was her husband. He didn't have to reject her like that. Make her feel cheap and dirty. Still, she should have known better. Joe would be appalled at the idea of her wanting to make love in the scullery and her father dead in the next room; she would have dropped another notch in his estimation.

When her mother had finished her tea, the sleeping tablets Rosaleen had insisted she take soon worked and she fell asleep.

'Joe, will you carry her over to the settee? She'll rest better there.'

After she had placed a pillow at her mother's head and gently tucked blankets around her prone figure, she turned to face him.

He looked so worn out that she wanted to go to him and hold him close, tell him everything was all right, but the rejection in the scullery still rankled and she found she could not make herself move towards him. She knew he needed to be held and comforted, and it was her duty to attend to him, but she had needs too . . . and he always left her wanting.

'Joe, you can sleep in me mam's bed, I'll sleep with Annie, all right? That is . . . unless you want to go home to Iris Drive? I must stay here in case I'm needed.'

'I'll stay here too. That is, if you don't mind?'

His look was pleading for understanding but she

refused to meet his eye. Keeping her gaze on his shirt front, she shook her head and moved over to the coffin to say goodnight to her father.

'Ah, Da, if you can see us, if you know what's going on . . . please help us through tomorrow,' she whispered, before heading towards the stairs. 'Come on, Joe. I'll show you where you can sleep.'

He followed her up the stairs and on the landing she motioned him into her mother's bedroom. There was such a wealth of sorrow in his eyes that she felt compassion block out all the other mixed-up, hurt feelings. It was like seeing a child in pain. And wasn't that what he was to her . . . a child? And who could reject a child?

With a sigh she followed him into the room and closed the door. He watched her, a hopeful expectancy about him. Pushing him gently down on to the bed, she started to unbutton his shirt.

The happiness that radiated from him was her reward, and cupping her face in his hands, he whispered, 'Thanks, Rosaleen . . . thanks, love. You're too good for me.'

'It's all right, love,' she assured him, while her mind lamented. If only it was all right. If only it was.

When she undressed and crept into bed beside him, he gathered her close and she thought, ah, what the hell? We can at least cry together.

The next morning, Rosaleen awakened early and asked Joe to nip down to Iris Drive and light the fire so that later the water would be hot enough for her to bathe.

Early though it was, she discovered when she descended the stairs that Annie and her mother had beaten her to it.

They were both washed and dressed and although they were sipping tea, untouched breakfasts were pushed to one side.

'Did you sleep well?'

Annie's voice held an insinuation and Rosaleen realised that she was envying her Joe's return.

'Yes.'

Entering the scullery she reached for the pan and then hesitated. Would it look heartless to make Joe a fry? He must be hungry, he deserved a fry and one thing was sure . . . her da would be the last to begrudge him a proper meal.

She sat sipping a cup of tea and watched Joe wolf down the bacon and eggs, potato and soda farls. He must have lost stones in weight. Once she got him home she would soon fatten him up.

He'd be home for a week, she'd shovel food and vitamins into him while he was here. It would help to sustain him when he returned to war.

After breakfast, Joe departed for Iris Drive to carry out Rosaleen's wishes and as she washed his breakfast dishes, Annie joined her in the scullery.

'I dread the day,' she said mournfully. 'I just know it'll be awful.'

'So do I,' Rosaleen agreed with her. 'I wish it was over and done with. Although . . . mind you . . . me mam's coping better than I imagined she would.'

'Ah, but wait 'til they take me da away. Oh, the very thought of it fills me with dread. If I need you . . . if she's bad, will you stay the night?' Annie's voice was apologetic as she added, 'I know you'll want to be alone with Joe . . . but if I need you, won't you stay?'

'Of course I will. Joe'll understand,' Rosaleen assured her.

'Thanks, Rosaleen.'

However, things rarely go as expected and in the event it was Rosaleen who was worst affected.

Father Logan and the hearse were expected at eleven, and at twenty minutes to the hour the

188

mourners gathered in the house to say the rosary. Someone suggested that Rosaleen, being the older daughter, should lead the prayers and bravely she tried, but halfway through the first decade her voice broke. At once Joe took over; with a comforting arm around her shoulders he recited the prayers in a strong voice.

Rosaleen let the Our Fathers and Hail Marys go over her head. She was standing beside the coffin and as she looked down on her father's features, she was suddenly swamped with guilt.

This dear, kind man had been so good to her. He had lavished love and affection on her all her life and she had accepted it all without so much as a thank you. When she was young, she hadn't known any better, but what about when she was an adult? She had just taken everything he did for her, as her due. As if it was his duty to attend to her. Not once had she asked if he was happy; if there was anything that she could do to make his life easier. No, she had been too wrapped up in her own problems. And the worst thing of all . . . she could never remember telling him how much she loved him. Probably when she was young she had told him, but never once had she said so when she was an adult. It didn't seem possible that she could have been so remiss, but it was true.

She heard the words of Hail, Holy Queen resound around the room and moved closer still to the coffin, sensing rather than seeing Joe's look of surprise as she left the shelter of his arm. The rosary was almost over, but she still had time to tell her father how much she loved him, before they put the lid on the coffin.

He was heavy, she couldn't get her arms under him to hug him, but she gripped the front of the shroud and kissed him feverishly. 'I love you, Da. Honestly! Honest to God! I just forgot to tell you.'

She felt hands try to move her away, was aware of

the awful hush, but still, defying their efforts, she clung on.

'Da . . . Da? Can you hear me, Da?'

It was her mother who at last managed to get through the wall of guilt that surrounded her. Gently, she put an arm around Rosaleen's shoulders.

'Come on, love. Come on now. He knows you loved him . . . he knows.'

'Really, Mam? You're sure?'

'Yes, love. Really . . . really. I'm sure. Now we must let him go, in peace.'

With these words, Thelma led Rosaleen into the scullery, and whispering 'I'll be back in a minute,' left her with Amy and went to make her own farewell to her husband.

The next think Rosaleen was aware of was wakening in her own bed in Iris Drive. Joe was sitting at the bedside holding her hand and when she opened her eyes he smiled at her.

'How are you feeling, love?'

A frown puckered her brow as she looked around the room. 'What happened?'

'You passed out.'

She struggled to sit up but he pressed her back.

'You need to rest.'

'You don't understand . . . I promised Annie that I'd stay and help her with Mam.'

'It's all right . . . Sean's home. His ship was in port loading cargo, and he got three days' leave. He arrived just as the funeral was moving off. He'll look after your mam and Annie. Now you go back to sleep. I'll see to everything else.'

She stretched herself. 'I ache all over.'

'That's shock. The doctor says you received a shock to your nervous system and it only hit you yesterday, when you realised that you would never see your father again.'

190

'Yesterday? You mean I've been sleeping since yesterday?'

'Yes. The doctor gave you a sedative.'

'How's me mam?'

'She coped very well . . . surprised us all. Even came to the cemetery in one of the cars. Sean came down this morning to see how you are and he said she seems to have accepted Tommy's death . . . ye know what I mean.'

Rosaleen gazed at him blankly. She couldn't understand her mother, but then, she had always thought her strange.

'Where's Laura?'

'Round at me mam's. Shall I go and fetch her? Do you feel well enough?'

'Yes, I feel much better now. Bring Laura home. There isn't much of your leave left. Let's not waste any more of it.'

With a grin on his face, Joe rose to his feet.

'I won't be long, love.'

When he left the room, Rosaleen swung her feet to the floor and rose shakily from the bed, surprised at how weak she felt.

Imagine her carrying on like that. What must everyone have thought? Now if it had been her mam, everybody would have understood. She couldn't understand herself what had possessed her. She knew her father couldn't hear her, couldn't feel her kisses, but she had felt compelled to try to reach him. If only she had been a better daughter. Well, she would make sure that she would have no such regrets when her mother died. From now on, she would make a point of showing her how much she meant to her. That would please her da. Yes, it would. Help to make up for her neglect of him.

Now she must see to it that Joe enjoyed the next few days. He was far too thin; needed to be fed and loved.

191

Loved ... why did the word love make her feel desolate? There were all kinds of love. Joe was probably right. Sex was just one facet of marriage, and a minor one at that. It was up to her to work at her marriage, and when the war was over, Joe would go and see about himself, wouldn't he? She could only hope so. But for now? Life must go on.

Chapter 6

It was with horror that Rosaleen learnt of the damage that was inflicted on Belfast on the night that her father was killed. Devastated by his death and preoccupied with arrangements for his funeral, she had only half listened when neighbours spoke of the raid, and her mother forbade the radio to be played whilst her father's body was in the house; said it would be disrespectful. So it was after the funeral before she became aware that the shipyard had been devastated, with three-quarters of its buildings destroyed, three corvettes burnt to a cinder and a transport ship sunk at her moorings. Three other vessels were also destroyed and many others were damaged. Like the shipyard, Shorts and Harland aircraft factory received direct hits, and planes, some already on the assembly line, were destroyed.

But then, things like this were expected, had to be tolerated. After all, this was what war was all about. This was why the soldiers went to Germany, to destroy their ships and planes. It was the news regarding the number of dead and the destruction of the centre of town that dismayed Rosaleen. She could not take it in that the town was almost flattened. Shaftsbury Square, she knew, had been hit, remembering how the young hospital doctor had made a detour away from that part of the city when going to the morgue. He had taken the back streets over Sandy Row, to the Donegal Road and by-passed that part of town, but they had seen in the distance the fires that raged; had been aware of the severity of the fires from the dense smoke.

Now she was being told that Donegal Place, Chichester Street, Castle Lane, North Street and Bridge Street were all wiped out, and the left-hand side of High Street was completely gutted. All those beautiful shops like Arnotts, Thorntons and the Athletic Stores, to mention but a few, were no more. Fires were the main cause of the damage. The whistling fire bombs had shot balls of fire far and wide, and lack of water to put out the flames had helped to destroy the town. All this, in spite of help once more sent post haste from the south.

St Paul's parish escaped with only minor damage, a bomb at Beechmount and a few delayed bombs going off during the course of the next few days, but all, with the exception of her poor father (why did it have to be him?) and the family at Beechmount, without loss of life. It was hard to believe that the town was demolished, hundreds of people dead, thousands wounded and thousands more homeless. Indeed, she would have to go downtown and see for herself the devastation before she would be able to take it all in.

She also learnt that the City Hall had been hit, half of it demolished – the half that housed the beautiful banquet hall – and close by, the Water Commissioner's Office had received a direct hit.

Because of burst pipes, in some districts there was sewerage in the streets and water carts were touring the areas, delivering clean water. This meant that after spending nights in the fields, tired, depressed people had to queue, sometimes for hours, to have their buckets and pots filled, adding to the sense of hopelessness and despair. There was also an acute shortage of essential food, and many grocery shops were closed, with their owners lamenting that they were ruined. With nothing to sell and, because of another rush of refugees from town, unable to track down people who owed them money, they were in despair. How could they survive? Personally, Rosaleen thought that they should be grateful to be alive, and their shops still standing.

All this had been going on during the days of Joe's leave and she completely unaware of it. It was Amy who queued up at Hughes Bakery for bread and at the butcher's shop for meat, supplying them with their needs, and they were grateful to her for giving them these few short days to themselves. Even at night when the sirens wailed their warning, they had remained in the house, seeking refuge in the cubbyhole under the stairs, clasped in each other's arms; Laura asleep on the floor. They were content, if they must, to die together. However, after another slight raid on the 6th, no more bombs had been dropped, so far.

Joe needed a respite before returning to war and Rosaleen was determined to see that he got it, lifting and laying him, listening to his tales of hardship and, when he suffered nightmares, holding him in her arms and hushing him as she would a child, murmuring endearments, until the terror passed and he slept again. When he left to rejoin his regiment, she was glad to note that he was more relaxed, although she could detect the reluctance with which he departed.

'Surely it won't be long now?' she questioned him. 'Can the war last much longer?'

He hugged her close. 'I hope not. All I want is to be back here with you and Laura.'

Human nature being what it is, the retort hovered on her lips: 'Well, you didn't have to go! You didn't have to enlist!' But, hearing the misery in his voice, she bit back the words and defying the tears to fall, smiled brightly.

'If the Americans enter the war, it won't last much longer. We must pray that they join the fight against Hitler, and then you'll be home in no time,' she consoled him.

He nodded, but it was a mournful sight. He put her firmly away from him as the taxi drew up to the door. Lifting a weeping, bewildered Laura up in his arms he kissed her fiercely, then thrusting her at Rosaleen, hurried from the house. Rosaleen rushed to the window. Lifting the net curtain, she watched him enter the taxi. Then, with a final wave, he was gone.

Later that afternoon, Annie and May arrived together. Rosaleen greeted them warmly, but with a surprised, questioning look in her eyes.

Seeing the look, Annie explained, 'We met at the corner, so we did.'

'Rosaleen . . . imagine me not being at your da's funeral!' May exclaimed. 'But I didn't know. I only heard last night that he was dead. Ye see, we don't get the *Irish News*.'

'It's all right, May,' Rosaleen assured her kindly. 'I guessed that's what happened.'

She turned to Annie. 'How's me mam?'

Annie rolled her eyes towards heaven. 'Oh, Rosaleen, you don't know the half of it. Sean and I spent his entire leave roaming the streets looking for her. And he only got three days' leave, so he did. He wouldn't have got home at all only his ship was in port for repairs.'

Concerned, Rosaleen pressed her: 'What do you mean? Roamed the streets? Why did you roam the streets?'

'Every time we left me mam alone for a minute, she took off. The first time was the day after the funeral. When Sean was down here telling Joe how well she was, she took off . . . just a coat over her nightdress, and slippers on her feet. It was three hours later that she was found, wandering on the Shankhill Road, and we had to go to the Shankhill Road police station to collect her.'

Rosaleen groped behind her for a chair and sat down. 'Oh, my God! Why on earth didn't you come for me and Joe?'

'You weren't very well.' Annie examined her face intently. 'How are you now?'

'I'm fine.' Rosaleen felt colour rush to her cheeks as she recalled her behaviour on the day of her father's funeral, and overcome with embarrassment, she muttered, 'I feel such a fool. I don't know what came over me. Imagine me getting on like that.'

'Well, you were always closer to me da than I was. You were his favourite,' Annie said sadly, and Rosaleen was dismayed. Had her father favoured her?

But her sister was continuing: 'Mam was great at the funeral . . . and afterwards. When people came back to the house she sat and chatted, praised me da to the heavens, but the next day . . . oh boy! She went berserk. The thing that surprised us most was that every time she took off, it was always the Shankhill Road she headed for. Imagine! Her that hated the Shankhill. Wouldn't set foot on it when she was normal.'

Rosaleen's breath caught in her throat at these words, and she whispered fearfully. 'What on earth do you mean . . . normal?'

Annie grimaced. 'She's in a bad way, Rosaleen. Sean told Joe that she was coping, but she wasn't. We thought that she would improve, but she hasn't. I haven't been able to get to work. I'm afraid to leave her alone.'

'Huh! You should've come for me. She's my mother too. I'd a right to know.'

'I waited 'til Joe's leave was over because . . . well, God knows when you'll see him again.' She watched Rosaleen covertly as she added, 'Doctor Hughes wants us to put her into Grahame's Home.'

At Rosaleen's start of dismay, and seeing her mouth open to protest, Annie hurried on, 'Just for a short while, Rosaleen. He says she'd be well cared for, so he did.'

'And what did you say to that? Did you agree?' Rosaleen's voice was indignant, her look threatening.

Annie shook her head. 'No . . . I said I'd have to talk it over with you first.'

'I'm glad to hear that. 'Cause no way is she going into that madhouse.'

Annie's head reared back defiantly. 'Hey, hold on now! It's all right you talking like that, Rosaleen, but I've to go to work.' The face she thrust at her sister was flushed with anger. 'Will you be able to look after her during the day, eh? Will you?'

'You don't have to go to work,' Rosaleen retorted, her face matching Annie's for bright colour. 'I'm sure Sean sends you plenty of money, and me mam has some insurance left, and . . . she'll probably be back to work in no time. Anyhow . . .' her lips tightened and her eyes flashed '. . . we'll work something out between us. No way is she going into Grahame's Home. No way! Do you hear me? Good God, do you want to send her around the bend? It's only natural that she's upset at the moment. Give her time to get over the loss of me da.'

'Doctor Hughes says it's not an asylum . . . just a hospital for nervous disorders and people unable to cope. People like me mam who've had a bereavement. He says it would give her a chance to recover.'

May squirmed uneasily in her chair; she didn't want to sit listening to this private business. At the first lull in the conversation, she rushed in.

'Look, Rosaleen, I'll go down and see me mam and come back later, O.K.?'

Rosaleen came back to reality with a start, and turned to her friend.

'No! No, May. That won't be necessary. You'll have to excuse us, getting all het up in front of you. I'll go up and see me mam tonight. That's what I intended doing anyhow.' She glanced across and nodded at Annie. 'We'll talk then. Meantime, I'll make us all a cup of tea.'

Annie rose quickly to her feet. 'Not for me, thank you. I'll leave you and May to have a chat. I don't want to be away too long. Me mam's in Mrs Murphy's.' She turned to May with a wry smile. 'Wish we were meeting under happier circumstances, but that's life. Hope your mother recovers.'

May jerked her head in a hopeless gesture. 'We can only keep our fingers crossed, Annie. See you soon.'

When the door closed on her, Rosaleen turned to May.

'What did she mean about your mother?'

'Me mam's had a stroke, so she has. She's bad, Rosaleen, paralysed from the neck down.'

'Ah, May, I'm sorry to hear that.'

May blinked furiously to hold back the tears. 'I wish it'd been me da,' she ground out through clenched teeth.

'Oh, don't say that. Whatever you do, don't say that,' Rosaleen begged her. 'Never wish ill on anyone. It always rebounds on you.'

May grunted. 'Huh! You sound like Father Docherty. When I said that to him, he nearly ate me.'

Picturing the big, stern parish priest of St Peter's, to which May belonged, Rosaleen gasped, 'You said that to Father Docherty?'

'Why not? It's what I was thinking.'

'What did he say?'

'Huh . . . he said me mam was ready to meet God and me da wasn't. He said I should pray for me da. Pray for him? I pray all right. I pray he'll roast in hell!'

'Oh, May, don't . . . don't,' Rosaleen whispered, and

a shiver ran down her spine. She wasn't really superstitious, but still . . . 'Will your mam recover?'

May's head swung slowly from side to side and the tears could be contained no longer. 'A couple of weeks . . . maybe a couple of months. She knows nobody, can do nothing for herself, and the worst of it is . . .' great sobs choked her and tears ran unheeded down her cheeks, to fall on her tightly clenched hands '. . .me da won't let me stay to look after her.'

'Is he back in the house then?'

'Oh, yes. He arrived the minute he heard about it, playing the concerned, doting husband. But he fools nobody. Everybody knows that he tortured me mam. And, Rosaleen . . . I just know he won't look after her properly.' Once more sobs caused her to pause. 'The lads will do their best, but they're on shifts and a woman's touch is needed. Our wee Jenny's too young.'

'Ah, May.' Rosaleen's arms stretched out and clasped her close.

After a few moments, May wiped her eyes and pushing Rosaleen back, grimaced at her.

'It's me who should be comforting you. At least my mam's still alive. Your da's dead. I cried when Billy came home last night and told me. Your da was such a good, caring man. No wonder your mam's had a breakdown.'

Rosaleen shook her head sadly and went to the bureau in the corner. She didn't want to talk about her da. It was too soon; the pain too close to the surface, ready to fill her with guilt and remorse. Forcing it into the back of her mind, she opened the bureau and produced a bottle of gin.

'I think we need something stronger than tea, May, a wee drink, eh? Widow's ruin.' She held the bottle, which was half full, up for May's inspection. 'It's all I have. Do you fancy a drop?'

May was looking at her, a comic expression on her

face, and Rosaleen, in spite of the misery that engulfed her, laughed aloud when her friend exclaimed, 'I never thought I'd see the day that you'd drink gin! But I'll be glad to join you.'

'Oh, I'm a changed girl, May. You'd never believe half the things I get up to.'

'No, I wouldn't!' May bestowed a wry smile on her. 'Your conscience wouldn't let you go far wrong.'

Rosaleen smiled grimly and changed the subject. If only May knew! Why, she'd be horrified.

'Where's the child, May?'

'Mrs Mercer has him. She's awful good, so she is. Says I'm to stay as long as me mam needs me, but that aul bugger won't let me. He got a great kick out of showing me the door, but I'll go back tonight when Colin's there. He won't take any nonsense from him.'

'Stay here, May. I'd be glad of your company and you'll be able to nip down to Spinner Street any time you feel like it.'

'You mean . . . bring Ian here?'

Rosaleen nodded her head excitedly. 'Of course! Why not? Billy can come and stay as often as he likes, and I'll be glad of your company.'

'Billy's only working half time, ye know. You might be fed up looking at him.'

'Not working? I thought the Falls Flax had plenty of orders.' Rosaleen's eyes were wide with wonder. What on earth was wrong?

'They have! Loads!' May assured her. 'But the raw material's not getting through, what with the docks and the railways being bombed, so they're working a three-day week, until further notice.' The look May gave Rosaleen was puzzled. 'All the engineering works are either closed down or on short time. There's hardly anybody working. There's thousands on the outdoor relief. Only the like of Mackie's is working full time. They've taken over orders that Shorts and Harland can't do and they're working around the clock. I can understand Annie wanting to go back to work. If she doesn't, she'll lose her job. They'll give her a wee breathing space on account of your da dying in the blitz, but the work has to be got out. If she delays too long, someone else will be only too glad to fill her shoes.

Rosaleen sighed. 'May, I'm not with it. With Joe being home, I haven't been out of the house. While he was here Amy kept us supplied with food and I didn't realise it was so bad.'

'We'll take a walk downtown this afternoon and let you see just how bad it is. Or . . .' May grimaced, '. . . on second thoughts maybe we shouldn't, it's enough to depress a saint. You wouldn't know where one street ends and another starts. Honest to God, Rosaleen, you can stand in Castle Street and right down to the Albert Clock at the bottom of High Street is flattened.' Her gaze was vacant as if seeing the ruins in her mind's eye. 'The right-hand side of High Street is still standing, but Bridge Street's rubble . . . so is Lower North Street and Donegal Street. All those big beautiful shops destroyed. And the clock itself is tilting to one side. Maybe it'll have to come down and all.'

Rosaleen took a gulp of the gin, grimaced with distaste, and proffered the bottle to May.

'No, thank you, I've enough here, I'll have to stay sober. Did you mean what you said just now? About me staying here?'

She watched Rosaleen closely, ready to back down if her friend looked dismayed. In case she had made the suggestion on the spur of the moment, and now regretted it.

She need not have worried, Rosaleen replied quickly, 'Of course I mean it. I tell ye, I'll be glad of your company.'

And they touched glasses and drank to that.

However, they had not reckoned with Billy. When May put the idea to him, he hit the roof.

'Are you mad? Do you think I'd let you take Ian over to live beside Mackie's? Wise up, woman.' He saw her lips tighten and softened his tone. 'Look, I know you want to be near your mother, but Ian must come first. Eh, love?'

May's face crumpled, and she wailed, 'I have to go . . . can't you see? I ran off and left me mam in the lurch once before when she needed me. I can't leave her lying there, helpless, and that aul bugger . . .' She turned aside and fought for control. At last she wiped her eyes and faced him again. 'I'm sorry, Billy, but I just can't stay. I'll leave Ian with your mam, and you can take him to the fields at night. All right?'

She watched him draw himself to his full height, his face a tight, angry mask, and gasped in dismay when he growled, 'No, it's not all right. I forbid you to go. You're my wife and your place is here with me and Ian.' Surprise was etched on her face as she gaped at him. Never before had he denied her anything, and that he should start now when she most needed his understanding, hurt her.

'Ah, Billy, you don't mean that.'

He nodded. 'Oh, but I do. I'd be a fool to let you stay over beside Mackie's. My God, May, they've hit everywhere else. If they come back, it's Mackie's they'll be looking for.'

'Billy . . . I have to go.' Her voice was soft, pleading.

His lips tightened and he played his trump card. She might leave him, and the indications lately were that she would like to, but she would never leave Ian.

'If you go, Ian stays. And I don't want you coming every other day upsetting him.'

He watched her head rear back; her chin jut out.

'Don't blackmail me, Billy,' she warned, her voice tight with emotion.

He ignored the warning. 'That's the situation, May. If you love Ian, you stay and look after him.'

He was ashamed of himself, bargaining with his son, but he had nothing else to bargain with. Lately May had withdrawn into herself. She who had been so loving and warm was building a wall between them and he couldn't penetrate it. He was at a loss as to what to do, and the uncertainty was killing him. Had she met someone else?

They stared at each other, a hard, bitter look, then with a sad nod of the head, May moved towards the stairs.

'I'll pack me bags.'

Billy watched her climb the stairs, hurt and humiliation a tight ball in his chest, Well, he'd no intentions of backing down. Let her go! He wasn't going to beg. He'd gotten over the loss of one wife, he could do it again.

But you didn't love Diane, an inner voice taunted him, and in spite of his resolutions he followed her up the stairs.

Standing at the door of the bedroom he watched her remove clothes from drawers and wardrobe and pack them into a suitcase. He avoided looking at the bed where she had given him so much joy. This plain, homely girl who held his heart in the palm of her hand. What had gone wrong? They had been so happy. He had let her have her way in everything. As long as she was content, so was he. Perhaps he had been too easy going. Perhaps he should have shown her who was boss long ago. Now it was too late.

May avoided looking at him. She longed to feel his arms around her, to beg for his understanding, but she was aware that sooner or later this had to happen. They could not go on as they had lately, and she would be the first to admit that it was her fault. She was the one who had changed, and the worst of it was, she couldn't tell him why. No. She had given him her solemn promise and she could not break it. When she had made the promise, everything in the garden was rosy; love had overcome all obstacles. However, the blitz had changed all that and she couldn't help how she felt now.

When the case was full, she pressed it shut. Raising her head she met his eyes.

'May, don't do this to me, please. I beg you.'

'I'm sorry, Billy, but I have to go.'

As she waited for him to move aside, he reached out and his arms gripped her close.

'Well, if you must . . . you must, but I didn't really mean what I said. You know, about upsetting Ian. You can come back anytime and see him.' He drew back and his eyes begged her forgiveness. 'Every day if you like. And when your mam recovers, or the worst comes to the worst and she . . . You'll come home, won't you?'

She nodded mutely, to show that she understood. The need for him was rising and knowing that it would serve no real purpose should she submit, she exerted pressure on his chest, indicating that she wanted to be free from his arms.

Silently, he released her and moved to one side.

Entering the back bedroom, May stood and gazed down at her son, tears blinding her. Billy was right. Ian should be looked after here. He would take him to the fields at the first sign of danger whereas she would probably want to stay with her mam. But she would have seen that the child was safe. Yes, she would have made sure that Ian was safe. She would have made Kevin take him and Jenny up to the Falls Park at the first sign of danger. No, he had been wrong to blackmail her like that. That hurt.

When she left the room, Billy sank down on the bed.

Ears strained, he listened to her descending the stairs. Hoping against hope that she would change her mind and come back. When he heard the outer door close on her, he buried his head in his hands.

Where had he gone wrong? What had changed May?

Rosaleen's visit to see her mother started in fear and apprehension. Thelma had cut herself off from reality and when Rosaleen entered the room she ignored her and stayed huddled over the fire. Annie nodded in her direction and mouthed the words: 'I told you so. Maybe now you'll believe me.'

Then, touching her mother gently on the shoulder, she said softly. 'Mam . . . here's Rosaleen to see you.'

Thelma made no sign that she had heard her and once more Annie bestowed on Rosaleen a knowing look.

Pulling a small stool close to her mother's chair, Rosaleen sat down. Taking her mother's hand between her own two, she exerted pressure on the cold, limp fingers until Thelma slowly moved her head and focused her eyes on her.

'How are you, Mam?'

After a short silence, Annie whispered with a shake of the head. 'She won't answer you. She hardly ever speaks.'

'I'm all right, Rosaleen.'

Thelma's words caused Annie to gape in amazement and Rosaleen had to smile when her mother added, 'Make Rosaleen a cup of tea, Annie. I'm sure she'd like one. It's cold outside.'

Grinning widely, in a happy, relieved, agreeable voice, Annie teased her. 'And how would you know that, eh, Mam? You haven't been out of the house for days.'

A confused frown gathered on Thelma's brow. 'I

thought . . .' She turned and bestowed a worried gaze on Annie. 'Surely I was over in Mrs Murphy's today?' she queried.

Annie clasped her hand to her head.

'Of course you were, Mam. It's me that's confused . . . not you.' She grimaced at Rosaleen's broad smile and headed for the scullery. 'I'll make the tea.'

And that was the turning point. Although Thelma was quiet and withdrawn, and her days were spent sitting gazing into the fire, she agreed to go to Rosaleen's house when Annie was working, and Grahame's Home for the mentally disturbed was mentioned no more. Rosaleen sometimes wondered if her mother had heard the doctor speak about Grahame's Home and perhaps this had hastened her recovery. Not that she had fully recovered, far from it, but whatever the reason, the wandering up the Shankhill Road stopped.

It was some days before Rosaleen realised that all was not well with May. When she arrived alone to stay Rosaleen had thought it reasonable that Billy did not want his son staying over in the shadow of Mackie's Foundry. And it was only natural that May be depressed. Wasn't her mother at death's door? Still, there was something else. Something was drastically wrong, she could sense it. Why hadn't Billy brought Ian to see his mother? Why did May change the subject when she inquired after Billy? Rosaleen was at her wit's end when at last things came to a head.

Kate Brady lasted just over two weeks and it was after her funeral that Rosaleen learned May and Billy were separated.

Billy was at the funeral and returned from the graveyard to Spinner Street to the wake.

It was late in the evening when the last mourner departed and Rosaleen, who had stayed back to help with the washing up, made her excuses and prepared to go home.

At once May was on her feet. Bidding her brothers goodnight, she made it obvious that she was accompanying Rosaleen. A tight-lipped Billy, in a voice that would not be denied, declared that he would walk them home.

The short journey through the dark, deserted streets was a nightmare to Rosaleen as she and Billy made inane conversation and a silent May walked some steps ahead of them.

At the door, in a dilemma, Rosaleen said tentatively, 'Look, I'll nip round and see how Laura and Amy are. It'll give you two a chance to talk.'

Amy had offered to look after Laura, and Rosaleen was aware that, like the rest of the Falls Road, she stayed awake even when the sirens didn't wail their warning, just in case of a raid. Although fewer people trekked up to the Falls Park and countryside every night now, they didn't retire until about two in the morning, when it was assumed that the danger of a raid was past, so Rosaleen was confident that she would find Amy still awake.

'No!' May's voice rang out sharply in the still night air. 'Billy won't be coming in. He's a busy man. He won't have time to talk to me.'

'May!' His voice was, if possible, sharper. 'Stop this nonsense. Of course we must talk. We've arrangements to make.'

'We can do that through the solicitors, Billy. Now that Mam's dead, I can start to put my affairs in order.'

With these words, she brushed past them and entered the house.

Standing on the pavement, Rosaleen gaped at Billy in dismay. 'I'm sorry, but I can't ask you in.'

'It's all right, Rosaleen. It's all right . . . don't upset yourself. Goodnight.'

Sensing the deep unhappiness in him, she gripped his arm as he closed the gate of the small forecourt.

'Billy, I don't mean to be nosey . . . but what on

earth's wrong?'

'Hah! I wish I knew, Rosaleen. I wish I knew. I've wracked me brains and I'll be damned if I can see what I did wrong. I gave her everything and this is the result.' He paused a moment, hating himself for asking the next question. 'Rosaleen . . . is there anybody else? Another man?'

'Good Lord, Billy, of course there isn't. The past few weeks have been devoted to looking after her mother. I thought that's why you didn't come. I thought you were giving her a breather while she nursed her mam. All this has come as a shock to me.'

'You mean she hasn't talked about us?'

'Not one word, Billy. Not one wee word.'

'Oh.' He looked perplexed, then, 'Here, I almost forgot.' He plunged his hand into his inside jacket pocket, and produced a bulky envelope, which he thrust into her hand. 'I intended to give this to her, but I didn't get a chance . . . couldn't get her alone. And, Rosaleen . . . if she's ever in need, you'll let me know, won't you?'

'I can't make any promises, Billy. May is very proud and independent, you know that. If she doesn't want you to know how she is, well . . . she's my best friend and her wishes come first. I hope I don't get into trouble for taking this.' She wagged the envelope in his direction, sorry that she had been so ready to accept it. May would probably be angry with her.

'I understand, Rosaleen, but make her take that. After all, she is still my wife. Goodnight.'

With these words, he turned on his heel and strode down the street, a picture of misery.

When Rosaleen entered the house, May had already retired to the back bedroom and although Rosaleen tapped on the door, there was no reply. The next morning she was gone from the house before Rosaleen descended the stairs and it was lunch time when she returned.

'When on earth have you been?' Rosaleen greeted her reproachfully. 'I've been worried stiff about you.'

'Afraid I might commit suicide?'

A wry smile crossed Rosaleen's face. 'No, never that. You're too strong a person to give into despair.'

'You're right. Mine isn't the first marriage to flounder, and it won't be the last.' She squared her shoulders and proudly declared, 'I've been out getting meself a job. Our Colin told me that Mackie's were looking for two learners and I start work there on Monday.'

This news didn't come as a surprise to Rosaleen. May was not one to let the grass grow under her feet.

'Good for you,' she praised her, and going to the bureau, retrieved the envelope Billy had given her the night before. Tentatively she proffered it to her friend. 'Now, May, don't be angry with me . . . he made me take it.'

May opened the envelope and peered inside. Rosaleen could see that all the notes were big and white. Fivers! And quite a lot of them.

May's face twisted in a grimace as she fingered the notes. 'These'll help pay for the divorce, so they will. It means he can get rid of me sooner.'

'May, don't say that. Billy's terribly upset. I doubt if he wants to be rid of you.'

'Well then, explain this to me, Rosaleen. Explain this to me.' Her voice choked with emotion. 'Why did he not bring my son down to see me? Eh? I've been out of the house three whole weeks and he never once brought the child to see me. He knew I was stuck in the house, looking after me mam, and still he never came. I'll never forgive him for that. Never!'

Unable to think of a suitable reply to this accusation, Rosaleen groped about in her bewildered brain and at last said haltingly, 'Perhaps Ian was poorly.'

'All the more reason why he should've been in touch

with me,' May interrupted her angrily. 'No, it's all over between me and Billy.' A harsh laugh left her lips. 'The neighbours in Spinner Street will be glad. They'll be able to say: "We told her so! She should have listened to us." '

She turned away for a moment. 'He didn't even mention Ian to me yesterday . . . not one word. He was there for hours and hours and he never mentioned Ian once. Never told me how the child is.'

'Ah, May now . . . be fair! You didn't give him a chance. You avoided him all day. Remember, I was there. I saw the way you kept him at arm's length. And he was probably waiting for you to inquire about Ian. How come you didn't ask about him, eh? Your only child, and you haven't seen him for three weeks, and you didn't ask about him.' The look she bestowed on May was scornful. 'It seems to me you were both at fault.'

May reacted angrily to her criticism. 'Don't you preach to me! You don't know the circumstances.'

Ignoring her anger, Rosaleen moved closer and beseeched her, 'No, May, I don't know the circumstances, but it seems to me that you should give Billy a chance to put things right.'

Tentatively, she placed a hand on her arm. 'May . . . what went wrong? You and Billy were so close. I used to envy you, you were that close. What on earth happened?'

Even in her misery, May gaped at Rosaleen in astonishment. '*You* envied *me*? You, who had everything, envied me?' A hand covered her chest. 'Me . . . living in sin on the Shankhill Road. Ah! Don't mock me, Rosaleen. You always thought that this would happen. Come on now, admit it. Right from the start you thought that Billy and I would break up.' She thrust a red, angry face close to Rosaleen's. 'Didn't you?'

Aware that, at the start, she had expected the

211

marriage to flounder, Rosaleen answered honestly.

'You're right, May. At first I had deep misgivings about your marriage but, against all the odds, you and Billy made a go of it. You were so happy, so close. It was your closeness that I envied. With different backgrounds, and different beliefs, you were still so happy. It was a joy to watch the two of you together. But it was your closeness that I envied most. Not many couples are as much in harmony. You're a fool if you don't fight for your happiness.'

Seeing May's eyes go round with wonder, and guessing that she was wondering just why she and Joe weren't close, Rosaleen hurried on. 'You really should talk it over with Billy. I'm sure things can be sorted out.'

May's mouth opened to speak but shut without uttering a sound. How could she tell Rosaleen about her change of heart. Why, she would laugh at her. Tell Rosaleen that she, who had never been gospel greedy, was afraid of losing her soul?

'If you don't mind, Rosaleen, I don't want to talk about it.' And to change the subject, she confided. 'I'm moving back home to Spinner Street, so I am.'

'Will your da allow you back?'

'No way! But he's not staying there. It seems some fool of a woman has been looking after him while he's been out of the house.'

'Really? You know, May, I felt sorry for him yesterday. He seemed so lost . . . so unhappy.'

'Huh! So he fooled you too? My da's crafty. There'll always be some idiot there to care for him. He must have some kind of charm, but I never saw it displayed in our house. No bloody fear. All I ever saw was scorn and dislike.' A puzzled frown knitted her brows. 'Do you know something, Rosaleen? I sometimes thought my da hated me. Even when the boys were young, he never hit them as hard as he hit me. Is it any wonder I hate him?' She paused and thought for a few moments. 'He used to shout at me: "If it wasn't for you, I wouldn't have married yer ma." It was a long time before I understood what he meant. Imagine blaming me on that, Rosaleen. Imagine me mam going through life, getting that thrown at her every time he was drunk.'

'Ah, May . . . you've had an awful hard life. You've been through the mill, so you have.'

The tears clung to May's lashes and the smile she gave was more a grimace, but there was no doubting her sincerity when she proudly declared: 'I've had over two wonderful years with Billy Mercer. Some people don't even get that, so I consider myself lucky.'

And as she turned away towards the bathroom, Rosaleen knew the tears were falling. But what could she do if her friend wouldn't confide in her?

With so many mills and engineering places shut down, there was a rush of young men to join the army, and it came as no surprise when, two weeks later, Billy arrived at Rosaleen's house to announce that he had joined up. He had Ian with him and as May hungrily reached for her son, Rosaleen lifted her coat and slipped quietly from the house, sending a prayer heavenward that things between Billy and May would be sorted out.

However, when she returned some hours later there was no sign of Billy and Ian and she found May huddled on the settee, crying as if her heart would break.

Taking May in her arms, Rosaleen sat and rocked her in silent sympathy. At last May drew back and, blowing her nose, confided, 'He's joined the army because of me, Rosaleen. He thinks I don't love him and he's joined up.'

'I wish I knew what to say. I wish I could help you.'

'Nobody can help me now, Rosaleen. I've made a

mess of everything, and if it was only me that was suffering, I wouldn't care.' She started to sob. 'But Billy's unhappy, too, and Ian's fretting.'

Rosaleen gripped her by the shoulders and shook her roughly. 'Oh, May! You make me want to scream! If you love Billy ... GO SEE HIM! Tell him you love him.'

But May just shook her head in a hopeless gesture and Rosaleen slumped back on the settee in despair. How could she help if May wouldn't listen to her?

'Rosaleen?'

May's head was buried in her hands and her voice was so low Rosaleen had to lean closer to hear it.

'Yes?'

'If I tell you what's wrong ... promise you won't laugh?'

'May, I never felt less like laughing in my life.'

Voice stronger now, she continued. 'Well, do you remember the night your da died?'

Rosaleen nodded. Would she ever forget?

'Well, there had been so many false alarms, we didn't bother trekking up to the fields. We stayed in the house ... in the coalhole.' May's head lifted and she turned to Rosaleen. 'It was awful, remember? Those whistling fire bombs.' Her eyes were vacant and her lips trembled as she relived the experience. Then, with an abrupt shake of the head, she continued, 'Well, the row of houses behind ours was hit. I'll never forget it ... it was awful. The screeching whistle ... the thud ... and then our house shook. I thought it was going to fall in on top of us. I was sure that we were all going to die ...' Her voice trailed off and Rosaleen sat silent, not wanting to interrupt the flow of May's words. She could picture the scene. The whistling bombs had been terrifying, even from afar, but it must have been awful to have been enclosed and one fall nearby.

May gave a grimace and continued, 'I kept thinking

214

of how I was living in sin, and the fact that Ian wasn't baptised . . . that tortured me, so it did.' Her head rose and she fixed Rosaleen with a shamefaced look. 'You must think me a right hypocrite.'

When Rosaleen shook her head and smiled sadly, denying May's accusation, she continued: 'Well . . . I was so worried, I promised God that I would put things right. And I really meant to . . . but, you see, when Billy and I discovered that we shared a lot of interests and he began to get serious about me . . . he asked me to make him a promise that I'd never badger him about bringing any children we had up in the Catholic faith.'

A harsh laugh left her lips as she thought of how naive she had been. Born in the shadow of Clonard Monastery, practically reared by the Redemptorist fathers, how could she have convinced herself that the church didn't matter to her?

'Anyhow, I promised. I vowed I would never mention the Catholic faith to Billy. And to tell you the truth, at that time I wasn't worried. I was actually amused and surprised when you said that you were worried about my soul. Everything in the garden was rosy, and I was glad to get away from me da.'

'May, why didn't you confide in me?' Rosaleen was reproachful. 'We're best friends.'

'Now, honestly, Rosaleen, tell the truth – do you tell me everything, hmmm?'

Sean's face rose before Rosaleen's mind and she was glad that dusk was falling and May could not see her blush, as she admitted, 'Well . . . not everything.'

'I thought so. Mind you, I don't blame you. When you're married . . . well, your husband comes first and you just don't talk as freely. The worst of it was we'd just heard that Billy's ex-wife was one of the people killed in Percy Street . . . remember the sixty victims? Well, she was one of those. He would have thought that I was

215

suddenly remorseful about the church because he was now free to marry me in it.' She shook her head. 'I couldn't break my promise, but at the same time I was uneasy. What if there was another raid? What if I died in a state of mortal sin?' She threw another wry smile at Rosaleen. 'Imagine! Me of all people worried about my soul. I didn't realise that at heart I was a staunch Catholic. I began to avoid Billy . . . you know what I mean.' A smile flitted across her face. 'I never had so many headaches in my life before. I think he thought I'd gone off him. That I fancied somebody else.'

At Rosaleen's start of surprise, May fixed her with an intent look and she found herself offering the information that Billy had indeed thought so. May's sigh was heartfelt. 'Poor Billy. Poor, poor Billy. He can't figure out what's wrong . . . but at least I put something right. Do you know what I did, Rosaleen?' She leant forward and held Rosaleen's eye. 'On the morning after the fire raid, I baptised Ian.'

'*You* baptised him?'

May laughed, and admitted, 'I can smile at the idea now, but at the time I was deadly serious. I was shaking like a leaf . . . afraid of not doing it properly. I nearly drowned the child . . . he screamed blue murder, so he did. If anyone had come in, they would have had me up for cruelty.'

'May!' Rosaleen found herself laughing softly at the idea. 'Ah, May.'

'Aye, I know. You may well laugh, but I kept thinking that if we were all to die in a raid, at least Ian would go to heaven with Billy, and I deserved to join aul Nick down below.' The look she gave Rosaleen was questioning. 'Rosaleen, truthfully now, have you ever wished that you'd been born a Protestant? I mean, if they do something wrong . . . but they don't realise it's wrong . . . well then, it's not a sin. But if we do something wrong, we're damned, if you see what I mean.'

Rosaleen nodded her head. 'I see what you mean, but no . . . I've never wanted to be a Protestant. But listen, May, you'll have to tell Billy the truth. You can't let him go to war thinking you don't care . . . thinking you fancy someone else. You just can't do it. When does he leave?'

'In two weeks' time, but I can't back down on my word, Rosaleen. I just can't.' May was adamant, and Rosaleen had to admit defeat.

Not that she had any intention of giving up. She hadn't made any promises, and just in case May got the idea of extracting one from her, she changed the subject.

'What about Ian? What's happening to him while Billy's away?'

'Billy's parents are moving to Newry. His aunt has a house there and they're taking Ian with them, until the war's over. I'm glad, Rosaleen. It's all for the best. I can't have him with me, what with me working. He's safer away from Belfast, and sure thousands of children are evacuated away from their parents. And this way . . . at least he's with his grandparents.'

A glance at the clock brought her to her feet. 'Look at the time. I've wasted your evening, but I'm glad I was up here when Billy called and not down in Spinner Street. I'd have hated him to go there. And it was good of you to leave us alone. Thanks, Rosaleen. Thanks for everything.'

Although it was a warm evening, Billy came through the gates of the Falls Flax, his step slow, shoulders hunched up around his ears as if from the cold. Rosaleen's heart went out to him, and when she hailed him and saw alarm fill his face, she felt like weeping. He hurried across the road and stopped in front of her, his eyes questioning.

'It's all right, Billy. Don't look so worried . . . May's

217

all right,' she hastened to assure him. 'Look, can we talk?'

'I'll walk you home.'

He fell into step beside her, his look still intent and questioning. All day she had been rehearsing what she would say to him, but now her mind was blank. She did not know where to start.

Suddenly, he smiled down at her. 'Well now, Rosaleen, I'm sure you didn't meet me just for the pleasure of my company. Is May well?'

'As well as can be expected.'

At once he stopped in his tracks and gripped his arm. 'What do you mean . . . as well as can be expected. Is she ill?'

'She's suffering from a broken heart, Billy.'

'Hah!' His head went back and he looked down the length of his nose at her. 'And just who's breaking her heart? Eh, Rosaleen?'

'Come off it, Billy. You know there's no one else.'

'Well then, what the hell's goin' on, Rosaleen?' he cried in exasperation.

Haltingly, she tried to explain May's change of heart towards her religion, how the blitz had brought home to her that she could die in mortal sin. To her surprise, Billy heard her out in silence and then shrugged his shoulders.

'So that's what was wrong. A big change of heart, eh? It wouldn't have had anything to do with the fact that my ex-wife was killed, I suppose?'

'No. That's why she didn't tell you. She said you'd think that.'

He shrugged these words aside. 'What about Ian, eh? She spent weeks away from him. Showed no interest whatsoever in his welfare. Our son . . . and she didn't give a shit whether he was alive or dead. Can she explain that away? Eh, Rosaleen? What has she to say about that?'

Deep dismay filled her. She had expected Billy to fall over himself to go to May, had pictured a happy reunion before he left for the army, but here he was deriding May.

'Billy, May dotes on that child! She's letting him stay with you because she knows that you can look after him better at present than she can. It will be different when the war's over. She'll want him back, and believe you me, she'll fight you tooth and nail for him. And another thing – May doesn't know that I'm here. I did this off my own bat. I thought I was doing the right thing. I thought you loved her . . .'

He interrupted her sadly. 'I do love her, Rosaleen, indeed I do, but, personally I believe Ian will be better off if I rear him alone. He'll have less hangups away from the Catholic faith. And as for getting married in the Catholic Church . . . no way. There's no way that I can do that. I made that clear to May before I married her and I haven't changed me mind. Ye see, Rosaleen, my da's in the Orange Order and it would break his heart if I married in the Catholic Church . . . he'd have to leave the order. I couldn't do that to him. I'm all they have and I've loved my parents longer than I've loved May. So, as far as I'm concerned, unless May comes back on my terms, which, after all, are what she agreed to in the first place, she needn't come back at all.'

In the face of such determination, Rosaleen was dismayed. She could only hope that May never heard about her attempt to win Billy back.

They had reached the corner of Springfield Avenue and she stopped and offered him her hand. She had allowed him to walk with her in this direction, picturing May maybe being on the dayshift and coming along, and she and Billy having a wonderful, happy reunion while she looked benignly on. Now she was afraid of May coming along and Billy sighting her. Why, May would never forgive her for interfering.

'I'm sorry, Billy. Seems I should have minded my own business. Sure you won't mention it to May, if you happen to be talking to her?'

He put his hands on her shoulders and kissed her on the cheek.

'Thanks, Rosaleen. Thanks for caring. But as you can see it's a hopeless case. Ye know, it's right what they say. You should stick with your own kind.'

Mackie's workers were starting to trickle down the Springfield Road and Rosaleen drew away from him.

'I'd better go now, Billy.' She nodded towards the workers. 'Just in case May comes along. God, but she'd never forgive me for interfering! So long, and safe home from the war.'

She hurried down Springfield Avenue and Billy watched her out of sight. Then, aware that he might see May if he waited, he walked down the road and sheltered in the doorway of Hughes Bakery.

At last he saw her approaching and drew back out of sight. She looked awful – thin and haggard, and she obviously wasn't bothering about keeping her hair blonde, the roots showed black for about four inches.

He examined her critically. She looked common. Common as muck. Was this what he was breaking his heart over? His lips tightened angrily. He must need his head examined. Even so, as she passed by, it took all his willpower to stop him from hailing her. After all, who was he to think anyone looked common? With a mug like his, he was in a position to criticise no one.

He waited until she had passed by, deep in conversation with Colin, and then he headed back up the Springfield Road, his thoughts in a whirl.

Rosaleen was right; he knew in his heart that May doted on Ian. She would put his welfare first, before her own feelings. It was unselfish of her to let him have the child. It would be only right to let her see him before he went to Newry. Yes, he would have to

220

arrange that. Even his mother thought his attitude towards May was hard. But then, she didn't understand. The next two weeks could not pass quickly enough for him. After that he wouldn't have time to brood. And if it wasn't for Ian, he wouldn't care whether or not he returned.

On Saturday morning Rosaleen was making her way down to the Post Office when May hailed her from the tram stop at the Falls Road junction.

'You're out early,' Rosaleen greeted her, and her eyes took in her friend's appearance. From the neat brown court shoes to the top of the pale, ash-blonde hair, she was pleased with what she saw. May had been letting herself go, but today she was back in form. Dressed in a dark blue suit and white blouse, with a beret tilted to one side on her head, she looked smart.

May waited until Rosaleen had finished her inspection and then jested: 'Well, do I meet with your approval?'

'You certainly do. You look smashing. Have you a date?'

May's eyes danced with laughter and she nodded her head.

Rosaleen was dismayed, she had been jesting, and May's smile broadened when she saw her friend's face drop.

'I've a date with a young lad called Ian,' she explained. 'Billy sent word in to work that if I liked – Imagine! If I liked – I could meet him in town to say goodbye to Ian. He's moving to Newry tomorrow.'

A smile of delight appeared on Rosaleen's face. 'I'm glad, May. Really pleased for you. I'm sure you're all excited.'

May grimaced, and confessed, 'I'm a bundle of nerves, so I am. I'm more worked up now than I was on my first date with Billy.'

221

Her eyes grew anxious. 'Do I look all right?'

'You look lovely. Billy's sure to be impressed,' Rosaleen assured her.

'Oh, here's the tram. I'd better run.' She gripped Rosaleen's arm. 'Say a wee prayer for me, won't you?'

'I will. And you let me know how you get on.'

'Oh, I will . . . I will. I'll come up the night and tell you about it.' She swung on to the platform of the tram and shouted over her shoulder, 'Bye for now.'

And she did come that night, subdued but happy. Billy had asked her to write to him while he was away and he had also arranged for his mother to keep in touch with her to let her know how Ian was progressing.

When she heard this news Rosaleen sent a thankful prayer heavenwards. There was hope for them yet.

Chapter 7

It was discovered that the damage to Harland and Wolff was not as bad as at first appeared. Although a vast number of the buildings and sheds at the shipyard were demolished, a number of important structures had survived the bombings. These included the power station, the building slips, and the pumping station, so although work was halted completely while unexploded bombs were hunted for and dealt with, urged on and supported by the ministry, work commenced building more ships much more quickly than expected. This was a blessing, taking hundreds off the outdoor relief, and as buildings were erected to house the homeless and accommodate the soldiers stationed in Belfast, more work still was available and unemployment fell dramatically.

Shorts and Harland also got off lighter than at first thought, and determined not to be caught with all their eggs in one basket again, spread their processes across Belfast and outlying districts.

The King's Hall at Barmoral was taken over for the making of fuselages and components, and aircraft wings were produced at Long Kesh. At Lambeg, a linen mill was converted and tail planes and flaps were made there. Sheetmetal pressings were made on the Newtownards Road, and all over the north other factories and buildings were converted and used as stores for supplies.

As work got underway in these places, unemployment, although not wiped out, was lower than it had been for many a year, and even Joe's small business flourished, obtaining plenty of orders for repairing houses that had been bombed but were sound enough for repairs.

Proud and happy, Owen Black approached Rosaleen to ask her opinion about taking on a man to help him and someone to look after the yard and take orders while he was busy. He emphasised the fact that his wife would take on the job of looking after the yard if she didn't have the kids to worry about, and Rosaleen realised that, in a roundabout way, he was suggesting she look after it. She turned the idea over in her mind.

Why not? She wasn't stupid; she could answer the phone, write down orders . . . she could even, with a bit of tutoring, do the books. And Amy was always willing to look after her beloved granddaughter.

Owen gave a nod of approval when she offered to look after the yard four mornings a week, and soon Rosaleen was caught up in the running of the business while the months slipped away unnoticed. The sirens were going off less frequently as Hitler's assaults on the west coast of England had decreased. The reason given for this was his decision to break his pact with Russia and launch an attack on them. However, to their surprise, the Germans were encountering far more opposition than they had bargained on from the Russians, and the planes that had formerly blitzed the west coast of England and the east coast of Northern Ireland were now turned on Russia.

The Russians, once regarded as those terrible communists, those awful reds, were suddenly regarded by all as gallant allies, calling forth praise from all sides, as they put up a fierce battle against Hitler.

And then, the day everyone was praying for – the day America entered the war. It was the Japanese bombing of Pearl Harbor on December 7th 1941 that caused America to join the fight against the Germans, and everyone was convinced that with their help, the fighting would not last much longer.

With hope of an early end to the war and the long lull, free from air-raids, the refugees started drifting back from the countryside. With plenty of jobs going, the people of Belfast were better off than they had been for many years, and this in spite of shortages and rationing. In the midst of war and ruin, the ordinary, poor people of Belfast never had it so good; never before had wages been so high.

The I.R.A., although still fighting fiercely against De Valera's government in the south, had been dormant for some time in the north, and in spite of constant fear of air-raids, peace reigned in Belfast itself.

This was not to last. To the surprise of all, America chose Northern Ireland as their base from which to launch an attack on Hitler's Europe. On January 16th 1942, welcomed by the Governor, the Duke of Abercorn, and the Prime Minister, the Americans landed on Irish soil. They disembarked on Dufferin Quay to the strains of 'The Star Spangled Banner' and the cheers of the crowds who had gathered, although their arrival was supposed to be a well-kept secret.

The Yanks brought with them Hershey bars and comics for the children, silk stockings and charm that would have put the Blarney Stone to shame for the young women.

The girls of Belfast lapped it all up, surging in their hundreds down to the Plaza Ballroom every night. The Catholics, not wanting to miss anything, ignored warnings from the pulpit that they were in danger of losing their immortal souls and joined the throngs.

The arrival of the Americans also galvanised the I.R.A. into action again, as they strove to show the Yanks how powerful they were.

In St Paul's parish heartbreak was to result because of this.

On Easter Sunday, a few short months after the arrival of the Americans, Constable Murphy of the R.U.C. force was shot dead. Rosaleen was on her way home from visiting her mother, coming down the Springfield Road with Laura by the hand, when it happened and all hell broke loose. First there was a great surge of people and Rosaleen thought, My, but the road's busy, so it is! And everybody's in a terrible hurry. Then premonition filled her with terror, turning her legs to stone as police cars screeched past and turned down Oranmore Street. She stood rooted to the spot, unable to move, Laura's head pressed protectively against her body as the crack of gunshots pierced her ears.

Then some man, a stranger to her, gathered Laura up in his arms and urged Rosaleen down Springfield Avenue. He knocked on a door and when it opened tentatively, pushed it roughly ajar and quickly thrust her inside, pushing Laura after her. She gripped her child close, he was gone, and the door was closed.

Rosaleen and the man of the house gazed at each other. His face was familiar to her, and she realised that she probably saw him at mass on Sundays.

Now she apologised. 'I'm sorry, I have no right to be here . . .'

'Never mind, missus . . . never you mind. Sure, you're welcome to stay 'til the shootin' stops. Do you know what's goin' on?'

Mutely, she shook her head, then voiced her impression of where the shooting was. 'It's in one of those streets off Oranmore Street . . . maybe . . . Cawnpore Street.'

'Come in and sit down, missus. I think you'll be here for a while.'

With these words the man led the way into the living room and they joined his wife and young daughter at the fireside.

'Maura!' Laura greeted the girl with delight, and Rosaleen recognised the child as one who sometimes played with her daughter when they visited the Dunville Park. She also recognised the woman of the house and nodded in her direction, and everybody relaxed as Laura was led away to see Maura's toys. Now that the man realised that they were practically neighbours, he introduced himself as Bill Hanna and his wife as Rose. After all, one had to be careful. One never knew to whom one was talking. Now their conversation centred around the shooting.

'After all these months of peace,' Rosaleen lamented. Then, realising how absurd this sounded considering that they were at war with Germany, she added with a wry grimace, 'You know what I mean.'

With a laugh, Bill agreed with her. 'You're right! I know what you mean.' And Rose smiled and nodded to show that she too understood.

'As if we hadn't enough to worry about,' Bill continued. 'Sure they're just showing off. Putting on a show for the Americans, that's what they're doing. The bloody fools!'

The shooting was long over before Bill judged it safe to allow Rosaleen to venture out, and she hurried down Springfield Avenue and arrived in Iris Drive to find a distraught Amy waiting at the door for her.

'Oh, thank God you're safe! I was worried stiff about you, so I was. I knew you'd be returning home about the time the shooting started.'

Rosaleen recounted her experiences, bringing gasps of concern and dismay from Amy, and asked, 'Have you heard anything about it?'

227

'Just a rumour on the grapevine that someone's been killed. A policeman!'

'Oh, sweet Jesus.' Rosaleen bowed her head in reverence when she took the holy name in vain. 'You know what that means. More retaliations . . . more innocent people suffering for things that they have no control over. You'd think the I.R.A. would catch itself on, now that there's plenty of work for everybody,' she said, and gaped in surprise when Amy retorted: 'It's all right you saying that, Rosaleen. But you were too young to realise how bad it was during the 1920s. It was awful then . . . you ask your mam. She'll tell you how bad it was. Then the I.R.A. was all we had between us and the Black and Tans, and those bloody "B" Specials picked up a thing or two from the B&Ts, and if anything they're worse now.'

It was the first time Rosaleen had heard Amy volunteer an opinion on something as touchy as the I.R.A., and she found herself apologising.

'I'm sorry. It's just that things have been going so well, in spite of the war . . . or should I say because of the war?' And she smiled tentatively at Amy who, appeased, shared the smile. The I.R.A. were not mentioned again.

On Easter Monday morning it was May who called and brought Rosaleen the news that a policeman had been shot dead, and that six young I.R.A. volunteers had been arrested and charged with his murder. It was alleged that they had fired on a police car, and when chased had sought refuge in Cawnpore Street. In the gun battle that followed, the young constable lost his life.

'Do you know any of them?' she asked May apprehensively.

'No . . . our Kevin went to school with two of them. Their families must be in an awful state, so they must. It's awful. They're only kids.'

When she heard their names Rosaleen realised that she knew some of their families and her heart bled for them. It was awful to think that your child could bring such sorrow to your door. She agreed with May; they really were just youngsters, five boys and a girl, all gullible fools, and they all but one belonged to St Paul's parish.

There wasn't a dry eye in church the following Sunday when the priest prayed for the widow and children of the young constable, who was also a member of the parish. He then prayed for the families of the six who now stood accused of his murder. He went on to say that it was an act of folly for the youngsters to fire on a police car, and that those who had given them the firearms and sent them out on such a mission had a lot to answer for.

'Remember, "Thou shalt not kill!" is one of the commandments of God and must be obeyed!' he thundered from the pulpit.

Once more Belfast was put under curfew, and the streets were patrolled by armoured cars and 'cage' lorries. While on foot, patrols of the 'B' Specials strutted about, displaying their guns, egging the I.R.A. on.

To everyone's horror, the six young offenders were condemned to die and the I.R.A. retaliated with assaults on British army barracks and police stations, bringing misery and unrest once more to the streets of Belfast. The attacks only led to more and more arrests and the worst activists were either sentenced or interned in Crumlin Road Jail. Meanwhile, petitions were got up begging for mercy for the six young offenders. The Eire government took the matter to heart, and in Dublin a petition was launched and over 200,000 signatures collected. The American, Canadian and British Ambassadors in Eire added their voice in support of the plea for clemency.

The British government wanted the six to hang as a deterrent to the I.R.A. during the remainder of the war, but with so many crying out for mercy, the sentences were commuted except for one young man. (An eye for an eye?) Tom Williams, from Bombay Street, was hanged in Crumlin Road Jail on September 2nd. It was a day of terrible depression, and black flags were flown from many windows. All day long prayers were offered up for the repose of his soul, and people lamented, 'It's the ones who gave them the guns that should hang!'

However, the Falls Road was used to these atrocities and once more the burden was shouldered and life went on as normally as the curfew would allow.

The curfew from 10 p.m. to 6 a.m. was always a curse, but as far as Rosaleen was concerned, it spoilt her life. Saturday night was her night out with either May or Annie (whoever happened to be on the right shift) and they went to the pictures. With the curfew starting at ten, there was only one show nightly and this began at half-past six or seven. It also meant that it was crowded and they had to go early and queue up, no matter what the weather was like. Then the show was over at half-past eight or nine and with being home so early, it spoilt the night out. She felt as if she had not been out at all.

Mostly they frequented the Broadway Picture House, further up the Falls Road, which was quiet and respectable, but sometimes they were lured to the Clonard Picture House by reports of a good film. The crowds that went to the Clonard every night were rough and ready, and although they went to the stalls, Rosaleen never felt comfortable there. She was not amused when May and Annie teased her, calling her a snob; remarking that they all came from the same district. Sometimes they even suggested that they go to the Diamond Picture House, which was down the Falls

Road on the corner of Cupar Street and was nicknamed the 'flea pit', falling about laughing at her outraged dignity when she refused.

The rest of 1942 dragged on, and she had no idea where Joe was. She received his letters via the ministry and it broke her heart to read them. May was in the same boat as her as far as Billy was concerned, but Rosaleen was pleased to note that when she did receive letters, May was all sentimental and happy. Hopefully things would work out for them. As promised, Mrs Mercer sent her news of Ian, and May had even made one flying visit to Newry to see him.

Sean fared better than Joe and Billy. Being in the Merchant Navy, he managed to get a forty-eight- or thirty-six-hour pass each time the ship was in a convenient port loading cargo so at least Annie was happy, and how Rosaleen and May envied her.

Although at the beginning of 1943 Hitler's bombers had still not returned to Ireland, the war still raged in Europe and Rosaleen wondered why everybody had been so keen for America to join the fight against Hitler. They had been fighting over a year now and still there was no sign that the war would end in the near future, and many a heart was broken as the girls who were foolish enough to take the Yanks seriously, learnt to their cost how silly they were.

Easter Saturday saw Rosaleen, Annie and May all together for a change, due to the Easter holidays, at the Broadway Picture House. They queued up outside for half an hour and then settled down to enjoy the film: a musical, starring Betty Grable. Each had used some of their precious sweet coupons on a quarter of a pound of their favourite confectionery and when the lights went out and the film whirred to life, they wriggled down in comfort and sighed contentedly.

They were sitting in the back stalls and as the film progressed gradually became aware that there was a disturbance in the front stalls, near the screen. Then the lights went up, and to their amazement they saw that two armed men had the staff gathered together and were holding them at gun point.

Someone behind Rosaleen whispered, 'Oh, dear God . . . it's Hugh McAteer. Ye know . . . him that escaped from the Crumlin Road Jail a couple of months ago. And that's Steele with him.'

Only then did she realise that it was two I.R.A. men, and fear made her heart bang against her ribs. Four had escaped . . . were the other two behind them? A swift glance over her shoulder reassured her that the space at the back was empty.

What did they want? Was there anybody important in the audience? Were they going to shoot someone? She was not left in doubt for long as the two men forced the audience to take part in an Easter commemoration for 'The dead who died for Ireland'.

In the silence that followed, Annie and May exchanged worried glances with Rosaleen. They were only too aware that if anyone tried to apprehend the fugitives, blood would be shed. The men appeared nervous and it was awful to think of shaky fingers on the triggers of guns. They prayed that no one was foolish enough to do anything provocative.

After the short silence, when the men thanked them for their co-operation and left the cinema, everyone breathed a sigh of relief and burst out into excited conversation. This was brought to a halt by an agitated manager announcing in a shaky voice that the film would continue immediately. Then the lights went out and the film recommenced.

Later, as they sat in the ice-cream parlour at Broadway, eating sundaes, they expressed worried thoughts that Easter Sunday might once again bring trouble. 1941 had brought the blitz, 1942 the shooting of the policeman, and now this display in the

Broadway tonight. Was anything else planned to stir up the troubles over the holiday?

To their relief, the rest of the Easter holiday, at least in St Paul's district, passed without incident, and later in the year they read in the *Irish News* about the recapture of McAteer and Steele.

By the end of 1943 it was estimated that there were 100,000 American troops in the province. Rosaleen's mind baulked at the thought of so many (where on earth did they all stay?) but the newspapers quoted that number, so it must be right.

On her outings to town with Annie, she could well understand the young girls being bowled over by the Yanks. Unlike the Irishmen, the Americans showed their appreciation of a pretty girl. Wolf whistles followed them everywhere, and she and Annie could have had dates galore if they had been that way inclined.

The Yanks were also a great source of money, being open-handed and ready to spend, and the shops and places of entertainment never had it so good. In 1944, when they were moved to England to prepare for D-Day, Belfast seemed empty and dull and many a girl shed tears.

It was apparent that the war was on the wane when it became common knowledge that the anti-aircraft guns around Belfast had been dismantled and the barrage balloons around Northern Ireland withdrawn. And when the British Air Ministry removed Northern Ireland's allocation of night-fighters, it seemed certain that the Germans would soon be defeated. Joe, Sean and Billy should be home soon.

It was amidst this feeling of well-being that the dreaded yellow telegram arrived at Rosaleen's door.

Amy was with her the day she received it; she had witnessed others receive one and had prayed that her turn would never come, but now it had. With hands that shook, she tore it open, but was dismayed to find that her eyes would not focus on the typescript.

As she stood gazing blindly at it, Amy gently took the slip of paper from her hands, and in a voice that shook, read aloud the printed message.

' "We are sorry to inform you that Private Joseph Smith has been wounded in action. Letter to follow with further details." '

'He's alive, Rosaleen. Thank God, he's alive.'

'Thanks be to God,' Rosaleen whispered, and then they were crying in each other's arms.

It was two long drawn-out weeks later that the promised letter at last arrived. In it she was informed that in one week's time, Joe would be in Belfast, but that he would be taken direct to the Royal Victoria Hospital as he required further treatment for his wounds.

Full of apprehension, Rosaleen and Amy reported to the hospital the day that Joe was due to arrive. At the reception desk they were directed to a ward and then a young nurse escorted them to Joe's bedside. Rosaleen warned herself to try to appear normal as shock registered at the sight of him. His face was grey and gaunt and he looked like a tired old man.

She heard Amy's intake of breath, and bent to kiss Joe to block out the dismay on his mother's face and give her a chance to get her features under control.

'How do you feel, love?'

As she spoke, her eyes ranged over the bed and relief flooded through her when she observed that he had all his limbs.

For the past three weeks she had been tortured by thoughts of Joe legless or armless, but although he was worn and ill-looking, he was at least whole.

'A lot better . . . now I'm home.' He lifted her hand to his face and held it against his cheek. 'I'm so glad to be home, Rosaleen. I could never, ever explain to you how glad I am.'

Holding his other skeletal hand out to his mother, he said, 'Don't look so worried, Mam. I'm going to be all right.'

Having regained her composure, Amy quickly agreed with him.

'Of course you are, son. We'll soon have you back on your feet. Won't we, Rosaleen?'

Mutely she nodded and smiled through her tears. She was glad when the nurse told her that the doctor wanted to speak to her; glad to escape from this skeleton with dark orbs sunk far back in his head. After the shock of his appearance, she needed a breathing space to get a grip on her emotions. When she entered the doctor's office, he rose to his feet, offered her his hand and introduced himself. She acknowledged his introduction with a nod of her head and then he motioned for her to take a seat.

'Your husband is a very sick man, Mrs Smith,' he said, and his voice and face were grave.

'I can see that!' Rosaleen answered sharply. Did they think that she was blind? 'Is he going to recover?'

'Well . . . let me explain. Joseph had a lot of shrapnel in his body. So far he has undergone surgery four times. All successful . . . but each operation takes a lot out of him. There are still two pieces to remove. One we'll remove when he has regained his strength from the last operation, but the other piece we can't touch. It's lodged close to his heart, too close for surgery.'

'Does that mean he's going to die?' Rosaleen asked fearfully, dismay in her heart. Her voice was shrill and she saw the doctor's eyes narrow.

'Are you feeling all right, Mrs Smith?' he asked solicitously.

Inwardly, Rosaleen fumed. Why didn't he just come out and tell her the truth? Not keep her on edge like this!

'I'm all right. Tell me! Is he going to die?' she insisted.

'No. At least, we don't think so. It's like this . . . we have experienced casees like this before, and most times the patient has lived to a ripe old age. However, some patients have died young. We shall keep an eye on Joseph, and if the shrapnel moves away from his heart, we will operate. Meanwhile, once we operate on his leg, he can go home and live as normal a life as possible.'

Rosaleen wanted to question him, ask what would happen if the shrapnel moved towards Joe's heart, but she held her tongue. After all, didn't she already know the answer to that?

It was a further three months before Joe was allowed home from hospital, and when all the well-wishers who had gathered to welcome him home had departed, he lay back on the settee, drained and tired, but happy.

'You know something, Rosaleen? I never thought that I would survive the war. It's great to be home . . . and soon I'll be able to go back to work. I'm proud of the way you've been helping Owen to keep the business going.'

'It'll be a while yet, love, before you're able to work,' she said, as she tucked a blanket around him. 'A long time. But the work's still rolling in. We'll never be rich, Joe, but if things keep on the way they're going, we'll never want, either.'

'What's the new man like, Rosaleen? Tell me about him. Is he handsome?'

Rosaleen looked at him in amazement at these words. What difference did it make whether or not the new man was handsome?

'He's nice . . . quiet, and a good worker. He has two children and another on the way.'

Joe sighed with relief. The new man was married. He could relax.

Thoughts of children made Rosaleen sad. Laura was now five, and she longed to give her a sister or brother.

Joe had been through so much, had spent such a long time in hospital, would he ever want to go see about his problem? She doubted it very much.

By the autumn of 1944, Joe was back at work, looking pale and frail, but except for the recurring nightmares, he seemed to be slowly making a full recovery. To be truthful, he wasn't able to do much work, just got in the way, but it pleased him to potter about, sort nails into different boxes, plane pieces of wood, and Rosaleen didn't mind – he was company for her when Owen and Andy, the new man, were out on jobs.

He attended the hospital once a month, but so far the shrapnel near his heart remained lodged in the same spot and the doctors were inclined to think that it was there for good, and once more assured Rosaleen that her husband would probably live to a ripe old age.

By the end of 1944, he was more or less back to normal but still pitifully thin, and Rosaleen had become aware that the reason he attended the yard each day was to keep an eye on her. It wasn't that he felt able for work. No, it was jealousy that brought him down to the yard each day. His jealousy was becoming overbearing.

He was full of plans for after the war; plans to build a house on the Upper Falls Road, a house with a garden for Laura to play in. When he had first arrived home from hospital, Rosaleen had settled him in the back bedroom, using the excuse that he needed a bed to himself for a while.

She could see that he didn't agree with her, but in the months that followed, after a few unsuccessful attempts at love making, he bothered her no more and they lived as brother and sister. Rosaleen refrained from pestering him to go and see a specialist, hoping that as his health improved he would suggest going himself, but she waited in vain.

Billy was invalided out of the army early in 1945, and Rosaleen was not surprised when May confided in

237

her that they were going out to Canada. Billy had two uncles out there and if they liked it, they were going to settle.

'I'm happy for you, May, but I'll miss you,' she wailed, as she pictured the lonely life ahead of her. May was her only chance of a night away from Joe. He was so possessive and jealous, and only her nights out with her friend and her rare outings with Annie kept her sane.

'Listen, Rosaleen.' May was only too aware of Joe's jealousy. 'You keep on going out. Do you hear me? Get Amy to go to the Broadway with you every week.'

Rosaleen had to smile at this idea. Amy was being courted by Bobby Mackay and had very little time to spare.

May saw the smile and realised at once the cause of it. 'Oh, I forgot. Any word of a wedding yet?'

Sadly, Rosaleen shook her head. 'No. I think she's letting Joe influence her. He doesn't like Bobby.'

May's face grimaced in disbelief and she cried, 'Doesn't like Bobby? Sure, you couldn't dislike Bobby if you tried. He's a wonderful person, and so good. Joe needs his head examined,' she finished in disgust.

'I think Joe's jealous of him. You see, he has always been the only one in Amy's life and he doesn't like coming second. And there's no doubt about it . . . Bobby comes first with Amy now. She'd be mad at me for saying so, but she's like a teenager in love.'

'And why shouldn't she, eh? Why shouldn't she? She's been a widow a long time. Joe should be glad that she has met someone to keep her company in her old age. Not that she's all that old! She can't be fifty yet.'

'No, forty-seven! She must have married young. I'm surprised that she never remarried. She's a fine-looking woman . . . must have been a beauty in her day.'

'Aye, indeed. Anyhow, Rosaleen, it'll be a while before I go, so let's not worry until we have to.'

As usual, May had underestimated Billy. Once he got

238

an idea into his head he neither stopped nor stayed until all arrangements were made, and soon Rosaleen was wishing May a tearful farewell.

'You'll write, won't you, Rosaleen?'

'Of course I will.'

'And if we like Canada and decide to stay after the war . . .' May's head swivelled to where Joe stood with Billy. 'Joe . . . after the war . . . you'll bring her to visit us, won't you?'

'That's a promise, May. I'll bring her out to visit you. I've always wanted to see Canada and America,' he assured her and, bathed in tears, May allowed Billy to propel her towards the customs, to enter the plane.

May's departure left a great gap in Rosaleen's life. With Annie being on shifts, she saw little of her, and her mother had got herself a part-time job in Mackie's Foundry. Four mornings a week she packed ammunition into cartons. Rosaleen was glad to see her filling out, see a bit of colour return to her cheeks, but they could not get her to go out and enjoy herself. Once home from work, she remained indoors and brooded.

To Rosaleen's surprise, Amy volunteered to accompany her to the pictures once a week.

'Ah, Amy . . . I don't want to come between you and Bobby.'

Hot colour rushed to her face and Rosaleen thought how lovely she looked. Why had she never remarried? Unthinkingly, she voiced the question.

'Amy . . . why did you never get married again? I'm sure you must have had plenty of chances.'

'Oh, yes . . . they were queuing up, so they were,' Amy jested. 'Look, Rosaleen, Bobby won't mind. In fact, he'd be only too pleased to accompany us. So how's about it, eh?'

'Thanks, Amy. It's kind of you to think of me. To tell you the truth, I need to get out on my own, now and again.'

239

'I know you do, love. I know you do. So come round to my house on Saturday night at six sharp and we'll go down to the Classic.'

'Oh, how lovely. I haven't been in the Classic for years.'

Amy smiled at her, glad to see the despair lift, if only momentarily.

If Joe wasn't careful, his jealousy would drive them apart. She knew just how obsessive his jealousy could be. Hadn't he ruled her life until Bobby came on the scene?

In his heart, Joe had been relieved to see May go to Canada. She was a bad influence on Rosaleen, expecting her to go to the pictures with her every Saturday night. Now Rosaleen would stay at home at the week-ends, keep him company. So anger was in his heart as he watched her prepare for her night out with Amy and Bobby. What on earth did his mother see in that man? She was making a fool of herself and every opportunity he got, Joe told her so. Now he chastised his wife.

'You know, Rosaleen, you shouldn't encourage me mam to go out with Bobby Mackay.'

'Why not?'

Rosaleen's voice was reasonable, she had no intentions of agreeing with Joe about Bobby. He was a wonderful man and he adored Amy.

'Because she's too old for that kind of thing.'

'What kind of thing? Bobby treats her like a lady, and I think that if you would unbend a little . . . we could soon be hearing wedding bells.'

'Good God! You don't think she'd really consider marrying him, do you?'

'Why not? They're both old enough to know their own minds! I think they make a lovely couple. Just what have you got against Bobby? Eh?'

240

Rosaleen frowned at Joe and his lips tightened as he glared back at her. 'Nothing . . . so long as he keeps out of my way.'

Rosaleen shrugged and refused to be drawn into an argument. Putting the finishing touches to her make-up, she put on her coat. 'I'm off . . . see you later.'

The film in the Classic Picture House in the centre of town was a comedy, and as they left the theatre after the show they were all relaxed and happy.

It was a lovely, warm night and Bobby suggested that they walk home and call into Victor's in Divis Street for some ice-cream. As she walked along, licking away at her ice-cream cone, Rosaleen remembered the night that Sean had walked her home from the Club Orchid. Thoughts of the events at the Dam returned to haunt her and sadness enveloped her. If only she had been wiser, how different her life might have been.

When they arrived at her corner, she invited them in for a cup of tea. At once Amy demurred, but Bobby gently over-ruled her.

'A cup of tea sounds lovely, Rosaleen.' He turned courteously to Amy. 'Do you not fancy a cup of tea?'

She gazed at him, and whatever she read in his eyes caused her to change her mind.

'Why not . . . why not indeed?'

The expression on Joe's face when Bobby entered the room made Rosaleen seethe with anger, and the look she threw him stopped the protest that hovered on his lips. He acknowledged Bobby with an abrupt nod.

'Your mam and Bobby have come in for a cup of tea, Joe. Would you like one?' she asked him, and even to her own ears her voice sounded false. She hated him for placing her in a position where she had to playact. They eyed each other but Joe found that even to please her he could not make 'that man' welcome in his home, so rising to his feet he headed for the stairs.

'No, thank you. I was just about to retire. Goodnight.'

As the door closed on him Rosaleen turned to Bobby. 'I'm sorry . . . I'll make the tea.'

He reached out and caught her by the arm as she passed him on her way to the kitchen.

'Hey now, don't you be upset. He's a sick man, Rosaleen. I keep telling Amy that we'll have to wear him down. So just keep inviting me in and let me do the rest, O.K.?'

Rosaleen looked at the big, long face that still seemed sorrowful even when he was smiling. He had been so good to her since her dad's death that it hurt her deeply that Joe should slight him; now she nodded, she would do as he asked.

'I'll make a pot of tea and we'll enjoy it,' she vowed, 'even if it chokes us.' And they all laughed at the idea.

When they had departed, Rosaleen climbed the stairs two at a time and burst into Joe's room without knocking. He was sitting up in bed reading a book and the look he gave her was venomous.

'Don't you ever again treat a friend of mine like that. Do you hear me?' she hissed at him.

'You're forgetting that this is my house, and I'll treat people any way I like in it,' he hissed back at her.

'Oh, yes? Well, the next time you let me down, in *my* home . . . remember it's your house, but I have to live here . . . I'll leave you. And that's a promise!'

With these words she left the room and it was a long time before she got control of her temper.

The next day she made a point of calling in to see Amy when she knew that she would be alone.

'I came to apologise, Amy. What Joe did was unforgivable.'

'Bobby didn't take offence . . . he's not like that. He could find excuses for Aul Nick himself. He's a wonderful person, Rosaleen.'

'I know that, Amy. That's why I can't understand

242

Joe's attitude.'

Amy eyed her and gave a long drawn-out sigh. 'Sit down, Rosaleen. I think it's about time I explained something to you.'

Mystified, Rosaleen sat down on the settee beside Amy and eyed her questioningly.

A grimace crossed Amy's face and her voice shook.

'This isn't easy for me to talk about. I'm not proud of my actions . . . my only excuse is that I was very young when it happened.'

Rosaleen sat silent, watching her gravely.

'You see, Rosaleen . . . I've never been married.'

She felt her jaw drop, and gulped to close it. Amy had never been married? That meant that Joe was . . .

As if she had followed her thoughts, step by step. Amy nodded sadly.

'Yes, that's right. Joe's illegitimate.'

Unable to think of anything to say, Rosaleen just repeated, 'Illegitimate?'

'Yes. That's why he's so bitter towards me. Why I let him rule my life for so long. But not any more. I told Bobby about my past and he advised me to tell you. Really I should have told you sooner, but I was embarrassed and ashamed.'

'No, Amy. There's no reason why you should have confided in me. Your past is your own business . . . it has nothing to do with me,' Rosaleen assured her.

'It would have helped you to understand Joe better had you known, but you see . . . he didn't want you to know.'

Rosaleen's face was a picture of confusion and Amy explained: 'To Joe it was a terrible stigma. And it is a stigma . . . I know that, but Joe took it even more to heart than others. It was my fault. I should have told him when he was young, but I kept putting it off. You see, when I was expecting him, I moved here to be near our Belle. You know, Bill Murry's mam? It was near the end of the '14-'18 war and everybody thought that I was a war widow, so I didn't enlighten them. There were a lot of young pregnant war widows about, and I was only too glad to hide my shame. The man I was in love with got me this house to rent.' Her voice became bitter. 'Payment for favours received!'

She sat silent for some moments and Rosaleen's heart went out to her. She heard herself whisper, 'What about your parents?'

'They were both dead, and our Belle did not want to advertise that I was a fallen woman so she encouraged the widow idea.' She looked Rosaleen in the eye and laughed. 'It got to the stage where I nearly believed I was a grieving widow. I was grieving all right.'

Once more her voice trailed off and Rosaleen gripped her arm. 'Amy, don't torture yourself opening old wounds . . . I don't need to know!'

'It's all right, Rosaleen, I want you to know.' And she continued, 'I led Joe to believe that his father had died when he was a baby, and when he started school I was glad that I had. You see, kids are cruel. There was one young lad who was illegitimate and the other youngsters tortured him about not having a father, so I kept up the pretence. It was such a shock to Joe when he found out.'

'How did he find out? Who told him?'

Rosaleen could imagine just how shocked Joe had been. He was so strait-laced; forgiveness would not have come easy to him. Poor Amy! She was even more dismayed when Amy continued her story.

'He found out when he tried to enter the ministry. You see, from when he was no age he wanted to become a priest.' Seeing Rosaleen's mouth gape open, she asked, 'He never told you that he once wanted to be a priest?' Her eyes rounded in disbelief.

'No . . . never.'

'Ah, Rosaleen . . . Well, I was over the moon. My

soon a priest? I couldn't believe it. I never dreamed it would matter that he had been born out of wedlock, but it did.' She paused to wipe away the tear that had trickled down her cheek and then wailed, 'It was awful. He was accepted and all, and so happy, and then they asked for his birth certificate.' She grimaced at Rosaleen before continuing, 'It shows you how thick I am. Even then, I didn't think it would make any difference. I was worried about what Joe would think, but I thought that he would be understanding. But the minute Joe saw it, he knew. He knew it would prevent him from entering the priesthood. He went berserk! Would not speak or eat. This went on for some time and I was in despair. And then, he started speaking to me, but it was as if the episode had never happened. The priesthood was never mentioned again, and when he met you and you agreed to marry him, he made me promise never to tell you. I thought that you must know. When you were married, you must have seen the birth certificate . . .'

At her look askance, Rosaleen shook her head. 'Joe attended to all that.'

So many conflicting emotions were fighting for control of Amy's features, Rosaleen clasped her arm tightly.

 'Don't torture yourself. Please, Amy, don't.'

Her heart was breaking at the thought of how Joe had kept his mother at arm's length all these years. How could he? How could he have been so cruel?

'He made me promise that I'd tell no one . . . but Bobby said he was wrong to extract a promise like that from me. He said that you had the right to know.'

'Is his father still alive?'

'Oh, no. He died when Joe was about ten. He left some money in his will . . . that's how Joe was able to start his own business.' She turned and looked Rosaleen full in the face. 'This may seem strange to you, but Thomas was a good man. It was just that he had so many commitments, and when I became pregnant . . . he couldn't leave his wife.' She smiled wryly at Rosaleen's start of surprise. 'That's right! He was a married man. A prominent figure in the church. The scandal would have ruined so many lives. I was very bitter at the time but I agreed to move away from the district, and as a reward Thomas granted me a small allowance so that I need never want. I wasn't quite seventeen and I loved Thomas dearly . . .' Her voice trailed off and Rosaleen moved closer and took her in her arms.

'I'm sorry, Amy. I'm so sorry for you.'

'That's life, Rosaleen. I've never wanted to marry. Joe was my life and I was so happy when he met you. I'm glad you're my daughter-in-law. However, I'm very fond of Bobby and I'll not let Joe spoil it for me.'

'I should think not! We'll do as Bobby says and wear him down. Eh, Amy?'

She smiled and they nodded at each other, but neither was very hopeful of success.

The long anticipated victory in Europe caused a festive air as the people of Belfast waited for the government to specify which day the celebrations would be held. In due course May 8th was named as a day of festivities to celebrate the Allied victory in Europe, V. E. day! The crowds went wild in the streets, and for the first time in six years the sky was aglow with lights from the bonfires. Buntings were strung across the streets, drums were beaten, and effigies of Hitler were burnt or strung up on lampposts.

On the 8th no work was done, and Joe and Rosaleen took Laura with them and joined the throngs that were heading for the City Hall to hear Churchill's speech relayed over the air by loudspeakers.

At three o'clock, everyone stood silent as he gave

details of the German capitulation. When he had finished, the city rang with cheers. Then the church bells rang out loud and clear, and the factory horns blared in accompaniment, while bin lids were rattled to add to the din. Hoarse but excited they returned home for dinner, but that night they were there again to witness the floodlighting of the City Hall for the first time in six years, and to join in the singing and dancing in the town centre.

It was late when they made their way to where Joe had parked the works van. Laura was asleep in his arms and he placed her on the floor of the van, rolled up his coat as a pillow for her head, and with Rosaleen in the cab beside him, drove slowly and carefully home so as not to jar the sleeping child.

The feeling of well-being persisted as Joe rekindled the fire and Rosaleen put Laura to bed. Afterwards, as she prepared a light supper, her thoughts turned to the future. The war was over and Joe was making good progress. Surely now she could broach the subject of more children without making him huffy or angry?

She could but try; she owed it to Laura to attempt to give her a sister or brother before she got much older.

With this thought in mind, she eyed Joe covertly as he ate the sandwiches she had made. He still looked frail, but contented and happy. When they had finished eating she retired to the kitchen to wash the cups and plates, all the while going over in her mind the things she would say; how she would broach the subject.

Returning to the living room, she sat on the floor beside Joe's chair and rested her head against his knee. He had an appointment at the hospital on Friday. Surely he was well enough to ask for advice about his problem? She was ashamed of the way she had settled him in the back room when he arrived home from hospital, using the same excuse he had offered her

247

when she was pregnant with Laura: that he needed a bed to himself for a while. At the time she had felt justified in what she was doing, and when he needed her she was always out of bed and in with him, the minute he had one of his nightmares, to hold him close until it passed and he slept again. But she could not bear to lie beside him night after night, frustrated and unhappy. Now, with the war virtually over, she felt uneasiness about the future. She wanted a full married life, but Joe seemed content with things as they were. After the few unsuccessful attempts at love making he had tried no more, and seemed content for them to live like brother and sister. However, she must make it plain to him that she wanted more out of life than a house up the Falls; that she didn't want the chains of jealousy to tie her to the home. She must make it plain to him that she wanted more children.

She pressed closer. Surprised, Joe placed his arm across her shoulders and drew her between his knees, his hand ruffling her hair.

It was a long time since she had shown any open affection towards him, and he was not fooled, he could guess what was on her mind.

'Joe . . .' Her voice trailed off. How should she phrase it?

'It's all right, Rosaleen. I know what you're going to say.'

Her head twisted round and she looked at him with brows raised inquiringly. He answered her look. 'You want me to go and see about myself, don't you?'

She laughed softly. 'How did you know what I was thinking? Are you psychic?'

He sank his face down against the silky softness of her hair, breathing in the sweet perfume of it.

'I think it's the relief that the war's over at last. Tonight, I bet everybody's making plans for the future . . . so why not you?'

'Yes, and . . .'

He interrupted her. 'Let me finish. Yes, I do intend seeing about myself. I promised you I would, and I'll keep my promise.'

When she raised a happy, bright face for his kiss, he cupped it with his hands and whispered against her lips. 'Can I sleep with you tonight, Rosaleen?' And as if afraid of rejection, he rushed on, 'I just want to hold you . . . be close to you.'

At the longing in his voice, shame engulfed her. This man was her husband; she should have been holding him every night, but it had been so frustrating. From now on things would be different, she vowed silently.

'Yes, love. I'll go on up and move Laura into the back room.' She rose to her feet and kissed his brow. 'Don't be long.'

A half hour passed and at last Rosaleen rose from the bed, pulled on her dressing gown and descended the stairs again.

He had fallen asleep . . . probably the heat of the fire had made him drowsy. In sleep, he looked young and contented, his head back against the top of the armchair, his eyes closed. His hair had tumbled down over his forehead and she gently pushed it back. He needed to have it cut, she'd make him go to the barber's tomorrow. Then awareness came over her and her hand shook as she touched his shoulder.

'Joe? Joe . . . wake up, love. Please Joe, don't tease. Joe, wake up!'

She realised that she was shaking him roughly and forced herself to stop, aware that he would never open his eyes again.

For some minutes she knelt beside him, explaining that she hadn't meant to be hard, that she had thought it best he slept alone. That in her own way she loved him dearly.

Well then, why hadn't she told him so? Why hadn't

249

she held him each night?

It was as if Joe had said the words, and tears of regret blinded her as she rose to her feet. Realising that it was too late for excuses, she tightened the sash of her dressing gown around her waist and went to awaken her neighbour. They would need the doctor and the priest. The shrapnel had moved the wrong way.

Chapter 8

The journey back from the graveyard seemed endless and when the car turned down Cavendish Street, Rosaleen moved restlessly to the edge of her seat, preparing to get out when it arrived in Iris Drive. Everyone had tried to persuade her not to go to the graveside but she had felt compelled to; had imagined that Joe would want her to be there.

She found it hard to convince herself that it was Joe in the coffin she had seen lowered into the wet clay. She could not believe he was dead, that she would see him no more; even though she had helped wash him and dress him in the shroud, and had kissed him for the last time before they put the lid on the coffin. Somehow, it was as if she was a bystander and someone else was going through the motions. Had she been a good wife to him? Plagued by guilt, she had started to shake uncontrollably as she peered down at the coffin. Did her father know what was going on? Was he aware that Joe was joining him in that dark hole? Oh, how she hoped they would be company for each other. Afraid that she would break down, Annie had ushered her away from the grave and into the car, and it had left the graveyard immediately.

At last it slid to a halt, and glad to escape her tortured thoughts, leaving Annie to deal with the driver of the limousine, Rosaleen left it and hurried to the door, hoping the neighbours would give her a few minutes to herself before calling to pay their respects for the last time. Although her hand was shaking, the key slid into the keyhole at first try and she quickly entered the house, darkened and cold, just as it should be after death had claimed the master.

Tea . . . she must make tea for the mourners coming back from the graveyard. The neighbours had been marvellous. Early that morning they had arrived at her door with freshly cut sandwiches and savoury dishes, and it was all laid out on a table in the kitchen. How they had managed it, in the face of all the food shortages, she did not know, but manage they had and she would be forever grateful to them. Now all she had to do was make tea. Soon, in a few short hours, she would be alone to face the doubts and regrets that kept tormenting her, but now . . . now she must brew the tea.

Glad that they were the first to arrive, Annie raised the roller blinds, which had been down for the past three days as was the custom, letting the daylight into the cold room. Then, after removing the black bow from the door knocker, she pulled out the damper at the back of the grate to set the fire glowing and followed Rosaleen into the kitchen.

Taking her by the arm, she led her gently out again and pushed her down on to the settee.

'You sit down and rest . . . talk to people when they come. People will want to talk to you and Amy. Mam will be here soon and she and I will attend to the tea.' She turned with a weary sigh at a knock on the door. 'And here's the first of them now.'

She was relieved to see that first to arrive were her mother and Amy, accompanied by Bobby Mackay. Bobby was kind, he would answer the door and let people in, and he would look after Rosaleen and Amy while she and her mam made the tea. Poor Amy. She was bearing up well under the strain, but then, Bobby had a lot to do with that. He was taking care of her.

When someone came to Rosaleen and clasped her hand, murmuring words of comfort and praising Joe's goodness, she must have made the right replies because they moved on to Amy and someone else took their place until, in due course, her duty was fulfilled and tea was served. There were so many mourners; men she had never seen before, assuring her that if she needed anything, just to let them know. Some Joe had lent money to, to start up in business. Others he had done work for; honest work. Everybody sang his praises, many shed tears.

To her surprise she noticed that some of the men were drinking beer, and her eyes sought Bobby's. He winked and nodded at her. How good he was. She had not even thought about beer. Funny how attached Bobby was to her family now. Even Joe had welcomed him towards the end. Hopefully, this would make Amy put him out of his misery and marry him. It was obvious that she loved him, but Joe had been the stumbling block. Poor Joe, so ashamed of his illegitimacy.

At last the mourners started to drift away and soon it was just family and close friends that were left. When Rosaleen slumped back in the corner of the settee like a wilted flower, Annie eyed her in dismay and then turned to her mother, a worried frown on her brow.

'Mam, will you be all right if I stay here with Rosaleen tonight?'

At once Thelma nodded her approval but Amy quickly interrupted with the suggestion that Thelma accompany her home. They had supported each other at the graveside when Joe had been laid to rest on top of Billy, and Amy had felt the tremors that had coursed through Thelma's body. In a way, looking after her had helped Amy. Helped her to keep at bay the pain that it was her only son who was being buried. Now, if Thelma accompanied her home, they would be a comfort to each other. However, Thelma demurred, shaking her head emphatically at this idea. Amy, catching Annie's eye, shook her head also.

Annie knew what she meant. Her mother had insisted on going to the graveyard, but it had upset her to see the grave opened, to be aware that her husband's body was down there. She had yet to come to terms with her loss and this could start her wandering again. No, she couldn't be left alone. Annie stood undecided and it was Rosaleen who solved the problem. Rising shakily to her feet, she said, 'I just want to be alone. Just Laura and me . . . please? Will you fetch Laura for me?'

'Ah, Rosaleen, I don't like leaving you.'

If only Sean were here, Annie thought, he would take charge. Poor Sean, he would get an awful shock. Perhaps his ship was in the middle of the ocean and he would not get home. They could only hope. He had been sent for but had yet to arrive. Joe had gone so quickly, everyone was still in a state of shock. Why, Rosaleen had yet to shed a tear. She looked so tense, so drained, that Annie was afraid to leave her alone, to brood.

'Please, Annie? I'll be all right. All I want is to be alone. Just me and Laura . . .' Rosaleen's voice trailed off forlornly, and this decided Annie.

'All right! If that's what you want,' she said resignedly. 'I'll fetch Laura.' And with these words she went next door to bring the little girl home. Before they left, Bobby built the fire up.

'That should last you 'til bedtime, Rosaleen. An' later on, see and make yourself something to eat, won't ye?'

'Yes, Rosaleen, promise me you'll make yourself a bite to eat,' Annie backed him up. She could not remember when she had last seen Rosaleen eat.

'I promise, Annie. I promise.'

She would promise them anything to be rid of them. If only they would get out and leave her alone. Her soul was crying out for solitude. She had not been alone since Joe died. Someone was always there keeping her company, preventing her from thinking. Did they not realise that she needed to grieve?

At last Amy and Bobby prepared to leave, and as she hugged Amy she envied her the tears that flowed. When at last she closed the door on her mother and Annie, she stood with her brow pressed to the smooth, cool wood. Now she could think; now she could grieve.

A small hand being pushed into hers brought her back to reality, and lifting Laura up in her arms, she hugged her close. Poor child, so bewildered and confused. Sitting on the armchair close to the fire, she took Laura on her knee.

Normally, Laura would have slid off, considering herself too big for cuddles, but now, as if as much in need of comfort as her mother, she pressed close.

'Would you like something to eat, love?'

'No. Mrs Gray gave me dinner. Mammy, is Daddy in heaven, or will he have to stay in purgatory for a while?' Laura asked, her eyes keen and searching, causing Rosaleen to pause and think before answering her.

'I don't know, love,' she answered truthfully. Had anyone ever came back to verify that there was a purgatory? 'I honestly don't know. I imagine he's in heaven. He was a good daddy, wasn't he?'

Laura nodded and big tears welled up and rolled down her cheeks. Glad to see them, Rosaleen encouraged her to cry, wishing she could join her, but she felt that there must be no moisture left in her body, otherwise surely she would have cried before now. When Laura sagged exhausted in her arms, Rosaleen gathered her up and climbed the stairs with her. And when she was snug in bed and asleep, she wearily descended the stairs again and sat huddled over the fire. If only she could get relief in tears it might help her, but she felt nothing. She was so cold. Perhaps if she took a hot bath she would be able to unwind. This thought brought her to her feet, and entering the bathroom she ran the bath full of hot water, but all to no avail. Even after a long soak, she still felt numb and tense. Wrapping herself in Joe's old dressing gown, she hugged her arms around her body and pressed her cheek against the shoulder of the dressing gown, desperately seeking warmth and comfort.

'Joe, I'm sorry – I'm so sorry. I failed you, didn't I?'

She had tried to love him. In a way she had loved him, dearly, just as she would have loved a brother. And he hadn't wanted anything else. Had he? Had she been fooling herself that he was happy the way things were? She must have been; he had sounded so sad the night he died, when he had asked to sleep with her. If she had tried, could she have made his last months happier?

Had she been a comfort to him? She had done her duty, comforting him when he had a nightmare, nursing him and caring for him after his operation, but had she successfully hidden her frustration and despair? Doctor Hughes had thought that she was the perfect wife, but what about Joe? How had he regarded her? Had he found her wanting in warmth and understanding? Had he guessed the way she secretly yearned for a normal life, for love and companionship free from jealousy?

When the knocker was lifted and dropped gently, breaking in on her misery, she ignored it. Let them go away. She could not bear to listen to any more platitudes. When it sounded again, she covered her ears and buried her head in the cushions to block it out, but when the knocking persisted and became urgent, with a sigh of regret she slowly rose and entered the hall.

Remembering Joe's warning never to open the door

at night without first making sure it was someone known to her, she whispered. 'Who's there?'

'It's me, Rosaleen. Sean!'

The key was icy to her touch but at last it turned in the lock and her cold fingers struggled with the bar at the top of the door, then the one at the bottom. Then Sean was in the hall, and the door was closed, and she was clasped to his breast, the tears free to flow at last.

There was infinite tenderness in the way he lifted her in his arms, inwardly lamenting at how light she was, and carried her to the settee where he sat with her on his knee.

'There now, love . . . that's right. Cry it all up.'

He held her close, rocking her gently, murmuring endearments, until the last shudder trembled through her body, and the last hiccup left her lips. Then, tilting her face up to his, he tenderly wiped the tears from her cheeks.

Taking the handkerchief from him, she blew her nose. 'I'm sorry . . . imagine greeting you like that.'

He smoothed the hair back from her damp brow and assured her, 'My shoulders are wide enough to bear your grief.'

She gazed back at him, sad-faced. Her hair was lank and lifeless, her nose and eyes swollen and red, but to him she was beautiful.

Embarrassed at the look in his eyes, she turned aside.

'I must look awful.'

He wanted to tell her that she could never look awful to him, but there lay danger, so instead he asked, 'Have you eaten anything today?'

When he had arrived home an hour earlier, after a bite to eat, Annie had urged him straight out again, and pressed on him the need to make Rosaleen eat something.

A guilty look passed over her face and she shook her

head. 'Sure, you won't tell Annie?' she pleaded. 'I promised her I would eat something, but when Laura said she had eaten next door, I couldn't be bothered to cook for meself. Besides, I'm not hungry.'

'Have you any eggs?'

At her indifferent nod of the head, he eased her gently on to the settee and rose to his feet. 'I'll make you an omelette.'

When the omelette was ready, he buttered crusty bread and poured a cup of strong tea. Pulling a small table over close to the fire, he made Rosaleen sit at it and watched until she had finished every last crumb of the meal and washed it down with the tea.

'Now, do you feel any better?'

With a faint smile she had to admit that she did. 'Thanks, Sean. You're very kind.'

KIND! The word struck into the depths of his being. If only he was free to show how he felt . . .

He poured her a small sherry and a whiskey for himself, and sat facing her. 'I'm sorry I was too late for the funeral. It must have been awful for you.'

She nodded and took a sip of sherry. Then to his dismay, with a hand that shook, she placed the glass on the table and buried her face in her hands.

'Ah, Rosaleen . . . Don't torture yourself, love.'

He fought the desire to go to her and hold her close again. He was only human and her need for comfort was putting a great strain on his self-control.

Her muffled voice barely reached him.

'I feel so selfish . . . Here I am, filling my face, and Joe's down a hole in the damp earth on his own.'

Suddenly her head jerked up and she gazed imploringly at him. 'Do you think me da and Joe will be company for each other?'

'Of course they will!'

He would tell her black was white if he thought it would ease her pain. His resolve to keep away from her

258

crumbled. Moving to the settee, he ordered, 'Come here. You still look frozen.'

She also was aware of the danger but she needed to be held, wanted to feel his arms around her, so she rose slowly from her seat and joined him on the settee.

His arms opened to hold her. When he tenderly pressed her close, she melted against him and felt all the tension flow from her body as his hands warmed and caressed her.

It was without surprise that she found herself naked in his arms on the rug in front of the fire. His face above hers was full of love and awe, bringing a lump to her throat at the wonder of it. Then Annie's face rose before her mind's eye and she tried to demur, to push him away as her conscience smote her, but he would not let her.

'Hush, Rosaleen . . . don't think, just feel.'

Mesmerised, she obeyed him, and all else was forgotten as for the second time in her life, she reached for heaven.

They lay for a long time at peace. If only they could stay like this forever. If only he was hers, to have and to hold, how wonderful life would be. If she had listened to him at the beginning, how different her life would have been. But then she had been so naive and innocent. Innocent? Ignorant was more like it!

At last he broke the silence. 'Rosaleen . . . we must tell Annie the truth.' He felt her body jerk in revulsion at the idea, and hastened to add, 'Not right away, but eventually. You know how it is between Annie and me. She doesn't care . . . all she thinks of is having a baby and I can't give her one. She'll be hurt for a while, but we must tell her.'

When she would have pushed him away, he tightened his grip on her. She had sent him away once before. This time he was determined to win her over.

'Listen, love. There's no point in everybody being

miserable, now is there? That would be stupid, wouldn't it? We'll go down south or over to England . . . anywhere you like. I'll leave the navy and get a job, and together we'll make a home for Laura.' His eyes held hers fearfully as he asked the next question. Would she mind having only one child?

'*You won't mind if you don't have any more children, sure you won't?*'

Mind? Even if he really was sterile, if she was childless, she would not mind. Just to be with him was all she desired. His words washed over her. He made it seem so easy. Just grab their happiness and take off. If only they could. Oh, if only they could. Why, it would be heaven to know that he was hers to have and to hold, to depend on forever. But that kind of romance was just for novels. Life wasn't like that! There was Annie to consider. In spite of what he thought, Annie loved him. She was just letting her desire for a child get in the way. If she had to choose between him and a child, she would choose him. This Rosaleen knew; this she was sure of. Besides, there could be no divorce. Annie would be tied to him for life, and they would be living in sin. No, she did not believe that happiness could be found at other people's expense. They would come to hate each other. No matter where they went, they would not be able to hide the truth from Laura. To her he would always be Uncle Sean, and she would be bound to inquire where her beloved Aunt Annie was. And to tell her and Sean the truth? No! That must never happen. How could Laura ever cope with that? No, she must not be swayed. She must convince him that she did not care enough to go away with him.

Gently, she extricated herself from his arms and sat up, her arms around her knees, her back to him.

Propped up on his elbow, he watched her in silence, determined not to let her send him away as she had before. They were two halves of a whole. They were

260

meant to be together. He should never have married Annie. Why had he been in such a rush? It was the war. Wanting to keep the family name going. Hah! That was a laugh. Well, many a hasty marriage had been entered into during the war. Three of his mates in the navy were getting divorced. But Catholics could not get divorced. That was the snag! He would have to persuade Rosaleen to live with him. He was very much aware that she would call it 'living in sin'.

He remained silent. Let her weigh the pros and cons. Let her measure life with him against life on her own. Surely she could not fail to see that they were meant to be together? With or without the church's blessing.

Rosaleen gathered all her resources about her. She had to convince him that she did not love him, that she had used him. Only if she convinced him of that would he leave her alone. There was no way she could square her conscience and go off with him. Hurt Annie? Bring shame on her mother?

No! It could never be.

When she was sure she could control her voice, she spoke. 'Sean, you've got it all wrong. I'm grateful to you for being here when I needed you . . .'

'Don't talk a lot of bullshit!' he interrupted her angrily. 'You love me! I know you do, and I won't be sent away again.'

'You listen to me, Sean Devlin,' she whispered fiercely, afraid of a bawling match. What if Laura awakened and came down? 'I admit that I needed you. Oh, yes, I needed you. And I know I shouldn't have used you, but I was missing Joe so badly . . .' Her voice broke as she uttered these lies to the man she loved above all others. But to Sean it sounded as if it was because of her longing for Joe and he rose from the floor in a fury. Gripping her by the shoulders, he hauled her to her feet and shook her roughly.

'Look me in the eye and tell me you don't love me!'

he ordered. 'Come on . . . look me in the eye.'

He gripped her chin and pulled her face towards his. Unable to do as he asked, she pulled angrily away from him, but his arms tightened around her and he pressed her closer still against the hard muscles of his body, defying her to deny her need.

As always, when close to him, she went weak at the knees and passion welled through her, causing her to tremble in his arms.

He smiled grimly in triumph. 'Go on. Deny you want me,' he growled.

Fear filled her mind. She must not let him take her again or all would be lost. There would be no turning back.

'You're despicable!' she hissed. 'You're taking advantage of my vulnerability, my unhappiness. Go home to your wife. Annie trusted you to come here alone to help me . . . and look how we repaid her trust.' She put her head high and looked him in the eye. 'I'm so ashamed of my actions . . . but it will never happen again, Sean. Believe me, it will never happen again.'

'I don't believe you. After how you behaved just now?' He saw the hot colour spread across her face, down her neck, and laughed harshly. 'Ah no, Rosaleen . . . you'll have to do better than that.'

Her heart sank. She must convince him.

'Lust, Sean?' She hardly recognised her own voice, it was so cold. 'You don't recognise lust when you experience it?' She forced a light laugh from her lips. 'Mad animal lust? Hah! You surprise me. It's all I know.'

He winced, and slowly relaxed his hold on her. His eyes examined her face and she returned his look without blinking. She sounded so sincere. Was she speaking the truth? For her, was it lust that lifted them above all reason; above right and wrong? Was it because he loved her so much that he'd believed she

262

felt the same? Had she just used him to assuage her longing for Joe?

Free of his grasp, she groped for the dressing gown and thrust her arms into it. As she tied the sash around her waist, she felt better, stronger. He had murmured over and over again how the sight of her bare body set him on fire. How he had pictured her often; longed to caress her milky skin. But now she must put out the fire. Try to deny her love for him.

Stunned and bewildered, he stood uncertainly, examining her face through narrowed, searching eyes. Head back she returned his look and just when she thought that she would break down, he reached for his clothes and started to get dressed. Unable to watch the hurt and pain on his face, she turned away, her heart aching. She had burnt her boats all right. He would never bother with her again.

When he was dressed, he stood silent, waiting, until she was forced to turn and face him. A ghastly smile twisted his lips and she cringed inside at the contempt in his eyes.

'Well . . . you know where to come when you need to be serviced. I enjoy it, Rosaleen, and I'll oblige anytime.'

With these cutting words, he turned on his heel and left the house.

In despair, she slowly sank to her knees and huddled in front of the fire. If only he hadn't married Annie! If only . . . She stayed on her knees for a long time but there was no relief in tears. The hurt went too deep.

The light was bright, and coming from the darkened house, Rosaleen shaded her eyes as she gazed up at the tall, young man in army uniform, standing on the pavement.

He returned the look, unblinking, noting the signs of grief and pain etched on her delicate features.

'Well, can I do anything for you?' Rosaleen's voice was sharp; it was the second time she had asked the question.

With a start of dismay, the man straightened to attention.

'I beg your pardon. Are you Rosaleen Smith?' he asked. He didn't need to ask the question. He knew who she was; had seen many photographs of her. None of which had done her justice.

She nodded and he delved into the pocket of his overcoat and extracted a letter, which he handed to her.

'Your father asked me to give this to you.'

'My da? You knew my da?' she asked in wonder. How could this soldier know her da?

'Yes, I knew him well ... very well indeed,' he replied gravely.

She gazed at him in bewilderment. 'He's dead, you know.'

Once more he surprised her. 'Yes, I know. I was informed. I would have come sooner but I've just returned from abroad.'

Her bewilderment grew and swelled. He had been informed?

She fingered the bulky envelope. From her da? Sure, he had hated writing. Would have done anything to avoid putting pen to paper. She examined the envelope; it was his scrawl all right.

Still looking bemused, she stood aside and with a jerk of her head motioned him into the house, closing the big outer door before following him into the living room. Since Joe's burial she kept the big door shut. The neighbours were very kind, but she couldn't think with them popping in and out at all hours and she needed to think, to face up to her shame. Besides, she was afraid of Sean coming back, she had to keep him at bay. She must never be alone with him again.

Once inside the living room, she tore open the envelope and counted the pages. Six! She found it hard to believe that her father would ever write six pages, but here they were in black and white.

Becoming aware of the bulk of the man standing watching her, she said abruptly, 'Here . . . gimme your coat, and take a seat.'

He struggled out of the army overcoat and her arms sagged under its weight as she took it from him and hung it at the foot of the stairs.

'Sit down. Go on . . . sit by the fireside,' she ordered, and when he obeyed her, she sat on the armchair facing him and turned her attention once more to the letter.

Tears stung her eyes as she read. In her head she could hear her father's voice. It was as if he was talking to her, a voice from the grave.

My dear, lovely Rosaleen, when you read this letter, I'll be gone. Gone to meet my Maker and receive my sentence. It will also mean that I have died before your mother, so I want to put the record straight. You see, Rosaleen, it's my fault that your mother is the way she is. My fault! Mine alone, and I shoulder the blame gladly. I have seen you look at me in surprise from time to time when I apparently let your mother walk all over me, but you see, Rosaleen . . . I deserved it. Your mother will never defend herself, she's a very private person and she'll let you go on believing that she is cold and hard. This is far from the truth, because behind that rough front your mother shows the world, is a very shy, passionate, loving woman.

Sharing a bed as we had to, she could not always deny her need for me, because in spite of what I did, in spite of the pain I caused her, she still loves me. That surprises you, doesn't it? But she does love me, and although I'm sure she had her chances (a lovely woman like your mother?) and she may have been tempted to get revenge, I know she never betrayed me. Besides, her good Catholic upbringing would never have let her commit adultery, so sometimes she needed me, and it was when she needed me that she scorned me most. For me, those were the moments that made up for everything else.

When I first met her, your mother was like a breath of spring. Very like you in looks, and pure and good. She could have had her pick of any man in the neighbourhood and she chose me. I couldn't believe my luck when she agreed to walk out with me. Me! Tommy Magee, a mill worker, when she could have had an electrician or a joiner or a schoolteacher. They all fancied her, but right from our first meeting there was a bond between us. I hope you and Joe are experiencing this bond. I've watched you together and sometimes I've been uneasy for you, but I hope and pray that you are happy, Rosaleen.

She paused, startled at these words. Imagine her da sensing that all was not well between her and Joe. Perhaps if she had talked to him about their difficulties at the start of their marriage, things might have worked out differently. Ah, but sure you couldn't talk to your da about a thing like that. Besides, although she had not been aware of it, she was already pregnant. When she had found out, would she have gone to her da and told him that? That she was expecting another man's child? No way! There was no way she could have admitted that to her da. Sad for chances lost, she continued reading.

But to get back to me. The day your mother married me, I was the happiest man in the world and I swore that she would never regret it. That I'd spend the rest of my life making her happy. And I meant it, Rosaleen. I wanted no other. All I wanted was to care for her and when you came along, my happiness was complete. But I was weak and the promises so easily made, were even more easily broken. I didn't mean to betray your mother's trust . . . ah no, I didn't set out to do it, but betray it I did.

Let me explain. We were invited to a party. A mate of mine got the key to a house in Leeson Street and threw a house-warming party.

Your mother was expecting Annie at the time and the day before the party she was confined to bed for a couple of days. Her blood pressure was giving concern. Nothing serious, but she had to rest, and going to a party wasn't allowed. I didn't want to go without her but she insisted. Said I must give the happy couple the wee present she had bought for them. So I went alone – and, oh, how I lived to regret it.

It was like this . . . it was a long night and there was plenty to drink. I didn't realise I was drinking so much, and I wasn't used to it.

Anyhow, I got drunk and was foolish with a girl. We were thrown together because we were both on our own, and later, it seemed only good manners to walk her home. I don't remember much about that night and I don't want to put the blame on her. It takes two. But one thing I did know – I knew I'd done wrong and I prayed your mother would never find out. As time passed and I never set eyes on the girl again, I breathed a sigh of relief. It was going to be all right and I had learnt my lesson. I would never get drunk again. And in spite of what your mother often implied, I never did. Tipsy, now and again, but never blind drunk. Ah, no, it had cost me too dearly.

Alas, our sins have a way of catching up with us,

Rosaleen, and mine did. Just when I thought that I could breathe easy, thought that I'd got away with my misdemeanour, there she was one night, waiting for me coming out of work. Pale and tense-looking, she told me that she was pregnant and that I was the father, and I remember grabbing hold of the gate of the mill to steady myself, I was so shocked. I stood in a daze and wished that the ground would open up and swallow me. The one thought in my mind was . . . how on earth was I going to tell Thelma of my betrayal?

Rosaleen paused once more and gazed blankly at the page for some seconds. She couldn't take it all in. She glanced at the stranger; he sat leaning forward, elbows on knees, gazing into the heart of the fire. What had he to do with it? As if aware of his scrutiny, he slowly turned his head and met her gaze; his eyes sharp, probing orbs. Flustered, she looked away and gave her attention once more to the letter.

The girl was in an awful state. She wasn't young, about thirty, and plain. She was actually grateful to me for giving her a child, said it would make her life worthwhile. I didn't know where to turn, Rosaleen. So when she explained that she was an only child, born late in life to elderly parents and she would not have approached me at all but for the need of help during the pregnancy, I could have wept with relief. She did not intend to cause a scandal and, living on the Shankhill Road as she did, with a bit of luck, if I was careful, your mother need never know. The relief, Rosaleen . . . never in this world could I explain the relief I felt.

To get more money, I gladly gave up smoking. My lungs were starting to bother me even then, so your mother was delighted when I stopped. Funny

... she never inquired what I did with the extra money, but then it wasn't much, I wasn't a heavy smoker, and Annie was only a couple of weeks old and she was preoccupied with the two of you. So every now and again, I met Ruby and gave her as much as I could afford towards the birth.

Then tragedy struck. Ruby died giving birth to my son. You can imagine how I felt ... I felt as if I had killed her. Her parents were wonderful, said that they would rear the boy, said it would give them something to live for now that Ruby was dead, but I decided that the time had come to confess to your mother and to ask her to adopt the baby boy.

It was awful! I had diarrhoea for two days with the worry of it, and there was your mother worrying and fussing over me, while I was trying to find the courage to admit my guilt. I'll never forget the look on her face when I told her. The look of horror, dismay, and ... rejection. It was like a physical blow. Of course she didn't believe that it had only happened once. She thought that I had been playing around with Ruby when she was carrying Annie and I could not convince her otherwise. I know it's hard to believe, Rosaleen, but it was only the once.

She closed her eyes and swallowed deeply. She believed him all right. Oh, yes, she believed him!

It was as if an invisible wall was between us and I never really got close to her again. Physically, yes, but spiritually, no. It was the end of happiness for me.

She refused to adopt the boy. Would not even see him. I was hurt, but in my heart I didn't blame her. I was the one at fault. Your mother had done no wrong. No wrong at all.

Once more Rosaleen looked towards the man and this time he was waiting.

'You're . . . you're my half brother?'

He nodded. 'Yes.'

Her eyes scanned his face. Yes, now she knew the truth, she could see the resemblance. The planes of his face, the dark chestnut hair. He was her father's son all right.

Not knowing how to react, she gave him a weak smile and returned to the letter.

However, one thing I couldn't do, not even to please your mother, and that was to sever all connections with my son. Every Thursday night I visited George. I watched him grow up and I contributed all I could to his upkeep . . .

Rosaleen recalled how she couldn't understand her mother's attitude when her father went to visit his old friend every Thursday night. Her bitterness and anger. How could she have been so blind? How did she not realise that something was wrong? Very wrong.

Rosaleen, be kind to him, please. He's a good lad and his grandparents are now dead. He has no one to call his own. Befriend him. For my sake, love, please befriend him. I know that during your mother's lifetime you will not be able to call him brother, but let him visit you and get to know you . . . and Joe and Laura. I leave it up to you whether or not to confide in Annie. She's different from you and might not take kindly to keeping a secret from her mother, so use your own judgement. I hope you never have to read this, but if you do, pray for me.

Goodbye, love.

Your loving dad

270

Rosaleen folded the letter and sat fiddling with the pages. How on earth had her father managed to keep this secret all these years? He must have been very, very careful, or the neighbours would have found out.

Covertly, she examined the man. His face in repose was sad and weary. Compassion filled her; here he was home from the war and no one to greet him. But he was from the Shankhill Road. They would have nothing at all in common. Nothing! Still, for her father's sake she would have to try to befriend him.

Unknowingly, she sighed, a long deep sigh, and the man's heart sank as he watched her. He grew more apprehensive, afraid that she did not want to know him.

At last she spoke. 'I'm afraid you're too late to meet my husband. He was buried a week ago.'

On his feet instantly, he was full of apologies.

'I'm sorry. Oh, I am sorry. I didn't know or I would never have come. I'll leave now. Not intrude any longer on your grief.'

He hesitated before asking haltingly, 'Perhaps you will allow me to come back at a later date?'

As he reached for his coat, her voice stayed him.

'No! Don't go. I'm glad of your company. Sit down.' She smiled kindly at him. 'I'll make us a cup of tea and we'll have a chat.'

In the sanctuary of the kitchen as she waited for the kettle to boil, she smiled wryly to herself. At least now she knew who she took after. Like father, like daughter. However, unlike her father, she could not blame drink. Each time she had been with Sean her senses had been her own. Very much her own.

Her poor mother . . . no wonder she nearly went out of her mind when Da was killed. Now it was clear to her why Thelma had been in such a state. To have withheld her forgiveness until it was too late. It must have been awful for her. All those wasted years when they could have been so happy. What had held her back? Pride? Probably ... pride, and fear of what people would think was an awful thing. That was what her mother would have dreaded most, the neighbours finding out.

To her surprise, once the first awkward moments were over, she and George got on like a house on fire. They discovered that they had a lot in common, and she learnt of a side to her father that she had never known. She enjoyed watching the different expressions flit across George's face, bringing her father close, and she noted that he had the same dry humour, being funny without realising it.

They had been talking for about an hour when a glance at the clock brought her to her feet. It was almost time to go and fetch Laura from school. When she voiced her thoughts, he looked so disappointed that she found herself asking him to accompany her and he eagerly agreed.

'But first I must change.' Embarrassed colour tinged her cheeks when she glanced down at the old soiled skirt and jumper she wore. She had been so careless of her appearance of late. 'What must you think of me? I look awful.'

Gallantly, he assured her that she looked lovely, and fetching clean clothes, she retired to the bathroom.

For the first time since before Joe's death she took trouble with her appearance, and she was pleased at the admiration in his eyes when she returned to the kitchen. Somehow, he made her feel at ease and she was grateful to him.

As they passed down the street, she greeted neighbours and was puzzled when her greetings were returned with abrupt nods.

Dismayed, she realised what they must be thinking. They would be saying, 'Now we know why she keeps the big door closed!' And they would also be thinking that she must have been carrying on before Joe died. How cruel people were, to condemn without knowing the whys and wherefors.

In the following weeks, George visited her regularly and they became close friends. Rosaleen grew to rely on him. She had decided not to tell Annie about George. Her sister was kind, very kind, but a bit of a blabbermouth, and it would be her mother who would suffer if Annie failed to hold her tongue. Not knowing the truth, she joined the neighbours in their condemnation, and a hurt Rosaleen refused to offer any excuse for her friendship with George. While her mother lived, they would have to think what they liked; she would not risk having Thelma hurt again.

How she would have survived without George, when morning sickness sent her retching to the bathroom every day, she did not know.

TWICE! Twice in her life she had been with a man and each time had resulted in a child. How could life be so cruel? Annie longed for a child and was unable to conceive, while Rosaleen certainly did not want this one! How would she manage to rear two children on her own? Especially with the business to run.

George comforted her; told her he would do all he could to help. He assumed that the child was Joe's and she realised that in ordinary circumstances it could be his. But try telling the neighbours that!

And Sean . . . what would he think when he heard?

George had just left the house late one night when a knock on the door brought her back to it, a smile on her face. He must have forgotten something.

When the door was knocked out of her hand she reared back in alarm, and then Sean closed the big door and bundled her into the living room.

'How dare you! What do you think you're doing?' she cried as she twisted out of his grasp. She could smell the drink on him and was afraid.

273

'Who is he? WHO IS HE?' he ground out through his teeth, and his words were slurred. It tore at his guts to think that she could have someone so soon after Joe's death. What kind of a woman was she?

'Shush! It's none of your business. I'm not accountable to you for my actions, Sean Devlin, so get out of here. Go on!' She flapped her hand at him. 'Go on . . . get out!'

What if he made a scene and the neighbours heard him? Oh, no, she couldn't bear that. They had enough to talk about already.

He swayed on his feet, shook his head and then sank down on to the settee.

'I'll not go 'til you tell me who he is.'

'It's none of your business!' she hissed. Then, softening her tone, she coaxed, 'Go home, Sean. It's very late.'

'Hah!' He scowled at her. 'That's a gag. I've been waiting out there.' He jerked his head towards the street. 'For him to leave. And you tell me it's late. Why didn't you tell him that, eh? Why didn't you tell him that?'

He looked so unhappy her heart was torn with pity, and as she gazed at him, temptation reared its ugly head. The urge to go to him in his misery and comfort him, as he had so often comforted her, was strong. To put her arms around him, hold him close and ease away the pain. To get lost in that wonderful well of passion that he inspired. As her emotions rose, the longing for him grew and swelled, blocking out all rational thought. As every nerve edge came alive, she argued with herself. Would it be so wrong? Annie need never know, and wouldn't he be easier to live with if he was contented? They could be careful . . . she would just see him now and again. That way the neighbours need never suspect. Her hand reached out tentatively to him and then commonsense prevailed.

274

Who did she think she was kidding? WOULD IT BE SO WRONG? It would be a mortal sin! And she was not the type to keep running back to confession with the same sin. She would be cut off from God's grace! How could she live like that? And no matter what he might say now, he would never be content with an affair. He wanted to own her, body and soul, and if he was free, he could own her body and soul. But that was the snag . . . he was not free! He watched the different emotions flicker across her face and when her hand dropped limply to her side, felt that he had been judged and found wanting.

Glaring up at her, he taunted, 'Were you enjoying his company too much to notice the time? Come on, talk to me, Rosaleen! Talk to me!'

'You're drunk, Sean. Come on.' She leant down to assist him to his feet, and when her face was close to his he caught and held her gaze appealingly.

'Why, Rosaleen? Just tell me why?' His hands stretched wide in despair. 'If you must be serviced, why him? Why not me? Eh? Why not me?'

Anger straightened her back and the full weight of her body was behind her hand when she slapped his face.

Taken unawares, without thought he was on his feet, retaliating. His slap sent her spinning and to her amazement, she found herself on the floor, gaping up at him.

At once he was on his knees beside her, cradling her in his arms, begging her forgiveness. 'I'm sorry, love. Oh, please forgive me . . . I'm so sorry.'

Great tears welled up and slid silently down her cheeks, and frantically he kept mopping at them.

'Ah, Rosaleen . . . don't cry, love. Please . . . please . . . I'm sorry. I didn't think. Ah, Rosaleen, sure . . . I wouldn't hurt you for the world.'

At last the well dried up. Relieved, he mopped her

275

face for the last time, and rising clumsily from his cramped position, assisted her to the settee.

She sat curled up, for a long time her face in her hands, and he watched her anxiously. Rosaleen drew a deep breath and straightened as she came to a decision. She had examined her predicament from all angles and could see no way out. There was no alternative. If she didn't want him to think badly of her, she would have to tell him the truth about George. It didn't matter what anyone else thought of her, she could not bear for him to think that she was a whore.

With another long sigh, she rose resolutely to her feet. 'I have something to tell you. But, first, I'll make us a cup of coffee.'

He pushed her gently down on to the settee again and put a cushion at her head, a stool at her feet.

'I'll make the coffee.' He held out his hands for her inspection. 'Look, steady as a rock. I won't break anything. I've sobered up.'

And he had. The shock of lifting his hand to Rosaleen had sobered him. When he handed her the cup of coffee, his fingers touched hers and they were icy. Placing the cup on the table, he took her hands in his and chaffed them until they felt warm, and then handed her the coffee.

They drank in silence. She trying to form words to tell him about George and that she was pregnant, without rousing his suspicions, and he putting off the moment when he heard from her own lips that she loved this other man.

At last, unable to bear the silence, he took the empty cup from her, placed it on the table, and said gently, 'You were going to tell me something?'

She nodded and rose once more from the settee. Going to the desk in the corner, she removed her father's letter from the drawer and thrust it at him.

'Read that.'

Mystified, he withdrew the sheets of notepaper and started to read, glancing up at her now and again in growing concern.

When he had finished reading, he folded the letter and returned it to the envelope before speaking.

'Then this man's your half-brother?'

She nodded.

'Why on earth didn't you tell us?' he cried in surprise. 'Why, Annie thinks you've a . . .' His voice trailed off in embarrassment and she smiled grimly.

'I know what my sister and my mother and the neighbours think. They think I've a fancyman, and I bet they think I've been carrying on before Joe died.' Her voice rose accusingly. 'Even you thought . . . thought . . .'

'I know. I'm sorry, but you should have told us. Ah, Rosaleen . . .' his voice broke on the words '. . . you don't know what I've been through.'

'You read the letter! Me da left it up to me whether or not to tell Annie, and I decided not to. She's a blabbermouth. You know she is and I won't have mother hurt any more. She must have been too proud to forgive me da all those years ago. We can't let her know that we know her dark secret. It would send her over the edge. Annie said that she's been in a state since the grave was opened again.'

'I know, I know. But why didn't you tell me?' His look was full of reproach. 'You nearly sent me over the edge.'

'I haven't seen you since George came on the scene, remember?'

He nodded sadly. This was true. He had been avoiding her, until listening to her mother and Annie discussing the 'other man', his jealousy could be contained no longer. His leave had been extended by the celebrations of D-Day but now he had but one week's holiday left and, fortified by a couple of drinks, here he was.

277

For some time he sat deep in thought and she watched him in silence. Drinking in the look of him. Longing for his touch. Loving the way his hair tumbled boyishly over his forehead. Admiring the strong jaw, the straight nose, the sensitive lips. Those wonderful lips . . . wonderful! His voice brought her back to reality and she gulped to regain control of her emotions.

He spoke haltingly. 'Rosaleen, do you not think . . . that . . . perhaps you should tell your mother about this man?'

She reared back and her brows climbed her forehead in amazement. 'And send her round the bend? Remember how bad she was when me da died?'

She was shocked; could not understand his reasoning.

'Ah.' His finger wagged. 'Listen, now. Listen to me, Rosaleen. Where did we always find your mother when she wandered off? Eh?' He nodded his head. 'Just you think about it.'

Comprehension dawned and she gazed at him open-mouthed.

'You mean . . . you think Mam was up the Shankhill looking for George?'

'Maybe not knowingly, but yes, I think guilt drove her up on to the Shankhill Road.'

She continued to gape at him and he smiled faintly at her expression.

'Tell you what . . . why not bring him up to meet her? Just introduce him as a friend and see what happens.'

'He might not come. She rejected him, remember.'

'What kind of a person is he?'

She thought of George – big, easygoing, kind – and smiled.

'He's a wonderful person. Me da all over again.'

Sean returned her smile. 'Well, if he's like your

278

father, he won't hold spite. When will you see him again?'

'He's calling tomorrow night.' Now was her chance to let him know. 'You see, he's been trying to cheer me up. I've discovered that I'm pregnant.'

He tensed and she saw his fists clench as he gazed at her in amazement. She held her breath. Would he twig or would she be able to convince him that Joe was the father?

Stunned, he sat silent, then his head bowed and he examined her closely from under drawn brows. 'You mean Joe . . .?'

'Of course! Who else? But the neighbours will never believe that he's the father. You can see the pickle I'm in. They'll swear George is the father, unless me mam claims him as her stepson, which I can't really see happening, but I can bear it if I have to. I don't want me mam hurt any more. She's suffered enough already.'

She watched him, her heart in her mouth. Would he believe her? She knew it was only Annie's strong belief that he was sterile that made him so naive. Would he twig on?

Sean gulped deep in his throat as pain seared through him. To think that a wreck of a man like Joe was able to give Rosaleen another child and all these years a big fellow like him had been unable to make Annie conceive. Feverishly, he pushed all self-pity from his mind. Time enough for that later, now he must think of Rosaleen.

'Well then, she'll have to be told,' he said determinedly. 'Does this George fellow look like your father?'

'Yes . . . well . . . he's not the spit of him or anything like that, but once you know who he is, you can see the resemblance.'

'Try and get him to come up with you tomorrow

279

night. Just introduce him as a friend, and we'll play it by ear. Your mother knew your father better than anyone else, so she should recognise him.'

'Will you be there?'

'I'll be there,' he promised. He continued to linger, and rising to her feet, she said, 'You'd better go now. Annie will wonder where you are ... and the neighbours will wonder what we're doing.'

On his feet, he faced her. His eyes examined her face, the eyes heavy from weeping, a bruise already discolouring her jaw, and shame smote him.

'Rosaleen, I'm sorry. Can you ever forgive me?'

He made to draw her into his arms but with a deft movement she eluded him.

'Sean, I'm tired. I want to go to bed.'

The old teasing look came into his eyes. 'Now is that an invitation ... or is that an invitation?' he whispered softly, and love flowed between them. He was relieved to see a slight smile drift across her face and she waved her hand at him.

'Away you go. Go on.'

'Good night.'

Still he lingered, and with a slight push she sent him in the direction of the door.

'Good night, Sean.'

As she climbed the stairs to bed, she was weary in mind and body. Was she doomed to spend the rest of her life alone? Even if she was lucky enough to meet another man who attracted her, who would want to take on a woman and two children?

The rain was cool on his cheeks as he walked home and he was glad it hid the tears. Imagine a skeleton of a man like Joe being able to give Rosaleen another child, while a big fellow like him could not make his wife conceive. He felt so helpless. So inadequate. Other couples were childless, but the women didn't go on like

Annie. Wait until she heard this latest bit of news . . .
her tongue was as sharp as a razor when she scorned
him, but wait until she heard about this! He supposed
she was right. He should listen to her and go see a
doctor. Annie had done all she could, and the doctors
could find no fault with her. So the defect must lie
within him. If only she had been patient just a little
longer. He had been talking himself into going to have
the tests done, but she had to jump the gun. He would
never forgive her for setting everything up and then
expecting him to perform. What did she take him for
. . . some animal?

He wiped his cheeks with the back of his hand. Why
was it considered unmanly for a man to cry? He felt
better for it. He would have to decide what to do with
his life. Perhaps this George fellow would be a blessing
in disguise. If Thelma was to recover enough to live on
her own, Annie might at last agree to buy a house
somewhere far away from Rosaleen. Not that Annie
would know that he was running away from Rosaleen,
but if they could just get away on their own, perhaps
then he would go and see the doctor. And if hardy
came to hardy, he would even consider adoption . . .
but first things first. For all their sakes, Thelma must
recognise and accept George. He could not live his life
hoping for crumbs from Rosaleen's table. No! He
owed it to Annie to try and make her happy.

As Rosaleen walked by George's side up the
Springfield Road the next evening, she was in a dither.

Watching her covertly, George smiled. Reaching for
her hand, he pulled it through his arm and pressed it
close to his side. 'Relax, everything will be all right.'

Easing her arm free, she gave him a grateful smile.
He didn't know what was at stake. It would never dawn
on him that the neighbours would think him the father
of her child, and it would never do to arrive arm in

arm with a strange man at her mother's. Annie would have a fit. Besides, the neighbours had enough to gossip about without that.

The hall door was open, and tapping on the kitchen door she entered the room. From the scullery, Annie looked at her in surprise and her jaw dropped with amazement when she saw Rosaleen motion George into the kitchen.

Where was Sean? He had promised to be here. Even as she thought of him, he was on the stairs, his voice welcoming as he greeted George.

Annie gaped at him. He had been as much against Rosaleen's fancyman as the rest of them, yet here he was fawning all over him. And how come he knew him?

'George, this is my wife Annie, and her mother Thelma.'

Good manners forced Annie to greet George civilly but she would have something to say to Rosaleen when she got her alone. Imagine bringing her fancyman into their home and parading him in front of their mother. Who would have thought that their Rosaleen would become such a shameless hussy? Thelma was in her usual position at the side of the fire and paid little attention to them, but at the sound of her name she glanced in their direction.

After a brief nod of acknowledgement at George, she returned her gaze to the fire. Rosaleen looked beseechingly at Sean. What were they going to do? Her mother didn't recognise the visitor.

'Sit down, George. Here, sit here by the fire.'

Sean deliberately motioned him to the chair facing Thelma's. Tommy Magee's chair. 'The throne' it had been called when Tommy was alive, and well dare anyone sit in it when Tommy was in the house.

'How's about a cup of tea, eh, Annie?'

It was with bad grace that she entered the scullery.

Sitting beside Rosaleen on the settee, Sean gave her arm a reassuring squeeze and spoke across to George.

'You live on the Shankhill Road, don't you?' he asked, and was relieved to see that Thelma was watching George covertly. Would she see the resemblance? He could see Tommy so plain in this young man, but he knew the truth. Would Thelma guess who he was?

'Have you always lived on the Shankhill, George?'

'All my life.'

'And your parents . . . did they always live on the Shankhill Road?'

'My mother was born and reared on the Shankhill. She died when I was born, but my father was a Falls Road man. He died during the blitz.'

Thelma tensed, and Sean pressed on. 'You're something the age of my wife, aren't you?'

Before replying, George examined the woman his father had loved. She must be about forty-nine but she looked sixty. Snow white hair was pulled back severely from a skeleton face, and the green eyes had a wild look about them. They were examining his face, and he saw a flicker of disbelief pass over the pale face.

It was obvious that she was far from well. Why, he had seen men look like this when shell-shocked. There was nothing that he would like better than to help this woman, but supposing they were wrong and it went the other way? Could they afford to take the chance? Shouldn't a doctor be present? However, Sean was nodding encouragingly at him so he replied, 'I think there's about six months between your wife and me.'

Annie heard his words as she entered the kitchen carrying a tray, and gasped aloud. How did this man know what age she was? Had Rosaleen told him?

Sean took the tray from her and placed it on the table, then lifting a cup of tea, he approached Thelma.

'Here, Thelma . . . here's a nice cup of tea for you.'

He placed a comforting hand on her shoulder as she

283

gazed beseechingly at him. Would she believe what her mind was telling her, or would she choose to close her mind and retreat even further from the world? It was in God's hands. They could do no more.

Rosaleen sat on the edge of the settee, clasping her cup of tea, and prayed. It would make so much difference to her if her mother accepted George, but she was afraid to hope.

Conversation flagged, and an uneasy silence reigned.

George felt Thelma's eyes on him and he moved slightly, bringing his face round so that the light from the window fell on it. However, he kept his gaze averted. The brightness of the woman's eyes worried him. He sensed that she was treading a narrow line between sanity and madness. Rosaleen had explained how the opening of their father's grave to receive Joe's body had knocked her back into despair. His father had stressed that he was sure that she loved him. Would she want to come face to face with the result of his sin?

At last the silence was broken by a great shuddering sob and at once George was on his feet, hovering anxiously over this poor, tormented woman.

To his relief, he saw that the madness had left her eyes and she was weeping quietly.

'Tommy sent you . . . didn't he? He's forgiven me . . . hasn't he?'

On his knees by her side, he gathered her hands in his.

'Yes, he sent me. He's forgiven you.'

As Thelma tentatively reached out a hand to touch George's face, Rosaleen released her long-held breath. And when a bewildered Annie would have broken the hush, Sean, with a finger to his lips, ushered her and Rosaleen out of the house, having the presence of mind to pick up their coats on the way out.

Once outside, Annie rounded on them. 'What's going on? Who's that man? I thought he was your . . .' Her voice trailed off and Sean and Rosaleen shared a happy smile. Annie could be told the truth.

It was Sean who spoke first. 'Rosaleen has something to tell you, Annie.'

Her eyes swung from him to Rosaleen.

'You're in for a bit of a shock. George is me da's son.'

'Me da's? You mean . . .?'

Rosaleen laughed at her shocked expression. 'Yes, that's right! Me da had an illegitimate child.'

'I don't believe you!' Annie cried indignantly. 'Me da loved me mam too much to have a fancy-woman.'

'You're right . . . he didn't have a fancy-woman. But he did have a one-night stand and George is the result.'

Still Annie looked scandalised. 'I don't believe you! Me da was too good-living to do anything like that.'

'I'm not saying me da wasn't a good man. He was wonderful. The very best. But even the best can fall, so they can.'

Rosaleen was unprepared for the picture of her actions with Sean that chose at that moment to rise in her mind, and turned away, confused. For the first time she was actually aware of the enormity of what she was doing to her sister. When she was with Sean it all seemed so natural, but no matter how right it felt, it was adultery. What if Annie ever found out? She had turned her anger on Sean. 'And you knew all about this, and you never said a word to me?'

'No! No, I didn't know until last night,' he defended himself, only to find that he'd jumped out of the frying pan into the fire.

'You were at our Rosaleen's house last night?' Annie's eyes darted from one to the other of them suspiciously. 'I thought you were at the pub with Jim Gourley.'

'I was at the pub . . . but I was a bit drunk, and you

know how you hate to see me drunk, so I called into Rosaleen's for a cup of coffee to sober me up,' he blustered.

'Oh, indeed?' Annie's voice dripped with scorn. 'So you don't mind if our Rosaleen sees you making a spectacle of yourself?'

Sean's voice was bitter when he answered her, 'Rosaleen's kind! She's not like you! You take after your mother.'

They had reached the corner of the street and Sean turned and strode up the Springfield Road, a hurt, vulnerable set to his head and shoulders. Rosaleen longed to go after him and assuage the pain, but she had not the right.

'Go after him, Annie!' she urged. 'He's hurt!'

Tight-lipped, her sister stubbornly shook her head. 'No! It wouldn't do any good. We're always at each other's throats. It's got to the stage where we can't look at each other without snarling.'

Seeing the misery on her face, Rosaleen slipped her arm through Annie's and led her gently down the Springfield Road.

'I know what we need . . . a drink. Come on, I've a bottle of sherry. Let's go drink it.'

'You don't . . .' Startled out of her misery, Annie drew back and gazed in open-mouthed amazement at her. 'Surely you don't . . . do you?' she gasped. Rosaleen smiled grimly when she realised what Annie was thinking.

'Tut! Of course I'm not a secret drinker. I haven't reached that point . . . yet. It's a bottle left over from the wake.'

Still uneasy, Annie said, 'What about me mam?'

'We can safely leave her in George's capable hands. You'll like George once you get to know him, he's me da all over again.'

'I can't take it in. Me da doing that . . .'

Rosaleen laughed softly. 'I know how you feel. I couldn't believe it either. No wonder me mam nearly went out of her mind when he died.'

'Me poor mam,' Annie said softly. 'To have lived with that knowledge all her life. How could me da have been so cruel?'

'He didn't set out to hurt me mam,' Rosaleen defended him.

'He must have known what he was doing!' Annie interrupted her. 'He was far from stupid. He must have guessed that there could be consequences, and that me mam would be heartbroken.'

'It was only a one-night stand, Annie. He explained in a letter to me. He was drunk.'

'Still . . . I can't believe that me da would do a thing like that.'

They had arrived at Rosaleen's house, and opening the door she ushered her sister inside.

'Let's have a drink and forget all about it,' she said as she filled two glasses and joined Annie on the settee. 'Here! Cheers!'

After a couple of glasses of sherry. Annie was mellowed enough for Rosaleen to risk questioning her.

'Annie . . . do you not think that you're making too big an issue out of not having children? I mean, lots of couples don't have children, but they don't get on like you do.'

To her astonishment, Annie rounded on her angrily. 'Would you not be mad if your husband refused to go see about himself? That's all I ask of him. And then . . . if we can't have a family . . . fair enough. But the big fellow won't even go to the doctor, and then he's mad when I make all the arrangements . . .' Her voice trailed off and Rosaleen was surprised to see a blush stain her cheeks.

'All what arrangements?'

Annie shrugged, and sighed. 'Oh, I suppose I can

tell you. I made arrangements to go see a specialist . . . all Sean had to do was perform before I went. That's all he had to do, and I'd have done the rest. But no . . . he hit the roof! Stormed from the house.'

A puzzled frown furrowed Rosaleen's brows. 'I don't understand.'

'It's simple! He performs . . . I go straight to the hospital . . . and they can take a sperm count without even seeing him. But he went mad, said I should have discussed it with him first. Said he was no performing animal. Well, as far as I'm concerned he'll never perform again.'

'You mean, you set all this up and never told him?' Rosaleen cried, aghast. 'No wonder he was mad. You'll be driving him into another woman's arms, so you will.'

'Huh . . . you don't know what it's like being married to him. He's away so often and I thought I was doing him a good turn, setting it all up. I honestly never meant to offend him, but now it's as if a brick wall is between us.' There was an edge of tears in her voice. 'I've tried,' she admitted, 'but he doesn't want to be friends again.'

'Annie, will you take a bit of advice from me?'

Her reply was sulky. 'Maybe.'

'Put on your sexiest nightie and make it up with him before he goes back to sea. Swallow your pride or you'll lose him. He's a very handsome man, and very passionate.' Horror made her pause at this blunder. 'At least, I imagine he would be passionate. Many a girl would be glad to accommodate him.'

She breathed a sigh of relief when Annie answered her. Obviously, she had not noticed the slip of the tongue. Funny how you trusted your own. Would not dream that they would betray you.

'I suppose you're right. Not that I'm worried about other girls. As you say, he is very handsome and girls are inclined to throw themselves at him, but never once have I seen him show a flicker of interest in return. And, strange though it may seem, I trust him.' She lapsed into silence. Then: 'I think maybe he cared deeply for someone before he met me, but she must have died or maybe she was already married. He never confided in me. I respect his privacy. Anything that happened before we married is water under the bridge as far as I'm concerned. I had my moments too.'

Observing Rosaleen's start of surprise, she laughed. 'Oh, nothing serious. Just some mad passionate embraces. But the monastery fathers soon put me back on the straight and narrow when I went to confession. And I'm glad, mind you. Sean married a virgin, so he did! No matter how fast me mam thought I was.'

'Forget about a baby, Annie. Just love him wholeheartedly and maybe you'll conceive.'

'Fat chance! There's nothing wrong with me.' She glared at Rosaleen. 'I've seen a specialist and he could find nothing wrong.'

'But sometimes the doctors are wrong. Maybe you're trying too hard.'

'Hah! Listen to you. I suppose you think you know better than the doctors?' Annie sneered.

'No, but give it a try, Annie. Show him you love him. Tell him it doesn't really matter whether or not you have children. Or, mark my words, you'll lose him.'

'Do you know something that I don't know?' Annie's voice was shrill and her eyes suspicious again. 'Has he been talking to you about me?'

'No, he hasn't Oh . . . I give up. I'm away to the loo and then we'll go up and see how things are with Mam. And I forgot to tell you . . . I'm pregnant!'

In the bathroom Rosaleen faced herself in the mirror. She would stay here until Annie got over the shock of her being pregnant. How she wished that she could change places with her. Everything would be okey-dokey if it was Annie who was pregnant.

Why was she trying to get Annie and Sean to hit it off? Because if they should part, she did not want to be the cause. If they parted with no help from her, then and only then . . . She pulled her mind back to reality. Now she was treading dangerous ground. Maybe when the baby was born she would have no choice in the matter and everybody would know the truth. It might be a boy, the picture of Sean. She was hardly likely to produce another green-eyed daughter. Then, if Annie chose not to forgive them, then and only then would she feel free to go away with Sean. Live in sin. Damn her soul. All she could do was wait and see. She might never get the chance.

Annie was still sitting on the settee when she returned to the living room. She turned an anguished look upon Rosaleen.

'Is it Joe's baby?'

'Of course!' Fear gripped Rosaleen's heart. Would Annie guess? But then, she thought Sean was sterile. Would this make her doubt her belief? 'You can understand why I'm so grateful that mam has accepted George, otherwise everyone would think that he was the father.'

Annie smiled wryly at her. 'I'm ashamed of the way I acted towards you, you know . . . about George. I should have known that you wouldn't do anything underhand. Am I forgiven?'

Embarrassed, feeling a traitor, Rosaleen avoided looking at her and headed for the door. 'Come on. Let's go and see how me mam and George are getting on.' And when Annie joined her and squeezed her arm, Rosaleen gave her what she hoped looked like a forgiving smile, inwardly hating herself.

Sean had already returned to the house, and when they entered the kitchen, glanced quickly at them and away again.

Amazed at the change in her mother, Rosaleen perched on the arm of her chair and hugged her.

'It's wonderful to see you looking so relaxed and contented, Mam.'

'I've you to thank for that, Rosaleen.' She smiled across at George. 'You brought him to me. How I've longed to see him, but I didn't know where to start lookin'. And . . . I was too ashamed to ask for help.'

'Ashamed? Why ashamed? You didn't do anything wrong, Mam,' Rosaleen assured her.

'Oh, but I did! I committed the worst two sins of all. My pride got in the way of my love for your da, and I wouldn't forgive him. That's the worst sin of all – to hold spite. I made his life a misery.'

Seeing that she was getting all het up again, Rosaleen said earnestly, 'Mam, me da loved you dearly. He was happy just to be with you, but he will be pleased . . . wherever he is . . . to know that you have accepted George.'

Thelma gripped Rosaleen's hand. 'You think he'll know?'

'I think he'll know,' Rosaleen muttered, and squeezed her tight. In her heart she really did think her father knew. 'But now I'll have to go down and collect my Laura. Amy'll think I'm lost.'

She eyed George and he stood up. At once Thelma was on her feet, eyeing him beseechingly.

'You'll come back, won't you?'

He smiled kindly at her. 'Just let anyone try to keep me away. You'll be fed up looking at me, so you will.'

'Never! Never, son, and I mean that.'

During this conversation, Rosaleen had been covertly watching Annie as she sat beside Sean on the settee. She saw her take his hand and whisper in his ear, and saw Sean nod and return the pressure of Annie's hand, and she breathed a sigh of relief. Perhaps everything would work out all right. Only time would tell!

Chapter 9

It was with apprehension that Annie stepped from the trolleybus and eyed her surroundings. It was one thing coming out the Antrim Road to Bellevue Zoo or the Cave Hill for a day's entertainment, but another matter entirely to consider living out here, so far away from her mother and Rosaleen. It was all right for Sean, he was away for months at a time, but she would be here day in, day out. As her eyes took in the lush, vivid green of the grass, and the yellow of the gorse, and her ears picked up the sounds of the countryside, she had to admit that it was lovely, and so quiet and peaceful. It was hard to believe that on their journey down they had passed through districts with streets missing and work still going on razing condemned buildings to the ground. A reminder of the past few years. It would be a long time before Belfast was back to normal.

The Cave Hill reared up behind them. So close, she felt that if she reached out her hand she could touch the legendary Napoleon's nose, etched sharp against the skyline. It struck her as strange that she had stood on that nose not so long ago and looked down over these fields and houses, out over the lough, and now Sean wanted to buy a house out here. Wonders would never cease!

In front of them, the fields and hedges tumbled

down steeply to the small village of Greencastle. Beyond that, in the far distance, Belfast Lough could be seen, shimmering and sparkling in all its glory, and away to the right of it, the cranes of the shipyard were prominent. Even the sky seemed brighter out here, with clouds scurrying across a curtain of deep blue, and the spring sun was a pale, yellow, hazy blur. But then, there wasn't much of the sky to be seen on the Springfield Road. Out here, there was no built-up area to obstruct your view. No mills and foundries casting dark shadows, so you were more aware of the sky and its beauty.

Sean watched her intently. It meant so much to him that she should like it here, and agree to live on the Serpentine Road. He knew he was asking a lot of her. She was used to living in the heart of the city; shops, churches, schools all close at hand. Out here, there was no tram at the corner and the nearest shop was in Greencastle, some distance away. The houses were spaced out and secluded, although the one he wanted to buy was semi-detached so perhaps the next-door neighbour would be nice, and good company for Annie. He realised that the cards were stacked against him, but they needed to be alone, to try and make a go of their marriage. He would just have to persuade her to give it a try. Now that Thelma was so much better and George was a constant visitor to see her, they could leave her to live alone without feeling guilty. And he needed to get away from Rosaleen.

He wanted a settled life, a home of his own, the chance to make Annie happy. And, God willing, maybe some day they would have a child. Slipping his arm through hers, he hugged it close to his side and led her across the Antrim Road, over to where the Serpentine Road started its meandering down to Greencastle.

'Wait 'til you see the house. It seems huge compared to your mother's,' he explained excitedly. 'It's semi-detached and there's a wide driveway. Maybe one day . . . who knows, we'll be able to afford a car, and we'll have room to build a garage. Now the war's over, anything's possible.'

A happy laugh left his lips and rang out on the still air and Annie laughed in return, pleased to see him so relaxed. It was a long time since he had laughed spontaneously; during his past couple of leaves he had been morose, if not actually unhappy. But then, that was her fault, not his. He had tried to please her. Any other woman would have been beside herself with joy at the flowers and gifts bestowed upon her, but she could see no further than the fact that after years of marriage, she was still childless. Ignoring Rosaleen's warning, she had nagged him often.

She could not help herself. All she wanted was for him to go and see about himself. Was that asking the earth, when so much was at stake?

Now she rubbed her cheek affectionately against his sleeve, and was rewarded with a quick kiss.

The Serpentine Road sloped gently down, winding in and out, just like the river it was named after. They dandered along, pausing now and then to admire the houses set back off the road. Some were detached, some were sprawling cottages, but all had one thing in common – they were well maintained, with rockeries and lawns a delight to the eye. And always, around each bend, to their right in the distance was the lough, calling for admiration.

At last Sean drew her to a halt. 'There it is.' He pointed upwards to two houses, set on an incline, looking very imposing. 'It looks all right, doesn't it?' he asked, nodding towards the right-hand house.

She smiled and nodded in return and followed him slowly up the drive, her eyes examining everything around her.

The garden was overgrown, but that could soon be

put right. The house was not very old. It had belonged to an aunt of one of the sailors on Sean's ship, built by an uncle who had died at war, and when his aunt died suddenly, to his surprise Sean's shipmate had inherited it. It was quite by accident that Sean had heard it was going on the market, and going at a bargain price for a quick sale.

Sean's letters had been full of it, and once home on leave he had gone straight to view the house. Having fallen in love with it, he was now praying that Annie would like it; would consent to live out here. Covertly he watched her reaction to the house. He just had to persuade her to live here. It was a beautiful house. They would never get a bargain like it again. Normally it would be beyond their pocket, and once it went on the market it would be snapped up.

They left the drive and climbed four steep steps, passing the big bay window. Annie noted as they did so that the top panes of glass of the window were lead-lighted and the fanlight above the door likewise. From here they paused and turned to survey the scene before them.

The house was well up off the road, and opposite it green pastures soaked up the peaceful, warm sunshine. In the distance, the lough could be seen, shimmering and gleaming. And to the left, the road meandered on, sloping in and out between secluded houses.

'Isn't it lovely?' Annie whispered, as if to raise her voice would shatter the stillness. 'It's like being in a different world.'

With a nod and a grin, Sean happily agreed with her, before turning and mounting another step up to the entrance of the house.

The big door was of hard wood and varnished, and the upper half of it framed a beautiful leadlight window.

He was surprised to note that his hand shook when he put the key in the lock, and smiling wryly, he admitted to Annie, 'I'm as excited as a child visiting Santa Claus.'

Pushing the heavy door open, he turned and smiled down mischievously at her.

'Hows about me carrying you over the threshold?'

With a quick glance at the next-door house, Annie grinned and declined his offer with a shake of her head. Stepping around him, she entered the house.

They stood close together and surveyed the hall. Annie was aware just what he had meant when he said that the house seemed huge compared to her mother's. Why, you could set her mother's hall in the corner of this one. It was wide, more than twice the width of the hall in Colinward Street, and ran almost the full length of the house. To their right two doors opened off the hall, and facing them at the far end was another door. A wide staircase rose to the floor above. Sean opened the first door and ushered her in. It was a wide, spacious room, with a high ceiling, a deep frieze and a big bay window. The floor boards had been sanded down and varnished and gave off a dull glow. In the wall facing them a slate mantelpiece commanded attention, the light from the window reflecting on its muted shades of blue and grey and making the marble hearth glisten just like washing soda. That was what came to Annie's mind, the rough washing soda, white, shot with colours.

'Well, what do you think?'

'Lovely . . . very nice indeed,' she replied cautiously, amused at his impatience.

The next room off the hall also had a bay window which looked out on the drive at the side of the house. Smaller than the first room, it was nevertheless larger than her mother's kitchen or Rosaleen's living room. Here there was a smaller grate with a wooden

296

mantelpiece and a tiled hearth. Sean pointed to the back of the grate.

'That's the back boiler, for heating the water. Just imagine, Annie, hot-water at the turn of a tap. No waiting for kettles to boil, to have a wash.'

'Now that would be nice,' she replied, and saw by his smile that he was pleased at her answer.

There was also bright oilcloth covering the floor and a small armchair at each side of the hearth. At her querying look, Sean nodded.

'Yes, they go with the house. They're not bad. They'd do until we decided what kind of furniture we want.'

The last door led to the kitchen. It was the width of the house but not very deep. An old, well-scrubbed wooden table took up a lot of the floor space. The window was to their right, above a deep sink with cupboards built around it. Annie was surprised to note that what she would call the 'back' door was actually at the side of the house, leading out on to the drive, and was relieved to see that the enamel stove was gas. A step down from the kitchen led to a small back hall and here, on the left side, facing the 'back' door, was a small room lined with shelves. This, Annie decided, must be the larder. It was much bigger than Rosaleen's, you could walk right into it.

Sean opened the door and stepped outside to survey the back garden, rolling his eyes heavenward when he saw the jungle that it had become.

'Dear God, Annie. You could lose half of Colinward Street in here,' he jested, as his eyes, bright with happiness, travelled the length and breadth of it.

'I'll soon get that mess cleared up,' he promised.

Silently, she wondered when he would find the time to clear it, he was away so often. Really, a house this size was too big for a couple on their own, and it was so cut off, so out of the way. What if the neighbours hated

297

them? Besides, time enough to buy a big house if they ever had a family.

Aware of her silent contemplation, Sean escorted her back through the house and up the wide staircase, all the while pointing out the advantages and beauty of the hall. At the top of the stairs was the bathroom. Here, the ceiling and walls had been fitted with light oak tongue and groove panelling and the bathroom suite gleamed, obviously well cared for. There were four doors off the landing; three of these opened on to bedrooms and the fourth was an airing-cupboard and contained the hot-water tank. One of the rooms overlooked the back garden, and from the window there was a breathtaking view of the Cave Hill. Annie stood entranced and Sean relaxed. It was obvious that she liked the house. However, he would not have been so happy if he had been aware of her thoughts. She was warning herself not to fall in love with the house. It was too big, too isolated. She would be out here on her own for weeks on end, depending on Rosaleen, her mother or George taking pity on her and paying a visit.

The other two bedrooms overlooked the front of the house and from these the view of the lough was breathtaking. The smaller of the rooms immediately sprang to Annie's mind as a nursery. She could picture murals on the walls, a big cot in the corner, and tears came to her eyes. Would she ever have a child?

She pushed these thoughts from her, knowing Sean would not want to hear her lament about a child, and as they descended the stairs, she smilingly agreed with him that the house was indeed a bargain.

'Well . . . what do you think?' His voice was apprehensive. She was too quiet, too unenthusiastic, and he feared the worst – that she did not want to live here. 'It's going for a fraction of its real price, Annie. We'll never get a chance like it again,' he pleaded.

Their tour of the house completed, they sat side by

side on the bottom step of the stairs, admiring the spring sunlight coming through the leaded light in the door and casting coloured rays over them. He waited anxiously for her reply, and after some moments of thought, she answered him.

Tentatively, not wanting to just dash his hopes, she countered, 'It's lovely . . . very nice . . . but do you not think it's a bit big for two people?'

Abruptly he rose to his feet, his face flooding with hot, angry colour, and glared down at her, causing her to draw back in dismay.

'Could you not let one leave go by without harping on that?' he cried bitterly. 'Eh? Are children the beginning and end of all for you?'

'No, but. . .'

'Oh, but YES. I'm sick of listening to you harp on about being childless. I'm sick watching you drool over other people's kids.' As suddenly as his temper had flared, all the fire left him. His shoulders slumped and his hands stretched out in a wide, hopeless gesture. 'I've been giving our marriage some thought, Annie, and I've come to the conclusion that perhaps we should try for an annulment.'

She was aghast. This was a bolt from the blue. 'What on earth do you mean?' she asked, and it was her turn to be apprehensive.

'I mean . . . since we can't get divorced, and since we're so incompatible, perhaps the church will grant an annulment. Set us free of each other. We can at least ask.'

'The church would never do that!' Annie cried, amazed that he could think such a thing. 'We married for better or worse, so we did. The church doesn't grant annulments just because you can't have children. That's God's will! You have to learn to live with it. You can only get a marriage annulled if it's not consummated.'

299

His finger pointed accusingly at her, and his eyes scornfully raked her face. 'But *you* can't live with it . . . sure you can't, Annie,' he taunted. And turning on his heel, he strode down the hall, through the kitchen and out of the door, to stand gazing blindly in front of him. The back garden, about seventy feet of it, stretched before him and the Cave Hill loomed high above it. He eyed it bleakly. Annie was right. This was a house to rear kids in. That big garden was made for swings and slides, the tree made for tomboys to climb. He'd been a fool to think that a house like this could ever belong to him.

Alone on the stairs, Annie sat stunned. She wanted children, yes, but Sean was her world . . . from the first moment she had set eyes on him, she had loved him, and no other man had ever received a second thought from her. Why, without him she would die. Slowly, she rose to her feet and followed him, pausing at the door.

'Sean?'

He remained outside, his head averted. His cheeks were wet with tears that he did not want her to see. He felt ashamed. Imagine crying over a house.

Going to him, she put her arms around him and pressed her cheek against his sleeve, delighting in the smell of him, the feel of the rough tweed of his sports jacket under her cheek.

'Sean, I'm sorry,' she said softly. 'I realize that I've been a selfish fool. If you want this house, buy it, and we'll give it a try.'

Astounded, tears forgotten, he turned to face her. 'You mean that? Honestly now, you're willing to give it a try?'

The sight of his tears dismayed her, tore at her heart.

'Ah, Sean . . . Sean. Forgive me. I've been blind.' Her fingers smoothed his cheeks, wiping the tears away. 'I've been a blind fool, so I have.'

'Listen, Annie, I've been selfish too. I should've gone and seen about myself long ago, but I was afraid.' A tense silence yawned as he gripped her tighter still. Then the fear that was constantly with him poured out. 'What if I can never father children?'

Regret gnawed at her mind. She had been so wrong. She had been blaming him, thinking that he didn't care enough about children, and all the while . . . he had been afraid of the result of the tests.

'It won't matter, Sean. Honestly, love. Just so long as we have both tried.' Her voice was earnest, compelling. She must make him understand that he came first. 'Much as I want children, I can live without them as long as I have you. But, love, don't you think it's worth a try? A visit to the doctor? That's all I ask. That we both try.'

Feeling humble, he vowed. 'On my next leave, once you know just when I'm coming home, you can set up an appointment for me with the doctor, and I promise I'll go.'

And as his lips claimed hers, hope was deep in their hearts.

Both Rosaleen and Annie gazed adoringly at the baby lying on the rug in front of the fire. He was a beautiful child, his chubby limbs flailing the air, gurgles being emitted from his widely yawning mouth.

On her knees beside him, Annie tickled him under the chin. She was rewarded with a lovely, gaping, toothless grin and a gurgle of pure happiness.

'He's lovely, Rosaleen . . . beautiful. Such a good baby. I wish he was mine.' She gave a long, heartfelt sigh. 'You don't know how lucky you are to have two lovely children.'

Rosaleen leant forward in her chair, the better to enjoy the beauty of her son. She agreed wholeheartedly with Annie. Her son was beautiful. The

301

pregnancy had been hard, the child spending most of his time lying on a nerve and causing her unending pain and misery, but the result was worth waiting for. Her eyes examined him intently. The chestnut hair, just like her father's, the big blue eyes . . . Would Sean see the resemblance? No one else had noticed. If he did notice, what would he do? Could she bluff him? Did she want to?

Annie continued gently to tickle the child, and as he gurgled and kicked, she examined him.

'Do you know something, Rosaleen? My desire for a child must be affecting my mind.' With a wry grimace she raised her gaze to Rosaleen's. 'I can actually see Sean in young Liam.'

Leaning forward as she was, their faces just inches apart, and taken completely unawares, there was no way Rosaleen could have controlled her expression, her change of colour.

Open mouthed, Annie gaped at her in dawning horror. She saw the colour flood her sister's face and creep down her neck, the guilt and dismay register in her eyes. Aghast, her eyes returned to the child and feverishly examined each feature. He had her colouring . . . just like his grandfather. He even resembled his grandfather in features, which meant that he favoured her. Why, this was how a child of hers and Sean's could look, chestnut-haired, blue-eyed. But then, thousands of children had blue eyes, she assured herself.

Not this shade of blue! her mind shouted back.

Such an unusual shade. She had noticed the eyes before but had assumed that they were inherited from Joe's father. Perhaps they were, she warned herself. She must be cautious, not accuse Rosaleen. Perhaps she was wrong. Once more her eyes returned to her sister but Rosaleen now had her emotions under control, her features schooled, and gazed innocently back at her.

Annie blinked in bewilderment. Had she imagined that look? No! No . . . she had not imagined it. But she must have. Surely she must have? There was no way that Sean could be the father. Wasn't he sterile? Besides, he wouldn't . . . not with Rosaleen, not with her sister! Would he? Would he do that to her?

Afraid to speak in case she said the wrong thing and made matters worse, Rosaleen watched Annie grapple with her doubts.

Confused, she shook her head as if to clear it and stumbled to her feet. Towering over Rosaleen, she wailed piteously, 'Tell me it's not true. Oh, Rosaleen, tell me I'm wrong. Please tell me I'm wrong,' she begged. 'Don't let this happen to me.'

'What? What's not true? I don't know what you're talking about.' Rosaleen replied, looking bewildered.

And all Annie's doubts fled. She knew! She was sure. How she didn't know, but she was sure that Rosaleen lied. Her voice was too easy . . . her manner too innocent.

Blinded by tears, she groped for her shoes and pushed her feet into them, all the while her mind insisting that it could not be true. It just could not be true! How would she be able to bear it if it was true? With shaking hand, she reached for her coat and shrugged it on.

Rosaleen watched her in silence, afraid to speak, flailing about in her mind for words that would make everything right, but none were forthcoming. At the door Annie turned and gazed wildly around the room.

The peaceful scene of mother and child by the fire enraged her. Her world was falling apart and nothing had changed. Everything still looked the same.

With a cry of pain, she lifted a vase that sat in pride of place near the door, and crashed it against the wall. As it shattered, Rosaleen was on her feet.

'Now wait a minute . . . just what do you think you're doing?'

'Don't you come near me, you mealy-mouthed, sanctimonious bitch, or I won't be responsible for my actions,' Annie hissed, her fist lifted threateningly in the air. 'You slut! You dirty, rotten wee slut!'

'I don't know what you're talking about,' Rosaleen blustered. 'But that was an expensive vase, and I'll see that you replace it. You're right. You are crazy. You need your head examined.' Then, her voice softening, she implored, 'Look . . . sit down. Let's talk this out.'

'Sit down? Are you nuts? I'll never sit in this house again. Never again.'

Pain was etched sharply on Annie's face and her voice broke on a sob that tore at Rosaleen's heart when she asked, 'Does he know?'

'Does he know what? I don't know what you're talking about, so I don't.'

'Oh, you know! You know all right! You lying cat!'

As the door settled back on its hinges and the sound of Annie's footsteps storming up the street receded, Rosaleen sank slowly down on to the settee, shame and regret tearing her apart. It was awful to hear Annie call her a slut, but wasn't it the truth? And didn't she still covet her sister's husband? What would Annie do? Would she confront Sean? If so, how would he react? Swamped with unhappiness, she argued with herself. Was it so wrong of her to want Sean? Perhaps Annie was meant to notice. Perhaps it was fate and at last she was going to get a chance at happiness. Was she not entitled to some happiness? All those wasted years married to Joe, frustrated and unhappy. And most of the time Annie and Sean were at loggerheads. Annie longed for a child and obviously she was barren. Sean was miserable married to her. He was right! She should have listened to him. Why should everyone be unhappy? Still, was she brazen enough to cause a big scandal? Run off with him and live in sin?

Annie's feet hardly touched the ground in her mad race up the Springfield Road. She kept her gaze straight head, ignoring people who spoke to her, not in a fit state to converse with anyone, very much aware that some stopped to look after her in amazement. And why wouldn't they? She must look demented. At the corner of Colinward Street her feet faltered, then continued on up the Springfield Road. George would be with her mother and she just didn't feel able to see him, make conversation.

George was so good and kind, her mother doted on him, treated him as the son she never had. It had surprised everyone the way she proudly introduced him as her stepson. Deep inside it must have hurt her to announce to one and all that her husband had sinned against her, but she seemed intent on punishing herself. She probably looked on it as penance, and her brave act brought her nothing but admiration.

Young Maureen Murphy also doted on George, but he kept her at arm's length, and Annie was aware that this was because his religious beliefs differed from hers.

Annie knew that she was just thinking of George to keep her mind off . . . Sean. There, she had let his face surface. How could he have done this to her? Him and Rosaleen. Her mind baulked as she tried to picture them together. Where had they met? Sean had been home so rarely during the war, and for such short periods . . . how had they managed to have an affair? Was he leaving Rosaleen and coming directly to their bed? But then, hadn't she been rejecting him? It had been wrong of her to withhold sex, to try to compel him to see a doctor. Was this why he had turned to Rosaleen? Hadn't she, hypocrite that she was, warned Annie that she would lose him? That some other girl would be glad to accommodate him. And all the while *she* was accommodating him, was already pregnant by him. She remembered how surprised she had been when Rosaleen had told her that she was expecting another child. The idea that a physical wreck like Joe could father a child, and a big healthy man like Sean could not, had stuck in her guts; made her, in her mind, scorn her husband. And all the time it was Sean's child that Rosaleen was carrying, and gullible fool that she was, she had believed Rosaleen that it was Joe's.

Pain seared through her, bringing sobs to catch at her throat. Angrily she choked them down. This was no time for tears. What she needed to do was think. She must have been blind! But then, wasn't the wife always the last to know? It's a wonder that the neighbours hadn't dropped hints. They delighted in doing that, and they must all have known. They must have been nudging each other and laughing at the idea of it. Well, what the neighbours thought had never bothered her before, so she would not let it matter to her now. No, she would not let it hurt her!

It was her own fault! She had been obsessed with the idea of having a baby. She had nagged and repulsed Sean and driven him into Rosaleen's arms. No, it was Rosaleen's fault. Good-living Rosaleen!

She, who cringed with distaste when a smutty joke was told. She, who would never take the Holy Name in vain. *She* had been letting Sean get his leg over. Oh, now, wouldn't Rosaleen be shocked at that expression? Wouldn't she just be shocked at anything so crude? How had she squared her conscience with committing adultery? Pure, holy Rosaleen! And what about Sean? It took two! But didn't the priests say that if there were no bad girls, there would be no bad boys? Didn't the women always get blamed. Weren't men weak, and wasn't it up to the women to keep them at arm's length? As for Rosaleen . . . how Annie had admired and looked up to her. All her life, because Rosaleen was such a good, pious person, she had thought it right that her mother and father should favour her, hold her up as an example. She had always been second best; only with Rosaleen and Sean had she felt that she came first. Rosaleen had been her friend as well as her sister, and look how she had betrayed her. How was Annie ever going to face her again? Her mouth trembled at the thought of her loss. Hurt and pain once more brought tears to her eyes, but she brushed them angrily away. She had no intention of wallowing in misery; she wasn't going to give in to self-pity. If Rosaleen thought that she was just going to walk off with Sean, she had another thought coming. He was her husband, and she would fight tooth and nail for him, child or no.

At the Dam she paused, then slowly made her way down the grassy bank, off the road. She could sit here for a while, gain control of her emotions before facing her mother. It was a lonely place, and as she gazed down on the water she shivered. Many nasty rumours circulated about the Dam, but the way she felt, it wouldn't matter if someone finished her off and pushed her in. Indeed, they would be doing her a favour.

As her anger abated, the house on the Serpentine Road came to mind, like a sanctuary in a storm. Sean had set things in motion the day after she had consented to live there and now it belonged to them, lock, stock, and barrel. So why not go there? But sure she couldn't. Except for the table and two armchairs, it was empty.

They intended moving in during Sean's next leave, but why wait? George would help her. He had a car; she could depend on him. First thing tomorrow morning she would go down and order a bed. It being a Saturday, the first day she could expect it to be delivered was Monday, but meanwhile she could sleep on the floor. It wouldn't kill her to live rough for a few days. Not after the nights spent in the Falls Park during the war. What about the chimneys? They needed to be swept. Sean had been warned not to light a fire until the chimneys had been swept. Well, it was just at night that it got chilly. The weather was changeable for June, but not really cold. She would survive. They had been told that a man in the village swept chimneys. Tomorrow she would find out where he lived and go and ask him to sweep them as soon as possible.

Now that a course of action was open to her, she turned and quickly retraced her steps up on to the road. She must catch George before he left to go home, make arrangements for him to help her move cooking utensils, bed linen and her wedding presents.

Once she had moved into the house on the Serpentine Road, she would be able to think, to decide what to do.

George and her mother had finished their inspection of the house and were now enjoying a cup of tea in the kitchen. Sitting at the old wooden table on two dining chairs borrowed from her mother, surrounded by pots and pans and boxes.

'It's lovely, Annie. You must be real proud to own a house like this.'

'Your mam's right . . . it's a beautiful house,' George agreed with Thelma. 'Well-built and sturdy. But will you be all right here on your own?'

There was a worried frown on his brow, and from her perch on the edge of the draining board, Annie smiled reassuringly at him.

'Yes. Once I get the gas and electricity turned on, I'll be fine. Meanwhile I have your Primus stove and oil lamp. I'll be all right.'

308

'You should have asked Rosaleen to come and stop with you for a couple of nights, just 'til ye get settled in. I'd have minded the kids, so I would. Surely you knew that?' Thelma admonished her. 'I don't know what the big rush was for. Ye said you'd move during Sean's next leave . . . what changed your mind?'

'Oh . . . I thought I may as well be doing some decorating . . . have some of the rooms ready for Sean coming home,' Annie replied airily. 'Anyhow, Rosaleen's too busy looking after her wee business, and to be truthful, I prefer to be alone.'

'Rosaleen'll be surprised when she hears about your movin'. She'll probably come down t'morrow t'see the house.'

'No. Tell her that I don't want her to come down. She'll understand, so she will.'

George watched her from under drawn brows. There was something wrong here. He sensed a deep unhappiness in Annie. Had she and Rosaleen quarrelled? Surely not. They were such close friends.

When they were ready to leave, and Thelma was in the car out of earshot, he whispered to Annie, 'I'll come down tomorrow afternoon and help you start cleaning out the rooms. I'll bring some food, so don't worry about cooking on the Primus stove. But do make yourself plenty of hot drinks.'

'Thanks, George. Thanks a lot,' she whispered back, 'I'll look forward to seeing you.'

Cold and unhappy, she was unable to sleep. Early next morning, an orange glow radiating from the front of the house brought her from the back bedroom to investigate – to stand at the window in awe and gaze entranced at the sun rising on the lough. Everything was orange and gold. The sky dazzling her eyes with its glow, and the lough shimmering and glowing like a thick gold chain brought a sigh of pure rapture to her lips. The sun was free of the lough and lightening the sky, and some sort of normality was apparent before she turned away from the beauty of it all. Imagine waking to that every morning. Wait until Sean saw the beauty of it, he would be enchanted. Thoughts of Sean dampened the joy that engulfed her. Would she ever be able to think of him without pain? Only time would tell, time and Sean's introduction to his son.

She had bought some ceiling white, and making up a thin paste with this, whitened the window panes. The house was high up and back off the road, and so far she had witnessed little traffic, but she still felt exposed by the curtainless windows, and the whitened panes made her feel easier, more private. With earning good money in Mackie's, she had some savings of her own. Tomorrow she would measure up for curtains and go into town to see if she could get any bargains. Something cheap to tide her over until the house was decorated and she knew just what kind of curtains she needed. They had decided that they would furnish the house slowly. Buy things as they could afford them. Only the best would do.

She had sent in word to her supervisor that she was ill. That gave her a week's breathing space, but could she travel to Mackie's every day? It would mean taking two trams . . . she would wait and see how she felt at the end of the week before making any decisions.

She had just finished her breakfast when there was a knock on the door. To her surprise it was the chimney sweep. Small, wiry, grinning from ear to ear.

'I couldn't let you spend another night without a fire, missus, so if it's all right with you, I'll clean yer chimneys now. Will ye allow me t'work on a Sunday?'

His infectious grin brought an answering smile to her face as she answered him.

'Of course, of course! I'm grateful to you for thinking of me.'

As she led the way into the sitting room, she said

over her shoulder: 'I'll be glad to get the chimneys swept.' She gave a slight laugh. 'But as for lighting the fires, I haven't any coal, so I'll have to wait until tomorrow to light them.'

'You've no coal, missus?' he cried, aghast.

When Annie smiled wryly and shook her head, the small man cried, 'Well now, we can't have that. Sure we can't. It gets chilly at night, so it does. There's a shop in the village that sells everything, an' it opens on a Sunday. When I've done the chimneys, I'll fetch you a small bag of coal and some kindlin' t'tide ye over. But I've t'go t'mass, so it'll be about lunch time before I get back.'

Annie smiled at him; she loved his strong brogue. Much broader than the Belfast tongue. Even stronger than the older folk like her mother.

'Oh, thanks very much. That's kind of you. Is the Catholic church far away?'

'It's just down in the village. Have ye not bin down?'

Once more Annie shook her head. This man would think her a fool. 'I just arrived here yesterday . . . ' she began apologetically.

He interrupted her. 'Never you worry. I'll take ye down t'mass, that's if ye don't mind travellin' in the van, an' then, sure, ye can buy yer coal and sticks yerself an' I'll run ye home again. I'll be finished in time for ten a'clock mass, so I will.'

He waved her thanks away and started to connect his brushes, preparing to sweep the chimney. Not wanting to stand over him, she left him to it and went to get ready for church.

Annie turned the bend in the road that brought her house into view and shock brought her to a standstill. Monday had dawned brisk but sunny, just right for walking, so when her bed had been delivered earlier that morning, she had decided to walk down to the

311

shops for some fresh milk and bread and meat. She had enjoyed her tour of the village and was in an easier frame of mind as she dandered up the Serpentine Road. Now she stood undecided, unrest once more agitating her. A figure sat on the step outside her door, a child in her arms and another youngster playing on the lawn. Rosaleen was gazing out over the lough, and Laura had her back to Annie. Should she turn back before they became aware of her? Should she stay away until they tired of waiting and departed for home?

Anger bubbled inside her. How dare she? How dare she come here, to Annie's home, to contaminate it. How dare she! With steps that dragged, she continued on up the road and was at the gate before Rosaleen, lost in a world of her own, became aware of her. As she closed the gate behind her, Annie tried to form words to tell Rosaleen that she did not want her in this house, would prefer her not to come visiting, but her mind was blank, and when an excited Laura threw herself into her arms, she hugged her close.

'Auntie Annie . . . Auntie Annie . . . we've come to see your new house, so we have.'

'Have you, pet? That's kind of you.'

Rosaleen had risen to her feet. Clutching the baby to her breast, she watched Annie fearfully. She had every right to refuse to let her in. Would she? As Annie drew close to Rosaleen, the baby, with a happy gurgle, held out his arms to her and she instinctively reached for him and hugged him close, her cheek softly caressing the silky hair of his head. Her actions surprised her. She had thought that she would never be able to look at this child again, yet here she was, hugging him.

Over the child's head their eyes met. Annie was pleased to see by Rosaleen's ravaged face that she too had suffered. Rosaleen looked how she herself felt: miserable beyond description.

'Annie, it was only the once.'

312

These words brought a howl of protest from Annie's lips.

'Don't you add insult to injury!' she cried. 'On Friday night you didn't know what I was talking about, and now you dare to insult my intelligence . . . me mam didn't believe me da, and I certainly don't believe you. Do you think I'm soft in the head?'

She stopped her tirade to glance down at Laura who was pulling at her skirt for attention. 'All right, all right, Laura,' she said testily. 'Let's go around the back. I've the back door key.' And with these words, she was committed to entertaining Rosaleen in her home, having to laugh when Laura exclaimed: 'This isn't a back door . . . have you no back door, Auntie Annie?'

'No, love. I'm rich, so I am . . . I've a side door.'

Begrudgingly, she showed Rosaleen over the house, receiving tight-lipped her obviously sincere words of praise.

When they retired to the kitchen, Rosaleen produced an apple tart from her shopping bag and proffered it to Annie. 'I'm hoping you'll offer me a cup of tea. And, Annie . . . we've got to talk.'

However Laura, who had kept the conversation going while they viewed the house, disappeared out into the back garden and the tea was drunk in silence. Both of them sat deep in thought, and the apple tart lay untouched. Once finished, Annie suggested that they sit out in the sun. That morning she had rescued two old deckchairs from the shed and they retired to these.

Rosaleen was having difficulty forming words to explain to Annie how she came to be pregnant. She had decided not to mention that Sean and she had been friends before he met Annie. If she once heard that, there was no way Annie would believe that it was only the one time and she must never learn about the first time, never! No one must ever learn about the

313

night up at the Dam. Annie must be convinced that it had been a one-off event. It was the only way that her marriage could be saved. The vague ideas and longings Rosaleen had harboured, that maybe Liam would bring Sean and she together, had slowly died in the face of her sister's awful desolation. Annie loved Sean . . . And he?

Well, she must not put him to the test. Sean must never learn that Liam was his son. Only she, Sean and May knew that they had dated, and only Sean and she knew about the night up at the Dam. May was in Canada. Somehow she must get word to Sean, and he must warn Betty never to mention to Annie that he had once been interested in her sister.

Now she began, choosing her words carefully. 'Annie . . . honestly . . . it was only the once.'

The hope in the look that Annie turned on her made her want to weep, but it was quickly replaced by scorn.

'I don't believe you.'

'Well, I can't help that!' Rosaleen cried in exasperation. 'I've come here to explain . . . I don't want you picturing Sean creeping down to my house every now and again.' Her head jerked from side to side in denial. 'It just wasn't like that. It wasn't like that at all! It was just the one time. Sean's not like that. You must know that he would have come out in the open about it . . . if . . . we'd been having an affair.' Her eyes begged Annie to believe her. 'It happened just after Joe died. I was unhappy and vulnerable. Sean comforted me . . . and one thing led to another.'

Annie desperately wanted to believe her. Accidents did happen and she remembered how devastated Rosaleen had been when Joe died. And hadn't she herself pushed Sean out of the house? Insisted that he go to see Rosaleen, and him just home after months at sea. Long, lonely months without a woman. Nevertheless they shouldn't have, they had no right . . . he was

Annie's husband. But if they did, and if it was only the once, was there an excuse for them? Angrily, she pulled her mind back to reality. Rosaleen was trying to fool her. Once? And there was a child? No, it was hardly likely.

'I don't believe you.'

But seeing that Annie was weakening despite herself, Rosaleen asked, 'Well, if you don't believe me . . . what do you intend doing about it?'

'What do you mean?'

'I mean, I want to know where I stand. Are you going to acquaint Sean with the knowledge that he's a father, or shall I?'

'He doesn't know?'

'Tut, Annie! Do you think he would just look the other way if he knew?'

Annie felt this was true. Sean had no inkling before he left that the child Rosaleen had just given birth to was his. She had already convinced herself of this. There was no way he would have asked her to make an appointment with the doctor if he had known that there was nothing wrong with him. Rosaleen had fooled him as well.

Now Rosaleen had her attention. 'Do you intend telling him?' Annie asked fearfully.

'Not unless *you* are going to act stupid. Sean is a wonderful person . . . as you well know. Are you going to let him go?'

'No, I am not!' Annie's voice was shrill. Imagine Rosaleen thinking she could walk off with Sean! 'I'll fight you tooth and nail for him.'

'You don't have to fight me,' Rosaleen interrupted her. 'Sean need never know about Liam, if you keep your mouth shut.'

Annie turned the words over in her mind, then her head swayed from side to side in despair.

'He'll know. The minute he sets eyes on Liam, he'll know.'

'Why?' At Annie's surprised look, Rosaleen repeated, 'Why? No one else has noticed.'

'I did!'

'Only you noticed. Look at him.' She pointed to where Liam lay sleeping on a rug. 'He's not the picture of Sean, is he?'

In sleep, Liam looked like the Magees. To Rosaleen's relief, Annie shook her head. Not a very definite shake, but a shake nevertheless, and she pressed on: 'He could have inherited his blue eyes from Joe's side of the family, couldn't he?'

A nod this time from Annie, and Rosaleen knew she had won – or lost? – her case.

'You have the right to maintenance, so you have,' Annie said mournfully.

Rosaleen tossed her head in disgust. 'Huh! I don't want maintenance. I'm far from rich but the business keeps me in comfort. I promise . . . I swear . . . that Sean will never hear from my lips that he's Liam's father.' She spread her hands wide. 'I can do no more.'

Annie looked at her intently. At the heavy, pale gold hair, the classic high cheek bones, the wide-spaced green eyes, so like her own, and without thinking, she asked, 'Are you in love with him?'

The colour rushed to Rosaleen's face and then receded, leaving her deathly pale.

'Of course I'm not!' And Annie was sorry that she had asked, because it was obvious to her that her beautiful sister was indeed in love with Sean.

The following day, Annie met her next-door neighbour. She was in the back garden gathering rubbish up and putting it in a pile at the bottom of the garden to burn, when a light voice hailed her from the other side of the hedge. The hedge wasn't very high and at first Annie thought her imagination was playing tricks on her, then the branches were parted slightly and she saw a small pale face with twinkling blue eyes.

'Hello, I'm Minnie Carson.'

'Hello. My name's Annie Devlin and I'm very pleased to meet you. Can you come in for a cup of tea?'

'I'd love to. I won't be a minnit.'

A few minutes later Minnie arrived around the side of the house, her arms full of flowers. The bunch was so big it almost dwarfed her. She was five foot tall, if that, about sixty years old, and bright and cheerful-looking.

'Thank you very much.' Annie sank her nose into the flowers and cried: 'Oh, they're lovely! Let's go inside and I'll put them in water.'

As they sat at the kitchen table, Minnie told Annie all about herself. She was a widow, with two married sons who lived on the opposite side of town. 'I was away at the week-end and I was going to call on you yesterday but you had company,' she explained.

'That was my sister and her children,' Annie replied, and Minnie nodded her head.

'I thought so . . . you are very alike.'

'You think so?'

Annie had always thought that she and Rosaleen were as different as chalk and cheese, but Minnie disagreed with her.

'The planes of your face are the same . . . and your eyes, it's just your colouring that's different.'

Annie grew silent. This tiny woman had noticed a lot, considering Rosaleen and she had been completely unaware of her. Had she overheard their conversation?

Minnie realised that she had given away more than she had intended, and sought to put matters right. From what she had overheard yesterday, fate had handed this young girl a bitter blow. She needed to be admired and her courage bolstered up.

'I saw you from the back bedroom,' she lied, with a nod up at the back of her house. 'I've a sewing machine up there . . . I was making curtains.'

'Oh, I see.'

'Do you sew?'

'I was a stitcher before the war, but I haven't a sewing machine,' Annie said regretfully.

'You can borrow mine. I'm away every week-end. You can have it any time you like. I visit the boys alternate week-ends.'

'Oh, that's kind of you. Curtains are so expensive. I would love to make my own. You must get on well with your daughters-in-law to visit them so often.'

'I do. But to tell you the truth, I'd prefer to stay in my own home. But since my husband died last year, the boys worry about me, and they insist I visit them.' Her face lit up. 'Perhaps, now that this house is occupied, I won't have to trek across town every week-end. And before I forget, I'll tell you another thing. I can get you material very reasonably. I've a friend in the business.' She drained her cup and rose to her feet. 'I'd better go now, but tomorrow you come and visit me.'

They beamed at each other, and Annie said softly, 'I'm glad to have you for a neighbour.'

'And I'm glad you're my new neighbour. I was dreading strangers coming, but I can tell that you and I are going to become friends. See you tomorrow . . . about eleven.'

Coming out of the docks, Sean flagged down a taxi, too excited to wait for a tram or trolleybus. He sat in the front of the taxi, beside the driver, and directed him to approach the Serpentine Road via the Shore Road. He wanted to see what Greencastle looked like. As they approached it, his eyes took it all in. It was bigger than he expected: a row of small shops and a pub, the Railway Bar, on the right-hand side of the road, and another row of shops and whitewashed cottages on

318

the left-hand side. This was all he had time to note as the car turned off near the start of the village and travelled up the Whitewell Road. Here, on the left-hand side, there was a housing estate and he observed that Greencastle had not escaped the blitz scot free. No, some streets were partially demolished, but he also noted that as they left the Whitewell Road and climbed the Serpentine Road, it was barely touched.

When his house came into view, he breathed a sigh of utter contentment, his eyes darting all over it in admiration as they approached. He had been surprised when Annie had written to tell him that she had decided to move into the house. Surprised, but pleased.

She had been living there for over three months now. Had left Mackie's a month ago to devote herself to decorating. Was she happy? Her letters were different. Not so demonstrative. All about the house . . . he had been perplexed, but soon would be able to judge for himself whether or not Annie regretted buying the house. He hoped not. He could picture them growing old together happily in this house.

When he had paid the taxi driver and turned to enter the driveway, he was puzzled that Annie had not come out to meet him. Perhaps she was busy?

He walked along the side of the house and stopped in amazement when he saw the changes made in the back garden. Annie was there, awaiting his reaction.

'You've been a busy wee woman!' he exclaimed, as he walked along the lawn, admiring the shrubs that had been trimmed, the borders bright with flowers. Even the big tree had been pruned. 'It's lovely, Annie. Very nice.'

She, too, looked lovely . . . beautiful, even . . . standing there. The late September sun highlighted the chestnut hue of her thick hair, showed up the

319

spattering of freckles that spanned the bridge of her small, straight nose, and turned her eyes to hazel. The short, yellow cotton dress she wore showed off her long slim legs and honey-coloured skin, and he found himself examining her intently. Gone was the cocky young teenager that he had married, and in her place was a beautiful, composed woman. All this hadn't happened overnight. How come he hadn't seen the changes taking place? His conscience would not let him escape from the truth. It wasn't because he was away so often. No, he had been too busy thinking of Rosaleen. Too preoccupied to see the beauty that his wife had become.

'You look lovely,' he told her sincerely, his eyes still on her face. She had made no effort to greet him. No face proffered for his kiss.

'Thank you.' She smiled wryly, and flapping her hand at the garden, confessed, 'Not all my work. I had a handyman in, an afternoon each week. I thought we'd better not let it go another winter.'

As he approached her, she turned and led the way inside, saying over her shoulder, 'The kitchen's pretty much the same as it was . . . just a lot cleaner.' She smiled at him, but he was aware that it didn't reach her eyes. 'Come see the sitting room.'

Slowly he followed her through the kitchen, along the hall, to pause on the threshold of the sitting room. As before she kept her distance from him, and awaited his praise.

And she deserved it; obviously long hours of work had been put into the room and the result was lovely. The high ceiling was snow white, as was the frieze, and the picture rail and deep skirting board and framework of the wide bay window a warm cream. The walls were papered with a flowered paper, a mixture of blues and greys, and a dark blue border, about three inches deep, ran along under the picture rail. At the window hung heavy damask curtains, a mixture of darker hues of blue and grey. All highlighting the beautiful colours in the slate mantelboard and contrasting with the pale grey of the marble hearth.

'I thought perhaps you would like to help choose the suite and carpet and a picture or two?' Her head tilted and her brows rose. 'Am I right?'

He nodded, and with a sweep of the arm embraced the room. 'All your own work?'

'Well, now. I have to confess that George helped me with the ceiling, but I did all the papering and painting,' she confessed proudly.

'It's lovely, Annie, you must have worked hard,' he praised her, but he was preoccupied. He was vaguely aware that something was wrong.

Any other time when he came home, if they had the house to themselves, they were straight up the stairs. Yet today, in this big empty house, she seemed to be avoiding him. Of course, she was anxious to show him the result of her labours. Still, she could just as easily have done so from the shelter of his arm. Not keep a wide berth between them.

'How's about showing me the bedroom, Annie,' he teased, and was surprised to note her dismay.

'Oh, I haven't decorated the bedroom yet!' she exclaimed, and he saw her squirm uneasily.

'I would still like to see it,' he insisted, and putting his arm around her waist, drew her out of the sitting room.

Annie allowed herself to be led up the stairs. His hand was gently moving along her ribcage, setting her aquiver, and when his other hand cupped her breast she thought she would faint with the longing and need that he was arousing in her. How could she let him? She should be ashamed of herself for wanting him so. After the way he had betrayed her. And with her sister. God, how it hurt, even after months of mulling it over.

321

Would she be able to pretend that she didn't know? She'd have to if she wanted to save her marriage, she would have to hold her tongue. Something that she was not noted for. Blabbermouth was her nickname, but once he knew he had a son . . . oh, it didn't bear thinking about. She was the one who was barren. There was nothing wrong with him. And she had gone on and on at him, making him miserable and afraid.

As he slowly undressed her, Sean kept his eyes on her face. She flinched each time his fingers touched her bare skin, and he thought he detected tears on her long dark lashes. What on earth was wrong with her? He felt as if he was seducing her. He let his hands grow still, and she stood there unmoving, gazing down at them.

'Annie? What's wrong?'

Her head swung in a wide arc, causing the tears to slip over and slide silently down her cheeks.

'Annie . . . look at me,' he commanded.

Slowly the dark, wet lashes rose and he gave a start of dismay. Never before in his life had he seen such despair. Did she hate living out here so much?

'Annie, is it because we bought the house?' he asked anxiously, his hands cupping her face, thumbs wiping away the tears. But as fast as he wiped them, more fell. 'Do you hate living out here so much?'

She gasped in alarm. 'No! Oh no . . . I love this house. It's the loveliest house in the world.'

How would she have survived without this haven?

He was bewildered and showed it. 'Then why on earth are you so miserable?'

Pulling free, she wiped the tears from her cheeks with the back of her hands, and grimaced.

'I'm just tired. I couldn't sleep last night, and I've a headache.'

The music hall excuse. Would he believe her?

He did not. 'That's strange, coming from you.' He

reached for her again, drawing her near, but not allowing their bodies to touch. 'But anyhow . . . it's not your head I'm interested in.'

Putting his finger under her chin, he tilted her face up and gazed deep into her tear-filled eyes.

She was trembling, and aware that she wanted him, he asked gently, 'Do you really want me to stop? I will, if that's what you want.'

She shook her head, her eyes clinging to his, and for the time being the cause of her misery was forgotten as he clasped her to him, and they responded to the urgent need created by months apart.

Once their reunion was over, Annie was more at ease. She blossomed under his teasing as together, the next day, they stripped the paper from the walls in the bedroom.

However, Sean was aware that things were far from well, so he questioned her.

'Did anything happen while I was away?' he asked, watching her intently.

'No . . . nothing important.'

Her eyes fell away from his. What a lie. Her world had fallen apart and the worry of what would happen when he saw Liam was with her night and day . . . and she was telling him nothing important had happened.

It was obvious to him that she lied, but he let it pass; she was still in a tearful mood and he did not want to upset her.

'Have you made an appointment for me to see the doctor?'

'Yes . . . yes, I have. I have to go next Wednesday.'

'*You* have to go?' His voice was sharp.

Her lip trembled and her voice shook when she replied, 'Please, Sean, do it my way . . . please? You're a Catholic. You know masturbation is a sin. I want to go to a specialist who is a Catholic, and that's the way he works things.'

323

It was a source of wonder to him just how good-living Annie was. When he had first met her, her forwardness, her cocky sureness, had convinced him that she was easy. Not cheap, oh, no, never cheap, but he had thought that she would be easily won over. He could not have been more wrong. Even with the engagement ring on her finger and war in the background, she had kept him at bay. Kisses and hugs, yes, she did not object to close embracing or long kissing, which were forbidden by the church, but anything else . . . no way. He had to wait until they were married, and he had been surprised at how proud he had been of her for sticking to her principles. And now, she preferred to go through the hassle and embarrassment of being examined herself rather than let him go.

'All right, all right . . . don't be upset.' He pulled her into his arms, and lightly rubbed his nose against hers. 'We'll do it your way,' he consoled her, and was rewarded by a wobbly smile.

On Wednesday morning, he walked to the top of the Serpentine Road with her. She had refused point blank to let him accompany her to the hospital, and as he assisted her on to the tram, he said, 'I'll keep my fingers crossed.'

She smiled and nodded at him, feeling a traitor. She knew that there was nothing wrong with him and she was letting him worry needlessly, but what else could she do? She had no choice. At least once the results came through he would know that there was nothing wrong with his sperm count. If Rosaleen was telling the truth, it would be high. Very high.

Thoughts that were never far from her mind returned to haunt her as she waited to see the specialist. Would Sean see the resemblance Liam bore him? He was owed a lot of holidays now the war was over, and he would be home for four months this time.

324

He had seen Liam on his last leave, but the baby had just been a few weeks old and had slept the whole time. There was no chance that he would not see the child this time, even though they lived so far away. Already he was planning on having her family down to spend Christmas Day with them. How would she survive it? The worry of it was having an awful effect on her; she was a bundle of nerves. She could see herself ending up in Grahame's Home, unless she got control of her emotions.

When the result of the tests eventually arrived, Sean greeted them with a great sigh of relief.

'Phew!' He took her in his arms and held her eye gravely. 'Now, Annie, there's nothing wrong with either of us. So let's just take things a day at a time and see what happens. Eh, love? Remember what you said? If it's God's will, we'll have a family. If not . . . well, we'll just have to live without them.'

And as she raised her face for his kiss, Annie was only too happy to agree with him.

Chapter 10

Pressing her forehead against the window, Rosaleen peered out into the gathering dusk to where, in the far distance, passengers were descending from the plane.

George watched her; he was worried about her. Since Annie's mad gallop down to live on the Serpentine Road, Rosaleen was a changed person. Withdrawn and touchy, she had even Thelma, usually unaware of undercurrents, muttering about her moods and easily aroused temper. On the journey down to Aldergrove Airport to meet her friends who were coming home from Canada to attend a funeral, he had tried to pump her. Tried to find out what had destroyed the close friendship shared by the two sisters, but she had evaded his leading questions, assuring him that nothing was wrong between Annie and herself. He was equally fond of both these girls who had welcomed him into their homes and hearts, and it dismayed him to sense the deep unhappiness within them. What on earth could have happened to cause such a rift?

Many times, he had gone over in his mind the week preceding the change in the girls but could think of nothing to account for their behaviour. He remembered that Annie had been distraught the night she had asked him to help her move things into her new home, but he had thought that whatever was wrong would soon blow over. But no . . . Annie had made it clear, at least to him, that she did not want Rosaleen visiting her. He had thought that when Rosaleen had gone down to Greencastle in spite of Annie's obvious rancour, all would be well, but alas, no. Rosaleen had obviously not been invited back, and Annie never came near her mother's, content to see her during working hours at Mackie's.

Suddenly Rosaleen turned to him, her face wreathed in smiles. He grinned happily back at her, glad to see the strain gone from her face. It was a long time since he had seen her smile spontaneously. Perhaps this friend they were meeting would take her out of herself; maybe even help to breach the great divide between Annie and her.

'I can see her! I'd know her from any distance!' Gripping his arm she pulled him close to the window. 'See the big tall guy, halfway up the steps? That's Billy! And there's May behind him . . . in the blue coat.'

They watched until all the passengers had disappeared into the tunnel leading to the Custom Offices, and then made their way down to the waiting room.

Her eyes fast on the door through which May would come, Rosaleen confided in him, 'You'll like her, so you will! Billy too.'

'I feel as if I already know her!' he exclaimed. 'I've heard so much about her. You two must have been very close.'

'We're like sisters.'

Pain shadowed her face at these words and he guessed that she was thinking of Annie, but it passed and then she was rushing across the room to embrace a small, obviously pregnant, young woman.

'May . . . ah, May! Here, let me look at you.'

Pushing May away from her, Rosaleen examined her critically. 'You look marvellous!'

And she did. Her hair was pale silvery blonde, obviously cared for by an expensive hairdresser, and even after the long journey, the bloom of pregnancy gave a glow to her skin. Lucky May! No morning sickness for her; she just sailed through her pregnancies.

'I wish I could say the same for you!' May eyed her in dismay. 'You must be about six stone. Does she not eat?' she demanded, turning to George.

'Not very much, from what I hear.'

'Oh, never mind about me, I'm all right. Billy . . .' Rosaleen's voice trailed off in confusion when she realised that he had a companion with him.

'Rosaleen, this is my cousin Andrew. And . . .?' He glanced in George's direction, his brow raised.

'Oh, excuse my manners.' Taking George by the arm, she pulled him forward. 'This is my brother, George,' she announced with a wide smile, and her pride in him was apparent to all.

'I feel as if I know you, George.' May gave him an impish grin. 'By . . . everybody must have got an awful shock when you turned up!'

'MAY!' Billy gave her a reproving look, dismayed at her audacity.

George just laughed. He had just been warned that May didn't pull her punches. 'Likewise. I've just been saying to Rosaleen I feel as if I already know you.' And after shaking each hand in greeting, he grabbed one of the cases and led the way out to the car park.

As they crossed over to George's car, aware of the other man examining her, Rosaleen thrust out her hand towards him.

'I'm sorry . . . I neglected to greet you. You must think me awful, but I wasn't expecting anyone else.'

'He made up his mind at the last minnit, Rosaleen.' May threw him an exasperated glance. 'I hadn't time to warn you.' But the smile she bestowed on him showed

328

how fond of him she was.

Rosaleen felt suddenly shy as Andrew held her hand longer than was necessary, and when he leant towards her and said, 'I'm very glad, now, that I decided to come.' She felt the colour rush to her face and was glad that the artificial lighting would conceal it. Imagine behaving like a schoolgirl!

In the car, she suddenly remembered the reason for this visit home and turned in dismay to Billy.

'I'm sorry about your father. You must think me awful but I was so pleased to see you, I forgot the reason you were here.'

'Don't worry your head, Rosaleen. The state me da's heart was in, it came as no surprise. He's been on borrowed time for years. I'm just sorry he didn't last long enough to see Canada. He'd have loved it out there.'

On the journey home, each time Rosaleen turned to speak to May or Billy in the back of the car, she met Andrew's eyes, dark and intense, examining her face, smiling faintly at her discomfort.

When they arrived at Iris Drive, Rosaleen dished up the supper she had prepared beforehand and once it was consumed George suggested that the two men would be better getting a move on. He was driving them over to the Shankhill Road to Billy's mother's and did not want to arrive in the early hours of the morning. Strange cars were suspect at all times on the Shankhill Road, but in the early hours of the morning – well, then you were really taking a chance.

May was staying with Rosaleen, and as the men donned their coats and bade them goodnight, a grave-faced Andrew assured Rosaleen that he would be back to see her, bringing bright rosy colour once again to her cheeks.

Annoyed at herself, she just gave him a curt nod. Who did he think he was? And just why was she blushing?

He was not someone that she would normally have given a second glance! Just an inch or so taller than herself, he was ordinary . . . ugly, even. The nicest thing about him was his eyes, the colour of dark chocolate and warm as velvet.

When they were curled up in armchairs each side of the fireplace, a gin and tonic in their hands, prepared for a long natter, May winked across at Rosaleen.

'Andrew is smitten.'

'Huh! Don't be silly!'

'He is . . . he is! A blind man could see it.'

'He's quite old, so he is. Is he not married?'

'He hasn't had time to bother with women. Not that they don't chase him, mind. Believe you me, they do! He's quite a catch . . . has his own small publishing business. And he's not all that old . . . he's only forty. You could do worse, so you could.'

'May, you haven't changed a bit! You always thought you knew what was best for me.'

'Well, I was right about Joe, wasn't I?'

Her eyes leaving May's searching gaze, Rosaleen gave a brief nod before retorting: 'Well, I'm not interested in any men at the moment.'

And to change the subject, she asked, 'How's Ian?'

'Great. Andrew's sister has him. She has two of her own so he won't be lonely.' Her hand fell to her bulging stomach. 'I hope this is a girl. Billy would love a daughter.' She grinned across at May. 'I can't wait to see your wee son . . . and Laura. I bet she has grown inches. I've a wee present for her.'

'She *has* grown . . . and cheeky with it!' But Rosaleen smiled as she said the words; she was very proud of her daughter. 'I don't know what I'd do without Amy. She's always willing to look after the kids, even at a moment's notice.' Suddenly apprehensive, she wondered what May would think of Liam. Would she see the resemblance he bore Sean? She hadn't thought of that. Best to try and keep them apart, but it would not be easy.

Now she said, 'You'll have to wait until after the funeral. Do you still want me to accompany you tomorrow?'

'Please . . . I'm not looking forward to it. Billy's worried about his mam. Thinks she'll want him to stay in Belfast, although, thank God, she has agreed to move in with one of her sisters, 'cause there's no way he'd leave her on her own.'

'How would you feel about that . . . staying home?'

'To be truthful, I want to stay in Canada. It's a better way of life over there. You'd love Canada, so you would.'

'There's not much chance of me visiting you, now that Joe's gone and I've two kids to rear.'

'It was awful sad him dying so young. I wish I could have been with you.'

'It was terrible, but your letters were a comfort to me, and Bobby Mackay was a tower of strength. I honestly don't know what I'd have done without him.'

'You must have had an awful shock, Rosaleen, when you discovered you were pregnant after Joe's death . . . especially after such a long break.'

'That's life. I wanted a brother or sister for Laura, but not the way it happened.' Her lips twisted wryly as she repeated inwardly: NO! Definitely not the way it happened.

'What are you smiling about?'

'What?' Rosaleen blinked and came back to reality. She had been smiling at how amazed May would be if she knew the truth of Liam's birth. Now she blustered, 'I'm not smiling.'

'It looked very much like a smile to me. Did I say something funny?'

'No . . . no. Tell me, what do you think of George?'

May gave her a reproving, 'You're not fooling me'

look, but condescended to change the subject.

'Oh, he's lovely. You can see your da in him, all right. There's no mistaking that he's your da's son.'

Her eyes grew round with wonder. 'Imagine . . . your da of all people! I nearly died when you wrote and told me. How on earth did he keep it a secret?'

'I don't know! I have often wondered that meself. In spite of visiting George every week, he managed to cover his tracks. Perhaps if George's mother had lived, he'd have been caught on.'

'He wouldn't have been able to keep it a secret in Spinner Street, I can tell you that. Old Ma Rafferty knows everybody's business.'

'There's one in every street, so there is. In Colinward Street it was Mrs Mullen, God rest her soul. But me da still managed to keep his secret.'

'All the same . . . it must have been awful for your mam. I don't know what I'd do if Billy suddenly confessed that another woman was expecting his child.' May lapsed into silence for a few moments. 'I think I'd murder him,' she confessed. 'Yes, it must have been awful for your mam, living with the knowledge that your da had a son.'

'That's life. We all get our crosses to bear.'

'Oh, listen to you! Like you've had crosses to bear?' She grimaced in dismay. 'Sorry . . . I know you were widowed young. But other than that, you were born lucky. And I'm sure Joe left you comfortable, eh?'

Rosaleen laughed outright. May didn't believe in beating about the bush.

'Yes, he left me comfortable,' she said, deliberately not telling May what she wanted to know. 'Now, how about you?'

'You'll never believe it . . . but Billy has consented to make an honest woman of me. Before this child is born,' she patted her bump, 'he's going to marry me in the Catholic Church.'

332

'Ah, May, I'm glad to hear that.'

'He's not turning, mind, but he has agreed the kids can be brought up Catholics. Ye see, it's different out there! Nobody cares what religion you are, so he doesn't have to worry about the effect it will have on his relatives, 'cause they'll be none the wiser. It's only here that Catholics and Protestants distrust each other, Rosaleen.'

Noticing the fatigue around May's eyes, the tired droop to her mouth, Rosaleen rose to her feet and relieved her of her empty glass. 'Do you want another one . . . or do you want to go to bed?'

'I think I'll retire, Rosaleen. I can hardly keep my eyes open.'

'It's great to have you home, May. Two whole weeks! Think of the fun we'll have.' Her voice trailed off. 'You know what I mean,' she finished lamely, thinking of the funeral.

'I know what you mean. It's sad . . . but once the funeral's over, we'll be free to enjoy ourselves. Seeing that Andrew enjoys himself will help Billy cope with his grief. He'll want Andrew to see all over the north. He was only seven when his parents emigrated. You'll not mind Andrew tagging along, sure you won't?'

'No . . . just as long as you don't try any matchmaking. Promise?'

'I can promise that with a clear conscience,' May assured her. 'Andrew doesn't need any help.' She grinned impishly. 'In spite of his ugly mug, he's a charmer. So, you have been warned. Come on. Let's go to bed, or I'll never make it to the funeral tomorrow.'

Once the funeral was over, Billy, with Andrew in tow, spent another two days attending to his mother's insurance policies and settling all accounts attached to the funeral. Then his mother went to stay with her sister, shooing Billy off to show Andrew around Northern Ireland.

Meanwhile May and Rosaleen shopped in town, May, having obtained some precious coupons from Billy's relatives, determined to buy some Irish linen gifts to bring back to Canada.

Then Billy, burying his pain deep within, determined that Andrew would enjoy the first break he'd had in years, and set about arranging a good time for him.

Although he and Rosaleen were thrown together a lot, Andrew never again expressed any romantic interest in her. In spite of all May's warnings, he never put a foot wrong; never said a word out of place. This pleased Rosaleen; it meant that she was able to relax and enjoy herself, and they became friends.

Billy hired a car and the four of them toured all over the north, showing Andrew around the Glens of Antrim, the stark splendour of the Giant's Causeway, the beauty of Cushendun and Cushendal, and wonderful Ballycastle where the Auld Lammas Fair was in progress.

Then, in Belfast itself, they took the tram out to the Zoo at Bellevue and then climbed the Cave Hill and stood on Napoleon's Nose, admiring the scenery for miles around, Rosaleen pointing out a winding road far to the left and explaining that it was the Serpentine Road and that Annie now lived there. The Botanic Gardens and Ulster Museum also received a visit, and the pride of Belfast, the Castle itself, was toured and exclaimed over by an admiring Andrew.

Then in the evenings they visited the Opera House and St Mary's Hall, and the Empire Theatre, where Andrew was delighted at the variety concerts. The two weeks went past in a flash and to Rosaleen's amusement, on the night before they were about to fly back to Canada, May and Billy had some very important business to attend to, leaving Andrew and she alone. Rosaleen realised that Billy would want to spend the day with his mother, but not his last night in Belfast. And May had apparently decided to spend the night with Billy at her mother-in-law's house. Rosaleen could see that she and Andrew were being set up.

She was a bit embarrassed, it was so blatant! Surely May could see that she and Andrew were not attracted to each other? At least not in that way. She found him a wonderful companion, felt contented in his company, but there was no physical attraction. During the past fortnight he had been kind and courteous, treating her like a lady, and it was true she would miss him. Life would be dull when he returned to Canada.

After first checking with her that it would be all right, he booked a table for a meal in one of the posh hotels in town and arranged to pick her up at seven o'clock.

She spent the afternoon preparing for their date, grateful to Amy for looking after the kids yet again; she'd had them so often since May's arrival, leaving Rosaleen free to enjoy herself. First a long, leisurely bath, perfumed with bath oils brought over by May. Then she shampooed her hair and rolled it in curlers. While it was drying, she manicured her nails and varnished them her favourite pale pink.

As she stood in front of the mirror smoothing her best petticoat down over her slim hips, she had to admit that May was right − she was too thin, except for her bust which was firm and full and swelled seductively over the lace at the top of the petticoat. She could do with some new underwear! But now that she could afford the best, there was not enough clothing coupons to buy them. Although the war was over, its effects were still being felt, and she had used all her coupons on a new coat for herself and clothes for the children.

Not that it would make any difference. Andrew had no chance of seeing her underwear . . . no chance at all!

She wore the suit and blouse that she had worn for her first date with Sean. Pre-war but that didn't matter. Everybody was wearing dated clothes, and this was the first time she had worn the suit since that evening and she knew it became her.

Once ready, she viewed herself from all angles, pleased that her hair just failed to meet her shoulders and swung like a bell around her face, casting shadows on her cheeks and making her eyes dark and mysterious-looking. The jacket of the suit, being boxed, was all right but the skirt didn't hug her hips as snugly as before; nevertheless, it swung seductively around her calves and called attention to her slim ankles, so what more could she ask for?

Satisfied at what she saw, she gave a wry smile. Anyone would think that she was going out with a lover. But still . . . she wanted to do Andrew proud, wanted him to remember her looking her best.

When he arrived, he stood inside the doorway and his glance slowly swept over her from head to toe, full of delighted admiration. She lapped it all up; it was a long time since she had seen such admiration in a man's eyes.

'You look beautiful,' he said sincerely, and she nodded in acknowledgement of the compliment. Lifting up her handbag, an exact match for her smart court shoes, she indicated that she was ready to go, aware that he had kept the taxi waiting to take them to town.

Once at the hotel, Andrew came into his own. Not used to dining in such opulence, Rosaleen asked him to choose for her, and this he did competently, conferring with her to be sure that she liked what she chose. In fact, Rosaleen noticed a touch of arrogance in his manner and guessed that he was used to being in charge, and often dined out. It was with surprise that she found herself wondering if he had a special woman friend. May was right; he was charming, and any woman would be proud to be seen with him.

When they were settled, waiting for the prawn cocktails he had ordered for starters, the wine waiter having poured the wine of Andrew's choice, he leant towards her.

'You know, I'm going to miss you,' he said softly.

'I'll miss you too,' she whispered back.

At this admission, he smiled and his hand reached across the table towards hers. His eyes were warm and caring and reminded her of her father's.

Without thought she said, 'You remind me of my da.'

It had been meant as a compliment but the minute the words left her lips she regretted them. She could see that he was hurt and offended. The smile slid from his face and his hand was slowly withdrawn.

However, he quickly recovered his composure and her muttered 'I'm sorry,' was waved aside as he raised his glass to toast her.

'I wish you all the best in the future, Rosaleen. May you meet somone you can be happy with.'

'Andrew . . . I'm really sorry.'

'Don't be! We can't help how we feel. Look, let's just enjoy ourselves. I'll probably never see you again after tomorrow and I want to remember you smiling and happy.'

But her words had put a damper on their spirits and the delicious meal was eaten in comparative silence.

Andrew had arranged for the taxi to return for them at half-past nine and as they awaited its arrival, they sat in the foyer and sipped brandy. Once more Rosaleen tried to breach the gap that was yawning wider between them with every minute that passed.

He was sitting, head bowed, swirling the brandy round and round in the glass. Impulsively, she reached across and touched his knee.

At once he was full of apologies. 'I'm sorry. How ignorant of me.'

'Andrew,' she interrupted him. 'Please let me explain . . . please!'

His hand covered and squeezed hers. 'There's no need. I was foolish to think you liked me.'

'I do! I do!'

'As a father figure?' He smiled slightly. 'That's not quite what I had in mind.'

'I was paying you a compliment. My father was a wonderful man . . . just like you. Kind and understanding . . . comfortable to be with.'

His grip on her hand tightened and he leant towards her. 'Rosaleen, are you telling me that you care for me?'

This brought her up short. She liked him, but obviously he wanted more. Just how did she feel towards him? She hadn't really given it any thought; had just enjoyed his company. Not wanting to lie, she groped about in her mind for words that would not give offence.

As the silence lengthened he relaxed his hold on her hand and with a sigh, drew back. Unable to think of anything to say, she was glad when he nodded towards a man hovering in the doorway.

'I think our taxi has arrived. I'll just check that it's ours.'

As she waited for him to return, she berated herself. She could have assured him that she was fond of him! What difference would it have made? Tomorrow he would be gone. She could have put on an act. But would it have been an act? She was all mixed up, hadn't thought of him in that way. Hadn't expected him to become serious.

The journey home was strained and when they arrived at Iris Drive, she turned to him.

'Don't send the taxi away. You must have packing

and things to see to. Thank you for a lovely meal. I'll see you tomorrow.'

He threw her an angry glance and followed her from the cab. When he had paid the driver his fare, he faced Rosaleen. 'I think the least you can do is offer me a cup of coffee or a drink.'

At his tone of voice, her head reared in the air.

'Of course!'

Inside the house, she headed for the kitchen, leaving him to hang up his own coat, should he care to remove it. She was angry, very angry.

So she had compared him to her father! So he had taken offence! Well, she had done all the placating she intended to do. The sooner he drank his coffee and left, the better she would like it. On second thoughts . . . it would be easier to pour him a drink. What had she to offer him? There was some Old Bush, left since God knows when. Would it be all right? Yes, of course! Whiskey matured with age, didn't it? But did it keep once the bottle was opened? She had no idea. Ah, t'hell! she'd risk it. It was all she had . . . besides a little gin for herself.

He had removed his coat and loosened his tie and was sitting sprawled out on one of the armchairs, making the chair appear too small for his bulk. Avoiding his eyes, she handed him the glass of whiskey and then sat down on the settee.

'Rosaleen, we got off on the wrong foot tonight. Will you accept my apology? I was childish to take offence.'

For the first time since they had entered the house, she looked him in the eye. They were full of pleading and her anger, already on the wane, disappeared altogether.

'We were both at fault, but I was honestly paying you a compliment.'

'I realise that now . . . and thank you. I didn't mean to throw it back in your face.'

339

'It's all right.'

Now that she was relaxed and the warmth of the fire warmed her limbs, the gin, following so swiftly on top of the wine and brandy and more than she usually consumed, took hold of her, sending her floating on a happy cloud. The room was slowly revolving around her and she closed her eyes to stop it, but that only made it go faster. She stared hard at the fire which helped.

In her dreamlike state, it came as a surprise to her when, prising the glass from her reluctant fingers and placing it to one side, he said, 'Come on . . . it's bed for you.'

Gripping her hands, he pulled her to her feet. 'Come lock the door after me. I'll see you tomorrow.'

He reached for his coat, but without his support she swayed and he drew her gently into his arms to steady her. Her eyes, almost on a level with his, were inviting and her lips swayed tantalizingly near.

Aware that she was not in command of her actions, he started to put her from him, but then she licked her lips as if anticipating his touch and he was lost.

For the second time in her life Rosaleen found herself on the rug in front of the fire, naked in a man's arms. His kisses were long and soul searching, his touch thrilling. She wanted him. How she wanted him! But even through the blur of pleasure that was lifting her towards fulfilment, warning bells rang. Was she prepared to carry another child? No! Oh, no! She couldn't take the risk.

Feverishly, she pushed at his chest; he drew back and looked deep into her eyes. 'What's wrong? Do you . . .'

'I don't want another baby . . . I can't have another child. You see, Joe isn't here to blame it on. Everybody will know I'm a whore.'

He gave her a slight shake. 'Rosaleen, listen to me . . . I promise you that there'll be no baby. Do you hear me? There'll be no baby.'

340

Her eyes sought and found reassurance in his and she nodded, and as his mouth lowered once more towards hers, her arms closed around his waist and gripped him tight.

Sounds downstairs awoke Rosaleen the next morning and she opened her eyes fearfully. Was it a prowler? Or Amy? Her eyes sought the bedside clock. Six! Too early for Amy . . . it must be a prowler.

Then, when she heard him mount the stairs, whistling happily, memory came rushing back.

Had he stayed the night? Had she really made love with him? It wasn't a dream then?

When he entered the room she was sitting up in bed, the bedclothes pulled up under her armpits, her eyes wide and wary.

'Good morning. I've brought you some tea and toast.'

He settled the tray across her legs and stood looking down at her, a wide grin on his face.

'My, but you'd be a sight to awaken beside every morning.' His grin became rueful. 'Pity I can't say the same about myself.'

Still she didn't speak. She wished she could remember all that had happened the night before; she couldn't even remember coming to bed.

'Eat your breakfast and then we'll talk.'

Obediently she lifted the cup of tea, but waved towards the tray to indicate that she did not want the toast.

He lifted it. 'Would you mind if I smoked? I don't usually smoke in the bedroom but I want to talk to you and at the moment I need a cigarette.'

She nodded her consent and he left the room.

When he returned he sat on the edge of the bed, drawing smoke into his lungs, deep in thought.

He was naked to the waist and as she sipped her tea

341

she examined him covertly. Thick black hair covered his arms and chest. At last he lifted his eyes and met hers.

'How much do you remember about last night?'

'Not much,' she admitted, her eyes fearful.

'Rosaleen . . . I want you to believe something. I didn't take advantage of you. You were all for it.'

She gulped in her throat. So they had made love. Had she conceived?

As if reading her mind, he continued, 'But I can assure you, there will be no baby.'

The relief that flooded through her sent all the tension from her body and she relaxed, slumping back on the pillows with a sigh.

He was in a dilemma. She had made some statements the night before that he would like enlightenment on but obviously she had forgotten them. Should he pursue the matter or let it go?

A whore! She had called herself a whore. Well, he had met many whores, and having spent the last two weeks constantly in her company, knew she was not one of them. But there was something bothering her . . . he decided to try and find out what it was.

'Rosaleen, you said some things last night that puzzled me.'

The fear was back in her eyes. What had she said? She shouldn't have drunk so much.

'What did I say?'

'You called yourself a whore.'

Her face blanched and at the stricken look in her eyes, he reached for her. She pushed him roughly away and turned her head from him.

'If you must know . . . I spoke the truth.'

Cigarette crushed out, he sank to his knees beside the bed, and endeavoured to pull her round to face him.

'You did not! You're not even promiscuous!'

Slowly, she turned her head towards him. 'How would you know? Eh? We've just met.'

'I know women and you are no whore. You said Joe wasn't here to take the blame . . . am I to assume one of your children wasn't fathered by him?'

'Neither of them are Joe's.'

She laughed bitterly at the stunned look in his eyes.

'Now do you believe me?'

Speechless, he gaped at her, his mind in a whirl.

Tears were swelling in her chest, and determined not to let him see her weep, she once more pushed at him.

'Would you mind leaving me now, please? I want to get dressed.'

Bewildered, he rose to his feet, trying to sort out his jumbled thoughts. Then he saw the tears spill over and slide silently down her cheeks and he sat down on the bed again. Ignoring her efforts to evade him, he gently gathered her into his arms, cradling her head against his chest.

'Cry it all up . . . get it out of your system and then tell me about it. Because no matter what you are. I've fallen in love with you.'

The shock of these words stopped the tears falling and in the comfort and warmth of his arms, with the kindness in his voice soothing her, she found herself telling him things she had told no one but the priest in the confessional.

Everything came tumbling from her lips: her night with Sean; Joe's impotence; her relief when he accepted Laura as his own. Her anguish when Sean married Annie. How, after Joe's funeral, she had again conceived Sean's child.

He interrupted her one time only.

'Is this Sean fellow stupid? Did he not guess?'

'Annie had him convinced that he was sterile, it was easy deceiving him.' She wiped her eyes dry on the

343

corner of the sheet and grimaced at him. 'Now you can see how evil I am.'

'No . . . no.' Tenderly, he pushed the damp hair back from her brow. 'Ah, Rosaleen, no . . . you are a victim of circumstance. What about other men? Is there anyone you see?'

'Just Pat McDade.'

'Who is he?'

'He lives around the corner in Oakman Street. It's not serious . . . well, not on my part. He wants to marry me.'

'But you don't want to marry him?'

She shook her head. Handsome though Pat was, he had never inspired any deep emotion in her; they were just friends.

'Is it a relationship?'

Uncomprehending, she looked blankly at him, then the penny dropped.

'Oh, no . . . no. I told you it wasn't serious!'

His look was full of sadness. So much of her life had been wasted. She was so sensual, so passionate. And she called herself a sinner!

He glanced at his watch. 'I'll have to be going soon. Look, Rosaleen . . . will you write to me?'

'Of course! If you really want me to.'

'I really want you to. And . . . I know that Sean is the great love of your life. I don't begrudge you that. But it's over! You must look to the future. I'll take anything you offer . . . it's up to me to teach you to love me, because *you* obviously need someone to take care of you.'

Wide-eyed, she stared at him and then her jaw slowly dropped when he rose and started to remove his trousers.

'Move over . . . If you don't remember last night, then I'll have to refresh your memory. I want to be sure you think of me often.'

Smiling at the eager way she made room for him, he slid into bed beside her. And proceeded to love her, teaching her as he went along, opening new avenues of pleasure for her. Stopping only when she was completely sated.

'I wish you had a shower, Rosaleen. That bath is going to be a tight squeeze for us.' `

'You mean ... us ... us ... bathe together?' she squeaked.

His great throaty laugh filled the room. 'Yes ... us ... together!'

Then he gathered her up in his arms and descended the stairs, satisfied that he was leaving her plenty to remember him by. He was only glad that he had been in time to catch her. She was ripe for the picking and if that fool McDade hadn't been so slow, she would have been lost to Andrew forever.

The following weeks were lonely for Rosaleen, but with each letter she received from Andrew a warm glow enveloped her and she walked around in a contented haze. Memories of him were constantly with her. Often she recalled the day she and George had driven them to the airport. When all their goodbyes had apparently been said, Andrew led her away from the rest and kissed her long and ardently.

Then he had whispered, 'Remember you're mine and I'll be sending for you.'

And hugging these words close to her heart, she had returned to the company, rosy with happiness; to delighted grins from May and Billy and a pleased smile from George.

There was only one cloud on the horizon now. Annie! The awful sin she had committed against her sister festered like an open wound.

If only Annie had not guessed the truth, they could still be friends and Rosaleen would be able to discuss with her the great change Andrew had made in her life. And now Sean was home, would they come visiting? Would he see the resemblance?

May had! It had been with apprehension that she had watched her friend's first encounter with Liam. Stunned incredulity had showed on her face, but Rosaleen had been ready for her.

Smiling and at ease she had said, 'Isn't he lovely? I think he's like me da, but Amy say's he's the picture of Joe's father,' she lied, and must have sounded convincing because May relaxed, and if she doubted Rosaleen, managed to hold her tongue. But what about Sean? What would happen if he guessed the truth?

To think that a few short months ago she had been hoping that he would recognise his son and persuade her to run off with him to live in sin. Imagine her contemplating living in sin! As if that was the answer to anything. In time, the shame would have tarnished their great love for each other and they would have been unhappy cut off from family and church.

Soon it would be Christmas. The family always gathered together then. What would Annie do?

For the first time in her life Rosaleen dreaded the festive season, and her gratitude to Andrew increased. His letters kept her from despairing. Though he never mentioned marriage. But then, he was up to his eyes in work. He wrote about his business . . . about launching books . . . but she didn't understand. It only made her aware that he had a hectic social life, and she felt jealous. It was obvious that he was a passionate man. Was he sharing his bed with someone? Oh, she hoped not! What if, in his case, it was out of sight out of mind? He had certainly made sure that she remembered him.

At night she hugged herself as she relived the feel of his arms around her, the rapture of his touch, and prayed that he would send for her. It would solve all her problems. Meanwhile, there was Christmas to get over, but that was out of her hands. It all depended on what Annie decided to do. She could only hope and pray everything worked out all right. Her sights were set on Canada; it was her only hope of a happy, fulfilling life. Please God, don't let anything spoil my chances, she prayed.

Chapter 11

For Sean, the following weeks flew past as, weather permitting, he toiled in the front garden each day building a rockery. He would disappear for a time and then arrive back, weighed down by a huge boulder; laughing at Annie when she chastised him, afraid of him wrecking his back. They were lucky to have Minnie living next door. She had *connections*, and even though wallpaper was like gold dust, managed to obtain some for them. None of the current paint and stippling for their rooms, and as Sean papered walls and painted woodwork he was contented and happy. He even built shelves in the alcove beside the hearth in the living room, displaying a talent for decorating to equal Annie's own. She assisted him in every way she could and each evening as they relaxed for an hour or two in the living room, before retiring for the night, there was a closeness and harmony between them such as they had never experienced before. Nevertheless, Sean was aware that Annie was not completely at one with him. There was a shadow in her eyes that all his teasing could not banish, and behind which he was not allowed to see.

He watched her sitting across the hearth from him, the light from the table lamp turning her hair to burnished copper, her face pale in its shadow; knitting needles clicking away as she knitted a pullover for him.

The wool had been salvaged from a pullover of Tommy Magee's. She had ripped it out and wound it into hanks. These had been washed and dried and then rolled into balls, and now a new pullover was appearing on the needles. Annie was a wonderful homemaker; thrifty and wise, she flourished where others would have foundered, and most pleasing of all . . . the house was coming alive under her influence. What pleased him most was the fact that she really must love the house, because not once had she suggested that they go out visiting, seeming content to remain at home with him. Knowing how close she was to her mother and Rosaleen, this surprised him. Different from him; a flying visit to his parents was sufficient for him, but then, daughters were closer to their parents than sons. However, was he not being selfish, shouldn't he offer to go visiting? Didn't she need to see her family? While he was feeling generous and willing to waste some of his precious leave visiting, he suggested: 'How's about you and me going out tomorrow night, Annie?'

Her head jerked up and she queried, 'Out? Out where? Where would we go?'

For a moment, the guard in her eyes slipped and he thought he saw fear there. But what would she be afraid of?

'Well, I thought perhaps we could go up and visit your mother and Rosaleen. Take them out for a quiet drink.'

Her gaze swerved away from his and he saw her knuckles grow white as her hands tightened on the knitting needles.

'Do you particularly want to go out?' she asked, the shadow back in her eyes as they gazed at him.

Bewildered at her attitude, he replied, 'Well, yes . . . why not? You know what they say . . . all work and no play makes . . . even someone as fascinating as me a

349

dull boy.' He grinned as he teased her, but her figure remained tense, her face serious. He continued, 'While we're up there, we can invite them down for Christmas Day. Let's invite George as well, shall we? And perhaps he has a girl friend he could bring. The more the merrier.'

Fear was welling up inside her. Before it could swamp her and he became aware of it, she agreed with him.

'All right . . . let's go visiting,' she said resignedly, and to turn the knife in the aching wound that was her heart, added, 'Young Liam will be quite a big boy now, almost ten months. He's a lovely child.' Her voice trailed off as she gazed into his eyes and remembered that Liam's were identical. She bit on her lip before finishing: 'He's beautiful, so he is.' After all, Sean had to see the baby sometime or other and better tomorrow than to have an almighty row when they came on Christmas Day.

Hearing the misery in her voice, Sean regretted his impulsive suggestion. Obviously, that was why Annie was staying away from the Springfield Road – she could not bear to see Rosaleen's children. He wished that he had not opened his big mouth, but he had committed himself now. Should he back down? No . . . she should not retreat from reality! It wasn't right that she should avoid children.

It was brought home to him just how wrong he had been to suggest visiting the Springfield Road when, that night, for the first time since he had arrived home, Annie stayed rigidly on her own side of the bed. He had been stupid to think that she was happy here. She was still fretting for a child, and it looked like they were doomed to be childless. What was to become of her? She could not avoid children for the rest of her life. Perhaps he should broach the idea of adoption?

He had been thinking about adoption for some time

now, but was reluctant to take the final step; to admit to himself that they were apparently doomed to be childless. Now he dithered. Not yet . . . not just yet . . . he would wait another while.

There was a sharp frost the next day and this increased as it wore on. The thought of the steep climb up on to the Antrim Road and then the hanging about in the cold waiting for a tram or trolleybus, followed by another wait in town for a tram up the Grosvenor Road to the Springfield Road, sent Sean out to the nearest phone box to order a taxi to take them to Colinward Street.

Sitting hunched up in a corner of the car, Annie felt physically sick as it drew up to her mother's front door. Would Rosaleen be there? Would she have Liam with her? To her relief, she was reprieved. Her mother and George were alone in the kitchen.

'Why . . . come on in, come on. It's nice to see ye, Sean. I was beginnin' t'think that I'd done something to annoy you.'

Sean answered her mother's greeting by lifting her up in his arms and giving her a bear's hug.

'We've just been awfully busy,' he informed her. 'We're getting the house ready, so that you can come down and spend Christmas Day with us.'

'Oh, but we're goin' down to Rosaleen's house for our Christmas dinner, so we are. Ye know how it is, Sean, we want to see the kids' faces when they see what Santa Claus has left them.'

'Oh, don't you worry about that. We're inviting Rosaleen down too. You can see the kids open their presents at home and then come to us. Santa will have visited our house with toys as well. We want to see the kids' faces and all.'

A sudden thought made his eyes seek Annie's face as he spoke. Had he done the wrong thing again? Did she want the kids down at Christmas? Not once had he asked her opinion. He had just assumed that she would love having them all down, had thought that he was pleasing her. However, Annie had her back towards him, she was busy hanging their coats at the foot of the stairs, and he did not know how she was reacting to his suggestions. He was stupid; he should have talked this over with her, not just rushed in where angels feared to tread. But the damage was done, his invitation received with a smiling nod.

The moment passed as George welcomed him and soon they were settled close to the fire and were brought up to date on all the news.

When Thelma rose to make a cup of tea, Sean stopped her.

'How's about something stronger? Do you fancy going down to the Clock Bar for a drink?' he asked. 'I thought we could call into Rosaleen's on our way down, and if Amy will babysit she can join us.'

George was on his feet instantly. 'That's a smashing idea, Sean. Let's not waste any more time. Come on, Thelma.' He lifted her coat, and before she had time to demur, assisted her into it.

'He looks after me well, so he does.' Thelma smiled fondly at George before adding, 'Did ye know that George lives here now? He's being instructed in the faith, so he is.' At Annie's start of surprise, she grunted, 'Huh! Of course ye don't know! You haven't been here since ye left Mackie's. Did we do something to offend you?'

'No, Mam. I've just been very busy, so I have.'

Although she was happy for George, this news dismayed Annie. At the back of her mind was the idea that if Sean recognised young Liam as his son and wanted to leave her, she could return to her mother's home until such time as she made other arrangements. Now where would she go? There were only two bedrooms in her mother's house.

Seeing Annie's dismay, Sean covered up for her, although he could not fathom why she should be unhappy at the idea. Wasn't she very fond of George? Glad that he had come into their lives?

'That's the best news I've heard in a long time,' he said. 'Tommy will be pleased.'

At once Thelma's eyes swung to meet his. Was he jesting? 'You think he'll know?'

And when Sean nodded his head vigorously and said, 'I think he'll know', she sighed contentedly and her smile stretched from ear to ear.

The two men walked ahead as they made their way down the Springfield Road. Annie was left to walk with her mother.

'Our Rosaleen's not a bit well lately, so she's not,' Thelma confided in her. 'She's lost an awful lot of weight. Wait 'til ye see her. Her clothes are hangin' on her. I think she works far too hard at that wee business. It's not worth it! I keep tellin' her money's not everything, but she doesn't listen to me. Will you have a word with her, Annie? She'll listen to you, so she will.'

'I don't think she'll listen to me, Mam. I'm the stupid one of the family, remember.' And inwardly she added, Stupid and blind!

At this Thelma drew back and looked at Annie in surprise. 'Stupid, my foot . . . you were the brainier of the two of ye. You took after your da.' A deep sigh left her lips. 'Your da was wasted, ye know. With a bit of education, he could have gone places, made something of hisself. It broke his heart that we couldn't afford to keep you on at school. You were so bright.'

'I didn't even know I was good enough,' Annie said, her voice full of disbelief. Had they really thought that much of her? Well then . . . why hadn't they told her? Made her feel as beloved as Rosaleen!

'Oh, did ye not?' When Annie shook her head, Thelma continued, 'I thought ye knew . . . we probably made light of it because we couldn't afford to let you go to St Dominic's. How your da regretted that he hadn't a better job! But even with my wee cleanin' job, we just couldn't manage it.'

This was all news to Annie, but it was too late for regrets. However, her mother sounded so sorrowful, she hastened to reassure her.

'Well, I didn't do too badly, did I?'

These words made Thelma laugh. 'No, ye did not. You'd go far to get better than Sean, so ye would. And now ye have that posh house.'

They had arrived in Iris Drive, and to Annie's relief she was reprieved again: Rosaleen was not at home. It was Amy who answered their knock on the door and informed them that Rosaleen had gone out for a few hours. Where she did not know.

After an exchange of greetings and a bit of a chat, they bid Amy farewell and continued on down the Springfield Road and along the Falls Road to the Clock Bar. Situated at the corner of Lower Clonard Street, this was one of the popular pubs and the lounge was crowded. And who should be sitting in one of the corners but Rosaleen.

Both Annie and her mother gaped when they saw who Rosaleen was with – tall, handsome Pat McDade, well known for his womanising and gambling. What on earth was she doing with him?

Rosaleen did not see them, and glad that the lounge was packed Annie made her way to the only empty table, in the opposite corner from Rosaleen and her companion, glad that they did not have to sit beside them.

Once the women were seated, Sean and George went to the bar for drinks and Annie watched Rosaleen, her eyes taking in the new coat that she wore. It had obviously cost a bob or two, not to mention clothing coupons, but then, Rosaleen's business was doing well.

354

Annie sighed. She had felt quite attractive in her dark brown two-piece wool suit, even though it was pre-war. Now she felt dated, mousy. It was all right for Rosaleen, her house had been furnished before all the rationing started; she didn't have to use her coupon allowance for curtain material and soft furnishings.

She found herself envying Rosaleen her new coat. Emerald green in colour, it highlighted her fairness, darkened the green of her eyes. Completely unaware of them, she was deep in conversation with Pat, laughing into his eyes, obviously teasing him. She looked beautiful, her hair a soft, shining, silvery cloud, her eyes glinting like emeralds. Annie agreed with her mother, Rosaleen had lost a lot of weight, but this just emphasised the high cheek bones, the small pointed chin, and when she threw back her head in laughter, her teeth gleamed, even and white. Even as Annie watched, she saw her glance at the bar, and the amazement and joy with which she met Sean's eyes brought fear rushing to Annie's heart. Sean was gaping back at her in surprise and a lump gathered in Annie's throat, threatening to choke her.

Rising abruptly to her feet, she made her way to the Ladies' room and was relieved to find it empty.

In front of the wash-hand basin she gazed mournfully at her reflection. Her eyes, dark and haunted, stared sorrowfully back at her. How was she going to get through the evening? Before she had time to regain control of her emotions, Rosaleen arrived on her heels and their eyes, green on green, met in the mirror.

'This is a surprise,' Rosaleen greeted her, and Annie's throat was so tight with unshed tears, she found that she could only nod in reply.

It was obvious to her that her sister was very much in love with Sean, but how did he feel?

'Were you up at my house?' Rosaleen asked, and when Annie once again nodded, she sighed. 'I wish I'd known that you were coming . . . I'd have stayed at home.'

Then she would not have been taken unawares and gaped at Sean like that. He would always have the power to lift her on high, but she knew that she would be better off with Andrew. He knew all her secrets and she would not have to watch her words or actions with him. Now she was worried that Annie had seen her greet Sean.

At last Annie found her voice and her look held disbelief. 'And missed your date with Pat McDade? Eh? What on earth are you doing with him?' she asked, and was glad to find that her voice sounded composed.

'What's wrong with Pat?' At Annie's incredulous look, Rosaleen added, 'He's good company, so he is, and I'm lonely. What with you sulking down in Greencastle and May in Canada. . .'

'Sulking?' Annie interrupted her angrily. 'Sulking?'

'Well . . . aren't you? Why can't you just let bygones be bygones?'

Annie was saved from answering her by the door opening to admit their mother. She had to make do with a withering look. Bygones, indeed! And Sean the father of her child?

'Are you all right, Annie?'

'Of course I'm all right, Mam. Why shouldn't I be?'

'Well, ye rushed away from the table so suddenly, without so much as an "Excuse me", that I thought ye must feel unwell.'

Aware that both women were eyeing her, Annie retorted, 'Sorry . . . but nature called. It's this cold weather, I'm always running, so I am.'

And although Thelma examined her face intently and noted how pale she was, she accepted the excuse, and they all returned to the lounge together; a worried Rosaleen well aware that Annie had not visited the loo.

Had Annie seen her greet Sean? That was the second time she had been taken unawares. She would have to find some way to warn him. Obviously Annie had not confronted him, but after the way she had gaped at him . . . who knew what Annie might do! If only Andrew would send for her, before all her guilty secrets were unmasked. That was if he intended to send for her. It was three weeks since he had written, and when questioned, May was noncommittal about him in her letters. She just dismissed him airily, writing that he was very busy and they saw little of him. She was urging Rosaleen to sell up and join her and Billy, and Rosaleen was sorely tempted. What did it matter if Andrew thought that she was chasing him? Even if he had changed his mind about her . . . well, she needed to get away from Belfast. In Canada she could start afresh. Until then, she would have to be more careful when she met Sean, and to keep her attention away from him, she turned all her charm on Pat.

The next two hours were the most miserable Annie had ever spent. She tried not to watch Sean, tried to keep her attention general, but it's hard to smile and chat when your heart is aching, and her nerves were stretched to breaking point, as the time crawled by.

After her first greeting, Rosaleen ignored them, giving all her attention to Pat. He was obviously lapping it all up, although a trifle perplexed looking.

Annie was aware that Sean covertly watched Rosaleen, a frown puckering his brow now and again, and when he went over to buy her and her companion a drink, Annie found that she could not bear it and escaped once again to the toilets, unable to watch them together. She returned to the lounge to find that it was her turn to be covertly examined by Sean, and this worried her. Was he comparing her with Rosaleen? Dismay filled her heart. How could she do other than come out second best?

Relief flooded through her when, near closing time, Sean refused an offer to return to her mother's house for a bite of supper, saying it was too late and that they would get a taxi straight home from the pub. She had been dreading returning to her mother's or Rosaleen's, couldn't bear to prolong the agony, and for the first time in hours relaxed, glad that her ordeal would soon be over.

When she saw them preparing to leave, Rosaleen came over to say goodnight, kissing Annie on the cheek, shaking Sean's hand and accepting his invitation to spend Christmas Day with them.

The journey home was conducted in silence. Sean reached for Annie's hand and held it between his own, but it was obvious to her that his thoughts were miles away. Was he thinking of Rosaleen? Wishing that it was she who was returning home with him?

Sean was indeed thinking of Rosaleen. The small piece of paper that she had pressed into the palm of his hand when saying goodnight was now burning a hole in his pocket. What was Rosaleen writing to him about? Why all the mystery?

When they arrived at the house, while Sean paid the taxi driver, Annie used her own key and entered the sanctuary of her home. Immediately, she felt calmer and with swift steps hastened to the kitchen and busied herself preparing a pot of tea. Sean always had a cup of tea before retiring, and while he drank it, she would plead a headache and escape to bed.

From the doorway of the kitchen, Sean watched her. He noticed the sad droop to her wide, sensuous mouth, the shadows under her eyes, and unable to bear it, he turned abruptly away. If only he could make her happy. But how could you please someone who kept a barrier between you?

'I'll be down in a minute . . . just going to the loo.'

Once in the bathroom he bolted the door and sitting

on the edge of the bath, took Rosaleen's note from his pocket and opened it out. There was no greeting, just four lines squeezed on to a small scrap of paper.

'Sean, Annie knows about us. She guessed . . . I told her it was just the one time, after Joe died. She must never know that we were friends before you met her. Never!'

Stunned, Sean read and re-read the small scrap of paper. How, after all this time, had Annie guessed? He sat for some time trying to figure out how she could have learnt about him and Rosaleen. It was Annie's voice, hailing him from the hall, that brought him back to reality.

'Sean, your tea'll be cold! Come on down.'

'I'm coming now.'

He tore the paper into small strips and putting it down the toilet, flushed it away before descending the stairs. It wouldn't do for to leave that lying about!

Annie passed him in the hall on her way up to bed.

'Sean, I've an awful headache. I think it was all the cigarette smoke in the small lounge tonight. I left your tea in the living room, it's warmer in there.'

He gave her a small, tight smile and she blushed, knowing that he was not in the least fooled. He was aware that she was avoiding him, but she could not help herself. Tonight she could not bear for him to touch her. Not after seeing him and Rosaleen side by side. How could he prefer her? Rosaleen was beautiful!

The cup of tea on the mantelpiece was ignored as Sean stretched out on the armchair, his feet on the hearth, almost touching the grate where the fire was banked down. It would be silly to disturb the coal, start it blazing, when he would be retiring soon. Now, casting his mind back, he reflected on the evening's happenings.

First, the surprise of seeing Rosaleen with that big good-looking guy, and not feeling in the least bit jealous. The joy that had radiated from her, when he caught her eye in greeting, had embarrassed him and he had been glad that he was not sitting beside Annie when it occurred.

Then when she had pushed the note into his hand, he had felt dismay. Had she changed her mind about him? If she had . . . well, it was too late! He had all he wanted in the house on the Serpentine Road. That was where he belonged, his niche in the world; he was happy with Annie.

He had been in a dither coming home in the taxi. Clinging to Annie's hand like a drowning man. Unable to make conversation. Then when he had read the note, he had wanted the floor to open up and swallow him. He remembered reading Tommy Magee's letter and knew just how he had felt. As if the bottom had fallen out of his world.

What puzzled him most was Annie's attitude. Now, he could understand her reluctance to let him make love to her when he first came home. It must have been awful for her, picturing him and Rosaleen together. He could imagine how he would have felt if he had heard that Annie had been with someone else. But . . . the big but . . . why had she not challenged him? She was so forthright, he could not imagine why she had not. A fleeting smile touched his lips at the next thought. Why had she not hit him with something? It would not have been the first time. Her temper, once roused, was fierce, but once the air was cleared she never held spite; never referred to past quarrels. He would have expected her to rant and rave, shout and yell, clear the air as it were, but no, without a word, she had suffered him to make love to her. Not that she hadn't enjoyed it . . . . oh, yes, indeed she had, but against her will. Very much against her will. Was that how it had been between Thelma and Tommy? Now he knew why each time they made love, she was quiet, not her usual joyous self. Was he doomed to be like Tommy Magee? Doomed to live in the shadow of his sin for the rest of his life? If only she would challenge him . . . then he might be able to convince her that he wanted no other but she.

Meanwhile, Rosaleen was coming down on Christmas Day, just a week away, and he would have to pretend that he was unaware Annie knew the truth or she would know that Rosaleen had told him, and would torture herself with thoughts of him sloping off to meet her sister. She would be hurt, and he had hurt her enough already, so he would have to make sure that she didn't realise that he knew.

Dear God, why had he suggested that they go visiting? Now he was in a quandary. He would have been better living in ignorance.

He remained downstairs for a long time, wanting Annie to be asleep when he retired. However, she was still awake when at last he crept up the stairs and into the bedroom. He knew by the deep, even breaths that she was faking, that she was awake but wanted him to think her asleep, and as he lay beside her still figure, he agreed with Tommy Magee. Your sins did catch up with you. Aye, and when you least expected it.

Once she was sure that Sean slept, with a sigh of relief Annie rose from the bed and flexed her limbs, cramped by trying to lie motionless, and feign sleep. Shrugging into the silk kimono Sean had brought her from abroad, she quietly left the bedroom and entered the small room. From the window, she stared out over the frost-covered hedges and fields to the lough, sparkling like a diamond necklace as it reflected the lights on the opposite shore. Each season gave the view a new beauty. She had seen the summer, the autumn and now winter. Each view different, each beautiful in its own way. Now, not a mark sullied the virgin whiteness. Not a cloud marred the moonlit sky. Even the lough was still, like a bright diamond band lying in the frost. She was surprised at how easily she had adapted to life out here, cut off from all the things she had once thought necessary for happiness. Indeed, the two trams to and from work every day had taken up too much of her time. She had given up her job when Sean's leave drew near, anxious to decorate the sitting room, wanting to spend all her time in the house. She could not picture returning to live on the Springfield Road. This was where she wanted to rear her child. Here in the fresh air of the countryside, far away from the smog of the mills.

Protectively, her hands cradled her stomach. Was her child to be the one without a father? She was sure that she was pregnant. There had been no morning sickness and, when she missed her second period, she had not dared to hope, having been disappointed so often in the past.

Now, she was sure; she had missed her third period and her breasts were swollen and tender, her nipples darkened. Funny how once she had stopped striving to conceive, she had been caught right away. Tomorrow she would go to the village on some pretext or other and go on down to Whitehouse, the next village down the Shore Road, where Minnie had told her Doctor Canavan lived. She had recommended him and told her to mention her name, so she must know him personally. Then she would know for definite, one way or the other.

'Oh, Sean. You startled me.'

Sean's hands circling her waist, brought her back to reality.

'It's beautiful, isn't it, Annie?' he whispered as he gazed over her shoulder at the lough.

When she nodded, he continued, 'It never looks the same twice.'

His hands slid up and cupped her breasts, as he

362

nuzzled the nape of her neck. Cradling their weight in his palms, he chided her, 'You're putting on weight, Mrs Devlin. I'll have to keep an eye on you, or you'll become a wee roly poly.'

Annie's breath caught in her throat. Would he guess? Before he could ponder, she replied, 'Ever hear tell of middle-aged spread? Mm?'

He laughed 'You're a bit young yet for that.' Then, in a more serious voice, he asked, 'Are you all right, Annie?'

'Yes. Just restless.'

She relaxed against him, glad that he had not guessed. First she must find out how he felt about Rosaleen. Only if she was sure that he didn't love her sister would she tell him about the baby.

Now his voice was husky, as, haltingly, he whispered, 'Annie . . . I've never tried to tell you how much you mean to me.'

Her heart gave a skip and she waited breathlessly. Was she about to hear the words she dreamed he would say to her?

Sean continued, 'I love this house. You'll never know how grateful I am that you consented to live out here. How much I appreciate the work you've put into. . .'

With a vicious twist and push she was out of his arms and facing him, her eyes flashing green with anger.

'Yes! Oh, yes, but indeed I *do* realise how much you love this house. You're making it your god!' she hissed at him, disappointed that he had not said what she wanted to hear. Building her up like that, for nothing. 'But never you fear, I'll continue to slave away making it into a home. Think of the money you're saving. Why, if divorce had been allowed by the church you would have got rid of me long ago, wouldn't you, Sean? Eh? And then you'd be out a fortune in housekeeper's bills. Or . . .' Dismayed, she bit on the words that hovered on her lips, and turned abruptly away. She had been

363

about to say: 'Or our Rosaleen would be living here.'

The words were spat at him in fury and he could only stand and gape at the empty doorway when she had turned on her heel and left him.

He stood still, dismay seeping through him. Wasn't it true what she had just said? If divorce had been allowed by the church, wouldn't he have asked her for a divorce after Joe died? Annie had every right to be angry at him, to keep him at a distance; he had never been a true husband to her. He had enjoyed her body, whilst longing for Rosaleen. What a fool he had been! Was it too late to win her over?

Rejected, he went down to the living room, and dawn was breaking when he at last judged it safe to return to bed.

On Christmas Eve as they returned from Midnight Mass it started to snow. Arm in arm they climbed the Serpentine Road, more at ease that they had been all week. It had been a miserable time, with Annie finding fault at the slightest provocation, and Sean biting on his tongue to keep the peace. Mass in the tiny Star of the Sea church, set on a hill on the outskirts of Greencastle, had been beautiful and peace had settled in Annie's heart, as she placed her happiness in God's hands. God's will be done. Why was she fretting and worrying? Had God ever let her down before? Whatever happened would be for the best. This she must believe.

Side by side, Sean and she had received Holy Communion and she knew him well enough to know that if he was doing wrong, he would not commit the sacrilege of receiving the Holy Host, so there was peace in her heart as they climbed the Serpentine, the snow flakes settling on and around them.

Once home, they discarded their wet outer garments and retired to the sitting room. Arms entwined, they stood at the big bay window and watched the snow fall, slowly at first, great, large flakes drifting gently down to lie and amass on frost-covered hedges and fields. Then thickening and swirling, until a blizzard beat against the window panes, obscuring their vision completely.

With a happy laugh, Sean squeezed her close and confided, 'It looks as if God has answered my prayers. Now that sledge I bought for Laura won't go to waste.'

Annie smiled happily up at him. Perhaps her prayers would also be answered.

Christmas Day dawned crisp and clear, with about eight inches of snow covering the land as far as the eye could see, and the lough a heaving silver necklace. Behind the house, the Cave Hill rose like a giant iced cake. Sean went out to clear the steps and driveway for their visitors, and Annie dusted and tidied the sitting room. This was the only room that was completely redecorated with new furniture and she was proud of it. Disliking the utility furniture made during the war, they had decided to wait and save until such time as changes were made before tackling the kitchen and bedrooms, making do with wardrobes and chests of drawers bought second-hand and painted white by Sean, and she had to admit that he had done a good job; their bedroom was quite presentable. Now, plumping up the cushions, she surveyed the sitting room with pride. They had decided not to cover the polished floor boards completely, and these glowed around a great square Persian carpet, brought home a long time ago by Sean, who had been unable to resist its beauty. Cream and blue, it lay in the centre of the floor and was soft and thick beneath her feet. After much discussion, and through one of Minnie's many contacts, they had chosen a dark blye velvet-covered suite. The settee they placed against the wall behind the door, facing the hearth, and the beauty of the mantelpiece was complimented by the two armchairs placed on either side of it. Annie had brightened the suite with pale cream satin cushions, and near the window the Christmas tree rose to the ceiling. Below the window a long, dark oak table reflected the lights of the tree, and under it, gaily wrapped parcels were piled. The fire, built high and burning brightly, threw a warm, cosy glow over everything. Pleased at the result of their labours, Annie uttered a satisfied sigh and retired to the kitchen to prepare the dinner.

Sean, once his task in the snow was finished, covered the old table (now in the living room) with a linen cloth and arranged the chairs, four of which they had borrowed from Minnie who had gone to spend Christmas with her youngest son. Then he set out their best cutlery, before joining Annie in the kitchen.

They worked side by side in harmony, Annie surprised at how calm she felt. She had dreaded this day, worried herself sick over it, but now that it had arrived, she was quite calm. It was probably because she now knew for sure that she was pregnant. Whatever happened today . . . whatever she lost – she would have a child. Sean had said it was all she wanted out of life; he was wrong. Without him, she would be only half alive, but at least now she would not be alone.

Liam was sleeping in Rosaleen's arms when they arrived in George's car, and after Sean had admired him and exclaimed at how he had grown, Annie led the way upstairs, and Rosaleen laid the child on the bed. The sisters eyed each other, and then Rosaleen held out her hand.

'Please say you forgive me . . . please, Annie.'

Slowly, she reached for Rosaleen's hand and clasped it, but her heart wasn't in it. Rosaleen had caused her too much heartache to forgive and forget, and what if Sean recognised Liam? She and Rosaleen were of the same flesh, the same blood ran in their veins, and how she wished things could have been different, but the damage was done; they could never be close again. Rosaleen had hurt her too much. Not only had she committed adultery with Sean and bore him a son, she had also done Annie out of the joy of sharing the knowledge of her pregnancy with Sean. Together, they should be able to confide in her mother and sister that at last they were about to become parents. Instead, she had to hide the fact and pray Sean would not realise that Liam was his son. If it was up to her, she would never see Rosaleen again ... would avoid having to watch Sean and her together.

'Annie, I want you to know that I've decided to sell the business. I made up my mind during the week and discussed it with Owen Black and he's going to buy me out. I'm putting the house up for sale and Bobby is going to look after that for me. So I'll be emigrating to Canada as soon as possible. May's been urging me to come out. Billy Mercer's uncle is willing to claim me and the kids.'

Annie's heart lurched in her breast; Rosaleen going to Canada could solve a lot of problems. Still, in spite of her relief, she found herself lamenting. 'Ah, Rosaleen, how I wish things could be different.' And suddenly she did. But it was too late for regrets.

Rosaleen gave a wry smile. 'Perhaps it's just as well,' she teased. 'If I don't go ... you might end up with Pat McDade for a brother-in-law, and I don't think you'd relish that.'

Annie knew she was jesting to relieve the tension, and smiled through her tears.

'Oh, well then, you'd better go. You're right! I could never bear that.'

The meal was a happy, leisurely occasion, everyone eating too much, and Annie's cheeks were warm with

367

the praise lavished on her for her cooking. She knew that she deserved it. Everything had been cooked to perfection. The turkey succulent, the vegetables just right, not too soft yet not undercooked, the roast potatoes crisp, and the creamed potatoes fluffy. And her gravy, usually a bit lumpy, had been creamy and smooth. The plum pudding, which she had baked months ago to allow it time to mature, was rich and moist, and covered in brandy cream had finished the meal off to a 'T'. Yes, it had been worth the sacrifice of doing without while Sean was at sea and saving her meat and bread rations for the Christmas spread.

They retired to the sitting room to drink their coffee, and afterwards, Thelma, unable to keep her eyes open, asked permission to retire upstairs to join Liam in a nap. Then, as if on cue, he signalled by a loud wail that he was awake.

Sean rose to his feet at once. 'I'll fetch him. I've yet to see him awake.'

They could hear him talking to the child as he descended the stairs, and both Annie and Rosaleen eyed him fearfully when he entered the room, but Sean was unconcerned as he knelt on the carpet near the tree and started to open the presents they had bought for Liam. With a relieved glance at each other, they relaxed. George joined him on the floor, and as they laughingly vied with each other for Liam's attention, Rosaleen caught Annie's eye and smiled encouragingly at her.

'Uncle Sean . . . Uncle Sean . . . you promised me that after dinner we'd go sledging, so ye did. Mam, you take Liam. Please!'

'Now, Laura, don't be impatient. Wait until Liam sees his toys,' Rosaleen admonished her daughter, and when at last Liam clutched his woolly lamb and small car to his breast, she held out her arms for him.

As Sean was about to lift the child and carry him to

her, she said, 'No, let him be. Let him walk.'

'You're joking!'

'No, he's toddling about.'

Carefully, Sean set Liam on his little chubby legs and they all laughed when he promptly sat down.

Once more Sean stood him upright and this time Rosaleen encouraged him. 'Come on, love. Come to Mammy.'

He swayed for some moments and Sean hovered anxiously over him, then Liam tottered across in a rush into Rosaleen's arms.

'Ah, imagine! Ten months old and he's walking. Oh, he's a wonderful child, Rosaleen,' Sean praised him, and added, 'He's the picture of your father, so he is.' Then seeing the hurt look on Laura's face at all the attention that Liam was receiving, he cried, 'But now I must take your wonderful daughter out and let her push me on the sledge.'

'No, Uncle Sean!' All smiles now, Laura giggled at the idea. 'You and Uncle George are going to push me!' she explained, and rushed to the hall to get her coat and mittens.

'Put on your hat, Laura,' Rosaleen warned, 'or you'll get an earache.'

Sean assured her as he followed Laura out into the hall, 'Don't worry, Rosaleen. I'll take care of her.'

And sadness settled on her at his words. If only he could take care of them all, but alas it could never be.

Once they were gone and Rosaleen and Annie were alone in the sitting room, with a raised eyebrow, Rosaleen said softly, 'Didn't I tell you he wouldn't notice?'

Annie nodded and sighed. 'I wish you weren't going to Canada,' she whispered. Then, in case Rosaleen was tempted to change her mind, hastily added, 'But it's all for the best, so it is.'

And Rosaleen nodded sadly, in agreement with her.

369

Children changed, as they grew up, and perhaps one day Liam would look more like Sean than he did at present. Her decision to emigrate had also been influenced by the fact that Laura was beginning to act like Sean. She didn't resemble him in the slightest, no . . . but a turn of the head, a raised eyebrow, brought him to mind. So, yes, it was all for the best that she should go to Canada. If only Andrew had kept his promise to send for her everything would have been fine. Now she would have to do everything herself.

'May will be glad to see you,' Annie consoled her and asked, 'How is she?'

'She's fine . . . being married in the church has made a big difference to her. The new baby is a girl. They're calling her Rosaleen.'

'Ah, that's lovely. I'm sure you're pleased.'

'Yes, as a matter of fact I am.'

'I'll miss you, Rosaleen.'

'Not once your baby's born.'

Annie gasped in dismay at these words. 'How did you guess?'

'It's obvious.'

'Sean doesn't know yet. And, mind, I want to tell him myself,' Annie warned.

'I was about to say it's obvious to me . . . there's a bloom about you. No one else seems to have noticed, and I certainly won't tell Sean.'

'When do you leave?'

'Not for a while. These things take time, but the fact that someone is claiming me should hurry things up a bit.' Not wanting to start talking about Andrew, whom Annie had never met, Rosaleen changed the subject. 'When's the baby due?'

'June.'

'I think I'll be away before then.'

Sadness settled on them, and to try to dispel it, Annie asked, 'Why didn't George ask Maureen

Murphy to come down with him?'

'He's not ready for a relationship yet, and somehow or other I don't think it'll be Maureen he'll pick. I think he fancies Mary Mitchel. I think that's why he's being instructed in the faith.'

At these words Annie gasped, 'Mary Mitchel? Her that lives in the big house up on the front of the Springfield Road? The builder's daughter?' Her eyes flashed derision. 'She'd never look twice at him. Why, she can pick and choose! No, I know her. She's got big ideas . . . he'll never get his boots under her bed.'

'I think you're wrong, but time will tell.' Rosaleen smiled at Annie's amazement and confided, 'He's been out with her a couple of times.'

'Well, I never! Good luck to him. She's not short a bob or two.'

'Ah now, Annie, you know that doesn't count where George is concerned,' Rosaleen chastised her.

'No . . . no, of course you're right. Still, it'll be a feather in his cap if he marries her.' She nodded her head and repeated, 'Aye, a big feather!'

There was relief in Annie's heart as she watched them all bundle into George's car that night, to travel home. The day had been enjoyable and Sean had treated Rosaleen as he would a sister. What more could she ask for? Still, she was glad to see them go.

The relief that Sean felt as he waved them off was heartfelt. It had been a strain, being careful how he looked at Rosaleen. Not that he wanted to ogle her. No, he was relieved to find that those days were gone. But he was worried in case she . . . He brought his thoughts to a halt. Did he really think that Rosaleen might ogle him? She was the one who had turned him down. But remembering her joyous look in the Clock Bar, he had been a bit worried, and was glad to see them go, glad to be alone with his lovely wife, in his beautiful house.

It was after tea on Boxing Day when Sean was washing his hands at the sink that Annie blurted out the news about Rosaleen going to Canada. She had been bracing herself all day to tell him, wondering how he would react. Now she saw his body go still as he paused in his task, and she berated herself.

Coward! Weak, stupid coward.

Why hadn't she told him face to face? Because she was afraid of what she might see in his eyes?

Annoyed at herself, she asked, 'Well, what do you think of that?'

Sean let the relief that this news created seep through him and when she spoke again, he commenced washing his hands.

His voice when he answered her was mild. 'I think that's a good idea. A very good idea. May and Billy are out there. They'll take care of her. And with her looks, she'll soon meet another man. What do you think?' he queried, as he lifted the towel and turned to face her.

Annie's eyes searched his face; it was calm, he was relaxed. There was no sign that he cared where Rosaleen went. But . . . would he have been the same if she had told him face to face? If she had taken him unawares? Well, fool that she was, she had missed her chance. Now she would never know.

To her surprise, unable to let the matter drop, she heard herself reply, 'It's not what I think that counts. It's what you think.'

He let his hands drop slowly to his sides, the towel trailing the floor unheeded, and eyed her through narrowed lids.

'Now just what's what supposed to mean?'

Was he going to get a chance to clear the air? Plead his case? His innocent demeanour made Annie throw caution to the winds. Rising to her feet, she bawled across the table at him: 'Stop looking so bloody innocent! I know about you and Rosaleen . . . do you

372

hear me? I know that you and Rosaleen had an affair.'

He breathed a sigh of relief. Annie in a temper he could handle. It was the cold, silent treatment he could not penetrate.

'And just who says that Rosaleen and I had an affair?' he asked, his voice still mild.

This infuriated Annie more. 'I got it straight from the horse's mouth, so I did. So there!'

Annie was warning herself to be careful, she must get a grip of her temper; she must not mention Liam. Not if she wanted to keep Sean. But did she want to hang on to him? Hang on to someone who had never even pretended to love her. Who, not once in their years together, had said he loved her. It had cut her to the very core when, mulling over the past, she had realised this. Oh, he made love to her as if he cherished her (was it better with Roslaeen?), and he called her 'love' and 'sweetheart' and 'darling', but these were endearments that he lavished on everyone. Not once had he said, 'I love you, Annie.' And she, fool that she was, had thought that because he had married her, he loved her. Whereas he had probably just wanted someone to call his own when he was away fighting during the war.

'Rosaleen told you?' Sean felt shock register in his brain. Had she confessed? No. In her note she had said that they had been together once. He must be careful. Not say something that might betray how he had once loved Rosaleen.

This thought startled him. Once loved? Leave that for now, he chastised himself. Pay attention to what Annie's saying.

'Yes, Rosaleen told me.'

'If she told you that we had an affair, she lied, and I can't see why she should.'

'Well, she did tell me . . . she admitted that you and she . . .' Her voice broke and clamping her lips tightly together, she blinked furiously to contain the tears and headed for the door. He was there before her, barring her escape.

Gripping her tightly by the arm, he said in a controlled voice, 'Now listen here . . . don't think that you can throw accusations like that at me and run away, and then tomorrow act as if nothing's different. You've been doing that a lot lately . . . starting to say things then ignoring me for a while, and I won't have it, Annie. Do you hear me? I won't have it. So . . . just what did Rosaleen say?'

Annie's head reared back and she fixed a hard gaze on him. 'You tell me! You were there!'

'It was only once.'

He made himself hold her eye, feeling ashamed. He became aware that he would prefer to tell her the truth, right from the beginning. Clear the air, once and for all. But Rosaleen had set the stage for this conversation and he could only play it by ear.

'When?'

Dismayed by her persistence, he released his grip on her and his eyes held contempt.

'After Joe died . . . do you want graphic details?'

In spite of herself, the tears that filled her eyes spilled over, but as they streamed down her cheeks, her head rose proudly in the air. 'No, Sean, that won't be necessary. I've pictured it often,' she replied proudly, and there was dignity in her walk as she left the room and climbed the stairs. After all, as she reminded herself, she had done no wrong.

Pain closed like a fist around Sean's heart. Pain for the hurt Annie was now feeling, hurt he had inflicted on her. He started to follow her, but changed his mind. What good would it do? He had thought that if it was once out in the open, he could explain, put things right, but he found that he could not tell more lies.

In the back hall he pulled on his wellingtons and waterproof coat, and tugging his cap down low on his brow, left the house.

From the bedroom window, Annie watched him plough through the snow and leaving the drive, turn up the Serpentine Road. He would be frozen, she fretted, catch his death of cold, but then . . . she was frozen, and she was in a warm room.

As he battled against the elements, Sean tried to sort out his emotions. How come Rosaleen, whom he had loved dearly for years, now failed to raise a flicker of passion? For a moment he felt bereft at the loss of his first love; it had been a part of him for so long. When had he stopped dreaming about her? When had Annie eroded her way into his heart? He didn't know! All he knew was that he had made a terrible mess of his life. Was he to lose Annie too?

He was very much aware that without Annie he would feel lost. Somewhere along the way, she had become the pivot of his life, the heart of his home. What would he do if she left him? Turn to Rosaleen? He was so confused. Less than two years ago he would have jumped at the chance of starting afresh in Canada with Rosaleen. Would have, at a nod from Rosaleen, taken off. Now it looked like Annie held his happiness in her hands and he could not reach her. He didn't deserve her; all these years while she had longed for a family, he had ignored her need. He should have paid attention to her, gone to the doctor, found out about adoption. Would Annie consider adoption? Would she give him another chance to try to make her happy? Despair engulfed him. Why should she? When she had needed him most, he had been pining for Rosaleen. God forgive him!

When he returned to the house, he was not surprised to find blankets and pillows piled on the settee. He smiled wryly as he gathered them up, remembering how Annie had vowed that no one would ever sleep on her beautiful settee. Was this her answer? Was there no hope of a future together for them?

He tossed and turned most of the night, and as a result slept late. Annie had already breakfasted when he entered the kitchen. She rose from her seat at once to prepare his breakfast.

'I'm not hungry. Just a bit of toast . . . that's all I want.'

While he was eating, Annie poured herself a cup of tea and sat facing him. Her face was pale but calm, and he noted that there was no sign of tears. She, obviously, had had a better night than he.

Annie sat pondering for a few moments before speaking. After much soul searching, she had decided that Sean must be free to make up his mind just what he wanted out of life. If he would be happier with Rosaleen, well . . . had she the right to keep him tied to her? She was aware that they would still be tied to each other as far as the church was concerned, but she felt sure that she would not want to marry again, and it was Sean and Rosaleen's own business whether or not they wished to live in sin.

Now she started to speak, tentatively. Although she wanted him to be free to choose, she did not want him to feel that she wished to be rid of him.

'Sean . . . I've been thinking about us.'

He paused, toast halfway to his mouth, and eyed her from under raised brows. 'Mm?'

'Well, I'm all mixed up. I can't offer you a divorce . . . I haven't the right. And divorced or not I'd still feel married to you, but I'll understand if you want to feel free.' Her voice trailed off and she waited expectantly. When he remained silent, disconcerted she continued, 'I would like to remain in this house for awhile, until I can make other arrangements. Will that be all right with you?' Again she paused. Why didn't he speak? 'I'll try to be gone before your next leave.'

The toast reached his mouth and his voice was muffled when he at last answered her. 'Yes . . . stay as long as you like.'

He tried to keep his voice airy, unconcerned. After all, she had already made up her mind. Obviously she had ceased to love him and he had no one to blame but himself, but there was no need to let her know how much he hurt.

With an abrupt movement, Annie rose from the table. She was in despair. He did not care. Did not even question her reasons. Was probably glad of the chance to be rid of her.

'Thank you . . . thank you very much. I'll make sure that I'm out before you return.' And with these words she quickly left the room, fearing her composure would crack.

Breakfast finished, Sean toiled out the back clearing snow, his heart and mind as heavy as the mist that obscured the top of the Cave Hill. Annie's rejection of him cut deep. This was the third time that he had been rejected, but it didn't get any easier. Especially when knowing that he was his own worst enemy, had brought all his troubles on himself, made it harder to bear. He would have to sell the house. It would be an empty shell without Annie's warm presence. How could he have been so stupid? To have won Annie's love and lost it by his indifference. He was a fool.

It was a long time later that he climbed the stairs in search of her. He had wrestled with his desire to hide his pain from her, and the chance to try one more time to make her change her mind. What if she rejected him again? She had every reason to. Would he be able to bear it? Rejection or no, he had to try one more time.

As usual, she was in the small room, leaning on the windowsill, gazing out over the snow-covered beauty of the fields to the lough. The amount of time she spent in this room surprised him. From their bedroom she could look out on the same view, and sit in comfort while doing so, but she preferred to stand in this small, empty room. She was unaware of him until he spoke her name.

'Annie?'

Slowly she straightened up from her bent position but did not turn to face him. He knew from the way her head tilted up that her chin was thrust out, ready for battle.

'Yes?'

A great, deep sigh left his lips. He was going to throw himself on her mercy and he had no idea, no idea at all, how she would respond.

'I don't know how to begin. Look ... I know I haven't been the world's greatest husband, but you have had some good times with me, haven't you?'

The chestnut hair bobbed forward in a nod, and he continued, 'I was wondering, Annie, would you not give me another chance? I've been thinking ... you want a child. Well, what about adoption? Would you consider adoption? Would that please you?'

Slowly, she turned to face him, her eyes wide and questioning. 'You'd consider adoption?'

He nodded eagerly, 'Yes, I would.'

'Does ...' She paused, now knowing how to phrase the next question. Why couldn't he be more explicit? 'Does this house mean so much to you?'

His brows gathered in a frown. 'The house?' Then comprehension dawned, and he bawled, 'Have a titter of wit, Annie! Do you really think that I'd consider adoption to remain in this house?'

It was her turn to frown. 'Well, why?'

'Look, Annie, I love this house, I admit that, but without you it'd be an empty shell. If you want to move back to the Springfield Road or even the Upper Falls, I'll move gladly. If only you'll give me another chance.'

378

She was in a dilemma; she wanted nothing more in the world than to believe him, but Aul Nick was whispering in her ear. Did he want to move to be near Rosaleen? Was he holding on to her while he sought to win Rosaleen over? His betrayal of her had made her wary.

'Annie.' He moved closer and reached for her hands, clasping them against his breast. 'Please give me a chance to prove how much I love you. How much I need you.'

For some moments she stood motionless, her eyes tightly closed, and let his words wash over her, balm to her tortured heart.

He loved her . . . HE LOVED HER! A great bubble of joy welled up and burst inside of her and his voice trailed off in amazement when she pressed close to him, eyes ablaze with happiness.

As his lips claimed hers, her kiss was full of joy, like it used to be. He gripped her closer still, unable to believe his luck, and when at last she freed him, he sank his face in her hair.

'Ah, Annie, Annie . . . I thought I'd lost you. I was in despair. Please don't ever shut me out again. You're my world . . . the heart of my home.'

Eyes brimming with happiness, she drew back and looked at him. 'Ah, Sean, you've just made me the happiest woman in the world. Listen . . .' A wave of her hand embraced the room. 'I've pictured this room often as a nursery. I'll paint the walls white and get some prints of nursery rhymes and flowers . . . and Minnie has a lovely cot that she is willing to lend me.' Her voice was excited and happy. 'It'll be lovely in this room, I can just picture it. It's huge . . . it will do a child until it's three years old. It would cost the earth to buy. Isn't Minnie kind?'

Still afraid to believe his luck, he clung to her, but fear penetrated his heart. He wished now that he'd mentioned adoption before, but she must be made to realise that it took time. She was going too fast.'

'Annie, please love, don't set your hopes too high. I've been asking around about adoption and it can take years . . . and sometimes you can be turned down for no apparent reason.'

'Sean, we don't have to adopt.' Her eyes teased him. 'You were right. I am too young for a middle-aged spread.'

Her hand drifted down and patted her stomach.

He stared at her uncomprehending, and she repeated slowly, her eyes holding his, her head swaying from side to side, 'The weight I'm putting on isn't a middle-aged spread.'

His brows drew together. 'You mean . . .'

She nodded, and watched his jaw drop with amazement.

'You're pregnant?'

'I only found out for sure last week.'

'And you never told me?'

Her eyes held his steadily. 'I didn't know what you wanted out of life, Sean. You might have wanted to join Rosaleen in Canada, and I didn't want you to feel tied. You see, I was convinced that you didn't love me.'

'But you must have known that I do.'

'No . . . you never said.'

Her voice was sad and he squirmed inwardly when he realised that what she said was true. How could he have said it? He had thought he still loved Rosaleen.

'Ah, Annie. Annie, my love.' The back of his hand caressed the curve of her cheek, her jaw, her throat; sending shiver after shiver of anticipation coursing through her. 'Annie . . . you'll be fed up listening to my declarations of love from now on.'

'Never . . . never! That's something I'll never tire of, and don't you ever stop.'

His hands cupped her face. 'I love you, Annie

380

Devlin. I love you so very much.'

The shadow had gone from her eyes and he felt humble as he gazed into her very soul, at the love shining there. Overcome with the wonder of it, wanting to hold back the tears that threatened to overwhelm him, he asked gruffly, 'When's the baby due?'

'June.'

'It'll be born before I come home again,' he lamented. 'Will you be all right, out here on your own?'

'Minnie will look after me.' Her eyes danced with happiness. 'She's adopted me. Says I'm the daughter she always longed for. And remember, she has a phone. I'll be all right, so I will.'

'Annie, there's something else I've been thinking about but I couldn't mention it while you were so distant.'

'Yes?'

Her eyes clouded over. Was there a snag?

'Well . . . do you think you could bear to have me under your feet all the time? I want to leave the navy, get a job ashore. What do you think?'

'Oh! I think that's wonderful . . . wonderful.' To think that he loved her that much, to want to leave his beloved sea and stay at home with her. A warm happiness enveloped her and her look became mischievous. 'I think I could just about bear to have you at home.'

With a happy laugh, he bent towards her and as his lips closed on hers, she felt a flutter as the child in her womb moved noticeably, for the first time, and sent a prayer heavenward that Rosaleen would find happiness in Canada and never, ever, return to Ireland.

Sean gently led Annie from the 'nursery' and into their bedroom. Now he knew why she spent so much time there. Soon they would have a child, and perhaps in a few years they would have another one. This house would need at least three children.

He voiced his thoughts to her. 'Annie, once this child is born, we'll space our family . . . say two years apart.' His voice trailed off as Annie's hand covered his mouth.

'There'll be no birth control, Sean. We'll live up to our religion. God will take care of us.' Her words dwindled away and her eyes grew fearful. 'Do you agree with me?'

'Anything you say, Annie. For my part, I would like at least six,' he assured her.

She smiled happily and nodded, relaxing contentedly against him.

'Ah, Sean . . . Sean.'

He held her close and settled her against his body. There now . . . that was where she belonged. Slowly, he began to undo the buttons down the front of her dress.

'Let's have an early night, eh, Annie my love?'

She giggled softly. 'Sean . . . it's nearly lunch time.'

He smiled at her amusement. 'Well then, let's have a mid-morning nap. Eh, love?'

Her arms crept up around his neck and her eyes danced with laughter. 'We might miss lunch, mind.'

'I think I could bear that,' he whispered, and at the look in his eyes, her heart turned over and no more words were needed as he gently lowered her on to the bed.

Wrapping Liam in a blanket, Rosaleen rubbed her nose gently against the sleeping child's before laying him on the settee. She sighed as she looked out of the window. Unlike the Serpentine Road, there was no large expanse of virgin snow here. Grey slush littered the footpaths and snowladen skies seemed actually to sit on the rooftops, darkening the rooms as if it was evening instead of early morning.

She had promised to take the children to spend Boxing Day with Amy and Bobby but she felt so depressed all she wanted to do was stay at home and weep. God forgive her! She should be counting her blessings instead of giving in to misery. And she had so many blessings: a lovely daughter, already on her way to visit her granny and Bobby. A beautiful healthy son. No money worries. Just why was she so depressed?

It must be the aftermath of spending Christmas Day at Annie's. The strain of being in Sean's company now that Annie knew the truth. The knowledge that Sean was uneasy and afraid in her company had filled her with a great aching pain. To think that Sean could fear her; be afraid of her spoiling things between Annie and him. As if she would! That's why she was unhappy.

Then on top of all that, the fact that Andrew had let her down deepened her unhappiness. She had been so sure he cared for her, but it appeared she had been wrong. Three weeks ago a doll had arrived for Laura, and a huge soft cuddly bear for Liam, but since then, nothing! Not one letter in answer to hers. And she had written twice! She squirmed when she thought of the drift of her letters. She had not actually asked him his intentions . . . but she may as well have. And he had not been man enough to answer her. Tell her he had changed his mind. And tonight she had to face Pat and tell him that she had decided to emigrate to Canada.

Her actions in the Clock Bar a week ago had given him the wrong idea and she knew he thought that his long, careful courtship was paying off. At the beginning of their friendship she had warned him that she wanted nothing more from him, but she had seen his hopes rise when she had fawned all over him in the pub and guessed that he was just biding his time. Now she had to dash his hopes, and dreaded how he would react to her news.

As she tidied the kitchen, determined to leave everything spotless before joining Laura at Amy's, dismay filled her when she heard the living-room door open and close. It must be Pat. She would have preferred to confront him at night. Not so early in the day, when she felt weepy. But so be it. She may as well get it over with.

'Is that you, Pat? Take a seat . . . I won't be a minnit.'

As the silence stretched, she turned slowly towards the living room, a frown on her brow. There was no way Pat McDade could stay so quiet.

The figure standing near the door was very still; large snowflakes melted on his dark hair and on the shoulders of his black Crombie overcoat, and Rosaleen felt the colour leave her face and her knees go weak at the sight of him.

'You are expecting . . . Pat?'

She longed to throw herself into his arms, feel the comfort of them around her, weep all over him, but the look in his eyes kept her motionless at the kitchen door. As usual when she was ill at ease, she resorted to sarcasm.

'What's it to you? Has another death brought you over?'

His face was stern, his eyes no longer warm and caring but dark and probing, but before he could answer her there was a light knock on the door and Bobby Mackay entered the room.

Startled and confused, he shuffled his feet in embarrassment and looked from Rosaleen to Andrew and back again.

'I'm sorry if I'm interrupting something, but the footpaths are in an awful state, Rosaleen. That snow coming down on top of the hard slush is treacherous so I came round to carry Liam for you.'

'That's kind of you, Bobby. He's ready to go.'

She nodded towards the sleeping child. To reach him she would have to pass close to Andrew and her feet would not obey her and move in his direction. It was Andrew who lifted the child and placed him gently in Bobby's arms.

'Bobby, I don't think you met Andrew when he was last here. He's Billy Mercer's cousin. Remember he came home for his uncle's funeral?'

'Of course . . . of course. No, I never did have the pleasure. Pleased to meet you.'

The two men shook hands but Andrew never spoke, just nodded in acknowledgement of Rosaleen's introduction, and Bobby quickly turned to leave the house. As he said to Amy later, the tension was so thick it was like waiting for the thunder to roll, heralding a storm.

'I'll go on round, Rosaleen. You take your time . . . there's no hurry. We'll expect you when we see you.' And with another nod at Andrew, he hurried out.

When the door closed on him, Andrew moved slowly towards Rosaleen but when he reached for her she hissed at him: 'Don't you touch me!'

She had endured weeks of torment because of this man, and he thought he could just walk in and take up where he left off.

Unable to stop herself, she let her tongue run away with her. 'You're too early! I've not had any drink yet,' she taunted him.

He drew back as if she had slapped his face. Was that the only way she could stomach him? Had all the plans and preparations he had made been in vain?

Had Pat McDade won Rosaleen over? Well, May had warned him not to delay too long. Hadn't she sung the praises of tall, handsome Pat? Everything that he was not. She had cautioned him not to keep Rosaleen in the dark about his plans. He should have listened to her, but he had wanted to surprise Rosaleen. But it had back-fired . . . he was the one who was being surprised.

He dragged his eyes from the cold, haughty beauty of her and glanced at the clock. 'What time are you expecting him?'

'I'm not really expecting him . . . when I heard the door open, I just thought it might be him. I certainly didn't expect to see you.'

'Oh.' He frowned. Why had she not expected to see him? Had she sent him a letter telling him not to come and it had gone astray? At a loss to understand, he sighed. 'Well, I'm very tired, Rosaleen. Do you think you could give me a cup of coffee before you show me the door?'

'Of course. I'm sorry . . . look, take off your coat and sit down. Are you hungry? Will I make you a fry?'

'No . . . no, I'm not hungry. Just a cup of coffee.' It wasn't food he was hungry for. He had hungered for her for long months, but it seemed he had delayed too long.

As she prepared sandwiches while the kettle was boiling, she chastised herself. He had travelled half-way across the world and look how she had greeted him. Not one kind word! As usual, she had let her hurt pride rule her tongue. She should have thrown herself into his arms and let nature take its course. God knows she had wanted to, but the look in his eyes had stopped her. There had been contempt in their depths . . . how could he look at her like that. Surely he didn't think that she was playing about with Pat? Would she be able to put matters right?

Drawing deep breaths into her lungs, she sought to compose herself. However, in spite of her efforts, her hands still shook as she placed a plate of sandwiches and a pot of coffee on a tray to carry into the living room, only to find him stretched out in the armchair, completely relaxed, his eyes closed, apparently asleep.

'Andrew . . .' she whispered, but he was out to the world, and returning the tray to the kitchen, she fetched a blanket and gently covered his prone figure.

He looked exhausted and shame once again smote her as she recalled the way she had greeted him. Well, when he awoke she would make amends, but first she must see Amy and ask her to mind the children, yet again. Then she would call in and see Pat McDade and inform him of her intentions to emigrate; she did not want him calling around and upsetting the plans she was going to set in motion. With these thoughts in mind, she quietly left the house.

It was two hours before Andrew showed signs of awakening.

Stretching, he craned his head this way and that, and it must have hurt because he grimaced as he opened his eyes. Awareness came slowly to him, as his eyes took in the room and at last came to rest on her.

Rosaleen watched him from where she sat curled up on the settee and smiled as she observed the surprise in his eyes as they roamed over her figure. The oyster-coloured silk pyjamas that she wore were very fine and hid nothing. Amy had supplied the coupons for them and Rosaleen had saved them for when Andrew should send for her, but now she felt the need to woo him. She had brushed her hair and it framed her head like a bright halo while her skin gleamed luminous in the dim firelight. Desire raged through him as he watched her rise from the settee.

Never having set out deliberately to charm a man before, she felt shy as she approached him.

Leaning over him, the pyjama coat open and revealing, she said softly, 'I'll make that coffee, now you're awake.'

He gripped her hand and motioned her to her knees beside his chair. They both started to speak at once.

'We must . . .' He stopped.

'It seems we . . .' She also paused and he nodded for her to continue.

'It seems to me we got off on the wrong foot again,' she whispered, and her eyes begged his forgiveness.

He smiled wryly. 'I must admit I've had better receptions.'

'I'm sorry . . . but I was so surprised to see you.'

His grip on her hand tightened. 'That's what I can't understand. Didn't you receive my letter?'

'No. It's almost four weeks since I received a letter from you.'

'It must be because of the Christmas mail. I wrote and told you that I would be arriving on Christmas Eve . . . but then the plane was delayed.' He pulled her closer against his thigh. 'I've spent forty-eight hours sitting at the airport dreaming about you. I thought I'd never get here! So you can understand how I felt when you seemed to be expecting Pat.'

Her gaze was compelling. 'I thought you had changed your mind. Even May's letters were so strange. She wrote that she rarely saw you. Then she urged me to sell up and go out to her and Billy. Is it any wonder that I thought she was warning me off? I was sure you had a woman out there and that May was trying to break the news gently to me.'

'That's my fault, Rosaleen. May was under threat of what I'd do to her if she told you what I was arranging. As for urging you to sell up and . . . well, I imagine she was trying to help me, by getting you ready to move.'

'Oh.'

'You see, I was buying a house. May assures me that you'll love it. I hope she's right. But I realise now that I should have asked you how you felt about it.'

She reached up and touched his cheek. 'You're sweet, Andrew . . . but yes, you should have warned me.'

He leant closer. 'Have you missed me?'

She nodded shyly. 'Awfully! I've thought of you often. Longed for you to send for me . . . when you didn't, I thought you had abandoned me.'

'Ah, Rosaleen, how could you think that?'

'It was very easy to doubt you. Thousands of miles away and no word of sending for me . . . no offer of marriage . . .' Her voice trailed off in embarrassment. 'At least . . . well . . . are you offering me marriage?'

'Of course!'

He released his hold on her and, twisting in the chair, felt in the pocket of the jacket draped over the back.

'May also assured me that you would love this. I chose it because it reminded me of your eyes.'

She opened the small jeweller's box and gasped in delight at the ring nestling within. A large emerald surrounded by diamonds.

'It's beautiful,' she whispered. 'May's right, I love it.'

'If it doesn't fit, it can be altered.' His hands cupped her face and there was reverence in his voice. 'Will you marry me, and make me the happiest man in the world?'

At her shy nod, he removed the ring from the box, but when he lifted her hand to place the ring on her finger, he hesitated, eyeing the wedding band that Joe had placed there almost nine years ago.

Slowly, Rosaleen slid it from her finger. 'I shall keep the rings Joe gave me, until Laura grows up,' she said, and stretching up she placed the wedding band on the mantelpiece.

Then she held out her bare hand to Andrew. The ring fitted perfectly and she raised her face for his kiss.

'Have you been drinking?' he asked, dryly.

Hot colour blazed in her cheeks.

'I'm sorry . . . that was an awful thing to say. Can you forgive me?'

She was tugging at his arm, indicating that he join her on the rug. Instead he rose to his feet. Gripping her hands, he pulled her up to face him.

'Rosaleen, much as I enjoyed my romp on the rug with you, I prefer the comfort of the bed.'

Her lips twitched in amusement, and laughing, he bent and kissed them hungrily. 'Does that make me

389

sound old?'

She shook her head. Gazing down into her passion-filled eyes, he said softly, 'Ah, Rosaleen . . . you are so beautiful. I can't believe my luck.'

His hands pushed the pyjama jacket off her shoulders and down her arms. For some seconds he gazed on the loveliness of her then, with a smothered exclamation, swept her up in his arms and headed for the stairs.